PRAISE FOR

BY ARRANGEMENT

"Hunter leaves the reader ⬛⬛⬛⬛⬛⬛ the
lives of her e⬛⬛⬛
—*Pub*⬛

"Layered with intrigue, history, passion, multidimensional characters, this book has it all. Quite simply, it's one of the best books I've read this year." —*Oakland Press*

"Ms. Hunter has a true gift for bringing both history and her characters to life, making readers feel a part of the danger and pageantry of the era." —*Romantic Times*

"Splendid in every way." —*Rendezvous*

BY POSSESSION

"Brimming with intelligent writing, historical detail and passionate, complex protagonists. . . Hunter makes 14th-century England come alive. . . . For all the historical richness of the story, the romantic aspect is never lost, and the poignancy of the characters' seemingly untenable love is truly touching." —*Publishers Weekly*

"Madeline Hunter's tale is a pleasant read with scenes that show the writer's brilliance. *By Possession* is . . . rich in description and details that readers of romance will savor." —*Oakland Press*

"This is another breathtaking romance from a talented storyteller." —*Romantic Times*

"With elegance and intelligence, Ms. Hunter consolidates her position as one of the best new voices in romance fiction." —*Romance Journal*

BY MADELINE HUNTER

MADELINE HUNTER

BY ARRANGEMENT

—

BY POSSESSION

DELTA TRADE PAPERBACKS

Delta
Trade Paperbacks

MADELINE HUNTER

BY ARRANGEMENT

—

BY POSSESSION

DELTA TRADE PAPERBACKS

BY ARRANGEMENT/BY POSSESSION
A Delta Trade Paperback / October 2005

Published by
Bantam Dell
A Division of Random House, Inc.
New York, New York

ISBN-13: 978-0-385-34007-6
ISBN-10: 0-385-34007-9

These titles were originally published individually by Bantam Dell.

Printed in the United States of America
Published simultaneously in Canada

www.bantamdell.com

OPM 10 9 8 7 6 5 4 3 2 1

BY ARRANGEMENT

FOR PAM,
WHO KNOWS WHY

CHAPTER 1

IF YOUR BROTHER finds out about this, I'll be lucky to walk away with my manhood, let alone my head," Thomas said.

The moon's pale light threw shadows on the walls of the shops that lined the street. Ominous movements to the right and left occasionally caught Christiana's attention, but she didn't fear footpads or nightwalkers tonight. Thomas Holland, one of the Queen's knights, rode alongside her, and the glow from his torch displayed his long sword. Christiana expected no challenges from anyone who might see them in the city out after the curfew.

"He will never know, I promise you. No one will," she reassured him.

Thomas worried with good reason. If her brother Morvan found out that Thomas had helped her sneak out of Westminster after dark, there would be hell to pay. She would take all of the blame on herself if they were discovered, though. After all, she could hardly get into any more trouble than she was in right now.

"This merchant you need to see must be rich, if he doesn't live above his shop," Thomas mused. "Not my business to pry, my lady, but this be a peculiar time to be visiting, and on the sly at that. I trust that it is not a lover I bring you to. The King himself will gut me if it is."

She would have laughed at his suggestion, except that her frantic emotions had left her too sick to enjoy the dreadful joke. "Not a lover, and I come now because it is the only time I can be sure of finding him at home," she said, hoping that he would not ask for more explanation. It had taken all of her guile to slip away for this clandestine visit, and she had none to spare for inventing another lie.

The last day had been one of the worst in her life, and one of the longest. Had it only been last evening that she had met with Queen Philippa and been told of the King's decision to accept a marriage offer for her? Every moment since had been an eternity of hellish panic and outrage.

She was not opposed to marriage. In fact, at eighteen she was past the age when most girls wed. But this offer had not come from Stephen Percy, the knight to whom she had given her heart. Nor had it been made by some other knight or lord, as befitted the daughter of Hugh Fitzwaryn and a girl from a family of ancient nobility.

Nay, King Edward had decided to marry her to David de Abyndon, whom she had never met.

A common merchant.

A common, *old* merchant, according to her guardian, Lady Idonia, who remembered buying silks from Master David the mercer in her youth.

It was the King's way of punishing her. Since her parents' deaths she had been his ward and lived at court with his eldest daughter, Isabele, and his young cousin Joan of Kent. When he had learned about Stephen, he must have flown into a rage to have taken such drastic revenge on her.

Stephen. Handsome, blond Stephen. Her heart ached for him. His secret attentions had brought the sun into her sheltered, lonely life. He was the first man to dare to pay court to her. Morvan had threatened to kill any man who wooed her before a betrothal. Her brother's size and skill at arms had proven a depressingly effective deterrent to a love match, just as her lack of a dowry had precluded one secured by property. Other girls at court had admirers, but not her. Until Stephen.

This marriage would be a harsh retribution for what had occurred on that bed before Idonia had found them together. And not one that she planned to accept. Nor would this old merchant want it when he learned how the King was using him.

She and Thomas followed the blond head of the apprentice whom they had woken from his bed in the mercer's shop. The young man had agreed to guide them to his master's house. He led them up the lane away from the Cheap and then over toward the Guildhall before stopping at a gate and rapping lightly. The heavy door swung back and a huge body filled it.

The gate guard held a torch in one massive hand. He was the tallest person Christiana had ever seen, and thick as a tree. Whitish blond hair flowed down his shoulders.

He spoke in a voice accented with the lilting tones of Sweden. "Andrew, is that you? What the hell are you doing here? The constables catch you out after curfew again . . ."

"These two came to the shop, Sieg. I had to show them the way, didn't I?"

The torch pointed out so that Sieg could scrutinize them. "He be expecting you, but I was told it was two

men," he said warily. "*Ja*, well, follow me. I'll put you in
the solar and tell him you are here."

Thomas turned to her. "I will go up with you," he
whispered. "If anything happens . . ."

"I must do this alone. There is no danger for me
here."

Thomas did not like it. "I see a courtyard beyond this
gate. I will wait there. Be quick, and yell if you need me."

She followed the mountain called Sieg. Doors gave
out on either side of a short passage, and she realized that
this was a building with a gate cut into its bottom level.
They crossed the courtyard and entered a hall set at right
angles to the first. She caught the impression of benches
and tables as they filed through, turning finally into yet
another wing that faced the first across the courtyard.
Here a narrow staircase led to a second level.

Sieg opened a door off the top landing and gestured.
"You can wait here. Master David be abed, so it might take
a while."

She raised a hand to halt him. "I didn't expect to disturb him. I can come another time."

"I was told to wake him when you came."

That was the second time that this man had suggested
that they expected her. "I think that you've made a mistake . . ." she began, but Sieg was already out the door.

The solar was quite large, and a low fire burned in the
hearth at one end. The furniture appeared as little more
than heavy shadows in the moonlight filtering through a
bank of pointed arched windows along the far wall. She
strolled over to those windows and fingered the rippled
glazing and lead tracery. Glass. Lots of it, and very expensive. This Master David had done well over the years selling his cloths and vanities.

It didn't surprise her. She knew that some of the
London merchants were as rich as landed lords and

that a few had even become lords through their wealth. The mayor of London was always treated like a peer of the realm at important court functions, and the families that supplied the aldermen had a very high status too. London's merchants, with their royal charter of freedoms, were a proud and influential group of men, jealous of their prerogatives and rights. Edward negotiated and consulted with London much as he did with his barons.

Sieg returned and built up the fire. He took a rush and lit several candles on a table nearby before he left. Christiana stayed near the windows, away from the light in her shadowed corner.

A door set in the wall beside the hearth opened, and a man walked through. He paused, looking around the chamber. His eyes found her shadow near the windows, and he walked forward a few steps.

The light from the hearth illuminated him. She took in the tall, lean frame, the golden brown hair, the planes of a handsome face.

Humiliation swept her. They had come to the wrong place!

"My lady?" The voice was a quiet baritone. A beautiful voice. Its very timbre pulled you in and made you want to listen to what it said even if it spoke nonsense.

She searched for the words to form an apology.

"You have something for me?" he encouraged.

Perhaps she could leave without this man knowing just who had made a fool of herself tonight.

"I am sorry. There has been a mistake," she said. "We seem to have come to the wrong house."

"Whom do you seek?"

"Master David the mercer."

"I am he."

"I think it is a different David. I was told that he is . . .
older."

"I am David the mercer, and there is no other. If you
have brought something for me . . ."

Christiana wanted to disappear. She would kill Idonia!
Her kindly old merchant was a man of no more than thirty
years.

He had stopped in mid-sentence, and she saw him
realize that she was not whom he expected either. He took
another few steps toward her. "Perhaps if you would tell
me why you seek me . . ."

Young or old, it made no difference. She was
here now and she would tell her story. This man
would not like playing the fool for the King no matter
what his age.

"My name is Christiana Fitzwaryn."

They stood in a long silence broken only by crackle
of the new logs on the fire.

"You had only to send word and I would have come to
you. In fact, I was told that the Queen would introduce us
at the castle tomorrow," he finally said.

She knew then for sure that there had been no mistake.

"I wanted to speak with you privately."

His head tilted back a bit. "Then come and sit yourself, Lady Christiana, and say what you need to say."

Three good-sized chairs stood near the fire, all with
backs and arms. Suppressing an instinct to bolt from the
room, she took the middle one. It was too big for her, and
even when she perched on the edge, her feet dangled. She
felt the same way that she had last night with the Queen,
like a child waiting to be chastised. She reached up and
pushed down the hood of her cloak.

A movement beside her brought David de Abyndon
into the chair on her left. He angled it away so that he

faced her. Close here, in the glow of the fire, she could see him clearly.

Her eyes fell on expertly crafted brown high boots, and long, well-shaped legs in brown hose. Her gaze drifted up to a beautiful masculine hand, long-fingered and traced with elegant veins, resting on the front edge of the chair's arm. The red wool pourpoint was completely unadorned by embroidery or jewels, and yet, even in the dancing light of the fire, she could tell that the fabric and workmanship were of the best quality and very expensive. She paused a moment, studying the richly carved chair on which he sat and the birds and vines decorating it.

Finally, there was no place else to look but at his face.

Dark blue eyes the color of lapis lazuli examined her as closely as she did him. They seemed friendly enough eyes, even expressive eyes, but she found it disconcerting that she could not interpret the thoughts and reactions in them. What was reflected there? Amusement? Curiosity? Boredom? They were beautifully set under low arched brows, and the bones around them, indeed all of the bones of his face, looked perfectly formed and regularly fitted, as if some master craftsman of great skill had carefully chosen each one and placed it just so. A straight nose led to a straight wide mouth. Golden brown hair, full and a little shorter than this year's fashion, was parted at the center and feathered carelessly over his temples and down his chiseled cheeks and jaw to his shirt collar.

David de Abyndon, warden of the mercers' company and merchant of London, was a very handsome man. Almost beautiful, but a vague hardness around the eyes and mouth kept that from being so.

A shrewd scrutiny veiled his lapis eyes, and she suddenly felt very self-conscious. It had been impolite of her to examine him so obviously, of course, but he was older and should know better than to do the same.

"Don't you want to remove your cloak? It is warm here," that quiet voice asked.

The idea of removing her cloak unaccountably horrified her. She was sure that she would feel naked without it. In fact, she pulled it a bit closer in response.

His faint smile reappeared. It made him appear amiable, but revealed nothing.

She cleared her throat. "I was told that . . . that you were . . ."

"Older."

"Aye."

"No doubt someone confused me with my dead master and partner, David Constantyn. The business was his before mine."

"No doubt."

The silence stretched. He sat there calmly, watching her. She sensed an inexplicable presence emanating from him. The air around him possessed a tension or intensity that she couldn't define. She began to feel very uncomfortable. Then she remembered that she had come here to talk to him and that he was waiting patiently for her to do so.

"I need to speak with you about something very important."

"I am glad to hear it."

She glanced over, startled. "What?"

"I'm glad to hear that it is something important. I would not like to think that you traveled London's streets at night for something frivolous."

He was subtly either scolding her or teasing her. She couldn't tell which.

"I am not alone. A knight awaits in the courtyard," she said pointedly.

"It was kind of him to indulge you."

Not teasing. Scolding.

That annoyed her enough that she collected her thoughts quickly. She was beginning to think that she didn't like this man much. He made her feel very vulnerable. She sensed something proud and aloof in him too, and that annoyed her even further. She had been expecting an elderly man who would treat her with a certain deference because of their difference in degrees. There was absolutely no deference in this man.

"Master David, I have come to ask you to withdraw your offer of marriage."

He glanced to the fire, then his gaze returned to her. One lean, muscular leg crossed the other, and he settled comfortably back in his chair. An unreadable expression appeared in his eyes, and the faint smile formed again.

"Why would I want to do that, my lady?"

He didn't seem the least bit surprised or angry. Perhaps this meeting would go as planned after all.

"Master David, I am sure that you are the good and honorable man that the King assumes. But this offer was accepted without my consent."

He looked at her impassively. "And?"

"And?" she repeated, a little stunned.

"My lady, that is an excellent reason for you to withdraw, but not me. Express your will to the King or the bishop and it is over. But your consent or lack of it is not my affair."

"It is not so simple. Perhaps amongst you people it is, but I am a ward of the King. He has spoken for me. To defy him on this . . ."

"The church will not marry an unwilling woman, even if a King has made the match. I, on the other hand, have given my consent and cannot withdraw it. There is no reason to, as I have said."

His calm lack of reaction irked her. "Well, then, let me explain my position more clearly and perhaps you will have your reason. I do not give my consent because I am in love with another man."

Absolutely nothing changed in his face or eyes. She might have told him that she was flawed by a wart on her leg.

"No doubt an excellent reason to refuse your consent in your view, Christiana. But again, it is not my affair."

She couldn't believe his bland acceptance of this. Had he no pride? No heart? "You cannot want to marry a woman who loves another," she blurted out.

"I expect it happens all the time. England is full of marriages made under these circumstances. In the long run, it is not such a serious matter."

Oh, dear saints, she thought. A man who believed in practical marriages. Just her luck. But then, he was a merchant.

"It may not be a serious matter amongst you people," she tried explaining, "but marriages based on love have become desired—"

"That is the second time that you have said that, my lady. Do not say it again." His voice was still quiet, his face still impassive, but a note of command echoed nonetheless.

"Said what?"

" 'You people.' You have used the phrase twice now."

"I meant nothing by it."

"You meant everything by it. But we will discuss that another day."

He had flustered and distracted her with this second scolding. She sought the strand of her argument. He found it for her.

"My lady, I am sure a young girl thinks that she needs to marry the man whom she thinks that she loves. But your emotions are a short-term problem. You will get over this. Marriage is a long-term investment. All will work out in the end."

He spoke to her as if she were a child, and as dispassionately as if they discussed a shipment of wool. It had been a mistake to think that she could appeal to his sympathy. He was a tradesman, after all, and to him life was probably just one big ledger sheet of expenses and profits.

Well, maybe he would understand things better if he saw the potential cost to his pride.

"This is not just a short-term infatuation on my part, Master David. I am not some little girl," she said. "I pledged myself to this man."

"You both privately pledged your troth?"

It could be done that way. She could lie. She desperately wanted to, and felt sorely tempted, but such a lie could have dire consequences, and very public ones, and she wasn't that brave. "Not formally," she said, hoping to leave a bit of ambiguity there.

He at least seemed moderately interested now. "Has this man offered for you?"

"His family sent him home from court before he could settle it."

"He is some boy whom his family controls?"

She had to remember with whom she spoke. "A family's will may seem a minor issue for a man such as you, but he is part of a powerful family up north. One does not defy kinship so easily. Still, when he hears of this betrothal, I am sure that he will come back."

"So, Christiana, you are saying that this man said that he wanted to marry you but left without settling for you."

That seemed a rather bald way to put it.

"Aye."

He smiled again. "Ah."

She really resented that "Ah." Her annoyance made her bold. She leaned toward him, feeling her jaw harden with repressed anger. "Master David, let me be blunt. I have given myself to this man."

Finally a reaction besides that impassive indifference. His head went back a fraction and he studied her from beneath lowered lids.

"Then be blunt, my lady. Exactly what do you mean by that?"

She threw up her hands in exasperation. "We made love together. Is that blunt enough for you? We went to bed together. In fact, we were found in bed together. Your offer was only accepted so that the Queen could hush up any scandal and keep my brother from forcing a marriage that my lover's family does not want."

She thought that she saw a flash of anger beneath those lids.

"You were discovered thus and this man left you to face it alone? Your devotion to this paragon of chivalry is impressive."

His assessment of Stephen was like a slap in her face. "How dare such as you criticize—"

"You are doing it again."

"Doing what?" she snapped.

" 'Such as you.' Twice now. Another phrase that you might avoid. For prudence' sake." He paused. "Who is this man?"

"I have sworn not to tell," she said stiffly. "My brother . . . Besides, as you have said, it is none of your affair."

He rose, uncoiling himself with an elegant movement, and went to stand by the hearth. The lines beneath the pourpoint suggested a lean, hard body. He was quite tall.

Not quite as tall as Morvan, but taller than most. She found his presence unsettling. Merchants were supposed to be skinny or portly men in fur hats.

He gazed at the flames. "Are you with child?" he asked.

The notion astounded her. She hadn't thought of that. But perhaps the Queen had. She looked at him vacantly. He turned and saw the expression.

"Do you know the signs?" he asked softly.

She shook her head.

"Have you had your flux since you were last with him?"

She blushed and nodded. In fact, it had come today.

He turned back to the fire.

She wondered what he thought about as he studied those tongues of heat. She stayed silent, letting him weigh however he valued these things, praying that she had succeeded, hoping that he indeed had a merchant's soul and would be repelled by accepting used goods.

Finally she couldn't wait any longer.

"So, you will go to the King and withdraw this offer?" she asked hopefully.

He glanced over his shoulder at her. "I think not."

Her heart sank.

"Young girls make mistakes," he added.

"This was no mistake," she said forcefully. "If you do not withdraw, you will end up looking a fool. He will come for me, if not before the betrothal, then after. When he comes, I will go with him."

He did not look at her, but his quiet, beautiful voice drifted over the space between them. "What makes you think that I will let you?"

"You will not be able to stop me. He is a knight, and skilled at arms . . ."

"There are more effective weapons in this world than

steel, Christiana." He turned. "As I said earlier, you are always free to go to the bishop and declare your lack of consent to this marriage. But I will not withdraw now."

"An honorable man would not expect me to face the King's wrath," she said bitterly.

"An honorable man would not ruin a girl at her request. If I withdraw, it will displease the King, whom I have no wish to anger. At the least I will need a good reason. Should I use the one that you have given me? Should I repudiate you because you are not a virgin? It is the only way."

She dropped her eyes. The panicked desolation of the last day returned to engulf her.

She sensed a movement and then David de Abyndon stood in front of her. A strong, gentle hand lifted her chin until she looked up into his handsome face. It seemed to her that those blue eyes read her soul and her mind and saw right into her. Even Lady Idonia's hawklike inspections had not been so thorough and successful. Nor so oddly mesmerizing.

That intensity that flowed from him surrounded her. She became very aware of his rough fingers on her chin. His thumb stretched and brushed her jaw, and something tingled in her neck.

"If he comes for you before the wedding, I will step aside," he said. "I will not contest an annulment of the betrothal. But I must tell you, girl, that I know men and I do not think that he will come, although you are well worth what it would cost him."

"You do not know *him*."

"Nay, I do not. And I am not so old that I can't be surprised." He smiled down at her. A real smile, she realized. The first one of the evening. A wonderful smile, actually. His hand fell away. Her skin felt warm where he had touched her.

She stood up. "I must go. My escort will grow impatient."

He walked with her to the door. "I will come and see you in a few days."

She felt sick at heart. He was making her go through with the farce of this betrothal, and it would complicate things horribly. She had no desire to play this role any more than necessary.

"Please do not. There is no point."

He turned and looked at her as he opened the door and led her to the steps. "As you wish, Christiana."

She saw Thomas's shadowy form in the courtyard, and flew to him as soon as they exited the hall. She glanced back to the doorway where David stood watching.

Thomas began guiding her to the portal. "Did you accomplish what you needed?"

"Aye," she lied. Thomas did not know about the betrothal. It had not been announced yet, and she had hoped that it never would be. Master David's stubbornness meant that now things were going to become very difficult. She would have to find some other way to stop this betrothal, or at least this marriage.

David watched her cross the courtyard, her nobility obvious in her posture and graceful walk. A very odd stillness began claiming him, and her movements slowed as if time grew sluggish. An eerie internal silence spread until it blocked out all sound. In an isolated world connected to the one in the yard but separate from it by invisible degrees, he began observing her in an abstract way.

He had felt this before several times in his life, and was stunned to find himself having the experience now. All the same, he did nothing to stop the sensation and did not question the importance of what was happening.

He recognized the silence that permeated him as the inaudible sound of Fortune turning her capricious wheel and changing his life in ways that he could only dimly foresee. Unlike most men, he did not fear the unpredictable coincidences that revealed Fortune's willfulness, for he had thus far been one of her favorite children. Christiana Fitzwaryn of Harclow. The caves of Harclow. There was an elegant balance in this particular coincidence.

The gate closed behind her and time abruptly righted itself. He contemplated the implications of this girl's visit.

He had understood King Edward's desire to hide the payment for the exclusive trading license that he was buying. If word got out about it, other merchants would be jealous. He had himself suggested several other ways to conceal the arrangement, but they involved staggered payments, and the King, desperate for coin to finance his French war, wanted the entire sum now. Edward's solution of giving him a noble wife and disguising the payment as a bride price had created a host of problems, though, not the least of which was the possibility that the girl would not suit him.

His vision turned inward and he saw Christiana's black hair and pale skin and lovely face. Her dark eyes sparkled like black diamonds. She was not especially small, but her elegance gave the impression of delicacy, even frailty. The first sight of her in the fire glow had made his breath catch the way it always did when he came upon an object or view of distinctive beauty.

Her visit had announced unanticipated complications, but it had resolved one question most clearly. Christiana Fitzwaryn would suit him very well indeed.

He had been stunned when the King had chosen the daughter of Hugh Fitzwaryn to be the bride in this scheme, and had pointed out that she was too far above him. Even the huge bride price that everyone would think he was paying did not bridge their difference in degrees.

The King had brushed it aside. *We will put it about that you saw her and wanted her and paid me a fortune to have her.* Well, now he knew the reason for the King's choice of Christiana. A quick marriage for the girl would snuff out any flames of scandal regarding her and her lover.

It was good to know the truth. He did not like playing the pawn in another man's game. Usually he was the one who moved the pieces.

He walked across the courtyard to Sieg.

"It is done then?" the Swede asked as he turned to enter his chamber off the passageway.

"It was not them."

"The hell you say!"

David laughed. "Go to sleep. I doubt that they will come tonight."

"I hope not. There's more visitors here at night than the day, as it is." Sieg paused. "What about Lady Alicia's guard?"

David glanced to the end of the building, and the glow of a candle through a window. "He knows to stay there. I will bring her to him later."

He turned to leave, then stopped. "Sieg, tomorrow I want you to find the name of a man for me. He is a knight, and his family is from the north country. An important family."

"Not much to go on. There be dozens . . ."

"He left Westminster recently. I would guess in the last day or so."

"That makes it easier."

"His name, Sieg. And what you can learn about him."

CHAPTER 2

CHRISTIANA SPENT a desperate night trying to figure out how to save herself. By morning she could find no course of action except writing to Stephen, bribing a royal messenger to carry the letter north, and praying that he received it quickly. But the betrothal was in a week, too soon for Stephen to get that letter and come for her.

The only solution was to speak with the King. She would not refuse the marriage outright, but would let him know that she did not welcome it. Perhaps, at the very least, she could convince him to delay the betrothal.

Steeling her resolve, she left the apartment that she shared with Isabele and Joan under Idonia's watchful eyes, and made her way through the castle to the room where the King met with petitioners. When she arrived, its anteroom had already filled with people. She gave her name to the clerk who sat by the door, and hoped that her place in the household would put her ahead of some of the others.

Some benches lined one wall. An older knight gave up his place, and she settled down. The standing crowd walled her in while she concentrated on planning her request.

As she waited and pondered, the outer door opened and a page entered, followed by her brother Morvan. She saw his dark head disappear into the King's chamber.

The King was going to tell him about the match now. What would her proud brother say? How would he react?

She had her answer very soon. Within minutes the measured rumble of a raised voice leaked through wall that separated the anteroom from the chamber. She knew that it was Edward who had lost his temper, because Morvan's worst anger always manifested itself quietly and coldly.

She had to leave immediately. With the King enraged, there could be no benefit in speaking with him today, and when Morvan left that room, she did not want him to see her sitting here.

She was rising to leave when Morvan hurried out, his black eyes flashing and his handsome face frozen into a mask of fury. He strode to the corridor like a man headed for battle.

She still needed to leave, but she dared not follow him. He might have stopped in the passageways leading here.

She glanced around the anteroom. Another door on a side wall gave out to a private corridor that connected Edward's chambers and rooms. It led to an exterior stairway, and there were rumors that secret guests, diplomats, and sometimes women came to him this way. Without it ever being formally declared off limits, everyone knew that it meant trouble to be found there. Even the Queen did not use that passageway.

She pushed through the crowd. She would slip away and no one would know that she had even come.

Opening the small door a crack, she slid through. The passageway stretched along the exterior wall of the castle lit by good-sized windows set into shallow alcoves. She scurried toward the end opposite the one with the staircase.

The sound of a door opening behind her sent her darting into one of the alcoves. Pressing into the corner, she prayed that whoever had entered the passageway would go in the other direction. She sighed with relief as she heard footsteps walking away.

Then, to her horror, more steps started coming quickly toward her from the direction in which she had been heading. Crushing herself into the alcove's shallow corner, she gritted her teeth and waited for discovery.

A shortish middle-aged man with gray hair and beard, sumptuously dressed like a diplomat, hurried by. He did not notice her, because he fixed all of his attention on the space ahead of him. It seemed that he tried to make his own footsteps fall more softly than normal.

"Pardon. Attendez," she heard him whisper loudly.

The other steps stopped. She heard the men meet.

They began speaking in low tones but their words carried easily to her ears. Both spoke Parisian French, the kind taught to her by the tutors, and not the corrupted dialect used casually by the English courtiers.

"If you are found here, it will go badly for you," the other man said. His voice sounded very low, little more than a whisper, but the words reached her just the same.

"A necessary risk. I needed to know if what I had heard of you was true."

"And what did you hear?"

"That you can help us."

"You have the wrong man."

"I do not think so. I followed you here. You have the access, as I was told."

"If you want what I think you want, you have the wrong man."

"At least hear me out."

"Nay."

The men began walking away. The voices receded.

"It will be worth your while," the first man said.

"There is nothing that you have that I want."

"How do you know if you don't listen?"

"You are a fool to speak to me of this here. I do not deal with fools."

The voices and footsteps continued to grow fainter. Christiana listened until their sound disappeared down the stairway. Lifting her hem, she ran back to her chamber.

She was sitting on her bed in Isabele's anteroom, fretting over whether to approach the King another day, when Morvan came storming into the chamber still furious from his meeting with the King.

He stomped around and ranted with dangerous anger. Rarely had she seen him like this, and keeping him from doing something rash became her primary concern. She felt guilty calming and soothing him, since she knew that everything was her fault and he, of course, did not. Morvan laid all of the blame on the King and the merchant.

"This mercer did not even have the decency to speak with me first," Morvan spat out, his black eyes flashing sparks as he strode around. He was a big man, taller than most, and he filled the space. "He went directly to the King! The presumptions of those damn merchants is ever galling, but this is an outrage."

"Perhaps he didn't know how it is done with us," she

said. She needed him calm and rational. If they thought about this together, they might have some ideas.

"It is the same with every degree, sister. Would this man have gone to his mayor to offer for some skinner's daughter?"

"Well, he did it this way, and the King agreed. We are stuck with that part."

"Aye, Edward agreed." He suddenly stopped his furious stride and stared bleakly into the hearth. "This is a bad sign, Christiana. It means that the King has indeed forgotten."

Her heart went out to him. She walked over and embraced him and forgot her own disappointment and problems. She had been so selfishly concerned with her own pride that she hadn't seen the bigger implications of this marriage.

Fleeting, vague memories of another life filtered into her exhausted mind. Memories of Harclow and happiness. Images of war and death. The echo of gnawing hunger and relentless fear during siege. And finally, clearly and distinctly, she had the picture of Morvan, ten years old but tall already, walking bravely through the castle gate to surrender to the enemy. He had fully expected to be killed. Over the years, she came to believe that God had moved that Scottish lord to spare him so that she herself would not be totally alone.

When they had fled Harclow and gone to young King Edward and told him of Hugh Fitzwaryn's death and the loss of the estate, Edward had blamed himself for not bringing relief fast enough. Their father had been one of his friends and supporters on the Scottish marches, and in front of Morvan and their dying mother Edward had sworn to avenge his friend and return the family lands to them.

That had been eleven years ago. For a long while thereafter, Morvan had assumed that once he earned his spurs the King would fulfill that oath. But he had been a knight for two years now, and it had become clear that Edward planned no aggressive campaigns on the Scottish borders. The army sent there every year was involved in little more than a holding action. All of the King's attention had become focused on France.

And now this. Agreeing to marry her to this merchant was a tacit admission on the King's part that he would never help Morvan reclaim Harclow. The ancient nobility of the Fitzwaryn family would be meaningless in a generation.

No wonder the Percys did not want one of their young men marrying her. But Stephen's love would be stronger than such petty concerns of politics property. And once they were married, she hoped that the Percy family would help Morvan, since he would be tied to their kinship through her.

The chance of that had always increased Stephen's appeal. The redemption of their family honor should not rest entirely on Morvan's shoulders. It was her duty to marry a man who would give her brother a good alliance.

Morvan pulled away. "The King said the betrothal is to be Saturday. I do not understand the haste."

She could hardly confide to her strict older brother that the haste was to make sure that her lover could not interfere. And maybe also to avert Morvan's anger. If he learned what had happened with Stephen, he would undoubtedly demand satisfaction through a duel. King Edward probably wanted to avoid the trouble with the Percy family that such a challenge would create.

Her attempts at soothing him failed. The storm broke in his expression again. He left as furiously as he had entered. "Do not worry, sister. I will deal with this merchant."

✦   ✦   ✦

David stood at the door of his shop watching his two young apprentices, Michael and Roger, carry the muslin-wrapped silks and furs out to the transport wagon. A long, gaily decorated box on wheels, the wagon held seats for the ladies and had windows piercing its sides. Princess Isabele sat at one of the openings.

The arrival of Lady Idonia and Lady Joan and Princess Isabele today had amused him and awed the apprentices. The ladies ostensibly came to choose cloth for the cotehardie and surcoat that Isabele would wear at Christiana's wedding, but the princess was not his patron. The news of the betrothal had just spread at Westminster, and he knew that in reality Christiana's friends had come to inspect him.

They had almost been disappointed, since he hadn't arrived until they were preparing to leave. His business extended far beyond the walls of this shop now, and he left the daily workings of it to Andrew. He smiled at the memory of tiny Lady Idonia throwing her body between Isabele and Sieg when he and the Swede had entered the shop, as if she sought to save the girl from Viking ravishment.

The boys handed their packages in to Lady Idonia. They peered into the wagon one last time as it pulled away surrounded by five mounted guards.

They had a lot to peer at, David thought, glancing at the crowd of onlookers that had formed on the lane when the wagon drew up. A princess and the famous Lady Joan, Fair Maid of Kent, cousin to the King. Members of the royal family rarely visited the tradesmen's shops. It was customary to bring goods to them instead.

Christiana had not come, of course. He wondered what ruse she had used to avoid it. He was sending a gift back to her with Idonia, however, a red cloak lined with black fur which the tailor George who worked upstairs had sewn at his bidding. The one that she had worn to his house four nights ago looked to be several years old and a handspan too short. Being the King's ward clearly did not mean that she lived in luxury.

She would probably feel guilty accepting his gift. In that brief time in his solar, he had learned much about her character and she had impressed him favorably. Her beauty had impressed him even more. The memory of those bright eyes and that pale skin had not been far from his mind since her visit.

She waited for her lover. How long would she wait?

Unlike most men, he liked women and understood them. He certainly understood the pain Christiana felt. After all, he had lived eighteen years near a similar anguish. Was he fated now to spend the rest of his life in its shadow again? Was that to be the price this time of Fortune's favor? This girl seemed stronger and prouder than that.

He had briefly lost awareness of the street, but its movements and colors reclaimed his attention. He pushed away from the doorjamb. As he turned to enter the building he noticed a man walking up the lane from the Cheap, wearing livery that he recognized. He waited for the man to reach him.

"David de Abyndon?" the messenger asked.

"Aye."

A folded piece of parchment was handed over. David read the note. He had expected this letter. In fact, he had been waiting for the meeting it requested for over ten years. Better to finish it quickly. Betrothal and marriage probably had a way of complicating things like this.

He turned to the messenger. "Tell her I cannot see her this week. Next Tuesday afternoon. She should come to my house."

He entered the shop. Michael and Roger were closing

the front shutters, and Andrew came in with cloth from the back room.

"I put the tallies from Lady Idonia and Lady Joan up in the counting room," Andrew said as he settled his burden down.

David clapped a hand on his shoulder. "So. A whole afternoon with the Fair Joan. Your friends will buy you ale for a month to hear your story."

Andrew smiled roguishly. "I was just thinking the same thing. She *is* very fair. As is Lady Christiana Fitzwaryn. I have seen them together in the city. You might have told us about this betrothal. It was very awkward finding out from them."

The boys stopped and listened. Sieg stood by the door.

"It was just decided."

They all waited silently.

"Let us close and go home. I'll explain all there."

Explain what, though? Not the truth. No one would ever learn that, not even Christiana. He would have to come up with a good story fast.

They were almost ready to leave when the sounds of a horse stopping in the lane came through the shutters. Michael ran over and peered out the door. "A King's knight," he said. "The same one who came looking for you this morning, David."

David knew who this would be. "All of you go back to the house. You too, Sieg. I will take care of this."

The door opened and a tall, dark-haired young man entered. He paused in the threshold and looked around. He wore the King's livery and a long sword hung from his knight's belt. Bright black eyes, so like those others but brittle with a colder light, came to rest on David.

The apprentices filed out around the big man, clearly

impressed with his size and bearing. Sieg glanced meaningfully at David. David shook his head and Sieg left too.

"I am Christiana's brother Morvan," the knight said
when they were finally alone.

"I know who you are."

"Do you? I thought that perhaps you mistakenly
thought that she had no kin."

David waited. He would let this brother make his
objections. He would not assume that he knew what they
would be, for there was much to object to.

"I thought that we should meet," Sir Morvan said,
walking down the passageway. "I wanted to see the man
who buys a wife like she is some horse."

David thought about the two hours he had spent this
morning with one of the King's clerks drawing up the
marriage contract. It had been impossible to keep out the
terms of the supposed bride price completely, because
only Edward and he knew its real purpose. Still, David had
tried, and finally negotiated only a reference to its amount
involving a complicated formula based on the price of last
year's wool exports. Only someone very interested would
ever bother to make the calculations.

Morvan must have been shown the contract for
approval and not missed that particular clause.

"The King insisted on the bride price, as in the old
days. I would have been happy to pay nothing."

Morvan studied him. "If she were not my sister, I
might find that amusing. You go to a lot of trouble to
marry a woman whom you do not know."

"It happens all of the time."

"Aye. If the dowry is satisfactory."

"I have no need of a dowry."

"So I am told. Nor are you much in need of a woman
to warm your bed, from what I hear. So why do you pay a
fortune for my sister?"

David had to admit that it was a damn good question. He realized that he shouldn't underestimate this young man. Morvan had been asking about him, just as David had been asking about Morvan. Perhaps the King's proposed explanation would work. *We will put it about that you saw her and wanted her and paid a fortune to have her.* Not, he suspected, that a man lusting after his sister would appeal much to this young knight.

"I saw her several times and asked about her. The King was receptive to my inquiries."

"So you offered for her just on seeing her?"

"I have these whims sometimes. They almost always work out. As far as the rest, the lack of dowry and the payment, things just developed as they often do in such negotiations." It sounded almost plausible. It had better. He had nothing else to offer.

Morvan considered him. "That would make sense if you were a fool, but I do not think that you are. I think that you are an upstart who seeks to buy status among his people through this marriage, and who sees his children raised above their natural degree through their mother's nobility."

Another plausible explanation. But if Morvan had spoken with the right people, he would know just how wrong it was.

"You are Christiana's brother, and are thus unaware of just how foolish she might make a man who is otherwise not a fool," David said.

A fire flashed in the young man's dark eyes. Nay, he did not like the idea of a man lusting after his sister.

"I will not permit this marriage. I will not see Christiana tied to a common tradesman, no matter what his wealth. She is not a brood mare to be purchased to ennoble a bastard's bloodline. She does not want this either."

David ignored the insults, barely, except to note that Morvan had been checking up on him quite thoroughly. "She and I have already spoken of that. She knows that I will not withdraw. I have no reason to."

"Let me give you a reason, then. Go to the King and say that the lady has a brother who has threatened you with bodily harm unless you withdraw. Explain that you did not anticipate that when you made this offer."

"And what of the King's displeasure with you if I say this?"

"If need be, my sword can serve another man."

"And if I don't do this?"

"The threat is not an idle one."

David studied his resolute expression. An intelligent man, and probably an honest one. "Do you know why your sister does not consent to this marriage?"

"That is obvious, isn't it?"

So Morvan did not know about Sir Stephen. She had claimed that he didn't, but he may have discovered it nonetheless and been planning to force things with Percy.

"Is it?"

"She is the daughter of a baron. This marriage is an insult to her."

David fought down a sudden profound irritation. He had long ago become almost immune to such comments, and to the assumptions of superiority that they revealed. But he had accepted more from this man in the last few minutes than he normally swallowed from anyone. He leaned against the wall and folded his arms and met Morvan's fiery eyes.

"Will you withdraw?"

"I think not."

Morvan looked him up and down. "You wear a dagger. Do you use a sword?"

"Not well."

"Then you had best practice."

"You plan to kill me over this?"

"I cannot stop this betrothal, but I will stop the wedding. A month hence, if you have not left London or annulled the match, we will meet."

Anger seeped into David's head. He almost never lost control anymore, but he was in danger of it now. "Send word of when and where. I will be there."

He knew that Morvan's own cold fury matched his own. But he also saw the surprise that the threat had been met with anger and not fear.

"We will see if you come," Morvan said with a slow smile. "I think that time will show that you are like most of your breed. Rich in gold but without honor."

"And you are like too many knights these days. Rich in pompous arrogance but without land or value," David replied sharply. It was unworthy of him, but he had had enough.

Morvan's eyes flashed dangerously. He pivoted on his heel and walked the twenty paces to the door. "My sister is not for you, merchant. You have a month to undo this."

Something snapped. As Morvan disappeared into the street, David uncoiled himself with a fluid, tense movement. His hand went to his hip, and a long steel dagger flew down the passageway, imbedding itself into the doorjamb directly behind the spot where Morvan Fitzwaryn's neck had just been.

A blond head moved in the open door's twilight, and Sieg bent into the threshold. He glanced at David and then turned and yanked the still-quivering dagger out of its target. He came down the passageway.

"I suppose that it is still early to congratulate you on this marriage."

David took the dagger and sheathed it. The worst of his anger had flown with the knife. "You heard."

"*Ja.*"

"I told you to leave."

"His sword and face told me to stay. I thought that I would have the chance to repay my debt today."

David ignored him and began walking away.

"Do you want us to take care of him? The girl need never know. There be all of these rivers around. A man could fall in."

"Nay."

"The sword is not your weapon."

"It will not come to that."

"You are sure? He looked determined."

"I am sure."

They walked up the lane toward the house. Sieg kept looking over at him. Finally the Swede spoke. "It is an odd time to be getting married."

"Aye." And it was. Any number of carefully cultivated fields were awaiting harvesting in the next few months.

"It could make things harder," Sieg said.

"I've thought of that."

"You could put the wedding off until next winter. November maybe. All should be settled by then."

David shook his head. He realized that he was not inclined to give her lover a whole year to come back. He also already knew that he had no intention of waiting that long to take the beautiful Christiana Fitzwaryn to his bed. "Nay. It will be safer to have her at the house."

"And if there are problems . . ."

"Then the girl is doubly blessed. She gets rid of a husband whom she does not want and becomes a rich widow."

✦   ✦   ✦

A fine cold mist shrouded the Strand as the little party rode up its length. John Constantyn sat straight and proud on his horse, his fur-trimmed and bejeweled velvet robe barely covered by the bright blue cloak thrown back over his shoulders. He glanced at David's own unadorned and austere blue pourpoint.

"Thank God you at least wore that chain," John said, grinning. "They might mistake you for some gentry squire otherwise. Under the circumstances you might have fancied yourself up some, just this once. It is an odd statement that you make with your garments, David."

David would like to claim that he made no statement at all with his clothes, that their plainness merely reflected his taste, but he knew that wasn't entirely true. Refusing to compete in the nobility's game of luxury was, he supposed, a tacit repudiation of the nobleman's assumption of superior worth.

He felt the heavy gold chain on his chest, arching from shoulder to shoulder. He had even worn this with reluctance, and finally put it on only for Christiana's sake. Her friends would know its value. He would not make this day any harder for her than it promised to be already.

"You should have seen your uncle Gilbert's face when I told him what I would be doing today," John said. "By God, it was rich. Right there outside the Guildhall, I asked him if he would attend, aware that he knew nothing of it. I made him worm the details out of me bit by bit, too. At least twenty of the wardens must have overheard." John's hearty laugh echoed down the Strand. " 'Aye, Gilbert,' I said, 'didn't you know? The daughter of the famous Hugh Fitzwaryn. By the king's pleasure, no less. In the royal chapel with the royal family in attendance.' His face looked the color of ash before I was done."

David smiled at the thought of Gilbert's expression when he learned that David would marry a baron's daughter. It was the first time that this betrothal had given him any pleasure.

He hadn't spoken to any of the Abyndons since he was a youth and had fully realized what they had done to his mother. He also refused to trade with them, and never sold them any of the goods that he imported. It was a childish revenge, but the only one open to him right now. Eventually the chance would come to plant that particular field in a more appropriate way.

John smiled more soberly. "Would that my brother could see this."

Aye, David thought. *But it is just as well that he cannot.* He thought a moment about his dead master and partner, the man who had probably saved him from a life in the alleys. A good man, David Constantyn, whose faith in his young apprentice had made them both rich and permitted David to become the man he was today. He had loved his master more than a son does a father.

It was out of respect and love that he had bided his time and waited. Waited for his master's death before planting those fields that waited to be harvested now. *Better that he is not here, for there is much that honest man wouldn't like*, David thought. *But then, he was shrewd, and might not be so surprised. He probably knew what he had in me.*

They rode through the town of Westminster to the castle and buildings that housed the court and the government. David led the way to the royal chapel.

People milled around outside its doors. The King's approach caused no commotion or even much attention. Edward and Philippa led their children and their closest retainers in for the daily mass. David had no trouble locating Christiana in the group, because she wore the red cloak. Her eyes did not seek him out as she silently between Joan and Lady Idonia.

A page had reserved space for David behind the royal family. At the other end of his row stood the rigid form of Morvan Fitzwaryn. In front of him Christiana focused her attention on the priest at the altar, not once turning her head.

The mass was brief and after it the priest came down from the altar and called Christiana and himself forward. Christiana, her cloak still on to ward off the chill in the chapel, went to her brother, then the two of them joined David in front of the priest. He looked over at her and saw a vacant expression in her eyes as she trained her gaze on a spot somewhere in the distance. She looked noble and calm and emotionally void.

Morvan took her hand and placed it in David's. It felt incredibly small and soft. One slight tremble shook her arm, and then they listened to the priest's prayer before pledging their troth. She recited the words like a school lesson, her expressionless chant suggesting that they held no meaning, if indeed she even heard them.

She turned for the betrothal kiss, lifting her face dutifully but keeping her eyes downcast. David felt an odd combination of sympathy and annoyance.

In the law of the church and the realm, she belonged to him now, but she had carefully managed not to see or acknowledge him since her arrival. It had been subtle, and he knew that she had done it for her own sake and to control her own pain. She had not deliberately tried to insult him. He simply didn't matter. He doubted that anyone but Morvan had even noticed.

He suspected that Christiana sought to turn this betrothal into a dream so that she could wake when her lover came and find that it had conveniently never really happened. That he understood this girl did not mean, however, that he felt inclined to indulge her illusions with the dutiful kiss that she now offered and expected.

He did not care that the King and Queen stood nearby, nor that the angry brother watched. This was solely between him and her.

He stepped close to her and laid his hand on her cheek. A small tremor awoke beneath his touch.

The hood of her cloak still rested atop her head, hiding her hair. He could tell that she wore it unbound, a symbol of virginity, as was traditional for the ceremony. With his other hand he pushed the hood away. The thick black locks cascaded down her back, and his hand followed until he embraced her.

"Look at me, Christiana," he commanded quietly.

The black lashes fluttered. The creamy lids rose slowly. Two diamonds flashed startled alertness and fear.

He lowered his head and tasted the soft sweetness of her trembling lips.

CHAPTER 3

CHRISTIANA STUDIED THE chessboard propped on the chest between her and Joan. She shifted a pawn.

Joan quickly took one of her knights. "You are playing badly today," she said.

They sat by a window in Isabele's bedchamber. The princess had gone to visit a friend in another part of Westminster, and Lady Idonia had accompanied her.

Christiana tried to concentrate on the game and not think about her betrothal three days earlier. In particular she worked hard not to reflect on David de Abyndon, but his intense eyes and warm touch kept intruding on her memory in a distressing way. He had handled the ceremony and dinner very kindly, almost sympathetically. With one stunning exception.

"You never told me what it was like getting betrothed," Joan said.

Christiana shrugged. "I don't remember much. I was most unsettled."

Joan tossed her blond curls and her eyes twinkled. "What was the kiss like? It looked like a wonderful kiss."

Christiana stared at the chessmen scattered on the board. She had been working especially hard not to think about that kiss.

What should she say to Joan? What *could* she say? How could she explain that only the most necessary part of her had paid attention to either the mass or the pledge? That she had deliberately dulled her mind so that she would get through the morning without panicking. That she had filled her heart with Stephen and the trust and knowledge of his love, and that the whole scene in the church had only been a restless dream that would quickly fade.

Until there had been that hand on her face in a gesture of intimacy, forcing her awake as surely as a shake during the night. A voice commanding her to look reality in the face. An embrace and a kiss of masterful possession.

What was that kiss like? Confusing. Frightening. Longer than necessary. Long enough to make clear that one of them intended to treat this betrothal seriously.

The sensation of a streak of warmth flowing through her body licked at her memory. She shifted restlessly and forced all of her attention on the chess game.

Aye, she did not want to think or talk about that kiss very much at all. "It was nice enough."

At least that part of this travesty was over. Now she had only to wait for Stephen to come.

"Have you ever been kissed before?" Joan asked.

Christiana wished that she could confide in her friend, but Joan was a notorious gossip. It had, of course, crossed her mind that if Joan did gossip, and Morvan learned about Stephen, then maybe her brother would encourage the Percys to change their mind. She had immediately felt guilty for that unworthy thought. After all, she didn't want

Stephen offering for her at the point of a sword. That wouldn't be necessary anyway.

The memory of Stephen's mouth crushing hers fluttered in her mind. David's kiss hadn't been at all like that, but then they had been standing in a church in front of a king and a priest. Still . . . nay, she didn't want to think about that kiss. "I have been kissed before. Frankly, didn't like it. I think that I am one of those women who doesn't."

Joan's expression contained a touch of pity. "He is very handsome," she said after a pause. "If you have to marry a merchant, he may as well be a rich and handsome one."

Christiana knew that Joan echoed the opinion of the whole court. *Poor Christiana. A sweet girl. Too bad about the King giving her to a common merchant, but at least he is rich and handsome.* It reminded her of the encouraging sympathy offered to a maimed knight. *Too bad that you will never walk right again, but at least you are not dead.*

"Lady Elizabeth buys from him, you know," Joan added very casually. "And Lady Agnes and a few others."

Joan always managed to find out such things. In the last week she had probably learned all there was to know in Westminster about David de Abyndon. She would drop tidbits like this here and there as it suited her.

"They prefer to go to his shop, which is quite wonderful. You really should have come with us, Christiana. He brings in silks from Italy and as far away as India. There are tailors there too. The women who use him treat him like a secret and will go nowhere else. Lady Agnes says that Lady Elizabeth's whole white and silver style was his idea. I'm surprised that you never saw him before this happened if Elizabeth is one of his patrons."

Lady Elizabeth, a widow, had been a special friend of Morvan's for a number of months a year ago. She was at least ten years older than him but exquisitely beautiful. Her most notable features were her prematurely white hair and her translucent white skin. Court rumors had predicted a marriage, but then Elizabeth had accepted the offer of an elderly lord and suddenly her friendship with Morvan had cooled.

For two years now, Elizabeth had affected a highly personal style that enhanced her unique beauty. She wore only white and silvery grays. Even her jewels were reset in silver.

"Isabele is convinced that he will make you work for him," Joan giggled. "Idonia has explained that wealthy merchants don't do that, but Isabele sees the women working in the shops and thinks that you will have to as well."

Dear saints, Morvan would kill her to protect the family honor before he swallowed *that*. "It is your move, Joan," she said, deciding that it was time to end the subject.

A page entered a short time later. "My lady, your husband is in the hall and bids you to attend on him," he said to her.

She stared at the boy as if he had spoken gibberish. "Is that the message as he sent it?"

"Aye, my lady."

"I do not much like this message," she said to Joan.

"It sounds common enough to me."

"He is not my husband yet."

"Oh, Christiana, you know that betrothed couples are often referred to as husband and wife. Saturday was the first part of the ceremony, and the wedding is the conclusion. It is half done."

Not for me, she wanted to shout. *And this man knows it.*

She also didn't like, not one bit, being "bidden" to do anything by David de Abyndon. When Morvan put her hand in David's, it was symbolic of handing over authority and responsibility, but under the circumstances of this particular betrothal, that was meaningless too.

She turned to the page. "Tell my betrothed that I regret that I cannot attend on him this morning. I am grateful that he has visited, but I am not well. Tell him that I have a headache and am feeling dizzy."

"I hope that you know what you are doing," Joan said.

More to the point was the importance that David know what she was doing. She had told him that they would not see each other, and if he mistakenly thought that she meant only before the betrothal, then this should clarify it. She had no intention of explaining to Stephen when he came that she had been playing out this farce more than necessary.

A short while later their door flew open and the page reappeared, red faced and winded from running.

"My lady, your hus . . . that man is coming here."

"Coming here!"

"Aye. I handed him over to another page and sent them the long way, but he will be here soon."

She looked desperately at Joan as the page left.

"I thought that you knew what you were doing," Joan said, laughing.

She jumped up. "Help me. Quickly." She ran into the bedchamber's anteroom and threw back the coverlet on her bed. "Tuck me in and close the curtains. Try not to let any of my gown show."

"This isn't going to work." Joan giggled as she poked the coverlet around her neck and sides.

"Tell him that I am resting and send him away."

Joan grinned and pulled the curtains.

Christiana lay absolutely still in the dark shadows of the bed. She could hear Joan walking around, humming a melody. She felt a little ridiculous doing this, but something deep inside her said that she should not see this man again.

Even though her curtains muffled the sounds, she heard the boots walking into the room.

"Master David!" Joan cried brightly.

"Lady Joan. You, at least, appear to be well."

Christiana sighed. This man's quiet, beautiful voice had a talent for putting a lot of meaning into simple words without so much as changing its inflection. It was very clear that he knew that she lied about being ill, but then she had counted on him seeing that. She just hadn't counted on him coming to confront her and thus forcing her to pretend that she hadn't lied.

"Indeed I am very well, David. And you?"

"Well enough, my lady. Although I find myself recently more short of temper than is normal."

"No doubt it is something that you ate."

"No doubt."

Boots paced across the floor. "I am told that Christiana is ill."

"Aye. She is resting, David, and really should not be disturbed."

"What is the malady?"

"It was really quite frightening. When she awoke this morning she was overcome with dizziness. She almost fell. We put her right back to bed, of course, and that seems to help. She could be abed for days, even weeks."

Don't overdo it. Christiana prompted silently.

"It sounds most serious," David said. "Such an illness is not to be taken lightly. Perhaps I should pay the abbey monks to say masses on her behalf."

"We are very worried, but I trust all will be well soon. We will be sure to send word to you when she is better."

"Is this her bed? I will see her before I go."

"I really don't think that will be wise, David," Joan said hurriedly. "The light seems to make it worse."

A clever touch, Christiana thought approvingly. But not clever enough. "I will be quick."

Even with her eyes closed, Christiana saw the light flood over her as the curtains were pushed back.

She gasped as he took her firmly by the waist, lifted her up, and dropped her on her back.

She lowered her lids as if the light hurt them, and moaned for effect. She hoped that she looked suitably pale and ill.

David gave her hip a gentle whack, gesturing for her to move over. Biting back her indignation, she scooted a little and he sat on the edge of the bed.

"Well, Christiana, I am very concerned. A headache and dizziness. You seem to have a serious illness indeed."

That hardness around his mouth seemed a bit more pronounced. Something in his expression suggested that he was capable of being the exact opposite of the kindly merchant whom she had first expected.

He rubbed her cheek with the backs of his fingers. "No fever. All the same, I think that we should have a physician see you at once."

"I am sure that isn't necessary." She tried to make her voice a little weak but not too much so. "I am feeling better, and I am sure that this will pass."

He ignored her. "I will have to ask around and see which of the ones at court are any good. Some of these physicians immediately want to bleed the patient, and that is so painful. We would like to avoid it if possible, don't you think?"

She had been bled once when she was eleven. She thought that avoiding it was an excellent idea.

"On the other hand, headaches and dizziness are probably caused by the humors that require it."

"I really find that I am feeling much better. The light doesn't bother me at all now."

"The idea of being bled always makes one feel better, my girl, but it doesn't last. However, if you think that you are recovering a little for now, I would really prefer to get you dressed and take you to see a Saracen physician whom I know in Southwark. He is an expert in ladies' illnesses, and treats all of the whores in the Stews. He is very skilled."

"A Saracen! A whores' physician!" She completely forgot to make her voice weak at all.

"Aye. Trained in Alexandria. Saracen physicians are much better than Christians. We are barbarians in comparison."

"I assure you that going to Southwark is not needed, David. Truly, I am feeling enormously better. Quite myself, in fact. I am confident that I am completely cured."

He smiled slowly. "Are you? That is good news. However, you must be sure to let me know if these spells return. I will be sure to get you to a physician immediately. I am responsible for you now, and would not have your health neglected."

She glared at him. This "husband" who had "bid her attend on him" was reminding her of his rights and warning her not to play this game again. She could think of nicer ways to have made the point without threatening to have her arm cut open.

He rose. Apparently his oblique scolding was finished, and Christiana felt confident that he would leave. She glanced at Joan triumphantly.

David looked down at her. "The day is fair. Perhaps all that you need is some fresh air to clear your head."

"I'm not at all sure . . ."

His gaze lit on the closest ambry. "Are your things in here? We will get you dressed and I will take you out for a while."

She narrowed her eyes at David's handsome face. One farce after another. She couldn't claim to be too dizzy to go out but also too well to see a physician. He had cleverly, elegantly manipulated her ruse against her.

"I am already dressed," she announced, throwing back the coverlet and sitting up, admitting defeat.

"So you are," he said quietly, coming toward her with a vague smile on his face and her old cloak in his hand. "What a disappointment. I was looking forward to that part."

That smile made her very uncomfortable. She would admit defeat, but not surrender. "Unfortunately," she said regretfully, "I cannot go with you. It is a rule. None of us can be with a man alone."

Joan nodded her head vigorously in support.

"Lady Idonia is gone, and unfortunately Joan has to meet with her brother soon," she added.

Joan continued nodding even though she had no such plans.

"It is a most serious prohibition," she emphasized. "As you can imagine, the consequences for disobeying are dire."

"Dire," Joan echoed helpfully.

David gave them both a look that indicated he thought that consequences had not been nearly dire enough for the two of them over the years.

"I might risk it, except that the Queen is most strict and . . ." She threw up her hands.

David flipped the cloak out and around her shoulders. He bent to pin the brooch under her neck. His closeness, and his hands working near her body, made her yet more uncomfortable.

"I am not just a man, I am your betrothed. What is the worst that can happen? If I ravish you, it simply means that the marriage is finalized that much earlier. Perhaps they would thank me for taking you off their hands. Besides, it is for me to punish your future bad behavior and not Lady Idonia and the Queen."

He was talking to her like a child again. In fact, he was dressing her like a child. Furthermore, this was his second reference to *that*, and she really could do without his innuendos. They prodded at something inside her that she didn't want to think about. Since they insinuated a familiarity that simply wasn't going to develop, she thought that it would be nice if they didn't even jest about it.

This merchant's presumptions indicated that he was taking his betrothal rights far too seriously. She did not want to be alone with David de Abyndon any longer than necessary, and she had ruined the chance of getting Joan to come with them. While he put on his own cloak, she caught Joan's attention.

Idonia, she mouthed.

She stood up to leave. With a smooth movement David bent and scooped her into his arms. She cried a startled "Oh!" and stared at him.

"I can walk." She fumed when he laughed.

"There are steps. If you get dizzy again, you might fall and break your neck."

"It is more likely that you will drop me."

"Nonsense. You are very light."

"Oh, dear saints," she groaned, letting her head fall back in exasperation. "Well, at least go down the back stairs to the entrance there. I don't want the whole court to see this."

As he carried her out, she turned her head and looked desperately back at Joan.

Send Idonia, she mouthed again.

He set her down at the back entrance that led to a small courtyard beneath Isabele's windows.

"There are some benches here and the sun is warm against that wall," she suggested. "Let us sit here."

"I think that we would prefer to take a ride."

Idonia would never find them and rescue her then. "*I* would prefer to sit here."

"Soon the shadows will move over that wall, and then you will get chilled. A ride in the sun will be better."

Walking beside him around the corner of the manor, she wondered if all men got so willful after one got betrothed to them. Would Stephen stop speaking pretty words when they were married? Was that just something done beforehand to lure women? The chansons weren't much help with this question. The couples in those romantic songs were never married. She immediately felt guilty for equating Stephen with this merchant. Stephen was a chivalrous knight, and poetry and romance flowed in his blood.

David took the reins of his horse from the young groom who had been holding them.

"I will send for a mount from the stables," she said.

"You will ride with me. One of the problems with being dizzy is that you cannot ride a horse unattended for a while." He lifted her up to the front of the saddle and swung up behind her.

She had never sat on a horse with a man before. The perch up front was a little precarious, especially if one leaned forward as she strained to do. This promised to be backbreaking and her mood did not improve.

They rode out the castle gate and turned upriver. The road grew deserted once they moved away from the castle and town. A few carts straggled past, and in the river an occasional barge drifted by. They were less than two miles from London's wall, but suddenly a world away.

They rode in silence for about a quarter of a mile. Christiana focused her attention on avoiding any contact with the man a hair's breadth behind her. Her back ached from the effort.

Suddenly and without warning, David pushed the horse to a faster walk. That did it. The gait threw her backward against his chest and shoulders. His arm slid around her waist. She tensed in surprise as that peculiar intensity flowed and embraced her more surely than his arm.

She noticed the solidity of his support and became acutely aware of his arm resting lightly across her waist. She looked down at the beautiful masculine hand gently holding her, and felt the soft pressure of his fingers as he steadied her. There was something tantalizing about his warmth along her back.

The oddest tremor swept through her. She tensed again.

"Are you afraid of me, Christiana?" he asked.

His face was very close to her head, and his voice barely louder than a whisper. His breath drifted over her temple, carrying his words. The warm sound mixed with the warm air and caressed her as surely as if fingers had touched her. Despite that warmth, a chill trembled down her neck and back. A very peculiar chill.

"Of course not."

"You act as if you are."

He had noticed the tremors, she thought, a little horrified but not sure why.

"I am a bit cold is all."

In response he drew the edges of his own cloak around her.

He seemed closer now. She could feel the muscles of his chest all along her back. His breath grazed her hair, making her scalp tingle. He was virtually a stranger, and the subtle intimacy of being cocooned inside his cloak with him did make her a little fearful now, but of what she couldn't say. She squirmed to let him know that she wanted him to let go.

He did not release her. Instead he bent his body over hers. Soft hair brushed against her cheek before he turned his head to kiss her neck.

The heat of his lips against her skin produced an incredible shock. He kissed her again, increasing the pressure, and the warmth of that mouth penetrated her skin, flowed down her neck and arms, and streaked through her chest and belly. The pure physicality of the sensation stunned her.

His arm pulled her tighter. His lips moved up her neck. Quivering, delicious tremors coursed through her. He nipped lightly along the edge of her ear. A hollow tension exploded, shaking her, and she gasped.

The sound woke her from the sensual daze. She turned her head away from his mouth. "Now I am afraid of you," she said.

"That was not fear."

She pushed against his arm. "I want to get down. This familiarity is wrong."

"We are betrothed."

"Not really."

"Very really."

"Not in my mind, and you know it. I want to get down. Now. I want to walk for a while."

He stopped the horse and swung off. She braced herself for his anger as she turned to be lifted down, but he only smiled and fell into step beside her.

Even walking apart from him, she could still feel the pull of that unsettling intimacy. This man had made her feel uncomfortable and vulnerable from the first time she had seen him, and it wasn't getting any better.

She felt an urgent need to banish the last few minutes from their memories, and took refuge in conversation to do so.

"Lady Idonia told me that the Abyndons are an aldermanic family in London."

"My uncle Stephen was an alderman about ten years ago, at the time that he died. I have an uncle Gilbert who would like to be."

"He did not come Saturday."

"We are estranged."

"And your parents did not come. Are they dead or are you estranged from them too?"

He didn't answer right away. "They did not tell you much about me, did they? My mother is dead. I do not know my father. Abyndon is my mother's name."

He was a bastard. Of all of the topics to choose for conversation, this had probably been the worst.

"Your brother knows of this," he added.

"It is a common thing. He would not find it worthwhile to comment upon it to me." That was a courteous lie, of course. It wasn't *that* common.

"Is there anything else you want to know about me?"

She thought a moment. "How old are you?"

"Twenty-nine."

"And you were an apprentice until twenty-five?"

"Actually, twenty-four."

"So how did you get so rich so fast?"

He laughed a little. A nice laugh. Quiet. "It is a long story."

"Not too long, if you are only twenty-nine."

He laughed again. "My master, David Constantyn, bought his goods from traders who came to England. Italians mostly, from Genoa and Venice. When I was about Andrew's age, twenty, I convinced him to send me to Flanders to purchase some wool directly. The prices at which we sell are regulated, so the only way to make more profit is to buy more cheaply."

"Your trip was successful?"

"Very much so. We did that for a year. Then, one day he came to me and agreed on another idea I had proposed. He gave me a large amount of money to try my luck elsewhere. I was gone for three years, and visited many of the ports around the Inland Sea. I sent back goods, became friends with men who became our agents, and established a trading network. We had a large advantage after that."

He told his tale as if men did this all of the time, but of course they did not and even a girl like her knew it. "You were still his apprentice then?"

"In the eyes of law. But he had been more like a father to me for years. As soon as I received the city's freedom and citizenship, he made me his partner. He was a widower and had no children, and left me his property upon his death. His wealth went to charity and for prayers for his soul."

She hadn't thought of a merchant as an adventurer. In her world only a knight errant or crusader might wander thus. "Where are some of the places that you traveled to?"

"I went by ship down the coast of the Aquitane and Castile and into the Inland Sea through the Pillars of Hercules. Then along the coast of the Dark Continent first."

"Saracen lands!"

"One must trade with Saracens to get anything from the East."

"It must have been dangerous."

"Only once. In Egypt. I stayed too long there. The ports welcome traders and depend on them. No one wants to discourage commerce by killing merchants. After Egypt, I went up to Tripoli and Constantinople, then sailed to Genoa. I came back through France."

She pictured the maps of the Inland Sea that she had seen. She imagined him riding through deserts and passing over the Alps. She glanced at the daggers he wore. One was a decorative eating tool, but the other was large and lethal looking.

"It still sounds dangerous. And very risky." Actually it sounded wonderfully exciting and adventurous.

"The risk was real enough, but mostly financial. David Constantyn was probably a bit of a fool to agree to it. Only as I see Andrew approaching the same age do I see the faith that he had."

"Will you have Andrew do as you did?"

"Nay. But I will send him to Genoa soon, where the agents send their goods for shipment here. I need a man there, I think, so that I do not have to travel down every other year."

There were many Florentine bankers and Italian traders in London, and tales of that sunny land had filtered through the court over the years. She felt a little envious of Andrew. The idea of spending her years embroidering in one of Stephen's drafty castles suddenly seemed very dull.

"I came to speak with you about something, Christiana," he said. "I was at Westminster to discuss the wedding. The spring and early summer are out of the question. There will be times when I will be out of London unexpectedly."

Spring and summer were the times when many trading fairs were held. Presumably he would need to attend some.

"Next fall, then," she offered. "October or November."

"I think not. Before Lent. The end of February."

"Five weeks hence! That is too soon!"

"How so?"

She glared at him. They had been having such a nice talk, too. He knew "how so." She marched on a little quicker, her gaze fixed on the road ahead.

He kept up by simply lengthening his stride. Finally his quiet voice flowed around her. "I said that I would step aside if this man comes, but you cannot expect me to arrange my life for his convenience. If he wants you, he will be here very soon."

She turned on him. "You are conceited and arrogant and I hate you. You are deliberately doing this to make things difficult for me."

"Nay. I only seek to avoid difficulties for myself that might complicate my business affairs. Five weeks is enough time for a man to decide that he wants a woman. I made my decision in a matter of days. A man in love should be even quicker."

He didn't think that Stephen would come, and now he had created a test for him. How dare he claim to know the heart of a chivalrous knight! How dare he compare himself to him! Stephen was as different from this mercer as a destrier from a palfrey. The same animal, but different breeds with different duties.

"Five weeks, my lady," he repeated firmly. He glanced up at the sun. "Now we must ride back. I have a meeting this afternoon."

He brought up the horse and lifted her up. She kept

her back very straight all of the way home to West-minster.

In the back courtyard they found Lady Idonia sitting by the wall. She rose at once and came toward them.

David dismounted and brought Christiana down. He turned to the guardian. "You decided to take some air, too, my lady? The day is fair, is it not?"

Lady Idonia did her best. "You should not have taken Christiana out with her illness. Her dizziness was most severe."

David slung an arm around Christiana's shoulders. It was a casual gesture, but it very effectively kept her from bolting. "Your solicitous concern for my betrothed moves me, my lady. But I have something to say to Christiana in private. Perhaps you would wait inside the entrance for her."

Idonia flustered in response to this blunt dismissal, glanced sharply at Christiana, and stomped off.

David dropped his arm and turned to her. "I will visit you next week."

Stephen would come soon, but not that soon. She really did not want to spend more time with David. It felt like a betrayal of her love. "That is not necessary," she said.

"It may not be necessary, but for your sake it is pru-dent. You expect your lover to come, but what if he does not?"

"He will come."

"And if not?"

His insistence irritated her. "What of it?"

"Then in five weeks you wed me, my girl. Just in case, shouldn't we spend this time getting to know one another? It is what betrothals are for."

But I am not really betrothed, she thought, eyeing him obstinately. *Not in my heart or mind.*

"Christiana, if you do not want to meet again until the wedding, that is how it will be. Yet think about it, girl. Going to bed with a stranger will not bother me at all, but you may find the experience distressing."

Her mouth fell open in shock at this blunt reminder of the marriage bed. Memories of herself with Stephen flew rapidly through her mind. He had not been a stranger, and she quickly relived the shock of his ferocious passion, the crushing insistence of his kisses, the almost horrible intimacy of his hand on her nakedness.

She stared up at David de Abyndon, noting the frank and open way that he watched her. It was cruel of him to make her think about this and face the possible conclusion of this betrothal. All the same, her mind involuntarily began to substitute him for Stephen in those memories. She was appalled that it had no trouble doing so and that the strange feelings that he summoned tried to attach themselves to the ghostlike fantasy. She shook those thoughts away. The whole notion was indeed distressing. And very frightening.

Five weeks.

"Am I supposed to wait upstairs for you to come and 'bid me to attend'?" she asked sarcastically.

"Let us say that I will come on Mondays. If I cannot, I will send word. If you are ill again, send a message to me."

She nodded and turned toward the door. She wanted to be done with this man today. She wanted to cleanse her mind of what it had just imagined.

He caught her arm and pulled her back. With gentle but firm movements he clasped her in an embrace.

A surging desperation claimed her. She remembered the betrothal ceremony and she knew, she just knew, that it was vital, essential, that he not kiss her again. She struggled against his arms and almost cried out for Idonia. As his head bent to hers, she twisted to avoid him.

His lips found hers anyway and connected with a grazing brush that wasn't even a kiss. She felt that same, warm soothing lightness again and again on her cheek and brow and neck. In spite of her love for Stephen, in spite of her anger at this man's intrusion into her life, she calmed beneath the repeated caress of his mouth as ripples of sensation flowed through her. Her awareness dulled to everything but those compelling feelings.

When he finally stopped, she wasn't struggling anymore. A little dazed, she looked up at him. The perfect planes of his face appeared tighter than usual, and he looked in her eyes with a commanding gaze that seemed to speak a language that she didn't understand. She knew that he was going to kiss her and that she should get away, but when he lowered his mouth to hers, she couldn't resist at all.

It was a beautiful kiss, full of warmth and promise. It deepened slowly and he held her head in one hand, the other arm lifting her into it. The waves of sensation flowed higher and stronger, carrying her toward a delicious oblivion.

He released the pressure on her mouth and took one lip, then the other, gently between his teeth. A sharper warmth shot down the center of her body. It was a stunning quiver of pleasurable discomfort that seemed to reach completely through her. Less gently, he kissed each pulse point on her neck, and it happened again and again, each time stronger, the compelling discomfort growing.

He lifted his head and looked down at her, his mouth set in a hard line with the lips slightly parted. He looked gloriously handsome like that.

"You make me forget myself," he said, his fingers stretching through her hair.

Their surroundings slowly intruded. Her position,

arching acceptingly into his embrace, suddenly became apparent, too.

Horrified, she abruptly disentangled herself. He let her go. With a very red face she hurried to the door. Lady Idonia waited there. She looked up sharply. " 'Send Idonia to save me,' " she mimicked. "I sat out there almost an hour, worried for you, although why I don't know, since you are marrying the man. Then you return and what do I see? Keep that up, girl, and there will be no need for a wedding at all."

Christiana blushed deeper. A profound sense of guilt swept through her. She loved Stephen. How could she be so faithless? How could she let this man kiss her like that? Even if he forced her to it, how could she let those feelings undo her so outrageously?

She followed Idonia up the stairs, more confused and frightened than she had been on her betrothal day. This was wrong. She must never let it happen again. She must be sure that she was never again alone with this merchant.

At the second-level landing, she paused and looked out the small window to the courtyard below. David was just mounting his horse to leave. As he began riding away, a movement at the end of the courtyard caught her attention. A man stepped away from the building and toward David's approaching horse.

David stopped and spoke with the man for a moment, then made to move on. But the man followed alongside, speaking and gesturing. Finally David dismounted. He tied his reins to a post and disappeared behind the building, following the man.

Christiana frowned. They had been some distance away, but she felt sure that she recognized the man. He was the French-speaking diplomat who had passed her alcove in the King's passageway the morning after she had met David.

CHAPTER 4

DAVID STOOD AT the threshold between the solar and the bedchamber and studied the woman whom Sieg had just brought upstairs. She was still an attractive lady, but thirteen years take their toll on anyone. He hadn't realized back then how young she must have been. No more than twenty-five at the time, he would judge now. Still, he would remember her anywhere.

She hadn't noticed him, and he watched her glide around the solar, fingering the carving on the chairs and examining the tapestry on the wall. She touched the glazing in the windows much as Christiana had done that first night.

He would not think about Christiana now. If he did, he suspected that he might not go through with this. He had already spent more time the last week thinking of those diamond eyes than about the carefully planned harvest of justice that he would reap this afternoon. The last thing he wanted now was the thought of a good woman making him weak with a bad one.

The woman's face looked paler than her hands, and he could tell that she used wheat flour to make it so. An artful touch of paint flushed her cheeks and colored her lips. If he gave a damn, he would find a kind way to tell her that the coloring was a bit too strong for the honey hair that had begun to dull with age. He suspected that this was one of those women who looks in the mirror a lot but never really sees what is reflected there.

He shifted his weight silently but it drew her attention anyway. Amber cat eyes turned and regarded him. He saw the brief scrutiny and then the slow relief. *Aye*, he thought, *if this woman whores for a man, she prefers him young and handsome*. She continued looking at him and he noticed the total absence of recognition.

"David de Abyndon?" she asked. Her eyes narrowed and a thin smile stretched her mouth.

"Lady Catherine. I'm sorry that I could not see you sooner."

She misunderstood and, flattered, smiled more naturally.

He gestured and she joined him at the doorway. When she saw it was a bedchamber, she glanced at him, reproving him for his lack of subtlety.

She entered slowly and again she took in the details of the room, calculating their value. Time and again her gaze rested on the large tub set before the hearth. It had been brought in by the servants before David dismissed all of them for the afternoon. If they wondered why he wanted it here and not in the wardrobe where it belonged, they hadn't said so.

It had been filled with water, and more water was heating by the hearth. David lifted the buckets and poured them into the tub.

She watched him with amusement. "Perhaps I came too early."

"This is for you."

"You thought that I would be unclean?"

You are so unclean that all of the water in the world would not cleanse you. "Nay. But I remember how much you enjoy baths and sought to indulge you."

She frowned and looked at him more closely. A spark of memory tried to catch flame, but he watched it die.

"My husband assumed . . ."

"I know what your husband assumed. But we do it this way or not at all." He leaned against the hearth wall and waited.

A little flustered, but not too much so, she began to remove her clothing. She carefully folded the bejeweled surcoat and placed it on the nearby stool. The beautiful cotehardie followed. Rich fabrics. He had no trouble calculating how many of her husband's debts were devoted to her wardrobe.

She untied her garters and peeled off her hose. He noted her lack of embarrassment. He was by far not the first stranger she had stripped for.

The shift dropped to the floor and she looked at him boldly. He gestured to the tub and she stepped in with clear irritation.

She settled down. She was childless and her body was still youthful. Her full breasts bobbed in the high water.

"Well?" she asked.

"Your husband sent you here to ask something of me. To negotiate for him, did he not?"

She gestured with exasperation at the tub.

David smiled. "I only do this to give you every advantage, my lady. I remember that you negotiate best when you are thus."

Again that scrutiny. Again the flame of recognition that died before it caught fire. She became all business.

"My husband says that you have bought up all of his debts."

The man had amassed debts to merchants and bankers over the last few years. When he had resorted to borrowing from one to pay another, when the financial market in London had realized that he tottered on the edge of ruin, David had bought the loans at a deep discount. He had not even gone looking for today's justice. It had simply fallen into his lap, one of Fortune's many gifts to him.

"He needs time to repay them."

"They are long overdue, as I have explained to him."

"He thought that you might be more reasonable with me. I have come to ask for an extension. The properties have been less productive of late, but that should improve."

"They are less productive because they are neglected and mismanaged. Already the ones that I hold have improved."

"The loans were made with the promise that the property you hold now would be returned to us."

"Only if the loans are repaid." He paused. "I think that we might be able to work something out about the loans and the property, however. Is there anything else that you require?"

Her face lightened. It was going better than she thought it would. "Aye. We need a further loan. A small one. As a bridge until things work out."

This husband placed a high value indeed on his wife's favors. "You are asking me to throw good money after bad."

"You will be repaid in full."

"Madam, your husband gambles. You are extravagant. Both vices are rarely conquered. I will consider the extension of the old loans, but in truth you will never repay them. Why would I now give you more?"

She looked at him boldly and a small smile formed on her tinted lips. Slowly, expertly, she shifted in the tub so that he had a full view of her body.

The years fell away. He was in another chamber standing in front of a younger woman. She was a frequent visitor to the shop, but when she had come this day, David Constantyn had not been in. She bought expensive cloths and paid with a tally as was the habit of such women, but then insisted that the young apprentice deliver the goods that afternoon to her manor in Hampstead where the tally would be made good.

He had gone. Like others before him, he had innocently ridden the five miles north to Hampstead.

She had received him in her chamber, lying in a tub much as she did now. Pretending to ignore his presence, she had demanded that her servants open and examine the purchases while he waited. All the while she had bathed herself, slowly and languidly, occasionally looking at him with a challenging stare that dared him to react to her nakedness.

He did not. He was randy enough at sixteen and not inexperienced, but he held his body in check. At first his dismay and shock helped him. His knowledge of females consisted of the happy servant girls with whom coupling was a form of joyful play. Instinctively he knew that this woman was nothing like that and that she tempted him to something other than pleasure.

But as she continued displaying herself, it was anger that kept him in control. He turned away from her. He did not like playing the mouse to this cat woman. He resented her using her position and degree to humiliate him.

Finally he could tell that she grew angry too. She addressed him directly and began to renegotiate the price of the goods. She pursued the subject a long while, refusing to pay the whole tally, demanding his attention. Finally, he had to look at her, and as he did she raised one leg to the side of the tub and exposed herself.

He lost control then, but not in the way that she expected. He let his face show what he thought, but it was not the desire she demanded. He looked down at her and let her see his utter disgust before he walked out.

He had almost reached the road before her men came and dragged him back. They tied him to a metal ring set in the trunk of an oak tree in the garden. Before the lash fell, he looked over his shoulder and saw her honey hair at a window.

"You do not remember me," he said. "But then, there were a number of us, why would you remember one?"

Over the years, they had found each other, the boys now grown to men whom she had ensnared in her web. The woman's unhealthy appetite was not discussed openly, but it was not unknown. It was why David Constantyn had never let his apprentices serve her or deliver goods.

But he was the one who had not played her game as she wanted it, and so the lash fell harder on him than those others whose only crime had been to show the lust that she demanded and then punished while she watched from her bower window. He had been flogged once in Egypt, but it was this first time that had scarred his back. His youth had been beaten out of him that day.

He regarded her impassively, watching her study him hard. This time the spark of memory caught hold and her eyes flamed with recognition. Her gaze slowly swept the room as she calculated her danger. She collected herself.

"You were compensated," she said coolly.

Aye, he had been compensated. When he staggered back home and his master saw his condition, that good man had done what no other master or father had done. Going to the city courts the next day, he petitioned against this woman and forced the mayor to address the issue. After a long while, the husband had been made to pay fifty pounds. David had refused to touch the money.

"The others were not. And it is not a debt that money settles anyway."

She glared at him angrily before calming herself. She glanced at the bed and then eyed him with a question.

"Aye, that too. But if you want this extension, I have other terms. I will extend the loans in return for the Hampstead manor and property, and for one hour of your time."

"The Hampstead lands belong to me, not my husband. They were not pledged as surety for any loans."

"I know that they are yours. In return for them, however, I will in fact forgive the loans, not just extend them." He smiled. "See how well you negotiate? Already I have conceded much more than I had planned."

He saw her weighing certain ruin against the property. If he called the loans, she would have to sell it anyway.

"Why do you want that house? Why not another? Are you going to burn it or something?"

"Nay. We merchants are very practical people. We rarely destroy property. It is a very beautiful house and I have admired it. I will have need of a country home near London soon. I hold no grudge against a building."

"And the hour of my time?"

"That is for the other debt. You will go to a place that I tell you. There a man will flog you just as you watched others flogged for your pleasure. Ten lashes."

Her eyes flew open in shock. He noted her reaction with relief. Those who took pleasure in pain often went both ways, and he did not want her to get perverse enjoyment out of this.

"I didn't realize that we had so much in common," she finally said.

"We have nothing in common. I will not be there, although some of the others might be. They will be told of this and may want to see it. I would demand your husband do it, as he should have long ago, but he knows what he has in you, and if he started he might not stop. It is justice we seek, not revenge or your husband's satisfaction."

She abruptly rose from the tub. She stepped out and began to dry herself. Her hurried, angry movements gradually slowed, however, and the expression on her face changed. He saw her considering, calculating, planning the final negotiation that, if executed well enough, might change everything.

He realized with surprise that he had totally lost interest in taking her humiliation any further.

He removed a small purse from the front of his pourpoint. It contained exactly the difference between the value of the loans and the Hampstead property. He dropped the purse on top of her garments. "It is the money that you seek but not a loan. That would be bad business. However, I always pay for my whores whether I use them or not."

He walked to the door. "A week hence, madam. The time and place will be sent to you. Afterward husband can contact me about settling the loans and property."

Her voice, harsh and ugly, ripped across the chamber. "There will be a new debt to settle after this, you bastard son of a whore!"

He paused. Justice, not revenge, he reminded himself. Still . . .

"Fifteen lashes, I think now, my lady. The last five for the insult to my mother."

He strode out through the solar and hall and left the house.

✦   ✦   ✦

The sky had clouded over and a light snow was falling by the time David reined in his horse outside the tavern. To his right, along the Southwark docks, small craft of all types bobbed. Stretched out in front of them rose the small houses where the prostitutes of the Stews plied their trade. Even at night these docks would be full, for the city discouraged crossing the river after dark and it was traditional for these women to have their customers stay until dawn.

The rude tavern was dark and musty with river damp. David let his eyes adjust, and then walked to a corner table.

"You are late," the man sitting there said.

David slid onto the bench. "Oliver, you are the most punctual whoremonger I have ever met."

Oliver passed him a cup of ale, drank some of his own, and wiped his black mustache and beard on his sleeve. "I am a busy man, David. Time is money."

"Your woman's time is money, Oliver, not yours. How is Anne?"

Oliver shrugged. "She doesn't like the winter. The nights are too long in her opinion."

She would probably move to Cock Lane soon. It was right outside the city wall and the women there worked differently than here in Southwark. But then, they also had to deal with the city laws. Southwark, across the Thames from London, was a town apart and close to lawless.

He looked at Oliver's wiry thin body and long black hair. They had known each other since boyhood, when they had played and scrapped in the streets and alleys together. On occasion during those carefree days, they had met danger side by side. But then Oliver's poor family had moved up to Hull and David had been plucked from those alleys and sent to school and into trade.

They had met again when Oliver returned to London several years ago. David had recognized at once that he had found a man whom he could trust. Like Sieg, Oliver might do a criminal's deeds sometimes, but he lived by a code of loyalty and fairness that would put most knights to shame. Since then, they had again on occasion met danger side by side.

The decision for Anne to become a prostitute had simply been the easiest of several choices available to them when they had come back to London. Anne had already decided that the winter nights were too long when he had met them a short while later. Still, she probably earned three times as much on her back than she and Oliver could together through honest labor. The odd jobs Oliver did for him and others helped some.

He wondered how he was going to explain Oliver and Anne to Christiana. Sieg's story would be strange enough when she finally realized that he wasn't a typical servant.

"Has he spoken to you?" Oliver asked.

"Twice. The last time just this morning."

"I have followed him like you said. He spoke to a ship's master yesterday. I think that he will sail back soon."

"He will need to. I expect that he will seek me out one more time, though, and delay his trip until I will talk to him at length. He has only felt me out so far, and has not achieved what he came for."

"You think that it is set, then?"

"I think so. I refused him, but I left the door open."

Oliver shook his head. "I am not convinced. His actions have been very normal. He goes to merchants and other places of business. That is all."

"His offer to me has been subtle so far but unmistakable. He appears to be a merchant because he is one. Except for the letter for Edward and his mission with me, he is here for trade. It is the whole point. Whenever

I go to France or Flanders, I go for trade, too." He stretched out his legs beneath the table. "Speaking of which, tell Albin that I will need to go over in about a week or so."

"Running from your duel?" Oliver asked with a grin.

"Before that. After he talks with me but before my wedding. I want to sail along the coast."

"You are pushing things, my friend," Oliver said, laughing. "Wait until after you marry this princess. Tempt fate and you might find yourself caught in bad seas for a week and miss the ceremony. That will take some explaining, I'll warrant."

David looked away. Sieg had been right. It was a bad time to be getting married. Oliver was right, too. He should wait until after the wedding to sail the coast. But it needed to be done soon, and he had no intention of leaving Christiana for a while after she came to him. This girl, and the growing desire he felt for her, were complicating things.

Her eyes were faceted jewels full of bright reflections. A man could lose his soul in eyes like that.

For one thing, he had begun to lose interest in these subtle and dangerous plans that he had laid and in which Oliver played a role. He had finally admitted that to himself as he rode over here today, and had been astonished to discover it. After all, he had been slowly planting this particular field for almost two years. A piece of information here, a deliberate slip there. It had worked because people like himself were quick to notice mistakes and weakness and potential advantage, and he knew that he dealt with a man very much like himself. In fact, matching wits with him should be a pleasure in itself, and the final justice much more satisfying than the rather thin contentment he had felt with Lady Catherine today.

Instead, he was losing interest and even considering cutting things short just as they reached the critical moves. His own plans and Edward's had become so intertwined that he had pondered at length whether it would be possible to extricate one from the other. That he even considered such a thing had to do with Christiana. She had him thinking of the future more than the past. He already felt responsibility for her. He considered far too often what it would mean for her if in the end he lost this game.

He had changed his testament so that she would be a wealthy widow if something went wrong. Funds would be on account with Florentine bankers too. When the time came, he would give Sieg and Oliver instructions for getting her out of the country if that became necessary. But all of that would never compensate her if he failed.

Her gestures were full of elegance and poise, her hands and arms beautifully angled like a dancer's. It was the way that she moved that made her appear fragile.

She still expected that her lover would come for her. He didn't doubt her resolve on that for one moment.

Stephen Percy. Learning the man's name and something of his character had been easy enough, but the knowledge only confirmed David's initial instincts about the affair. Christiana was in for a bad disappointment.

That her heart would break soon went without saying, but when would she see the truth behind illusions? Two weeks? A month? Never? The last possible. A girl's first love could be a blind thing, and she was convinced that she was in love with this man. Accepting the truth could well be impossible. God knew he had seen that before.

So young Percy doesn't come for her. Then what? A marriage full of cold duty? He smiled thinly at the thought. He knew well what happened in such unions. The men found mistresses quickly or spent too many nights with the prostitutes on Cock Lane. The more honest wives absorbed themselves with religion or their children.

And the braver and bolder women ... well, they eventually found their ways to the beds of men like David de Abyndon.

He felt her thin, lithe body against his. He sensed her responses to him, and her fear of them. A tremor flowed through her and into him, and he had wanted to kiss her again and again.

He had enough experience to recognize the possibilities which those tremors had revealed. But then, he had already sensed them that night in his solar.

In his memory's eye he saw her sparkling eyes and pale skin and the wide mouth that he couldn't see without wanting to kiss. He imagined her walking toward him, naked and inviting, that beautiful face and mouth finally turned up willingly to his.

But then her image grew hazy and dim, and another woman's face replaced it. Gaunt and tired, this face was beautiful too despite its weariness. Resting on a pillow with golden brown hair encircling it like a halo, its eyes were finally closed to disappointment and disillusion.

The image fell away and he could see the entire chamber with its flickering candles and the white sheets on the bed. Clothes hung on pegs along a wall and a fire burned too hotly in the hearth. And sitting on the bed, his graying head buried in that lifeless breast, bent the anguished figure of David Constantyn.

He hadn't realized until then how much the man had loved her. At night when the house was dark, did he go to her? Did she go to him? Had she slept with him? God, but he hoped so.

He firmly set aside consideration of the risks that had meant nothing before he met Christiana.

For both of them, then, he thought.

"If you refuse this merchant, do you think the other will come?" Oliver asked.

"He will come," David said. "I would come. Keep your ears and those of your listeners open, Oliver. Not just for that, by the way. Stay around the pilgrims' taverns. I seek news from Northumberland."

"Any particular news?"

"There is a knight named Stephen Percy. If he comes to Westminster, I want to know right away. Or if you hear anything else about that family."

Oliver raised an eyebrow. "And if this man comes?"

David saw the look and knew at once that Sieg had already told Oliver of his interest in Sir Stephen. No doubt they guessed that he had something to do with Christiana.

He remembered Sieg's offer to deal with Morvan, and knew that Oliver was making the same suggestion now. It was not in their natures to do such things, but out of friendship for him they would do them anyway. Their loyalty could be burdensome at times. He had enough trouble battling his own inclinations without having to worry about the souls of the men who served him.

He thought about his promise to step aside. It had been a moment of weakness while gazing at a lovely face. His eye for beauty drove him from one bad bargain to another sometimes, especially when he negotiated for something that he wanted to keep for himself. Fortunately, Percy would not return and test his honesty to that promise. All the same . . .

"Just let me know at once," he said. "I will decide then."

CHAPTER 5

CHRISTIANA REMAINED FIRM in her decision not to be alone again with David. The next Monday she insisted that they sit in the garden, where Lady Idonia just happened to find and join them. It was a pleasant visit as he entertained them with stories from his travels.

During dinner a few days later, Sir Walter Manny stopped by her table. Sir Walter was one of the Queen's men from Philippa's native land of Hainault. During their conversation he mentioned that he knew David and had even introduced him to the King two years ago when Edward had a letter for the mayor of Ghent and David was planning a trip to Flanders.

"Are you saying that David delivered the letter for the King?" she asked.

"It is done all the time, my lady. Why send a messenger if a trusted merchant makes the trip? Sometimes it is even better this way, especially if you do not want to draw attention to the communication. For example, everyone knows that there is currently a Flemish trader in

Westminster who is partial to the French alliance of the Count of Flanders, unlike his fellow burghers who support England. We just assume that he might have brought a private letter from the Count to our King. A formal exchange would be awkward since they are adversaries, but still negotiations occur." He scanned the hall and pointed. "There he is with Lady Catherine. His name is Frans van Horlst."

Christiana looked to where a gray-haired man fawned over Catherine. It was her "diplomat," the one she had seen speak with David that first Tuesday after the betrothal.

And then, out of the corner of her mind came another memory, of the first time that she had seen that man in the King's private corridor. Two voices speaking Parisian French. One soft and low and barely a whisper.

David? The voice had been too quiet to tell. He knew the King well enough to offer for the daughter of Hugh Fitzwaryn, and yet no one had ever seen him around court. The access of that private passageway would explain that contradiction. Had it been David there that day? If so, what was he to the King that he entered and left by that special route? And what had Frans van Horlst wanted of him?

"Do you know if David still performs such favors for the King?"

Sir Walter shrugged. "I suggested him that once and introduced them. Whether the relationship continued I cannot say."

"How did you come to know my betrothed?"

Sir Walter grinned and bent his fair head conspiratorially. "You no doubt know that he is an accomplished musician? Taught himself, too."

She nodded dutifully, although she didn't know that at all.

"We both belong to the Pui," he confided.

The Pui was one of many secret fraternities in London. The only thing truly secret about it was the date and location of its annual meetings. Besides drinking all night, the men of the Pui performed songs that they had composed, and one of the songs was chosen to be "crowned." Sometimes when a jongleur played a new chanson, one might hear references to it being from the Pui.

"Has he played the lute for you? His preferred instrument is that ancient Celtic harp of his, but it often doesn't suit the songs and so he has had to learn the lute. Still, two years ago he beat me out for the crown, and I still swear it was only because of the novelty of that damned harp," Walter said.

Christiana suddenly thought of the perfect way to be the exact opposite of alone with David that upcoming Monday. She confessed that her dear betrothed had never had the chance to play for her. Would Sir Walter be willing to help remedy the situation?

When David arrived Monday morning, she greeted him happily. She even smiled when he kissed her.

"I have called for a mount from the stables for you," he said. "We will go to my house for dinner. You should meet the servants, and the boys need to get to know you."

The last thing she wanted was to go to his house and meet the people involved in his life. They would be greeting her as their future mistress, while she would know that she would never see them again.

"Let us go out through the hall," she suggested. "I need to see if Morvan is there. I have something to tell him."

Of course Morvan wasn't there as she knew he wouldn't be. But Sir Walter was, sitting in a corner surrounded by seven young girls. He sang a plucky love song as he played his lute, raising his eyebrows comically at the more romantic parts. The girls giggled at his exaggerated expressions.

"David!" he called, breaking off his playing as they crossed the hall.

"Walter," David greeted him warmly. He glanced down at the girls sitting on the floor. "I see that you are living an Englishman's fantasy."

The girls turned and assessed him. Christiana watched them react to his handsome face. They were all unmarried and younger than her.

"I am trying out a new lute," Walter explained, holding up the instrument. He gestured to another on the bench beside him. "But I think that I prefer the old one."

"It is always thus at first," David said. He took Christiana's arm and began to guide her away.

Christiana glared at Walter.

"Let us see how they sound together, David," Walter said quickly.

The girls clapped their hands in encouragement. David looked at Walter. He looked at the second lute. He looked at Christiana.

She smiled and tried to make her expression glitter like Joan's. She let her eyes plead a little.

With a sigh of resignation he stepped through the girls and sat beside Walter, taking the lute on his lap. Walter mumbled something and they both began playing a song about spring.

They played a long while, until the hall began filling for dinner. Whenever David attempted to finish, the girls would whine and cajole. There came a point when Christiana could tell that he had given up, that he knew that he was trapped for the duration. After that he even enjoyed himself, trading jokes with Walter and finally singing a song on his own.

It was a love song that she had never heard before. The melody was lyrical and slow and a little sad. Christiana closed her eyes and felt her own sadness stirred by it.

Her thoughts turned to Stephen and the melancholy swelled. She lost track of the next few songs as her heart and worry dwelled on him. Then the girls moved around her and she became alert again. The merry group broke up and Walter insisted that David dine with him. David accepted and then helped her to her feet. Briefly he looked at her, then smiled and shook his head in amusement.

They did not go to his house. She did not meet the people there. More importantly, they were not alone all day. When she finally returned to Isabele's apartment, Idonia and Joan had returned, and so his departing kiss was as light and discreet as his greeting.

Christiana stepped out of the silvery pink wedding gown and handed it to the tailor, who managed adroitly not to see her standing in her shift.

This marriage business did wonders for a girl's wardrobe. She could not feel excited about this new cotehardie, however. The cost made her feel guilty because she knew that it would never be worn. It would be in extremely poor taste to run off with Stephen in defiance of the Queen but still take the gown that the Queen had purchased.

What really bothered her about this gown, however, was its relentless progress toward completion. These fittings had become unwelcome but unavoidable reminders that time kept passing far too quickly. Half of the five weeks had passed, and still she had no word from Stephen Percy.

A servant helped her into her plain purple cotehardie

and blue surcoat. She sent the woman off to find Joan while she slipped on some low boots.

It was Friday, almost three weeks since her betrothal, and she would be seeing David this afternoon instead of next Monday because he would be out of the city then. They were going to the horse fair and races at Smithfield, which she thought might be fun.

Before they got there, however, she had a thing to two to say to Master David de Abyndon.

David rode into Westminster flanked by Sieg and Andrew.

Sieg was frowning. "Now, if pretty young Joan comes out with her, I leave and Andrew stays," he said. "But if the little bit of fire from hell, that Lady Idonia, shows up, it's the other way around."

"I'm afraid so, Sieg," David said. On his left Andrew smirked.

Sieg frowned some more. "And whoever stays is to distract the other female so she's not in the way."

David nodded. He had used Christiana's own lie about the Queen insisting that the girls not be alone with men to explain his need of Sieg and Andrew today. He was almost thirty years old, but this girl had reduced him to games that he'd given up at eighteen. She had avoided being alone with him since that first Tuesday and had been very clever about it. He was amused and not annoyed, but then he was growing fascinated with her and would probably excuse anything.

Their mutual attraction simply did not fit in with her plans. Her response to his kiss and embrace had badly frightened her. She acted as confused and inexperienced as an untouched virgin. That effect of innocence had charmed him almost as much as her quick passion had enflamed him.

He could avoid this game. Eventually, soon in fact, she would be his. But he found himself picturing those eyes and tasting those lips in his memory far too often for complete retreat. Besides, he did not want her rebuilding her defenses too well. He didn't relish the notion of having to choose between continence or rape on his wedding night.

"The problem as I see it," Sieg continued, "is what if Lady Idonia won't be distracted? She's like a lioness protecting her cubs."

"Hell, Sieg, you're three times her size, for heaven's sake," Andrew muttered. "Just pick her up under your arm and walk off with her."

Sieg's frown disappeared. "*Ja?* That was how I did it back home, of course, but I thought that here in England . . ."

"Andrew is jesting, Sieg."

The frown returned. "Oh. *Ja.*"

David had agreed to meet Christiana in the back courtyard. She and Joan stood by two horses being held by grooms. Sieg turned his horse away and David slipped a delighted Andrew some coins. "Keep Lady Joan busy at the races and the stalls."

The grooms got the girls mounted. Christiana looked meaningfully in Andrew's direction.

"He will ride with us. He needs to see a man at the fair for me," David explained.

She seemed to accept that, and they rode together in silence. By the time that they reached the Strand, Joan and Andrew were four horse lengths ahead and Christiana didn't seem to mind.

"People have been talking about you," she said at last. David got the impression that she had waited for exactly the moment when Joan was too far ahead to hear what she said.

"People?"

"At court. Talking about you. Us. Everything."

"It was bound to happen, Christiana."

"Not these things. They weren't bound to be talked about because they are very unusual."

"You needn't turn to the court gossips. I will tell you anything you want to know."

She raised her eyebrows. "Will you? Well, first of all, some ladies have spoken to me on your behalf. Told me how wonderful you are."

"Which ladies?" he asked cautiously.

"Lady Elizabeth for one."

That surprised him. He and Elizabeth had an old friendship, but it was not her style to interfere in such things. "I am honored if Lady Elizabeth speaks well of me."

"And Alicia."

Hell.

Christiana's face was a picture of careful indifference. "Are you Lady Alicia's lover?"

"Did she say that?"

"Nay. There was something in the way that she spoke, however."

When he had offered to tell her anything, this was not what he had in mind. "I do not think that we want to pursue this, do you? I did not press you for the names of your lovers. You should not ask me for mine."

She twisted toward him abruptly. "Lovers! How dare you suggest that I have had lovers! I told you of one man."

"You told me of a current man. There may have been others, but as I said, I have been open-minded and not asked."

"Of course there were no others!"

"There is no of course to it. But it matters not." He

smiled inwardly at her dismay. "Christiana, I am almost thirty years old and I have not been a monk. I do not plan on being unfaithful to you. However, if our marriage is cold, I imagine that I will do as men have always done and find warmth elsewhere."

He had deliberately broached a topic that she would not want to talk about. As he expected, she had no response. So much for Lady Alicia. She would change the subject now. He waited.

"That is the least of what I have heard," she said.

"Somehow I thought so."

Her lids lowered. "Did you buy me?"

He had been wondering when she would hear of it. "Nay."

"Nay? I heard that Edward demanded a bride price. A big one. Morvan says it is true."

He had been waiting for this. He was ready. "A bride price is not the same as buying someone. Bride prices have an ancient tradition in England. Women were honored thus in the old days. With dowries, the woman is secondary to the property. It is as if a family pays someone to take her off their hands. If you think about it, dowries are much more insulting than bride prices."

"Then it is true?"

He chose his words carefully. If she found out the truth twenty years from now, he wanted to be able to say that he hadn't lied. "Your brother has seen the contract, as you will soon. There is no point in denying that there is a bride price in it."

"And instead of being insulted, you say that I should feel honored."

"Absolutely. Would you prefer if the King had just given you to me?"

"I would prefer if the King had continued to forget that I existed," she snapped.

They rode in silence for a minute. "How big is it? This honorable bride price?" she finally asked.

So Morvan had not told her. She would see the contract soon. David thought of the complicated formula it contained.

"How good are you at ciphering?" he asked casually.

"Excellent."

She would be. "One thousand pounds."

She stopped her horse and gaped at him. "One thousand pounds! An earl's income? Why?"

"Edward would hear of no less. I assure you that I bargained very hard. I personally thought that three hundred would be generous."

Her eyes narrowed suspiciously. "Morvan is right. This marriage never made any sense. Now it makes less."

"Aren't you worth one thousand pounds?"

"You must have been drunk when you made this offer. You will no doubt be relieved when I get you off the hook."

"He has come then?"

She ignored that. "Just as well for your health, too, that I will end this betrothal soon. I have heard about my brother's threat to you."

"Ah. That."

"Wednesday, they say."

"I expect Thursday," he corrected calmly. "Does your brother know that you have heard of this?"

"Of course. I went to him at once and told him that I wouldn't have it."

"Your concern touches me."

"Aye. Well, he wouldn't hear me. But, of course, you won't meet him."

"Of course I will."

She stopped her horse again. Joan and Andrew were far in the distance now. "You cannot be serious."

"What choice do I have?"

"You will not be in town Monday. Can't you extend your trip?"

"Eventually I must come back."

"Oh dear." She frowned fretfully.

He looked at her pretty puckered brow. "He will not kill me."

"Oh, it isn't that," she replied with ruthless honesty. "This just makes a messy situation messier. First a duel, then an abduction, then an annulment . . . well, it will make a terrific scandal."

"Perhaps someone will write a song about it."

"This is not humorous, David. You really should withdraw or leave. Morvan's sword is not a laughing matter. He may not kill you, but he may hurt you very badly."

"Aye. One thousand pounds is one thing. An arm or a leg is another. I certainly hope that you are worth it."

"How can you jest?"

"I am not jesting. But let me worry about Morvan, my lady. Are there any other rumors and gossip that you need to discuss?"

They had approached the city and began circling around its wall to the north. "Aye. Not all of the ladies who know you were so complimentary. Lady Catherine spoke with me. And with Morvan."

David waited. He would not assume what story Lady Catherine had given them.

"She told me that you are a moneylender," Christiana said quietly, as if she didn't want to be overheard by passing riders.

He almost laughed at her circumspection. The girl lived in a world that didn't exist anymore, full of virtuous knights and honored duty and stories of King Arthur's roundtable. King Edward carefully nurtured these illusions at his court with his pageants and festivals and tournaments. A mile away, within the gates of London, time moved on.

"It is true. Most merchants loan money."

"Usury is a sin."

"Perhaps so, but moneylending is a business. It is widely done, Christiana, and none think twice about it anymore. England could not survive without it. One of my sinful loans is to the King at his demand. Two others are to abbeys."

"So you just loan to the King and abbeys?"

"With others I purchase property and resell it back later at an agreed-upon time and price."

"At a profit?"

"Why else would I do it? I have no kinship or friendship with these people. However, often when I sell it back, my management has improved the income, so perhaps the profit is theirs."

"When the time is up, what if they cannot repurchase it?"

He had been trying to put a better face on this for her sake, and he cursed himself now. He had sworn he would not make excuses to this girl for being what he was. "I sell it elsewhere," he said bluntly.

She chewed on that awhile. "Why not keep it?"

It wasn't the argument he had expected. He thought that she would upbraid him for unkindness and chant sentimental pleas for the poor borrowers.

"I don't keep it because of King Edward's damned decrees saying any man with income from land over forty pounds a year has to be knighted. He has almost caught me twice."

"What do you mean, caught you? To be a knight is a wonderful thing. They are more respected than merchants, and of higher degree. You would better yourself if you were knighted."

She said it simply and innocently, stating a basic fact of life. She was oblivious to the insult and so he chose to ignore it. This time.

"Well, I am a merchant, and content as such."

One would have thought that he told her that he would rather be a devil than a saint. "You mean this, don't you?" she asked curiously. "You really don't want to be a knight."

"No one does, Christiana, except those born to it. Even many born to it avoid it. It is why Edward issues those decrees. The realm doesn't have enough knights for his ambitions. The position holds less and less appeal, so Edward plays up the chivalry and elevates the knights higher to compensate." He paused. He would be marrying this girl. He would try to explain. "It is not cowardice or fear of arms. Every London citizen swears to protect the city and realm. We must practice at arms and own what armor we can afford. I have a whole suit of the damn plate. We defend our city and send troops on Edward's wars. Many apprentices are excellent bowmen and Andrew has even mastered the longbow. But if you think about the military life honestly, it has little to recommend it."

"It is a glorious life! Full of honor and strength."

"It is a life of killing, girl. For good causes or personal gain, in honor or in murder, knights live to kill. In the end, for all of the pretty words in the songs, that is what they do. Their wars disrupt trade, ruin agriculture, and burn towns and villages. When they are victorious they rape and they steal all that they can move."

He had lost his patience and this tirade simply poured out. She stared at him as if he had slapped her, and he regretted the outburst. She was young and had lived a sheltered life. It shouldn't surprise him that she had never questioned the small protected world in which she had dwelled.

He had been too hard on her. It was her father and brother whom he described, after all. "I have no doubt that there are still many knights who are true to their honor and their vows," he said by way of a peace offering. "It is said that your brother is such a man."

That seemed to release her from the brutal reality he had thrown at her.

"Did Lady Catherine say anything else that concerns you?"

"Not to me. She said that she told Morvan something important. He said that it was nothing of significance, and then lectured me about not being friends with her."

"Good instruction, Christiana. I do not want you having anything to do with the woman."

"I think that I am old enough to choose my own friends."

"Not this one. When we are married, you are to avoid her."

Her irritation with him was visible, but she held her tongue. She turned her attention to the road as they approached Smithfield.

CHAPTER 6

SMITHFIELD ABUTTED LONDON'S north wall. Around the periphery of the racing area, horse traders had their animals tethered and lively bargaining was underway. Buyers often asked to have the horse run before purchasing, and that was how the informal races had developed. The crowds attracted to this spectacle in turn drew hawkers, food vendors, and entertainers, and so, every Friday, Smithfield, the site of London's livestock markets, was transformed into a festival site.

They found a man with whom to leave the horses and plunged into the crowd. Andrew immediately guided Joan off in a separate direction. Christiana, still thoughtful over their discussion, did not notice. She walked with her hands and arms under her cloak, her pale face flushed from the cold.

"Let us look at the horses," David said. "You will need one once you leave the castle."

"I don't want you to buy me a horse, David."

"You will not be using the royal stables after we are wed. We will find a suitable horse today."

"After I am wed, I will not be riding your suitable horse, since I will not be wed to *you*."

"Then I will sell it. For convenience, we will see if there is one while you are here to choose. Just in case."

She suppressed the urge to get stubborn and fell into step beside him as they went to survey the animals.

As they walked around the field examining and discussing the horses, they found several possibilities. Toward the end of their circuit they came upon a most suitable horse, a beautiful small black palfrey. The owner produced a saddle, and Christiana tried him out. While David came to terms with the man and arranged for delivery to Westminster's stables, she scanned the crowd for signs of the long-absent Joan and Andrew. The field was too big and busy for her to find them. Just like Joan to forget the reason for coming in the first place.

A bear baiter and some dancers arrived to entertain. Christiana had no interest in the bear, but the dancers fascinated her. At court she tried never to miss dancers of any kind. This group was fairly rustic and unschooled compared to others she had seen, but still she followed their movements to the simple music for a long while. A part of her envied these women who were permitted to let the music entrance them, whose bodies swayed and curved and angled like moving pictures.

"I would have liked to be a dancer."

"You dance at banquets and feasts, do you not?" David asked.

She blushed. She hadn't even realized that she had spoken out loud. "Aye. But that is different. That is like a dinner conversation." She gestured to the women. "This is like a meditation, I think. Sometimes I will see one who looks to be in ecstasy, who is not even aware of the world anymore."

She felt his gaze and tore her eyes away from the performance to look at him. His face held that penetrating expression that he directed at her sometimes. There was something invasive about this focused awareness, and it never failed to make her uncomfortable.

It is like I am made of glass, she thought. It wasn't fair that he could do this. He knew how to remain forever opaque to her.

"I think that you would be a beautiful dancer," he said. "If you think that dancing thus will give you pleasure, then you should do it."

Finally the dancers took a break and the crowd that had formed drifted away.

"We should find Joan," she said, peering at the crowd.

"I'm sure that we will cross paths. If not, we will meet at the horses."

She joined him and they examined the wares that the vendors sold. She wondered what Joan was up to with that apprentice, and what Lady Idonia would say if she found out that Christiana had lost track of her.

One of the vendors offered savories of fried bread dipped in honey. The smell coming from the hot oil was delicious, and she glanced over longingly as they walked by. It was messy food and just the sort of thing that Lady Idonia had never let her buy when they went to festivals.

David noticed and went to purchase some.

"It is sure to stain my clothing," she said, echoing the reason Idonia had always given for avoiding such food.

"We will manage."

He took one of the doughy savories, and gestured for her to follow him behind the stall to some trees. The vendors edged the crowd and field, and there was no one back here.

He broke off a piece of the honey-covered bread and held it out. She reached for it but he pulled it away.

"There is no reason for us both to get covered with it," he said, and placed the dough near her lips.

It smelled warm and yeasty and sweet and wonderful. Baring her teeth to avoid the fingers that held it, she stretched her neck forward and took the morsel in her mouth. It tasted heavenly and she rolled her eyes at the pleasure.

He laughed and broke off another small piece. She stretched for it. "I must look like a chicken," she giggled with her mouth full.

Those long fingers fed her again. She felt some honey dripping down her lip and licked to catch it. He gently flicked it away, the pad of his finger grazing the edge of her mouth. Her lower lip quivered at the sensation, and her face and neck tingled.

The last piece was too big and she had to bite into it. Her teeth nipped his fingertips and she blushed, awkwardly conscious of the contact. He still held out the rest of it, and her gaze stayed on that beautiful hand as she chewed quickly and then hesitantly took the last of the savory.

His hand did not move away this time, but followed her head back. His fingertips brushed her lips and rested there. The dough suddenly felt very thick in her mouth.

She looked up at his face and saw the slight hardness around his mouth. His lids lowered as he watched her lips move beneath his hand. An odd stillness descended, and she swallowed the last of the sweet dough with difficulty.

With a deliberate movement and watchful eyes, he ran his finger around the edge of her mouth, collecting the errant honey, and then wiped the sweetness onto her lips.

She had a sudden shocking urge to lick the last of the

honey off those fingers. He looked in her eyes as if he understood. One by one, he wiped his fingers across her mouth like a repeated invitation to her impulse, layering the sticky remains on her lips.

The gesture mesmerized her. The sounds of the field and races receded to a distant roar. In the still silence that engulfed her, she could hear her heart beat harder with the light pressure of each small caress. The exciting intensity that she always sensed in him spread to surround her.

He looked at her a long moment when he finished. Then he abruptly took her hand and pulled her back amongst the trees. She stumbled after him, not really cooperating but not resisting either. Breathless anticipation claimed her as they left the sanctuary of the field. She told herself that she did not want to do this, that she would not go with him, but she went anyway.

He dragged her behind a large oak. With his arm, around her shoulders he pulled her into an embrace. The other arm slid under her cloak and around her waist, pressing her body to his body as he kissed her.

Those new sensations that had snuck up on her so insidiously the last time suddenly exploded all at once. It was if they had been carefully corralled for two weeks but now he had opened the gate and waved them to a frenzy. The intimacy of the embrace felt exhilarating, and a thundering tremor full of sharp sensual spikes shook her from her neck to her thighs.

He gentled his kiss and began biting and licking the honey off her lips in an unhurried way, pulling her yet closer to him. She became very alert but only to him and each touch of warmth on her mouth. Awareness of everything else washed away beneath the stunning waves of slow, tight heat that coursed over and over through her body.

His tongue grazed against her lips, inviting her to open to him. With the one thread of reason still left, she kept her mouth resolutely closed. He smiled before moving his mouth down.

Did she deliberately throw her head back so that he could reach the hollow at the base of her neck? She didn't know for sure, but his mouth was there suddenly and her arms were up and around his shoulders, and both of his hands grasped her beneath her cloak, holding her, bending her up to his kisses.

She grew acutely aware of every touch, every kiss, every wonderful strange reaction that she felt. Her upraised arms brought her body closer to his, and through the stretched fabric of her clothing she could feel his muscles and warmth tingling her breasts. The pressure of his hands around her felt both dangerous and comforting. Her awareness became full of something else, too, something commanding and expectant and connected to the hollow tension that spread through her belly. It was that as much as the exquisite feelings that kept her from stopping him. Vaguely, dully, her mind considered that he was luring her toward something that she did not really understand.

He kissed her mouth again, and his hands moved. Slowly, gently, he caressed down and up her sides beneath her cloak, his fingers splaying around the outer swells of her breasts. Shockingly, insistently, they moved down her back and over her buttocks and up her hips. The tightness in her belly ached and somewhere low inside her a throbbing demand pounded.

One hand stayed on her hips but the other moved up. She knew what he was going to do. She remembered Stephen's crushing grip and tensed, almost finding her senses, almost finding the strength to push him away.

But he did not crush her. His fingers stroked around

the edge of her breast in a gentle, delicate way, tantalizing her to an excruciating anticipation of she knew not what. Her breath quickened to a series of short gasps as her whole body waited.

When he finally caressed her breast, she bit back a moan. The pleasure startled her. She tried to pull away.

He would not let her go. Kissing her beautifully, caressing her softly, he summoned delicious feelings. His fingers touched her as if no cloth lay between them and her skin, finding her nipple and playing with it until that throbbing sensation low by her thighs became almost unbearable. He took the yearning hard bud between his thumb and finger and rubbed gently. This time she could not catch the small cry before it escaped her.

His mouth went to her ear and kissed and probed before his quiet voice flowed into her.

"Come back to my house with me. It is but a few minutes from here through the gate."

"Why?" she muttered, still floating in the sensual stupor that his hand created.

"Why? For one thing you should visit and meet the people who live there," he said, lifting his head to kiss her temple and brow. His hand still caressed her and she found it hard to pay attention to what he said. "For another, I am too old to make love behind trees and hedges."

Naming what they were doing intruded like a loud noise on a dream. The sounds of the races instantly thundered around her. His hand on her body suddenly felt scandalous. Burning with shame, she looked away.

"This is wrong," she said.

"Nay. It is very right."

"You know what I mean."

His hand fell away from her breast, but still he held her.

"Did your lover give you such pleasure?" he asked softly.

She blushed deeper. She could not look at him.

"I thought not."

"It was different," she said accusingly. "We are in love. This is . . . is . . ." What? What was this horrible, wonderful thing?

"Desire," he said.

So this was desire. No wonder the priests always preached against it. Desire seemed a very dangerous thing indeed.

"Well, girl, if I had to have one without the other, I would choose this," he said. "Desire can grow into something more, but if it isn't there at the beginning it never comes, and love dies without it."

He was lecturing her like a child again. She truly resented when he did that. "This is wrong," she repeated firmly, pushing a little, putting some distance between their bodies. "You know it is. You are luring me. It isn't fair."

"Luring you? Why would I do that?"

"Who knows why you do any of this? Why offer for me in the first place? Why pay the bride price?" She studied him. "Maybe you want to bed me so that when he comes, the betrothal cannot be annulled."

"It is a good idea. But that never occurred to me, because I know that he is not coming."

He had said that since the first night. Calmly, relentlessly he had repeated it. "You cannot know that," she snapped. But there had been something in his voice this time that terrified her. As if he did know. Somehow.

"He is not here, Christiana. He has had your message a long time now."

"Perhaps not. Maybe the messenger couldn't find him."

"I have spoken with the messenger whom you hired. He delivered the letter into the hands of the man to whom you sent it ten days after you wrote it."

"You spoke . . . you interfered in this? How dare you!"

"It is well that I did. Your messenger had no intention of leaving at once for your mission. He planned to wait until other business took him north. It could have been weeks. Even then he might have handed it off to any number of other people along the way and spared himself the trip."

"But he went at once for you? And delivered it directly?"

"I paid him a lot of money to do so. And to offer to bring a letter back."

She had been given no return letter. A frightening sadness tried to overwhelm her. She didn't want to hear what David was saying, didn't want to consider the implications. The messenger had been back for a while. If he could return in this time, so could Stephen. He could have at least sent a note. But perhaps the messenger had admitted doing her betrothed's bidding and Stephen did not want to risk it.

Fortunately her anger at David defeated her forebodings, or she might have been undone right there. She glared up at him. "Do you enjoy this? Destroying people's lives?"

He gave her a very hard look, but it quickly softened. His hand left her side and stroked her face. "In truth, it will pain me to see you hurt."

"Then help me," she cried impulsively. "Set me free and help me to go to him."

He looked at her in that way that made her feel transparent. "Nay. Because he does not want you enough to hold on to you, girl, and I find that I do."

For an instant, while he looked at her, she had

thought that she saw wavering, that he might actually do what she asked. His words crushed the small hope. Petulantly she shook off his arms and moved away. "I want to go back to Westminster now."

Wordlessly he led her back to the vendors and over to a woman selling little bits of lace. He spoke a few words to the woman, and then turned to her. "This is Goodwife Mary. Stay with her while I go and find Andrew and Lady Joan. Do not move from here," he ordered before walking away into the crowd.

She got the impression that he wanted to get away from her, and she was glad that he was gone, too. He gave her commands the way that Morvan did, and she resented it. *We will ride north. We will buy a horse. Stand here and do not move.* She was glad that they would not be marrying. Living with him would be like having her brother around all of the time, picking at her behavior. Lady Idonia could always be tricked and subverted. This man would be too shrewd for that.

She was glad that he had left for another reason. She never had any peace with him nearby. She knew now that it had to do with what had just occurred beneath the tree. Something of that excitement, of that anticipation, was there between them even when they just rode down the Strand and talked. Merely thinking about those wonderful feelings could call up her tingling responses again.

Desire, he had called it. She did not much like this desire. She did not like the invisible ties it wove between them. The excitement she had felt with Stephen seemed a thin and childish thing in comparison, and she didn't like that either.

Stephen. He had not come yet, had not sent a letter back. . . . A horrible, vacant ache gripped her chest. She would not think about that, would not doubt him. She especially would not contemplate what it might imply about her and David de Abyndon.

"There you are!" Joan came skipping toward her with Andrew.

Christiana glanced at her friend. Joan looked flush-faced and beautiful. A piece of hay stuck out of her hair.

"Aye, here I am. David has gone looking for you and ordered me to wait here like a child." She eyed the hay and plucked it out. "Where have you been?"

"Oh, everywhere," Joan cried. "This is much more fun if Lady Idonia isn't with us."

"I can only imagine." She held up the hay and raised her eyebrows. Andrew flushed and moved away.

Joan shrugged. "There was a hay wagon beneath a tree and we climbed the tree and jumped in. It was a lot of fun."

"I thought that you were in love with Thomas Holland."

"I am. We just played."

"Joan! He is an apprentice!"

"Oh, you are as bad as Idonia. We only kissed once."

"You kissed . . . for heaven's sake!"

Joan's eyes narrowed. "It was only one kiss. It isn't as if I am going to marry him."

She said it lightly, but the warning was unmistakable. David had been an apprentice like Andrew, and Christiana *was* going to marry *him*. *I love you*, the voice and eyes said, *but you are in no position to criticize me*.

A new, sad emotion surged. Joan pitied her. They all pitied her, didn't they? All of the desire and pleasure in the world could not balance that out, could it?

David emerged from the crowd then. He silently collected them and led the way to the horses.

"He looks angry," Joan whispered. "What did you do?"

It was more a matter of what she didn't do, Christiana suspected. Still, she found herself rather pleased that he was angry. Maybe because this was the first clear emotion that she had ever seen in him. It was the first time that she knew what he was thinking.

They retrieved the horses and headed toward Westminster. Joan and Andrew fell back and began talking again, but David tried to move at a fast pace. At first Christiana kept up with him, but then she simply slowed her horse and let him pull ahead. Shortly he slowed as well and rode beside her. She rather enjoyed making him do that.

His silence became oppressive, and after noting with a sigh that he brooded when angry just like Morvan, she stopped paying him any attention. She occupied herself with speculation about Stephen's home in Northumberland. The worry that David had given her about Stephen quickly disappeared as she found a variety of excuses for his delay in writing or coming back.

"You are thinking about him again, aren't you?" His voice, hard and quiet, intruded on her.

"What makes you say that?" she asked guiltily.

"The look on your face, girl. It is written all over you."

She was very sure that her expression showed nothing when she thought about Stephen. In fact, she worked at it. But then, David always seemed to see and know more than she wanted him to.

"You are a coward, Christiana," he said quietly, but the angry edge was unmistakable. "It would seem that I am too real for you. You refuse to see the truth. Not just about your lover not coming and this marriage really happening, but about us."

"There is no reality to face about us."

"I want you and you want me. That is very real. But it doesn't rhyme with the song that you have composed, does it? You continue to live the lyrics that you wrote in ignorance about this man and yourself."

"I do not live according to some song."

"Of course you do. Duels and abductions are the stuff of songs, not life. Do lutes play when you think of the man who used you? Are your memories colored like the images on painted cloth and tapestries?"

She looked away, trembling at these harsh words that spoke an understanding of her mind that no one should have. She suddenly felt helpless again against the fears those words raised in her. He was horrible to say that Stephen only used her. Cruel. She hated him.

His voice sounded raw and angry when he spoke again. "I should send you to him and let you see how your song ends."

"Why don't you then?" she cried.

He stopped both their horses. His hand came over and took her chin. She resisted its guiding turn.

"Look at me," he ordered.

She deliberately turned away. His hand forced her head around to him. His blue eyes flashed with something dangerous.

"Because he would use you again before he is honest with you. The past is one thing, but you belong to me now. I will let no one else have you so easily. Do not ever forget that."

She suddenly realized that his mood had to do with more than her refusing him. It involved something bigger. It was about her and him and Stephen.

Was he jealous? Of Stephen? It was so unlike him to show his reactions, and this anger flamed hot and alive and visible. Was this emotion one that he was not accustomed to controlling?

Anger unleashed something frightening in this man, and it made her especially unsettled that the fear itself seemed touched with that other tension that always seemed to exist between them.

Westminster looked like a haven from a storm when they finally arrived. She hopped off her horse before anyone could help her and ran inside without so much as glancing back at David de Abyndon.

CHAPTER 7

CHRISTIANA LIFTED HER knees and rested her head on the edge of the large wooden tub. The warm water almost reached the top, and positioned like this, she could float a little in the soothing heat. A circular tent of linen enclosed the tub and held in the steam, creating a humid, sultry environment that loosened her tense muscles.

The castle had been practically empty when she called for the servants to prepare this bath. A rumor spreading through Westminster that Morvan was to meet David on London Bridge had drawn the bored courtiers like flies to a savory. Idonia had stayed behind with her, but Isabele and Joan had attached themselves to a group including young Prince John and Thomas Holland.

Not everyone approved of this duel. Some of the older knights considered it unchivalrous to challenge a mere merchant, but even they understood Morvan's anger. Since the duel was to be so public, everyone assumed that Morvan meant only to humiliate David, and that made it more acceptable, too. After all, these merchants often forgot their place. In overwhelming David, Morvan would be reminding all of London that wealth could never replace breeding and nobility when it really mattered.

She closed her eyes and tried to get the knot in her stomach to untie. She prayed that David had delayed his return to London as she had advised. She had offered a number of such prayers during the last few days as this duel approached. She wouldn't want to see David harmed. He had become a friend of sorts, and she had rather grown to depend on his presence.

She had been thinking about him a lot since that day at Smithfield. Sometimes she listened to the remembered quiet voice in the King's private corridor. The more she thought about it, the more it sounded like David who had been approached by Frans van Horlst that day. Other times her mind drifted to the two of them under the oak tree. Those memories were both compelling and disturbing, and tended to sneak up on her when she least expected them.

Which would be worse? If David had returned from his journey, he would face her brother in front of hundreds of people and be made to look a fool. If he had not returned, the whole world would know him for a coward. Morvan and the court would probably prefer the latter. The lesson would be taught without a sword ever being raised.

Her brother did this out of love for her and concern for the family's honor, but she really wished he had stayed out of things. He was only making a complicated situation worse, and he might well ruin her plans completely. Did Morvan think that the humiliation would make David withdraw? In all likelihood it would only make him more stubborn. He might even refuse to honor his promise to let her go with Stephen.

Of course, Stephen wasn't here and the wedding was only twelve days away. She tried not to think about that, but it was becoming difficult. It was one thing to wait patiently and another to see the sun relentlessly set every day on your unfulfilled dreams. Lately she had found herself listening for horses whenever she went outside. Perhaps he planned some dramatic abduction soon. She imagined him riding down the river road with his boon companions in attendance, maybe on the day before the wedding itself. Would he wait that long? How would he get to her and get her out? There were always so many people about.

She sat up abruptly.

There were hardly any people about right now.

Morvan had been nowhere to be found this morning as the rumor of his duel on London Bridge spread. Who had started those whispers? Morvan himself? Or someone else who wanted Westminster emptied of all but the essential guard?

A heady excitement gripped her. Was Stephen coming for her today? If so, the plan was audacious and brilliant. She couldn't be sure, but it suddenly all made sense. If he had learned of the duel and its location from one of his friends here, he might well make use of it in this way. She hadn't realized that he was that clever.

Smiling happily, she quickly washed herself. She felt the knot of hair piled high on her head and considered whether she had time to wash and dry it.

Her arm froze at the sound of boot steps entering the wardrobe where the tub sat in front of a hearth.

She couldn't believe it! Finally! She eagerly parted the drape to greet her love.

Her gaze fell on beautiful leather boots and a starkly plain blue pourpoint. A sword hung from one belt and two daggers from another. Deep blue eyes regarded her, reading her thoughts like she was made of glass.

"You were expecting someone else?" David asked. He undid the sword belt and placed the weapon on the top of one of the chests that lined that walls of the wardrobe.

She let the drape fall closed and sank into the water.

"Nay. I just wasn't expecting you," she responded through the curtain of cloth.

"I said that I would come. But perhaps you thought that I would be dead."

"Badly wounded at least, if you were fool enough to meet him. Why aren't you?" That didn't come out the way she had planned, and she grimaced. It sounded like she was annoyed that he was whole.

"Edward stopped it as I knew he would. He is counting on that bride price, you see."

She heard him walk over to the wall by the door. He didn't leave.

What if she was right and Stephen came now? He would find David here. Morvan may not have drawn blood, but Stephen just might.

"You have to go, David."

"I think not."

"I must finish my bath. I will attend on you in the hall shortly."

"I will stay here. It is warm and very pleasant."

She splashed the water angrily.

"You are giving him too much credit for drama and intelligence, my girl. Stephen Percy is not in London or Westminster. His is not coming today or any day for a long while."

She sank her shoulders down under the water. *He knows what I am thinking. He knows Stephen's name. Is there anything that he doesn't know?*

"I sent the court to London Bridge, Christiana. I

wanted no one to follow your brother to the place where we really met."

"Why? So that no one would see him best you?"

"Nay. So if he forced me to kill him, I could lie to you and you would never know the truth of it."

The chamber became very still. It was absurd, of course. David could never hurt Morvan. When it came to skill at arms . . . and yet . . .

Footsteps came over to the tub. The drape parted and he handed her a towel through the slit. "Enough of this for now. The water must be cooling. Get out and dry yourself."

She grabbed the towel and jerked the drape closed. She waited as he walked away.

The water was indeed cooling and the steam had disappeared. It was getting chilly in the bath.

"Call the servant, please. She is in the chamber."

"I sent her away."

She looked down at her nakedness. She listened to the silence of the empty castle. She thought of her clothes piled on a stool by the hearth. The bath was losing its warmth quickly, but the chill that shook her had nothing to do with the water.

"Idonia should be returning soon, David. It will embarrass me if she finds you in here."

"Lady Idonia decided to take a ride with Sieg. A very long ride, I should think."

Her annoyance flared at this game he played with her. She grabbed the towel and stood in the water, drying her arms and body with hurried movements.

She would show this merchant what noblewomen were made of.

She draped the large linen towel around her, catching its ends under her arm. She stepped out of the tub and kicked aside the drape. Water from her legs began pooling on the wooden floor.

He sat atop a high chest next to the hearth, his back against the wall and one arm resting on a raised knee. His cool gaze met hers and then drifted down in a lazy way. She fought down the alarm that rose in her chest.

He had placed another log on the fire, and the small wardrobe, crowded with chests that held Isabele's gowns and furs, felt warm enough. She sat on a stool by the tub and patted the ends of the long towel against her legs to dry them.

She did not look at him but she knew that he watched her. She worked hard not to let him see that it unsettled her.

"How did you know his name?" she asked, proud of how casual her voice sounded. Almost as casual and placid as his did all of the time. Except when he was jealous. She groaned inwardly at her stupidity. Perhaps it would be best to avoid talk of Stephen Percy under the circumstances.

"I've known who he was from the beginning. Don't look so surprised. You all but told me his name that first night. I also know that you are not the first innocent girl whom he has seduced, nor will you be the last. Some men have a taste for such things, and he is one of them."

His words probed at forbidden thoughts buried deep in her heart, thoughts that tried to surface late at night as she lay in her bed and counted days passing and days left. She had walled those worries into a dark corner, and she rebelled at this man going near them.

She glared at him. *He sits there so damned calmly*, she thought. *He looks at me like he has a right to be here. Like he owns me.* She braced herself against the feelings of vulnerability and tension which that look summoned.

"I hate you," she muttered.

His lids lowered. "Careful, girl. I may decide to encourage your hatred. I find that I prefer it to your indifference."

He hopped off the chest. The movement made her tense.

"You still wait for him," he said. "After all of this time and when the truth is so clear. It is well that Edward gave you to me. You would have spent your whole life waiting and living in a faded dream."

"Perhaps I still will." She spoke the words like a bold threat.

"Nay. You wake up today."

He stepped toward her. She rose from her stool at once, clutching the towel around her and backing up. He stopped.

She didn't like the way he watched her. Even worse, she didn't like the way that she was reacting to it. For all of her annoyance, that exquisite expectation branched through her. Sharp and vivid memories of the pleasure she had felt at Smithfield forced themselves onto her thoughts and her body.

"I demand that you leave," she said.

He shook his head. "Your brother is out of this now. So is Stephen Percy. There was no duel and there will be no abduction. Finally it is just you and me."

Her heart pounded desperately. "You are frightening me, David."

"At least I have your attention for a change. Besides, I told you before. It is not fear that you feel with me."

"It is now." And it was. A horrible, wonderful combination of fear and anticipation and attraction and denial. Like the lines of a rope twined in on each other, they twisted and twisted together, pulling and stretching her soul. If he didn't leave, she was sure that something would snap.

"If you won't leave, I shall." Somehow she found enough composure to speak calmly.

He gestured to the clothes on the stool to his right and the door to his left. "I will not stop you, Christiana."

She had to pass him to leave. Was it her imagination that his blue eyes dared her to approach? *He is enjoying this,* she thought, and the vexation surged in her again, vanquishing those other feelings for a moment and making her brave.

The daughter of Hugh Fitzwaryn need not be afraid of a tradesman, she thought firmly. A noblewoman could walk naked down the Strand and her status would protect her and clothe her as surely as steel. How many tailors and haberdashers of David's degree had seen her dressed in no more than a shift as they waited upon the princess and her friends? This towel covered her more. Such men did not exist if one chose to have it so.

Aye. It would even be thus with David de Abyndon.

She lowered her eyes and collected herself. She imagined that he was a mercer who had come to show his wares. She let her spirit withdraw from him and from those strange feelings that he summoned so easily, and she wrapped herself in the knowledge of who she was and what he was.

Lifting her gaze, she looked more to the hearth than to him. Holding the towel around her, she calmly walked over to the stool and bent her knees so as to reach the garments.

Fingers stroked firmly into her hair and twisted. The clothes fell from her hand as he yanked her up. Gasping with shock, she found her face inches away from flaming blue eyes.

"Do not do that again," he warned. "Ever."

She was looking into the face of danger and she knew it. She did not move. She barely breathed.

Slowly, as he held her and looked at her, the flames cooled and the hardness left his eyes and mouth. She could see when he regained control and the anger fell from his perfect face.

The expression that replaced it was just as dangerous in its own way, though. His hand did not release her hair. If anything, it gripped a little tighter.

He looked over her face slowly and then down at her bare shoulders and neck. She watched his gaze drift to the damp towel clutched against her body. She had never been so thoroughly looked at in her life. His unhurried possessive inspection left her as breathless and tingling as a caress.

He pulled her toward him. A tremor of fearful anticipation quaked through her. Her legs almost wouldn't support her as her body followed her head. He lowered his mouth to hers.

She fought the emotions. She battled them valiantly with every bit of her strength of will. But her defenses had never been very strong against his kisses, and as this one deepened and his other arm embraced her, she melted against him as those wonderful sensations took control of her.

His mouth moved beautifully over her face and neck and ears and shoulders, kissing and biting gently, drawing softly at the pulse points. He played at the lines of tension stretching through her like they were the strings on a lute, luring her toward acceptance. She knew what was happening, but the pleasure of the heated shocks that spiraled from each kiss made her want more, and the gentle waves flowing through her from his caress on her back promised an ocean of oblivious delight.

He tugged gently at the back of the towel. She fought to the surface of her sensual sea.

"Nay," she whispered.

"Aye," he said.

The towel's edge dislodged from under her arm and fell away from her back. That fear that wasn't fear shrieked and she clutched the edge of the linen tighter to her chest, her arms crossing her breasts.

He did not try to remove it. Untangling his hand from her hair, he embraced her tightly so that her arms were imprisoned between their bodies. He lowered his mouth to the skin just above her hands while his embrace moved down her back.

The feel of his warm hands on her bare skin exhilarated her. Even her awareness of his kisses dimmed as all of her senses focused on those heated caresses. Her whole being waited and felt and savored the progress of that touch. Low and deep in her body that strange pulse began throbbing.

He took her mouth again and his hands went lower, down to her hips and lower back, down finally to her bottom. She started in surprise but he kissed her harder and his hands stayed there, following the swells of her body. That secret pulse grew aching and hot, and she dully realized that it was deep in her belly near her thighs and his hands were very close to it.

The feelings were too exquisite, too delicious to stop him. The voice of her mind grew very quiet and weak. That rational awareness only observed, noticing the scent of the man who held her and the sound of her gasping breaths. The waiting expectation she had first felt at Smithfield obliterated any real thought and grew now into something demanding and impatient and slightly painful.

His hands drifted lower. He cupped her lower buttocks

in a caress of commanding intimacy. She gasped aloud as that throbbing center of pleasure exploded with a white heat.

His fingers rested at the very top of her thighs where they joined. She felt as she had when she waited for him to touch her breast, only the anticipation had a frantic, desperate quality to it and the pulsing expectation possessed a physical reality that stunned her.

Suddenly the fear that had always been there when he kissed and touched her rose from the depths where the pleasure had banished it. The small voice of her mind considered that something was occurring here that had never happened with Stephen.

"David . . ." she whispered, beginning a feeble protest.

He lifted his head and looked at her with a face transformed and more handsome than ever. The glowing warmth in those eyes left her speechless.

He pulled her hips closer to his. Her arms still held the towel to her chest, and she didn't stand of her own will now. The fingers near her thighs shifted as he moved her closer yet.

Her belly pressed against him. She felt warmth and hardness. That hidden place, so full of ache and yearning and so close to his hand, responded forcefully.

Her eyes flew open wide.

He bent to kiss her again. "Aye," he said quietly.

A very peculiar notion teased at her mind and then forced itself on her.

Outrageous, really.

Impossible.

As if reading her thoughts, he slid his hand between the back of her thighs and gently touched her. Effortlessly his fingers found that hungry ache.

She cried out from the shock of the pleasure. Twisting

violently, she jumped out of his arms and just stared at him.

His own reaction was just as strong. She watched breathlessly as surprise gave way to perplexity and then finally to anger. Pulling the towel back around her, she moved away, trying desperately to sort her confused thoughts and emotions.

She didn't want him angry. She wanted to explain. But explain what? That a bizarre, unnatural idea of what he wanted from her had unaccountably lodged in her mind and suddenly seemed . . . logical? She was probably wrong, and if she spoke of this to him, he would think her perverted. All the same, she didn't want him touching her again, especially like that, until she found out for sure that she hadn't grossly misunderstood everything.

He just looked at her, the beautiful warmth dimming from his eyes and the placid expression reclaiming him. She felt like a fool standing there in her towel, but she didn't know what to say.

"Very well, Christiana. If you do not want to give yourself to me now, I will wait," he finally said, walking over to pick up his sword.

Her mind reeled. *Give yourself to me*, Stephen had pleaded that day on the bed. She thought he meant in marriage. But it meant something else, didn't it? Had she gotten absolutely everything wrong?

She needed to talk to someone. Now. Soon. Who? Joan. Would Joan know?

David walked back over to the door. *Today you wake up*, he had said. Dear God, but she felt awake now. Horribly so.

"I will not return here, Christiana. We will do it your way. Today I learned that Edward will attend our wedding. Your brother and the King will deliver you to me two

Tuesdays hence. If you have need of me before that, you know where to find me."

He turned to go. Out of the jumbled confusion of her mind a question that she had pondered leapt forward. Without thinking, she blurted it out. "Who is Frans van Horlst to you?"

Perhaps because it was so unexpected and so irrelevant to what had just occurred, it startled him. He quickly composed himself.

"He is a Flemish merchant. We have business together."

He was lying. She just sensed it. *Dear God, I don't know him at all. Twelve days and I don't know him.*

The shock to her emotions had made her very alert, very awake. Inconsistencies about David suddenly presented themselves. She had never noticed them before. She had never paid attention.

There were a lot, and her suspicions about Frans van Horlst only added to them. What were these trips he took? How did he have access to Edward? Why offer for her and pay a huge bride price? Why did he have a servant who looked like a soldier? How did he know that Stephen was not coming?

He knew that for sure. She just felt it.

Finally she spoke. "Who are you? Really?"

The question startled him anew. For the briefest instant the mask dropped, and in those eyes of lapis lazuli she saw layer upon layer of shadowed emotions. Then his careful expression returned and he smiled at her. It was a faint smile that revealed nothing.

He opened the door. "You know who I am, my lady. I am the merchant who paid a fortune for the right to take you to my bed."

She stood with her arms embracing herself in the

towel and listened to his steps recede through the anteroom.

He had responded to the last question just as she had
asked it, in perfect Parisian French.

Christiana waited until the deep of night when the apartment and the castle were silent before slipping out of her
bed. At the end of the room, Lady Idonia slept the sleep
of the dead. Christiana wasn't surprised. Idonia had
returned from her ride with Sieg flush faced and bright
eyed, looking very young for her thirty-eight years.
Kerchief gone and hair disarrayed, she had only halfheartedly mumbled some criticisms of David's presumptuous
servant and of David himself, who had ordered Sieg to
carry her off.

She padded the few steps to Joan's bed and slipped
between the curtains. She sat on the bed and jostled her
shoulder. Total darkness wrapped the bed, and that suited
her just fine. She felt like an idiot and didn't need to see
Joan's amusement during this conversation.

She sensed Joan jolt wake and heard her sit up.

"It is I," Christiana whispered. "I need to speak with
you. It is very important."

Little stretches and yawns filled the tented space. Joan
shifted over to make more room. Christiana crossed her
legs and pulled part of the coverlet over them.

"Joan, I need you to tell me what happens between a
man and a woman when they are married."

"Oh my goodness," Joan said. "You mean . . . no one
ever . . . Idonia didn't . . ."

"Idonia did. When I was about ten. But I think that I
misunderstood." Christiana remembered well what Idonia
had said to her. In its own way it had been quite straight-
forward, up to a point, and had struck her at the time as

very peculiar and not very interesting. She suspected that Idonia had assumed that over the years common sense would fill in the essential gaps, but until this afternoon her imagination had failed her.

"You marry in less than two weeks, Christiana."

"Which is why I need to know now."

"I would say so. The notion usually takes a while to get used to."

"How long?"

"For me, about three years."

Wonderful.

"So tell me."

Joan sighed. "Let's see. Well, haven't you ever seen animals mating?"

"I have lived at court since I was seven. Where in these crowded castles and palaces do animals mate? The stables? The kennels? Not the dinner hall or the garden. I didn't grow up on a country estate like you, Joan."

"Dear saints."

"Tell me bluntly, Joan. Plain language. No gaps."

Joan took a deep breath and then explained quickly. Christiana felt more the fool with each word that she heard. Deep in her heart she had known since David touched her that it was thus, but her mind simply wouldn't accept the appalling logic of it.

Jokes suddenly made sense. Vague lines in songs abruptly became clear. Stephen's hand pushing apart her thighs . . .

He had not done this thing to her, but he had planned to. Only Idonia's arrival had saved her from that brutal shock. She hadn't even known what he was about.

David . . . good heavens.

"Can a man tell if you have done this before?" she asked cautiously.

She could feel Joan's eyes boring through the blackness. "Usually." Joan explained how they could tell. Christiana winced at the description of pain and blood.

"Are you saying that you did this and didn't know it, Christiana? That doesn't make sense."

"Nay. I thought that I had . . . I told David that I had."

Joan barely suppressed a giggle. "Well, that is a switch. Normally girls need to make excuses why there *isn't* evidence of virginity. You, on the other hand . . ."

"Don't laugh at me, Joan. This is serious."

"Aye. He may think that you lied to get out of the marriage, mayn't he?"

Aye, he may, Christiana thought dully.

Joan's hand touched her arm. "Who was it? I didn't realize there was someone. No wonder that you have been so unhappy about this betrothal. I never saw you even speak with a man more than once or twice, except maybe . . ." Her hand gripped tighter. "Is that who it was? Stephen Percy? Oh, Christiana."

She neither agreed nor disagreed. Joan knew she had guessed right, though, and in a way she was glad. It felt good to finally share that agony, even if the pain had been dulling for some time now.

Joan's hand sought hers in the dark. When she spoke, her voice was low and sympathetic. "I must tell you something. You will hear it soon, for it will be all around the court in the next day or so. Stephen's uncle was on the bridge, and Thomas and I spoke with him. He received a messenger today from Northumberland." She squeezed Christiana's hand. "Stephen was betrothed ten days ago. The match had been made when he was just a youth."

A huge, deep fissure opened up inside her, slicing through her soul as if it were carved by hot steel. It reached down to the deepest reaches, releasing at last all of those fears and suspicions and forbidden doubts. They surged and overwhelmed her.

"I am sure that he loves you," Joan said soothingly. "His family no doubt forced him to this. It is common enough when early matches are made."

Aye, common enough. Men married women they did not love or want and amused themselves elsewhere as they pleased. She suddenly and clearly saw Stephen's wooing of her as the insincere, dishonorable thing it had been. A game of seduction to pass the time even while he knew his future wife waited back home. Had Morvan's threats made the siege more interesting, more exciting?

She thought of the letter she had sent him. Had he laughed? Her ignorance about men and women had been making her feel like a fool this evening, but that was nothing compared to the devastating desolation this news of Stephen caused. Her body shook and her heart began burning and shattering. She released Joan's hand and scooted off the bed.

"I'm so sorry, Christiana," Joan said.

Controlling her emotions by a hairbreadth, she pushed through the drapery and rushed to her own bed. She threw herself on her stomach and, biting a pillow to muffle the sound, cried out her humiliation and bitter disappointment.

CHAPTER 8

SHE REMAINED IN bed for two days. During the first one, she wallowed in a bitter pain full of memories suddenly seen anew. Stephen's words and face had not changed in them, but different meanings now became terribly clear. The truth mortified her, and by day's end she was close to hating Stephen Percy for having used and humiliated her.

The next day she lay in a dumb stupor, floating mindlessly through time. The numb daze was soothing and she considered staying forever in it.

On Sunday she rose from her bed and dressed. She managed not to think about Stephen much at all, but on the few occasions that she did, a raw sore of pain and anger reopened before she pushed his memory out of her mind.

By Tuesday she felt much better and more herself again. She even laughed at a little joke that Isabele made while they dressed in the morning. The glances of relief that Idonia and Joan exchanged made her laugh again.

And then, right after dinner, the tailor arrived for the final fitting of her wedding gown, reminding her abruptly that in exactly one week she would marry David de Abyndon.

That reality had been neatly obscured by the violent emotions that had ripped through her upon hearing the news about Stephen. As she stood motionlessly in the silvery pink gown, however, she knew that it was time to face the facts about this marriage.

It was going to happen. In a week Morvan would literally hand her over to him. She would live in the house that she had refused to visit, and be mistress to a household whom she had refused to meet. The center of her life would move from Westminster's court to the merchant community of London. Her life would be tied to and owned by this man forever.

Nothing would be the same. She looked at Joan and Isabele. Would they remain her friends? Perhaps, but they would drift apart because her life would not be here. She thought about the animosity between Morvan and David. Would her husband let her see her brother again? It would be in his power to refuse it.

During her years at court, she had always been a little adrift, but her brother and her few friends had served as anchors for her. After she married, she would have only David for a long while. Without him she would be completely alone in that new life that awaited.

As she turned this way and that while the tailor inspected his work, she contemplated David. She desperately wanted to hate him for being right about Stephen, but she could not. If David had not pointed the way to the truth, would she have ever seen it? How much easier to make excuses for Stephen like Joan had done. How reassuring to avoid the real pain and continue the illusion of a true love thwarted.

She didn't know David very well, but she had come very close to not knowing him at all. In the face of her indifference to him and blind loyalty to Stephen, he had tried to prepare her.

She had left things badly with him. True to his word, he had not come back to Westminster. She had insulted him that day in ways that she didn't fully understand.

The tailor left, and she walked over to a window and gazed down into the courtyard. She pictured David riding in and dismounting, and imagined his steps coming toward the apartment. In her mind he kissed her and her skin awoke with the warmth of his lips. She let the memories fuse and progress, and she felt his firm hand on her breast. She clenched her teeth against the desire that phantom touch awakened. Finally she forced herself to picture the joining that Joan had described.

Her imagination failed her and the image disappeared as if a drape had dropped in front of it. Pain and blood the first time, according to Joan. Lured by pleasure into horror.

He would not come. *You know where to find me*, he had said. An invitation. To what, though? His company or his bed?

It surprised her what these thoughts were doing. Her heart yearned to indeed see him appear in the courtyard below. She missed him, and the knowledge that he waited for her went far to ease the pain of these last days. The fear of what he awaited could not obscure the images of his kind attention to her. Thinking of Stephen still opened hollows in her soul, but David's memory soothed the devastation.

It was whispered that he wanted her so much he had paid that bride price to have her. The idea of the marriage bed filled her with dismay, but at least David had pursued her honorably. He hadn't tried to steal what he wanted in a dusty room in a deserted passageway as Stephen had.

He had a right to know about Stephen. More importantly, she needed to explain the stupid mistake that she had made about that other thing. The world treated virginity as very important, and so she suspected that such things mattered much to men.

It would not be easy to go to him. She steeled her will. They faced a life together. She could not meet him at the wedding with what stood between them unresolved.

Tomorrow she would go and find him. She would ride her black horse and wear her red cloak. She would also deal with one other problem as well.

That evening she went down to the hall well before supper and sought out Morvan. She found him with a young widow who had recently come down from the Midlands to visit Philippa. His black eyes sparkled with their dark fire. The poor girl looked like a stunned animal caught in the light of a torch. Christiana knew well this feminine reaction to him. Now, however, she understood exactly what he was about. Marching over, she interrupted his seduction with a loud greeting and a rude dismissal of the woman.

"Later, Christiana," he snapped.

"Now, brother," she replied. "In the garden, where we can be alone, please."

Fuming silently he took leave of his helpless prey and followed her through the passageways to the garden. The sun had set and twilight dimmed.

He was still annoyed. She didn't care. The stories about her brother were some of those things that made far too much sense all of a sudden. He was little better than Stephen from what she could tell, except that he didn't ruin virgins.

"Tomorrow I want to go and see David in the city," she explained. "I want you to take me to him."

"Send word to him and let him come here."

"He will not come. I left things badly when last we met."

"Then let him wait until the wedding to see you."

"I must speak with him, Morvan. There are things that I need to discuss."

"You will have years to talk, thanks to the King. I will not take you to him." He turned to leave.

She stomped her foot and grabbed his arm. "He thinks that I am not a virgin, Morvan."

That stopped him. He regarded her carefully. "Why?"

She faced him bravely. She understood her brother now, and his overbearing protection. Like David, he knew men well. He protected her from such as himself.

"Because I told him that I was not."

"You lied about such a thing? Even to avoid this marriage, Christiana, such a lie . . ."

"I thought it was the truth."

The implications sank in. "Who?" he asked quietly. Too quietly.

"I will not say. Do not think to bully me, Morvan. It is over and done with and thanks to Idonia I am whole. It is partly your fault, brother. If you had not scared off every boy, I might have had some experience in knowing a man's intentions. As it was, I was helpless against them and, until three days ago, didn't even know what he wanted from me."

He stood silently in the gray light. "Good God," he finally said.

"Aye. Eighteen and as ignorant as a babe. I came close to learning the hard way, didn't I? And almost went to my marriage bed a complete innocent."

"Hell."

"So, I did not lie to David. What had occurred between me and this other man seemed to fit all of the requirements as I stupidly understood them."

"And this merchant, knowing this, still took your hand?"

"Aye. I told him before the betrothal. He said that repudiation would ruin me."

He shook his head thoughtfully. "This marriage never made any sense."

"Nay, but I cannot worry about that now. I must see him before the wedding. I want to explain this."

He brought his arm around her shoulders and began guiding her back toward the castle door. "It is well that you explain. He might hurt you more than he has to if he doesn't know."

The very frank way he said this surprised her. So did this new ambiguous piece of information. Perhaps she should have talked to Morvan instead of Joan. She smiled, picturing her brother's distress as she demanded blunt descriptions with no gaps.

"If you go to him, he will misunderstand why you have come," he said. "It is said that he wants you badly. Perhaps that is the explanation for everything after all."

"Then I wish I had not been so unworldly. I might have traded my body for my freedom that night."

"It doesn't work that way, Christiana."

How does it work? she wanted to ask. "Well, I marry him in less than a week. When he hears what I have to say, he will not misunderstand why I have come. I must go, and I want you to bring me."

A torch by the doorway illuminated his handsome face. "So you go to him before the wedding, and I take you there? Of your own will, prior to the King's command? Having just learned what this man expects from you?"

"I face a life with him, Morvan. I want to see him and start it well. And I want him to know that you accept it, so that perhaps he will not stand between us. Aye, I go of my own will and I want him to see that I do."

He sighed with resignation. "In the morning then. Although it will kill me. Never have I brought such a precious gift to a man I disliked so much."

They stopped their horses at the end of the lane and looked up at David's shop. A large cart stood outside laden with large cylinders wrapped in rough cloth. Sieg pulled strenuously on a rope running up to a round wheel projecting from the beam of the attic. One of the cylinders dangled from the other end of the rope while he hauled it up the side of the building, his large muscles rippling under the strain as he yanked the rope hand over hand.

The cylinder reached the open attic window. Christiana caught a brief glimpse of golden brown hair as a strong arm reached out and grabbed the rope, pulling the load in.

Her courage had been slowly leaking away since yesterday evening and now she debated turning back. If David was busy today . . .

"He will stop his work when you come," Morvan said. He moved his horse forward.

She fell in beside him. "I don't know, Morvan. Perhaps. . . ."

"He wants you and nothing else will matter. Trust me on this, sister. I know of what I speak." He gave her a wink.

Morvan helped her to dismount. Sieg was busy

tying another cylinder to the rope and did not notice her.

"I will come back in a few hours. Early afternoon," Morvan said.

"Maybe tomorrow would be better."

He kissed her brow. "You made your decision with a clear head and an honest heart, Christiana. You were right. This marriage cannot be stopped and it is best that you see him. Courage now."

She nodded and entered the shop.

Two apprentices served patrons inside. The younger, dark-haired one, a youth of perhaps fourteen years, approached her.

"My name is Michael, my lady. How can I serve you?"

"I am Christiana Fitzwaryn. I have come to see your master. He is upstairs?"

Michael nodded, his expression awestruck.

"My horse is in the lane," she said, handing her cloak to him. "Perhaps when you are free you will move him for me."

She marched valiantly down the passageway. She climbed the steep steps to the second level and the sounds of tailors talking and working in the front chamber. Along the wall of this passage rose another set of steps, very steep and open like a ladder. She walked down to their base and, gathering her tattered courage, lifted her skirt to mount them.

She held on to the wall to keep her balance. The treads were narrow and treacherous. Her concentration distracted her and so she was almost at the top before she realized that her way was blocked. A little sound caught her attention.

On the third step from the top perched a small black kitten. It wailed faintly and helplessly as it surveyed its precarious position. Somehow it had gotten itself here, but it knew not how to get back up or down.

She tottered on the stair. She hadn't seen many cats before. Most people were afraid of them. This one, with its puny little sounds, was adorable. And in her way.

She lifted the kitten into her arms. At first it curled against her chest as if grateful for the security. But when she tried to climb the next step, it shrieked in terror and stretched up, clawing into her chest. She gasped as tiny spikes dug into her skin.

Footsteps approached the top of the stairs. Andrew, stripped to the waist, gazed down at her.

"David," he called over his shoulder.

David walked into view. Like Andrew he was naked to the waist, and a slight sheen of sweat glistened on his shoulders from his labors in the warm attic. She noticed with surprise the taut definition of the muscles of his broad shoulders and arms and chest. He looked lean and hard and athletic.

She was unaccustomed to seeing men undressed. In the summer, knights and soldiers stripped thus when they used the practice yards, and some of the girls made it a point to walk by, but Lady Idonia had forbidden it and lectured them about impure thoughts. David's very apparent flesh stunned her. She stared speechlessly up at that handsome face and body.

The kitten decided to move. She cried and tottered as the little paws dug their way up until the furry body straddled her shoulder.

"Steady now," David said. He stepped down and sat on the landing, reaching toward the kitten. He pried its claws out of her skin, removing them carefully so that the fabric of her surcoat and gown would not snag. He lifted the howling animal away.

It curled up contentedly, soft and furry against his chest. He stroked it absently and turned his blue eyes to her. Those beautiful hands holding that black fur against the hard chest struck her as incredibly alluring.

"You are busy. I should have sent word first," she said.

He twisted and placed the kitten on the floor behind him. The action made his muscles stretch with sinuous elegance. "Go find your mother," he told the cat. The little black face closed its eyes and rubbed against his back before scampering off.

He looked at her again and smiled. "I am not so busy. I am glad that you came."

He rose and stepped down toward her. "I will help you back down." He squeezed past and aided her as her feet blindly sought each step. Halfway down he jumped to the floor and plucked her off by her waist, setting her beside him.

"Go downstairs and wait for me."

There had been no greeting. No courtly pleasantries. He had not asked why she had come, and simply acted as if he knew. She scurried down to the invisibility of the lower passageway.

David watched her hurry away. She had surprised him by coming here. He had underestimated her.

Andrew hopped down the steps, carrying both of their shirts. He glanced at Christiana's disappearing skirt. "She's going to bolt," he observed casually.

David took his shirt.

Andrew gestured to the stairs. "By the time you are washed and dressed, she'll be gone."

"Are you giving me advice on women now?"

Andrew laughed. "Women? Hell, no, I wouldn't think of it. But then, she's not a woman, is she? She's just a girl.

I wager I've had more experience with them than you have recently." He pulled his shirt over his head. "One moment they are brave, the next they are shy. First it's aye, then nay. Remember? She used all of her courage to come, and now she is telling herself to leave. Unless, of course, your warm welcome reassured her. Smooth, that."

David looked at the empty stairs. Andrew's sarcasm was justified. He hadn't greeted her well and it *had* taken a lot of courage for her to come.

He went into the counting room and grabbed Andrew's pourpoint and threw it at him. "Then get yourself down there, boy, and stall her until I come," he said. "Block the damn door with a sword if you have to."

Andrew grinned and pulled the garment on. "Aye. And I'll tell Sieg that we'll take a break with the last carpets. He and I can get it done before dinner without you." He sidled to the doorway. "I assume this means that we will forget about that last nightwalking fine."

"Go!"

He followed Andrew down the stairs and watched him head in search of Christiana. He slipped out the back to the well and began washing off the dust in the crisp air.

She had heard about Percy's betrothal, of course. Almost a week ago probably. How bad had it been for her? He didn't like to think of her hurt, but he didn't want her making excuses for the man either. A woman could fill a lifetime with excuses to avoid the truth.

His head had been full of her since he had left her last Thursday. He rarely second-guessed himself, but during the days and long into the nights as he thought about her, he had considered how he had handled this girl and whether he hadn't made some miscalculations. He wasn't used to them so young, of course. He forgot sometimes that there was still something of the child in her. Even his greeting today . . . an Alicia would have welcomed his frank acceptance of her arrival. But Christiana was not like Alicia.

He had visited Westminster on Monday and almost gone to that apartment. He felt pulled there, and only a long inner debate had kept him away. *Let her come to me*, he had decided. *Either on her own or for the wedding.* He had stuck to that resolve until last night, when Oliver had appeared late at the house with some news. And then he had known that he couldn't wait for her to come any longer.

He dried himself as he went back upstairs to dress. But for the early arrival of that ship from Spain and its cargo of carpets, he would have spared her this cost to her pride. He had planned to fetch her from Westminster this morning, and only this work had delayed him. She had come to him first, however. A small gift to him from Lady Fortune. It was better for Christiana this way, too.

He went back downstairs. He could see a bit of red near the entrance of the shoproom. She had already reclaimed her cloak. Andrew's body stretched casually against the threshold, his foot resting across the space on the opposite jamb. He hadn't blocked the way with a sword exactly, but the red cloak could not pass.

He walked toward them and Andrew looked up in a meaningful way. Dropping his leg, he let the cloak ease into the passageway, right into David's arms.

"You are ready to go then?" David asked.

"Go?" she asked, flustered by his sudden presence.

"We will go to the house. John Constantyn is coming

for dinner but first we need to get some salve for the cat scratches. They might make you ill if you aren't careful."

She smiled weakly. "Your house . . . aye, I would like to see it."

There had been the possibility, small but real, that she had come to ask for the annulment. He allowed himself one breath of relief that the request would not come and that he would not have to refuse it.

"How did you get here?"

"My horse is in the alley, I think. Morvan brought me. He comes back in three hours or so."

Interesting. "We will walk. Let me tell the boys to bring the horse."

He went back into the shop and gave the apprentices instructions, then returned to her. He guided her up the lane with his arm about her shoulders, enjoying her warmth beside him and the feel of her arm beneath his hand.

Nothing could hide in this sunlight and he studied her face. She looked as exquisitely beautiful as ever, but subtle changes were apparent. He knew her face well, had memorized its details and nuances, and could read the anguish of the last days in it.

She turned her head and her sparkling eyes regarded him. He saw a change in those dark diamonds as well. Their glitter had dimmed very slightly, as if one facet of trust and innocence had dulled.

I will obliterate your memory of him.

She kept glancing at him and parting her lips as if she planned to speak. Finally the words poured out.

"You were right. About Stephen. He is betrothed as well. An old match. But you knew that, didn't you? You knew on Thursday that I would hear of it soon."

How long before she could read him as clearly as he

did her? She was by nature intelligent and perceptive. The girl often misunderstood what she saw, but the woman would not.

"I knew."

"Why didn't you tell me?"

"It was not for me to do so."

"You knew before the court. Even his uncle only heard that morning."

"Merchants and pilgrims arrive every day from the north. They bring gossip and news."

"You were asking them?"

"Aye."

"I feel like an idiot," she said forcefully. "You must think women are fools and that I am one of the worst."

"I do not think that. And if it makes you feel like an idiot, let us not speak of it."

They turned onto the lane with his house. She stopped and turned to him. Her brow puckered as she looked in his eyes.

"Will you tell me now? Why you marry me?"

He glanced away from her confused curiosity. Sore and wounded, she thought she had nothing to lose from blunt questions and frank answers. How would she react if he told her the truth?

What was the truth?

It had been weeks since he had thought about the bizarre bargain that had given her to him. In his mind, Edward's story had become real, and the license and its payment the deception. He had indeed seen her and wanted her and offered a fortune for her. The money had been for her and the license had become the gift and not the other way around. If the King tomorrow demanded another thousand pounds to let him keep her, he would pay it without a second thought.

He wanted her. Not for one night or a few months. He did not think of her that way and never had. Perhaps the inevitable permanence of marriage had woken this deeper desire in him. He wanted her body and her soul and her loyalty and her joy. He did not question why he wanted her. It just *was*.

"I marry you because I want to," he said.

CHAPTER 9

THE GATE TO the courtyard stood open. She paused in the passageway and then walked bravely into the sunny yard full of laughing women and fluttering cloth. Two large tubs stood side by side, one over a low fire.

Laundry day.

David strolled into the melee. A thin old woman with a kerchief on her hair hustled in their direction. He embraced the crone and kissed her cheek.

"They said you was out for a shipment, and I didn't expect to see you," the woman said, smiling.

"Slow down so you can have dinner with us, Meg," he said. "John is coming." He turned and pulled Christiana forward. "This is Christiana, Meg. My wife."

Meg peered at her with filmy eyes. Her toothless mouth gaped in a grin. "A beauty, David." She winked at Christiana. "Watch yourself. He's been nothing but trouble and mischief since he could walk."

David led Christiana away. "You and the women will stay, Meg. I will tell Vittorio."

Christiana followed him into the hall. "The laundress Meg has known you a long time," she said as she took in the large chamber's furnishings. Nice chairs. A handsome tapestry. Beautiful copper sconces to hold the wall torches.

"My mother worked for her when I was a child."

A middle-aged woman opened a door at the far end, and tumultuous sounds of pots banging and male cursing poured out at them. The plump woman carried a stack of silver plates in her arms. She looked Christiana up and down. David introduced her as Geva, the housekeeper. Geva smiled, but Christiana saw criticism in her sharp gray eyes.

David pushed open the door to the kitchen attached to the side of the hall. "And this is Vittorio." He gestured to a rotund, round-eyed man barking accented orders to a girl and man who assisted him. Worktables laden with knives and chopped food lined the room, and copper pots hung in the immense hearth. Vittorio bent his head to one of the pots, sniffed, and raised his thick black eyebrows in an expression of reluctant approval.

"Vittorio," David called.

The fat man straightened and looked over. "Ah! *La ragazza! La sposa!*" he announced to the assistants. They stopped their chores and smiled greetings.

He clasped his hands effusively. "*Finalmente!* Signorina Christiana, eh? Beautiful name. *Bellissima*, David." He made a comical look of approval.

"Lady Christiana will dine with us, Vittorio. And Meg and her women as well."

Vittorio nodded. "*Si, si.*" He turned back to the kitchen and gestured for the assistants.

David took her into the building across from the gate. She knew from her last visit that the solar was upstairs, but he led her past the steps to a simple bedchamber. "I will have Geva get the salves," he explained before leaving.

She removed her cloak. This chamber held some items of a personal nature. A simple cloak hung on a wall peg. A silver comb lay on a table. She sat on the bed and waited for Geva.

It was David who returned, however, and not the housekeeper. He carried a bowl of water and a rag and a small jar. He placed them on the table.

His long fingers pushed aside the shoulder of her surcoat. She glanced down at that hand and the scratches it uncovered. He moved to her other side and began unlacing the back neckline of the sleeveless outer garment. She glanced up at him in surprise.

"The salve will stain it," he explained, gesturing for her to stand and helping her to step out of it. The intimacy of the simple, practical action unsettled her.

"Is this Geva's chamber?"

The neck of her cotehardie was cut low and broad and exposed the scratches. He dipped a rag in the water and began wiping the little streaks of blood from her skin. "Geva lives in the city with her family and comes by day. This was my mother's chamber. She was David Constantyn's housekeeper for ten years before her death. He met her through Meg. She did laundry here with the others, and when his housekeeper died he gave her the position."

"And later made you his apprentice?"

"Aye."

He carefully cleaned the scratches on the back of her shoulder. She tried to ignore his closeness and the attention he gave his ministrations. She noticed again the objects on the table. They seemed to still hold something of the dead woman's presence.

He picked up the jar. "Don't worry. You are not intruding on a shrine. This chamber is used by visitors."

He soothed some of the salve over the scratches, and she sat very still with the warmth of his fingertips on her skin and the slight sting of the medicine in the sores. She lifted her gaze and saw him looking down at her. She thought that she knew that look.

She had better explain why she had come. Soon. They needed a place to talk alone, but not here in this room.

"Is there a garden?" she asked, rising.

He lifted her cloak to her shoulders. "This way."

The garden stretched behind the building and the kitchen. A high wall enclosed it. It was barren now except for some hedges and ivy, but she could tell that in summer it would be lush. Flower beds, crisscrossed with paths, flowed back to a little orchard of fruit trees. A larger bed near the kitchen would be planted with vegetables.

"There is a smaller garden back here," he said, leading her to a door in the wall.

The tiny second garden charmed her. Ivy grew everywhere, covering the walls and ground and creeping up to form a roof on a small arbor set in one corner. Two tall trees filled the space. In summer this enclosure would be cool and silent. An outer stairway led from the garden to the second level of the building.

She doubted that she would find anyplace more private than this. "Can we sit down? I need to tell you something."

They sat on a stone bench nestled deep inside the ivy covered arbor. Sunlight broke through the dense covering, mottling the shadows with little pools of yellow light.

She bent over and plucked a sprig of ivy from the carpet at her feet. She nervously pulled the little points off the leaves. Probably best to just plunge in.

"When we first met, I told you . . . I indicated that I was not . . . that Stephen and I had . . ."

"That does not matter now."

"It does, though. I must explain something." She tried to remember the exact words that she had rehearsed.

His voice came low and quiet. "Are you saying that there were others?"

"Heavens, nay! I did not lie about that. I am trying to say that there was no one, not even Stephen. It seems that I was wrong. I made a mistake." She thought that she would feel less awkward once it was said. It didn't work that way.

For a long while he didn't move or speak. She concentrated on pulling the ivy leaves off their branch.

"It is a difficult mistake for a girl to make, Christiana. Impossible, I would think," he finally said.

Saints, but she felt like a fool. "Not if she doesn't know what she is talking about, David."

His motionless silence stretched longer this time. She suffered it for a while, and then snuck a glance at him.

"Are you angry?"

"You have it backwards. A man is supposed to get angry when he learns of his new wife's experience, not her innocence."

"You might be angry if you thought that I lied on purpose. To discourage you."

"I don't think that. In fact, what you have told me explains much. When did you realize your mistake?"

She had assumed that she could just blurt this out and be done with it. She hadn't expected a conversation.

"Last Thursday night."

He stayed silent and she knew that he was remembering the two of them in the wardrobe. His body pressed to hers. That intimate caress. Her cry of shock.

"I must have frightened you very badly."

He regarded her with a warm and concerned expression. He could be a very kind man sometimes. Perhaps he even understood how distressing all of this had been. Maybe . . .

"Nay," he said with a small smile.

"Nay what?"

"You are wondering if, under the circumstances, we might put off the wedding or at least that part of it. I think not."

She blushed from her hair to her neck. It really was discomforting to have him read her thoughts like that.

He reached over and lightly touched her hair. "Although, considering this stunning revelation, I probably won't seduce you today as I had planned."

She almost gushed relief and gratitude before she caught herself. Her face burned hotter yet. His fingers on her hair and head felt very nice, though. Comforting.

"Who spoke with you?"

"I asked Joan."

"She is unmarried herself. Are you sure she got it right? That you know what I expect from you?"

"I doubt that Joan gets much wrong where men are concerned."

He laughed. "Aye, I suspect not."

Never in her life had she felt this awkward and embarrassed. She wished that someone would come and announce that John Constantyn had arrived.

"How often were you with him?"

Dear saints. She stared at her lap, covered now with little bits of ivy leaves and branches. She brushed them off.

"Just that once. Do not be too hard on him, David. He had reason to believe that I agreed. My misunderstanding of his intentions and actions was boundless."

"Were you unclothed?"

Her mouth fell open. She continued staring at her lap,

and as she did, his hand appeared and he placed another sprig of ivy there. The gesture and its understanding of her embarrassment touched her. All the same he waited for her answer. It seemed odd that when he thought her experienced, he had requested no information, but now that he knew her not to be, he wanted these details. She had opened a door and he seemed determined to examine the entire chamber behind it.

"Partly. He ripped one of my surcoats." Stephen's carelessness there had assumed a symbolic quality these last few days.

His hand still gently touched her head, brushing a few feathery hairs away from her temple. "Did he touch you?"

"We were on a bed together. He couldn't avoid touching me," she sharply. "I don't want to talk about this. Why do you ask me these things?"

"So I know how careful I must be with you."

She took a deep breath. She realized that there was such a thing as being so embarrassed that it couldn't get any deeper and that she had reached that point. There was a certain freedom in knowing that it wouldn't get any worse.

"Not the way that you did . . . last time. Idonia came in first. Just in time, according to her. He touched my breast, though. He hurt me." It felt good accusing Stephen of that. She had thought at the time that it was the only way.

"I didn't like it," she added, honestly remembering her reaction to that crushing body. "I decided that I was one of those women who . . . who . . ."

"Is cold?"

"Aye. One of those."

"We both know that is not so, Christiana. Besides, I do not think that there are many cold women. There are, however, many men who are ignorant, selfish, or impatient. You will find that I am none of those things."

Deep in her heart, she knew that. It was what kept her from panicking when she thought about this marriage, so inevitable and close now. It was that which had given her the courage to come despite Morvan's warnings of what it might lead to. Still, she was glad that he had decided not to seduce her today.

She waited for his next question as he touched her in that soothing, vaguely exciting way. Her scalp tingled from the light pressure of his fingers. She gazed at her lap and the destruction she had absently wrought on the second sprig of ivy.

There were other things that she needed to say. She wanted to tell him that she accepted the marriage. He deserved to hear it after all of the times she had smugly insisted it would never happen. She needed to promise that she would try to be a good wife to him, whatever that meant. She would like to thank him for being so patient with her. She had expected all of those things to be easier to explain than this first admission, but she found now that they were much harder.

As she groped to phrase these other things and sought the courage to say them, his right hand came into her view and settled on her lap beside her own. He turned it palm up.

She smiled down at that beautiful hand waiting for her. Her gaze locked on its exciting, elegant strength. No kinsman or priest would join them today, but there was an offer and promise in his gesture far more meaningful than the official betrothal.

He understood. He was making it easier for her. Today is the real beginning, that hand said.

Forever. The immensity of it tried to suffocate her for an instant, but she pushed the fear away.

It was why she had come, wasn't it?

She placed her own hand in his. Of her own will.

He pulled gently and lifted her, turning her so that he could set her on his lap. The devastated ivy scattered down her cloak.

She looked into deep blue eyes full of kindness and warmth. It occurred to her that maybe she didn't have to say anything else at all.

Tentatively she placed her arm around his shoulders. A little awkwardly, she reached out and touched his face. It was the first time that she had touched him instead of the other way around. It felt different this way, and she marveled at the sensation of his skin beneath her fingertips.

She let her fingers caress the planes of his handsome face. They came to rest on his lips, and she lightly stroked their warmth.

He did not move. She lifted her gaze to his eyes and collected her bravery. After a little false start she leaned forward and kissed him.

She had never done this before, with him or anyone, and once her lips were on his she really didn't know what to do. It felt very nice though, and she pressed a little harder. His mouth smiled beneath hers.

She pulled away sheepishly. "You are laughing at me because I don't know how to do it."

His hand rose up and cradled her head. "Nay. I am thinking that was the most wonderful kiss I have ever had."

She blushed and kissed him again. He took over this time, responding to her artless start.

She loved the way that he kissed her. She always had. The sensations he awoke in her were always so powerful and sweet and heady. This time she didn't completely lose herself, though, but followed his lead, doing as he did, learning from him. Finally, when he gently bit the corner of her mouth, she parted her lips to him.

He did not choke and gag her as Stephen had, but instead gently stroked the inside of her mouth at first, sending chill upon chill down her spine. The intimacy startled her, and when he deepened the kiss she sensed a change in him and a rising passion that excited her as much as his warmth and touch. She had always been so caught up in her own reactions that she hadn't noticed his. Sharing the pleasure was much richer than just accepting it, and in a way this kiss moved her more than anything they had ever done before.

"Oh my," she gasped when they separated.

"Surely you have kissed like that before."

"It wasn't so nice."

"Ah. Well, perhaps it helps now that you know that it won't get you with child."

She closed her eyes and groaned in mortification. Burying her face into his shoulder, she muttered miserably, "How did you know?"

He began laughing. "You have always kept your lips locked like they were the gate to paradise itself, Christiana. I thought that you simply didn't like it. But it is the only misunderstanding that has any logic."

She laughed too. She lifted her head and wiped the tears brimming at her eyes. "Oh, dear saints. I assure you, it made perfect sense in light of what Idonia had told me when I was younger. You must think that I am the most stupid girl you have ever met."

He shook his head. "I think that you are the most beautiful girl whom I have ever met."

It was sweet of him to say that, but he had no doubt known many beautiful women. Still, it felt nice to be wooed with pretty words. He had never done that before.

"You don't believe me."

"I am pretty enough, David. I know that. But not really beautiful. Not like Joan."

"Lady Joan is like a sunbeam and is a beautiful girl, Christiana. You, however, are the velvet night. Dark sky"—he touched her hair—"Pale light"—his fingers stroked her skin—"Stars"—he kissed the side of her eye.

The sounds of voices intruded from the outer garden. She glanced resentfully in their direction. She wanted to stay in this hidden arbor longer, laughing and talking with David. Maybe kissing again.

"We must go back," he said regretfully. "John will be here by now."

They found John talking loudly with Sieg and peering around the garden for signs of the alerted lovers. He gave David a very male look as the couple emerged through the garden door and greeted him.

CHAPTER 10

CHRISTIANA ASSUMED THAT the dinner was more lavish than the household's usual midday meal. The visit of John Constantyn probably accounted for most of the extra dishes and savories, but she suspected that her own presence had inspired Vittorio to some last minute delicacies.

"He's one of the best cooks in London, I'll wager," John confided. "I wrangle an invitation to eat here whenever I can." He patted his thickening girth. "Better not let him cook for your wedding, David. The King will take him from you."

Vittorio made sure that everything was perfect on the table, and then took a seat with the apprentices and Sieg. Soon that whole table chattered in Italian.

"It is easiest for them to learn it at table," David explained. "They will need it for trade."

Christiana watched the boys. Andrew was older than her and Roger just two years younger. They would not find it odd, though, that a girl their own age married their master. Actually, child brides were more common and she was a bit old for the role.

John helped himself to some salmon. "I heard that you received a shipment today, David."

"Carpets from Castile."

"You have been taking a lot of winter cargo."

"They come when they come."

"Like hell. You expect trade to be disrupted in the spring or summer, don't you?" He lowered his voice. "He's going to do it, isn't he? Another damn campaign. Another army to France and every ship in sight requisitioned for it. I'm glad that I only deal in wool. He'll never interfere with that."

"If Edward keeps borrowing money, there will be no silver in the realm even to buy your wool, John, let alone Spanish carpets."

"You always sell your luxuries, David. You always know what they want." He leaned toward Christiana. "He has golden instincts, my lady. Wouldn't touch the King's monopoly for exporting raw wool a few years back and talked me out of it too. Saved my ass. Most everyone involved lost their shirt."

The meal was long, friendly, and relaxed. David and John chatted about business and politics, and they discussed Edward's policies more bluntly than the courtiers. On occasion certain opinions even sounded faintly disloyal. Barons and knights probably spoke thus amongst themselves, too, she realized, but not in the King's hall.

She surveyed the people sitting at the other three tables. In addition to Sieg, Vittorio, Geva, and the apprentices, four other servants worked here on a regular basis. David's household appeared large, well run, and efficient. He certainly didn't need a wife to manage things. She suspected uncomfortably that her own presence would be superfluous at best and maybe even disruptive.

Throughout the entire meal, David let her know that he had not forgotten her presence. His gestures and glances suggested that despite his attention to his guest, most of his mind dwelled on her. When they had both finished eating, his hand rested permanently over hers atop the table, the long fingers absently caressing the back of her palm while he conversed. In subtle ways he maintained the intimacy they had shared in the ivy garden.

She became very conscious of his touch and looks as the meal drew to a close. As the hall began emptying, the apprentices heading back to the shop and the servants to their duties, she sensed his awareness of her heighten even though nothing changed in his behavior or actions.

John Constantyn did not linger long after the other tables had cleared. They accompanied him into the courtyard.

"I will see you at the wedding, my lady," John said. "Is it true that the King attends, David?"

"So I have been told. Christiana is his ward."

"I hear that the mayor convinced you to move the banquet to the Guildhall."

Christiana tried not to embarrass David by letting it show that she knew nothing of the plans for her own wedding. They had never spoken of it. She had never asked, because she had never expected to be there herself.

She could not blame him if he thoroughly disliked her by now. Maybe he did. He would never let her know. He was trapped as completely as she, but would try to make the best of the situation. Is that all they were? Two people accommodating themselves to the inevitable?

"Aye. And the mayor made clear that if the royal family attended, all of the aldermen should be invited," David said. "We will have the mayor's dull, official banquet, and then another one here for the ward and household. Save your appetite, John. Vittorio cooks for the second one."

John laughed. "And your uncle Gilbert, David? Will he come?"

"I invited him. I borrowed a royal page to send the message, in fact. Gilbert's wife is a good woman and I would not insult her. She will make him attend." His eyes sparkled mischievously. "The decision will drive him mad. Decline and he misses the King. Accept and he honors me."

"Aye," John said, grinning. "His dilemma might be cause enough to get married if the best reason didn't stand by your side now."

She decided not to think about how David came to have use of a royal page.

John left then. The courtyard suddenly seemed very quiet.

David's arm slid around her waist. "Come. I'll show you the house."

They visited the stable first. Her black horse, unsaddled and brushed, stood in a stall beside David's two mounts. The groom was nowhere to be seen. She reached up and petted the black nose. She supposed that she could name him now that she would be keeping him.

In the building facing the street she saw the chambers used by Michael, Roger, and some of the servants. Andrew slept at the shop, she knew. It impressed her that each person had his own small room. The servants of this mercer possessed more privacy than the noble wards of the King.

Silence greeted them as they reentered the hall. Even the kitchen echoed empty. Vittorio was just leaving with a basket on his arm to shop for the evening meal. He smiled indulgently and slipped away.

As David opened the door to the last building, Christiana thought that there should probably be a little more household bustle going on. She realized with a jolt that everyone had left the premises.

She followed David to the storage rooms filled with wooden crates on the first level, beyond his mother's old chamber. The scent of cinnamon and cloves wafted toward her. Carpets and spices and silks. Luxuries. John's observation had been correct. David would always sell these things. They defined status and honor and many people would eat only soup in order to purchase them.

His arm circled her shoulders as he led her back toward the kitchen. The simple gesture suddenly seemed less casual than before. Had he dismissed the whole household, or had natural discretion made them all decide to become scarce so that the master could be alone with his lady?

They were alone, that was certain. The resonating silence had imbued this simple tour with a creeping intimacy. By the time they returned to the stairs leading to the upper level and David's chambers, her caution was fully alerted.

David began guiding her up. She balked on the second step.

His smile of amusement made her feel childish. He took her hand. "Come now, girl. You should see your house."

Her mind chastised her instincts. After all, she had been in the solar before. They would marry soon and, despite Morvan's warnings, he had not misunderstood her reason for coming. She let herself be cajoled upwards.

In the light of day she could see the solar's beauty. The glazed windows on one side looked down on the garden, and in summer the flowers' scents would drift into the square high chamber. David built up the fire and she walked around, admiring the furnishings. Each carved chair, each tapestry, every item down to the silver candleholders, possessed an individual and distinctive beauty.

She fingered the relief of ivy edging the chair on which she had sat that first night. What had this man thought of the child who faced him, her feet dangling as she announced her love for someone else?

Stephen. The thought of him could still open a hollow ache.

She looked up to see David regarding her. "Did these lovely things come to you with the house?" she asked.

"Nay."

She hadn't thought so. Like the severe cut of his clothes, they were, in their own ways, perfect.

"You must spend a lot of time looking for such things."

"Rarely. Something catches my eye and I buy it. It doesn't take long at all."

She gazed at one of the tapestries hanging beside the windows. Superb. She thought about Elizabeth's dependence on his taste. He had a natural eye for beauty. It must give him a tremendous advantage in his trade.

I think that you are the most beautiful girl whom I have ever met.

Her eyes slowly followed the sinuous lead tracery that held the pieces of glass together in the windows. She felt him watching her.

He saw her and wanted her and offered the King a fortune for her.

A small book rested on a low table near the hearth. She knew that if she opened it, she would find richly painted illuminations. Like everything else in this room, it would be exquisite.

Something catches my eye and I buy it. It doesn't take long at all.

Two doors flanked the hearth. She drifted to the one on the right and opened it. She found herself on the threshold to his bedchamber. Ignoring a qualm of misgiving at the way he watched her, she went inside.

The hearth in this chamber backed on the solar's and the windows also overlooked the garden. The chamber was simply furnished, with one chair near the fire and a large bed on a low dais in the center of the room. Heavy blue drapes surrounded the bed and formed a canopy, and one side was tied open to reveal a rich matching coverlet. A fire burned in the hearth.

She walked along the wall overlooking the garden and passed through a door at the far end of the chamber. She entered a wardrobe with chests and pegs for clothes. It included a small hearth and wooden tub just like Isabele's, and a door at its end led to a garderobe and privy. A spout in a wall niche, similar to ones seen elsewhere in the house, provided piped water.

She opened a door cut in the wall and found herself at the top of the stairs leading down to the small ivy garden. Besides the solar, this was the only other way into the apartment.

Back in the bedchamber, she looked around, trying to grow accustomed to this space. David stood at the threshold, his shoulder resting casually against the doorjamb. She smiled weakly at him, feeling like an intruder.

"Where is my chamber?"

"You mean the lady's bower? There is none. Merchants do not live that way. Your place is here with me."

He walked to the hearth. There was no need to build up this fire. It sparked and crackled with new logs. She stared at the hot bright flames and read their flickering significance.

Who had come and prepared this room? Geva? He

would not expose his intentions to a woman. Sieg, then. The big Swede had been the first to leave the hall. She doubted that David had said a word to him. It had simply been done. She managed not to glance at that big bed dominating the room. Of course, Sieg would not know of David's reassurances in the garden.

She could not just stand here forever. She searched for something to look at.

The solar stretched the width of the building and had windows over both the garden and the courtyard. This chamber was not so wide, and its court wall was solid. She spied a door at its end and strode toward it.

As soon as she saw the side chamber she stopped in her tracks. It was a study. She quickly surveyed the objects filling it and knew that now she definitely intruded. She began backing out and bumped into David's chest. His hand came to rest over hers on the door and he pushed it forward.

"This is your home," he said. "There are no doors closed to you here."

Home. She had not had a home since Harclow. Not really. As the royal household moved from one castle or manor to the next, she had never felt at home, not even at Westminster. For eleven years she had been something of a permanent guest.

This small chamber might not be closed to her today, but it obviously was to everyone else. No housekeeper tended this room, and a thin layer of dust covered some of the items on the shelves flanking the high window. Her gaze took in a stack of books and some scrolls of paper. A small painting in the Byzantine style and a beautiful ivory carving were propped at one end beside an ancient hand harp whose frame was inlaid with intricate twining lines of silver.

The only furniture was a large table covered with

parchment papers and documents. A chair angled behind it, and underneath she saw a small locked chest on the floor.

From the corner of her eye she noticed that the wall behind the door also bore shelves. She turned and gasped as a man's face peered back at her.

David laughed and stepped past her to the shelf.

"It is remarkable, isn't it?"

She approached in amazement. The man's face was carved in marble and its realism astonished her. Whichever mason had done this work possessed a god's touch. Subtle shadows modeled the skin so accurately that one believed one could touch flesh and feel bone beneath it.

"I found it in Rome," he explained. "Just lying there in the ancient ruins. I picked up a small section of a column and this was underneath. There are many such statues there. Whole bodies just as real, and stone caskets covered with figures that are used now to hold water at fountains. I saw some statues at the Cathedral of Reims recently that come close, but nothing else similar north of the Alps."

Reims. Near Paris. What was he doing there recently? Stupid question. He was a merchant, after all.

"You carried it all of the way home?"

"Nay. I bribed Sieg to," he said, laughing.

"You seem to like carvings and paintings a lot. Why didn't you become a limner or a mason?"

"Because David Constantyn was a mercer and it was he who gave me an apprenticeship. As a boy I sometimes dawdled around a limner's shop and watched them work, mixing their colors and painting the images in books. The master tolerated me and even showed me how to burn wood to make drawing tools. Fate had other plans for me, however, and I do not regret it."

She stepped behind the table. On its corner were some new parchments folded and closed with a seal showing three entwined serpents. Strewn across it were papers with oddly drawn marks. The top one simply showed jagged lines connected by sweeping numbered curves. Little squares and circles lined up along snaking borders. She glanced away carefully. It was a map. Why did David make maps?

Not today, she reminded herself.

She turned and examined the books on the high shelf. "Can I look at one?"

"Which one do you want?"

"The biggest one."

He lifted the large folio down, placing it on the table, covering the cryptic drawings. Christiana sat in the chair and carefully opened it. She stared in surprise at the lines and dots spread out in front of her.

"It is Saracen, David."

"Aye. The pictures are wonderful. Keep turning."

She flipped the large sheets of parchment. "Can you read this?"

"Some of it. I never learned to write the language well, though."

"Is this forbidden?" she asked skeptically. She knew that the church frowned on certain books.

"Probably."

She came to one of the pictures, and it was indeed wonderful and strange. Little men in turbans and odd clothes moved across a world drawn to look like a carpet.

"Will you teach me to read this?"

"If you wish."

He took down the harp and leaned against the table's edge beside her, looking down at the book while he plucked absently on the strings. The instrument gave a lovely lyrical sound. She continued turning the pages, glancing on occasion at the man resting close to her now and the compelling fingers creating a haunting melody.

Toward the back of the book she found some loose sheets covered with chalk drawings. Spare lines described tents on a desert and a town by the sea. She knew without asking that David had drawn them.

Beneath them, on smaller sheets, lay the faces of two women.

One of them riveted her attention. The face, beautiful and melancholy, appeared vaguely familiar. She realized that she studied an image of his mother. It felt eerie to be facing a dead person thus, but she examined the face closely.

"Will you tell me about her?" she asked quietly.

"Someday."

She turned her attention to the other face. "Who is she?" She gazed at the sloe-eyed exotic beauty captured forever with careful, fine lines. She knew that she pried but she could not ignore the worldly way this woman's face looked at her.

"A woman whom I met in Alexandria."

As with the likeness of his mother, there was much of the artist's feelings in the sensitive way this woman was drawn.

"Did you love her?" she asked, a little shocked by her own boldness but not too much so. He had become much less a stranger since she stepped into this chamber.

"Nay. In fact, she almost got me killed. But I was enchanted by her beauty, as I am by yours."

Something in his quiet tone made her go very still. She lifted her gaze and found him looking at her and not at the book and its drawings. Looking and waiting. He was good at that. Something in his eyes and in the set of his mouth told her that he contemplated waiting no longer.

He saw her and wanted her and paid the King a fortune to have her.

He had stopped playing the harp. Her pulses pounded a little harder in the renewed silence. Total silence. Not a sound in the whole house.

She returned to the book and very carefully turned the page, burying the drawings. Another painting loomed but she didn't really see it.

"Do you know that I have only seen your hair down once, at the betrothal," he said. She sensed his hand reach toward her even before his fingers fell on her head. "Even in the bath it was bound up."

The light pressure of his caress sent a tremor through her. The bath. The wardrobe. His hands and his touch.

"Take down your hair for me, Christiana."

His tone fell somewhere between a request and a command. She leaned back in the chair, away from him.

She would marry this man very soon. She shouldn't be afraid of him. But her quickening blood and unworldly spirit shouted to her that she should get away from him now.

She looked at him, silently asking him to remember their conversation in the garden and to understand and wait a little longer. "Morvan is probably at the shop, David. I should go and meet him."

"I left word that we were coming here."

"Then he most likely waits outside. He will not enter. I should not leave him there."

He gestured to the window. "It looks out on the courtyard. See if he awaits you."

She eased out of the chair and past him, and turned on her tiptoes to glance down at the deserted courtyard.

His quiet voice flowed over her back and shoulders. "He will not come. He accepts that you belong to me now. As you do."

She went down from her toes and looked up at the clear afternoon sky. A part of her wanted desperately to fly out that window. But his touch and words and the expectant silence of this house had awakened those other feelings, and that exquisite anticipation licked through her.

"You frighten me sometimes," she said. "I know that you should not and that you have said that it isn't fear, but a part of it truly is."

He was quiet for a moment. The house seemed to quake with its emptiness. "Aye," he finally said. "For a virgin, part of it truly is."

She sensed him move. She felt his presence behind her. She both awaited and dreaded his touch, her spirit stretched with tension like a string pulled taut.

His hands gently took her waist and she sighed at the feel of each finger. His head bent to her bare shoulder. He kissed the little scratches, and then her neck. She closed her eyes, savoring the delicious closeness of him.

"Take down your hair, Christiana."

She raised her arms and clumsily fumbled for the pins that held her hair. She pulled out the intricate twists and plaits, terribly conscious of how weak and vulnerable she felt, wonderfully aware of those fingers splayed around her.

The heavy waves fell section by section down her neck and back, all the way to his hands. She shook her head to release the last of them, placing the pins on the windowsill.

He nuzzled his face in her unbound hair, and his breath tingled her scalp and neck through the tresses.

His hands turned her to him and took her face, cradling

it gently like something precious and fragile. He kissed her tenderly, beautifully, and fully, and she trembled as his mouth made the low tension and excitement sharpen and rise.

He prolonged the kiss, taking her in an embrace that pulled her to his warmth. She held her arms open at his sides for one worried moment before accepting him.

She sensed a change in him after that. His kiss deepened, commanding her desire. His hand cupped her breast. She gasped and closed her eyes, waiting for the delicious sensations.

They undid her completely. Her limbs went languid as heat poured through her body. His soft hair brushed her face as he lowered his mouth to the skin exposed by her low-cut cotehardie, kissing the top swell of the breasts that his fingers caressed into peaks of yearning.

Fear told her to stop him but the desire would not let her. Rivulets of pleasure merged into a fast-running river, and struggling against its current seemed futile and impossible.

His fingers played at her and the pleasure became a little frantic. *I am drowning in it*, she thought as his mouth claimed hers again.

He lifted his head and looked down at her, watching her responses to his touch. She gazed at the parted lips and deep eyes and knew that there would be no help from him this day.

He began guiding her toward the chamber door.

She thought about where they were going and what he wanted. "I don't . . ." she whispered even as she took another step.

"It is why you came, is it not? For reassurance that this marriage need not be so terrible?"

She resisted at the threshold. His hand returned to her breast and his lips to her neck.

"You said . . . you said that today you wouldn't . . ."

"I said probably," he murmured. "And I lied."

He took her face in his hands again. "His shadow is between us and I would banish that ghost. Today we even the accounts and turn the page. It will be easier for you this way, too."

She read the decision in his eyes.

"Do not be afraid. I will wait until you are ready and until you want me. It will be all right. I will make it so," he promised.

I am helpless against these feelings, she thought. *It is unnecessary to fight them. This is inevitable anyway. I am his forever.*

She turned her face and kissed his hand.

He lifted her in his arms and carried her into the chamber.

CHAPTER 11

HER THIN ARMS encircled his neck and tightened as he approached the bed.

It will be all right. I will make it so. Brave words from a man who hadn't taken a virgin since he was sixteen. Still, he would indeed make it so. Whatever lies he told her today, that would not be one of them.

He should have known. *She's just a girl,* Andrew had said. *One moment they are brave and the next shy. Remember?*

He sat on the side of the bed and settled her into his lap. He kissed her until the arm grasping his neck loosened a bit.

Innocent and ignorant. All during dinner it had been all he could do not to stare in astonishment. While he ate and spoke, his mind had recalculated what this revelation meant. Perhaps it made today unnecessary and he should wait. Perhaps it made it essential. In the end his own desire chose the course. He would not let her leave without claiming her. He wanted her and there was only one way to possess her securely.

She touched his face in that tentative way, and his desire surged. He took her mouth hungrily and fought back the cataclysmic storm that threatened to thunder through him. Slowly and simply, he reminded himself again.

He caressed her breasts and when her arms tightened this time it was not in fear. Her body relaxed into his. She tried to imitate his deep kiss and probed cautiously and delicately. The artless effort almost undid him.

The joy he found in her innocent passion surprised him. He had never sought it in other women. It shouldn't matter with Christiana either, but it did. He felt her body responding to him and listened to her sharpened breathing. He delighted in her awkward embrace and in her startled gasps when his hands raised a new pleasure. He reveled in the knowledge that despite what had occurred with Percy, no man but himself had ever aroused her.

He kissed her again, savoring the soft taste of her and the compliant arch of her back. His hand sought the lacing of her cotehardie, and he began undressing her.

The virgin stiffened for an instant as the garment loosened, but then those glittering eyes watched his hands ease the gown off her arms and down to her waist. Her mouth trembled open and her eyes closed as he touched her breast through the thin batiste of her shift.

A small hand left his shoulders and caressed down his chest, and the thunder tried to erupt again. Her fingers slid under the flap hiding the closures to his pourpoint. He watched her earnest expression as that hand fumbled down his chest. Aye. Having chosen to yield, the sister of Morvan Fitzwaryn would not play the reluctant victim.

He slid the straps of the shift down and uncovered her beautiful breasts. His gaze followed the path of his fingers as he traced their high, round swells. Her breath quickened and she buried her face shyly in his shoulder.

She was beautifully formed, pale and flawless. Her skin was not translucent and white like so many Englishwomen, but rather had the opaque tint of new ivory. It was the color of the bleached beaches along the Inland Sea. He caressed her, whisking and grazing the tight nipples, and her whole body reacted. With a faint moan she arched into his touch. The light brown tips beckoned like an offering. He lowered his head and gently kissed one before taking it into his mouth.

She almost jumped out of his arms.

He held her firmly and looked at the startled shock in her eyes. He kissed her cheek reassuringly.

He lowered his kisses until that sweet breast was in his mouth again. Jesus, the man must have barely touched her. No thought to her at all. If Idonia hadn't found them, he would have brutalized her.

A picture of that formed in his mind, and his spirit reacted with a surge of protective anger followed by a wave of tenderness. He played at her with his tongue and teeth until her bottom pressed against his thigh in her search for relief. He reached back and pulled down the bed coverings. Slowly and simply, but before she left him he would show her the glory of the pleasure. She was all that mattered this time.

He rose with her in his arms and turned and laid her down. Dark eyes, liquid with passion, regarded him cautiously. He gazed down at her lying there, naked to the waist with her clothes falling around her hips, and he considered leaving her thus. She looked sweet and fresh and reminded him of the girls of his youth lying back in hay and grass. He thought of the carpet of ivy in the small garden below. If he lived until summer, the warm starlit nights promised a special ecstasy.

Gently he pulled the cotehardie and shift down her slender curves.

Christiana bit her lower lip as shock and excitement merged at the sight of him undressing her. She watched her naked body emerge. When the gown and shift were gone, he untied the garters at her knees and slid off her hose.

A prickly expectation twisted in her. The fear had not completely disappeared. It acted like a spice in the stew of emotions and sensations that boiled inside her.

He shook off his pourpoint and removed his shirt before lowering down beside her. She watched his hard body come to her, and sighed with relief when he was in her arms again.

She let her hands feel his shoulders and back, and she noted the ridges of scars there. He moved into her caress. The heady warmth and closeness overwhelmed her. That strange pounding need went all through her now, shaking her from shoulders to toes.

He kissed her deeply while his hand followed the tremor, sliding down her stomach and belly, reaching down her thighs and legs. Possessive, hot and confident, his caress took control of every inch of her. Her body arched into his touch and rocked to the rhythm of that hollow hidden pulse. Everything began to spiral into the need now. Her breathing, her blood, her awareness, even the pleasure flowed to and from it.

He cupped her breast in his hand and rubbed the tip with his thumb. "I am going to kiss all of you now," he said. "Do not be shy. Nothing is forbidden if it gives us both pleasure."

And he did kiss all of her, his mouth pressing and biting and drawing down her body, creating new pleasures and surprises and leaving her breathless. Down her stomach and belly, down even to her legs. Several kisses even shockingly landed on the flesh of her thighs and then on the soft mound above them and she cried out as long, hot streaks shot through her.

His lips closed on one breast while he caressed the other and the excitement rose to a frantic level. She grabbed desperately at his back and hair. His muscles felt tense beneath her fingers, and his breath sounded ragged to her ears.

He rose up and loosened the rest of his clothing. She reached down to help and her hand brushed his arousal. She felt a reaction all through him, and she bravely touched him again as he kicked off his clothes.

Fear spiked through the oblivion of desire.

Impossible . . .

He returned her hand to his shoulder and then stroked down her body to her legs. Teasing her thighs apart, he slid his hand up and under to her buttocks. His arm pressed up against her while his tongue and lips aroused her breasts.

The pounding need exploded, obliterating the renewed fear. She pushed down against the pressure of that arm offering relief but only bringing torture. Her whole body wanted to move in abandoned, base ways, and she controlled it with difficulty. Over and over she bit back wanton cries that threatened to fill the room.

The warm water of his voice flowed over her. "Do not fight it, Christiana. The sounds and moves of your desire are beautiful to me."

Gratefully she submitted to the delirium. When his hand came forward, she opened her legs without encouragement. She felt no shyness or shock as he caressed her, only a torturous desire that would surely explode into flames if it was not fulfilled.

The sensations of his magic touch led her into madness. Gentle caresses created streaks of concentrated pleasure. Deliberate touches summoned a wild and desperate excitement.

His quiet voice penetrated the wonderful anguish. "Do you want me now, Christiana?"

He touched her differently and she cried out. She managed to nod.

"Then tell me so. Say my name and tell me so."

In the distance somewhere she heard her voice say it. The frantic need completely took over and her hips rose to meet the body coming over hers.

She reveled in the feel of his long length along her and the total closeness of their bodies. She delighted in the concentrated passion transforming his face as he looked at her.

He took her slowly and carefully and she marveled at the beauty of it. With gentle pressure and measured thrusts he seduced her open. The feared pain was not really pain at all but only a stretching tightness lost in the wonderful relief of him filling that aching need. Without thinking, she rocked up to meet his gentle invasion.

She froze as a burning shock stopped her.

He kissed her softly and pulled back. "It cannot be helped, darling." He thrust and a sharp pain eclipsed the pleasure for a flashing instant.

His body didn't stop and the hurt and its memory quickly disappeared as he withdrew slowly and slid in again. It felt desperately good. Instinctively she embraced him with her legs, holding him closer, taking all of him to herself. She found his rhythm and rocked with it in a soundless chant of acceptance.

Nothing, not the songs or his touch or Joan's lesson, had prepared her for the intimacy that engulfed them. Skin on skin, breath on breath, limbs entwined and bodies joined . . . the physical connections overwhelmed her senses. Each time he withdrew, it was a loss. Each time he filled her, it was a renewed completion. It awed her and she sighed her amazement each time they rocked together.

He paused and she opened her eyes to see him looking at her. The careful mask was gone and those blue eyes showed the depths that he never let people see. She moved her hand and touched the perfect face, then let her caress drift down to his neck and chest.

He moved again and it was less gentle this time. He closed his eyes as if he sought to contain something, but if he fought a battle he lost it. "Aye," she whispered when he moved hard again. It hurt a little but the power of it awoke something in her soul. She wanted to absorb his strength and his need. She wanted to know him thus without his careful defenses.

He looked straight in her eyes and then kissed her as he surrendered. As his passion rose in a series of strong, deep thrusts and peaked in a long, hard release, she felt that she touched his essence and he hers.

She held him to her, her arms splayed across his back and her legs around his waist, and she floated in the emotion-laden silence, feeling his heartbeat against her breast. Her body felt bruised and alive and pulsing where they were still joined.

Slowly the chamber surrounded her again. She felt the reality of his weight and strength above her and his soft hair on her cheek.

Still half a stranger, she thought, wondering at this thing that could connect her in indescribable ways to a man whom she barely knew. Amazing and frightening to touch the soul when you did not know the mind.

Her awareness of the unknown half of him seeped around her. She suddenly felt very shy.

He rose up on his arms and kissed her gently. "You are wonderful," he said.

She didn't know what that meant but she was glad he was pleased. "It is much nicer than I thought it would be," she confided.

"Did I hurt you at the end?"

"Nay. In fact, I'm a little sorry it is over."

He caressed down her leg and removed it from his waist. He shifted off her. "That is because you are not done."

She thought of his almost violent ending. "I would say that we are most done, David."

He shook his head and touched her breast. Her eyes flew open at her immediate forceful response. His hand ventured between her legs. She grabbed onto him in surprise.

"I would have given this to you earlier, darling, but you needed to need me this first time," he said as the frenzy slammed into her again.

He touched and stroked at flesh still sensitive from the fullness of him, and a frantic wildness unhinged her. She called out to him, saying his name over and over as her mind and senses folded in on themselves and she lost hold of everything except the ascending pleasurable oblivion.

And then, when she thought that she couldn't bear it anymore and that she would die or faint, the tension snapped in a marvelous way and she screamed in the ecstasy of release rushing through her body.

She rode the eddies with stunned astonishment until they slowly flowed away.

"Oh my," she sighed as she lay breathless and trembling in his arms.

"Aye. Oh my," he said, laughing and pulling her closer. He reached for the bedclothes and covered them both, molding her against his body. His face rested on her hair, his lips against her temple. They lay together in a lulling peace.

The intimacy of their lovemaking had been stunning and poignant. This quiet closeness felt sweet and full and a little awkward. In the matter of an hour a connection had been forged forever. He had taken possession of her in ways she hadn't expected.

She slept and awoke to a darkened room, the twilight eking through the windows. Distant sounds of voices and activity drifted toward her. She turned and found David up on his arm, looking at her.

He liked looking at her. Like his carvings and books? It was something at least. It could have been a man who cared not for her at all.

"I should be going back," she said.

"You will stay here tonight. I will bring you in the morning."

"Idonia . . ."

"I sent a message that you were with me. She will not worry."

"She will know."

"Perhaps, but no one else will. I will get you back by dawn."

A shout from Vittorio echoed through the garden and into the windows. Everyone here probably knew, or would soon when she didn't leave. She thought of the sidelong glances that she faced from these servants and apprentices, from Idonia and even the whole court if word got out.

"You will stay here with me," he repeated. It wasn't a request.

He rose from the bed and walked to the hearth. His sculpted muscles moved as he stretched for a log and placed it on the fire. In the sudden bright illumination she studied his body, casual and unashamed of its nakedness, and noticed the lines on his back that her fingers had felt. Flogging scars. How had he come by them? His dead master did not sound like a man to do this. He returned to her and she watched him come, surprised by the thrilling pleasure she found in looking at him.

Pulling down the coverlet, he gazed at her body. He caressed her curves languidly. She watched that exciting hand move.

"Are you sore, darling? I would have you again, but not if it would hurt you."

Again? How often did people do this? For all of Joan's bluntness, a lot of information had been left out.

His frank statement of desire sent a tremor through her. She didn't doubt his concern for her, but she knew that his question also offered her a choice. "I am not hurt." She raised her arms to embrace him and the wonder.

Throughout the evening and night he forged an invisible chain of steel tying her to him. She felt it happening and wondered if it was something that he controlled. Links of passion and intimacy joined by pleasure and tenderness encircled her.

Late at night, while they basked in the hearth's warmth, she asked him about the wedding and learned that the ceremony had also been moved. They would wed in the cathedral with the bishop in attendance instead of in David's parish church.

"It is getting very elaborate," she mused.

"It couldn't be helped. Once the mayor found out that Edward was coming, the fat was in the fire. I had hoped no one would know and he could just show up."

He spoke of the King in a casual way. Why did she hesitate to just ask him about that relationship? Why did she feel that the topic was forbidden and that to pursue it would be prying?

She sensed that it would be, though, and tonight she did not want to knock on doors that he might not open. She changed the subject. "David, what else do you expect of me?"

The question surprised him. "What do you mean?"

"Considering how stupid I was about this, it won't surprise you to learn that I know little about marriage. I haven't had a very practical education."

"I expect you to be faithful to me. No other man touches you now."

His firm tone stunned her.

"Do you understand this, Christiana?"

"Of course. I'm not *that* stupid, David. I was referring to household things. Everything here is so organized."

"I hadn't really thought about it."

Then why did you go looking for a wife if you hadn't realized that you needed one.

"Isabele thinks that you expect me to work for you," she said, grinning.

"Does she now? I confess that it hadn't occurred to me, but it is a good idea. I shall have to thank the princess. A wife provides excellent free labor. We will get you a loom."

"I can't weave."

"You can learn."

"How much can you earn off of me after I learn?"

"At least five pounds a year, I would guess."

"That means that in two hundred years I will earn back my bride price."

"Aye. A shrewd bargain for me, isn't it?"

They laughed at that and then he added, "Well, the household is yours. Geva will be glad for it, I think. And the boys need a mother sometimes."

"One of the boys is older than me, David."

"It will not always be so, and Michael and Roger are far from home and could use a woman's understanding sometimes. And you will have your own children, too, in time."

Children. Everything he had mentioned could have been provided by some merchant's daughter who brought a large dowry. Children, too. But her sons would be the grandchildren of Hugh Fitzwaryn.

Morvan suspected that David sought their bloodline for his children with this marriage. Could he be right? She found that she hoped it was true. It would explain much, and mean that she brought something to him that another woman could not.

Late that night she awoke in his sleeping embrace. It seemed normal to be in his arms. She lay motionless, alert to his reality and warmth. How odd to feel so close to someone so quickly.

True to his word, he brought her back to Westminster by dawn. She walked through the corridors of a building that felt slightly foreign to her. She slipped into the hidden privacy of her bed while Joan and Idonia still slept.

A firm hand jostled her awake and she looked up into Joan's beaming face. "Aren't you coming to dinner? You sleep the sleep of the dead," Joan said.

Christiana thought that skipping dinner and just sleeping all day sounded like a wonderful idea, but she pulled herself up and asked Joan to call for a servant.

An hour later, dressed and coiffed, she sat beside Joan on a bench in the large hall, picking at food and watching the familiar scene that now looked slightly strange. Her senses were both alerted and dulled at the same time and she knew that those hours with David had caused this. Joan asked her some questions about David's house, and she answered halfheartedly, not wanting to share any of those memories right now.

Toward the end of the meal, Lady Catherine approached their table, her cat eyes gleaming. She chatted with Joan for a while and then turned a gracious face on Christiana.

"You marry quite soon, don't you, dear?"

Christiana nodded. Joan glanced at Catherine sharply, as if it was rude to mention this marriage.

"I have a small gift for you. I will send it to your chamber," Catherine said before leaving.

She wondered why Lady Catherine would do such a thing. After all, they weren't good friends. Still, the gesture touched her and left her thinking that Morvan, as usual, had overreacted to something in warning her off Catherine.

Thomas Holland spirited Joan away and left Christiana on her own. She returned to Isabele's deserted apartment, glad for the privacy. The court routine seemed intrusive when her thoughts dwelled on yesterday and the future.

She went into Isabele's chamber. *Four days and I leave here forever*, she thought, looking out the window. She no longer feared that. A part of her had already departed.

The sound of a door opening reached her ears. Joan or Idonia returning. She hadn't seen the guardian since her return. She wondered what that little woman would say to her.

The footsteps that advanced through the anteroom were not a woman's, however. Morvan had come. One look at her and he would know. Was she brave enough to say "Aye, you were right and it was magic and I liked it?" His strength had stood for years between her and all men, and now she had given herself to one whom he hated.

The steps came forward. They stopped at the thresh-old to the bedchamber.

"Darling," a familiar voice said.

Shock screamed through her. She swung around.

There in the doorway stood none other than Stephen Percy.

CHAPTER 12

"STEPHEN," SHE GASPED.

He smiled and advanced toward her, his arms inviting an embrace. She watched him come with an odd combination of astonished dismay, warm delight, and cold objectivity. She noticed the thick muscles beneath his pourpoint. She observed the harsh handsomeness of his features. His blond hair and fair skin struck her as blanched and vague compared to David's golden coloring.

She couldn't move. Confused, horrified, and yearning emotions paralyzed her. *Not now*, her soul shrieked. *A month ago or a month hence, but not now. Especially not today.*

Strong arms surrounded her. A hard mouth crushed hers.

She pushed him off. His green eyes expressed surprise and then, briefly, something else. Annoyance?

"You are angry with me, my love," he said with a sigh. "I cannot blame you."

She turned away, grasping the edge of the window for support. Dear God, was she to have no peace? She had found acceptance and contentment and even the hope of something more, and now this.

"Why are you here?"

"To see you, of course."

"You returned to Westminster to see me?"

"Aye, darling. Why else? I used the excuse of the pre-Lenten tournament."

The tournament was scheduled to begin the day after her wedding. Stephen loved those contests. She suspected that was his true reason for coming, but her broken heart, not yet totally healed, lurched at the notion that he came for her.

The pain was still too raw, the humiliation still too new, for her to completely reject the hope that he indeed loved her. The girl who had been faithful to this man desperately still wanted to believe it. Her heart yearned for that reassurance.

Her mind, however, had learned a thing or two from its agony. "When did you arrive?"

"Two days ago. I did not seek you immediately because I was with my friend Geoffrey. He is in a bad way with a fever. He lies in Lady Catherine's house in London."

"You are friends with Catherine?"

"Not really. Geoffrey is, however." He stepped toward her. "She told me all about your marriage to this merchant," he said sympathetically. "If Edward were not my king, I would challenge him for degrading you thus."

She glanced at the concern in his expression. It struck her as a little exaggerated, like a mask one puts on for a festival.

He reached out and caressed her face. The broken heart, aching for the balm of renewed illusions, sighed.

The spirit and mind, remembering last night's passion and David's rights, made her move away.

"You already knew of my marriage, did you not? I wrote you a letter."

"I knew. I received it, darling. But I never imagined that the King would go through with this. And Catherine has told me of your unhappiness and humiliation."

How kind of Lady Catherine, Christiana thought bitterly. Why did this woman meddle in her affairs? And how had Catherine known about Stephen and her?

Joan. Joan had gossiped. Did everyone know now? Probably. They would all be watching and waiting the next few days, maybe the next few years, to see how this drama unfolded.

"Perhaps I should not have come," Stephen muttered. "Catherine assured me that you would want to see me."

"I am glad to see you, Stephen. At the least I can congratulate you on your own betrothal."

He made a face of resignation. "She was my father and uncle's choice, my sweet. She does not suit me, in truth."

"All the same, she is your wife. As David is my husband."

"Aye, and it tears me apart that there is nought we can do about that, my sweet."

A candle inside her snuffed out then, and she knew that it was the last flame of her illusions and childish dreams. It did not hurt much, but something of her innocence died with it, and she felt that loss bitterly.

Through it all, she had saved a little bit of hope, despite knowing and seeing the truth. If he had not returned, it would have slowly disappeared as she lived her life and spent her passion with David, much as a small pool of water will disappear in the heat of a summer afternoon.

What if Stephen had spoken differently? What if he had come to plead with her to run away together and petition to have both of their betrothals annulled? It was what that reserve of hope had wanted, after all.

A week ago she would have done it, despite the disgrace that would fall on her. Even last weekend, such an offer might have instantly healed her pain and banished her doubts about him.

Now, however, it would have been impossible. Now . . .

A horrible comprehension dawned. Stephen's presence receded as her mind grasped the implications.

Impossible now. David had seen to that, hadn't he?

Last night had consummated their marriage. No annulment would be possible now, unless David himself denied what had occurred. And she knew, she just knew, that he would not, despite his promise that first night.

I expect you to be faithful to me. No other man touches you now.

All of those witnesses . . . even Idonia and her brother.

An eerie chill shook her.

David had known Stephen was coming. He had been asking the pilgrims and merchants. He could not know if Stephen came to claim her, however. Nonetheless, he had still covered that eventuality. Methodically, carefully, he had made sure that she could not leave with Stephen. If she did anyway, despite the invisible chains forged last night, despite the dishonor and disgrace, he possessed the proof necessary to get her back.

The ruthlessness of it stunned her.

She remembered the poignant emotions she had felt last night. Twice a fool. More childish illusions. Her stupid trust of men must be laughable to them.

A warm presence near her shoulder interrupted her thoughts. Stephen hovered closely, his face near hers.

"There is nought that we can do about these marriages, darling, but in life there is duty and then there is love."

"What are you saying, Stephen?"

"You cannot love this man, Christiana. It will never happen. He is base and his very touch will insult you. I would spare you that if I could, but I cannot. But I can soothe your hurt, darling. Our love can do that. Give this merchant your duty, but keep our love in your heart."

She wanted to tell him how wrong he was, how David's touch never insulted. But what words could she use to explain that? Besides, she wasn't at all sure that the magic would return now that she knew why he had seduced her. Perhaps the next time, on their wedding night, she would indeed feel insulted and used.

Well, what had she expected? David was a merchant and she was property. Very expensive property. She doubted that King Edward gave refunds.

Love, she thought sadly. She had thought that there was some love in it. Her ignorance was amazing. David was right. She did live her life like she expected it to be some love song. But life was not like that. Men were not like that.

"I am a married woman, Stephen. What you are suggesting is dishonorable."

He smiled at her much the way one might smile at an innocent child. "Love has nothing to do with honor and dishonor. It has to do with feeling alive instead of dead. You will realize that soon enough."

"I hope that you are not so bold as to ask for the proof of my love now. I wed in several days."

"Nay. I would not give a merchant reason to upbraid or harm you, although the thought of him having you first angers me. Marry your mercer as you must, darling. But know that I am here."

"I am an honest woman, Stephen. And I do not think that you love me at all. I think that this was a game to you, and still is. A game in which you lose nothing but I risk everything. I will not play in the future."

He began protesting and reaching for her. Footsteps in the anteroom stopped him. She turned to the new presence at the threshold.

Good Lord, was there no mercy?

Morvan filled the doorway, gazing at them both. For one horrible moment an acute tension filled the room.

"Percy, it is good to see you," Morvan said, advancing into the chamber. "You have come for the tournament?"

"Aye," Stephen said, easing away from her.

Morvan eyed them both again. "I assume that you are wishing each other happiness in your upcoming marriages."

She nodded numbly. There was no point in trying to explain away Stephen's presence. She saw in her brother's eyes that he had heard the gossip.

"It is a strange thing about my sister's marriage, Stephen," Morvan said as he paced to the hearth. "It is said that the King sold her for money, and I believed that too. But I have lately wondered if this didn't come about for another reason. Perhaps he sought to salvage her reputation and my family's honor, and not disgrace it."

She watched them consider each other. *Not now, Morvan*, she urged silently. *It doesn't matter anymore.*

"I must be going, my lady," Stephen said, turning a

warm smile on her. She gestured helplessly and watched him stride across the chamber.

"Sir Stephen," Morvan called from the hearth. "It would be unwise for you to pursue this."

"Do you threaten me?" Stephen hissed.

"Nay. It is no longer for me to do so. I simply tell you as a friend that it would be a mistake. Her husband is not your typical merchant. And I have reason to think that he knows well how to use the daggers that he wears."

Stephen smirked in a condescending way before leaving the apartment.

She faced her brother's dark scrutiny. He looked her up and down, and searched her eyes with his own.

"It is customary, sister, to wait a decent interval after the wedding before meeting with one's old lovers."

She had no response to that calm scolding.

"And since you spent the night in that man's bed, you are indeed truly wed now."

"David. His name is David. You always call him 'that merchant' or 'that man,' Morvan. He has a name."

He regarded her with lowered lids. "I am right, am I not? You slept with him. With *David*."

It was pointless to lie. She knew he could tell. She nodded, feeling much less secure about that decision now that she understood David's motivations.

"You must not see Percy again for a long while."

"I did not arrange to meet Stephen."

"Still, you should be careful. Such things are taken in stride if the woman is discreet or if the husband does not care, but you have no experience in such deceptions and your merchant does not strike me as a willing cuckold."

"I told Stephen that I am not interested in him anymore."

"He does not believe you."

He was just trying to help her. In this his advice was probably as sound as any man's. He'd certainly bedded his share of married women.

"Do you despise me?" she whispered.

A strained expression covered his face. He strode across the space and gathered her into his arms. "Nay. But I would not have you be this man's wife, and I would not have you be Percy's whore. Can you understand that? And I blame myself because I did not find a way to take you away from here."

She looked into his dark eyes. She read the worry there and thought that she understood part of it.

"I do not think that being David's wife will be so bad, Morvan. He can be very kind."

A small smile teased at his mouth. "Well, that at least is good news. I am glad that he is accomplished at something besides making money."

She giggled. He tightened his embrace and then released her. "Take your meals with me these last days," he said. "I would have this time with you."

She nodded and watched sadly as he walked away.

She never doubted that her brother had requested her attendance at meals because he wanted her company. She would be leaving him soon, and a subtle nostalgia hung between them at those dinners and suppers, even when they conversed merrily with the other young people at their table.

Morvan's presence beside her had other benefits, however, and she suspected that he had thought of them. Stephen did not dare approach her in the hall while Morvan stayed nearby, and the peering, glancing courtiers received no satisfaction to their curiosity about the status of that love affair.

Everyone knew. Stephen had only to rise from his bench and sidelong looks would watch to see if he would speak with her. It became abundantly clear that the court believed an adulterous affair with Stephen was probably inevitable at some point. She got the impression that many of these nobles accepted the notion with relief, as if such an affair would be a form of redemption for her. The marriage to the merchant would just be a formality, then, and much easier to swallow and even ignore.

Aye, Joan had gossiped. When Christiana confronted her, she tearfully admitted it. Just one girl, she insisted. Christiana had no trouble imagining that small leak turning into a river of whispers within hours.

She filled the next days with preparations for the wedding. Philippa came to the apartment to survey her wardrobe on Saturday and immediately ordered more shifts and hose made for her. A new surcoat was fitted as well. Haberdashers descended so that she could choose two new headdresses. Trunks arrived to be filled with linens and household goods for her to bring to her new home.

She spent most of her time in the apartment managing this accumulation, but her mind dwelled on David. They had agreed that he would not come before the wedding because of their time-consuming preparations and because he had his own affairs to put in order. All the same, she expected him to surprise her with a visit. It would be the romantic thing to do, but when he came it would not be for that reason, although he might pretend that it was. She expected him to check that Stephen had not persuaded her to run away or do anything dishonorable. He would want to make sure that his plan had worked.

He did not come. Saturday turned into Sunday and stretched into Monday. She began to get annoyed.

She felt positive that David knew that Stephen had returned. How could he just leave her here to her own devices when another man drifted about who wanted to seduce her? A man, furthermore, with whom she had been in love? Was he that sure of himself? That sure that one night could balance the ledger sheet of a woman's heart? Didn't he worry about what Stephen's presence might be doing to her?

She pondered this sporadically during the days. At night she chewed it over resentfully. But in the dark silence of her curtained bed, her recriminations always managed to flow away as other thoughts of David would flood her like some inexorable incoming tide. Images of his blue eyes and straight shoulders above her. The power of his passion overwhelming his thoughtful restraint. Her breasts would grow sensitive and her thighs moist and the thoughts would merge into wakeful dreams during a fitful sleep.

She awoke each morning feeling as though she had been ravished by a phantom but had found no release.

David did not come, but others did. Singly or in twos or threes, the women of the court approached her.

Aye, Joan had gossiped, and not just about Stephen. It seemed every lady felt obliged to advise the motherless girl who, rumor had it, was unbelievably ignorant about procreation.

Some of the servants joined in. While she bathed on her wedding day, the girl who attended her boldly described how to make a man mad with desire. Christiana blushed from her hairline to her toes. She seriously doubted that noblewomen did most of these things, but she tucked the tamer tidbits away in her mind.

Getting her dressed turned into a merry party with all of her friends there. They gave her presents and chatted as the servants prepared her. Philippa arrived to escort her down to the hall. The Queen examined her closely and reset the red cloak on her shoulders. Then with her daughters beside her, and with Idonia, Joan, and several other women in attendance, Queen Philippa brought her down to the hall.

Morvan awaited them. He wore a formal robe that reached to mid-calf. His knight's belt bound his waist but no sword hung there. "Come now," he said, taking her arm. "The King already awaits."

The doors swung open. She stepped outside.

She froze. "Oh, dear saints," she gasped.

"Quite a sight, isn't it?" Morvan muttered dryly.

The yard was full of horses and people and transport vehicles. She saw Lady Elizabeth entering one of the painted covered wagons, and other feminine arms dangling from its windows. Knights and lords waited on horses decked out for a pageant. King Edward, resplendent in a gold-embroidered red robe, paced his stallion near the doorway. A long line of royal guards stood waiting.

The presence of so many knights and nobles touched her. They came to honor her family and, perhaps, to reassure her. They also came for her brother's sake, and she was grateful.

The extensive royal entourage, and the obvious instructions that everyone should follow the King in parade, were another matter.

The King gestured and three golden chariots drove forward.

"Oh, dear saints," she gasped again, watching this final grandiose touch arrive.

"Aye, one is for you. The Queen herself will ride with you," Morvan explained.

"This retinue will stretch for blocks. All of London will watch this."

"The King honors you, Christiana."

She turned away from Edward's smiling gaze and spoke lowly into her brother's shoulder. "I am not stupid, Morvan. The King does not honor me, he honors London. He does not bring Christiana Fitzwaryn to wed David de Abyndon. He brings a daughter of the nobility to marry a son of the city. He turns me into a gift to London and a symbol of his generosity to her."

He grasped her elbow and eased her forward. "It cannot be undone. You must be our mother's daughter in this and handle it as she would have. I will ride beside you."

She let him guide her to the front chariot and lift her in. She bent and whispered in his ear. "I will think the whole time how I am not the virgin sacrifice they expect."

The parade filed out of the yard, led by the King and his sons. By the time they reached the Strand, thick crowds had formed. Inside the city gates it got worse. The guards used their horses to keep the people back. Slowly, with excruciating visibility, they made their way through to St. Paul's Cathedral.

Morvan lifted her off the chariot. "Well, brother, don't you have anything to say to me?" she asked as they approached the entrance. "No words of advice? No lectures on being a dutiful and obedient wife? There is no father to admonish me, so it falls to you, doesn't it?"

He paused on the porch and glanced through the open portal into the cavernous nave filled with noisy courtiers and curious townspeople.

"Aye, I have words for you, but no lectures." He bent to her ear. "You are a very beautiful girl. There is power for a woman in a man's desire, little sister. Use it well and you will own him and not the other way around."

She laughed. Smiling, he sped her down the nave.

David waited near the altar. Her heart lurched at the sight of him. He looked magnificent, perfect, the equal of any lord in attendance. The narrow cut of his long, belted, blue velvet robe enhanced his height. The fitted sleeves made the exaggerated lengths and widths of the other men's fashions look ridiculous and unmanly. Beautiful gold embroidery decorated the edges and center of the garment. She wondered who had convinced him to agree to that. The heavy gold chain stretched from shoulder to shoulder.

Morvan handed her over. Idonia fluttered by, took her cloak, and disappeared. David gazed down at her while the noise of the crowd echoed off the high stone ceiling.

"You are the most beautiful girl whom I have ever met," he said, repeating the words he had spoken in the ivy garden.

She had a long list of things to upbraid him about, and some deep hurts and misgivings that worried her heart. But the warmth in those blue eyes softened her, and the sound of his beautiful voice soothed her. There would be time enough for worry and hurt. This was her wedding and the whole world watched.

An hour later she emerged from the cathedral with a gold ring around her finger and David de Abyndon's arm around her waist. The chariot awaited but Sieg, looking almost civilized in a handsome gray robe, brought over a horse.

"You will ride with me, darling. With these crowds, those chariots may never make it to the Guildhall."

"You might have warned me about all of this, David," she said as pandemonium spilled into the cathedral yard and surrounding streets. "It was like the prelude to an ancient sacrifice."

"I did not know, but perhaps I should have expected something like this. Edward loves ceremony and pageantry, doesn't he?"

She wasn't convinced. He always seemed to know

everything. She glanced askance at his face as he lifted her onto the saddle and swung up behind. His bland acceptance of Edward's behavior irked her, but then he hadn't been the girl on public display.

"The King must think very highly of you to have brought such an entourage," she remarked dryly.

"I would be a fool to think so. This had nothing to do with you or me."

They joined the flow of mounted knights and lords inching toward the Cheap. David's arm encircled her waist, his hand resting beneath her cloak. She reached up and touched the diamond hanging from a silver chain around her neck. It had been delivered while she dressed. "Thank you for the necklace. It went perfectly with the gown."

"Edmund assured me that it would. I'm pleased that you like it."

"Edmund?"

"The tailor who made your wedding garments, Christiana. And your betrothal gown. And most of your cotehardies and surcoats over the last few years. His name is Edmund. He is one of the leading citizens of the town of Westminster and an important man in his world."

She felt herself blush. She knew the tailor's name. She had simply forgotten it just now. But David was telling her that she should know the people who served her and not think of them as nonentities.

Her chagrin quickly gave way to annoyance. She didn't like it that one of the first things her new husband had said to her had been this oblique scolding.

Other reasons for annoyance marched forward in her mind.

"I thought that you would come to see me," she said.

"We agreed that I would not."

"All the same, I thought that you would come."

She felt him looking at her, but he said nothing.

"He is back at court," she added. "But, of course, you know that, don't you?"

"I know."

That was it. No questions. Nothing else.

"Didn't you wonder what would happen?" she blurted angrily. "Are you that damn sure of yourself?"

"To have come would have insulted you. I assumed that the daughter of Hugh Fitzwaryn had too much pride and honor to leave her marriage bed and go to another man, especially after she had seen the truth about him."

"All the same . . ."

"Christiana," he interrupted quietly, lowering his mouth to her ear and running his lips along its edge, "we will not speak of this now. I did not come because my days were filled making ready for this wedding. In the time I could steal, I settled business affairs so that I could spend the next three days in bed with you. And my nights were spent thinking about what I would do when I had you there."

She would have liked to ignore the shiver of excitement that his lips and words summoned, but her body had been betraying her during the nights too and now it responded against her will.

She forced herself to remember his calculating seduction to claim his property. She resented self-confidence.

"What makes you think that I will choose to spend the next three days that way?" she asked.

"You are my wife now, girl. Surely you know that you only have choices if I give them to you." He pressed his lips to her temple and spoke more gently. "You will find that I am a reasonable master, darling. I have always preferred persuasion to command."

Beneath the full flow of her cloak, he reached up and caressed her breast.

Her body shook with a startling release of pleasure.

She glanced around nervously at the faces turned up to them in smiling curiosity.

He stroked at her nipple and kissed her cheek. She felt the urge to turn and bite his neck. She twisted her head and accepted the deep kiss waiting for her and those wonderful sensations flowed through her like a delicious sigh of relief.

All of London watched.

"David, people . . . they can see . . ." she whispered breathlessly when he lifted his head but did not move his hand. His fingers were driving her mad.

"They cannot. Some might suspect, but none can know for sure," he whispered. "If you are angry with me, you can upbraid me at will after the banquets. I promise to listen very seriously and take all of your criticisms to heart." He kissed her neck again. "Even as I lick your breasts and kiss your thighs, I will be paying close attention to your scolding. We can discuss my bad behavior between your cries of pleasure."

She was already having a very hard time remembering what she wanted to scold or discuss.

At about the point when she felt an unrelenting urge to squirm against the saddle, they arrived at the Guildhall. She worried that she would not be able to stand on her languid legs when he lifted her to the ground.

"That wasn't fair," she hissed.

He took her hand and led her into the Guildhall. "I only play to win, Christiana, and I make my own rules. Haven't you learned that by now?"

CHAPTER 13

DAVID LEANED IN the shadows against the threshold of the hall, watching the dancers whirl around the huge bonfire in the center of the courtyard. Couples romped together in a round dance on the periphery of the circle, but near the center a group of women performed an energetic exhibition alone. Oliver's woman Anne led the group, since she danced professionally on occasion when the opportunity and pay were convenient. Serving girls and women from the ward surrounded her. In the thick of it, her face flushed with delight and her eyes sparkling with pleasure, swung the elegant figure of Christiana Fitzwaryn.

The lights from the bonfire seemed to flame over the women in a rhythm that matched the beating drums. The whole courtyard and house glowed from that huge blaze and from the many torches lining the buildings and the back garden. The fires tinted the night sky orange, and from a distance it probably appeared that the house was burning. No doubt the priests would insist that the scene, with revelers giving themselves over to all of the deadly sins, resembled the inferno of hell itself.

People filled the courtyard, the gardens, and the rooms of the house. Men and woman perched on the roof of the stable. To his left several couples embraced in a dark corner.

A loud laugh caught his attention and he leaned back and glanced into the hall. The milling bodies parted for a moment and he saw the laughing man sitting by the fire with a girl on each knee. The gold embroidery on the red robe was the only proof that this man was a king, for Edward had shed his royal persona as soon as he slipped through the gate with his two guards after sending his wife and family home after the Guildhall banquet. He was well into his cups now, and long ago the party had stopped treating him like the sovereign and simply absorbed him into their merriment.

David returned his attention to his wife. He enjoyed watching her even when she didn't move at all, but her freedom and pleasure in this dance mesmerized him. Like her King, she had quickly succumbed to the unrestrained mood of this second party, and David had delighted in watching her joy as she feasted and drank and traded jests with the neighbors from the ward.

She moved beautifully, languidly, imbuing even this base dance with a noble elegance. Her lips parted in a sensual smile as she twirled around, enjoying at last the ecstasy of movement that she had vicariously felt so often before.

He watched and waited, suppressing the urge to walk to that fire and pick her up and carry her away.

He wanted her. Badly. He had wanted her for weeks, and their night together had only made the wanting more fierce. He had spent the last days in a state of perpetual desire.

Her innocence that day had disarmed him in a dangerous way. Her passion had no defenses, and her total giving and taking had burned down his own. Unlike the experienced women he usually bedded, she knew nothing about protecting herself from the deeper intimacies that could emerge in lovemaking, knew nothing about holding her essence separate from the joining, knew nothing about keeping the act one of simple physical pleasure. She had felt the closeness for what it could be and had simply let the power come and wash over them both. He had seen the wonder of it in her eyes and felt her amazement of it in her grasping embrace and had almost warned her to be careful, for there could be danger and pain in it for her, too. But he had not warned her, for that deep intimacy brought a knowing of her that something inside him craved and in the end he also proved defenseless against the magic that he hadn't felt in so many years.

His gaze followed her, his body responding to the seductive moves of her dance. In his mind's eye she looked up at him and touched his face and his chest and sighed an "aye" that asked for all of himself.

A figure strolled in front of him, mercifully distracting his heated thoughts. Morvan drank some wine as he walked, casually surveying the dancers.

The drums and timbrels beat out a frenzied finale and then the dance ended abruptly. All around the fire, bodies stopped and heaved deep breaths from their exertions. Christiana and Anne embraced with a laugh.

She thought that Anne was Oliver's wife. He would have to tell her the truth, he supposed.

Morvan caught Christiana's eye and gestured for her. She skipped over to him with a broad smile. He bent and said something, and David watched the happiness and pleasure fall from her face and her body like someone had stripped it off.

She threw her arms around him and spoke earnestly, entreating him no doubt to stay longer. Morvan shook his head, caressed her face, and pulled away.

He walked toward the gate. Christiana gazed after him, her straight body suddenly alone and isolated despite the crowd milling around her. David could see her composed expression but he had no trouble reading the sadness in her.

Her whole life, her whole family, her whole past was leaving the house now.

He pushed away from the threshold and went to her. He draped her cloak over her shoulders, and she glanced up with a weak smile before her gaze returned to the retreating tall man.

He smiled and shook his head. He strode after Morvan, calling his name. A part of him couldn't believe that he was going to do this for her.

The young knight stopped and turned. He came back and met David partway. They faced each other in the fire glow.

"You are leaving, Morvan?"

"Aye. It is best if I go now." He glanced at his sister.

"You must come and visit her soon. She will want to see you."

Morvan looked over in surprise.

"Her life will be much changed and it may be hard on her," David continued. "I would not have her unhappy. Come when you will. This house is always open to you."

Morvan looked more surprised yet. He nodded and smiled a little. "I thank you for that, David. For both our sakes."

David walked back to Christiana. The cloak was falling off and he wrapped her in it more warmly, embracing her shoulder.

"What did you say to him?" she asked, her gaze still on her brother.

"I told him that he must visit you whenever he wants."

"Did you, David? Did you really?" She turned to him with a bright smile. Her unaffected surprise and gratitude wrenched something inside him.

"I know that he is all that you have, darling. He only sought to protect you, and I can blame no man for that. I would not stand between you."

She nestled closer to him and looked into his eyes with an almost childish innocence. "Not all that I have, David. Not anymore. There is you now, isn't there? We have each other, don't we?"

He embraced her and she placed her head on his chest, her face turned to the shadows that swallowed her brother's tall body. David laid his face on the silky cloud of her hair.

All that she was, all that she was supposed to be, left through that gate. The life she had led and had been born to live, the position assured her by her blood, returned to Westminster tonight without her. He didn't doubt that she understood that. She knew what this marriage had taken from her.

He kissed her hair and closed his eyes. He could give it back to her. All that she was losing and more. It was in his power to do so. The offer still stood and would be made again, of that he was sure. He had only to play out the game as planned but change the final move. He knew exactly how to do it. He had been considering the possibility for weeks.

As if reading his thoughts, she tilted her head and looked up at him. "You are very good to me, David. I know that you will take care of me and do all that you can for me."

He bent to kiss her and her parted lips rose to meet

his. A tremor shook her and she pressed herself against him as she embraced him tightly. His mind clouded and the restraint of the last hours cracked.

She grasped him as desperately as he did her, her mouth inviting his deep kiss. Perhaps it was the wine and the dance. Maybe it was her gratitude over Morvan. He didn't care. He would accept her passion any way that it came to him.

They stood thus at the edge of the fire glow, two bodies molded together, banishing the separateness, the sounds of revelry echoing around them. He kissed her again and again, wanting to consume her and absorb her into himself.

He found the sanity to pull his mouth away. "Come upstairs with me now," he whispered, his face buried in her neck, her scent driving him mad.

"Aye," she said. "Now."

He turned her under his arm while he kissed her again. Somehow he found his way blindly across the courtyard, into the building, and up the stairs. A group of revelers discreetly poured out of the solar when they arrived, and he kicked the door closed behind them.

In his chamber he threw off their cloaks and fell on the bed with her, covering her with his body, feeling her pliant length bend up into him. His head emptied to everything but the feel and smell of her. He tried to check himself, tried to calm the thundering storm that controlled him, but the deep, probing kiss he gave her turned fierce and needful when she took his head between her hands and pressed him closer.

He managed to remove her surcoat without tearing it, but the cotehardie's lacing defied his practiced fingers. He plucked at the knot as he kissed and bit the tops of her breasts. Finally, in a fury of frustration, he moved aside, turned her on her stomach, and stared at the recalcitrant closure.

"Hold still," he muttered, pulling out his dining dagger and blinking away the obscuring passion. He rose on his knees and slid the blade under the lacings. "It is an old wedding trick. Your servants tied a knot that cannot be undone."

She laughed beautifully, lyrically, and then turned on her back, joyfully helping him push down the gown. When it was gone, she got to her knees and flew to him as if the separation had lasted an eternity.

He lost himself then. In a frantic whirlwind of caresses and kisses, they managed to pull off his clothes. With cries and gasps and little ecstatic laughs, her hands met his on his belt and shirt and finally poured heatedly over his skin. He pushed her shift down from her shoulders, uncovering her breasts, and bent her back so that he could revel in their sweet softness.

Her cries undid him and unraveled his last thread of control. He pushed the shift up her hips and felt for the moisture of her arousal.

"I promise that I will give you slow pleasure later," he said as he laid her down. "All night if you want. But right now I cannot wait, darling."

He spread her legs and knelt between them. She looked up at him, her dark eyes full of stars.

He gazed at her lovely face and her round white breasts. The shift bunched at her waist and the hose were still gartered at her knees. He pushed the bottom of the shift up higher, exposing her hips and stomach. He touched the pulsing, swollen flesh between her thighs and watched the pleasure quake through her.

The fantasies of his desire pressed on him relentlessly. Despite her ignorance and his need, he could not resist them all. He bent her legs so that she was raised and open to him. Her ragged breathing broke through his fog, and he glanced and saw the flicker of wariness and surprise in her eyes.

"Do not be afraid," he said as he lifted her hips. "I want to kiss all of you. That is all."

He knew that he could not indulge himself thus for long. His own body would not let him. Nor, it turned out, would hers. She writhed and cried out from the shock and intensity of this new pleasure, and soon he felt the first flexes of her release.

He left her and came up over her, bringing her legs with him, settling them on his shoulders. She thrashed in frustration that he had brought her to the edge of the precipice but no further.

"Soon, darling. I promise. When we are together," he said soothingly, and he rose up and entered her with one thrust.

His whole body shook from the torturous pleasure of it, but the tremor itself gave him back some of his control. Extending his arms, he stroked into her, his consciousness filling with the exquisite sensation that came from tottering on the edge of his own release.

She watched him as he moved, her hands caressing his shoulders and chest in that open, accepting way of hers, her sparkling eyes and soft sighs telling him that he filled other needs besides those of her body. The emotions seeped out of her and around him and embraced them both as surely as their arms had entwined moments ago.

He felt her tensing, stretching, for her climax. His own control began crumbling. He reached down between their bodies to give her release. As the frenzy possessed her she grabbed fiercely for him, arching her hips up against his thrusts, pulling him with her into the delicious oblivion.

He rarely sought a mutual release. In fact he avoided

them. Now, as their passion peaked and shattered to-gether, he felt her ecstasy even as his own split through him. For an unearthly instant the lightning of the storm melted them into one sharing completeness.

When they were done, he stayed with her, kissing her softly while he moved her legs down, letting himself enjoy the glorious expression on her beautiful face. He rolled over to his back, bringing her with him so that she lay on him. He held her there, her head on his chest and her knees straddling his hips, and watched his hand caress her pale back and hips.

After a long while she lifted her head and cocked it thoughtfully. "I hear lutes," she said.

"You flatter me."

She giggled and thumped his shoulder playfully. "Nay, David. I really do. Listen."

He focused his awareness and heard the lyrical tones amidst the distant noise of the party. He moved her off, got out of bed, and disappeared into the wardrobe.

Christiana waited, still floating in the wonder and magic of their passion. It seemed that the lutes got louder.

He returned and pulled the coverlet off the bed. "They are for you. You should acknowledge them." He draped the warm cover over his shoulders, and she got up and joined him in its cozy cocoon.

The door to the stairs leading to the ivy garden was open, and they went out on the stone landing. David lifted her up and sat her on the low surrounding wall, tucking the coverlet securely around her legs.

Below in the tiny garden she could see four men with lutes. They sang the poetic lines of a love song. She rec-ognized the deep bass of Walter Manny.

"Who are the others?" she whispered.

"They are all from the Pui. It is a tradition when one of them marries."

They began another song. Torches lit the larger garden, but here the singers were only dark forms in the shadows. Above them the clear night sky glittered with a hundred stars. David stood beside her, holding her under their cover, nuzzling her hair. There was something incredibly romantic about being with him in the cold night with the intimacy of their joining still hanging on them while the music played.

Walter sang the next song alone. It possessed a slow, quiet melody that she had heard only once before. It was the song that David had sung that day in the hall, the one she had found so sad at the time. Now she realized that it wasn't sad at all, just soft and beautiful. It had sent her off thinking of Stephen that day, and she hadn't really noticed the words, but this time she listened carefully.

It wasn't really a love song, but more a song that praised a woman and her beauty. The words spoke of elegant limbs and noble bearing. Her hair was described as black as the velvet night, her skin pale as moonlight, and her eyes like the diamonds of the stars. . . .

She grew very still. She listened to the rest of the lovely song that described her. David had written this. He had played it in the hall for her that day, and she hadn't even heard it.

Walter's voice and lute closed the melody. She looked up at the shadow of the man beside her. Her heart glowed warm and proud that he had honored her in this way, so long ago, even as she treated him so badly.

"Thank you," she whispered, stretching up to kiss his face.

They listened to several more songs, and then the four musicians walked forward and bowed to her. "Thank you, Walter," she called quietly.

"My lady," he replied, and the shadows swallowed him.

"What a marvelous tradition," she said to David as they returned to their bed. "Have you done that?"

"Aye, I've spent my share of cold winter nights in gardens singing to new brides. We stay until she acknowledges that she has heard us. On occasion the groom is so enraptured in bed that it takes hours. We give him hell afterwards then."

She laughed and rested her head on his shoulder.

"It was a wonderful wedding, David." A din still leaked through the windows from the continued revelry outside and below. "I had so much fun. Anne says that I dance very well for an amateur. She said that she will teach me more if I want."

"If it pleases you, you should do it."

"I like her. I like Oliver, too. He is an old friend?"

"From when we were boys."

"Have they been married a long time?"

A peculiar expression passed over his face. He looked so handsome now, his golden brown hair falling over his forehead, his deep blue eyes regarding her.

"Christiana, Oliver sells women. Anne lives with him but is not his wife. She is one of his women."

"You mean she is his whore? Anne is a whore? She does this with strangers, for pay? He lets her, and even brings the men to her?"

"Aye."

"How can he? He seemed to care for her, David. How . . ."

"In truth, I do not know."

She pictured Anne, with her pretty brown curls and sweet but worldly face. "It must be horrible for her."

"I suspect that most of her isn't really there with them."

Could people do that? Join like this and not even care about it, not feel anything? Or just take the pleasure and

206 ✦ MADELINE HUNTER

close their eyes to the person giving it? It struck her as a sad and frightening thought.

She turned her head and gazed up at the billowing canopy of blue cloth above them, feeling sorry for Anne and not much liking Oliver for expecting such things of her. They were poor, true, but surely there must be some other way.

And yet, she had to admit that this lovemaking obviously happened in all kinds of ways and for all kinds of reasons. In fact, she suspected that often love had nothing to do with it at all, especially for men. After all, the desire that she and David shared was mostly physical, wasn't it? For him, that was all that it was. And other women had been here, where she was now, experiencing the same thing. He had wanted them and now he wanted her. Whom would he want next?

The magic and wonder suddenly seemed a lot less special.

Did it last long, this desire? Perhaps if a man paid a thousand pounds for a woman, he felt obligated to desire her for a long time. But when the desire faded, what would be left for her? A home and maybe children. Not small things, but she wanted more.

The admission startled her and she didn't understand the feelings that it revealed. She realized, however, that there could be danger in this bed with this man, and the chance of disappointments far worse than she had known with Stephen Percy.

A strange emptiness opened inside her. It felt like a desolate loneliness, despite the man who held her. She had been having a wonderful time these last hours, laughing and dancing and being overwhelmed by their mutual passion. Nestling with him outside while the love songs played had been so romantic. She bleakly realized that she had been foolishly building another illusion, another dream.

She felt him shift and then those blue eyes were above her, studying her.

"What are you thinking about?" he asked.

Don't you know? she wanted to say. *You always know.*

She met his gaze and realized that he did know. At least part of it.

"I am thinking that there is more to all of this than I understand." She made a little gesture that covered the bed. "You must find me very childish and ignorant compared to the other women whom you have known."

Beautiful women. Worldly women. Experienced women. She could never compete with them. She didn't even know how. Why in God's name had he married her?

His hand caressed her cheek and turned her face to his. "I am most pleased with you, Christiana."

She felt a little better then, but not much.

"Alicia was your lover, wasn't she?" she blurted.

"Aye. But it is over."

"There were others, too, others whom I know and who know me," she said blankly.

He just looked at her.

"Elizabeth?" she asked, thinking of that exquisitely lovely woman and feeling a spike of infuriating jealousy. No one could ever compete with Elizabeth.

"Elizabeth is an old friend, but we were never lovers."

Protective indignation instantly replaced the jealousy. "Why not! You are better than most of the men she has been linked with. And that lord she married is old and ugly."

He laughed. "Now you are angry with her because we didn't sleep together? Nay, there was no insult in it. Elizabeth likes her lovers very young."

"You are young."

"Not young enough. She likes them still partly unformed. She wants to influence them."

"Young like Morvan?"

"Aye."

She thought about that, and those months when Morvan had attended on Elizabeth. A long time for him. Worrying about her brother relieved her of the worries about herself.

"Do you know about the two of them, and what happened? Some at court thought that they would marry, but then it just ended. Morvan would never speak to me about it."

He looked down at the pillow for a moment and she could tell that he did know.

"Oh, please, David, tell me," she cajoled. "He is my brother, after all. I am very discreet, you know. I am the only female at court who didn't gossip."

"A rare virtue that I should not corrupt."

"I always *listened*. I just never repeated what I heard," she said.

"Elizabeth didn't marry your brother because he never asked her to. Also, she loved him and he didn't love her. Not the way she wanted. Elizabeth would never bind herself to such an uneven love. Then there is the fact that she is barren. She has known it since girlhood. It is why only old men offer for her. They already have their heirs. One day your brother will be lord of Harclow again and he will want a son."

"Nay, David, I do not think he ever will be. The King swore to see it happen, but he has forgotten."

"Men do not forget the oaths that they swear."

She wondered what else David knew about the people with whom she had spent her life. Perhaps, if she proved very discreet, he would tell her sometime. This felt very pleasant and cozy, talking like this in the warmth of the bed. When he was up and walking about, he still remained a mystery to her, but the intimacy here temporarily banished that.

"I was surprised that the King came here this evening," she said, wondering how far she could push the mood.

"Even kings like to have some fun. Being regal can get tedious, and Edward is still a young man. He isn't much older than I am."

"He seems to know you well."

"We are of similar age, and he is more comfortable with me than with the city officials who are very formal with him. And I have done some favors for him. He sends me on errands. To Flanders mostly. I carried letters to the governor of Ghent on several trips."

"Do you still do this? These errands?"

"Aye. Some of the trips that I take are for Edward."

That was that. She smiled at her foolish hesitation. She should have just asked earlier. It all made perfect and innocent sense. Still . . .

"Are they ever dangerous? These trips?"

"They haven't been."

That wasn't the same as saying that they weren't. She decided to leave it, however.

She snuggled closer, enjoying the feel of his arm around her. She thought about some of the people she had met at the Guildhall banquet. In particular, she remembered the thin-lipped, gray-haired Gilbert de Abyndon, who had tried to ignore David's presence even while David introduced her.

"I liked Margaret, Gilbert's wife. I think that she and I could be friends. Do you think that he would permit that?"

Actually, she wanted to know if David would permit

it. Margaret was not much older than herself, and a friendly blond-haired woman. They had enjoyed their brief meeting and chat, even if their two husbands had stood there like frozen sentinels.

"Most likely. Gilbert is very ambitious. He will overlook your marriage to me because of your nobility and connections at court. Like most of the wealthier merchants, he wants to lift his family into the gentry."

"Still, he may object to her visiting me. It is clear that you and he hate each other very much."

Her comment was met with a long silence. She turned and found him gazing at the blue canopy much as she had done earlier. He glanced at her with a glint in his eyes. Had simply mentioning this uncle angered him? He kissed her hair as if to reassure her.

"I hate him for what he did to my mother, and he hates me because I am alive and use the Abyndon name. He is the worst of our breed, my girl. Judgmental and unbending. He is full of self-righteousness and attends church each morning before he spends his day damning people. If he had been at this house today, he would have seen nothing of the joy and pleasure but only sin and weakness. If you are going to befriend Margaret, you should know this, because that is the man she is tied to. Hopefully, for her sake, her old husband will die soon."

She blinked at his last words. Wishing someone dead was a dreadful thing. The dispassionate way he said it stunned her even more.

"We need to find a servant to help you with your clothes and such," he added. "Geva said that you would want to choose the girl yourself. In a few days, go and visit Margaret and ask for her help in this. See if Gilbert permits it."

He stroked her hair and her shoulder and she stretched against him as the tingling warmth of his caress awoke her skin. She suspected that he wanted to make love again. She waited for him to start, and was surprised when he began speaking, his quiet voice flowing into her ear.

"My uncles Gilbert and Stephen were already in their twenties when my mother was still a girl. Old enough, when she turned fourteen, to know what they had in her. She was beautiful. Perfect. Even when she died, despite everything, she was still beautiful. Her brothers saw her marriage for the opportunity it was. They had it all planned. A nobleman for her. Second choice, a merchant with the Hanseatic League. Third, a husband from the gentry. They settled a fat dowry on her and began pushing her in front of such men. Every banquet, they brought her with them, dressed like a lady."

"And did it work?"

"Aye, it worked. John Constantyn has told me what she did not. The offers poured in. Gilbert and Stephen debated the marriage that would be best for them, of course, and not her. They became too clever and played one man off against the other."

"Did she refuse their choice? Is that why . . ."

"Worse than that, as my body beside you proves. They had not been careful enough with her. Their parents were dead, and the servants who supervised her indulged her. She fell in love. The man was gone by the time she found herself with child."

"Was it one of her suitors?"

"Apparently not. Still, her brothers sought to solve the disaster in the usual ways. They demanded to know his name so they could force a marriage, but she would not give it to them. Gilbert tried to beat it out of her, and still she would not say. And so they found another husband who would accept her under those circumstances and sought to have a quick wedding."

Christiana grimaced inwardly. She remembered that first night in David's solar, and him asking if she was with child. He had thought that it was the same story, and that he was the other man whose quick wedding would cover up a girl's mistake.

"She would not have him," he continued. "She was certain that her lover would return for her. She went to the priest and declared that she was unwilling."

Braver than me, Christiana thought. *My God, what must have been running through David's mind that night as he faced me so impassively in front of the fire?*

"What did they do?"

"They sent her away. There are some relatives in Hastings and she went there. Gilbert told her to give up the child when it was born. If she did not, all of their support of her would cease and she would be as if dead to them. Under no circumstances was she to return to London."

"But she kept you. And she came back."

"She was sure that her lover would come, and she knew that he would not know where to find her if she wasn't here. And so she returned quickly. Somehow she found Meg and began working with the laundresses. Meg served as midwife when I was born. Those early years, we lived in a small chamber behind a stable near the river. Besides Meg and the other workers, I was my mother's only companion. Gilbert and Stephen never saw her, and true to their threat, did not so much as give her a shilling. She could have starved for all they knew or cared."

"And you? Did you know who she was and who they were?"

"Not until I was about seven. And then I would hear

of these men with my mother's name and I began to figure some of it out. Stephen began rising in city politics
then. And I knew by then that I was a bastard. The other
boys made sure I knew that. Several years later she became
David Constantyn's housekeeper and things got better for
her, although Gilbert and Stephen never forgave him for
helping her. In their minds she deserved all that had happened to her. Her misery was the price of her sin against
God and them. Mostly them."

He had told this story simply and evenly, as was his
way. But she sensed that many other thoughts were tied to
this tale, and that some of them concerned herself.

She remembered the drawing of this woman's face
which she had seen, and looking at his perfect bones now,
she could see his mother in him. But another face had
contributed to these planes and deep eyes. An unknown
face.

"What was her name? Your mother's name?"

"Joanna."

"And your father? Do you know him?"

"The only father I ever knew was my master. The first
time I saw him, he scolded me for stealing one of his
apples. He came out of the ivy garden as I sat beneath the
tree eating it while my mother helped with the laundry in
the courtyard. I talked fast and hard to get out of a beating, I'll tell you that. He gave me a good wallop anyway
and dragged me back to my mother. A few weeks later he
showed up while we were here and took me into the city
to see a thief hang. On the way back he told me that there
were two ways for clever men to get rich. One was
through stealing and the other was through trade, but that
the thieves lived shorter lives. By age eight I had done my
share of stealing, and the lesson was not lost on me."

She pictured the urchins whom she sometimes saw on
the city streets sidling up to carts and windows, running

off with food and goods. She imagined a little David amongst them. Never getting caught, of course.

"He offered to marry her, I think," he added thoughtfully. "I remember coming upon them one day when I was about twelve. They were sitting in the hall. Something important was being discussed, I could tell. I sensed what it was."

"She refused him, you think?"

"Aye. I assumed then that he offered because he wanted me. We had become close by then, much like father and son. We even shared a name. She had chosen mine from the Bible, but it is an unusual name in England and I knew from the start that it fascinated him that I had it. Even her position here— I thought he had accepted the mother to get the son. But I think now that maybe it was the other way around."

"Did she refuse him because of the other man, your real father?"

"Aye. Her heart waited long after her mind gave up. I despised her for that when I was a youth, but by the time she died I understood a little."

She thought of David's patient understanding during their betrothal, but also of his cruel, relentless prods about Stephen.

You still wait for him, after all of this time and when the truth is so clear. It is well that Edward gave you to me. You would have spent your whole life waiting, living in some faded dream.

In not repudiating her, he had taken a horrible, painful chance.

She pressed herself against the warm comfort of his body, feeling the texture of his skin against her length. It touched her that he had told her about Joanna and his early life. Little by little, in ways like this, perhaps he would cease to be a stranger to her. She also knew that it was not in his nature to make such confidences and that only the intimacy of their marriage and passion had permitted it.

Without thinking, she rubbed her face against his chest and then turned and kissed it. She tasted the skin and kissed again. Her desire to give and take comfort and revel in their new closeness changed to something else as she kissed him, and impulsively she turned her head and gently licked his nipple. He touched her head and held it, encouraging her. A languid sensuality spread through her, and she felt the change in him, too. Only then did she remember that this was one of the things that the servant girl had told her about during her bath this morning.

He let her lips and tongue caress him a while longer, and then gently turned her on her back.

"I think that I promised you slow pleasure," he said. "Let us see how slow we can make it."

Much later, for David could make the pleasure very slow when he chose to, they lay together on the darkened bed, the curtains pulled against the dimming sounds and lights from the wedding party. Christiana began drifting into sleep in his arms.

She felt him move, and sensed him looking at her nearly invisible profile.

"Did you speak with him?" he asked quietly.

She had forgotten about that. Had forgotten about Stephen Percy and her anger and hurt with David. This day and night had obscured her suspicions about his motivations with her, and she really wished now that he hadn't reminded her.

He lives with realities, she thought. *You are the one who constructs dreams and songs.* But he had written that song about her, hadn't he? Not a love song, though. He thought her beautiful and had written about it. Perhaps he composes such melodies about sunsets and forest glens too.

"Aye, I spoke with him."

"What did he want?"

"Nothing honorable."

He was silent awhile.

"I do not want you seeing him," he finally said.

"He is at court often. Are you saying that I cannot go back to Westminster again?"

"I do not mean that. You know what I am saying."

"It is over, David. Like you and Alicia. It is the same."

"It is not. I never loved Alicia."

She turned her head to his. He had opened this door and she felt a compulsion to walk through it now.

"You never planned to let me go with him, did you?"

"I did not lie when I said it, but I was sure it would not come up."

"And if it had?"

His fingers touched her face in the darkness. "I would not have let you go. Early on I knew it."

Why? Your pride? Your investment? To save me from your mother's fate? She could not ask the question. She did not want to know the true answer. A girl should be allowed some illusions and ambiguities if she had to live with a man. There was such a thing as too much reality.

"How did you know that I would come that day?"

"I did not expect it. I planned to go and get you."

"And if I wouldn't come and agree to your seduction?"

"I would not have given you much choice."

She thought about that.

"You were very clever, David, I will grant you that. Very careful. Lots of witnesses. Your whole household. Idonia. How thorough were you? Did you even save the sheets? Did you leave them on the bed until Geva had seen them the next day?" Her tone came out more petulantly than she felt.

He kissed her temple and pulled her into the curve of his body. "The first time I met you and every time after you told me that you loved him, Christiana. Up until last Wednesday itself. Despite what happened between us when I kissed you, despite his misuse of you. Aye, darling, I was thorough. And calculating and clever. I deliberately made this marriage a fact and bound you to me. I took no chances that he might tell the lies that your heart wanted to hear so that he could misuse you again. Would you have had me do otherwise? Should I have stood back from this knight like the merchant I am? Would honoring my promise to let you go have pleased you?"

She trembled a little at the blunt force of his words. It sounded very different when he put it that way, when she saw it through his eyes. It had been so easy to forget how she had been before last Wednesday.

"Nay," she whispered, and it was true. She would not have been pleased at all if he had proven indifferent and had simply let Stephen lure her away. Another reaction that she feared to examine too closely.

The silence descended again, and after a time she relaxed in his embrace. Sleep had almost claimed her when she heard him laugh quietly in her ear.

"Aye, my girl, I was thorough and took no chances. I saved the sheets."

CHAPTER 14

DAVID WAS DROWSILY aware of the curtains being pushed back. He turned his face away from the flooding light.

"Hell," a man's voice said, pulling him awake.

He opened one eye a slit. Unless he was still dreaming, his wife was gone and the King of England stood beside his bed.

"Damnation, David."

Not dreaming.

"My lord?" He rose up on his elbows.

The King stared down with a frown. "Will you be wanting to repudiate her? Philippa assured me the girl was whole, I swear. I told her we should have her examined, but she and Idonia . . ."

David looked to where the King gazed. The coverlet and sheets were bunched over to reveal a bloodless marriage bed.

Hell. The last thing he had expected was someone

looking for evidence of Christiana's virginity. What was Edward doing here, anyway?

"Do not let it concern you, my lord. There will be no repudiation."

Edward's frown relaxed. "Damn chivalrous of you, David."

"I am a merchant and we are apart from chivalry. That is reserved for your knights. I assure you that my wife came to me a virgin, though. If I had thought that someone would seek the evidence this morning, I would have bled a chicken."

Edward looked at him blankly.

The man was still half besotted. David noted the red robe. The King had been here all night. Where and with whom? David decided that he didn't want to know.

"Do you need to see the original sheets? I have them," he offered with a laugh, but as soon as he said it he realized that Edward's mind had moved on.

"I want to speak with you. It will save you a ride to Westminster."

David glanced around the bed. Christiana's and his clothes were still strewn around the posts and floor. "Perhaps in the solar?"

Edward nodded and drifted off.

David grabbed a robe off a peg in the wardrobe, threw it on, and followed. Edward stood by the solar windows with a speculative, hooded expression on his face. David joined him and glanced down at the courtyard. A redhaired serving woman from a nearby house lounged against the well, surrounded by the litter of the night's revelry.

Edward sighed. "I suppose I have to give her something, eh? Hell, I can't even remember." He patted his robe for evidence of a purse or coins.

"She is not a whore," David said. "Wait one moment."

He went back to the wardrobe and returned with a purple silk veil embroidered with gold thread.

Edward examined it. "Awfully nice, David. Don't you have something plainer? I don't even know if I enjoyed myself. This would be good for Philippa, though. Peace offering . . ."

David went to the wardrobe once again and fetched a blue veil with no embroidery.

"What, do you keep a whole box of them to give to your women?" the King teased as he stuffed them in his robe. "Best hide them from your wife. See my wardrobe treasurer about them."

David pictured himself arriving at Westminster without a debenture or tally to claim payment for two veils purchased by the King for his slut and his neglected wife.

"Consider them gifts," he said dryly. "You wanted to speak with me about something?"

"Aye. The council met two days ago. It was decided to embark right after Easter. I'll summon the barons shortly."

David waited patiently for the rest of it.

"We received word that Grossmont engaged with the French and has secured Gascony," the King continued.

David nodded. Gascony, below England's Aquitaine on the west coast of the continent, was territory held by Edward in fief to the French king. Among the many points of contention between the two monarchs had been the degree of control which France wanted to exert there. Henry Grossmont had been sent to stabilize the area.

"Furthermore, he has pushed as far north as Poitiers," Edward said. "The port of Bordeaux is secure now. We will go in that way, join with him, and head northeast. I'll not be needing that last bit of information from you after all."

"Poitiers is a long way from Paris. The spring rains will make movement difficult."

"The council considered all of that. Still, our army and Grossmont's will be a formidable force. And debarking at Bordeaux will be riskless."

Presumably the council of barons knew what they were doing. They were experienced soldiers. But it struck him as a fruitless strategy.

Edward watched him with an amused expression. "You do not approve. Speak your mind."

He knew that a merchant's mind was irrelevant, but he spoke it anyway. "Bordeaux is a seven-day sea voyage. A long way to take an army by boat, and you risk bad winds. The French already await you at Poitiers. Even with a decisive victory you will be a long way from Paris. If the French crown is your goal, you must take that city and the royal demesne, must you not?"

"I will have twenty thousand with me," Edward replied jovially. "We will cut through France like a hot blade through butter."

Like all armies paid with spoils, yours will slog through France like a feather through cream, David silently replied.

"Those weapons you offered me," Edward mused. "Where are they?"

"Nowhere near Poitiers. I have one here, outside the city. If you have room on one of your ships, it is yours. Send me some men and I will train them in its use."

"Ah well, one toy is probably enough. I will need the maps that you have been making of that region. Do you have them ready? We will want to know all of the possible routes and the best roads. Especially where to cross the Loire river during spring floods."

"They are in my study." The King followed him through the door by the hearth into the small chamber.

He took some rolled parchments off the shelf and placed them on the table. "This one is of the north. This other is Brittany, from Brest to the marches of Normandy. The large one shows the routes out from Bordeaux." He unrolled the largest parchment. "Remember that I was there in November, and the marked river crossings are based on conversations that I had with the people in the area, and not on what I saw for myself. The conditions of the roads were obvious even in late autumn, however." He pointed to one line. "This road is fairly direct for your purposes and lies on high ground, so it should be in better condition than the main one. It passes through farmland, and there are few towns along it." Few opportunities for looting. The barons would press for the muddy low road so that they could pay their retinues.

Edward admired the drawing. "You have a knack for this sort of thing. I told the council that you would do the job and none would be the wiser."

"Do you want them all?"

"You can bring the others later. This one I will take now. We are itching to begin our plans." He took the parchment and tucked it under his arm. "A clever idea, to have you map out three possibilities. I know your own mind on this, but it will be Bordeaux."

Aye, David thought. *The army will land and engage. Battles will be fought and towns besieged, and knights and soldiers will grow rich from the looting. And after a summer of fighting, you will come back and nothing will have been resolved. Until you take Paris, this will never end.*

What this decision meant to him and his own plans was another matter, and one that he would consider carefully later.

A sound behind made them both turn. Christiana

stood at the threshold to the bedchamber with a startled expression on her face. She carried a tray with food and ale.

"My lord," she said, stepping in quickly and placing the tray on the table. "My apologies."

They watched her go.

"Do you think that she heard?" Edward asked, frowning.

"If so, she will say nothing." It really didn't matter. One could hardly sail hundreds of ships down the coast of Brittany and France and not be noticed. There would be little surprise when this invasion finally happened.

Was it over? He smiled at his King, but already his mind began recalculating.

On the fourth morning after their wedding, David told Christiana that they would ride north of the city a ways.

"I recently acquired a property in Hampstead," he explained as they headed out the city gate side by side. "We will go there so that you can see it. I have to speak with some workers, and there are other matters to attend."

"Is it a farm?"

"There are farms attached to it, but it is the house that you should see."

"Many farms?"

"Ten, as I remember."

"Aren't you afraid that the income will put you over the forty-pound limit? That Edward will force knighthood on you?" she teased.

"Aye. That is why I put the property in your name."

"My name!"

"Yours. It belongs to you, as do the farms' rents."

She absorbed this startling news. Married women

almost never owned their own property. It went with them to their husbands. The only woman she knew who owned land outright was Lady Elizabeth. Joan had told her that Elizabeth always demanded property in her name as part of her marriage settlements to those old men.

"The dowry manor that Edward settled on you is yours as well, Christiana."

"Why, David?"

"I want you to know that you are secure, and without land you never will feel thus. I am comfortable with wealth based on credits and coin, but you never will be. Also, I take risks in my trade, sometimes big ones. I want to know that should my judgment fail, you will not suffer."

It made a certain sense, but still it astonished her.

"There is something that you should know about this house," he said later as they turned off the road onto a lane. "It came to me through moneylending. You should also know that it was owned by Lady Catherine. If you do not like that, you can sell it and purchase elsewhere. Near London, though. I want you to have someplace to go when the summer illnesses spread in the city."

The twinge of guilt that she felt at this news disappeared as soon as she saw the house. Wide and tall, its base built of stone and its upper level of timber and plaster, it sat beautifully inside a stone wall at the end of the lane, surrounded by outbuildings and gardens. A bank of glazed windows on the second level indicated its recent construction.

Workers were laying tiles on the hall floor when they entered, and David went over to speak with them. She explored the other chambers. Very little furniture had been left, and the building echoed with their footsteps. David explained that he would leave furnishing the house to her.

"We need to ride out onto the property," he said as they reclaimed their horses. "There are some men awaiting me."

The men worked half a mile away on an open field. Three of them stood around a big metal cylinder, narrower at the top than the bottom, propped and angled up on logs. A bulky man with black hair explained something to the others as they approached.

"What is that?" she asked.

"A toy. You will see how it works."

He tied the horses to a tree and walked over to the men. She wrapped her cloak more tightly around her and sat down on the dried grass near a small fire that had been built. David and the others fiddled and fussed with the toy a long time, and the black-haired man kept crouching behind the low end of the cylinder and spying along its length. Her eyes followed the man's line of sight, and in the distance she saw an old wooden building.

David poured some sand in it from a leather bag and stuck a stick down after it. He lifted a large stone from in front of it. A mason had clearly worked it, for the stone was perfectly round. He rolled the stone into the cylinder.

He came over to the fire and lifted a flaming torch.

"Cover your ears," he said. He lit a line of the sand snaking along the lower end of the toy.

A moment later the loudest clap of thunder that she had ever heard cracked the winter silence. Smoke spewed out of the cylinder and it jumped back. Across the deep field, a few seconds after the toy was fired, the farm building's roof burst into pieces.

She jumped up and crossed over to the smoking cylinder. The black-haired man drew the other two aside and began to explain something that sounded a lot like geometry.

"What is this?" she asked, peering into the hot hollow.

"The future. It is called a gonne."

She walked along its length, and noted the stack of round stones nearby. "It is a siege machine, isn't it?"

"Aye, that it is."

She knew more than she wanted about siege machines. As a child she had watched the towers and catapults built outside Harclow. She had seen the horrible damage that they wrought and had lived in fear of those flying missiles and baskets of fire. She looked at the farm building. Only the shells of its side walls remained. It had been old, and built of wood, but this toy possessed more force in hurling its small stones than any of the machines which she had seen at Harclow.

"Do you plan to make and sell these?"

"Nay. But they will be made by others. It is inevitable. I first saw them on my way home on my first trip. There was a demonstration near Pisa. They didn't work well, and never hit their mark then, but already they improve. They fascinate me, that is all. This one is for Edward. Other kings will have them, so he must." He walked toward the horses. "I am going to check the building You can come if you want to."

She wasn't at all sure that she wanted to, but she went nonetheless.

She gazed at the tatters of the building. No wonder David did not want to be a knight. Of what use were armor and shields against war machines like this?

There were other buildings nearby, all neglected. This had once been a horse farm with many stables.

"I should tell you that this section of the property is not yours," he explained as he dismounted.

She saw no signs of labor here. It appeared that David had kept the poorest portion for himself. "You need a field with old buildings to play with your toys?"

"Aye. And to collect that which makes them work."
He led the way into one of the stables.

The roof of this structure was in disrepair, and
splotches of sunlight leaked through its holes. David went
into one of the stalls and crouched down. He wiped his
fingers across the dried dirt and lifted his hand. A sandy
substance glittered.

"It is found in stables like this that have been used a
long time, and other places where animals live. The powder that makes the machine work requires it. It is said that
the secret was brought back overland from Cathay in the
Far East. It has no English name, although some translate
it to saltpeter."

"Are those men back there from the King?"

"Two are. The other brought the machine from Italy."

"Will Edward use it? Will he take it with him to
France? To Bordeaux?"

He did not answer her. They remounted and rode
back to the men who had already prepared the machine
again. David spoke in Italian to the black-haired one and
then led her away.

"I know that you overheard Edward in my study,
Christiana," he finally said. "You know, I'm sure, that you
cannot repeat such things. Even when every-
one else suspects and talks of it, you should pretend ignorance."

It was true, then. She had heard the King mention
Bordeaux and had seen the rolled parchment under his
arm. It was one of those maps she had noticed that day in
David's study. Her husband did not just deliver messages.
He did other things for Edward as well. Much more dangerous things. Dangerous enough and important enough
that the King told him about Bordeaux.

She prayed that now that Edward had chosen his

course, David would be out of it. He wasn't a knight or noble. It wasn't fair for the King to use him thus when he would see little profit and significant loss from such wars.

They approached the house from the rear. The tilers' wagon had left. A new horse was tethered by the side of the house, however, and a man stood beside it.

David stopped his horse. He gazed hard at the newcomer.

The stranger was a tall man with long white hair and a short beard. A dull brown cloak, no more than a shapeless mantle, hung to the ground. The horse beside him looked bony and old.

David dismounted and lifted her off her horse.

"Wait outside while I speak with this man."

"It is cold."

"I am sorry for it, but do not come in."

They had been out most of the day, and the chill had long ago penetrated her cloak. "I will go up to the solar and you can use the hall," she suggested.

"You are not to come into the house while he is here," he ordered harshly. His gaze had not left the waiting man. "I insist that you obey me on this, my girl."

His tone stunned her. She watched his absorbed attention with the figure by the house. His awareness of her had essentially disappeared. The withdrawal was so complete that she had never felt more separate from him than she did at that moment, not even the night when she first met him as a total stranger in his solar. This sudden indifference, contrasting so vividly with the constant attention that he had shown her since their wedding, sickened her heart.

Giving the stranger a more thorough examination, she strolled toward the garden.

✦   ✦   ✦

David walked slowly toward the house, and with each step the eerie internal silence grew more absorbing. Scattered thoughts scrambled through his mind, and odd emotions welled inside his chest. Emotions that he could not afford to either acknowledge or examine now.

Nor could he afford to indulge himself in the usual fascination with the sound of Fortune's wheel turning yet again. He shook off the silence.

The man waited and watched. He stood too tall and proud to make the worker's cloak an effective disguise, but David doubted that anyone else had paid much attention.

He had expected this man eventually, but not today and not here. Oliver had received no report yet, for one thing. That must mean that he had come by way of a northern port, and not one along the southern or eastern coasts. A long detour, then, to ensure safety. It was the sort of refined and careful strategy that David could appreciate. He had come alone, too. Either he was very brave or very sure of himself. Probably both.

He tied the horses' reins to a post near the stable building and then walked over to the man. The white head rose as high as his own. Deep brown eyes regarded him carefully.

They did not greet each other but David suspected that the odd familiarity which he experienced was felt by the other, too.

"How did you find me?" David asked.

"Frans learned from its previous owner that you had acquired this property. I thought that you might bring your bride here. A beautiful girl, by the way. Worthy of her bloodline. Worthy of you."

He ignored the compliment, except to note that it was

not one which a man like this would normally give a merchant. "Frans has a friendship with Lady Catherine? Is she one of yours? A watcher?"

The man hesitated and David had his answer. No doubt Lady Catherine would do anything for a price.

"You should have waited until my wife was not with me. I do not want her involved in any way."

"I could not wait forever. I am here at great risk to myself. If you had left her side for a few hours . . ."

The man's voice drifted away and a full silence fell. It held for a long time. They faced each other, both knowing that whoever spoke first again would be at the disadvantage.

David calmly let the moments throb past. He had much more experience in waiting than his guest. A lifetime of it, in fact.

"Do you know who I am?" the man finally asked.

"I know who you are. I assume that you seek what Frans sought, and since I told him I would not help, I wonder about the reason for this meeting."

The man reached into the front of his mantle and withdrew a folded piece of parchment. "This is one of yours. It was found amongst the papers of Jacques van Artevelde."

"Your man and I have already discussed my relationship with Jacques. My letters to him were matters of trade, nothing else."

"His relationship with you and others like you got him killed."

Jacques van Artevelde, the leader of Ghent's pro-English burghers, had become a friend. His death last year at the hands of a mob had been more than a political loss for David, and he resented this offhand reference to it.

It went without saying that the Count of Flanders had been behind that mob's murder. Had this other man been involved, too?

"We met for business and nothing more," David said blandly.

"Let us skip the games, Master David. As Frans explained, we know about you. Not everything, I'm sure. But enough. Besides, it was not the content of this letter that made him bring it to me. It was the seal." His long fingers played with the parchment. "An unusual seal. Three entwined serpents. How did you come to use it?"

"It was on a piece of jewelry that my mother owned. It was as useful a device as any other."

"This item of jewelry. Was it a ring? With a gray stone?"

David let the silence pulse as he absorbed this astounding question and its unexpected implications.

"Aye. A ring."

The man sighed audibly. He stepped closer and scrutinized David's face. "Aye, I can see it. The eyes, but not their color. His were brown. The mouth. Even your voice."

David met that piercing gaze with his own. "I, of course, have no way of knowing if you are right or if you lie. You want something from me. It is in your interest to claim a resemblance."

"I do not come here to trick you into treason."

"Merely meeting with you might be construed as treason. Your presence here compromises me. You should have given me a choice."

"It was essential that I see you. I had to know. Surely you understand that."

"I'm not sure that I do."

"Why did you never come to us?"

"I had no need of you, and you none of me."

"We have need of you now."

David examined the man's serious, expectant expression. "You must want this very badly, to appeal to a stranger."

Shrewd eyes met David's own. "Aye, I want it badly. I want it for my country but I want it for myself, too. You are not such a stranger. I have made it my business to learn about you. Your accomplishments in trade will not satisfy you much longer. Already those small victories seem thin and shallow, do they not? Especially compared to the politics of monarchies."

David glanced away, knowing even as he did so that the reflex signaled a certain defeat.

He gestured for the man to follow him into the house.

Christiana huddled in her cloak on the bench under a tree in the garden. She was not at all pleased to be stuck out here while David held this secret meeting. She was even less pleased with the way he had dismissed her, and his tone when he ordered her obedience.

That tall man's presence had obviously surprised him, and that explained some of it. Still, she doubted that this meeting had anything to do with trade or finance. The stranger was no merchant, despite his simple cloak and humble horse. He could no more hide his true status than he could hide his height. She had recognized him for what he was. Any time, any place, nobles knew each other when they met.

They were talking a very long time. Her hands felt a little numb from the raw chill, and she wrapped them in the billows of her cloak.

If David didn't come and get her soon, she was going to disobey him and go inside. It was one thing to be a dutiful wife, and quite another to sit out here and freeze like an idiot who didn't know when to come in from the cold.

She stomped her feet and huddled smaller. She tried to distract herself by thinking about that strange invention David had shown her earlier. For someone who didn't like knights and war, David had a peculiar fascination with siege machines.

Her eyes scanned the house, looking for some sign of movement. They were probably in the solar in front. From her vantage point she could see the rump of the stranger's horse tied by the side of the building.

David had ordered her to stay outside. He hadn't said where.

She got up and walked through the garden, heading to the sorry-looking animal. Not much of a horse for a nobleman. Perhaps it was someone down on his luck seeking a loan.

A bag lay over the animal's hind quarters. Soothing him with her hands and voice, she eyed the loose flap.

She really shouldn't. It was definitely none of her business.

Asking for forgiveness, she lifted the flap and peered inside.

The bag held clothes. Rich clothes. Expensive fabrics. Garments not at all in keeping with this horse and that worn cloak. The man had disguised himself to look poor.

Voices startled her. She let the flap drop and hurried away.

She had just turned the corner of the house when she heard David's voice.

"We must not meet again in England."

That stopped her. She pressed against the stones of the house.

"I leave tomorrow. Do not worry. I know your risk. I have no desire to jeopardize you," the stranger said. He spoke English, but the accent was unmistakable. This man, this nobleman, was French.

"Frans is not to return to England until this is over. The man is careless, and his long stay last time was noticed. His woman friend is a complication that I will not accept. Sever ties with her," David said.

Frans van Horlst. A French noble. Dear saints!

"He will leave with me tomorrow and not return. The lady will be out of it as well."

"There is one final condition. I will want documents from you. Witnessed."

Only the sound of her heart broke the silence that ensued.

"You do not trust me," the stranger finally said. "I suppose I can't blame you. How will I get these documents to you?"

"You will not. I will come to you."

Her mind scrambled to make sense of these cryptic statements. Documents? Why was David meeting in secret with a French noble and discussing such things? Her heart heaved as one horrible possibility sprang to mind. But if that were the case, David would be providing the documents, and not the other way around.

The sounds of a saddle creaking and a horse stomping reached her ears. She began easing away.

"I look forward to knowing you better," the stranger said. "In France, then."

The horse walked away. David would come looking for her now. She plunged away from the house and ran into the garden.

CHAPTER 15

AS SOON AS DAVID returned to his trade, Christiana presented herself at the house of Gilbert de Abyndon. No one seemed surprised at her going alone. She marveled at this and other new freedoms, so in contrast to the close supervision of Westminster. A childish exhilaration gripped her as she walked along the city streets, pausing occasionally to inspect the activities and wares in the tradesmen's windows.

Margaret appeared both delighted and flustered to see her. Hesitation briefly clouded her pale, delicate face before a very mature resolve took its place. "Does your husband know that you are here?" she asked after she sent a servant for some wine.

"He knows. It was his suggestion that I come. I am in need of a servant and he thought that you might be able to help me."

Margaret tilted her head and raised her eyebrows. "You know that they hate each other. Our husbands."

"I know. And it is always deep when kinsmen feel like that with each other. If my visit will cause trouble for you, I will leave."

Margaret sat on a cushioned window seat and patted the space beside her. Christiana joined her. "I will handle Gilbert. I recently learned that I am with child. I will tell him that I was feeling poorly and that your visit healed me." She smiled conspiratorially. "This child has already changed much and will change more. He will be like clay in my hands now."

Christiana blinked at this bald admission of manipulation. Margaret appeared so frail and sweet, it was hard to believe that a steel rod of practicality held her upright in this marriage.

She felt sorry that Margaret had a marriage in which only her breeding potential was valued. Then she reminded herself that was the likely reason for her own match.

Over the next few hours they formed a bond. The next day Margaret sent a girl named Emma to enter service. Although the daughter of a merchant who had fallen on bad times, Emma proved to be a willing and excellent servant. She arrived daily at the house before dawn and helped Vittorio and Geva until Christiana called for her.

Christiana learned about the fall in Emma's fortunes. Her father had been wealthy one day and poor the next because of one shipping disaster. She wondered if David's wealth tottered so precariously. He had suggested as much when he told her about the lands he had put in her name. Her consideration of this and of the household which she now directed led her to a decision. It was time to acquire a practical education, for the day might come when she had no servants. She set about learning how to cook from Vittorio and how to sew from the women. She learned from Geva how to be a housekeeper.

She had visitors, too, those first few weeks. Morvan came several times to take her for rides and to reassure himself that she wasn't miserable. Isabele and Idonia came once so that Isabele could examine Christiana's new home. Margaret visited at least once a week and they formed a fast friendship.

Toward the end of Lent, troops began arriving to muster for the King's French campaign. Most of the men lived in camps on the surrounding fields. During the days, they descended on the crowded city to pass the time while they awaited embarkation. David curtailed her freedom then, and told her not to leave the house alone.

The Tuesday before Easter, she returned from a trip to the market with Vittorio to find Joan waiting for her. The King's purveyors had been busy the last weeks requisitioning food throughout the countryside to feed the army, and the stalls in London had been hawking depleted meats and produce at inflated prices. She began her conversation with Joan by complaining about this.

Joan laughed. "You are sounding like some bootmaker's goodwife, Christiana. It is well that I have come. We will go to your chamber and I will teach your servant a new hairstyle which I learned. You can show me the things that your rich husband has bought you while I tell you the court gossip."

"How is Thomas Holland?" Christiana asked as she led Joan upstairs.

"He has been sent to Southhampton to help with the ships there. Have you ever seen anything like it? There must be two hundred in harbor here alone, and they say it is the same in the Cinque Ports and up the east coast as well. And no one knows where Edward plans to land once he gets to the Continent."

Bordeaux, Christiana almost said. *He goes to relieve Grossmont at Poitiers.* The ships were merchant ships, requisitioned by the King. Overseas trade had stopped. But Joan would not want to hear about the hardships that would cause.

"With Thomas gone, it has been lonely, but fortunately William Montagu has been very attentive, so I do not feel too dour," Joan giggled. "In truth, it would be hard for any girl to feel sad at court right now. Westminster is bursting with knights and barons, all here without their ladies. The few females around are surrounded by men. It is delicious."

"If I were still there, it would not be delicious for me," Christiana said, laughing. "I would die of thirst in that lake of male attention. Morvan would probably stand up at a banquet and issue a general warning and challenge."

"But he has no say now. You have to come and visit," Joan cajoled as she began working Christiana's long hair into thin braids that she then looped around her head. "Before the fleet leaves, while it is still busy and gay."

"I am married, Joan. My place is here now."

"You can come for a few days, can't you? It really isn't as much fun without you. At least come for the Easter banquet. Bring David with you. He can keep the men away."

Christiana thought about the elaborate banquet and tournament held to celebrate Easter at court. It would be nice to attend as an adult rather than a child.

That night she told David about Joan's invitation. They were sitting in the solar while she practiced the Saracen letters that he had taught her.

"You must go if you want to," he said.

She stared down at the shallow box of sand in which she traced the letters with a stick. They had been married five weeks and David had never accompanied her to court, even when she attended a dinner.

"Joan says that she will arrange for us to have a chamber for a few nights if we want," she said. "You don't think the boys will mind if we are gone for Easter?"

"The household can celebrate without us."

"We will go then?"

"As it happens, I must be out of London then."

"And if not, you still would not come, would you?"

"You had and have a life and place there, and I would not deny you that. But it is not my world. I will not be the upstart merchant who enters the King's court by hanging on to the hem of his wife's veil."

His frank admission that he would not share that part of her life saddened her. She missed him when she was at Westminster. A part of her remained removed from the gaiety, thinking about him. Sometimes she would find herself turning to comment on some entertainment or jest and be a little startled not to find him beside her.

She enjoyed those visits to the court, but she always returned to the city eager to see David and relate the gossip and news which she had learned. She realized that there could be no joy in anything unless she could share it with him in some way.

She looked over at the man gazing thoughtfully into the hearth fire as his long body lounged in the wooden chair. She thought about how she filled her days with activities but how, through them all, a part of her was always waiting for something. Waiting for him, for the sound of his horse in the courtyard and his footsteps in the hall. She was always so happy to see him that sometimes, without thinking, she would run to him and he would laugh and sweep her up into a kiss. She thought about how his return to the house for dinner and again each evening filled her with comfort and relief as if, upon his leaving, she had taken a deep breath and only released it when he came back. He was the center of this household, its very heartbeat. His presence brought security and joy and excitement.

"I need to speak with you about this trip, Christiana."

"Will it be a long one?" she asked, returning to her letters. She wondered how she would get through the nights without him.

"It could be. Two weeks, maybe longer."

"Where do you go?"

"West. Towards Salisbury. The King has received reports of corruption among royal purveyors in that shire. He has asked me to find out what I can before he orders an official investigation."

Another favor for Edward? The thing about secret trips for the King was that no one could ever check on them.

"It is the first time that you have left since our marriage."

"That is why we must talk. All journeys have some danger in them. I should explain some things to you before I go."

She glanced up sharply. He faced her impassively, but she had learned much about him these last weeks, and that perfect face could never be a complete mask to her again. Now she noticed the thin veil of concern that diffused the warmth of his eyes. A strange numbness began slipping over her.

"Before I go, I will be giving you a key. It is for the box in my study. There is coin there. I will also show you a trunk in the wardrobe that contains papers regarding properties and banking credits. The mercery accounts are at the shop. Andrew is well familiar with them. Should you ever need help with anything, John Constantyn will aid you." He paused. "He is the executor of my testament."

Somehow she managed to draw another letter despite her shock. "You only ride to Salisbury, David."

"You should know what to do. I have seen too many women who did not."

"I do not want to speak of this."

"Nor do I, but we must nonetheless."

She gritted her teeth and tried to ignore the appalling realization that forced itself into her mind. She knew, she just knew, that David did not go to Salisbury. He was going someplace very dangerous to do something very risky.

For Edward? She wanted to believe that was so, but the memories of Frans van Horlst asking a man for help in the King's secret corridor, and of a French noble meeting David in Hampstead, boiled in her mind.

I have no desire to jeopardize you. In France then.

He watched her with that deep gaze that always saw too much. Could he read these thoughts as he could so many others?

She was surely wrong. The very notion was unworthy of her. But he knew about Bordeaux and he played to win and used his own rules.

He could not do this. He would not. Their gold and silver would not tempt him. He was not ruled by such hungers.

"I expect that with John's help I will be able to manage things," she said. "Do not concern yourself."

"If something ever happens to me, the shop can be either sold or liquidated. Andrew could help with that. The mercers' wardens will see to placing the boys with other masters."

"And me, David? Will they seek to place me with a new master as well?"

"They have no authority over your life. But they will no doubt offer advice and counsel you to remarry and join your property and business with another merchant's."

"Is that the advice that you gave women as a warden?"

"Often. You, of course, need not look to merchants. You will be very wealthy."

He spoke as though that should reassure her. He was telling her that if wealthy, widowed, and noble, she could have the husband she was born to have. It hurt her that he could so blithely talk about her going to another man.

"I assume that the properties in my name are well documented? And there will be money enough to buy more. Perhaps, then, I will not remarry at all."

He reached over and stroked her cheek. "The thought of you living your life alone gives me no pleasure."

"Let us be frank, David. We are speaking of your possible death. Your pleasure afterwards will not matter. Now, are we finished with this morbid topic? When do you leave?"

"Two days."

Holy Thursday. Joan had said that the rumors called for the fleet to embark for France soon after Easter. Two days and then two weeks of empty chambers. She knew that a part of her would simply cease to exist while he was gone. Maybe it would cease to exist forever. She wouldn't believe that, she couldn't accept its possibility, but he had as much as warned her so just now. He would not have spoken thus unless he thought his danger very real.

A ripping ache filled her chest. Wherever he went, he must go for Edward. Surely he would not risk giving her such pain for anything else.

She set aside her box and stared at her lap. She tried not to care. She argued valiantly that if he was involved in something dishonorable, she would not want to see him again anyway. She told herself that if the worst happened and she became a rich widow, that would not be so bad. None of it helped relieve the weight around her heart.

Her throat burned and she fought to hold on to her composure.

Suddenly he stood in front of her. He lifted her up into his arms. Before she buried her face in his chest, she saw surprise in his eyes.

"I did not mean to upset you, my girl."

The warmth of his embrace made the tears flow. "Did you not?" she mumbled. "You speak to me of dying and widowhood as if you speculated about next year's wool shipments."

"That is because I do not expect to be harmed. I am just being practical for your sake. I have survived many worse dangers than I could possibly face on this little adventure."

There was much in this man that remained a mystery to her, but the parts that she knew she had come to know very well. And she knew now that he lied to her. He did not do that too much anymore, mostly because she avoided asking the sorts of questions that led him to it. And his lies had rarely been true lies. Usually they were ambiguous statements like this one.

She nestled her head closer and his embrace tightened. "Can you not stay? Let another do this," she whispered.

"None other can do it," he said quietly. "I have committed myself."

"Then I care not where or why you go," she said. "You are a merchant, and there will be many trips, some of them very long. Go where you have to go, David, as long as you promise to come back."

David and Sieg left Thursday morning. Christiana threw herself into a whirlwind of packing in order to distract herself. She chose and rechose her clothes for court until Emma was frantic. She tried not to think too much about the poignancy that had imbued David's lovemaking the last two nights.

He had hired two men to guard the house in Sieg's absence, and in the afternoon she had one of them escort her to Westminster.

She reclaimed her bed in the anteroom, and tried hard to pretend that it was just like old times. Sometimes it was, but often, as Joan and she lay on Isabele's bed and shared gossip and talk, her mind would suddenly drift away as she wondered where David was and whether he was safe.

Her suspicions about what he might be doing played over in her mind, and more than once she forced herself to analyze the evidence suggesting treason. That's what it was, after all. Treason of the highest kind, that would put people whom she loved in danger. She told herself that there was no proof that David was selling the French information about the fleet's destination and that she had let some overheard phrases work evils in her mind.

At the Easter banquet the King formally announced the embarkation to France, and the cheers in the hall greeted it as joyous news. Word spread that the troops would board the ships on Wednesday.

On Tuesday morning Joan roused her out of bed early. "There is to be a big hunt, and then lots of private parties in the taverns and inns on the Strand before tonight's feast. One last celebration before all the knights leave," she said as she went to Christiana's trunks and began choosing clothes for her. "You must come with William and me and be my chaperon so Idonia won't interfere. It will be a day of play to last everyone through the summer."

Christiana had been enjoying her stay at court, even

if a part of her kept worrying about David. Joan had been right, and Westminster bulged with knights eager to pay any female attention. They practiced their poetic flattery even on unattainable women. It was expected for women at court to accept the milder attentions, and she did so, in part because they helped distract her from her concerns and suspicions about David.

Like most of the women, she merely rode to the hunt and watched the men demonstrate their prowess with arrow and spear. She stayed close to Joan and William Montagu the whole morning. The young earl acted besotted with the Fair Maid of Kent. Joan flirted back enough to give more hope than she ought. Christiana thought about Thomas Holland supervising the loading of ships in Southhampton. First Andrew and now William and who knew how many in between. Joan's constancy hadn't lasted very long.

The hunting parties made their way to the Strand at midday, and Joan's group descended on a large inn close to the city gates. Usually inns did not serve meals, but most had brought in cooks to deal with the large number of visitors to the area. This one's public room became so stuffed with tables and people that one could barely move, and Christiana soon lost track of Joan. She found herself standing against a wall, searching the crowd for friends to join.

"There you are," said a soft voice at her shoulder.

She turned to find Lady Catherine edging up close to her.

The older woman's cat eyes gleamed. "This is horrible, isn't it? I expected as much and took a large chamber upstairs. Come and join my party for dinner, Christiana."

She hesitated, remembering David and her brother telling her to avoid Catherine.

"I expect Morvan to eat with us," Lady Catherine said.

She hadn't seen much of her brother these last days. The King's knights had been managing the troops provided by the city. It seemed odd that Morvan would dine with Catherine, but maybe whatever he held against her had been resolved.

The crowd pressed against her. Catherine touched her arm and gestured with her head. Christiana debated the offer. It would be nice to spend some time with Morvan before he sailed.

"Thank you," she said, deciding quickly. There could be no harm in it, and surely David wouldn't mind if Morvan was there, too.

She followed Catherine through the throng to the stairs leading to the second level. Even up there the bodies were thick, because others had shown Catherine's foresight and taken chambers. Lady Catherine continued up to the inn's quiet third level, led her to a door, and ushered her in.

The chamber had been prepared for a party of fifteen. Two long tables cramped the space between the bed and the hearth. It was a warm April day and the narrow windows overlooking the courtyard had been opened, but the thick walls obscured the sounds from below.

Only one person waited in the chamber. Stephen Percy stood near the farthest window.

"I must go and collect the others," Lady Catherine said brightly, turning to leave. "We will be back shortly."

Christiana stared at Stephen. He smiled and walked to one of the tables and poured wine into two cups.

"A fortuitous coincidence, Christiana," he said as he handed her one of them. "I feared that I would not see you before we left."

She glanced at the tables awaiting the other diners. How long before some of them arrived?

"You will ride with your father?" she asked.

"Aye. The King has collected a huge army. It promises to be a glorious war. Come and sit with me awhile before the others come."

She thought of David's demand that she not see this man. By rights she should leave. But they would only be alone for a few moments and there could be no harm in wishing him well. She took a seat across from him at one of the tables.

"How is your merchant?" Stephen asked.

"David is well."

"He is not with you. He did not accompany you on this visit or on the others." His tone lacked subtlety. He assumed she returned to court to avoid David. That she sought solace amongst her friends.

"He is a busy man, Stephen, and is out of the city now."

"Still, I expected him to welcome the entry to court that you provided."

"He has little interest in such things."

Stephen raised his eyebrows in mock surprise. He leaned forward and his gaze drifted over her face.

His attention evoked an utter lack of feeling. In a strange way she felt as if she were seeing him for the first time. The face which she had once thought ruggedly handsome now appeared a bit coarse. There was something ill defined in the cheeks and jaws, especially compared to the precision of David's features. The blond hair, she felt quite sure, would not feel very soft if she touched it. Those thick eyebrows contrasted so little with the fair skin as to be almost invisible.

"You are so beautiful," he said softly. "I think that you grow more lovely each time that I see you."

She raised the cup of wine to her mouth and watched him over its rim. His hand reached toward her face.

In that instant before he touched her, she suddenly knew several things clearly and absolutely. She knew them as surely as she knew that day would follow night. Although they came as revelations, they did not surprise her at all. Rather she took a step and there they were, new facts of life to be reckoned with.

She knew, first of all, that no other diners would be joining them. No one, least of all Morvan, would arrive at that door. Stephen had arranged this with Lady Catherine's help, or maybe Catherine had done it herself. The tables, the cups, were all a ruse to get and keep her here so that she and Stephen could be alone.

She also knew, as she regarded that suddenly unfamiliar face, that she had never loved this man. Infatuated, giddy, and excited, she had been those things, but those feelings would have passed with time if he had not tried to seduce her and thus disrupted her life. She had decided that she loved him in order to assuage her guilt and humiliation after Idonia found them. She had clung to that illusion in hopes of rescue from the consequences. But she had never really been in love with him, nor he with her, and now she felt only a vacant indifference toward that hand reaching for her.

And finally she knew, with a peaceful acceptance that made her smile, that the daughter of Hugh Fitzwaryn had fallen in love with a common merchant. A glorious burst of tenderness for David flowed through her with the admission.

She leaned back out of reach.

"Nay."

He dropped his hand and sat upright, his green eyes examining her own. She let him search as long as he wanted, for he would not find what he sought. He smiled ruefully and poured some more wine.

"You have grown up quickly. It is a woman's face that I see now."

"I have had little choice. Perhaps I was overlong a child anyway."

"Innocence has its charm," he said, laughing.

"And its convenience."

He glanced at her and shrugged. "Your merchant is a very fortunate man, my sweet."

She felt a vague affection for Stephen. He was a rogue to be sure, but no longer dangerous to her heart. "I know that none at court will ever believe this, Stephen, but I think myself fortunate, too."

It felt good saying that. It felt wonderful standing up for her husband against the pity and sympathy of these people.

Stephen glanced at her sharply and then laughed in an artificial way. "Then my quest is indeed hopeless."

"Aye. Hopeless."

He made an exaggerated sigh. "First your brother's sword and now your husband's love. This story is a tragedy."

Nay, it was always a farce. Written by you and played by me who thought it real life. But she found that she could not hold that against him anymore. It really didn't matter. He didn't matter.

Dinner actually arrived, brought by two servants, and she stayed and ate with Stephen because being alone with him held no betrayal now. Her love for David felt like a suit of armor, and she was sure that Stephen recognized the futility of trying to penetrate it. They spoke casually about many things, and the hour passed pleasantly.

Toward the end of the meal, however, she suspected that he again began weighing her resolve against his skill

252 ♦ MADELINE HUNTER

at seduction. His smiles got warmer and his flattery more florid. His hand accidentally touched hers several times.

She calmly watched the unfolding of his final effort with surprise and amusement. She rose to leave before he could act on his intentions.

He rose more quickly and stepped between her and the door. His slow, insinuating smile filled her with sudden alarm.

"The meal was lovely, and it was good to share this time with an old friend, Stephen. But I must go now."

He shook his head, and his green eyes burned brightly. "The duty that says you must go was not chosen by you. In this world and this chamber, it does not bind you, my love."

She cursed herself for thinking that she could treat this man as a friend. "It is not duty that takes me away, but my love for my husband," she replied, hoping to kill any illusions he might have that she pined for him.

A spring breeze, light and free, blew through her heart with this more blatant admission of her feelings for David. How long had she loved him? Quite a while, she suspected.

How ironic that the first person to whom she admitted her love should be Stephen Percy. Ironic and also fair and just. Now she must tell David when he came back. If he came back. Then again, maybe she would not have to. Maybe he will just look at her and know. Of all her thoughts and emotions that he had read, this would probably be the most obvious.

Stephen had not moved out of her path, and he considered her closely, as if he judged her determination. She looked back firmly. Her response did not evoke the reaction she expected. Instead of backing down, a subtle ferocity entered his eyes and twisted his mouth.

He suddenly reached for her. She tried to duck his grasp, but he caught her shoulder and pulled her toward him. Surprised by his aggressive insistence, she squirmed to get free. He imprisoned her in his arms.

"A woman such as you cannot love such a man. One might as well try to mix oil and water. You have told yourself that you do in order to survive your fall, my love. That is all."

"You are wrong," she hissed, narrowing her eyes at him. "I love David, and I do not love you. Now *unhand me.*"

"You may think you do not love me, but you will see the truth of it." His face and lips came toward her.

She leaned back until she could lean no further. She desperately turned her face away, but that bruising mouth found her cheek and neck. He grasped her hair to steady her darting head and forced a crushing kiss on her lips. His other hand slid down to grab her bottom. Her stomach turned. To think that she had cried over this lout! She began using all of her strength to break free.

Stephen laughed. "You are spirited. That will soothe my regret that you are no longer innocent. The memory of the passion that I awoke in you last time has filled my memory ever since, begging for completion."

"Passion? I felt no passion with you, you conceited fool! You hurt and humiliated me that day and you will not do it again! Loose me or I will scream and the whole court will know that you force unwilling women!"

"You are not unwilling, just afraid," he murmured, pressing her against his warmth and forcing a caress down her back. "I will show you the pleasure that love can be when you are with a real man. When you scream, it will be with desire and none will hear you. The walls are thick and the building noisy, so do not be shy."

Good Lord, his arrogance knew no bounds. No wonder Idonia never wanted them to be alone with men.

His hands began wandering freely over her body. She gritted her teeth against the repulsion she felt, and took advantage of his loosening hold. Frantically she groped behind her back on the table, feeling for some weapon. Her hand closed on a crockery pitcher.

Just in time, too. Stephen's breathing had grown ragged and heavy. He began pressing her backward against the table, trying to lay her down. His hand started raising her skirt.

She stopped her fight and leveraged her hips against the table's edge. She smiled at him. Stephen paused, looked at her triumphantly, and readjusted his stance. With a snarl, she lifted her knee with all of her strength up between his legs. Then she crashed the pitcher down on his head.

His face shattered in pain and surprise while he bent over. She roughly pushed him away.

"I am an honest woman who loves her husband," she seethed. "Do not ever touch me again."

She strode to the door. As she left she glanced back at the man in whom she had believed during the last days of her childhood.

As she flew down the stairs she heard his step behind her. On the second level he caught up with her. She shook off the hand with which he tried to restrain her. Pushing her way through the throng of revelers, she hurried to the public room below.

She noticed Lady Catherine in the crowd, and those cat eyes glanced at her smugly. Stephen had said that he was not friends with Catherine, and yet this woman had gone out of her way to help him. She wondered why.

"You might at least bid me farewell, my sweet," Stephen said lowly in her ear. His attempt at lightness could not hide an underlying anger in his tone.

She turned on him, furious at his persistence. Before she could speak, he bent down and kissed her, then smiled and melted into the crowd.

CHAPTER 16

THE FLEET SET sail. Westminster and London, emptied not only of the visiting soldiers but also of many of their workers, grew strangely quiet. Christiana returned home and impatiently counted the days until David returned.

Spring storms arrived and soon the news spread that the fleet was returning. Long before the first masts reappeared on the Thames five days after embarkation, everyone knew that ill winds had forced King Edward to cancel his invasion.

The city filled with soldiers again, this time passing through as they began their return to towns and farms and castles inland. Edward could not hold the troops indefinitely for better sailing and had dispersed them.

Christiana was stunned by the relief that she experienced when the news of the aborted campaign reached her. She thought that she had convinced herself that David indeed had gone to Salisbury, but her reaction spoke the lie of that illusion. Now she just felt gratitude that Edward's plans had changed and made the possibility of David's betrayal irrelevant.

The chance that he had done this thing, or had even tried to, should appall her more than it did. The potential dishonor should disgust her. But all she cared about was his safety and the fact that this turn of events would preserve him from the horrible consequences of discovery.

She longed to see him. Memories of him hung on her every moment of the day and filled the hours of the night. She realized that she had probably loved him for a long while. She had refused to see it because of her obligation of loyalty to Stephen. And, she had to admit, she had long denied her feelings because David was a merchant. Noblewomen were not supposed to love such men. She had been raised to think such a thing contrary to nature.

Did he love her at all? His joy appeared to match her own at his homecomings each day, and he had seemed sad about leaving her for this trip. During their lovemaking she saw more in his eyes than simple pleasure, but in truth she did not know how he really felt. She had no experience in such things, and he remained an enigma in many ways.

It didn't matter. As the days slowly passed she knew that there could be no hope of hiding her feelings. Surely when she gave him a child, some type of love would grow for her. In the meantime she felt confident that he would accept her love kindly. She did not plan when she would tell him. It would simply happen in the warmth of their reunion.

He rode into the courtyard a day early. She heard the sounds of his arrival while she sewed in the solar. She threw aside her needle to run down the stairs. Bursting through the door, she flew to him and jumped into his arms.

He caught her as he always did, and swung her around

as he embraced and kissed her. She clung to him while his scent and touch reawoke her soul.

Her blood raced with joy. "I am so glad that you are back and safe. There is something that I must tell you . . ."

The expression in his eyes brought her up short. He examined her with a haunted scrutiny. No affection reached out to her, despite his embrace. In fact, those arms closed on her in a restrictive way as if he sought to hold her in place while he studied her.

She noticed with misgivings the hard line of his mouth. Something dark and disturbing emanated from him. She had never seen this expression and mood. Indeed, for a horrible instant, she felt as if she had never seen this man before.

"What is it?" Had he been discovered after all? Was he in danger?

He turned her in his arm and guided her toward the hall. The grip holding her shoulder felt hard and commanding. "I have had a bad journey and need a bath and some food, Christiana. We will talk later. Send a servant up to me."

His arm fell away and he walked across the hall toward their chambers. His words and manner made it clear that he did not expect her to follow.

Flustered and hurt, she set about seeing to his needs. She sent Emma and the manservant up to prepare the bath and warned Vittorio to serve dinner as soon as possible. Then she paced the hall, absorbed with concern over this change in him.

Could this be his reaction at having his plans thwarted? If he had gone to France, and risked what he risked, had the turn of events angered him? For there had been anger in those blue eyes, and a cold distance that chilled her.

He joined the household for dinner. He sat beside her

and received reports from Andrew as he ate. Nothing specific conveyed his displeasure, but she could sense it distinctly. At the end of the table, Sieg ate his meal with a methodical silence that suggested he at least recognized David's mood.

She had assumed that they would tumble into bed at the first chance upon his return, but under the circumstances she didn't mind too much when he moved his chair to the hearth after the meal. The others left and she sat across from him and watched him stare into the fire.

A very strange silence descended. She bore it awhile and then tried to fill it with conversation. She described small events in the household while he was gone, and the reaction when the fleet returned. Chattering on anxiously, she told him about her sad leave-taking of Morvan and then her relief upon his unexpected return.

He turned those haunted eyes on her while she spoke. His steady regard made her uncomfortable. She had imagined his homecoming many times, and it had been filled with elation and joy and her newly discovered love. She found all of those emotions retreating from the dark presence sitting near her.

She began telling him about the Easter joust, but he interrupted with an abruptness that suggested that he hadn't been listening to anything.

"You were seen," he said.

She jolted in confusion. The frightening realization struck her that this change in him had something to do with her.

"Seen? What do you mean?" She instinctively felt defensive.

He rose from his chair. Grabbing her arm, he lifted her and began pushing her in front of him through the hall.

"What are you talking about?" She glanced back at the stranger forcing her to scramble up the steps.

He dragged her to the bedchamber and slammed the door behind them. She sensed his anger spike dangerously. Some anger of her own rose in response and mixed with her worry and fear. She shook off his grip and backed up to the windows.

He faced her with tense hands on his hips. "You were seen, girl. With your lover."

"There were men at court who paid me attention, David, but it was harmless. No doubt many saw me, but not with any lover."

Her light response only made it worse. His anger surged. "Men paying you attention are inevitable. Stephen Percy, it seems, was inevitable, too, despite your vows and your assurances to me. It did not take you long to find your way back to that knight's bed."

His crisp words stunned her. She had actually forgotten about that dinner with Stephen these last few days. Stephen Percy had ceased to exist for her as she reveled in her love for David. She stared at him speechlessly and knew that the truth, that she had met with Stephen, was written on her face.

"That was harmless, too," she said, knowing that her denial would not matter. The meeting itself was the betrayal and he would assume the worst.

"You have no talent for adultery, darling. You don't even know when to lie and how to do it. Harmless? Lady Catherine was seen taking you up to a chamber in that inn and then returning without you. An hour later you emerged with Percy. I am told that your kiss of farewell was chaste enough, but he could afford restraint and discretion by then."

"What you were told is true, but I did nothing wrong in that chamber," she explained with a calm she did not feel at all. She could offer only her word against the damning evidence. "Who told you of this, David? Many saw, I am sure, and I am sorry that I did not think how it would appear to them and what it might cost your pride. But who felt the need to tell you? Was it Catherine? She helped Stephen in the ruse that brought me to him unknowingly."

"No doubt Lady Catherine eagerly awaits letting me know," he said bitterly.

"Then who?" but even as she asked it she knew the answer. He had just arrived back in London. Whoever had told him this was someone he trusted. Her indignation at the implications helped beat back the desperation.

"Oliver," she gasped. "You were having me followed. Dear saints! All of the time? When I walked about the city, was he always there? Did he hide in the shadows of Westminster and follow us into the forest for the hunt? Did you trust me so little . . ."

"He followed you for your protection, and not to catch you thus. In this one thing I surely trusted you, or I would not have let you go back to court where he could not follow."

"He was there? At the inn?"

He advanced toward her, dangerous and tense, and she backed up until she bumped against the window.

"He tried to hide the truth from me, but I can read him as I read you, and I forced it out." He reached out and laid his hand against her face. There was nothing soothing in his quiet voice or reassuring in that touch. "So you have finally had your knight, my lady. Was it all that you expected? Like the songs and poetry of chivalry on which you were raised? Did that knight's hands give you comfort that you are still who you were born to be? That you had not been debased beyond redemption in the bed of a merchant?"

Nay, she wanted to say, *it was the other way around.* But admitting that Stephen had touched her would only throw oil on this fire.

He neither crowded her nor restrained her, but she suddenly felt extremely helpless. A sensual edge in his soft tone made her wary.

"I did nothing wrong . . ." She repeated, searching his eyes for belief and understanding. She saw only shadows and fire and something else that alarmed her.

When he lowered his head, she tried to turn away. His hand twisted into her hair and held her as his mouth claimed hers.

She loved him and missed him and wanted him, and at first her body and spirit accepted him gratefully. But as she felt his passion rise and his kiss deepen, she knew that it was neither love nor affection driving him but rather pride and anger, and this reminded her too much of Stephen's assault. She jerked her head away and struggled as he pulled her into his arms.

"Nay. Do not . . ."

"Aye, my girl. I have been two weeks without a woman. That is the best thing about marriage. One need not waste time wooing and seducing when it waits for you at home." He imprisoned her with his embrace and cradled her head steady with a forceful grip. "This is the problem with adultery, and you might as well learn it today. The man can avoid his wife if he chooses, but the woman must return to a husband who still has his rights."

He held her firmly and kissed her again. She desperately squirmed against those strong arms. Her shock eclipsed every other emotion. He might have been a stranger handling her.

"I feared that you might repulse me, knowing where you had been and what you had been doing the first time I left the city," he said as his hands moved over her body.

He smiled faintly but she could tell that his anger hadn't abated at all. "It would be ironic, wouldn't it? To have paid all of that silver for property and then found that I no longer wanted the use of it."

Her mind clouded with horror at hearing him speak so coldly of their marriage. There had certainly been evidence that he thought of her thus and had even seduced her to lay claim to what was his, but to hear the words bluntly spoken and to have the confirmation thrown into the face of her love sickened her.

"Property . . ." she gasped.

"Aye. Bought and paid for."

Her eyes blurred and she thought that her heart would shatter. But his words also insulted her pride and her fury flared.

"I don't choose to be property to be used at your convenience," she cried, twisting and kicking to break free. "You will not do this in anger and punishment."

Her struggle only infuriated him. With two rough moves he pinned and immobilized her against the window.

"You are my wife. You have no choices."

She screamed as he lifted her and carried her to the bed as if she were a carpet. When he threw her down, she rolled away and tried to scramble free. He caught her and pulled her to him, pressing his chest into her back and throwing a leg over hers.

He held her until her thrashing stopped. She emerged from her delirium of rebellion. He softly stroked her hair and back as if she were a skittish animal.

Devastation flooded her. She bit her lower lip and fought back tears. She thought of the stupid and trusting joy which she had carried down to him just a few hours before. Love, alive but battered, searched for shelter somewhere inside her.

He shifted off of her and ran his hand down her back. His fingers pried at the knot of her cotehardie's lacing.

"I'm sorry if I frightened you, but I share you with no man, least of all that one." His voice came quietly and gently, but anger still radiated from him, mixing with the passion of his body. "You must never go to him again. If you do, I will kill him."

He said it simply and evenly, in the voice of the David she knew. The hands that she relished stroked her back through the loosened garment, their warmth flowing through the thin fabric of her shift. Her foolish love glowed in response. Her bludgeoned pride pushed it back into a corner.

She turned onto her back. His mood had not improved much although he tried to hide it now. She gazed at that handsome face that could so easily make her heart sigh. His expression softened, and he caressed her stomach and breast. A pleasurable yearning fluttered through her and it horrified her that she could respond under these conditions. Her love started stringing through her, offering to weave an illusion for escape.

His blunt words repeated themselves in her head. She grabbed his wrist and stayed his hand. Love or not, she could not delude herself about what was about to happen and why he did it and what it meant to him.

"So, we are down to base reality at last," she said, narrowing her eyes. "How tedious it must have been to have to pretend otherwise with the child whom you married."

He stared at her. His lack of response and denial turned her anguish to hateful spite. "The merchant has need of his property, much as he rides his horse when it suits him? Well, go ahead, husband. Reclaim your rights. Show that you are equal to any baron by using one of their daughters against her will. Will you hurt me, too? To make sure that the lesson of your ownership is well learned?"

Still he did not react. Her heart broke with a suffocating pain and she threw out whatever she could to hurt him, in turn. "Do not bother with seduction and pleasure, mercer. Soil feels nothing when it is tilled, nor wool when it is cut. I will think about who I am and what you are and feel nothing, too. But be quick about it so that I can go cleanse myself." And then she looked at him and through him the way she had that day after her bath.

She thought that he was going to hit her. In that brief moment of his renewed anger, as he drew up and his eyes darkened, she rolled frantically off the bed and half ran, half crawled to the door of the wardrobe.

She slammed and barred it just as he reached her. A vicious kick jarred the door and bolt. She pushed a heavy trunk over against them and stood back fearfully as he kicked again.

Then came only silence. She ran to the door leading to the exterior stairs and barred it too. She waited tensely a long time but the quiet held and he made no more attempts to enter.

Heaving breaths of relief, she sank down on a stool and finally let the tears flow. She cried long and hard, awash in misery and shock, his cruel words echoing in her ears. Her pathetic love fluttered out of hiding and added to the agony.

Eventually a numb stupor claimed her. Only one thought came clearly, over and over again. She had to get away and leave this house and this man. She would not, could not, live with the reality he had forced on her this day. Not now. Not for a long while. Maybe not ever.

✦   ✦   ✦

The rain pounded relentlessly, its blowing spray stinging David's face. He stood on the short dock and watched the patterns that the drops made in the muddy Thames. Beautiful, rhythmic splashes, full of faint highlights of purity, existed for split instants before the dirty flow absorbed them.

He let the rain wash over him. It soaked his clothes and plastered his hair to his head. After a long while it cleansed the black anger from his mind.

And then, with the madness gone, he faced the memory of what had occurred. That would never wash away and he lived it all again. His spiteful words. Her harsh insults. His vicious debasement of her.

Thank God she had gotten away.

They knew each other well enough to point the daggers expertly and draw blood from each other's weaknesses. He would never forget what she had said, but he couldn't blame her for admitting those feelings and thoughts. Since the day she had come to him, she had tried valiantly to ignore what this marriage meant to her life.

He had never been as cruel and hard to a woman as he had been with Christiana this day. Oliver and Sieg had been right. He should never have returned home and confronted her while the knowledge of her infidelity still flared like a fresh log tossed on a fire. He had known that they were right even as he ignored their advice and entreaties.

He pictured Oliver sitting across the tavern table from him and Sieg, listening with studied absorption to their tale of waiting on the Normandy coast for signs of the fleet passing. David described how the days had turned dark with storms and how he had realized that this month at least he would be spared the decision awaiting him in France.

And all the time that Oliver carefully listened and prolonged the tale with questions, he had watched the signs of ill ease on his old friend's face. They betrayed him worse when David asked after Christiana. Poor Oliver. He had tried to lie and then to equivocate when he probed for details. David knew that his own expression had turned dangerous when he felt Sieg's hand on his shoulder and that lilting voice urging him to stay away from the house for a few more days.

Impossible, of course. He had to see her at once and look into those diamonds knowing what he knew. He wanted and expected to feel dead to her, to be free of the love that was complicating his life and making him suddenly indecisive.

For when he had stepped off Albin's boat this morning after two treacherous days at sea, he had known that he loved her. He had recognized the feelings for a long time, but in Normandy he had put the name to them. He had sought out Oliver before returning home, because he knew that when he entered that house he would not want to leave again for a long while.

In his mind he saw her running to him, face flushed and eyes bright. He had watched her exuberant greeting with dark fascination. He had not expected her to be so good at deception. And mixed with that initial reaction had been the appalling realization that he still wanted her.

A dangerous mix, he thought now as he raised his face to the rain. Anger and desire and jealousy. Why had he let her play the game out? Why had he permitted those hours to pass as she pretended that nothing had changed and his own rancor grew? He grimaced and wiped the water from his face. He had been watching and waiting and, aye, hoping. Waiting for a confession and hoping it included the admission that her infidelity had been disillusioning.

Waiting for her to beg forgiveness and say that she now knew that she no longer loved Percy.

Fool. Unfaithful wives never did such things. Even when cornered with the evidence, the prudent course was to lie. Honesty was too dangerous. Men reacted too violently. He had certainly proven that today, hadn't he? He had forced her into lies born of her fear.

He closed his mind to the memory of her shock and terror.

She had denied it, but he didn't believe her. She loved Sir Stephen and her knight had been leaving for war. Her own testimony suggested that Stephen had no skill as a lover, but that did not reassure him in the least. A woman in love sought more than pleasure in bed and would forgive any clumsiness.

He contemplated that denial as he walked back to his horse. One part rang true. *Lady Catherine brought me to Stephen unknowingly*, she had said. He believed that, and it was something at least. Christiana had not arranged that meeting on her own, but had been lured there. Considering how she felt about Stephen, perhaps the rest had been so inevitable as to make her practically innocent.

As for Lady Catherine and her role in this . . . Well, when he settled this new account, he would permit himself the pleasure of revenge and not just justice.

He couldn't stay away from the house forever, and so he rode back, not knowing what he would say to Christiana when he got there. The temptation presented itself to pretend that the whole day had never happened, that he had never confronted her in his rage.

Would she accept their behaviors as an effective trade? One infidelity and betrayal for one attempted rape? If it had just been that, the accounts might be cleared, but his words and manner had insulted her more than any bodily assault could. To hurt her, he had told her that she was only a noble whore whom he had bought. She would not quickly forgive him that.

He rode into the wet courtyard and handed his reins to the groom. As soon as he entered the hall, a corner of his soul suspected.

The house felt as it had before their wedding. It had been his home for years and he had found contentment in it and so he had never noticed the voids that it held after his mother and master died. Only after Christiana filled those spaces with her smiles and joy had he realized their previous vacancy. Now he heard his footsteps echo in the large chamber as if all of the furniture had been removed. He paced to the hearth, avoiding the confirmation of his suspicion.

Geva entered from the kitchen with crockery plates in her arms. She glanced at him and shook her head.

"You be soaking wet, David. Best get out of those garments," she scolded.

He turned his back to the fire. Geva hummed as she set out the plates for supper. She acted as if nothing was amiss, and his foreboding retreated. With one final glance at him, she disappeared back into the kitchen.

He looked at the tables. He counted the plates. One short. The foreboding rushed back.

He slowly walked across the hall and up to his chambers, knowing what he would find.

In the wardrobe, hanging on their pegs and folded in trunks, were all of the garments that he had given her, including the red cloak. He flipped through them, noting that her other things, her old things, were mostly gone. Not all of them, however. One trunk still held some winter wools. He lifted them to his face and savored her scent, and an invisible hand squeezed his heart.

He left the wardrobe and passed quickly through the

bedchamber, not wanting to look at that space that still held the vivid images of the wounds they had inflicted on each other.

Sieg squatted in the solar, building the fire. He raised his eyebrows at the soaked garments.

"Did you throw yourself in the river then?"

David ignored him.

"Did you harm her?"

He shook his head.

Sieg finished with the fire and then rose. "I told you to wait, David. Your mood was blacker than night. I've not seen you like that, even when the Mamluks first threw you into that hell with me after that slut sold you out to them. Not even during our escape when you killed the one who had flogged us."

"I should have listened."

"*Ja*, well you never have where this girl goes, so this is no different."

David hesitated. With any other man he would not have asked, but Sieg had seen him weak before.

"Where is she?"

Sieg's eyes flashed and his posture straightened. "Hell! You don't know? I swear she told me that you'd agreed to it or I'd not have taken her . . ."

"Where?"

"Back to Westminster." He turned toward the door. "I go and get her now. Hell."

"Do not. Leave her stay awhile."

"Do you mean to say that you will stand down to this fool of a knight who steals your wife? You will permit this?"

"If it comes to that, I have driven her to it," he said. "Do you think that she plans to remain at court? Did you sense that she intended to continue on elsewhere?"

"She promised to remain there, which I found odd, since she owes me no explanation."

"Sir Stephen left for Northumberland several days ago. Oliver told me. She knows that I will know, or find out. Her promise was to assure me that she does not go to him." He smiled thinly. "I said that I would kill him if she did. My behavior gave her reason to believe me."

Sieg threw up his hands. "It makes no sense, David. If this man is up north, why does she just go to Westminster? If she doesn't go to him, why run away at all?"

David didn't reply, although the answer was obvious. *She does not run to Percy*, he thought. *She runs from me.*

Christiana sat in a garden redolent with the scent of late May flowers. She gazed at the pastel buds and smiled. Being a woman instead of a child wasn't all bad. Last year she would have taken the flowers' beauty for granted. Today she carefully admired their fresh purity.

David had taught her this. To pay attention to the fleeting beauties in the world. Not a small gift.

She sighed into the silence. The garden was empty despite the warm weather because the court attended dinner in the hall right now. She had avoided those crowded meals and all other events where she would be required to chat and make merry. She had escaped to Westminster for sanctuary and to heal her heart and soul.

She had found welcome and sympathy when she arrived. Lady Idonia had taken one look at her and known the reason for the visit. That little woman asked no questions and settled her in as if they had been expecting her. Joan and Isabele, warned by Idonia no doubt, sought no explanations either.

They were the only family she had known for years, and they surrounded her and protected her in her pain. Even Philippa, on hearing of her extended stay, had come to see her. Alone together in the anteroom, the Queen had tried to be a mother to her for once as she explained the difficulties of marriage. Upon leaving, she had offered to write to David and say that she requested his wife's continued attendance. He would not dare come for her then, and Christiana would have more time.

More time. For what? To reconcile herself to living her life with a man who at most wanted her available to satisfy his needs? Who had purchased a well-bred and well-formed bedmate, much as he carefully chose his horses? A man who did not believe her now after she had always been honest with him to the point of cruelty? A man who barely cared for her at all, but whom she loved despite everything?

There lay the real problem, of course. The rest she could manage and accept if she didn't love him. It was the lot of most women, and she had even ridden to her wedding assuming that it would be hers. Mutual indifference would make it bearable. Wasn't Margaret surviving?

Aye, she needed time. Time to stop loving him.

She had been working hard at that these last few weeks. She kept the memory of his harsh indifference and his attempted rape sharp in her brain. She reexamined the evidence implicating him in some treasonous game. It hadn't worked and she was in a quandary. The love wouldn't die and he had robbed her of the chance to build illusions out of ambiguities.

She looked up from the flowers. More time. How much would it take? How long before she could return to that house and that bed as indifferent to him as he was to her? How long before he could touch her and she would feel no more than simple pleasure or, if not that, remove herself from the experience? Hadn't David said that Anne handled her whoring that way? What was she but some incredibly expensive whore?

Surely just being away from him should kill these feelings eventually.

A palace door opened. Morvan paused in the threshold. He looked at her a moment before walking over. He sat down and stayed there in silence with his arm around her back. She let her head rest on his shoulder.

She hadn't spoken with him all of this time and had actually avoided him. When they briefly saw each other, she turned away from the questions in his eyes. Now he had deliberately sought her out and she felt grateful. He possessed so much strength that there always seemed to be extra to spare for her.

She turned and looked at his profile and saw his concern. She also saw something else and suspected with a numb resignation that her time was up.

"Why are you here, Christiana?" he finally asked, demanding the information that no one else had required.

"I could not stay there."

"Why not?"

Because my husband does not love me at all. She could not say it. It sounded too childish. Like most nobles, Morvan probably thought the issue of love irrelevant in marriages.

"Did he hurt you? Abuse you?"

"Nay." Not the way that Morvan meant. If he had, she would have lied. She did not want her brother killing David.

"Does he use you too hard?" he asked softly.

"Nay," she whispered.

"Has he gone to other women? If it is that, Christiana, I must tell you that with men . . ."

"To my knowledge he has not, Morvan. He thinks that I went to another man. To Stephen. He does not believe me when I deny it. He was mad with anger and jealousy. We argued and said things . . . ugly things."

"All couples argue. Our parents had terrible fights."

"This was different."

"Perhaps not."

"Did our father love our mother?"

The question surprised him. "It was a love match. I think they still loved each other at the end."

"Then it was different."

"That is a rare thing, Christiana. What they had. I do not think that it is given to most. Not really."

"Not you?"

"Nay. Not me. Like most men, I settle for brief simulacrums of it."

She thought that sad. She remembered David saying that Elizabeth would not marry Morvan because of their uneven love. She understood Elizabeth now and knew why Elizabeth had chosen instead that old baron for whom she felt nothing. Marriage to Morvan would have torn her heart daily.

"You cannot stay here," Morvan said gently. "Philippa spoke with me. Edward has become aware of your presence and questioned her about it. She does not think that David said anything, but the King has some affection for your husband, it seems, and interfered on his own."

"I cannot go back there."

"There is no place else to go."

She closed her eyes.

"God willing, Christiana, the day will come when I will have a home. If you still need to leave, I will take you in forever and keep him from getting you back. But for now, there is no choice." He paused and added carefully,

"Unless you want to go north to Percy. Did Stephen offer to keep you?"

She uttered a short laugh. "Nothing so formal or permanent, brother. Even if he had, I would not go, because I do not care for him now and would not dishonor you thus even if I did. Also I would not go because David has said that he will kill Stephen if I do, and I believe him." She smiled mischievously. "Would you have let me go?"

"Probably not."

"I did not think so."

He smiled kindly at her. "I have asked Idonia to pack your things. Horses await. I am taking you home now."

Her stomach twisted. "So soon?"

"Whatever is between you and David will only be a day worse tomorrow."

He rose and held out his hand.

"I do not know if I can bear this, Morvan. The last time I saw him . . ."

The last time she saw him, he was about to hit her because she had spoken to him noble to commoner and implied that his touch would debase and dirty her. The last sound she had heard him make was that kick trying to break down the wardrobe door.

"He will probably be happy and relieved to see you," Morvan said as he raised her to her feet. "It occurs to me that this is the third time that I have brought you to him. The man should have great affection for me by now."

She forced a laugh at her brother's attempt at levity, but she didn't think for one moment that David would be relieved to see her.

David heard the horses enter the courtyard just as dinner ended. Andrew was leaving the hall and he glanced over meaningfully, confirming the riders' identities.

Michael, crowding in behind Andrew at the door, announced happily to the servants that their mistress had returned.

David gestured for everyone to go about their business. He went to the door and stepped outside. The apprentices greeted Christiana as they passed her on their way to the gate. She rode forward slowly beside her brother.

She had been gone for almost three weeks. No messages or notes had passed between them, and his option of fetching her back had been cut off by the Queen's interference. Three weeks and before that two more. He'd only had that horrible afternoon with her in all of that time.

They stopped their horses right in front of him. Christiana looked down impassively. Morvan tried to appear casual and amiable. He swung off his saddle and walked around to lift his sister down.

"Christiana asked me to escort her home," he said as he began untying the small trunks on the saddle. "She was finding Westminster tedious."

David waited. Christiana walked a few steps and faced him.

"He is lying," she said quietly. "He made me come."

"All the same, it is good to have you back."

She glanced at him skeptically. "Did you keep Emma?"

"She is inside."

"I will go and rest now," she announced. "I find that I have a headache and am a bit dizzy."

He let her pass, nodding acknowledgment of her old excuse for avoiding him.

Morvan set the trunks down near the door.

"I thank you, Morvan."

Morvan's face hardened. "Do not thank me. She is pained about something, although I know not what. If there had been anywhere else to take her, I would have done so."

He mounted his horse. "I will come in a few days to see her," he said pointedly.

"I will not hurt her over this."

He turned his horse. "All the same, I will come."

David crossed the courtyard and entered the side building. As he approached the stairs he saw Emma emerge from his mother's old chamber. She softly closed the door and eased over to him.

"She is most poorly, I think. She said that she could not make the steps."

He glanced at the door behind which his young wife hid from him. Would she ever open it again of her own will, or would he eventually have to tear it down? He would wait and see. He was good at waiting.

"She will use that chamber until she feels better, then. Make her as comfortable as you can, Emma."

CHAPTER 17

THE BED FELT a little strange. Christiana snuggled under the covers even though the June night was warm enough to leave the windows open. She gazed up at the pleated blue drapery.

She did not have to be here, she reminded herself, and she still had time to change her mind. He would not be back for several nights. No one knew that their sick mistress had stolen up these stairs and entered this chamber while the household slept. She could return to Joanna's room before morning and continue her deception.

She doubted that anyone continued to be fooled by her illness, except maybe trusting Emma. The concern with which she had been treated those first days had long ago dissolved into silent curiosity.

Her arm stretched out and slid over the cool sheets where normally David slept. Perhaps it had been a mistake to come here tonight. Even if she left now and never returned, he would undoubtedly sense that she had been here. It had probably been foolish to steal up to this bed and try to imagine whether she could return to him without being devastated.

He had supported her claim of illness. For three weeks he had treated her with concern in front of the others. He greeted her warmly upon returning to the house and placed his hand over hers while the conversations continued after the meals.

When they were alone, she had seen other things in those blue eyes, however. The knowledge that she deliberately avoided him. A forbearing but not eternal patience. Sometimes, perhaps, an intelligent male mind calculating his options with her.

Since she ostensibly could not climb the stairs, she had taken to sewing in the hall after the evening meals. After the first few days, he began joining her there. A subtle tension underlaid the stilted conversations which they held across the hearth, but recently its tremoring pulse had gotten worse during the long silences. She would look up from her sewing and find him watching her and the look in his eyes would summon that old fear that wasn't fear. She would curse herself and pray that he would leave her alone in peace and not remind her with his presence and his gaze how much she still loved and wanted him.

It had been deliberate. Every touch, every gentle kiss good night when she left the hearth to return to Joanna's room, had been intended to remind her of the pleasure she felt with him. He had been playing a slow, methodical melody on the strings of her desire.

It had succeeded. The last week as she lay in her lonely bed, she had begun considering that maybe she could live this life in which she had been imprisoned. She could take the pleasure for what it was. Why deny herself? It had become clear that this special hunger, once awakened, did not sleep easily ever again.

Since the day she had returned, she had lain in that

bed every night, unable to sleep quickly, listening for the step outside her door that warned that he finally came to demand his rights and her duty.

Last night she had barely slept at all. He had intended to leave in the morning to attend one of the trade fairs inland. She did not doubt the truth of his destination this time, because John Constantyn was going with him. It would not be a long journey, but their silent evening by the hearth had been heavy with the knowledge of his impending departure. Did his memories turn as hers did to his last emotional leave-taking and what had occurred upon his return?

His kiss when she finally left him had been long and less chaste, and his hands had caressed her while he embraced her. Hungry, aching feelings long denied had flooded her before he drew away. If he had lifted her up and carried her back to his bed then, she could not have stopped him.

He did not, though. He let her leave him as he always had these last weeks. She went to the small chamber that had become her home. She waited, praying this time that he would indeed come and end this even as she dreaded that he would. Her need for his closeness overpowered her. Her insulted pride and her hurt at his indifference ceased to matter. That her desire was totally entwined with her love did not frighten her so much anymore. She would manage those feelings somehow.

He had come, but not during the night. At first light her door had opened and she had turned to find him standing there, looking down at her. She rose up against the headboard and pulled the sheet around her naked shoulders.

He sat down beside her and she saw signs of weariness in his face that suggested he had not slept much either.

"You are leaving now?" she asked.

"Aye. John awaits outside. Sieg will stay here. There are rumors that Edward has summoned the army again, Christiana. If men start arriving in the city, do not leave the house without Sieg or Vittorio."

She hadn't known that Edward had renewed his plans about France, but then she hadn't left this house in weeks because of her illness. Margaret had visited her several times, but Margaret had no interest in court gossip or politics and so had told her nothing. Nor had David until now.

Perhaps there were no rumors yet. Perhaps David only knew because the King had told him.

He only travels to a trade fair, she told herself firmly. *John Constantyn goes with him, not Sieg.*

He placed his hand on her knee. She looked down at it, so exciting in its elegant strength, so warm despite the sheet between their flesh. That quivering intensity that always emanated from him seemed especially apparent this morning.

"This cannot go on," he said. "You cannot stay here."

They had never spoken of that day nor of why she feigned this illness. A part of her had hoped that they never would.

"That is what Morvan said. He came to me at Westminster and said I could not stay there. Now you say it about this house."

"Nay. I say it about this chamber. I'll not see another woman buried alive in it."

"Then give me some money to pay servants and I will go live in Hampstead. I will repay you from the farm rents."

A glint of anger glowed in those blue eyes before he suppressed it. He slowly shook his head.

His hand still rested on her knee, beckoning her with its warmth, offering her its pleasures. Better if he had just carried her upstairs last night. Better to have never put words to what was happening.

"What are you saying, David? Are you ordering me to my duty?"

"I am asking you to return to our marriage and our bed."

"What about Stephen Percy?"

"We will put that behind us."

"You still do not believe me, do you? But you kindly forgive me. That is most generous of you, but I neither want nor need your forgiveness."

"Perhaps I want and need yours."

"I do not know if I can give it," she whispered, as memories of that day drifted into the space between them. "Even now, as you ask me to come back to you, I know that you just find that you have need of your property and resent being denied it. It may be the way these things always are, but I do not think many women have to hear it so frankly stated and then live with the truth in such a naked way. Perhaps that is the reason for dowries. To give women some other value in marriages so that their dignity is preserved."

That exciting hand rose from her knee and stroked her cheek above the bunched sheet with which she shielded herself. It rested there, and its warmth flowed into her and down her neck. "We both spoke harsh things to each other. I think of no person as property, Christiana. Least of all you."

He leaned toward her. She knew that it would not be a simple kiss of parting and that she should turn away, but she could not even though the connection would bring her anguish. The warm touch, the quiet voice, the intense blue eyes had made her defenseless. Sensual memories during the night had left her tired body half aroused. His kiss lingered and deepened and she could not fight it because something inside her, apart from her reason and her hurt, hungered for him.

He kissed her as if the world had ceased to exist. Gently, almost lazily, he bit along her lips. The nips and warmth stunned her. He slowly pried his tongue into her and she parted her mouth stiffly, accepting him with a hesitation her trembling, anxious body didn't feel at all. The heady intimacy of this small joining washed over her and submerged her resentment and hurt.

A small internal voice cried a warning, but her appalling, forceful longing ignored it. She released one hand's hold on the sheet and awkwardly embraced the shoulders leaning toward her.

They kissed again tentatively, like first-time lovers finding their way. Then slowly, carefully, as if each touch revealed something precious, he pressed his lips to her neck and shoulders. Her whole body tremored with grateful relief at the repeated warm contact of that mouth.

She opened her eyes and found him looking at her, and she guessed that he could, as always, see everything and knew that her traitorous body had vanquished her resolve. She silently begged him to stay and also prayed that he would not.

"Come here," he said, reaching for her. He lifted and turned her and set her on his lap, resting her head and shoulders on the support of one arm while his other one embraced her to him. She still clutched the sheet and it followed her, trailing over her body as it twisted from the bed. Despite the sheet and his clothing, she felt his warmth and strength and sighed at the closeness. Her buttocks pressed against the hard muscles of his thighs and her hip felt the hot ridge of his arousal. It had been months since he had held her, and she lost herself in a mindless fog of connected warmth.

Cradling her in his arms, he lifted her to a hungry,

probing kiss. She felt his passion overwhelm his restraint
of the last weeks. Her barely controlled desire also broke
loose of her tenuous hold. Her last clear thought was an
indifferent awareness that she would pay for this pleasure
with pain.

With her free hand she encircled his neck and pressed
him closer, asking for more, encouraging him. Her long
abstinence had made her shameless, and she would not let
him end the deep, frantic kiss. His embracing arm loosened and she moaned into him as his wonderful hand
caressed her bare back and hip.

He broke the kiss and looked down into her eyes. His
gaze lowered and his fingers traced down to where she still
grabbed the top of the sheet.

"It did not help you much that day in the wardrobe,
darling," he said quietly. "Let go now."

He spoke of the sheet, but he also meant much more.
He softly stroked her clutching hand until her fingers
relaxed beneath his seductive touch. She turned her face
into his shoulder as he eased the sheet from her grip and
slid it away. Cool air alerted the skin of her entire body.

She knew that he looked at her as he so often had
done, only now she felt suddenly shy and stunned by a
furious anticipation. She gritted her teeth and buried her
face harder in his shoulder.

He kissed her neck and his quiet voice flowed with his
breath into her ear. "Do not hide your face from me,
Christiana. The desire that we feel for each other is a
wonderful thing. I want you to watch me as I give you
pleasure."

Gently he turned her face to his and forced her to
meet his gaze. He had not even touched her yet, but that
aching need already tensed her belly and a hot insistence
throbbed between her legs.

She watched as he demanded. Watched as he cradled

her and kissed her breasts and moistened their hard tips with his tongue. Watched as his fingers slowly traced along her breastbone and teased in a circle. Her breasts swelled beneath that wandering touch, anxious, begging, and her consciousness focused on nothing besides her silent, breathless urging. His fingers slid to one moist nipple. She saw her body arch toward that devastating touch, and then she saw little else. Incredible sensations and single-minded desire obliterated all thought.

He aroused her as if time didn't matter, as if no one awaited him in the courtyard and no journey beckoned. Her breasts had never been so sensitive, and his deliberate caresses raised excruciating pleasures. When his strong arm lifted her shoulders and his mouth replaced his hand, the delicious need he created with his lips and teeth became consuming and painful.

He lifted his head and looked down her body. Her own dazed eyes followed. His hand splayed over her belly, his light golden skin contrasting in a compelling way with her creamy whiteness. He pressed down, stilling the rock of her hips. He caressed her thighs and they both watched that hand's progress. Her breath shortened to a series of low sighs.

"I am thinking that it is in my interests to leave you ill contented," he said softly as his hand trailed over her body. "Abstinence is a powerful enhancement to passion. I do not think that you would remain ill too long after my return."

She barely heard this frank assessment of her condition and resolve. She watched and felt his hand follow the crevice where her legs joined. Stabs of heat distracted her.

"But I find that I cannot do it," he said, "I have missed your passion and would at least have that from you this day."

His gaze claimed her attention, and his words penetrated her stupor. He kissed her beautifully. "Open to me, darling," he said while his fingers touched the soft mound of hair.

She had been waiting for him to rise and turn and lay her down. She had been waiting for the intimacy of his body along hers and the obliteration of her choices. She realized that he had never intended to use her desire against her like that today.

She hesitated, and almost said, as he made her say that first time, that she wanted him.

"Open," he commanded gently. His fingers caressed so close to her need that her breathing stopped and that hidden flesh pulsed. "There is no defeat in taking pleasure from me thus."

She had no resistance. She closed her eyes and parted her legs and accepted the relief he offered. It did not take long. He touched her slowly and gently as if to prolong the ecstasy, but her body already cried for release and each touch sent lines of frantic sensations through her until soon she felt the incredible tension wind inside and she thrashed and stiffened and exhaled sounds of mounting desire. He pulled her shoulders to him and held her firmly, kissing her ferociously while he pushed her over the edge into fulfillment, taking her cries into himself when the violent climax finally crashed through her.

He held her in a tight embrace for a long while, his face buried in the angle of her neck and shoulder. She awoke from the delirium to find her hands clawing the garments at his chest. She doubted that he had found satisfaction in this.

He loosened his hold and looked down at her. She noticed a little blood on his lip where she must have bitten him.

Silently he rose and laid her down on the bed. He caressed her face and looked into her eyes. "I must go."

He had contented her, but her deeper desire still burned. She almost urged him to stay longer and to finish what had begun. The choice would not really be hers then.

He left. Left her with the proof that he possessed the power to seduce her back. Forcing would have never been necessary, this parting visit had said, because this gentler persuasion had always been available to him and would be in the future. For a while longer the choice would be squarely hers, though. He had left her to decide if she could live this marriage and come to him, once again, of her own will.

She gazed at the blue pleats billowing above the bed. Aye, maybe she could. During that brief submersion into pleasure she hadn't thought about anything else, not even what she meant to him. Only later, when he left, had the pain and doubts closed in. In time perhaps they would cease to torment her. In a few years maybe her love would only exist as an amusing memory.

She should leave this bed now, before she fell asleep. If Emma found her upstairs in the morning, the whole household would assume that her illness had ended and Joanna's room would cease to be an option. No choice then. She smiled at how greedily her soul grasped at the possibility for self-deception. *Stay here, fall asleep, and it is done. An accident rather than a decision.*

The bed had lost its strangeness and a delicious relaxation claimed her. Even as she admonished herself to leave, her lids lowered. She surrendered to the prideless love that would accept any pain to be close to him and would gratefully accept the small part of himself that he chose to give her.

She did not know how long she slept, but suddenly

her eyes flew open. A sound had penetrated her dream, prodding her out of her peace. She raised herself on an elbow.

A large dark shadow moved past the window nearest the wardrobe door.

"David?" she mumbled, wiping her eyes.

A strange presence filled the chamber. She heard soft, scuffling footsteps. The shadow moved, and two others joined it.

Suddenly alert with shock, she started to scream. The large shadow lunged toward her. Strong arms pinned her down while rough hands pried and shoved a cloth into her mouth.

She thrashed violently against the suffocating gag. More hands pressed on her until she became immobile. She stared up into strange faces barely visible in the moonlight while her heart pounded wildly in the renewed silence.

"Now you be calm, my lady, and no harm will come to you," a man's voice said softly, just inches from her ear. Not an English voice, she considered as she jerked motionlessly against the restraining hands. Scottish.

One hand released her and a glint of steel appeared in it and waved in front of her eyes. "Listen carefully. We will let you up, but there be three of us here and armed at that, so do as I say. You will go into the wardrobe and dress and pack some things for yourself."

Pack? These men planned to take her someplace. Where and for what possible purpose?

Her mind frantically assessed her danger. How had they gotten into this house with its surrounding wall? Where was Sieg?

"Do you understand? Don't raise your hands to the gag."

She dumbly nodded. The hands fell off her one by

one and the talking man eased away. Shaking with terror, she slid out of the bed, grateful that she had not lit a candle and that these men could not see her naked body very well in the moonlight.

She staggered on wobbly legs to the wardrobe, trying to control the panic that threatened to cloud her mind of all reason and sense. Despite their warnings, she wanted to run and run and let the terror consume her as she did. She rashly decided that in the blackness of the wardrobe she would remove the gag and scream for help.

Upon entering, she saw the door to the garden open. Enough light seeped through to make the lines of her shadow visible and her actions obvious.

They watched as she fumbled for a loose gown and pulled it on. One of the men found a small traveling trunk, and she stuffed clothing into it, not knowing what she grabbed.

Thrusting her feet into shoes, she turned to them. She tried to remain calm although the deathly panic still wanted to unhinge her. Her only hope was to keep her wits about her. If Sieg still lived, he would save her when they tried to leave. She would make as much noise as possible on the courtyard stones in hopes of awakening him and the others.

"Now we will walk down those steps out there and go to the back of the garden," the man said.

Her heart sank. They had come in over the wall, not through the gate. Sieg slept unknowingly in the front building. He and the others would never hear.

They surrounded her like a prisoner being moved and guided her down the stairs and out the gate to the main garden. At the back wall two of them disappeared up a crude ladder.

"Now you. There's another on the other side. Take care, my lady. The drop could hurt you," the Scot said.

She tottered up, turned her body blindly, and felt for the wooden slats on the other side. Hands plucked her off halfway down and set her on the ground. They walked up the alley to where horses waited. Someone tied her hands before lifting her onto a saddle. Being bound made her feel even more helpless. They trailed out through the city lanes, towing her along.

She watched the streets anxiously, hoping to see the flames of torches that indicated other night travelers or the ward constable. If they were stopped, would the constable notice her gag? Would these men use their steel if they were challenged?

No challenge came. Her fear grew as she noted their approach to the city's gate. To her anguished dismay, the gate guard let them pass.

The lead man continued straight ahead after they passed through the wall. She straightened in shock. They headed for the northern road.

North. Northumberland. *Stephen?*

The Percy family held lands in Scotland and on England's border in Northumberland. Was this Scot one of their retainers?

Stephen abducting her? Now? It would be madness. Nay, not Stephen. Unless his pride had been wounded because he had lost his game to a mercer. During tournaments, Stephen had never been especially gracious in defeat. And if not Stephen, then who? She could think of no other possibility.

As they rode silently through the night, she told herself that Stephen would never do something so absurd, but a part of her worried that in fact he might. He might even consider it chivalrous and romantic and a grand gesture of salvation.

Duels and abductions are the stuff of songs, not life. Unless you were dealing with some childish girl and a foolish knight. Stephen, she suspected, could be very foolish.

He had seemed in the end to accept her refusal at that dinner. Had he later reconsidered her resolve? Had his conceit led him to conclude that she fought him against her heart's true desire?

Dear saints. David would kill them both.

Her misgivings flared when, some miles north of London, she spied shadows on the road ahead. Her small group approached two other figures on horses and stopped.

"You made quick work of it," a woman's voice said.

Christiana's eyes widened and she peered in the dark toward the hooded cloak. She knew this voice. This *was* Stephen's doing. And once again he had enlisted Lady Catherine's help.

Catherine's arm stretched out. "Here is the coin you will need. Do it exactly as I told you, and do not delay. The man will pay you your fee. And remember, she is not to be harmed."

Christiana made a loud sound from behind her gag. Lady Catherine turned toward her. "You want to speak, child? Remove her gag."

Dirty fingers pried the wadded cloth out of her mouth. She gasped deep breaths of air before speaking.

"Where do you take me?" she demanded.

"You will find out soon enough."

"If you abduct me for ransom, tell me now. Name your price and return me home. I will pay it."

"A generous offer, but there will be no ransom," Catherine said.

"Then why? Who bids you do this? Stephen Percy?"

Catherine laughed lightly. "All will be explained in good time, my dear. In the end you will thank me for this."

Did Catherine assume, like so many others at court, that she must welcome redemption in Stephen's arms?

"My husband will kill you for this," she hissed toward the men who waited. She realized that it was the first time she had claimed David's protection instead of Morvan's. But David *would* kill them. The thing about property was that one didn't like it stolen.

"By the time he finds you, it may not matter so much to him," Catherine said. "He will have bigger concerns. Take her now, and remember that she is not to be molested or handled. Do not try to run away, Christiana, for they have their orders to deliver you and will tie you to the horse if they have to."

"This is madness—" she began to protest, but the gag suddenly filled her mouth again and she choked on the words.

Lady Catherine and her silent companion turned south while her captors tugged the reins and started north. Christiana held the front of the saddle with bound hands and swayed into the animal's quicker walk.

North. Of all of the times for Stephen Percy to finally decide to live out some chanson!

Didn't he remember that violent deaths and jealous murders often ended those long love songs?

CHAPTER 18

DAVID LET HIS father's blood flow. He unblocked it from the recesses and fissures in which he kept it dammed and controlled. He permitted all of its dark strength to wash through him.

Sieg walked beside him as he rode across the courtyard. He looked down on the Swede's furrowed brow. Sieg blamed his own negligence for Christiana's disappearance and would not rest contented until he had helped bring her back. David would welcome his friend's help in the end, but not right now.

"The swords, Sieg. Don't forget to pack them," he said. Sieg nodded and David passed to the gate. It was possible that he wouldn't need the preparations that he was leaving Sieg to make. Possibly he would find her elsewhere. He doubted it, however. Still, he would have to check.

He paused and looked back at the buildings where he had lived his youth and manhood. If things turned out as he expected, he would never see this home again.

His father's blood didn't give a damn. He smiled thinly. Nay, no sentiment there. Not when faced with a quest or a goal. Or revenge.

He had known for years that it was in him and what it could do. As a youth he had examined his face and soul to know what came from the Abyndons and what came from the other side. He had tried to reconstruct the image of his absent father from the disconnected pieces that bore no Abyndon legacy. The love of beauty. The emotional restraint. The dark calculations. The ability to kill. Even Gilbert's self-righteous cruelty could not match his own inclinations to cold ruthlessness. That in particular had always been in him, a strength to be used and a weakness to be feared, and it went far beyond the shrewd analysis taught as part of a mercer's trade. His mother's blood had tempered it some, but the real lessons in controlling it had been David Constantyn's greatest gift to him.

It had been his father's half that had hurt Christiana.

He would check London and Westminster first, just to be sure.

A short while later he rode into the courtyard of Gilbert de Abyndon's house for the first time in his life. A groom approached for his horse but he ignored the man and tied the reins to a post.

The household sat to dinner when he entered the hall. He had planned it this way. He did not want Margaret to have to confront her husband's wrath if he came when Gilbert wasn't home, and he wanted plenty of people around so that maybe he wouldn't smash his fist into Gilbert's face when his uncle insulted him, as the man was sure to do.

Gilbert looked up from his conversation as David approached his table, and one would have thought that the man had seen an apparition, so complete was his shock. Margaret visibly paled.

David simply nodded acknowledgment of his uncle and turned his attention to Margaret.

"I am seeking Christiana, Margaret."

She frowned. "Seeking?"

"She has left the house."

"She is better then?"

So Christiana had not confided in her new friend. "Aye. But she is two days gone, Margaret. Did she come to you?"

Realization took hold, but Margaret hid it from her expression. Gilbert proved less discreet.

"So your noble wife has left you so soon?" he jeered softly.

"Is she here, Margaret?"

She shook her head.

"You have never known your place, boy," Gilbert snarled. "The conceit of marrying such a woman! Of course she is gone. It is a wonder she stayed this long."

David managed to ignore him. "Do you know where she is, Margaret?"

Poor Margaret shook her head again. Distressed eyes flickered up to his. Her hand rested protectively on her slightly swelled belly.

Gilbert laughed. "It is a pleasure to see great pride humbled. Such are the wages of that sin. Look you to the beds in the castles of the realm for her, nephew. Those women have no morals."

His hand shot out and he grabbed his uncle by the neck. Gilbert cried out and fell back in his chair. David let his arm and hand follow until he had the man pinned against the wooden back. The hall fell silent and a dozen pairs of eyes watched.

"You will say no more, Uncle, or I will release your young wife from the misery of this marriage," he said. "Now, you will permit Margaret to accompany me to the door and you will not follow. Do you agree to this?"

Gilbert glared at him. David squeezed. Gilbert nodded.

Margaret eased off her bench and came around the table. David dropped his hand.

"I am sorry," he said as they walked across the hall. "There was nothing for it but to come here."

"I understand. Do not worry. He will sputter for a few days and speak ill of you to all he meets, but that is nothing new, is it?"

David paused at the door. "Did she ever speak of Sir Stephen Percy to you?"

Margaret's surprise and shock were genuine. "Nay, David. She spoke of no man to me except you and her brother. Even when she described a humorous event at court, the players had no significance."

He nodded and turned to go. "Be well, Margaret."

She stopped him, and stepped out into the courtyard so that she could speak privately. "Why do you ask me about this man, David? Do you think Christiana has run away?"

"It is possible."

"With this man?" She looked at him incredulously. "I always thought that you were the exception to the rule that men were fools, David. If she held another in her heart, then I did not know her at all. She spoke only of you, and with warmth and affection and respect. If she is gone, it is not of her will, I am sure." She frowned with distress. "She is in danger, isn't she? Oh dear God . . ."

"I do not think that she is in danger," he said soothingly. "Go back to your husband now. Tell him that I would not let you leave me until you answered my questions."

"You must find her . . ."

"I will find her."

David stood against the wall of the practice yard and watched Morvan Fitzwaryn swing his battle-ax and land it against his opponent's shield. A bright sheen of sweat glistened on Morvan's naked chest and shoulders.

David sensed a movement behind him and turned to see two women peering over the wall as they strolled past. They eyed the tall knight appreciatively and giggled some comments to each other behind raised hands before they moved on.

He waited. Morvan had noticed him already. Eventually this practice must end.

Soon it did. Morvan's opponent gestured a finish. The two knights walked over to a water trough and sluiced themselves. Morvan came over as he shook the water from his head.

"You want me?" he asked, his voice still a little breathless from his exertions.

"Aye. Three nights ago Christiana left the house. None saw her and she told no one where she was going."

Morvan had been in the process of wiping his brow. His hand froze there.

"Did she come here, Morvan?"

"Nay."

"You said that you would have taken her elsewhere if possible. Have you done so now?"

Morvan glared at him. "If I had taken her from you, I would have let you see me do it."

David began walking away.

"She has not gone to him," Morvan called after him.

He pivoted. "How do you know?"

"Because she told me she would not."

"Then you received more assurances than I did."

"Why give assurances to a man who does not believe them?" Morvan asked tightly as he walked up to him.

"I will know the truth of it soon enough, I suppose."

Morvan stared thoughtfully at the ground. "The last time she left and came here, she let you know where she was."

"Aye."

"But not this time. And she told me that she no longer cares for him. If she is with Percy, David, I do not think that it is her choice."

"I thought of that. You know the man better than me. Is it in his nature to do this? To abduct her?"

Morvan glanced blindly around the practice yard. "Hell if I know. He is vain and conceited and, I always thought, a little dull in the wits. The women say that he does not take rejection well. The men know that he is quick with a challenge if he thinks himself slighted."

David absorbed this. He should have met Sir Stephen or at least learned more about him. Pride had prevented it, but that had been a mistake. One should always know one's competitors' strengths and weaknesses. Even a green apprentice knew that.

"I will let you know when I find her."

"Do you ride north, then?" Morvan asked cautiously.

"Aye."

"I will come with you."

"I will go alone. For one thing, the King will need you here as the army musters. For another, I do not plan to do this in a knight's way."

He turned to leave, but Morvan gripped his arm. He looked into sparkling, troubled eyes so like those others.

"You must promise me, if you find her there, that you will give her a chance to speak. If there is an explanation, you must hear it," Morvan said.

David glanced down on the hand restraining him, and then at the intense bright eyes studying his face. Did he look as dangerous as Morvan's worry suggested?

"I will hear her out, brother."

He left then, to meet Sieg and Oliver and begin the journey to Northumberland. First, however, he made his way to the stone stairs that led to Edward's private chambers.

David and Oliver eased along the gutter of the inn, their backs pressed against the steep roof. Below them the lane that led to this hostelry appeared deserted except for the large shadow of a man resting casually against a fence rail. The shadow's head looked up to check their progress.

It went without saying that Sieg could not join them up here. He weight would have broken the tiles. He would wait below and then enter the normal way, dispatching in his wake any inconvenient squires or companions who might try to interfere.

"This reminds me of the old days," Oliver whispered cheerfully as they carefully set their steps into the gutter tiles. "Remember that time we boys got into the grocer's loft through the roof? Filled our pockets with salt."

"Nothing so practical, Oliver. It was cinnamon, and worth more than gold. They'd have hung us if they caught us, children or not."

"A great adventure, though."

"At least your mother used what you took. Mine knew it was stolen, gave it away, and dragged me to the priest."

"Her sensitivities on such things are no doubt why your life took a turn for the worse when you got older," Oliver said. "School and all."

"No doubt."

Oliver's foot slipped and a tile crashed to the ground. Both men froze and waited for the sounds that indicated someone had heard.

"I've a good mind to slit this knight's throat just to express my annoyance that he was so hard to find," Oliver muttered in the silence.

David smiled thinly. Percy had certainly been hard to find, and the length of their search had not improved David's own humor much. The man seemed to be hiding. Not a good sign.

They had ridden first to his father's estate, then his uncle's, and finally to the properties which Stephen himself managed. There had been no need to approach the castles and manor houses. A few hours in the nearest town or village gave them the information they sought. Young Sir Stephen had not been seen for at least a week. Finally, on the road south, a chance conversation with a passing jongleur had revealed that Percy had been resting at length at this public inn several miles north of Newcastle.

David surveyed the ground below him, dimly lit by one torch. Sieg glanced up and nodded. They were just above the window to Stephen's chamber on the top level of the inn. The warm June night had caused the window to be left open.

It was the dead of night and no sounds came from the inn or the chamber below. David turned to the roof, crouched, and grasped the eaves. He lowered his body down, slowly unbending his arms. His feet found the opening and he angled in, dropping with the slightest thud on the floor of the chamber.

He peered around at the flickering shadows cast by one night candle. Curtains surrounded the beds in this expensive inn, but here they had been left open. He saw a man's naked back and blond hair, and a strong arm slung over another body. Long dark tresses poured over the sheet.

His stomach clenched. A bloody fury obscured his sight. He unsheathed the dagger on his hip.

Oliver swung in the window and landed beside him. He gestured for David to be still, and then eased over to the door. Sieg waited on the other side.

With Sieg's arrival there could be little hope of keeping their presence a secret. The Swede stomped in, unsheathing his sword. Stephen Percy's head jerked up.

Sieg reached him before he had fully turned over. He placed a silencing finger to Percy's lips and the sword to his throat. Stephen froze. The woman still slept.

David found a taper near the hearth and bent it to the guttering night candle. He walked over and inspected the man who had caused him so much trouble.

Bright green eyes stared back warily over the shining blade. Stephen had rugged features and his skin appeared very pale, especially with all of the blood gone out of it now. David grudgingly admitted that women might find this man attractive.

"Who are you?" Stephen asked hoarsely in a voice that tried to sound indignant.

David leaned into better view. "I am Christiana's husband. The merchant."

Stephen's gaze slid over David, then angled up at Sieg and over to Oliver. "Thank God," he sighed with relief.

Sieg frowned at David. David gestured to Oliver. The wiry man moved to the other side of the bed.

Oliver pushed back the raven tresses spilling over a thin back. The girl jolted awake and turned. She managed one low shriek before Oliver's hand clamped down over her mouth.

Oliver stared. "Hell, David, it isn't her!"

"Nay. I never really thought it would be. She would not come on her own, and he never cared enough to abduct her. But I had to be sure."

The girl had noticed the sword at Percy's throat, its point not far from her own neck. She huddled herself into a ball and stared around wild-eyed.

David smiled down at Sir Stephen. "You thought we might be her kinsmen?"

Stephen gave a little shrug.

"Another virgin sacrifice to your vanity, Sir Stephen?"

Stephen's eyes narrowed. "Have you lost something, merchant? You can see she is not here, so be gone."

"Do you have her elsewhere?"

Stephen laughed. "She was sweet, but not worth that much trouble."

Dangerous anger seeped into David's mind. "Sweet, was she?"

A sneer played on Stephen's face. Sieg lifted the blade a bit, forcing Percy's chin to rise with it. Stephen glowered down at the sword and hesitated, but conceit won out.

"Aye," he smirked. "Very sweet. Well worth the wait."

"I kill him now, David," Sieg said matter-of-factly.

"Nay. If he dies, he is mine."

The girl had begun crying into her knees. Oliver sat beside her and patted her shoulder. She muttered something between her sobs.

"Considering your position, you are either very brave or very stupid to taunt me thus," David said.

Stephen laughed. "You are no threat to me, mercer.

Harm a hair on my head and you had best leave the realm. If the law doesn't hang you, my family will."

"A good point. Except that I had already planned to leave the realm, and so it appears that I have nothing to lose."

The smug smile fell from Stephen's face.

"David," Oliver said, "this girl is little more than a child. Look at how small she is. How old are you, girl?"

"Just fourteen this summer," she sobbed miserably. She glared at Stephen. "He was going to take me to London, wasn't he?"

Stephen rolled his eyes. "We will go, my sweet. After it is safe . . ."

"Nay, you won't," Oliver said to her. "He will leave you to the wrath of your kinsmen, and you'll be lucky to end up in a convent. What are you? Gentry? Aye, well, they won't press case against a Percy, will they? Nay, girl, it's a convent or whoring for you, I'm afraid."

The girl wailed. Percy cursed.

"So do we kill him now?" Sieg asked.

Quick. Easy. So tempting. David gazed impassively at the rugged face trying to remain brave and cool.

"I think not," he finally said.

Stephen's eyes closed in relief as Sieg cursed and sheathed his sword.

"Give me your dagger, David," Sieg said, holding out his hand. "The Mamluk one."

"What for?"

Sieg sniffed. "In honor of the love I feel for this country and in protection of the few virgins left in it, I'm going to fix this man."

Stephen frowned in perplexity.

"Remember that physician in prison, David? The one who had once worked at the palace? Well, he told me how they made eunuchs. It is a simple thing, really. Just a quick cut . . ."

Stephen's eyes widened in horror.

"Sieg . . ." David began.

"The dagger, David. You always keep it sharp. We'll be out of here as quick as a nick."

David looked at Sir Stephen's sweating brow. He looked at the crying girl and Oliver's gentle comfort. He thought about Christiana's pain over this man.

"If you insist," he said blandly.

"Aye. Oliver, help hold him down for me."

The girl saw the dagger approach and began a series of low, hoarse screams. Sir Stephen practically jumped out of his skin. He inched back on the bed, staring at the looming, implacable Sieg. He turned to David. "Good God, man, you can't be serious!"

"As I said, I have nothing to lose."

Stephen laughed nervously and held up a hand as if to ward off the dagger. "Listen. Seriously. What I said before about Christiana . . . I was lying. I never had her. In truth I never did."

"It is more likely that you are lying now."

"I swear to you, I never . . . I barely touched her! I tried, I'll admit, but, hell, we all try, don't we?" He turned wildly to Sieg and Oliver, seeking confirmation.

"Let's see. Kneel on his legs, David. Oliver, climb over and put your weight on his chest," Sieg said as he reached for the sheet.

"*Jesus!*" Stephen yelled. "I swear it on my soul, she wouldn't have me."

David smiled. "I already knew that."

Sieg took another step forward. Stephen looked ready to faint.

"How?" Stephen croaked while he stared at the ugly length of steel.

"She told me." He placed a hand on Sieg's shoulder. "Let us go, Sieg. Leave this man."

"Hell, David, he is disgusting . . ."

"Let us go."

Oliver got up from the bed and fetched some garments from a stool. "You wait outside, we will be down soon."

"*We?*"

"We can't leave her here, can we? He's ruined her if she's found. I told her that we'd take her to Newcastle and leave her at an abbey. She'll say that she got knocked on the head and lost her memory and wandered for days until some kind soul brought her to the city."

"Ah. The knocked-on-the-head-and-wandered-for-days explanation. A bit overused, don't you think?"

"Her family will believe it because they will want to. On the way, I'll tell her how to fake the evidence when she gets married."

"Oliver . . ."

"She's just a child, David. Too trusting, that is all."

"You are a whoremonger, Oliver. You are supposed to recruit girls who have fallen, not save them." He looked at the girl not much younger than Joanna had been. He sighed and went to the door with Sieg.

Hell. At this rate, he'd never get out of England.

But, then, that had been the whole point of forcing him to make this search in the first place.

CHAPTER 19

CHRISTIANA PULLED THE knotted sheets and towels tautly to be sure they held together. She slid her arm through the center of the coiled rope of cloth and draped her light cloak over all of it.

It will work, she decided. It has to.

Leaving the chamber and building, she walked across the courtyard to the hall. She sought out Heloise sewing with her servants and three daughters. Beautiful, blond Heloise looked up kindly as she approached.

"The evening is fair," Christiana said in the distant tone she had maintained since her arrival. "I will sit in the garden for a while, I think."

"The breeze is cooling," Heloise said.

"I have brought my cloak if I need it."

The woman nodded and returned to her conversation.

Christiana forced her steps to slow indifferently. Outside she nipped into the walled garden behind the hall. She meandered through the plantings so that her progress would appear accidental. Slowly, deliberately, she worked her way toward the tall tree in the back corner of the garden.

Five days. Five days she had been a prisoner, and she still did not know why they had brought her here. She doubted that Heloise knew either. Perhaps her husband, the mayor of Caen, in whose palatial home she now found herself, had the answer, but he had explained nothing. Since the day she had stumbled into that hall, filthy and disheveled from her journey on horse and sea, furiously indignant and ready to kill or be killed, no one had told her anything. They had welcomed her as a guest, however, and shown her every honor and hospitality.

Except one. She could not leave.

Well, she would leave now. Yesterday she had found this tree. It grew higher than the wall, and she had eagerly climbed it, praying that some structure to which she could jump abutted the wall on the other side. Hovering amongst the obscuring branches and leaves, she had looked down at the sheer twenty-foot drop awaiting her. Even as disappointment flooded her, however, she had laid her plans.

She glanced around cautiously while she backed up into the shadow of the tree. At least two hours before nightfall. Enough time to get away from this city and find shelter somewhere.

Hoisting the line of sheets up her arm, she climbed the tree. She found a strong branch overhanging the wall's crest and settled herself on it. Easing off the sheets, she tied one end to the branch and threw the rest over the wall.

She shimmied out over the precipice and looked down. The dangling white line reached within ten feet of the ground. If she hung near the end and dropped, she should be safe enough.

She eyed the sheets and their knots. If they failed to support her weight, this could maim her. She prayed that the mayor of Caen bought top-quality linen for his bedding.

Lowering her feet to the top of the wall, she grabbed the first knot. She stepped back.

She had hoped that she could basically walk down the wall, but it didn't work that way. She found herself dangling against it, her hands clawing at the white line that supported her. The muscles in her arms and shoulders immediately rebelled.

Only one way to go now. Grasping with all of her strength, she began to jerk her way down, hand over hand. Halfway to the ground, she began to hear a distant commotion. It grew and moved toward her.

Noises and voices resonated through the stone wall. A lot of people were in the garden, thrashing around. She continued her painful progress and stared up at the tree limb fearfully, waiting for the face that would discover her. The leaves must have hidden her rope's end, because the noises retreated.

She had tied some towels at the end to lengthen the rope, and she reached them now. The knot stretched against her weight. Just as her hands were about to give out anyway, she heard the rip that sent her crashing to the ground.

It had only been a drop of eight feet, but it still stunned her. She cautiously rose to her feet and glanced around.

Another wall, of another house, stretched in front of her. Between the two ran a very narrow alley where she now stood. At one end she saw a jumble of roofs that suggested it gave out on a city lane. The other way looked clearer.

Staying in the wall's shadow, she quickly walked

up the alley with a triumphant elation pounding through her. Whatever the mayor of Caen had planned for her, he could find another Englishwoman for the role.

She would cross the river and and stay off the roads and make her way to the coast and a port town. Maybe she would find an English fisherman or merchant there who would help her.

She stopped near the end of the wall and strained her ears for the sounds of the searchers. All was silent. She started forward again.

Suddenly a man stepped from behind the wall's end. He stood twenty yards in front of her with his arms crossed over his chest. She paused and stared at him in the evening light.

Definitely not the portly, short mayor. Too tall and lean, although the long hair was just as white and the clothing just as rich. Not one of his retainers either. She carefully walked forward, hoping that this man's presence had nothing to do with her, despite the concentrated way that he watched her approach.

She had just decided to smile sweetly and pretend that she belonged in this alley and neighborhood when she drew near enough to see his face.

She recognized him and, she knew, he recognized her. Her heart sank as her feet continued bringing her closer to the French noble who had disguised himself to meet with David at Hampstead.

She had not met him up close that day, but she stopped only a few paces away and faced him squarely now. She remembered more about his appearance than she had thought, for he looked very familiar to her in unspecified ways. Hooded brown eyes gazed down examining her. Between the white mustache and short beard, a slow smile formed.

"You have spirit," he said. "A good sign." He looked

down the alley to the swaying white line of sheets and towels. "You might have hurt yourself."

"Does it matter?"

"It matters a great deal."

"Well, that at least is good news."

He stepped aside. With a flourishing gesture, he pointed her back toward her prison.

Christiana plied her needle in the twilight eking through the open window. A low fire burned in the hearth, but the early July evening was very warm and the fire would not be built up when the daylight faded.

She glanced at the women and girls sitting around her, speaking lowly to each other as they bent to their own needlework. Occasionally one would look at her curiously. They still did not know why she had been foisted on them to befriend and entertain, and nothing beyond the previous polite courtesy had developed over the seven days since her attempted escape.

She looked down the hall to the other hearth and the four men gathered around it. Two of them were local barons from the region who had arrived during the last few days with their retinues at the French king's command. Others had come before them. The city was filling with knights and soldiers. Some camped across the river that served as a natural defense to this Norman city. A few had entered the castle, but most came here, to the mayor's house, and consulted with the tall white-haired man sitting by the other hearth.

She knew his name now. Theobald, the Comte of Senlis. Not just a noble, as she had surmised that day in Hampstead, but an important baron equal in rank to an English earl, and an advisor to the French king.

He had only spoken to her enough to ascertain that she had not been harmed or molested. He had ignored her demanding questions. She suspected, however, that she had been brought here at his initiative and command, and not the mayor's.

A prisoner still. *His prisoner.* To what end and what purpose? The women did not know. The Comte would not say. She sat in this house day after day, keeping to herself, refusing all but the barest hospitality, and watched the lords' arrivals and the daily consultations at the other end of the hall.

The light had faded. She rose and went to a bench below a window on the long wall of the hall. She would sit alone for a while and give the ladies time to gossip and speculate about her. Her unnatural and strained social situation did nothing to alleviate the chilling fear that she had carried inside her ever since those men had pulled her from her home. She admitted that the chill had gotten colder since she had faced the Comte at the end of the alley.

She had imagined during her first days here that David would come to rescue her. Perhaps he would bring Morvan and Walter Manny and some of the other knights to help. They would ride up to the river and across the bridge and into the city and demand her release. Like something out of a chanson.

She grimaced at her foolishness. If David were coming, he would have been here by now. In fact, he could have arrived before her. Returning home and finding her gone, he could have sailed from London and reached France before her own boat. Her captors had dragged her all the way north, almost to Scotland, before securing passage at a seaside port. A waste of time that made no sense, but then none of this did.

She had closed her eyes as she contemplated her situation, and the hall had receded from her awareness. A slight commotion intruded on her reverie now.

At the far hearth the Comte had risen from his chair and bent his ear to a gesturing man-at-arms. A broad smile broke over his face. He turned and said something to the mayor. One of the barons clapped his hand merrily on the other's shoulder.

The entrance to the hall swung open and she had a view of the anteroom beyond. Through the threshold to the courtyard she saw a man approach. Torchlight reflected off armor before the darkness of the anteroom swallowed him.

Another baron. They came to prepare for King Edward's invasion, of course. No doubt similar councils and musterings were taking place all over France.

One of the Comte's squires entered first, carrying a helmet and shield. She glanced at the newly painted and unscarred blue and gold coat of arms on it. Five gold disks over three entwined serpents, and the bar sinister of a bastard son.

Three entwined serpents . . . shocked alertness shook her. She sat upright and stared.

The knight entered the chamber. Tall and lean, he looked around placidly as he removed his gauntlets. His body moved fluidly in the clumsy armor as if he wore a second skin. He stood proudly with a touch of arrogance. Mussed brown hair hung around his perfect, weather-bronzed face. Blue eyes met hers intently.

She watched speechlessly. To her right, the women turned to regard the strong and handsome new man. To her left, the Comte strode forward, smiling, his hands outstretched.

"Welcome to France, nephew."

David de Abyndon, her David, her merchant, turned to the Comte de Senlis.

Nephew! Stunned, she looked from him to the Comte and then back again. She suddenly understood the odd familiarity she had felt when she looked in that older man's face.

She glared at David, standing there so casually and naturally in his damn armor, looking for all the world like a knight, accepting a kinsman's welcome from this French baron.

Of course. Of course. Why hadn't she seen it before? The height. The strength. The lack of deference. He hadn't told her. He had never even hinted. The urge to strangle her husband assaulted her.

The Comte spoke quietly and gestured David toward the hearth.

"I will see to my wife first," David said, and dismissing his uncle's interest, he crossed the space to her.

She glanced up the molded metal plates and looked him accusingly straight in the eyes. He looked straight back. Placid. Inscrutable. Cool.

"You are well and unharmed?"

"Aside from feeling like an ignorant and stupid fool who is married to a lying stranger, I am well."

He bent to kiss her. "I will explain all when we are alone," he said quietly. "Come now, and sit with me. Do not take to heart what I say to him, darling. I would have the Comte think that we are not content together."

"I should be able to help you with that."

The Comte wanted to speak with David alone. He had dismissed the barons and mayor, and frowned in annoyance when David led Christiana to the hearth.

"Thanks to you, I gamble with her life now as well as my own," David said. "She has a right to know my situation."

She sat in a chair. David stood near the hearth and she

watched him with confusion and shock and anger. In a strange way, however, a small part of her nodded with understanding. Something seemed appallingly *right* about seeing him like this, as if a shadow that had always floated behind him had suddenly taken substance and form. *Who are you really?*

She glanced at the Comte and could tell from that old man's approving gaze that he saw what she saw.

David turned to his uncle and let his annoyance flare. "I told you that she was not to be involved."

The Comte raised his hands. "You did not come in April. I sought to encourage you."

"I did not come because the storms rose as soon as I reached Normandy. Why deliver news that would have no value? The fleet barely made it back to England."

So he had come to France at Easter. But then, she had known that as soon as she saw him enter the hall.

"I had men waiting for you at Calais and St. Malo. You did not come."

"Do you think that I am so stupid as to put in at a major trading port where I might be recognized? Would you be so careless?"

The Comte considered this and made a face of tentative acceptance. "Still, you are late. I expected you weeks ago. The army is ready to move."

"I am late because my wife disappeared and I sought to find her."

"You knew where she was."

"I did not. I could hardly leave England without knowing her fate."

The Comte flushed. "They were to leave—"

"No note or word was left." David stared hard at the Comte. "You sent Frans to do this, didn't you? Against our agreement."

"He knew the people. He knows your habits."

"Aye. But he relied on Lady Catherine, who holds no love for me. Also against our agreement. And she had her own plans for me. I was lucky to get out of England alive."

The Comte reddened. "She endangered you?"

"You probably assumed that I would know, note or not, that you had taken Christiana. What other explanation could there be? What you did not know is that my wife has a lover who lives in the north country."

The Comte glanced in scathing disappointment at her. She faced him down. David had better have a damn good reason for telling his uncle that.

"Lady Catherine knew this, however," David continued. "And so she had the men whom she and Frans hired leave no note or sign, so I would wonder if Christiana had gone to this man. They even took her out of the country by way of a northern port, so that I could follow her trail toward her lover. All the while, time is passing and I am still in England." He paused and smiled unpleasantly. "And during that time, Catherine went to King Edward and told him about me. She had a lot to tell, because Frans had let her know of my relationship to you."

A very hard expression masked the Comte's face. Christiana drew back in alarm. She had seen that expression before, but not on this Frenchman's face.

"I will deal with them both. The woman and Frans."

"I have already done so."

"If the woman betrayed you to Edward, what you know may be useless. He may change the port."

She had been correct in her suspicions then. David planned to give the port's location to the Comte and the French. But not in exchange for silver and gold. And, as a son of Senlis, not even in treason. Every noble knew and respected the loyalties of blood ties. An oath of fealty bound one just as strongly, but a wise king or lord never asked his liegemen to make a choice between the two obligations.

"I thought of that," David said. "And it may happen. But before I slipped out, I learned that, even two weeks after hearing Catherine's tale, he had not changed his mind. He had already sent word to the English forces on the Continent, and there was no time to undo that. But he may hope that you expect him to, so that you resist committing all of your forces to the one place. I wonder if he did not let me escape with the news of Lady Catherine's betrayal in order to cast doubt on the value of this information in the event that I had managed to send it to you earlier."

All of David's attention was concentrated on his uncle, and those blue eyes never wavered in their scrutiny of the older man's face. The Comte's own eyes, brown rather than blue but so similar nonetheless, appeared just as piercing whenever he studied David.

Who are you really? Well, now she knew. She was too numb and confused to decipher how she felt about this startling revelation. She should be relieved. Her husband was not common. His father's blood, the important blood, had been noble.

So why did this anger unaccountably want to unhinge her?

The Comte paced and nodded to himself. "I think that you are right. The summer is passing quickly. If he comes at all, he must do so now. His army has been mustered. It is too late to change course." He pivoted toward David. "Do you have it, then?"

"I have it. More than he knows that I have. The roads he will take and the direction he will head. The size of his force. I have it all."

The Comte waited expectantly.

David smiled faintly. "Do you have the documents?"

The Comte gave an exasperated sigh. "Mine is here and witnessed. The constable brings that from the King when he arrives. But we waste time . . ."

"You have already broken most of our spoken agreement. And because of that, I have been left no choice but to do this. I cannot return to England, and although Edward may one day acknowledge Christiana's innocence and welcome her back, she is forced now to a future that she did not choose either. I do not plan to start life over with the little gold I brought with me. I go no further without the documents."

A very ugly tension seemed to paralyze the two men, and something threatening and dark flowed out of the Comte. Christiana sucked in her breath. She had felt this dangerous presence before, too. She wondered what the Comte contemplated. He was as unreadable as David.

Except to David.

"I was tortured once in Egypt," David said calmly. "The French mind cannot compete with Saracen invention on that. You will buy no time that way, and will have an heir who waits to see you dead."

Beneath hooded lids, brown eyes slid subtly in her direction. A horrible chill prickled her neck.

David's eyes narrowed. "Do not shame your name and your blood by even considering it. She knows absolutely nothing, as your wife would not under the circumstances."

But I do know, she thought frantically. She suspected that this uncle could read people as well as David. She lowered her eyes from his inspection and prayed that he saw only her palpable fear in her face.

The Comte considered her a moment and then laughed lightly.

"When do you expect the constable?" David asked.

"By early morning."

"You are too impatient then, and too quickly consider

dishonor. Is it any wonder that I demand written assurances?"

A dangerous scolding for a merchant to give a baron, kinsman or not. Laden with distrust and insult. But the Comte seemed more impressed than angry.

"All men consider things that they would never do, nephew. Recognizing one's options is not the same as choosing them."

David frowned thoughtfully and then nodded, as if he completely understood the Comte's explanation and had reason to accept it as sound.

The tension slowly unwound.

"I promise that there will be time enough to move your forces. The ships were not even half ready to sail when I left," David said.

That seemed to lighten the mood even more. The Comte smiled pleasantly, even warmly.

David walked over and took her hand. "Show me our chamber, Christiana. I want to get out of this steel that has broiled my body under the hot sun all day."

"I will send my squires to help you," the Comte said. "And tell the mistress to have servants prepare a bath for you."

Christiana wordlessly led David out of the hall and toward the tall side building that held the chambers.

"The man drains me," David muttered as they walked through the warm night. "It is like negotiating with the image I see in a mirror."

CHAPTER 20

THE TWO SQUIRES removed David's armor. They kept calling him "my lord." Christiana glanced with annoyance at her husband's tall body standing spread legged while the plate came off. One would think he had done this a thousand times.

Near the low-burning hearth fire, servants prepared the water in a deep wooden hip bath. One girl kept looking at David and smiling sweetly whenever she caught his eye. Christiana grabbed her by the scruff of the neck when the last pail had been poured.

"Out. I will attend my husband."

The servants scurried away. The squires finished their long chore and, calling merry farewells, drifted off. David stripped off his inner garments and settled into the tub.

The sight of his body stirred her more than she cared to admit. She cursed silently at her weakness and at her traitorous heart's independence from her will and mind. *Our life together has been one long illusion*, she fumed. *It was a mistake to think that I could find contentment in pleasure*

*alone. He will always be a stranger. I will always be the play-
thing who shares his bed but not his life. I will have it out with
him once and for all and then demand another chamber.*

She pulled over a stool, sat down, and faced him.

"Aren't you going to attend me?" he asked.

"Wash," she ordered dangerously, throwing him a
chunk of soap. "And talk."

"Ah," he said thoughtfully.

"And no 'ahs,' David. One more 'ah' and I will drown
you."

"I understand that you are angry, darling. Believe me,
I went through great trouble not to involve you. I intended
you to know nothing. Edward would never have blamed
you for my sins. The Comte surprised me with this abduction. Frankly, I am disappointed in him."

"Are you indeed?"

"Aye. I expected more chivalry of him. To abduct and
endanger an innocent woman . . . It is really very churl-
ish."

"He wants the name of the port, David. He would
probably kill me if he thought it would make you give it to
him a minute sooner."

"Which is why I want him to think that we are not
content together. I do not want him debating whether he
can use you against me. Once the Constable d'Eu arrives,
I will get his assurance of your safety before I speak with
them. The constable is reputed to be honorable to the
point of stupidity."

She rolled her eyes. "Let us start at the beginning. Is
the Comte in fact your kinsman?"

"It would seem so."

"How long have you known?"

"Almost my whole life. My mother told me of my
father when I was a child. So I would know that I was not
an ordinary, gutter variety bastard."

"Why didn't you tell me?"

"It is a claim easily made but hard to prove, Christiana. And unless a bastard is recognized, it has no value." He watched himself lather an arm. "Would it have helped, darling?"

She sorely wished that she could say not. "It might have. At the beginning."

"Then I am sorry that I didn't tell you."

"Nay, you are not. Your pride wanted me to accept you as the merchant, not the son of Senlis. You can be very strange, David. Not many men would think noble blood makes them less than they are instead of more."

He glanced at her sharply. She let him see her anger. "You lied to me," she said. "Over and over."

"Only to protect you. This began long before we met. I sought to keep you out of it, ignorant of it, so that you would be spared if something went wrong."

"I am your wife. No one would believe my ignorance."

"You are the daughter of Hugh Fitzwaryn and were a ward of the King. All would believe it. Neither Edward nor his barons would have blamed you for the actions of your merchant husband."

His bland excuses infuriated her. She raised her fists and slammed them down on her lap. "I am your *wife*! If something went wrong, I would have had to watch them tear your body apart even if I was spared. I still may have to, for all that I know. But worse, you hid yourself from me, hid your true nature, who you are."

That hardness played around his mouth and eyes. "You have not been my wife for months now. Should I have trusted the girl who lived in my home like a guest or a cousin?"

"Better a guest than some precious artwork. Better a

cousin than a piece of noble property purchased to salve the forgotten son's wounded pride."

His eyes flashed. "If you truly believe that, then there is no point in explaining anything to you. No matter what I said that day, you should know better of me."

"Know better of you? Right now I don't think that I know you at all, damn you. And do not insinuate that our separation led you to maintain your deception. You had no intention of telling me anything until this was over, no matter how dutiful I might have been. What then? Would you have stayed in France and sent for me? Written a letter that bid me to attend on you here?"

"It always was and still is my intention to give you a choice."

"Indeed? Well, your uncle has closed that door!"

"That remains to be seen."

She looked away until she regained control. She smoothed the skirt of her gown. "I want you to tell me all of it. Now. I would know my situation and my choices. From the beginning."

He told his tale while he washed. "It began simply enough. Edward had asked me to make the maps. It occurred to me that when the time came, I might learn the port that he chose from the questions that he asked me about them. I have never really forgiven my father for what he did to Joanna. He destroyed her and left her to the mercy of the world. Perhaps I also resented his ignorance and neglect of me. Anyway, not really expecting it to work, I began making enough mistakes in France so that anyone paying attention might suspect what I did there. And I began using the three serpents as the device on my seal. They were carved into a ring my father left with my mother. She thought it like a wedding ring, but I suspect he had intended it as payment for her favors."

He paused and lathered the soap between his hands. The gesture distracted him. Christiana watched him examine the white foam and then the cake itself. She had to smile. The merchant's wife had been similarly distracted during her first bath here.

"It comes from a town on the Loire," she said.

David smelled the foam. "Superior, isn't it? I wonder . . ."

"Twenty large cakes for a mark."

He raised his eyebrows. She watched him silently begin calculating the cost of importation and the potential profit.

"David," she said, calling him back.

"Aye. Well, my plan was to let the Comte know of me, realize our connection, and then approach me for the port. I would resist and let him cajole me by playing on the bonds of kinship. I would relent, accepting no payment so he thought that I did it for my blood and so trusted me. But I would give him the wrong port. The French army would go in one direction, Edward would come from the other, and the way would be clear for an English victory."

She looked at his expression. Matter-of-fact. Blasé. As if men calculated such elaborate schemes all of the time and spent years manipulating the pieces.

He enjoys this, she realized. He traveled to the Dark Continent and he crosses the Alps every other year. He needs the adventure, the planning, the challenge.

"And you would have punished that family for your mother's fate," she added.

"That too. I doubt that the Comte de Senlis would remain on the King's council after giving such bad advice. A loss of status and honor, but no real harm. Unlike Joanna's fall. Still, some justice."

"So what went wrong?"

"Nothing. It unfolded as planned. Except for a few surprises. Early on, Honoré, the last Comte, died, and his brother Theobald took his place. A more dangerous man, Theobald."

She stood up and paced slowly around the chamber. She waited for the rest. David waited longer.

"What did you mean when you said that about his heir wanting him dead?" she blurted.

"The other surprise. A very big one. He did not offer me silver. He offered me recognition and Senlis itself. Honoré's and Theobald's other sons are dead. He offered to swear that his brother had made secret vows with my mother. It would be a lie, but it would secure my right to inherit."

She stared at him.

David. Her merchant. The Comte de Senlis.

"Men have been tempted to treason by much less, my girl."

"You said that you had no interest in being a knight."

He laughed. "Darling, a knight is one thing. A leading baron and councilor to the King of France is quite another."

"You are going to do it then?"

"I have not yet decided. What would you have me do?"

"Nay, David. You began this long ago. You do not foist the choice on me now."

She began pacing again, thinking out loud. "There are many men who owe fealty to two kings or lords. Many English barons also have lands in France. Everyone understands that loyalties conflict sometimes."

He reached out and caught her arm as she passed. His grasp held her firmly and he looked up at her, shaking his head. "Let us not pretend that I face other than I do.

What you say is true, but there are rules that decide which way a man goes in those cases. This is different. If I help the Comte and France, if I do this, I betray a trust and a friendship and my country. For the prize that is offered, I am not above doing it, but I will not pretend it is prettier than it is."

Damn him. *Damn him.* There were enough ambiguities here for a bishop to rationalize his actions. He could at least let her find some comfort in them.

"France is your country, David," she pointed out. "Your father was French."

"In truth, I find that it is not England that concerns me. Or even Edward. He has had barons do worse by him, and he possesses a large capacity for understanding and even forgiving such things. Nay, it is London that has been on my mind. If not for my city, I do not think that I would hesitate."

He held up the soap. "Since you sent the servants away, you could at least wash my back."

She knelt behind him and smoothed the lather over his muscles. Despite her inner turmoil, she couldn't help but notice that it was the first time that she had touched his body in months. A slight tensing beneath her palm told her of his awareness of it, too.

"You lied to me in April. You came to France and did not go to Salisbury."

"I could hardly implicate you with the truth." He glanced over his shoulder. "That day in the wardrobe. Your questions. How much did you suspect?"

"Most of it eventually, but not about your father. I heard Frans's first approach to you. I was hiding in the passageway. But I wasn't sure that it had been you there. I learned that he was an agent for the French cause. I saw you meet with him again at Westminster. When the

Comte came to Hampstead, I heard his voice before he left. I knew that he was French and a noble."

"You thought that I might be selling Edward's plans for silver?"

"It was one explanation for these things. Actually, it was the silver that didn't make sense. You enjoy your wealth, but are too generous to be a man who would do anything out of greed."

He twisted around and looked down at her. "If you knew so much, I am surprised that you did not leave sooner, while I was gone, for your own safety and the honor of your family. You might have gone to Edward with your suspicions. Why didn't you?"

She looked away from his knowing eyes. She did not want the vulnerability that answering would expose. Besides, it was her turn for questions.

"You had said that you would come back in April and I believed you. Did you lie about that, too?"

He shook his head. "I had not decided what I would do once I got here, but I expected to come back in either case. If I had given the Comte the port of Bordeaux, and he had gone there, Edward would never have suspected me or anyone else even if the whole of France waited for him. Half of their army is already in the south dealing with Grossmont. The rest might have received reports of the ships sailing down the coast, or have gone to reinforce the siege at Angiullon down there. I fully expected to return, assuming that Theobald would permit it."

His steady gaze and quiet voice, his face so close to hers, disconcerted her. Her resolve began loosening. She pushed his shoulder so that she could rinse off the soap, and he turned away.

"But now Lady Catherine has told Edward about you,

and so you cannot go back. Why would she do this? Is she angry about the property in Hampstead?"

He didn't respond for several moments. She suspected that he debated his answer. She braced herself for more lies.

"Lady Catherine and I have a long history. The property is a small and recent part of it. She did me an injury when I was a youth. The evidence is beneath your fingers now. Some months ago I responded in kind."

She rocked back on her heels in shock. She looked down at the strong back and the diagonal scars on it. Despite her determination to treat him with the same indifference he felt for her, her heart tore.

She didn't need to hear the story, because she could imagine it. Her fingertips traced the thin, permanent welts. She pictured him being flogged as a boy. She saw Lady Catherine, secure in the immunity that her nobility gave her, ordering it for some perceived slight or crime. Not in London, of course. Even as an apprentice, he would have been protected there.

He had responded in kind. Did that mean Catherine's own skin bore scars now? She hoped so.

She felt a wave of tenderness for the youth who had been so harshly abused. She barely resisted the urge to kiss those welts.

This is madness, she admonished herself. *He wants no sympathy or tenderness from me. I am no part of his history or his revenge. I have no role in the pageant unfolding now, either. At best I am an inconvenience with which the Comte has complicated his plans.*

"You say that you have not decided what to do, David. What will happen if you will not give the port tomorrow?"

She was glad that she couldn't see his face. If he lied to her, she didn't want to know.

"The Comte has done everything possible to ensure that that isn't much of a choice anymore. Catherine did go to Edward as I said, but the Comte's surprise at the news was false. He sent her to betray me, to force my hand in this. Her plan to keep me in England so that Edward could capture me was all her own, however. Still, he sought to force me out of England, and he took you so that I would have to come here. With my life endangered in England, he knows that his offer becomes very attractive." He paused. "However, kin or not, I do not think that he will allow me to leave here alive if I refuse him."

She wished that he had indeed lied. "Then you have no choice."

"Of course I do."

She felt sick. On the one hand, status and wealth awaited. More than he had ever expected in life. Senlis was his right and his due and he should take it. But, dear God, men whom she knew and loved would ride those ships to France. Her brother, her King, Thomas and others . . . and now he had all but said that Theobald would kill him if he did not cooperate.

It should not matter to her. He should not matter.

She almost embraced him and begged him to find a way to take both choices and thus none at all.

She returned to the stool. "Were you truly almost captured?"

"No one challenged or questioned me. The armor proved a good disguise, since there are knights moving everywhere in England. Even here, it helped me travel without suspicion."

"The coat of arms on your shield?"

"Do you like it? I could hardly pass myself off as a knight with a blank shield. Fortunately, I met no heralds who would know it was new and unofficial."

"You followed me north, then?"

"Aye." He shot her a piercing look. "Do not worry. He was not harmed. Although when Sieg threatened to make him a eunuch, I thought he might die of fright. Since I saved him from that, he will probably be glad to lay down his life for me now."

She glanced to the hearth, not much caring if Sieg had made Stephen a eunuch, whatever that was.

"We were further delayed when Oliver insisted on taking the girl with Stephen under his wing and trying to save her from her family's wrath."

She barely heard him. She went over to the hearth. A bucket of water warmed there and she picked it up and carried it the few steps to the tub.

She noticed David looking at her.

"What?" she asked.

"Didn't you hear me? Aren't you jealous? I said he had a girl with him."

She narrowed her eyes. "For a clever man, you can be an idiot!" she shrieked, pouring the water over his head. She upturned the bucket, slammed it down to his ears, and stomped away.

She stared at the wall, blind with fury. She heard him leave the tub and dry himself. A few moments later he came up behind her.

He touched her shoulder lightly.

"You still do not believe me," she spat, shrugging off his hand. "You have told me lie after lie, while I gave you nothing but the truth from the beginning. Do you assume that everyone lives the kind of deceptions that you do?"

"I believe you. But I wonder if you still love him. You never said that you had stopped."

"I told you it was over."

"That is not the same thing."

"You should have just asked me, then, if you wondered."

He stepped closer and spoke quietly. "I did not ask you about this, just as you did not ask me about France, and for the same reasons. We have not spoken to each other about the things which might pain us. I never asked you, because I feared the answer. I hoped that time would deal with it. But we have run out of time and I am asking you now. Do you still love him?"

She closed her eyes and savored the sound of his beautiful voice and wished that its quiet tones were not asking questions which led down this path. She feared where it might lead.

Still, he was right. Finally, today, he had given her honesty. She should not start her own deceptions now. But honesty about them, the two of them, could well leave her bereft of everything even as it destroyed the fragile resolve with which her anger had conquered her passion and love.

"I no longer care for him at all and doubt that I ever loved him."

"Why do you doubt it?"

Because I know what love feels like now, she almost said.

The silence pulsed as he awaited her answer. She suddenly felt terribly vulnerable. This was the second question that if answered honestly would demand an admission of love from her.

Why not just tell him? Admit the truth, and then walk out the door. She grimaced. A grand gesture totally lacking the hoped-for drama and impact. He would simply let her go, and then proceed to live the life he chose for himself. He did not care enough to be touched by either the admission or the rejection.

"Why do you believe me now about that meeting, David? Did Stephen tell you the truth? Did you believe that fool when you hadn't believed me?"

"He told me, but he would have sworn to being chaste from birth under the circumstances. It did not matter because I already believed you. Whenever I thought about that day, I kept seeing a beautiful girl running into my arms. Full of joy, not guilt or fear." His hands gently took her shoulders. "What was it you wanted to tell me then?"

Again a probing question.

He suspects, she realized with shock. *His mind's reflection has seen what his anger did not.*

She became acutely conscious of his warmth and scent behind her. The silence tightened as something else flowed from him. Something expectant and impatient.

She ached to say it, but she thought about the things she had thrown at him that afternoon in their chamber. She remembered how she had avoided him and his affections during their betrothal. She imagined the apprentice being tortured at the will of the noble Lady Catherine.

She certainly could not tell him now. Even if he put some small value on her feelings for him, he would think that his change in fortune from merchant to baronial heir had made her find sudden love.

"I do not remember," she muttered.

He stayed silent, softly stroking her arms. She closed her eyes and absorbed his touch and closeness. His exciting intensity surrounded her in a luring, seductive way. Despite the knot into which the day's revelations had tied her emotions, despite her decision to leave this stranger, she drew amazing comfort from his slow caress.

"I need to know some things from you now," he finally said.

"No story I can tell will be nearly as interesting as yours."

"Were you harmed at all?"

"Nay. Not really. We rode for days and my rump

got sore from the saddle and my skin red from the summer sun, but that is all. At nights we stayed in rude inns and all shared one hot chamber, but the men did not bother me, although one looked at me too boldly for comfort. The food was horrible and the sea trip frightening, and I arrived looking like the worst peasant, and smelling too ripe for decent company, but I was not harmed."

He turned her around. He had thrown on a loose, long robe, like something a Saracen might wear. She looked up into his face and saw things hiding beneath his calm expression that she had never witnessed in him before. Worry. Indecision. Doubt. He looked much less contained than he had in the bath.

He touched her face. "If I do this thing, you need not stay. Very soon Edward will accept that you were no part of it. You can return home."

She gazed at him, her love twisting her heart. This small contact of skin on skin was enough to awaken all of her senses to him. "That is why you put the properties in my name, isn't it? So they could not be confiscated."

"Aye. There was always the chance that Edward would learn enough to suspect me, no matter what my intentions. I did not want you left dependent if this dangerous game went wrong."

"Why didn't you wait? To marry? You said that this began long before we met. Long before you offered for me. Why complicate things thus for yourself?"

Even as she said it, an eerie sensation swept through her. A knowledge that she did not want to face stretched and stood tall and presented itself squarely. An explanation for one of the first and most enduring questions she had ever had about this man stared at her.

Dear God. *Dear God.* Even that had been a lie, an illusion! It hadn't been much, but at least, as her love sought a compromise with her life, it had been something to hold on to.

His fingers still rested on her face. She looked desperately into his blue eyes and sought all the awareness she had ever had of him during their closest intimacy. She gazed through the veils and intensity, trying to see his soul.

"You never offered for me, did you?" she said. "It was Edward's idea. He proposed this marriage, for my sake perhaps, but also to get money out of you. You could not refuse him."

He took her face in his hands and bent closer. He looked straight back at her. The control and restraint fell away and he permitted her to see what she sought. He let her look through the shadows and layers, down to his depths. Naked of all defenses and armor he met her inspection. Her breath caught at the emotions suddenly exposed to her.

"Nay," he said quietly. "I saw you and wanted you and paid Edward a fortune to have you. And I did not wait because I could not. It was selfish of me." His thumbs stroked her cheekbones. "I am out of time, Christiana. I need to know my true choices, and what I gain and what I lose. If I do this thing, are you going to stay with me?"

She barely heard his words because the stunning truth written inside him made the events which had created this marriage suddenly irrelevant. She could not turn from his warm, binding gaze. She did not want to lose this soulful connection, this total knowing that he offered her. She doubted that he had ever before let anyone, even his mother, see him thus.

Everything was reflected in those deep eyes. Everything. His guilt at endangering her. His fear of himself. His hard hungers and conflicting needs and dark inclinations. But illuminating all of those shadows, warming their chilly depths, flowed a sparkling emotion that she recognized for its beauty and joy and salvation. Her own love spread and reached out to meet it gratefully. His lips parted and a glorious warmth suffused his gaze. An exquisite, anguished relief poured out of him.

"Will you stay?" he repeated, his face inches from hers.

"I will not leave," she whispered, for there could be no other answer after what she had just seen. "Noble or merchant, I will stay with you."

He pulled her into an embracing kiss. She grasped his shoulders and lost herself in a warm rush of poignant intimacy. For a breathless, eternal moment, their bodies seemed to dissolve within the dazzling brilliance flowing between them.

The connection and knowing was so complete that she felt no need to speak of it. But David did.

"What did you want to say to me that day, Christiana?"

"Couldn't you tell? I was sure that you would see it at once."

"My anger and pain blinded me to everything else. I stepped off that boat with a head and heart full of love for you, and Oliver's tale cut me like a dagger and made me a madman."

She lifted her eyes to his, rendered speechless by this calm articulation of what she had just seen and felt in him. In speaking first, he made it easier for her. He had always done that, every step of the way. Out of sympathy and understanding at first maybe, but later because of his love.

She touched his face. She let her fingers drift over the tanned ridges of his cheekbones and jaw, and caress his lips. "I wanted to tell you that day that I was in love with you. I realized it when Catherine delivered me to Stephen. The love was just there, very obvious and completely real. I knew that I have loved you a long while."

He kissed her again, so gently and sweetly that her awareness of his love filled her to the point of weightlessness.

His lips moved to her ear. "They took you from my chamber. Upstairs. Geva had touched nothing when I returned."

His quiet, beautiful voice warmed her as much as his breath and touch. A delicious peace flowed through her like a breeze. She was grateful that he knew that she had loved David the mercer long before she learned the whole truth about him. Glad that he knew that she had returned to him of her own will.

"Do you want me, Christiana? Will you come to bed with me now?"

"You know that I do. You know that I will."

He held her and let her innocent love and joy overwhelm him. Ever since he had returned to the house and seen that disheveled bed, his physical desire for her had beat a low, constant rhythm in his soul and body. Now, however, he resisted the movements that would take her to bed. Her loving embrace soothed him as no passion would.

Noble or merchant, I will stay with you. More than he had asked for or expected. Far more than he deserved.

She broke his long kiss and smiled up at him. "Has it been so long that you have forgotten how to do it?"

He laughed. "Aye. Perhaps I should have kept in practice."

Her brows rose in surprise and he laughed again. "There has been no one else. I found sitting near you at the hearth more compelling than seducing my way into some strange bed."

She frowned. "It is strange, David. I sat there loving you and you sat loving me and we didn't see it. Why not? You see everything. Can thoughtless, cruel words build such walls?"

"It is over. We do not have to—"

"I want to. I spoke to hurt you, and you did the same. We threw the other's fears and illusions at each other and we each believed the words even though the truth stared us in the face." She gazed intently at him. "If I had thought clearly then, as I have since, I would have known that you never thought of me as property. In fact, you behaved just the opposite. If you had bought yourself a noble whore, you certainly did not make much use of her, did you? Why?"

She surprised him. She was growing up fast, and her sharp intelligence, freed of its isolating shelter, had already learned to see to the heart of things.

He loved the girl. He suspected that he would worship the woman.

"You were very innocent, darling."

"Not so innocent. Women speak to girls before they marry. I knew that men usually expected more than you ever asked of me. I knew there could be more to lovemaking than you ever sought."

"We were not together very long, Christiana."

She bit her lower lip thoughtfully. "I do not think it was that. You knew your blood, but I did not. I think that you worried that I would indeed feel debased and used. For all of your pride, David, you did not meet me as an equal in our bed."

She astonished him. He had been very careful with her. He had never gone beyond the impulsive acts of their wedding night. The restraint had come naturally to him and he had never thought about it, but now he had to admit some truth in what she said.

A very worldly and determined expression flickered in those diamonds. "I have been jealous, you know. I do not like knowing that you did things with Alicia and others that we never did. Noble or merchant, I will stay with you, David, but not as some precious vessel that you fear to break."

Playfully, she pushed him back, up against the post of the bed. She leaned up into him, pressed her body along his, lowered his head with her hand, and kissed him. He accepted her erotic little assault. Lightning flashed through him and the tightness grew and spread.

She glanced up, very pleased with herself. He grasped her hips and pulled her closer and she deliberately rubbed against him. Weeks of need and waiting responded forcefully and he lifted her into a devouring, obscuring kiss. She gave herself over to it and their passion melted them together. But then her hands smoothed over his shoulders and down to his chest and she subtly pushed away.

"On my wedding a day, a servant gave me some very explicit lessons," she said, looking more to his chest than his face. "She said that men like to watch women undress. Would it please my merchant husband if I undressed now?"

She looked up at him and blushed. He thought his heart would tear his chest open. She turned and walked away, her hands plucking at the knot on her gown's laces. The simple gesture almost undid him. He leaned against the bedpost and crossed his arms over his chest.

He had seen her undress many times, of course, but not like this. She moved so beautifully, so elegantly, that her sudden awkwardness at finding herself watched thus almost wasn't apparent. But he could tell that she immediately found it harder than she had thought. He managed not to smile at the slight flush on her face and the hot look in her eyes as she turned to him and let the gown slide to the floor. She bent to her hose.

"Nay," he said. "The shift first."

She straightened. Crossing her arms over her chest, and appearing very much the shy virgin she had so recently been, she slid the shift off her shoulders. Her hands and arms followed its descent, unfolding to reveal first her breasts and then her hips and thighs.

The thin garment fluttered to her feet and she stepped out of it. She looked at the floor a moment before raising her eyes to his. The glint in those diamonds told him that she had discovered that this could arouse the woman as much as the man.

Her beauty mesmerized him as always. Her frank desire to give him pleasure transformed the pleasure itself. His storm of need subdued itself into a threatening but controllable gale. He knew that he could ride its wind indefinitely.

"Now the hose."

She bent and her graceful arms reached for the garter of one forward-stepping leg. He glimpsed the taper of her shoulder to her waist and the gentle flair of hips beyond. Her breasts, tight with need, hung for a moment like two perfect half globes as she rolled the hose off her leg.

"Turn for the other."

She glanced over in surprise, but then did as he asked.

The graceful curves of her hips and buttocks fell into erotic swells as she bent to untie the garter. She must have sensed her vulnerability, because her bravery deserted her and she made quick work with the hose.

She straightened and faced him with eyes like liquid stars. He let his memory be branded with her image. Not short and not even small, but beautifully formed in her slender fullness.

"Your hair, Christiana. Take down your hair for me."

Her arms rose as she sought the pins. The movement brought her breasts high and their hard tips angled upward. She unplaited her raven locks and they began spilling around her. He made no effort to hide what he felt from her gaze.

"Come here, my girl, and kiss me the way a bride in love should."

She walked slowly toward him, her expression a heart-stopping combination of passion and love and joy and invitation.

More than he ever expected. Far more than he deserved.

The morning was a lifetime away.

She stepped up to him and placed her hands on his chest. She stretched up toward him. He lowered his head and took her kiss with more restraint than he felt. He let her lead, biting gently around his mouth. Delicately, but not so artlessly, her tongue grazed his lips and then flickered more intimately.

He embraced her with one arm, reveling in the sensation of her skin beneath his hand. A slight sheen of sweat covered her and the warmth and moisture sent a flare through his whole body.

He caressed her face, and broke their kiss so he could watch his hand and her body as it traced down. His embrace arched her back, and her breasts rose to him. Her tremor when he touched her taut nipple flowed right into his hips and thighs.

Neither one of them succumbed to the waiting frenzy. They both sought to prolong the exquisite anticipation she had begun.

Her hands still lay on his chest and now they caressed at the loose lacing down the front of the long robe.

"It looks very exotic. Very handsome."

"Saracens know how to dress for hot weather."

She stroked his chest lazily. "The servant said that men like to be undressed by women, too."

He didn't answer, but watched as she carefully untied and pulled out the laces down to his waist.

She caressed him through the gap. He closed his eyes to the heat of that small hand. It had been too long since he had even this small connection and affection from her.

She pushed the garment open, almost off his shoulders, and laid her face against him. Languidly, deliciously, with a slow care that only increased the tension between them, she rubbed her cheek against his chest and watched her hand follow his muscles.

"You were right," she said as she turned to kiss him. "Abstinence is a powerful enhancement to passion. A part of me cannot wait and already screams for you, but another part wants to prolong this forever."

"You know how it will end. I have never failed you there. Let us enjoy the journey. We will never take quite the same path again."

She smiled sensually and nodded. Running both hands up his chest, she slid the robe off his shoulders and guided it down his back.

His control threatened to dissolve when she extended her caresses to his hips and thighs.

"What else did the servant tell you?" he asked, touching her as she did him, feeling tremors quake subtly through her.

"That men like to be kissed and touched, but I have already learned that is true." She proved it by mouthing at his chest. Rumbling shocks rocked through him with each kiss and nip. "Other things. I thought them shocking at the time. I do not find them so now."

The robe still hung from his hips. She gently shook

off his embrace. She caressed and kissed down his body as she lowered herself.

He watched and waited, his breath barely coming to him. An obscuring haze of passion clouded his mind and he saw both nothing and everything. Saw her hands push the robe to his feet. Felt her fluttering caress on his thighs and legs. Saw her fingers stroke his hard phallus while her lips pressed to his belly and hip. Her boldness both touched and stunned him. He wondered at the deceptive calm his body maintained, because desire began splitting him apart.

She caressed the back of his thighs and moved her head away. Questioning eyes glanced up at him. He bent and reached down for her and drew her up to his embrace. "Only if you want to, darling. And never on your knees."

She nestled into his arms. "Then take me to bed, merchant, so I can show you my love and honor."

He lifted her into a kiss that removed her feet from the floor. He turned and laid her down and lowered himself next to her.

The warm night air flowing through the window felt cool against the heat of their entwined bodies. He lost himself in the intimacy of her scent and swells and slick sweat.

He would show her such a journey as she had never imagined.

Slowly, deliberately, using all of his knowledge of her, he obliterated her shaky control. Never touching her below her hips, he drew her toward completion. Caresses on her inner arm, biting teeth on her nipples, consuming mouth on her neck—her passion rose with each knowing demand. She tried, despite her growing mindlessness, to give him pleasure in return, but he would not let her. He listened to her low sounds of abandon and felt her body climbing, shaking, toward its peak of sensation.

She grasped his shoulders. "David, I . . . please . . ."

He stilled his hands and mouth and held her. She twisted against him in rebellious frustration. Her eyes flew open.

"David!" she cried accusingly.

"Hush, darling. I said that I have never failed you."

"You mean to torture me to death first?" She pummeled his shoulder none too playfully.

He laughed lightly. "It is only torture if you think only about the release. Take the pleasure of the climbs for themselves, knowing that eventually you will fly."

Her passion had receded and the frenzy had passed. Her arms surrounded his shoulders and he turned his head to kiss the bend of her arm while his hand stroked down her body. "Again, then," he said.

She clung to him and opened her legs and accepted his touch. Her folds and passage already throbbed with her arousal, and he deliberately caressed her in ways that would bring pleasure but not fulfillment. She rebelled at first, and tried to move toward more productive touches, but then she relaxed and took the streaks of pleasure with joyful gasps and low moans.

He saw the glorious ecstasy on her face and nearly lost control himself. He touched her differently and watched her climb again, higher this time, as it would be every time. He took her to the peak and kept her there, tottering on its exquisite contracting edge, and let her taste the first tremor before he withdrew his hand.

Her nails had dug into his arm and shoulder. He kissed her and soothed her with soft caresses.

"That was wonderful," she whispered. "Does it keep getting better each time?"

"Up to a point."

"Do you plan to do this all night?"

He laughed. "I seriously doubt it. Love has made me very noble and chivalrous, but I have my limits."

She regarded him. "I think that two can play this game of yours, David. Would that please you?"

"Very much, if you desire it."

She rose up and pushed his shoulders down on the bed. She gave him a smug little smile full of unwarranted self-confidence. She kissed him fully before moving her hands and her mouth down his chest. He closed his eyes and stroked her back.

"Nay, David. You did not let me touch you, so you cannot touch me."

The luxurious spots of heat she created moved lower. He sensed her pause to consider the situation. Then he felt her turn and draw up her legs and lean against his stomach.

He had taught her to please him with her hands, and her caresses drove him close to delirium. When she paused again he opened his eyes just as she lowered her head.

He knew no thought after that. He looked through a cloud of engulfing sensation and pleasure at the erotic lines of her back and buttocks and the two delicate feet tucked beneath her.

He knew his limits but she did not. As he neared them he reached down and slid his fingers along the cleft of her bottom.

She groaned and shifted and accepted his touch. He rearranged their bodies so that his mouth could reach her. Bracing himself for control, he let them share the ecstatic pleasure a while longer as he brought her as far as she had him, to the very edge. Finally it was too much for them both and she sensed it. She released him and turned toward him and as she did he lifted her body and brought her down straddling his hips.

For an instant she seemed surprised to find herself there. Then wordlessly, instinctively, she rose up and took him into herself.

His sigh met hers in the space between them. She closed her eyes at the sensation, then slowly rose and lowered again.

Passion veiled her eyes when she opened them. She moved again and sighed. "This is incredible, David."

He reached up and caressed her breasts so she could see just how incredible it could be. He rubbed the taut nipples between his fingers. Her head fell back and she lolled sensually into a wonderful rhythm as she repeatedly drew him into her tight warmth and released him. Enhanced by abstinence and love, the pleasure moved him in ways he had never known.

He pulled her down toward him.

"Come up to me. Move forward a bit," he instructed.

She slid up but halted. "I will lose—"

"You will not. Come up to me."

She lowered and he eased her forward until he could take her breast in his mouth. She hovered above him breathlessly, her body barely still joined to his. He felt her grasping to absorb more of him, driving him mad with the mutual caress they created.

"David," she gasped, her body shaking from the combination of tantalizing pleasures at her breast and between her legs. He stroked her back down to its lowest curve and continued to arouse her breasts. He felt the first deep tremor and knew what it meant even if she did not.

"David," she cried again, frantically this time.

He released her and she slammed down on him with a needful cry. Burying her face in his chest, she moved hard again.

"Aye, it can happen thus, too," he reassured her, and

he held her hips firmly and took over and helped her find that different, more elusive fulfillment.

He had never seen a woman reach such a violent and complete release. Wonder, desire, and love echoed through her cries. She kissed him ferociously and gazed into his eyes as her passion peaked and her open acceptance of the magic made the intimacy fuse their souls as it always had. Her whole being seemed to fold in on itself, taking his own essence to its burning center, before flying out in all directions. At the end she rose up in a magnificent display of sensual ecstasy as she cried her abandon. Their mutual fulfillment momentarily obliterated time and space and consciousness.

She collapsed on him and he floated with her in their unity. Her love awed him and filled him with its innocent peace and grace. The hungry and needful response of his own soul astonished him.

Her face lay buried near his neck.

"Do you think anyone heard us?"

"Us?"

She giggled and playfully swatted his chest. "All right. *Me*?"

He thought about the open window and the silent city night. The whole household and half of Caen had probably heard her. So much for pretending that they were not content together.

It would not matter now. If the Comte thought to use her in that way, he would have already come for them both.

"I am sure that no one heard, darling."

She moved and settled down next to him. He had never known such peace and contentment, and he let himself savor it, knowing it would not last long and might never come again.

He probably should have told her everything.

Eventually he would have to. This love would not permit long deceptions, even for her sake.

"Have you ever been there?" she asked. "To Senlis?"

"Twice. The first time some years ago, and then again recently."

"Did you go inside?"

"Aye. The Comte was not there, and I entered as a traveling merchant with luxuries to sell. No one will remember. The vanities absorbed the women, not me."

"Do you want it? Senlis?"

"Who would not?"

She rose up and looked in his eyes. "*You* might not."

All the same, a choice awaited. "It is your fate that I decide as well as my own. I would know your will in this."

"I would have you with me forever, alive and whole. That is all that really matters to me, but I know that you will not make your choice for your own safety, and I will not ask it of you. As to the rest, there is no clear right and wrong here, is there? Both hold some pain and betrayal. England and France both have a claim on you. Both men, Edward and Theobald, deserve your loyalty." She paused, considering the dilemma. "I think that you should choose the life that you were born to live, whichever you think it was."

To the heart of things. Life with her would be fascinating.

"And what about you, Christiana? What about the life that you were born to live?"

She smiled and rested her face against his chest. "I was born to marry a nobleman, David. And you have always been one of the noblest men I have ever known."

CHAPTER 21

CHRISTIANA AWOKE TO an empty bed and the early morning light streaming in the chamber's window. The mellow memories of the night vanished at once. She rose and quickly dressed.

He was meeting with them now. It was being done. She could not pray for one outcome or another, even though she knew which she would prefer. He could give them the port, become the heir to Senlis, and live the life that few men had. Or he could refuse, be deprived of his old life but not given a new one, and maybe be killed. Not much of a choice to her mind, nor, she hoped, to his either. All the same, despite the status of Senlis and all that it entailed, she did not look forward with any enthusiasm to living in that strange place so far from home.

She paced the room but the confined space only increased her worry. She left the chamber and sought the stairs that led to the flat roof of this tall building with its many chambers for sleeping and storage.

Tubs of summer flowers and vines dotted the roof. As

she stepped out onto it she heard the sounds of activity floating up from the city below. The usual drone of commerce and movement had been replaced by a din of wagons and horses and men shouting orders.

David stood by the low wall surrounding the roof, looking down into the city streets to the west. Another man of middle years with a thick build and long brown hair watched beside him.

David turned and noticed her. He held out his hand. "My lord, this is my wife, Christiana Fitzwaryn. This is the Constable d'Eu, darling."

Christiana met the inspecting gaze of the chief military leader of France.

"I am Theobald's cousin, my lady, and so a kin of your husband's." He glanced at David. "The daughter of Hugh Fitzwaryn, no less. You did well for Senlis. Theobald is pleased that your wife brings such blood to the family."

Christiana stepped to the wall beside David. In the streets beyond, she could see the feverish activities of an army preparing to move.

It was done, then. She glanced at David's impassive face.

"My lady, your husband will be staying here in Caen," the constable said.

She looked from one man to the other. Something was wrong. She could feel it.

"Are you saying that I am still a prisoner?" she asked.

"You are free to go. I will arrange an escort to take you to Senlis."

"Then my husband is now a prisoner?"

"A guest. Until the English land. He can join you then. He is not trained in warfare, and this battle is not his."

"I would prefer to stay with my husband."

The constable looked at David. David didn't react at all. The older man smiled. "As you wish," he said, and he turned away and walked across the roof to the stairs.

She waited until he had gone.

"Why must you stay here, David?"

"He does not trust me. He fears that I have lied to them. But your choice to stay with me has reassured him a little."

"But why keep you here if the army moves?"

"Theobald will take the army. He has already left the house. But the constable has decided to remain in Caen with a small force, to be available in case Edward comes a different way. The King's chamberlain is here, too. He agreed that this would be wise."

"And your uncle agreed to this?"

"Even the Comte de Senlis does not stand against the constable and chamberlain of France. Theobald wanted me with him, so that I could see the glorious French victory that I have helped bring about. The constable insisted that I stay with him here, however, so that he would have me at his disposal if I betrayed them in some way. He thinks that I might steal away from the army during its march, or that, if it came to it, Theobald would not take vengeance on his heir." He smiled. "The constable does not know his cousin very well."

He embraced her and placed his cheek against her hair. He still looked down into the city. She felt conflicting emotions in him and wished that she could say something to comfort him. This decision had not been an easy one, no matter what prize it brought.

"Why doesn't the constable trust you? Surely the logic of your choice should be clear to him. It is the decision any man would have made, and there will even be English knights and lords who recognize the fairness of it."

"He explained it to me just now. Almost apologized. It seems that if I were a knight, he would have no doubts about me. It is the fact that I am a merchant, and a London merchant at that, which gives him pause."

"That is outrageous. Does he think merchants less honorable?"

"Undoubtedly, as all do. Still, in a way, he credits me with more rather than less honor. He told me that he knows burghers, and has met many from London. He knows that we owe our first loyalty to the city itself. He does not claim to understand men who give their fealty to a place rather than a man, but he knows it is so with us and he has seen its power. He could accept that I would betray Edward, or even the realm, but not London. And so, while he and the chamberlain agreed with Theobald that the army should move with speed, the constable will stay here to organize a defense if I lied to them."

A steady stream of knights and mounted soldiers streamed across the gate bridge from the other side of the river. They moved through the city toward its southern edges. Foot soldiers, carts, and workers plodded with them. The streets looked like colorful, moving rivers.

David's gaze followed the lines. "I should have insisted that you go to Senlis, but I feared never getting you out later. Theobald can be ruthless when angered, I suspect. Still, it would have been safer for you. The constable assured your safety, but there are limits to his protection."

"What are you saying, David? Do you think that Edward has indeed changed his plans and that the constable will blame you in some way?"

He pushed away from the wall and walked across to the southern view with his arm around her shoulders. In the distance, past the lower rooftops, they could see the field on which the army gathered. At the front, with gold and blue banners, no more than dots to their eyes, sat three men on horseback.

"Theobald?" she asked.

He nodded. "There are five thousand here with him. Others will join the army as they pass south."

"They go to Bordeaux, then?" she asked, even though the answer was obvious. She needed to hear it said, however, so that she could begin reconciling herself to the future he had chosen for them.

She wished that she felt some joy, but her stomach churned in an odd way. She thought about his question last night before they slept, and of her response.

He had misunderstood. She had sought to assure him that she loved him no matter what his degree, and had found him noble even before she learned about his father.

He has done this in large part for me, she realized. *To give me back the life which this marriage took from me.*

The Comte and Duke began to ride. The thick, undisciplined mass of the army oozed after them.

"Aye, they go to Bordeaux," he confirmed.

He wore a peculiar expression on his face. His eyes narrowed on the disappearing blue banners. "Edward, however, does not."

She gaped at him. His gaze never left the southern field.

"I went to Edward before Catherine did. I told him everything, and offered to finish the game as I had started it. I would give them one port, and our army would arrive at another one. I pressed for him to consider Normandy, since half the French army was already in the south and if I failed he would still only face an inferior host. His experience trying to sail to Bordeaux had already inclined him to change plans, and a Norman knight has been at court these last months, also telling him about Normandy's unwalled towns and clear roads."

She glanced in the direction of his gaze. She could still see reflections off the Comte's armor.

"Edward will debark in Normandy? Here on the northern coast?" Tremendous relief swept her, but with it came a sickening fear for David and what he now faced.

"Assuming that he doesn't get clever at the last moment, which is entirely possible. Or that he doesn't grow to doubt me. Catherine probably told lurid tales of my duplicity, but I am counting on Edward knowing what he has in her. Godefrey, the Norman knight, and I were able to give him three possible ports, small and out of the way. He will use the one which the winds favor."

"Does the King know about Senlis and what you were offered? If he does, he may well doubt you. He will not understand your choice."

"I told him everything. I could not be sure that Lady Catherine was involved in your disappearance, or that she planned to betray me, but I suspected it. I could not be sure that she remained ignorant of my relationship with the Comte. It was well that I spoke frankly with Edward. When I finally got a hold of Frans, I had my suspicions confirmed."

"So you were never in danger in England? And you can return?" *Assuming that he could get out of Caen alive.*

"Aye."

"Still, having convinced Edward on Normandy, you might have betrayed him. When did you decide what to do?"

He still looked to the flow of the army. "Early this morning. Knight or merchant, you said. I took you at your word."

"And if I had spoken differently? If I had said that I wanted to be the wife of a comte?"

"I would have given it to you, and learned to live with my conscience." He looked down and smiled. "I suspect that I could have rationalized it. The power and luxury of Senlis can probably obscure any guilt. Such a life has its appeal. I will not pretend that I was not tempted."

She embraced him tightly. "You have sacrificed much for your city and your King, David. Edward owes you much."

"He owes me nothing, Christiana. He gave you to me. The debt is all mine."

His gaze had returned to the distant field. The Comte was barely visible now. She saw that peculiar expression on his face again, and a flicker of yearning pass through those eyes.

He had executed a brilliant victory, a daring strategy, a magnificent game, but no triumph showed in him. She doubted his subdued reaction had anything to do with the danger he now faced. She snuggled closer under his arm and tried to comfort him.

"In time he will understand, David. He knows about honor and the hard choices it gives a man. He may not forgive you, but he will understand."

He tensed at this mention of the Comte and the blood ties which he had betrayed.

She tried again. "David, I know there is pain here. He is your uncle . . ."

His fingers came to rest on her lips, silencing her. "I should have told you last night," he said. "I feared your reaction to the truth, and also did not know if he would try to learn what you knew. I have spent the last hour wondering if I would ever tell you."

She frowned in confusion. She searched his face for some explanation.

"Theobald is not my uncle, Christiana."

His words stunned her. It took a few moments for the full implication to penetrate her dazed mind.

"Are you that clever, David?" That audacious? You found a man whom you resembled in some way and plotted this elaborate scheme? You fed me this story so that I could convincingly support you if I was questioned?"

That peculiar, yearning expression passed over him again.

He shook his head. "It is much worse than that, my girl." He glanced to the speck of a man being swallowed by sunlight and haze. "Theobald is not my uncle. He is my father."

Christiana did not know how long they stood there with his words hanging in the air, but when he spoke again the straggling ends of the army were passing out of the city.

"He did not even remember her name."

They still stood near the roof wall. He rested his arms against it and he looked south, but at nothing in particular now.

"He seduced her, took her love, left her with child, and destroyed her life. I use her name, but it meant nothing to him. Both he and Honoré had been to London several times as young men, and he assumed that I was the product of one of his brother's sins. It was the final mockery of Joanna's timeless trust."

She spoke to comfort him more than defend Theobald. "It was thirty years ago. When you are fifty-five, do you think that you will remember the name of every woman you bedded?"

"Aye. Every one."

"Perhaps only because he did not."

He appeared not to hear. "There had been two rings, one gray and one pink. He assumed that I had Honoré's, the gray one, and never asked to see it. At Hampstead, he looked at me and saw only his brother."

"He knew his brother's face better than his own. How often do we see clear reflections of ourselves in glass and metal?"

"She meant nothing to him. She was merely a beautiful girl with whom he amused himself for a short while. A merchant's daughter who counted for nothing in the life of a son of Senlis."

She didn't know what else to say. He had watched Joanna's misery and patience. He had lived in the shadow of her disillusionment. He had watched the master whom he admired love her in vain. She doubted that his anger at Theobald could be assuaged by words.

"Why didn't you tell him the truth? Why let him think you are his nephew?"

"At Hampstead, when I realized his mistake, it stunned me. Otherwise, my plan had unfolded perfectly. I told myself at the time that correcting him might complicate things. For all I knew, he might resent the sudden appearance of a bastard son, or even suspect that I sought revenge against him. But in truth, it was my own resolve that I questioned. Meeting him was much harder than I thought it would be. I had fully intended to despise him. And then, there he was, and suddenly a hundred unspoken questions that I had carried in my soul all of my life were answered. The answers were mainly unpleasant, but at least I had them." He smiled ruefully. "The connection, the familiarity, was immediate. Unexpected and astounding. If he had known me for his own, and appealed to me father to son, I do not know what I would have done. So, I let him think otherwise."

He did not have to tell her this. She would have never known or suspected.

"So, Christiana. You are married to a man who lured his own father into disrepute and betrayed him. It is a serious crime in any family, especially noble ones."

He searched her eyes for disapproval or disappointment. She knew that he found only understanding and love.

She thought about the yearning she had seen in him, and her heart swelled with sympathy. "Do you regret it? As you watch him ride off, would you change things?"

"Only for you would I have done it differently and changed course. Never for him. I wish that I could say that I regret having started this, but I do not. I am what I am, my girl, and a part of me, the Senlis part, is glad that I have revenged Joanna a little."

"Do you hate your father, David?"

He smiled and shook his head. "It would be like hating myself. But I hold no love for him either. Theobald may have given me life, but the only father I ever knew and loved was David Constantyn."

He took her hand and eased away from the wall.

"What now, David?"

He glanced around the roof, as if inspecting it. "Now I see to your safety." He grinned down at her. "The danger that I face from the Comte de Senlis and the Constable d'Eu is nothing compared to what Morvan Fitzwaryn will do if I let anything happen to you. I think that you should ask the lovely Heloise to show me her house. All of it. Tell her that I am curious to see how Caen's wealthiest burghers live."

David and Christiana had their tour. David peered around without subtlety and effused compliments, and Heloise beamed with pride at the appreciation of this handsome London merchant. Christiana thought that he overdid it somewhat, but his praise dragged the afternoon out and gave him the opportunity to examine every chamber and storage room, every window and stable. He seemed especially fascinated with an attic at the top of the main building. Loaded with cloth and mercery, it could only be reached by a narrow flight of steps angling along the inner wall.

They finally left Heloise at the hall and strolled into the garden.

"There does not appear to be any way out except the front gate, short of getting a ladder to the wall," David said.

"Is that what you looked for? I could have told you that. There is one way, but you will need rope." She began angling him in the direction of the tree. She smiled at this simple solution. David would escape, she would join him, and then . . . what? A run to safety, to Edward and his army. How long was the Comte's reach if he sought revenge? Perhaps they would leave both England and France behind and go to Genoa.

As they neared the garden's corner, her heart fell. Where the tall strong oak had stood, they found only its stump.

"I went out this way a week before you came," she explained. "Theobald caught me. He must have ordered it cut after that."

"It doesn't matter. I doubt that we would have made it through the bridge gate."

She sought the comfort of his arms.

"How long?" she asked, bravely broaching the subject that she had avoided. "When does Edward land?"

"I calculate five days, maybe six."

"You must get away. You cannot be here when they

find out. Tonight, I will distract the guards at the front gate and you—"

"I do not leave without you."

"Then we must find a way," she cried desperately.

"If there is one, I will find it. But I think that it is out of our hands. Who knows? When the English army begins ravaging Normandy, the constable and chamberlain may be so busy organizing the defense that they will forget about me."

He said it so lightly that she had to smile. But she didn't believe that would happen, and she knew that he didn't either.

When she awoke to an empty bed the Wednesday morning after the army departed, she threw on a robe and went in search of him. She found him on the roof, gazing toward the west. Dawn's light had just broken, and the city still appeared as gray forms below them. Despite the stillness, the air seemed laden with a strange fullness, as if a storm brewed somewhere beyond the clear horizon.

She drifted up beside him. His blue eyes glanced at her, then returned to their examination of the field beyond the river.

"Look there," he said. "Approaching the bridge."

She strained to see. The light was growing and a large shadow on the field moved down the far bank of the river. She watched and the shadow broke into pieces and then the pieces became people. Hundreds of them.

They moved quickly, carrying sacks and leading animals. The sun began to rise and she saw that the crowd included women and children. They poured through the buildings across the river, past the abbeys built by William the Conqueror and his wife Matilda, and then began massing at the far end of the bridge, shouting for entry to the city.

"Who are they?"

"Peasants. Burghers. Priests. They are refugees, fleeing Edward's army."

Additional guards ran to reinforce the watch at the bridge gate. The mob of refugees coalesced and their shouts rose. On the near side of the river, two men mounted horses and began riding through the deserted streets toward the mayor's house.

"Is the army nearby?" she asked.

"I would guess only hours away."

"It comes here? To Caen? You might have told me, David. I would not have worried so much."

"I could not be sure. In April, by accident, I found a port on the Cotentin peninsula just to the west. Sieg and I waited there for the English ships to pass before I met with Theobald here in Caen. During the storm, a merchant ship was pushed inland toward the coastal town where we waited. It came within one hundred yards of the coast and did not run aground. The sea must have shifted the coast over the years and the port gotten deeper. Perfect for the army's debarking. Still, the winds may have taken Edward further east to one of the other ports I had found earlier."

"You did not want to give me false hopes," she said.

"I did not want to give you more worry, darling."

"Worry? This is good news! Edward will obtain your release. The flower of English chivalry comes to save you," she said, smiling.

"If the city surrenders, it may happen that way."

"Of course the city will surrender. There is no choice."

"London would not surrender."

"*London has walls.*"

"I hope that you are right."

"What is it, David? What worries you?"

But before he could reply, the answer appeared on the roof in the persons of two knights from the constable's retinue.

CHAPTER 22

DAVID PACED AROUND the small storage chamber. The space reeked of herring from the barrels stacked against one wall. A small candle lit the windowless cell, and he tried to judge the time passing by its slowly diminishing length.

He was fortunate to still be alive. Upon confronting him in the hall about his betrayal, the constable had barely resisted cutting him down with his sword. The panic and confusion brought on by the English army's approach had saved his life. The hall had been in an uproar as the constable and chamberlain tried to organize a defense of the city while their squires strapped on their armor. Word had been sent east and south, calling back Theobald's army and rousing the general population to gather and fight this invasion. David had been imprisoned in this chamber to await hanging after the more pressing threat had been defeated.

Before being led away, he had tried to reason with the constable and chamberlain and convince them not to resist Edward. He had told them that the English army numbered at least twenty thousand, while the constable had at best three hundred men still in Caen. He had reminded them that surrender would spare the people of the city and only mean the loss of property. Only the mayor had listened, but the decision had not been his. The French king had told the Constable d'Eu to stop Edward, and the constable intended to fight for the honor of France despite the odds. Caen would not surrender or ask for terms.

He strained to hear the sounds leaking through the thick cellar wall. The house had quieted and the more distant activity only came to him as a dull rumble. The real battle would be fought at the gate bridge. If the city could retain control of that single access, the river would prove more formidable than any wall.

For Christiana's sake, he hoped that the gate bridge held. If the city fell, she would not be safe from those English soldiers as they pillaged this rich town. He doubted that they would listen to her claims of being English, just as they would not listen to him when they broke into this storage room to loot the goods that it contained. He grimaced at the irony. He would undoubtedly die today, but if he lived long enough to hang, if Edward failed to take this city, at least Christiana would be safe.

He pounded his fist into the wall in furious frustration that he could not help her. She had been sent to Heloise and the other women immediately upon his arrest. She had fought the knights who pulled her away. Those knights had not returned, and he prayed that they guarded the chamber in which the women waited. It would be some protection, at least.

He lifted the candle and reexamined his tiny prison. He wished it contained other than dried herring, and not just because of the smell. Whoever went to the trouble to break down this door would probably kill him out of resentment at finding nothing of value for their time and labor.

As if echoing his thoughts, a sound at the door claimed his attention. Not the crash of an ax or battering ram, though. The more subtle tone of metal on metal.

Perhaps Edward had decided to move on. Maybe it would be hanging after all. He moved to the far wall and watched the door ease open.

At the threshold, her face pale like a ghost's, appeared a haggard Heloise. Christiana stood behind her holding his long steel dagger at the blond woman's throat.

"She knew it was the only sensible thing to do, David, but she is one of those women who only obeys her husband, so I had to encourage her," Christiana said. She replaced the dagger into the sheath hanging from her waist.

Heloise looked ready to faint. She leaned against the wall for support.

"What has happened?" he asked.

"The bridge has been taken," Christiana explained. Her own face was drawn with fear that she tried bravely to hide. "The knights protecting us left long ago, and I have been watching from the roof. Our army is all over the town, like a mob. It is as you said. In victory they are taking all that they can move. The people are throwing benches and rocks down on them from the roofs, and that is slowing their progress, but not by much."

"No one is here," Heloise cried. "The gate is guarded only by some grooms and servants. When the bridge fell, the soldiers all left, some to fight in the streets, others to run."

Christiana moved up close to him and spoke lowly. "She wanted to take her daughters and run, too, but I convinced her that she was better behind these walls than in the city. They are not castle walls, and will not stop the army long, but the soldiers are killing all they meet. Even from the roof I could see many bodies fall."

He looked in her eyes and read her deep realization of the danger which she faced. He turned to Heloise.

"It is well that you released me, madame," he said soothingly. "Fortune has always smiled on me. Perhaps she will be kind today as well." He eased the woman away from the wall. "Let us go and assess our situation."

Bad news awaited in the courtyard. The servants guarding the gate had fled, and the entry stood open to the street. In the distance they could hear the screams of a city being sacked.

He ran over to close and bar the gate. A group of six women surged in just as he arrived. They looked to be burghers's wives and they threw themselves at Heloise.

"That devil of an English king has ordered everyone put to the sword," one of them cried. "They are stripping the bodies of their garments and cutting off fingers to get the rings. They are raping the women before slitting their throats."

The other women joined in with hysterical descriptions of the horrors they had seen. David barred the gate and looked around the courtyard. Christiana was right. These were not castle walls and they marked the house as that of a wealthy merchant. Eventually some soldiers would decide to batter down the gate or scale their heights. But they were better off here than outside in the city.

Christiana stood to the side, listening to the tales of mutilation and destruction with an ashen face. The sounds of the pillaging army gradually moved closer.

He walked over and embraced her. "Do you remember the attic storage above the bedchambers? The one reached by the narrow stairs? Take them there."

"And you?"

"I will join you shortly. It appears that I will need that armor after all. I never thought to wear it against Englishmen. It appears that my father will have his way in the end. It is an ironic justice that my betrayal of him has put you in such danger."

"Do not blame yourself for this. You did not bring me here," she said, instinctively knowing the guilt that wanted to overwhelm him.

"All the same, you are here." He hesitated, not wanting to speak of the horror that threatened. "If they come, let them know who you are. Speak only English. Claim the protection of your brother and the King."

"It will not matter," she said, turning to the knot of women nearby. "I have seen it before. At Harclow. It had begun before we left. My brother accepted defeat and possible death to save my mother from what we face today."

She approached the women and spoke to them. Grateful to have some instruction that at least offered hope, they fell in around her as she led the way to the tall building and the attic chamber.

David followed, but detoured to the room he and Christiana had shared. He slipped the breastplate of his armor over his shoulders and then lifted the pieces for his arms. He considered whether, with weapons and armor, he would be able to get Christiana alone out through the city streets. He shook his head. He had no jerkin that identified him as part of an English baron's retinue, and his shield bore no arms that these soldiers would recognize. They would think him French. In any case, he did not have it in him to abandon those other women and girls, nor would Christiana want him to. In death at least he could be the husband she deserved. Hoisting his sword with the other hand, he made his way to the stairway and the hiding women.

Christiana had already set the women to work. Lengths of cloth stretched on the floor, and they used his dagger to slice off sections of it.

"What are you doing?" he asked, setting down the armor.

"Banners," she said. "The white and green of Harclow. Thomas Holland's colors, and those of Chandros and Beauchamp. We will hang them from the windows. Who knows, it may attract someone who can help us."

She looked at the armor and stepped close. "I will do it." Her fingers began working the straps and buckles.

It took a long while to fit all of the armor, and he didn't even have the leg pieces. When they were done, she unstrapped the sheath from her waist and handed it to him, then retrieved the dagger from the women.

He looked a moment at the long length of sharp steel. Their eyes met.

"It will do me no good against armed men," she said, slipping it into its sheath on his hip. "And I am not brave enough to use it on the others and myself."

The women opened the windows and slid out the banners. The summer breeze carried the sounds of screaming death. As they closed the windows to secure the cloth, a crash against the gate thundered into the attic space. The noise jolted everyone into utter silence.

The air in the chamber smelled sour from the fear pouring out of its occupants. David glanced at the eight women and three girls. Their faces were barely visible in the room darkened now by the cloth at the windows. He drew Christiana aside and turned his back on the others.

He held her face with his hands and closed his eyes to savor the delicate softness of her lips. An aching tenderness flooded him, and her palpable fear tore his heart. "When I go to Genoa this fall, you will come with me," he said. "After this, crossing the Alps will seem a minor thing.

We will spend the cold months in Italy and travel down to Florence and Rome."

"I would like that," she whispered. "Perhaps we can even cross the sea to a Saracen land, and make love in a desert tent."

He kissed her closed eyes and tasted the salty tears welling in them.

Unmistakable sounds of the gate giving way pounded into the chamber.

"Look at me, Christiana," he said. Her lids lifted slowly and he gazed into those liquid diamonds and let her see his soul's love for her. She smiled bravely and sorrowfully and stretched up to kiss him.

The shouts and clamoring of men pouring into the courtyard bounced around them. Christiana lifted his sword and handed it to him. Behind him the attic chamber held complete silence. The women were beyond hysteria. Heloise's young daughters stared at him with wide-eyed solemnity.

With one last long look at his beautiful wife, he opened the door and took a position at the top of the narrow stairs.

The primitive noise of rampage and looting filled the building. David stood tensely at his post, his sword resting against the wall beside him, and waited for the soldiers to eventually find the passage that led to these steps and this attic.

The door behind him had been closed, but it could not be barred from the inside. Once he fell, there would be no protection for Christiana and the others.

The bedchambers and hall and lower storage rooms had kept them occupied for at least an hour now. It would not be long.

If he was fortunate, the men who had broken in might have closed the gate to others in order to keep the rich booty of the mayor's house for themselves and there might not be too many. If he was really fortunate, there would be no archers among them. If Fortune truly favored him, someone in authority might eventually arrive to secure the mayor's house for the King's pleasure and disposal.

He wondered if there were knights amongst them, and if appeals to chivalry would do any good.

He could not see the bottom of the stairs, for they rose up the side of the building to a landing before angling along the back wall to him. But he heard the scurrying below, and a man's shout to his friends when he discovered them.

They mounted the steps quickly, full of good cheer while they traded descriptions of the garments and jewelry and silver which they had already procured. He could tell that they were not knights from their speech. He waited.

Six men turned the corner of the landing. They began filing up. The first had reached the seventh step from the top when they finally noticed him. Six heads peered up in surprise.

"Who the hell are you?" the lead man barked.

"An Englishman like yourselves. A Londoner. A merchant."

"You don't look like a merchant."

"None of us looks or acts like ourself today. War does that."

They stretched and craned to see around each other.

"What is behind that door, merchant?" one of them yelled.

"Cloth. Ordinary and not of much value."

"He's lying," the leader said. "These stairs are hidden. This is the chamber with the spices and gold."

"I swear that neither spices nor gold are in this room."

"Step aside and let us see."

"Nay."

More footfalls on the steps. More faces joining the others. The line turned the corner and out of sight. David eyed the long daggers and swords while the word was passed that gold and spices awaited above.

The closest men eyed him hard, measuring him, trying to decide if the armor indicated superior skill. The narrow steps meant that they could not rush him all at once and the first to come might well die.

The long row began jostling around. A red head moved through them, pushing upward. "Stand aside!" a young voice commanded.

The others squeezed over and let the young man pass. He eased up next to the front man. A squire, David guessed from his youth and livery. Maybe twenty years old. Separated from his lord and enjoying his power and status in the hell that Caen had become.

The squire glanced to David's sword and unsheathed his own.

"We opened this gate. The spoils are ours," he said.

"Since I stand on the top step, it is clear that I arrived before you," David replied.

Agitated complaints and curses rumbled up the stairs. The men in the rear began calling for David to be dispatched so they could get to the gold.

David stared at the squire and the man beside him. The shouts rose and filled the stairway. Both men grew hard faced as their comrades urged them to action. He watched and waited, reading their resolve, bracing himself for the attack.

It will be the young one, he thought regretfully.

The red head suddenly surged upward. The long sword rose. David's hand went to his hip. Before the youth had climbed two steps he jerked upright. His shocked eyes glanced down at the steel dagger embedded in his throat. Then the body crumbled, blocking the stairs.

The mob of soldiers took a collective pause, and then the shouts and curses resumed at a louder, more insistent level. David reached for his sword.

He noticed an inexorable crowding forward, as if more men had joined the others and all pressed upward. The pressure on those in front became physical as well as vocal. Hands reached out and pushed the squire out of the way. The acrid smell of unleashed bloodlust permeated the closed space. He let the ruthless blood of Senlis flow to give him its cold strength.

And then, suddenly, silence began rolling up from the rear. The men on the landing looked behind them and then at each other. Bodies crushed against the walls, out of the way.

The tall, dark-haired figure of a knight wearing the King's livery stepped up into view.

Dark fiery eyes looked at David and flashed amusement and surprise. Sir Morvan waited calmly and silently for the soldiers above him to realize he wanted to pass. They jostled each other and pointed and cleared a path for him. He slowly mounted the steps until he came to the fallen squire. Glancing at David, he casually reached down and withdrew the dagger and blood began pouring from the wound. He wiped the weapon on his jerkin and joined David in front of the door.

"That is the problem with a dagger," he said lightly as he handed it over. "Once you have thrown it, you don't have a weapon anymore." His gaze raked over David's armor. "Nice steel. German?"

"Flemish."

"Aren't you supposed to be in England? Northumberland, wasn't it?"

"Other business led me here."

"And my sister?"

"I found her. Not with Percy."

Several of the men began muttering loudly about knights always taking the best portions for themselves. Morvan all but yawned as he unsheathed his sword. The grumbling stopped.

"You are in a bad position here," he observed.

"Aye. It is well that you arrived."

Morvan shrugged. "Once the bridge fell, the fun was over. Rape and looting don't appeal to me, so I decided to see about this house that flew the colors of Harclow." He glanced back at the door. "Whatever you guard, it is not worth it. Step aside and let these men have it. They cannot be controlled once they have smelled spoils and tasted blood. Thomas Holland and I have spent the last hours trying to keep women and children from being murdered or defiled."

"I cannot step aside."

"It is just a matter of time before they find an archer. Is it truly gold as they said below?"

David shook his head and gestured to the door. Morvan opened it a crack, peered inside, and stiffened. He frowned and peered in again. Hot eyes turned on David as he closed the door. "Tell me that wasn't my sister who I just saw among those women."

"If you insist. It wasn't your sister."

Morvan snarled, opened the door once more, then slammed it shut. "Hell's teeth. What is she doing here?"

"Visiting friends of mine in this city. Whoever expected our army to come and sack it?"

"Once I get her out of here, I am going to kill you."

"If you can get her out of here, you may do so." He gestured to the men. Impatient complaints and mumbling had resumed, and he suspected that plans were being laid. "How many are there?"

Morvan shrugged. "Twenty. Thirty."

"Which is it? I would say it makes a difference."

Morvan smiled wryly. "Hardly. Twenty against two or thirty against two is equally hopeless. I am damn good, David, but not that good, and my King's livery will only deter them for a while longer." All the same, he turned to the stairs and took a battle stance. With an exasperated sigh he reached over to David's sword hand and jerked it so the weapon pointed up rather than down. "Considering how you handle a sword, it is more like twenty or thirty against one and a half. You'd best stay on my right side. That is where we put the young squires."

Just then a quake shook the stairway. It repeated over and over. A series of grunts accompanied it, and the men on the lower landing looked behind themselves wide-eyed and then tried to melt into the wall. A massive body stepped up and a craggy face grinned at David.

"I correct myself," Morvan said dryly. "Thirty against ten."

"*Ja*, but it was hell finding you, David," Sieg said as he climbed toward them. Two men made the mistake of not peeling away quickly enough. Sieg calmly lifted them by their necks, crashed their heads together, and let them drop. "First I went to that castle across the river, but that bishop holding it has it sealed as tight as a coffin. I tried the Guildhall where the King has set up, then figured, hell, maybe they had her here at the mayor's house."

Indignation at Sieg's handling had made several men brave. Glinting knives were brandished behind him. Without missing a step, he reached back with his huge hand, grabbed the nearest fool, and smashed the man's head into the stone wall.

"Is Oliver with you?" David asked as Sieg joined them.

The Swede laughed and drew his sword to menace the threats forming below. His face positively glowed at the prospect of fighting all of these men. "I lost him in the streets. All these houses open and all these goods for the taking got the better of him. Said how it was a pity you weren't with him. Like old times, he said."

Morvan raised an eyebrow at this conversation. David smiled and shrugged.

"We still need some help to move these women out," Morvan said. "Now that your man is here, I will go and fetch some. Thomas should be nearby, and some others. You might cover my back with that dagger, David."

He wore a more dangerous expression leaving than he had when he came. No one challenged him.

"Did any messengers get through to warn the Comte?" David asked when Morvan had gone.

"Nay. Oliver and I stayed a few miles out on the road south as you said. They came right to us. When the King sent some men to block the news from following the French army, we finally left and gave the messengers to them. The Comte won't hear of Edward's landing for many days now." He gestured with his sword. "I clear these men out now."

"Try not to kill them all. They are supposed to be on our side."

Sieg descended two steps so that he could stretch to his fullest height. He raised his dagger in his left hand and his sword in his right, glared at the men facing him, and let loose a primitive Viking war cry.

The realization that a King's knight went to get more help had already subdued the soldiers. Sieg's display of strength thoroughly discouraged most of them. Heads began bobbing and shifting as men turned and tried to squeeze down the stairs.

By the time Morvan returned with Thomas Holland and two other friends, most of the soldiers had melted away. Their arrival took care of the rest.

David opened the door and led the way into the attic.

A hysteria of relief swept the women when they saw rescue walk through the door. Several began wailing with delayed shock. Christiana ran into David's arms.

"Thank God you are whole! You saved us all, David!"

"It was your banner that did it, darling. It seems that sacking cities bores your brother, and he came to investigate your colors."

She turned with surprise to the four knights. "Morvan!" she cried. "Thomas!"

Morvan sidled over and accepted his sister's embrace. He glanced over her shoulder dangerously at David. Christiana pulled back in time to see the look.

"Don't you dare, Morvan. He saved me, and all of the others here. The French knights and soldiers abandoned us and he put his own life between us and danger. You could not have done better."

Morvan's expression softened as he looked at his sister. "If that is how you say it was, then I will not kill him this time."

Thomas Holland walked over. "There is nothing for it but to take them all to Edward. Nowhere else will be safe. But it is some ways, and the city . . ."

David read his expression and concern. "We will keep them between us. Christiana, gather the women and tell them what we will be doing. Tell them to look to the ground as we move."

She nodded and went over to Heloise and her daughters first. David gestured for Sieg. "You will carry the youngest one," he said. "Do not let her see the bodies."

While his wife explained to the other women, David

approached Heloise. She hadn't moved since they entered, and she sat on a stack of cloth looking spent and numb. Her hands clasped something. A faint glitter dangled down her skirt.

She looked up at him. Her hands opened to reveal a gold and emerald necklace. "I thought maybe, if it came to it, I could buy my daughters' safety."

"They will be secure now, madame. I am sure that your husband is safe as well. He will probably be taken to England to await ransom like the rest of the wealthy burghers, but there is no profit in killing such men."

She looked down on the necklace. "Please accept it. To repay you for my husband's role in taking your wife, and for your help here today."

He had no trouble calculating the value of the gold and emeralds. But his role in the day's events was not nearly so chivalrous as the woman assumed, and he would not profit from them. "It was the arrival of my wife's brother that saved you. If you wish to express gratitude, show it to him." He lifted her to her feet. "We must go now. Follow the instructions my wife gave you."

The men led the ladies down the steep steps. In the courtyard they all drew their swords. Sieg had convinced the youngest girl to let him bind her eyes, and he lifted her up while she clung to him. David placed his left arm around Christiana. Then they began walking the women through the hell of death and destruction that had once been the great city of Caen.

Edward sat in the Guildhall, surrounded by clerks who carefully listed ownership of the spoils to be sent back to England. The arriving pageant of knights and women silenced the chamber. Along the way, other desperate women had attached themselves to the group, and

Thomas Holland had even broken away to rescue several. Twenty women marched in on the King, flanked by sword-bearing knights.

Whatever inclinations Edward might have had regarding the disposal of these females became irrelevant. In the face of his young knights, he had no choice but to display the chivalry which he had always celebrated in his court. He formally extended his protection to them and had them sent to another chamber for safety.

David turned to go with Christiana, but the King gestured for him to stay. He dismissed the men around him and faced David over a table strewn with maps, grinning broadly.

"A splendid plan, David! God, what a victory!"

David thought of the hundreds of bodies they had just passed. People of all ages and degrees, butchered and stripped naked. The streets were covered with blood.

"Is it true that you ordered everyone put to the sword?"

Edward scowled. "It was my right when they did not surrender, and they knew it. Hundreds of our men died from their resistance. Not just at the bridge, but in the streets. Those damn stones and benches . . . I have rescinded the order, however. Hell, they should have yielded."

When faced with twenty thousand, they should have. But London would not have yielded, David thought. *Nor would you have wanted her to.*

Edward waved off the destruction of Caen like so much flotsam of war. He beamed with delight and pointed to the map on the table. "We will be clear all the way to Paris. Their army cannot return in time and none will stop us now. No sieges will delay us once word of Caen spreads." He frowned a little. "Do you know the river

Somme, David? It worries me. We could find ourselves
trapped between it and the Seine, and there appear to be
no crossings except a few bridges. Damn, I should have
had you make this map as well. Yours are far better."

David walked over to procure a quill from a clerk. He
returned and bent to the map, and drew two lines across
the river. "Here. You can ford the river, but the water
moves like a tide, so you must cross when it is low."

Edward rubbed his hands together. "Splendid. We
have the constable and chamberlain, you know. Rich ran-
soms there. I am sending them and the other hostages
downriver in the morning, along with the spoils. Shipfuls
of it. By the way, where are those weapons?"

"Nearby in the town of Bayeaux."

"Excellent. We will be going there next."

"My man will come and show you their location."

"Not you? You must join us. This will be a glorious
campaign."

"My role is over. I would like to return to London
with my wife."

Edward regarded him, and a different expression
replaced his glee. "You sacrificed much to remain loyal to
me, David. I do not forget such things. During the last
two days I have been knighting men whom I never met
before. Let us do it now. Take the place assured by your
blood and earned by your loyalty."

"I am honored by the offer, but I prefer that you did
not."

Edward looked a little annoyed. David smiled amiably. "I do request some other favors from you, however,
if you feel moved to grant them."

The King's eyebrows rose.

"When I return to London, I will bring your treasurer
one third of the price of the license which you granted me.

The next third will come in two years, and the rest four years hence, as I first suggested."

"You have already paid . . ."

"Nay. That was the bride price for Christiana. I wish to turn that story into the truth, and I ask that you never reveal our original bargain. She is never to know."

Edward laughed. "The girl has won your heart, has she? Well, I would be fool to turn down another thousand pounds. It will be as you request. And the other favors?"

"I ask that you remember your oath to help reclaim Harclow, and aid her brother as you can when the time comes."

Edward looked down thoughtfully before nodding.

"Lady Catherine must be removed from London," David added. "She knows too much, and my continued value to you, should you require me, will be compromised by her."

Edward grinned. "I wish you could have been there when she came to tell her tale. I let her spin on and on. A clever woman, I suspect. I've never much cared for clever women. I have already sent her to Castle Rising to attend on my mother. She will be held in close confinement with her there. Those two can drive each other mad with their schemes. The merchant, Frans, is enjoying less comfortable accommodations until I return and he is ransomed. The disadvantages of being a commoner."

"I would like Christiana and myself to go downriver with your people in the morning."

"Of course. I will give you some documents to bring back. We found written plans for the invasion of Southampton. I will have the priests read it from the pulpits so the people know how close England came to seeing French troops on her soil."

The Earl of Warwick entered then, and Edward turned to greet him with a new spurt of excitement. David took his leave and made his way to the chamber which held the women. Sieg waited outside its door.

"You will go to Bayeaux with the King before heading south," David explained.

"*Ja.* You want me to show him where the gonnes are?"

David nodded. He reached into his pourpoint and withdrew some folded parchments. "Here is Theobald's recognition and the French king's permission for my succession at Senlis. You already have the ring and the drawing. Wait until he has already learned of my betrayal. You will not be safe if you bring that news. You may not be safe in any case once he sees that the ring's stone is pink, and is his and not his brother's."

"I know what to do."

"Will you come back to London afterward? Today you more than repaid that debt you always claim you owe."

"Hardly repaid, David. Those Mamluks were set to kill me. If you hadn't planned that escape . . ."

"Morvan and I could not have held them off today."

"*Ja,* well, I may join this war for a while. When the French finally catch this army, the battle should be wonderful. I will send word to you if I don't return by fall."

David looked to the documents held in the massive hand. "Be careful, my friend. In this one thing, I cannot guess how he will react."

CHAPTER 23

MEN CROWDED THE docks, carrying looted goods to the waiting boats. The spoils had been listed and assessed, and now it all headed back to England.

David stood amidst the fruits of war stacked on one of the piers. A river breeze offered some refreshment from the stench of death hanging over the city. An open box of silver plates glittered ten paces away in the summer heat.

He watched as Christiana walked down the dock to meet her brother. He could tell that this leave-taking weighed heavily on her. She had seen far too much of war's ruthlessness last night, and knew that Morvan might not survive this campaign.

David could not avoid contemplating the implications of that. He did not even try to. The son of Senlis was incapable of ignoring the fact that it was in his interest to have Morvan Fitzwaryn never return to England.

For with Morvan gone, Christiana became the heir of Harclow, and one day Edward would indeed reclaim the lands in the name of his dead friend Hugh Fitzwaryn.

With Morvan gone, David de Abyndon, bastard son of the noble Theobald of Senlis, would become the lord of Harclow as Christiana's husband.

Being an English knight was one thing, being an English baron was quite another.

But in truth, the land and status were the least of it. The merchant in him knew the real value of Harclow. He had been there, just as he had been to most of the estates along the Scottish border. He alone knew that in the hills of Harclow and other Cumbrian lands there were many caves, ancient caves, in which animals had lived since time began. And in the caves of Harclow alone there lay an earl's ransom of the rare stuff called saltpeter that was essential to make powder for gonnes.

And he had paid King Edward one thousand pounds for the right to be the crown's exclusive agent for the purchase and sale of saltpeter, and had taken Christiana Fitzwaryn to wife in order to hide the arrangement.

He watched brother and sister meet and embrace. His mind began involuntarily calculating the tremendous loss of profit when he actually paid Morvan for the contents of those caves.

Aye, it was very much against his interests to have Morvan return. In fact, having Sieg guarantee that Morvan fell during battle . . .

Christiana looked up at her brother with glistening eyes. Even at a distance, her worry was palpable.

Her sadness twisted his heart. His mind emptied of everything but the desire to comfort her.

Theobald had been right. Recognizing one's options was not the same as choosing them. He would turn his back on these golden opportunities which Lady Fortune had capriciously offered him.

He would do it for Christiana, because he loved her.

✦ ✦ ✦

Christiana and Morvan stood arm in arm while men burdened with booty jostled past.

This was what war was really all about. Profit, of the most primitive sort. All of the talk of chivalry and honor appeared very false to her today.

"Every farmhouse in England will have new cookware and cloth," Morvan said, surveying the boats riding low in the water.

"Is any of it yours?"

"Nay. My prize is your safety. It is enough for me." He glanced to where David waited fifty paces away. "And for your merchant, I think. This time, at least."

"David. His name is David."

"Aye. David."

"I know that you still do not favor him, Morvan, but he is a good man. You can not deny that he proved that."

"He has goodness in him, but much more too. Things that I do not understand. But he has proven that he can protect you. I can part from you today with an easy mind, if not an easy heart."

"It will not be such a long parting. This war cannot last once winter threatens."

He turned his attention from the boats to her. "However long it lasts, I do not think that we will see each other for many months. Knowing that you are safe and have a home frees me to leave the court. I may not return with the army. I think that I will seek some adventure when this campaign ends."

Her spirits had been battered by the destruction of Caen, and now a new sadness spread through her.

She embraced him. "I pray that you change your mind. My place with him does not dim my love for you. If you must seek adventure, let it be for a short while only. And my home is yours too. Please believe that."

"It will not be so long. But you have found your future, Christiana, and now it is time for me to find mine." He set her away, and smiled down at her. "I must leave you now. Edward has duties for me. No tears, sister. This is not forever. Go to your husband."

He walked away, and soon the sight of him became lost in the bustling crowd. She kept watching, hoping to see his dark hair one more time, praying that his words were true, and not the last that she would ever hear him speak.

David came up behind her. She felt his presence, and then the comfort of his arms surrounding her, holding her closely.

"I love you," he said.

How like him to know that she needed that right now. But then those blue eyes had always seen into her heart. She turned to him, and to the sanctuary that his declaration offered.

"I worry about him," she said.

"He is skilled and strong, Christiana. And in battles, they do not try to kill knights, but take them for ransom."

"Aye. But I know the value of a knight's ransom and there is no father to pay it. He could live his life in the hole of some French keep if Edward fails."

"If he is captured, I will get him out."

She looked in his eyes and knew that was true. Whether it took coin or a dagger, he would do it for her.

The horrible images of the last day receded. The brilliance of his love and care burned away the fog of melancholy that had thickened with Morvan's departure.

"Where is Sieg? Isn't he returning with us?"

"He decided to join this war. It is his nature to enjoy such things."

"But he has gone to your father first, hasn't he? You sent him to return the documents, didn't you? Your mother's picture was missing from the book in your study. You sent that too. So he would know who you really are and why you did it."

That surprised him. His smile showed amazement. And admiration. "You are becoming dangerously clever, darling."

"So how long do you think that we have?"

"I will be in England. He cannot harm me there."

"Of course he can, but that is not what I meant. How long do you think the Comte will live? How long before Senlis is yours?"

Not just surprise this time. Astonishment. That in turn astonished her. He had not considered this possibility. He truly had not foreseen how this would end.

"He is a nobleman, David, and the last of an ancient line. In this one thing I know him better than you. He does not want the line to die out and the lands returned to the crown. Such men will do anything to assure they have an heir. Despite what you did, he will not forget that you are all he has left once he learns the truth."

He stood very still while he absorbed that.

"So how long do you think we have?"

"He is about fifty-five. If you are right, and I think that you misjudge him, it should be a long while before I face that choice again."

He said it lightly, but she felt a change in him. She sensed his mind and emotions begin to churn. She knew him very well now, and easily recognized the quiet drama that his soul controlled and contained.

He had seen that she was right, and that Senlis could one day be his after all. He had begun waiting again. He was good at waiting.

She reached up to caress his face. "I love our life, and I am not sorry that it will probably be a long while. And I love you. I thank God for our love, David. There is beauty and goodness in it, and in you, always waiting for me."

"Whatever goodness you see in me is merely a reflection of yourself, my girl. You make me better than I was ever born to be."

"That is not true. For a man who sees so clearly, there are parts of yourself that you do not know very well."

"Parts I would have never known if you had not touched them."

She began to object. The intensity in his expression stopped her. Maybe he was right. Hadn't his love taught her things about herself that she might have never learned without him?

Two men carting a bed jostled by. The din on the docks intruded.

"Maybe love is all that stands against what we have seen here in Caen," she said. "That is sad."

He shook his head. "I understand the darkness in men like your innocence never will, Christiana, and the acts of war are the least of it. Trust me when I say that love is a formidable foe. Perhaps the only foe."

For a moment his gaze revealed his soul like it had the night of their reunion, and it was all there. The shadows that he spoke of, and the power of love to contain them. Aye, Morvan had been right. There was goodness in him, but other things too.

"Then let us love each other as well as we can, David. Let us build a life full of hope and light that never dims, no matter what the world brings us. I want our love to be the hearth at the center of our home, wherever it is, burning hotly forever. I never want to look back on what we shared here and wonder if it was an illusion that we embraced in our desperation."

"It was no illusion. You owned my heart long before I found you here, and it is yours forever. Our love is as real as the arms embracing you, and always will be. I am not a man who loses hold on something precious once it is in his possession."

He kissed her, his mouth lingering and claiming, a welcome reminder of the passion they had found. He held her so closely that they molded as one and made an image of love amidst the greed swarming the docks.

He turned her under his arm. "Let us leave this place now. Let us go home."

A few men had paused their hauling to watch the lovers. She met their eyes frankly, and hoped that the display had reminded them about the true value of things.

"Aye, David, let us go home. Take me back to our garden and our bed."

They walked down the pier side by side, with no prize in their arms except each other.

BY POSSESSION

FOR JEAN,
MY DEAR FRIEND AND MY FIRST READER

PROLOGUE

✦ *1324* ✦

ADDIS WAS SURPRISED BY the witch woman's summons. She normally only called him to service her on nights when the full moon rose. All the same he obeyed and left the corral where he tended her father's horses and walked to her house near the forest's edge. He would be killed if her father ever discovered their furtive coupling amidst the pine trees while the white disk hovered in the heavens, but still he went. He had learned to take the rare opportunities for human warmth no matter how strangely they came to him.

He found her outside, holding the reins of a horse. That surprised him more than the summons. The normal ritual was for her to make an excuse for his presence by giving him work to fill the evening hours of light.

During the first year of his enslavement she had called for him frequently, and sat by the door watching him while he fixed her house and dug her paths. She had taught him her language and demanded to learn his until they could communicate in a rough, blunt way. And in that rough, blunt way she had finally told him that she suspected he was a knight and not a groom, and that to fulfill her calling as priestess she had a special need of him. He had fully expected to be sacrificed amidst those trees, which was the occasional fate of Christian knights captured by these pagan barbarians, not stripped naked and joined with the witch woman while she chanted incantations to her moon god above.

Her face bore a hard expression which did not soften when he approached. The late afternoon light showed faint lines etching her skin near her eyes and mouth. Not a young woman, and thin in a gaunt way that spoke of the fasting and other self-denials that were a part of her magic.

"I did not expect this," he said in her Baltic tongue. The formalities between them had eased a little over the years. He might be a slave and she the daughter of a *kunigas*, a priest, but two people cannot make love repeatedly and remain strangers.

"I need some plants that grow only near the river. You will help me." Another surprise. She retrieved a large basket near the door and handed it to him. A cloth covered its top, but it was not empty.

Curious now, he lifted her into the saddle, then took the reins and led her toward the forest path that snaked to the river. She did not speak the whole way, and he wondered if anyone in the big house or in the scattering of huts had seen them leave and would follow. She had never been this careless with his life before.

They emerged by the river's edge, where the trees fell away and the boggy banks shot high with reeds and growth. He helped her down and tied the reins to a spindly sapling.

"Our king will refuse baptism," she said abruptly. "We heard this morning. He will wait until the papal legates come in the fall to say so, but he has chosen."

His chest suddenly felt hollow. He knew that her king had been negotiating with the Pope. It was to be a political bargain to ensure that the Pope stop the Baltic crusade led by the Teutonic Knights. It required that the king accept the Christian faith of Rome, and with him his people.

He had refused to hope, had dug out the seedlings of frantic hunger in his heart that yearned to grow toward the light of freedom, but all the same a few had flowered and spread, much like the wildflowers peeking through the late summer greenery at his feet. Conversion might have released him. Fingers in his soul grabbed the disappointment and dragged it into the shadows where he had learned to bury and hide every emotion.

"There will be much fighting again, worse than this last year," she said. "The knights will come once more on their crusade. And there will be other repercussions. Many are angry that our king considered such a thing. They will want to appease the gods who have been insulted, and the *bajorai* will not stop it now."

He heard a note in her low voice, a caution, a warning. "Does your father know?"

"About us, no. About you . . . maybe. He has said things sometimes. I mock the suggestion, and he does not pursue it, and he admires your skill with horses, but the skill itself, when you ride . . . he has wondered. And you do not look like a groom. Too big. I remind him that your people are larger, but . . ."

But his danger was real, more real than it had been since that day they found him six years ago amidst the dead killed in that *reise*. He had been conscious and seen them searching and managed to pull off his heraldic surcotte and most of his armor. If they had wondered they had put it aside because they had found another knight, unmarked and unscarred, to burn to their gods that night. Over the years his skill with the horses had gained him favor and safety. These people considered them sacred animals.

The witch woman named Eufemia walked away, her body a little stiff, her bony arms pressed to her sides. "Wait here. I will gather the plants and be back soon." Her voice sounded low and harsh. The growth of the high plants began absorbing her form. He looked down and realized she had not brought the basket. Lifting it, he called to her.

She turned, only her head and breast visible. Behind her the river roared, almost swallowing his voice, its force throwing up the fresh smell of water and earth. She looked at him, dark eyes glinting, and her gaze slowly drifted down his length. Ignoring the basket with which he gestured, she turned away, leaving him standing there alone.

Alone. Suddenly the sounds of the forest and river became deafening. The horse refooted itself, jostling his shoulder. The basket weighed heavy in his hands. She wouldn't . . .

His mouth dried with fear and hope. He looked at the horse, and then the path winding beside the river, and then at the spot where her black hair had disappeared. The blood of excitement beat in his head, a painful sensation which he hadn't felt in years. Grabbing at the cloth, he uncovered the basket.

Two daggers, some bread, and some salt pork lay within. Something glittered below the food and he rummaged and pulled it out. Two gold armlets that Eufemia wore during ceremonies slid down his fingers.

He looked for her again. Would she pay for this? She was a daughter of a *kunigas*, and a priestess of rites older than the moon god and the sky god. Perhaps they dared not disbelieve whatever story she gave.

He wished she had said something. He had never let himself care for her or anyone all these years because it would be a form of surrender, but she had been the closest thing to a friend and in this instant he experienced a nostalgic pain and gratitude.

She might be risking much for him. The final surprise, since she had made very clear that he wasn't really with her under those moons, that he only provided a body that the god Menulius used. Well, for whatever reason, she had decided to give him a chance for freedom, and he would take it.

The hope long suppressed scorched, moving him to action. He swung up on the horse, noting that it was one of her father's finest. He quickly tied the basket to the saddle, noticing some garments stuffed into a leather bag on the other side. Eufemia had provided well for him.

He paused, looking once more to the river. From his height he could see the top of her black head bending toward the water. Mouthing silent words of farewell, he dug his heels into the horse's flanks.

CHAPTER 1

Wiltshire, England ✦ 1326

MOIRA FELT THE DANGER BEFORE she heard it. It rumbled from the ground up her legs and through her back while she bent over the hearth setting some water to heat. She froze as a distant thunder began shaking the cool dawn air entering through her open door. She darted to the threshold as the sound grew stronger. Stepping outside she saw the men approach through the morning haze.

They poured down the hill from the manor house of Darwendon, aiming for the village, four dark shapes flying on fast steeds with short cloaks waving behind them. They looked like legged falcons soaring through the silver mist.

Rushing over to a pallet in the corner, she crouched and shook the small body lying there. "Brian, up now! Quickly."

Sun-bronzed arms and legs jerked and stretched and she yanked at one wrist while she rose. "Now, at once, child! And silence, like I told you."

Blue eyes blinked alert with alarm and he scurried behind her to a back window. She could hear the riders galloping toward the cottages now. Brian paused on the sill, his blond head out and his rump still in, and twisted with apprehension toward her.

"Where I showed you, and cover yourself well. Do not come out, no matter what you hear," she ordered, giving him a firm push. *Even if you hear my screams.*

She watched until he disappeared behind the shed in which she stored her baskets, then she closed the shutters and sat on the narrow bed. With quick movements she tied her disheveled hair behind her neck with a rag, smoothed her stained homespun gown, and stretched to move her darning basket near her feet. Lifting a torn veil, she pretended to sew.

She tried to remain calm while the horses clamored toward her with a violent noise. They were not stopping in the village. They were coming here, to this house. The sour bile of fear rose to her mouth and she sucked in her cheeks and forced it down.

Two horses pulled up outside in a mélange of hooves and legs and pivoting turns. Two men swung off and strode toward her. They barged in and peered around the darkened chamber.

"Where is the boy?" one of them asked.

"What boy? There is no boy here."

The man strode to the large chest against the wall, opened it, and began rummaging through the garments inside. She did not protest. Brian's things were not in there, or anywhere they would easily find them. She had prepared for this day, although the passing years had led her to believe him safe and forgotten.

The other man grabbed her arm and pulled her up from the bed. "Tell us where he is or it will go badly for you."

"I have no boy. No son. I do not know who you mean."

"Of course you know," a new voice said.

She twisted around to the doorway and the tall, thin man standing there. His long blond hair looked white in the dawn's glow.

"Raymond!"

Brian's uncle, Raymond Orrick, smiled smoothly and stepped inside, his knight's spurs glinting. He gestured lazily and the gouging grip released her arm. "Forgive them, Moira. It was not my intention to frighten you. We got distracted in the village and they moved on ahead. They thought . . ."

"They thought I was a peasant and undeserving of any courtesy."

He sauntered over to the hearth, glancing around the simple chamber, taking in her two chests and bed and table and stools. His eyes finally came to rest on the pallet. "He is safe?"

She moved up close to him, shooting cautious looks at the two others. Even if they were his liege men he should not speak of this in front of them. "Aye, he is safe."

Raymond smiled in the familiar way he had used too often since her fifteenth year. It was the smile that a magnanimous lord might bestow on a favored servant. But she did not serve him, least of all in the way he would most like.

"You have done well for us, but we have come for him," he said.

"Come for him?"

"It is time."

A sickening strumming began in her chest. She wished suddenly that she had claimed that Brian had perished in this summer's fever. Behind her she felt the presence of a fourth man enter.

"He is safer here," she said.

"It is time," Raymond said more firmly.

"Nay. It is unwise and you know it. Your sister, Claire, asked me to care for her son before she died. You agreed because you knew Brian could be hidden here. If you take him back to your home at Hawkesford now, the men who wish him harm will learn of it and take him from you. You cannot withstand those who invoke the king's name as they commit their crimes."

The latest man to arrive moved. He came around her, taking a place in Raymond's shadow near the hearth. "Where is the boy?" he asked in a commanding voice that expected a response.

She pivoted and peered at him. He stood taller than Raymond, and broader too, and she could make out similar long hair, but dark, not fair. He wore a peculiar garment on his legs, and no armor or sword. She could not see his face well in the shadow, but he did not appear friendly.

Raymond looked over at the man and seemed to shrink a little, as if in natural deference. That was not like Raymond at all. He counted his own worth very high.

"The boy," the man demanded.

Raymond caught her eye meaningfully. He stepped toward her, whether to signal that he relinquished responsibility for what occurred, or to protect her, she couldn't say. With his movement, the hearth glow suddenly illuminated the stranger.

She gasped. *Surely not. It was impossible!*

A handsome face composed of sharp planes emerged from the retreating shadows. Deep-set dark eyes met her gaping stare, the low fire highlighting golden sparks that brightened while he considered her. He turned slightly and she gasped again when she saw the pale scar slicing down the left side of his face from forehead to jaw, contrasting starkly with his sun-browned skin.

Impossible!

"You know who I am?"

She knew who he appeared to be, who the scar and eyes and dark hair said he should be. But that was all that reminded her of him. Certainly not the suspicion and danger quavering out of him and giving that face a harsh, vigilant expression. Especially not the crude garments that made him appear like some marauding barbarian. In the hearth light she could see that they were made of buckskin, not woven cloth. The hip-length sleeveless tunic displayed the sinewy strength of his arms. More leather clad his legs to the ground in two narrow tubes. The tunic was decorated with orange beads that picked up the fire.

"You spoke boldly enough before, woman. Do you doubt your own eyes?"

"I doubt them, since the man you appear to be is dead eight years now."

"Well, I am not dead, nor a ghost."

"If you are who you appear to be, you should know me as well."

The eyebrow bisected by the scar rose. "Come here."

She stepped closer and he scrutinized her face. She managed not to flinch as his gaze pierced hers, invading and probing with a naked contemplation. Still, he didn't look quite so fearsome up near, and her own examination revealed something of the handsome, blessed boy she remembered. Leaner and harder, but the same high cheekbones and strong jaw defined the face.

"In the last few years that I served Raymond's father, Bernard Orrick, as a squire, Bernard kept a serf woman named Edith as his lehman," he said. "You are Edith's daughter, but you are well grown these eight years, and not the plump child you were when I left." His intense gaze drifted down and then returned to her face until their eyes met in a frank connection of familiarity. She saw recognition and maybe something else in his expression. Her nape prickled.

Another count against him and she doubted anew. The man he claimed to be had never looked at her like that, and never would.

"Raymond no doubt told you who I am," she said.

"So you do not trust Raymond either? No wonder you have kept the boy safe. In these times you are smart to suspect everyone. But Raymond would not know the name I called you when you were underfoot and in the way, would he?"

Nay, Raymond would not know that name that spoke volumes about her youth, her appearance, her status in the Orrick household. Her insignificance.

He reached out and touched the tip of her nose as he had done on occasion when she was a child. "You are little Moira, Claire's Shadow."

A stunned acceptance swept her, splashed with relief and joy and heartbreak. Brian's father, thought dead these last eight years, had come for his son.

"Now, where is the boy?"

The heartbreak submerged the other emotions. She turned away, castigating herself. She had been keeping Brian safe for a reason, hadn't she? He was not really hers and did not belong here. This man above all others would ensure that he someday sat in his rightful place and lived the life he was born to live.

She should be happy, not devastated, but her spirit began a silent, grieving moan as she realized that she would lose Brian forever. "I will show you. Tell the others to stay here. They may frighten him."

Raymond and his men remained in the cottage while she led the way around to the shed in back. She called Brian's name when they approached the stacks of reeds drying for her baskets. The bundles shifted and a blond head stuck up. Young blue eyes examined the stranger cautiously.

"It is all right. Come out now."

He scrambled up and came over to her. Moira stepped away. Man and boy examined each other. She was glad that Brian had the good sense not to comment on the scar or garments, even though both obviously fascinated him. He looked so small and brave there, struggling not to shrink from the hard countenance above him. Her heart swelled at the image of them taking their mutual measurements.

She slipped back beside him and knelt, placing her hands on his shoulders, closing her eyes, and savoring the feel of his small frame under her palms. *Probably never again.* She wished she had known that it would be today. She would have taken him to the stream to play yesterday, and cooked him a special meal. Tears puddled in her eyes and she looked away, biting her lip for composure. Then she pressed his shoulders and smiled at his questioning face.

"This is Addis de Valence, Brian. This is your father."

"My father is dead. He died on the Baltic crusade."

"Nay."

He frowned up. Realization began dawning. Fear and panic masked his face and he lunged into her arms, burying his face in her breast. She embraced and rocked him and silently pleaded with her eyes for Addis to be patient.

The scarred face turned toward the house and she twisted and saw that Raymond and the others had followed. Perhaps they thought Addis de Valence needed help subduing one seven-year-old boy. She tried to disentangle Brian but he burrowed in deeper. Perhaps they were right.

Addis reached down and pried the boy loose. Brian squirmed in resistance but Addis lifted him and gave a sharp look that quelled the rebellion. He began walking away with little Brian's distraught eyes locked back on her. She reached out a reassuring hand to the boy who had been her son for four years.

Addis walked as if indifferent to the boy's tears. When he passed Raymond, he glanced back. "Bring the woman."

The solar of Addis's manor house at Darwendon rose above the eastern half of the hall. He stood on the stair landing in front of its door, looking down on the activity below. This property had been his wife's dowry when he and Claire had married. Its value lay in the surrounding farms, not the old house protected on its hill only by two circles of wooden palisades.

The boy had stayed close to Moira, but now some servant children whom he knew approached and he ran off with them. Moira's presence should reassure the child for a while, but Brian could not stay here, nor in that house outside the village. Addis would have to arrange for his safekeeping, and very soon.

"He looks like Claire," he said to his brother-in-law, Raymond, who stood beside him. Addis had not even known that Brian existed until several hours ago. The boy's similarity to Claire disturbed him. Seeing the boy evoked old memories, many of them bitter.

Raymond nodded. "He does at that," he said quietly.

Addis looked back at Raymond's nostalgic expression. They had known each other since childhood, both the eldest boys of two old friends who traded sons for fostering and training. He had served Bernard as squire and Raymond had served his own father, Patrick. His marriage to Raymond's sister, Claire, had been foreordained since the day she was born. A perfect match, everyone had said, and he and Claire had agreed. A beautiful girl and handsome boy fated to live out a romantic poem.

He would not think about Claire now, although he had contemplated her often during the two years since Eufemia had freed him. Had it been thoughts of Claire that delayed his return and led him to take passage up to Norway and sit out first one and then two long winters? Finally he had forced himself to come back, only to find that the problem that had sent him away had been solved by God, and that far bigger ones loomed. Maybe it had not been Claire at all. Eufemia would have said that his soul had foreseen what awaited.

Addis gestured to Moira. She had presumptuously sat in the lord's chair near the hearth, but then there were no stools or benches about. Still . . . "How did Brian come to be with her?"

"When your father died, Claire had the good sense to leave your family's home at Barrowburgh. She came back to us at Hawkesford. Moira attended her as in the old days, and when Claire took ill she asked Moira to care for your son. When your stepbrother, Simon, usurped your father's lands, we all knew that Brian represented a threat to Simon's hold on the estate, and that he might be in danger. Moira brought Brian here when Claire died. Your stepbrother would not have known Moira well, and never guessed Brian might be with her."

Servants hustled around quickly, occasionally glancing up at their watching lord. When he had approached the gate during the previous night they had almost refused him entry. They had secretly sent a messenger to Raymond, and Claire's brother had arrived just before dawn determined to throw the impostor out.

He looked down on Moira. She rested her head on the back of the chair and closed her eyes. She had changed much in eight years, and he almost had not recognized her. Raymond had not told him who had been caring for the boy, but she had looked vaguely familiar as soon as he entered that dimly lit cottage.

Her old green gown hung loosely from the shoulders, but the flowing fabric could not hide her thrusting breasts. If anything the drapery emphasized them. She wore no wimple or veil, and mussed chestnut hair fell over her shoulders, looking like the mane of a woman who had just been well bedded. Her skin wore a light golden bronze from the sun. While she had gaped at him near the hearth he had noticed the incredible clarity of her light blue eyes and their bright, intelligent sparkle. He imagined that if he smelled her hair it would be full of the scents of hay and clover. Her whole appearance spoke of sensuality and warmth and comfort. He didn't wonder that Brian had not wanted to leave the security of her breast.

Moira Falkner. Claire's Shadow. The quiet daughter of Edith, Bernard Orrick's whore. Moira's father had been an Irish falconer who had silently accepted the arrangement until the day he walked away from the estate forever. Moira . . . the easily ignored and forgotten playmate and confidante of perfect, radiant Claire.

Addis could barely remember anything specific about Moira. He had rarely even spoken to her during those years at Hawkesford while he served Bernard as a squire. But for some reason the buried memories that would not take form floated in their insubstantial way on a peaceful breeze through his spirit. She was the only person besides Raymond whom he had seen since he returned who belonged to the contented past of his youth.

Aye, she had been no more than a shadow to the pale brilliance of Claire. If lovely, lithesome Claire entered the hall right now, Moira would dissolve into a dark blur beside her. It had always been thus with his wife, and he had been as susceptible as the others. But right now, resting in the chair that he should whip her for touching, Moira looked very womanly and not at all insubstantial.

"She is still a bondwoman?"

"That house and a field are hers. You remember, when my father gave Darwendon to you as Claire's dowry, he noted the farms owned by freeholders. That was one, given to Edith, her mother. When Edith died, it passed to Moira."

"But the mother was a bondwoman, so she is also, property owner or not."

"She claims my father freed Edith and her descendants on his deathbed. I was not there, and the priest is gone." Raymond's lids lowered in a predatory way. Addis followed the calculating gaze down to its destination. Well, well. So the son of Bernard had sought to continue what his father began, but with the daughter. He had tried to lure her to his bed, but she had refused him. It explained the lack of comfort in that cottage. Raymond had withdrawn the Orrick largesse until she came to him.

"Unless she can provide proof, she is still a bondwoman and attached to this manor," Addis said. "With the little left to me, I do not intend to lose any more."

"There is still Barrowburgh, but you will have to fight for it."

Aye, he would have to fight for it, and against men favored by the king. A desperate quest, and unlikely of success. According to Raymond, Addis's stepbrother, Simon, was firmly in the camp of the Despensers, the family who controlled the king, and with their aid had managed to take Barrowburgh and its lands upon Patrick de Valence's death. He would not relinquish one hectare easily.

His spirit heaved with exhaustion. He had learned nothing but bad news since he stepped off that ship at Bristol. He returned to a realm torn apart, baron pitted against baron, laws ignored with impunity by the mighty, the people oppressed by unchecked brigandry. King Edward was continuing his reign the way he had begun it, ineffectually, a weak monarch who was wet clay in the hands of ambitious men who flattered and manipulated him.

An outright rebellion had occurred in his absence, led by his father's friend Thomas of Lancaster. Four years ago Thomas had been defeated and executed, and the taint of treason had smeared Patrick de Valence's name too, making Simon's grab that much easier when Patrick suddenly died.

His jaw clenched. They had all died during his absence. His father. Claire. Bernard. Edith. Even cousin Aymer, the Earl of Pembroke, had been murdered two years ago by men in league with the Despenser family. Only Raymond remained, resisting Simon's claim on Darwendon by arguing it had not been Patrick's land but Addis's, and before that Bernard Orrick's. He had insisted that with Addis dead it should be held by the Orricks for Brian.

His shifting gaze came to rest on the woman below. Nay, not only Raymond had survived.

"She sings, as I remember." The clouded image of a plump girl filling a hall with a sweet voice took form in his mind.

"Aye, but not for me," Raymond muttered. Addis raised one eyebrow and almost laughed. A strange sensation, wanting to laugh. "She makes baskets," Raymond continued. "It is said they are exceptional." He shrugged to indicate he wouldn't know himself. "She will probably want to leave now that you have returned and taken the boy. She spoke once of selling the house and land and using it for a dowry."

"She is unmarried yet?"

"Married twice. My father arranged the first. An old man. Gentry, actually. He died right after the wedding banquet. The second was not so old and lived a month." A leer contorted his features. "She is called the virgin widow. After two such deaths, none has asked for her that I know of."

"They think she killed them?"

"Nay. They think the sight of her naked body stopped their hearts. She is very . . ." He made a curving gesture.

Addis looked at the swells beneath the gown's drapes. Aye, she was "very." She had been, what, five and ten when he left? He couldn't remember noticing before.

She shifted and opened her eyes and looked around peevishly. Rising, she paced in front of the hearth with her arms crossed over her chest. The swaying fabric hinted at a narrow waist and curving hips and long striding legs. He had kept her waiting a long time while he spoke with Raymond and learned the worst of what he faced. She threw up her arms in annoyance and retook the chair.

"I will send word to the villeins and tenants that I will hold a court under the old tree tomorrow," he said, turning to the stairs. "How many men can you leave with me for now?"

"The six I brought, and I will send six more, but if Simon learns you are here and moves against you, it will not be enough. And I will send some proper garments so you do not look like a barbarian when you meet with your people."

His people. The few hundred who still served him on this patch of land that was all that remained of the great holdings that were his by birthright.

He knew what he was expected to do, what his family honor demanded, what his stepbrother, Simon, would anticipate and try to thwart. But he found that he had no taste for it. He felt unbelievably weary, and bitter that his old world had not been awaiting his return. He had expected to simply step through the gate of his family's castle at Barrowburgh and have those years in the Baltic lands disappear. It would take all of the will he could summon just to hold on to what was left, let alone fight for what had been lost.

He walked toward Moira, feeling sour about the course forced on him. She saw him approach and did not rise. Perhaps she meant no insult, but it annoyed him nonetheless. Her mother's place in Bernard's household and her own place behind Claire may have given her a lady's manner, but she was a bondwoman and should never forget her true place, which, at the moment, was certainly not in his chair.

The temptation to grab those brown locks and force her to kneel almost overwhelmed him. Only the memory of once being compelled to kneel himself stopped his hand. He forced down the rancor and his inner voice chastised that it had not arisen in reaction to her at all, but because of all the other insults and indignities to his person and status.

She met his eyes and he noticed that she did not look away from his face as most women did. Even in the cottage her gasps had come from the shock of recognition and not repulsion. He had grown used to the polite eyes that looked above or below his head or over his shoulder, had come to anticipate the extra coin demanded by the whores. And so her unwavering gaze had been a little unsettling in the cottage but right now, in his present mood, it struck him as insolent.

He looked pointedly at the chair. She flustered and rose. "You bid me wait here for you when we arrived," she explained. "It has been some hours, and the rushes on the floor are filthy."

They *were* filthy. The servants had grown slovenly with no lord or lady watching them. His first order had been that the entire manor be scrubbed and they hustled around now doing it.

He eased into the chair and she stood in front of him, her arms again crossed over her chest as if she sought to hide it.

"You will stay here a few days until the boy grows accustomed to me," he said.

Her cheeks hollowed as she bit their insides. She had not liked his tone. At the moment, with Raymond's tales still weighing on him, he didn't give a damn.

"If it will help Brian, I suppose that I could do so but my house is not far away."

"You will stay here."

"I will agree to it, but only for a few days."

Raymond had been right about her claims of freedom. He might be indebted to her for protecting Brian, but it was best to have it out now. "Your agreement is not required. You will do it because I bid it, and you will do it as long as I say. When I have no more need of you here, you can return to your house."

Her color rose. "You have been gone many years and can be excused for misunderstanding how it is with me now. I am a freeholder of that house and property."

"You may hold that property, but you are not freeborn. Your mother was a bondwoman of these lands. When Bernard gave them to me, he gave you as well."

She visibly struggled to control her anger. Not a beautiful woman, but clearly spirited, and her bright eyes made up for any deficiencies in her other features. As a youth he had never noticed the Shadow's eyes and spirit, but then his own eyes had lingered only on Claire.

"Sir Bernard freed my mother after you left. I was present and heard his words and he included me."

"Raymond told me you claim this. Are there any witnesses?"

"The priest. The woman Alice who served Claire. *Me.*"

"Raymond says the priest is gone. Where is Alice?"

"She left . . . London, I think . . . after Claire died. There were documents. I remember Bernard signing them. But if the priest took them, they would have been lost when the manor chapel burned a few years ago. . . ." She spoke disjointedly, verbalizing scattered thoughts and memories. "Perhaps Raymond has them."

"He did not speak as if he did."

She still looked angry, but also distraught. It would be an easy thing to accept her claim. After all, she had served him well even when she believed she had no obligation to do so. But something rebelled at the notion of releasing her, and not just his resolve to hold on to what little was still his. Raymond had said she planned to leave the estate. She was of his old world, and he would not permit yet another part of it to disappear.

Her arms unfolded and her fists clenched at her sides. "Ask in the village what I am, who I am. Everyone knows."

"Everyone knows your mother lived in Bernard's keep and slept in Bernard's bed. Everyone knows that she lived like a lady and that her daughter was treated like Bernard's own. But that is not the same thing as having the bonds of one's birth broken."

"You are calling me a liar."

"Nay, I am calling you my bondwoman. Even if Bernard spoke thus while he died, it is not legal without witnesses and documents."

Her eyes glinted magnificently. "Is this the thanks I get?"

"You have my gratitude, although you did not give

Brian care for my sake. For Claire's perhaps, or maybe for your own, but not for mine. I was dead. Remember?"

"I find myself wishing you had remained so!"

"Oddly enough, so do I. Now go and find the boy, and tell the women to prepare a chamber for you both. A man will take you back to the cottage later so you can get whatever you need for yourself and him."

She began walking away, stiff-backed and furious. He remembered Raymond's predatory look. Raymond was an old friend, but he knew the man's way of handling women, and he guessed that this one had been resisting his coercions for years. Perhaps that was why she sought to leave.

"Raymond will be staying for the midday meal," he said to her retreating form. "You will sing for him."

She froze in mid-stride, and turned her head slightly so he could see her profile. "Even bondwomen have rights," she said sharply, her visible eye sparkling like clear water reflecting sunlight. "In this I am not my mother's daughter. Do not expect me to whore for your brother, or for any other lord or knight."

The message was unmistakable. *Do not expect me to whore for you.* No doubt this attractive, voluptuous woman of uncertain status had fought off her share of men of every degree, so it was not really a presumptuous assumption.

As it happened it was also an accurate one, but he knew that he had given no indication of it. A slave learns to hide his desires as surely as he learns to bury his hopes. She could not know that images of having her in bed had been forming since he walked into her humble cottage.

"Bondwomen have rights, but they also have obligations for which they are paid with protection. You will sing for him, but at my command, and he will understand what it means. After today he will not bother you again."

She turned and faced him squarely, as she had in the cottage and when he approached her a few minutes ago in this hall.

Her gaze did not appear shocked or insolent now, but familiar and knowing, as if she were accustomed to seeing the scarred barbarian every day and knew him far too well to find him at all remarkable or frightening.

And, during that moment while their eyes met, Addis did not feel like a stranger in his own homeland for the first time since setting foot back in England.

CHAPTER 2

FOOTSTEPS SOUNDED BEHIND HER *in the twilight as long strides brought the youths closer. She tucked her chin down and hunched her shoulders, trying to become invisible, and walked a little faster toward the village. They laughed and jostled the way boys do, full of the horseplay that signaled squires freed for a while from their duties and out looking for trouble. She prayed that they would simply pass by.*

They closed in behind her, their presence prickling her spine. Silence fell, broken only by whispers and snickers. Boots and long legs stretched into step alongside.

"What do you have there, girl?"

She hunched further and ignored him, clutching the basket that held the bits of old ribbon Claire had given her.

"I'm talking to you, girl. What have you got there? Something you stole?"

"It's the daughter of the falconer. You have a gift for the husband of Bernard's whore in that basket? Payment from the lord? Some wine or meat?"

"If it's wine, let's have it. Will save us the cost of ale."

They had surrounded her and she was unable to walk forward. Despite the fear trembling like a plucked harp string, she dug in her heels and glared at them, "My mother is not a whore!"

"Ooo! Spirit. Too much for your place, girl. And your mother doesn't visit Bernard to read him the Hours. Maybe he'll share her with all of us. Make her a gift to us when we earn our spurs."

"Why wait for the mother when the daughter is right here?"

"Aye. She looks like a dumpling, but maybe there's more curves under that robe than it appears."

They all stepped toward her, enough to close the circle and intimidate her with their size and strength. A hand reached out and twitched the fabric of her garment with an insinuating taunt. Bright eyes and twisted smiles peered down at her, still just teasing, but approaching a dangerous line. "Leave me alone!"

One, bolder than the others, the first who spoke to her, gladly crossed that line in a way that showed in his eyes. "I don't like the way you talk to us, girl. Perhaps you need a lesson in what you are."

"Leave her alone, John," another voice said from behind. She twisted and saw him stride toward them, a little winded from running to catch up with the others, tall and beautiful with raven hair falling around his face. Some said he was the image of Adonis, whoever that was. Her heart made a little flip of relief and then rose to her throat.

"It's just a serf girl, Addis. Not a damsel in distress."

"She's a child. Leave her alone. What do you think Bernard will do if he finds out you molest Edith's daughter?"

On the warning of their lord's disfavor, all but John eased back. They stepped just enough to open the circle, suddenly looking bored and impatient to be off. She faced John defiantly, feeling much braver and almost indignant now that she had

*him one-on-one with Addis de Valence to back her up. "My
mother is not a whore," she hissed.*

*John sneered a laugh and turned on his heel. The others
walked off with him, leaving her to glare at their backs. Addis
made to follow, then paused and looked directly at her. It was
the first time, she was very positive, that he had ever done so.
"Get on home to your father, girl. It is almost dark and you
shouldn't be here."*

She awoke from the dreamy memory that had materialized while she awaited the dawn, annoyed that it had
surfaced to remind her of that childhood awe and infatuation. Other memories, of watching for any sign of his recognition during the next weeks, of elaborating on his
rescue in her imagination until she was in fact a beautiful
damsel in distress, tried to take form but she banished
them to the shadows of time. She turned on her bed, embarrassed by the recollections. Oh well, if a twelve-year-
old girl can't be foolish, who can?

Perhaps the supper yesterday had provoked the memory. He had made her sit at the high table, two places
down with Brian between them, so that she could care for
the boy. Raymond had sat on his other side, and she and
Brian had been ignored until the meal ended, when Addis
had turned and courteously asked her to sing.

She had risen and sung an old religious melody and had
seen Raymond's bright attention as he leaned forward to
watch. It was the first time that she had sung publicly in
years, and a full silence descended in the hall while she
continued. Out of the corner of her eye she noticed Addis
say a few words to Raymond that provoked a sharp expression and then a suddenly much duller contemplation
of her.

Perhaps he had given Raymond the message he intended. When Raymond left after the meal she had been

spared the usual insinuations with which he habitually took his leave of her. In fact, he hadn't taken his leave of her at all this time, but then a knight does not concern himself with courtesies toward a serf.

The first light leaked through the window slit and she sat and reached for her shift. If Addis thought that his gesture of protection was going to make her content, he was much mistaken. She had lived as a serf long enough to learn their few rights under the customs of the land. She did not need his help with Raymond. She had been handling that man almost as long as Addis had been gone.

She woke Brian and made him dress like a lord's son in tunic and hose. No sooner had he washed and dressed than he darted out of their chamber in search of friends.

The hall was already buzzing with activity when she entered. She spied Leonard the bailiff and walked over to him. Leonard had been Bernard's man, and the only authority on the manor during the last years. He collected the rents and saw to the villeins' service, but he was old, with filmy eyes that didn't see well anymore, and no steward or lord had been coming for visits to support his voice as was customary.

"Why are you wearing your best garments, Leonard? Those green velvets are too warm for a summer day."

"There's to be a hallmote. Word was sent out yesterday."

"So soon? Addis does not waste time."

"Long overdue. Haven't held one in years. Most of the cases are so old, it will be a wonder if anyone remembers the facts. Still, I've my records, all written down. Them that thought they'd never be called to a reckoning are in for a surprise." He smiled contentedly, proud to have done his duty despite the ambiguous ownership of the manor. "I spent several hours with him last night, showing him the accounts. In good order, he said. The fines should bring in some nice income today, but me thinks he needs more since the word has spread that he is willing to sell the freedom to any with the price."

That surprised her. It had become common for lords to sell their villeins their freedom, but his treatment of her yesterday had suggested that he preferred the old ways. Still, if he needed coin, it made sense. Even freed, those peasants would still work the land and accrue income for him, paying tenants' rents instead of bondmens' fees, and so their manumission meant extra funds in the short term and no real loss in the long.

His insistence on her bonded status suddenly made sense too. It would annoy her to pay for what she already owned, but if it would make short work of this misunderstanding it might be the smartest choice. If Addis just wanted a lord's fee, he should have simply named his price.

"What do you think the fee will be?"

Leonard shrugged. "Depends on the man and his worth. He won't set them too high. No one could pay then, could they? Wouldn't be any point to it."

Relief replaced the indignant anger that had been weighting her mood. The issue of her status was a small thing, some might say. There were villeins in the village who were wealthier and more respected than most freemen. But, for all of the changes, a bondman still belonged to the lord, and if that lord proved cruel even the rights accrued by time and custom would avail him little. Freedom had been one of Bernard's three important gifts to Edith, and the greatest by far.

The hallmote was held under the old oak tree just outside the village. The manor-house folk streamed there at midday to join the villeins and freeholders who had traveled from the other parts of the estate. Perhaps two hundred gathered around the benches set out for the twelve jurors. The lord's chair stood to one side.

Addis arrived last, impressive and frightening with his height and strength and scar. He appeared very much the lord in the long blue cotte that Raymond had sent in the morning. Moira sat in the grass with some women.

A stream of petty offenses filled the next few hours. Villeins shirking their day work and freeholders refusing to contribute to the harvest. Women accused of brewing weak ale, unmarried girls caught coupling, and a few cases of petty theft. The jurors assessed the fines with which most lords had long ago replaced physical punishments.

Leonard spoke for the lord's rights and Addis sat silently, only asking questions on occasion when explanations conflicted. The sun hung low in the sky when the legal debris of the years was finally swept away. Then it was time for petitions directly to the lord. The farmers and herders and craftsmen approached who sought to purchase their freedom.

She moved closer while Addis determined the worth of each man to the land and then set the fee. Most fell between three and ten pounds, but that would be a year's income or more for these people. Everyone thought him fair enough. She waited until all the rest finished and then approached herself.

She knelt as was customary, since she could hardly ask to buy a freedom that her actions implied was not his to sell. It hurt her pride to do so. She heard some gasps, for no one considered her a serf any longer. Looking to the ground she waited for his acknowledgment. It was a long time coming.

"You want to beg a favor or judgment, Moira?"

She looked up and saw that he was not pleased. A dangerous humor sparked in his eyes. "Aye, my lord. I too ask to buy my freedom."

"So you acknowledge publicly that you are indeed a bondwoman?" She did not answer and his eyes locked on hers. "You think that you have enough coin?"

"I think so. A woman's fee must be lower than a man's, and my value to you is negligible."

"You are wrong there, Moira. Your value to me is very high."

A low buzz scurried through the crowd. "Name the fee and I will pay it," she said tightly, thinking that she would like to strangle him for that unwarranted insinuation. He regarded her with a warm intensity that unsettled her further. A bit like Raymond, but more shielded and dangerous. He wanted to embarrass her as a punishment for daring this. Addis de Valence would never really have an interest in her like that. But the twelve-year-old girl inside her flushed from his attention and she cursed at that foolish, inner child.

"The fee for you is two hundred pounds."

Two hundred pounds! She almost upbraided him with scathing words that could earn her a public whipping. "Then I ask the amount of the merchet for a woman who marries."

"On the manor or off?"

"Off."

"Who is the man?"

"I will find one."

"Not from what I hear."

Laughter waved through the crowd. Her face burned. Dear God, he had already heard about that. Probably from Raymond.

"Not all men are superstitious."

"Indeed not. I, for one, am not superstitious at all."
Some women clucked their tongues at this more blatant
suggestion. "If you find another, on the estate or off, I
hope that he is rich and extremely enthralled, Moira. The
merchet for you is one hundred pounds."

Fury almost strangled her voice. "That is not within
the customs of the manor."

"Do not presume to instruct me, woman. If you marry
off the estate, it is the same as losing your services through
freedom. The price should be two hundred then, but since
you will pay a yearly fee while absent I have decided to be
generous. In the old days I could have refused permission
for you to marry at all, but the Church has interfered with
that. Still, it is my right to set the amount."

More for the crowd to chew on. The rumbling comments grew into a low roar. She rose with humiliated
exasperation and turned to the jurors. "I ask a judgment
then. My mother and I were freed upon the last lord's
death. You all know this."

The twelve men squirmed. Addis stood. "The woman
claims this, but even if it is so, it does not apply. Her
mother was bonded to Darwendon and even though Edith
moved to Hawkesford when she married the falconer, her
tie was to this land. And this land was given to me before
Sir Bernard died. This freedom, even if the woman speaks
the truth, is invalid."

Her jaw clenched and she faced Addis down. "My
mother was born here, but I was not. Bernard's freedom
may have been invalid for her, but not for me."

"At best your situation is ambiguous and you owe obligations to both Hawkesford and Darwendon. As to
Bernard's freedom, is there anyone here who will pledge
for you, Moira? Anyone who will swear that they know
you speak the truth?"

Even if there were, they would hardly come forward

with that hard countenance challenging them. "I will find a pledge. I ask time until the next hallmote to do so."

The jurors began agreeing with relief, glad for the delay. She waited tensely until Addis nodded. "It will be so, but until then, you will serve me any way that I order." Suggestive coos emerged from women at that. He stepped closer and spoke to her ears alone. "Until you find the proof or the pledge, do not challenge me again."

She made sure only he could hear her reply. "I will challenge you every way that I can about this, *my lord*, until I break these bonds that you have illegally placed on me."

"I am within the law and my rights and you know it," he said sharply. "You should be glad for my protection. Freedom has its perils for a woman alone."

"I managed well enough, and have no need or interest in whatever protection you imagine you can give. Until I can undo this outrage, I will serve you according to a villein's customary obligations, but do not interpret my doing so as acceptance. And if you ever think that I challenge your rights and power, then do your worst."

The words poured out in a seething whisper and when she had finished she glared at him. He looked at her long enough that her defiant stance began to feel a little ridiculous. Then his lids lowered over lights of surprising warmth. He found her dare amusing!

"I am pleased to find you so willing to submit. You will continue caring for the boy, and you will help Leonard by supervising the women in the manor house."

Submit! "I will gladly care for Brian. As to the rest, that is your lady's duty."

"I have no lady, so you will do it, and the women will obey you because I say so. I'm sure that you know how it is done. Your years at Hawkesford as Claire's Shadow should have taught you."

He was reducing her to a manor servant! It was the

final insult. She turned on her heel without waiting for his dismissal.

She halted with the first step, startled by the silence and rapt expressions surrounding her. A field of eyes had been watching their private confrontation with fascination.

He had claimed that he wanted her to care for Brian, but that became irrelevant when three mornings later he instructed her to pack the boy's garments. She listened to his abrupt order and her heart split.

"You are taking him away?"

"He is not safe here."

"Where is he going?"

"Only I will know where."

"When do you leave?"

"At once."

He stood at the threshold of the house, looking out over the yard, his unscarred profile facing her. A sickening anticipation of loss hollowed out her insides. She resented that this man did not feel the same thing. Easy for him to send Brian away. He had barely paid the boy any attention at all since he found him. She examined the unwavering expression that said he privately contemplated many things, but not his son or her grief.

He had changed more than time could explain. The smiling, happy youth had become encased in impenetrable layers, much like the insects captured in a few of the amber crystals that decorated his primitive tunic.

And yet she could see that boy in him still and could picture the fuller face before it had matured, could remember the generous mouth when it was mobile and quick to laugh and not an uncompromising line more frightening than the scar. And the eyes—how their golden lights had danced when he was young! Now they glinted with danger and caution, full of tiny bonfires no one could see behind.

They were all afraid of him. The servants, the peasants, even Raymond. The piercing regard could reduce them to puddles of obedience. The severe expression brooked no defiance. The lean strength of his body and the pale slashing scar eloquently announced that he had survived far worse than any of them could offer. He still wore the buckskin garments sometimes, but even when he donned woven cottes and tunics his aura remained slightly foreign and mysterious, as if the barbarian ways had seeped into him in ways he could not shed so easily as clothing.

They were terrified of him, but she was not. At least not in the ways that the others were. That, more than his orders, had established her authority with the women. It surprised them. Sometimes, when he spoke to her and she did not fluster and tremble, she wondered if it surprised him too. But she could never be afraid of a man after she had held his grief and despair in her arms, even if he did not remember that she had done so.

He turned suddenly. "You think that I should have told you sooner. The pain would have been no lighter if you had known."

Nay, no lighter, and certainly longer. Perhaps it had been a mercy that he hadn't warned her. She had been able to enjoy the few days' reprieve.

"When he is gone, I assume that this will be over?"

"Over?"

"My imprisonment and slavery here."

He looked at her much as he had at the hallmote, with a combination of anger and amusement and curiosity. Her throat dried. Nay, he did not terrify her the way he did everyone else, but this intense attention badly unsettled her and she worked not to show it.

His silent appraisal drew out and turned invasive, as if

he sought to learn something about her that his eyes could not quite see. She resented this inspection, but she could not turn away from it and sever the peculiar connection it created between them.

"You do not know what you speak of, Moira. Perhaps I should tell you what happens to women who are truly imprisoned and enslaved." He reached out and fingered a strand of her hair escaping the front of her veil. "Be glad I do not show you."

For a moment they stood there, his fingertips barely grazing the feathery hair, his arm spanning the space separating them. A frightening, thrilling tension throbbed through that instant. Then he stepped forward abruptly, away from her, so that she barely saw his face. Only then did she realize that she had frozen into breathless immobility.

"It is over when I say it is over. Now prepare the boy. It is time for him to leave here."

It is time. Raymond had said that in her cottage. Well, now it was truly time.

She packed Brian's things. His young eyes solemnly watched her while he comforted them both in his childish way, reassuring her bravely that his father had promised he would see her again.

Addis awaited with two horses. The privilege of being permitted to ride his own mount obliterated Brian's sadness. He joyfully let his father lift him up and became absorbed with the saddle, barely looking at her until their farewell kiss.

She watched them ride out with a breaking heart and stood at the gate almost an hour until their specks disappeared over the southern horizon.

And then Brian was gone, and with him her purpose in life.

She stayed there for a while longer, absorbing the numbing grief of what had just occurred so quickly. Then, since no one seemed inclined to stop her, she walked down the road to the village.

Cottages and longhouses angled this way and that off the lane, each with its small toft in front surrounded by a ditch or fence and filled with pecking poultry. Men were returning from the fields for dinner and their women appeared in the doorways to greet them. She pretended not to notice the unusual amount of attention that her presence raised.

Paul the cooper fell into step beside her as she passed the alewoman's house. A handsome young man with a lanky strength, Paul had been the one to coin the title "the virgin widow." One night some men had dared him to test the superstition he had helped create and he had come to her house in a drunken stupor, determined to prove his fearlessness. She had been forced to knock him unconscious with an iron pan.

"So you've the lord's favor now, have you?"

"Nay. Do not start on that, Paul."

"Two hundred pounds he put on you. Makes a man wonder what a woman could offer that's worth that much. No wonder those old husbands died."

"We barely speak. He has no interest in me in that way, nor I him. There is nothing like that between us."

She spoke with more conviction than she felt. To be sure, Addis had done nothing specific to raise her concerns. Unlike Raymond's, his eyes did not undress her and he did not find excuses to sidle too close. And yet, sometimes she would turn and find him there, looking at her with that intensity he had shown again today, contemplating her as if his mind followed some debate toward a judgment. A peculiar pull would tug between them that unnerved her more than any leer from Raymond ever could.

Her woman's instincts had grown alert even while her mind kept rejecting the possibility. This was Addis de Valence, after all, and she was Claire's Shadow. But all these subtle attentions had made her feel wary when he was present, and not nearly so fearless as she appeared, but for reasons that had nothing to do with his power as the lord and everything to do with those old feelings that kept wanting to surface.

"We all heard him under the oak tree. All saw him and you and how cozy things were," Paul said, leering.

"You are drunk again."

"Word is that he has you sit at the table with him and run his household. Quite the mistress of the manor, from what is said."

"I take care of Brian. I . . ."

"We men in the village aren't good enough for a fine lady like you, eh? First a gentry knight and then a towns-man and then the image of virtue for four years, but in a blink you go whore up the hill."

That, of course, was the crux of it and the reason for the looks and whispers that had followed her progress down the lane. The villagers took such things in stride if it was among themselves. A woman who coupled out of wedlock with a man of her own degree did so for love or pleasure, but if she went to the bed of a lord or knight it was probably for gain, and she was a whore.

That had been the assumption about Edith despite the affection she and Bernard had shared, and it looked as if it was becoming the judgment about her. If she ever re-turned to her cottage the men would probably start lining up in her garden, jingling the coin in their purses.

Well, she had already decided she would not return,

nor would she remain in the manor house. The reason for staying had just ridden through the gate. It was time to get on with her life, and not the life Addis de Valence had decreed with his insistence that she belonged to him.

She would simply leave. Others had done so. Her father, and Claire's servant Alice. Rare was the lord who pursued.

She shook off Paul's company, and strode past the last of the village and on to the cottage inherited from her mother. It was another of Bernard's three gifts. No time now to sell it or the field, but land made as good a dowry as coin, so that shouldn't matter.

Aye, she would leave, and she would go far away. Far from the stupid rumors about her husbands' deaths, far from the memories of Brian that tore at her composure, and very far from Addis de Valence, who wanted to own her for reasons she couldn't fathom.

Years ago I would have accepted shackles of iron, Addis. But I am not that awestruck girl and you are not the boy whom I admired.

She would speak with Tom Reeve tonight, and trade him the use of her own virgate and this house in return for his extra donkey and cart. She would leave tomorrow. Addis expected to be gone at least a week, but she wanted to be far away before he returned.

She bent to the hearth and probed at some rocks near its base. One shifted and she clawed it away. Feeling into the recess, her hand closed around a little leather sack. She pulled it out, then sat on the bed and emptied it.

A heap of coins fell into the fabric between her thighs. She didn't need to count them to know they amounted to eight pounds, five shillings, and ten pence, the profits from planting her virgate and selling her baskets and living very frugally for four years.

She sifted the coins away from what lay beneath them. She lifted the small object and a light beam from the window fractured its red watery planes into a display of brilliance.

A ruby. Bernard's third gift, easily worth two hundred pounds. The temptation after the hallmote to march to this cottage and retrieve this jewel and throw it into Addis de Valence's face had been intense. Two hundred pounds was too high a price for smug satisfaction, however, especially when she could easily escape for nothing. She had been saving this jewel for a purpose, but that purpose had just been severed from her life, and so now she would use it to find a new one.

She scooped the coins back into their sack, but held the ruby while she pulled over her sewing basket. It glittered warmly in her hand. She smiled. If Edith had been nothing but a whore to Bernard, she had been the most expensive whore in Christendom.

CHAPTER 3

SHE SLIPPED THROUGH *the croft toward the stream,
delighting in the faint sounds of crickets and animals and scraping branches. It was a perfect night, cool and breezy after a hot day, so clear that stars specked the sky as far as one could see. She followed the line of the gurgling stream, aiming for her favorite spot, the big flat rock where she could lie in total privacy and dream. On a night like this a girl could be anyone and anyplace on that rock.*

She approached the small clearing in the growth where the stream widened and the rock jutted out. Something moved and she paused. A dark form hunching on her rock took shape in the shadows. She stepped forward curiously.

"Who goes there?"

She recognized the voice and it took her a moment to find her own. She should probably run away, but it was her rock after all. "Just a village girl."

"Your father will beat you if he learns you are out this late." The voice, normally low and melodic, sounded tight and strangled.

Her father would do no such thing, since he had been gone three days now. It had finally occurred to her that he might not return, but she had not told anyone yet, not even her mother, who had not come down from the castle for over a week this time. She moved in closer. He sat with his legs drawn up, his arms resting on his knees.

"You should not be out this late either," she said, knowing a thing or two about the rules for the squires.

"They will not miss me. They still celebrate Claire's birthday."

An odd thing to say. Claire at least should miss him. She herself had been to the feast at midday, but had not been invited to the evening meal.

She thought about his expression at that earlier celebration, and his sober withdrawal amidst the revelry, and Claire's pique that he hadn't been as much fun as usual. Thoughtless Claire.

"I'm sorry about your mother," she whispered, wanting him to know that she understood why he was here. In a way it was why she had come too. Her own heart was heavy with the realization that her father had left for good and might as well have died.

He turned to her, the shadows barely showing his features except the lights in his eyes which burned like an animal's in the night. His silent regard lasted a long time, and she wondered if she had angered him. "Will you be going home?" she asked.

"Nay. She would be buried before I got there." He looked away and spoke bitterly. "It is a small thing to them. They hardly knew her, except Bernard, but even he . . . a person passes and life goes on. The day has been so damn normal. . . ."

"It is astonishing, isn't it? I remember when my little brother died. I felt the earth, the air, every plant had changed. After we buried him my mother came home and began cooking and cleaning like she did every day. I was furious with her. A momentous event had occurred, to my mind, one that changed

everything. But almost immediately the hole he had left just began filling in."

"At least you were among people who acknowledged his small significance. At least, for a few hours or days . . . Bernard has said the mass tomorrow will be for her, but I do not know how I can attend. People will chatter through it like a normal daily mass, and I will want to kill them."

She hopped up on the stone next to him. His words broke into odd groupings, as if his thoughts ran ahead of his tongue. His sadness subtly quaked the air around him and tore at her heart. He had come here to be alone with it, but he had not insisted that she go. "What was she like?"

At first she thought he would not respond, or do so angrily and indeed tell her to leave. Instead he stretched out one leg and rested his cheek against the knee of the other and spoke of her. He described scattered images and memories such as a child has of his mother, of small kindnesses and comforts and securities. He talked a long time. At first the words came haltingly, then more smoothly, but finally with a rough, throaty tone that said his composure was breaking. Without thinking she placed a hand on his shoulder.

She did not remember how they ended up lying on that warm rock with her arms around his large frame, cradling him the way her mother had comforted her when her brother died, his face against her breast. If he cried it had been silent, more soulful than physical. Her own sadness about her father was relieved by absorbing this higher grief.

They lay there a long while after it had passed with the sweet mood of exposed emotions binding them. She looked to the beautiful sky and savored the sound of the stream, thinking it was delicious to be close to someone like this, even if he was practically a stranger and if in the dark he didn't even know who she was.

In the oddest way the mood slowly changed and became imbued with something tense that she didn't understand. He rose up on his arm and gazed down at her. "How old are you, girl?"

"Thirteen."

He looked away into the night. "Too young."

"Too young for what?"

He laughed and her heart skipped with joy that he didn't sound so sad anymore. "Definitely too young." He rolled away and slid off the rock. "Run home now. If your parents find you gone they will raise the hue and cry."

She emerged from her reverie as she had entered it, watching the mesmerizing rhythm of the donkey's flanks as it pulled her cart down the road. She glanced back to check how far she had sightlessly traveled. Her pace must have slowed, because the wine merchant's wagon that she had followed most of the morning had disappeared ahead.

It was all coming back to her in memories like this, little pageants from her childhood that had become buried by time and blocked by grief. People die and life goes on and the memories of them are best put away since the grief never really dims otherwise. Still, details ignored are not details forgotten. If she let herself think of Claire or Edith she could still feel the anguish of losing them as if it had been yesterday.

And so it had been with Addis, except that now he had returned from the dead. These thoughts kept insinuating themselves into her mind, sometimes taking it over completely until they ran their course, forcing the old feelings to emerge even if he was no longer the youth on whom they had dwelled.

She looked back at the cart stuffed with trunks and baskets and reeds and stools. The coins were tied in their sack below its planks. The ruby was stitched into the lining of her sewing basket. The emotions of her recollections weighed on her.

A good thing that she had left. If this kept up, she

would have been unable to deny him anything, even seeing now what Claire had done to him and knowing full well the revenge he had taken on her.

She vaguely remembered passing the road south to Salisbury while she daydreamed. In her old plan, that city had been her destination when she finally left. Now it was too close and too small. She headed farther away than that.

The road had been active with travelers all morning, but it had become deserted. She switched her willow at the donkey's flank, thinking it would be wise to catch up with that wine merchant again.

She rounded a bend and, as if summoned by her vague foreboding, three men materialized on the side of the road ahead. Light reflected off their spurs, but then their postures alone bore the arrogance of knights. One crossed the road and they waited for her approach. She urged the donkey to a faster gait and looked straight ahead, hoping they would let her pass.

The two on the left seemed inclined to do so, but the one on the right stepped out and grabbed the donkey's bridle. Instinct alerted her caution.

"Where do you hail from, woman?" he asked. The heavy stubble of a dark beard shadowed his face and his cotte looked soiled by dirt and food.

"My home is far from here. I have just been to the markets in some towns back a ways."

"Did you stop at Darwendon?" another asked while he lifted one of her best baskets from the cart. She wondered if he could assess its value and hence his question. A basket like that, with its several colors and intricate weaving, was not the sort one sold at a town market but rather to the mistress of a manor.

"Nay. If you like that you may take it for your lady," she offered, hoping she could buy them off.

"Still, you must have heard talk at the towns. About Darwendon."

"I seem to recall some comments, but I was just passing through and paid little attention."

"What sort of comments?"

"This and that. The condition of the crops, the number of young sheep . . ."

"Nothing else? About the lord, perhaps?"

A pluck of apprehension scurried up her spine. These knights wore no livery that proclaimed their lord's retinue. Either they were without a liege lord, and possibly brigands living off the theft of travelers, or they sought to hide their identity. In either case they were dangerous. "The lord? Oh, you mean the one who returned recently. Aye, there was some talk of him. A hard man, they say."

"Is he there now? At Darwendon?" The knight holding the donkey peered at her. His eyes reminded her of a fox.

Which would be the better answer? If they knew he was gone, perhaps they would go and lie in wait for him. "Aye, he is there."

The fox released the bridle with a thin smile that said she had chosen wrongly. Hands on hips, with a swaggering authority that made her stomach churn, he paced around the cart eyeing its contents. "Others who passed said he left yesterday. You are lying. I wonder why."

"I do not lie. As I said, I did not pay attention. What do I care about the doings at Darwendon?"

He returned and gave her a look that suggested her truthfulness didn't really matter, that he had moved on to other considerations. The fox eyes glowed and drifted down her body. "Does a basket maker visiting markets always bring her chests and stools? Perhaps you came from there. Perhaps while the hard lord is gone you seek to escape him."

"Perhaps I do, or perhaps I come from one of the other manors or towns nearby. What difference does it make?"

He grinned at his friends. "None."

She flicked the willow switch and the donkey stepped forward. "Then I bid you good day."

Her dismissive tone usually did the trick with men. Certainly it always checked Raymond, but then Raymond at his core was an honorable knight. These three were not. A hand shot out and clutched the bridle again. She watched those fingers close on the leather and knew for certain that she was in horrible trouble. Raw fear gripped her.

"Where is your man?" the fox asked, looking up and down the road, toying with her, emphasizing their isolation.

She battled the panic that wanted to shriek. "Back a short ways. Just behind the bend. A wheel came loose on the other cart. He will be here shortly."

He smiled, charmed that she would even try such a ruse. "The road has grown very quiet," he said to the others. "It must be mealtime."

They laughed and stared at her like so many wolves cornering a chicken. Her stomach heaved. Blind desperation broke. She swung the switch around, slashing all of their faces, then brought it down hard on the donkey.

He lurched forward into an awkward gallop but a donkey leading a cart could hardly outrun them. Still she whipped and whipped, praying they would give up their game. Instead boots pounded up behind her and hands pulled at the cart's walls. The fox leapt up beside her and grabbed the reins with one hand while he twisted her veil and hair with the other.

"Bitch!" he growled, wiping the thin line of blood on his cheek with his arm. He shoved her out of the cart into the arms stretching up to grab her.

She fought like an animal, terror and fury giving her strength. She pummeled and twisted and kicked and bit in a blur of movement. An arcing hand landed hard against her face, snapping it back, but she still resisted. A fist swung into her stomach and the pain quaked through her whole body.

Resignation nearly defeated her then, but while they carried her into the trees the panic returned and she scratched at the eyes of the man who held her shoulders. Her rebellion slowed them and it took a long while to pull her into a clearing.

They hauled her over to a fallen tree trunk and threw her facedown over it. The hard bark pressed into her sore stomach.

"Hold her down. Christ, she's a hellcat."

"Aye, better that way though."

"Hold her still, damn it!"

One stepped over the tree and knelt facing her, pressing his weight onto her back with his hands. Other hands began pushing up her skirt. Senseless with terror, she twisted her head and bit an arm above her and the hold released.

"Damn bitch!"

Leveraging up she kicked blindly behind and her heel connected with a crotch. A guttural cry filled the clearing.

"Looks like you'll be last," the fox laughed. The hands pressed her to the log again and then the man bent over her, his whole chest immobilizing her torso and shoulders.

"Get her skirt up. I'll soften her up some so she's not so much trouble," the fox said.

She couldn't move. Her head was crushed into the stomach of the man holding her and she could barely breathe. What gasps she managed were full of the reek of him. He grabbed up her skirt, exposing her buttocks. She still struggled, but futilely.

The man she had kicked laughed. "God, now that's a sight. Give it to her good so's she learns her lesson."

The sharp sting of a strap landed on her buttocks. She clenched her teeth and her mind went black with rage. She tried to heave up the chest pressing into her back. They all laughed. The tip of the strap tickled at her skin, taunting her, then seconds later it struck again.

"Hell, it's making me hard as rock just watching," her captor groaned. "More."

She braced herself. She would kill them, *kill them*, even if it took her whole life to do it.

Suddenly he groaned again. More a garbled cry, actually. Weight collapsed on her back. Yelling and shouts and furious activity crashed all around her. She pushed up against his stomach and chest. When that didn't work she rolled her body until he slid off.

A chaos of violence assaulted her. Swords flashed and rang and pain-curdled cries echoed. At first it appeared that ten men fought in the clearing, but her befuddled mind slowly realized it was only three and then only two. She glanced down at the head lolling over the tree trunk. Blood dripped from its neck into a puddle in which she sat.

Abruptly a horrible silence fell. She stared wide-eyed at the carnage filling the clearing, unable to absorb it coherently. Blood everywhere, bright and garish, like gaping wounds on nature's bounty, flashed into her senses. With the danger past she succumbed to the terror and began shaking from a cold that arose from her core.

Strong arms lifted her up, crushing her face against a broad chest while the trees sped by. Then she was cradled on hard thighs near the ground, encased in human warmth and flooded with sunlight that began to banish the cold and calm her trembling.

Her senses slowly righted themselves and she found herself staring at a little amber crystal with a bug trapped inside. She lifted her head to a stony profile with a pale scar slicing from hairline to jaw. "What took you so long?" she mumbled.

He turned his eyes on her. Small quakes still shook her, but her gaze seemed to be clearing. Blood streaked her gown but he could not tell if it came from her. Her veil and wimple hung limply from behind one ear and her hair was half-unbound. "I decided to let them whip you to save myself the trouble later."

She pursed her lips. He had hoped for a more spirited reaction that might indicate whipping was all they had done.

"How did you . . . ?"

"I saw the cart left on the road and became curious."

"But the road was empty all the way east."

"I came from the west, around the bend."

Her brow puckered. "Not heading to Darwendon, but away from it?"

She still looked dazed and shocked. He rested his palm against her cheek. Still too cool, but warmth was flowing back. She seemed oblivious to the gesture, so he let it lie there a bit longer than necessary. "I must go elsewhere before I return to Darwendon."

He had almost ridden past that cart until the household goods had caught his eye. And then the baskets. *Exceptional* baskets, as Raymond had described hers. Not really believing she would be either so stupid or so bold as to run away by herself as soon as his back was turned, he had let curiosity lead him to the sounds in the trees.

He had known it was she even though he could see nothing but creamy buttocks and naked legs. Had just known it, and gone berserk. He had let them whip her again while he moved to a better position for first killing the one who held her. He remembered little of the rest. The rage still boiled in his head and in truth he hadn't been in much better shape than she when he carried her away.

She suddenly realized that she sat in his arms and pushed herself onto the ground. She grimaced when her bottom landed, and then rocked forward with an arm over her stomach.

"They asked about you," she muttered. "Maybe they were waiting for you." With disjointed words she told him about the questions.

"Wait here. Do not move. I will be back very soon." He gave her a glance of concern before walking back to the clearing.

He couldn't remember doing half of the damage waiting there. Not like him to lose his head like that, but since it had been three against one it was just as well that he had. He paced over to what was left of the man who had dared abuse her with that strap. He knew him. A youth back then, full of lewd talk when he visited Simon at Barrowburgh.

He doubted they had been lying in wait. Most likely, from their questions, they were just collecting information. But if he had turned that bend unawares he didn't doubt that they would have availed themselves of the opportunity to win Simon's further favor. They would have recognized him more quickly than he did them too. The scar was like a banner announcing his identity.

He returned to Moira. She rested on her hands and knees, getting sick under a bush. Her abuse had probably saved his life. How long had they had her? He couldn't tell from her behavior. He had seen enough slave women after their rapes to know that different ones dealt with it in different ways. She was tough-willed and might act as if nothing had happened and so her calm expression when she struggled to her feet didn't reassure him much.

He took her arm and guided her to the road where his

palfrey was tied to the back of the cart. He handed her a water bladder and she washed out her mouth.

"You are limping," she observed while she pulled the dragging veil and wimple from her head. "You haven't done so before. I thought your hip was fully healed and whole."

"Normally it does not trouble me, but it caught the broadside of a sword back there." He lifted her into the cart and climbed up alongside.

"We expected worse, of course. With the hip. When they brought you to Hawkesford it was corrupted and it looked like you might die or never walk again. Of course, you don't remember any of that. You were out of your head from the fever."

If speaking of ordinary things would help, he'd let her do it, although he would prefer any topic to this one. "Nay, I remember very little. I remember riding off to war newly knighted and newly betrothed, determined to win glory for my lady. I remember the glint of the sun flashing off the falling sword. And I remember healing at Barrowburgh." Actually he remembered much more.

"They brought you to Hawkesford first. It was closer."

He remembered that more than he'd like, even if they were fragmented recollections lost in black despairing fog. "You were there?"

"Where else would I be? Edith and I lived there then. She tended you. Reopened your hip so it could be cleansed. She sewed your face."

"I am indebted to her then. I have been told that I should have lost the eye and most of the movement on that side if it had been done less well."

She peered at the scar curiously. Reaching out, she ran her finger pads down its length, examining it as if it were a new basket weave. He almost recoiled from the gesture.

He couldn't remember any woman welcoming its sight let alone its touch.

"A clean line, not deforming at all. But it wasn't too deep. Edith said that made all the difference. You were lucky."

"Aye, I was very lucky. It only cut my face in half."

His sharp tone flustered her and she snatched her hand away. She looked around, suddenly aware that he sat in the cart too and planned to drive the donkey. "You need not take me back. I will promise to return to the manor."

"You will not travel alone."

"I can take care of myself."

"No doubt you think so. That is probably why I found you bent over that tree with your bare ass to the sky less than a day after you left the manor."

A blush showed beneath her tan. "Then continue on your way. When we pass the first wagon heading west, I will join them."

He'd had no intention of turning back, and he switched the donkey. "Where were you going?"

"To a town."

"A free town? Far away? Where I could not find you for the year and a day it takes to break the bonds?" He could not keep the annoyance from his voice.

She turned her head primly to the passing trees. Her hands rested on her bloodstained dress. Lovely hands, long-fingered and with delicate planes shaping the back of the palms. He could still feel their warm tips tracing the scar on his face.

"What did you plan to do in this free town? Find a husband?"

"Aye." Her blue eyes glinted and the return of their bright clarity heartened him.

"A particular man?"

She shook her head.

"What are your requirements? A proud woman like you probably has a whole list of them. Perhaps I will meet a man who fits your demands. I can reserve him for you. Assuming, of course, that he has one hundred pounds to spare."

She cocked her head. "A freemason, I've decided. Well established and highly skilled. Preferably on his way to becoming a master builder."

"Why a freemason?"

"The ones I have met are intelligent. They make good wages, are respected, belong to major craftsmen companies, and are almost always employed."

"When employed they are away from home most of the year."

"Aye, there is that benefit too."

Well, well. So the virgin widow was not a virgin but had decided she didn't like bedding much. Her choice of a mason made excellent sense.

She seemed back to normal. He had to know. "Back there, did they hurt you more than I saw, before I came?"

"Nay."

The firm response relieved him more than he expected. He didn't know what he would have done if the answer had been otherwise. He'd already killed them, so he could hardly track them down and kill them again.

They rode silently for some time. Moira twisted and grabbed a sack with some bread and cheese and offered him some. She forced herself to nibble, but had no appetite. Her stomach hurt and her buttocks still stung and the day's experiences had cast a pall over everything.

Those men had sapped her courage. Soon she would be headed back to Darwendon. It might be a long while before she found a way to leave that didn't include this kind of danger.

Maybe she would never find the heart to leave again at all. She certainly didn't feel strong enough to consider it now. In fact, the idea of living out her days at Darwendon, within shouting distance of Addis's sword, appealed to her. The size and strength of the man sitting close beside her offered a seductive comfort and his rescue and their shared danger had produced a raw intimacy.

She looked to the bloodstains on her garment. They would never wash out. It didn't matter because she would never wear it again anyway. It smelled of that man. *She* smelled of him.

"Were they from Simon?" she asked.

"Aye. I recognized one. He must have sent them when he heard, to see what they could learn. Simon is shrewd. He will take his time to decide what to do."

"How would he know?"

"Someone must have gone and told him. Many have seen me since I landed in Bristol. With this face, I cannot hide who I am."

His casual attitude toward his danger irked her. "He will try to kill you."

"Not necessarily. If he is secure in the king's favor, he may decide that I am a nuisance that can be ignored."

"He must know that you will move against him, king's favor or not."

"Why must he know that? I do not even know it myself."

"You cannot intend to accept this! Simon has taken what belongs to you, to your son. It would be a fine thing if I spent four years teaching Brian about the duty for which he must prepare only to have his father turn his back on their honor."

"Is that what you were doing? Raising the boy to be strong and true so that he could fight Simon when he was grown?"

His tone fell somewhere between fascination and sarcasm. It did sound foolish when he put it like that. "He had a right to know who he was, what rightfully belongs to him. You find that amusing?"

His mouth softened into a smile. It was the first one she had seen in all these days. "Not amusing. I find it ironic."

She noticed distant movement on the road ahead. A large wagon drawn by horses lumbered toward them, with a man and woman in front. They looked safe enough, and she could follow them most of the way back home. She raised her hand to hail them.

"Nay," Addis said. "If I send you back, you will just run away again."

"I would say that I have learned my lesson."

"For a day or two, no more. You are a stubborn, willful woman. Soon you will convince yourself it would not happen again. I may be gone for several weeks, and if you go back one less villein will be there when I return. I have decided that you will come with me."

"*You* are a very stubborn *man* if you saddle yourself with the inconvenience of a woman. . . ."

"It will be very convenient. Finding you has proven fortuitous. You want to go to a free town? I will take you to one. London. My mother had a house there, and it occurs to me that it will have been vacant for some years. It will need attention, and I doubt that any servants remain. While you serve me there you can look for your freemason."

"You go to London?" She tried to keep the excitement out of her voice. London, the biggest town of them all. London, with its royal charter of freedoms, beholden to no lord. London, with so many people and lanes that a woman could easily dodge anyone searching for her, for a year and a day if necessary. Claire's servant Alice had gone

to London, and it was to London that she had been heading when those men assaulted her.

Her spirits renewed immediately and all thoughts of
cowering at Darwendon disappeared. She smiled inwardly,
and glanced at the man who claimed to be her lord. She
would let Addis de Valence escort her to London, but
once they got there she would not serve him.

"Aye, we go to London," he said. "But first we go to
Barrowburgh."

CHAPTER 4

PEACE. THAT WAS WHAT he felt in her presence. He could not account for it. She did not have to speak, she did not even have to know he was there for the comfort to flow like warm water. He had experienced a peculiar strangeness since returning, as if he walked foreign ground during a distant time. Only when she was near did he feel properly centered inside his own body and existing in the world in the normal way.

He had almost turned back to Darwendon because of her. He had stopped where the road from Salisbury met this one and debated it. The peace waiting in one direction held much more appeal than the conflict promised in the other. She would not welcome his return or his demands for her presence, but the peace would still be his while she moved through the manor and sat aside at the table. He doubted that he could flatter or bribe her into more than that. She resented his claims, and the deformed Addis de Valence would hardly succeed where the handsome Raymond Orrick had failed.

He drove the cart until twilight began falling even though his hip pained him and Moira grew weary and uncomfortable. She was not an inconvenience, but the cart and donkey were. It would take much longer to make this journey now. But he also pushed on because he wanted them both exhausted before he made camp for the night. She would sleep then despite what had happened this day, and he would sleep too, despite the temptation of ultimate peace lying a few paces away.

It did not work that way. Sleep did not come quickly at all. He lay by the fire listening to her soft breaths carried to him on the night from the place he had made for her in the cart. He imagined that breath in his ear and on his body and felt himself sinking into her softness and warmth. He rose and walked into the trees, away from her, and forced himself to reconsider the decisions he had taken regarding Simon.

The man would not move against him publicly. He would not risk the king's disfavor by committing an open murder that might inflame the opposing barons. If the quiet opportunity came his way, that was different, but in that perhaps nothing had changed. The truth regarding that suspicion should be clear soon enough, but barring such a chance Simon would bide his time.

So the immediate future depended upon the king and the law and the customs of the realm. If those failed him then the choice would be faced squarely, but he suspected it would be a bigger choice than Raymond or Moira saw. At least he would face it in London, where he might better learn the odds and risks. He would face it while Moira's peace would help him to think more clearly. And Simon's quiet opportunity would be harder to find or arrange in London.

Contemplation of what awaited unsettled him, and he paced back to the fire. He paused at the cart and looked in.

She rested on her side, one hand in a loose fist by her face as a child might sleep, her dark hair making a nest for her head.

He had planned to make this a fast journey, but that would not be necessary now. He could stay in London for as long as it took, because the reason beckoning him back to Darwendon would be with him.

He should let her go when they arrived in the city, release her to the life she claimed as her right, but he could not. If she found her stonemason he should allow her to wed, but he would not. A man who had been enslaved should be sympathetic to her quest, and he was, even though her status was not that of a slave and he knew the difference all too well. For one thing, if she were a slave she would have been in his bed from that first night, and he would not be peering over a cart wall at her, battling his desire.

He might be sympathetic, but that weighed little against that desire, or the peace, or the inexplicable possessiveness that had made him kill three men for trying to defile her.

He roused her at dawn and got them back on the road in quick order. Moira found some dried grasses among the trees with which to make a cushion on which to sit. She looked like some harvest goddess perched on a bed of hay beside him, reminding him of ceremonies that he had seen in the Baltic lands. It was at planting and harvest that the oldest rituals were performed by Eufemia's people, rites that alluded to an ancient time when their supreme deity had been a woman and not a man, when the physical vitality of the earth had possessed more importance than the vast abstractness of the sky.

They rode past more woods, and he thought about those years among the Baltic people. The experiences seemed more familiar to him now than the memories of his own family and land. They believed that every shrub and plant, every stream and pool, even every rock, was a home to a spirit. After a few years he had come to understand. After he had lain with Eufemia he could sometimes sense the spirits quivering in the growth around him, speaking a primitive language to his soul.

The trees now flanking the road contained none of that. If there had ever been spirits in the land of England, they had long ago left or been silenced. Here the rocks were for moving or chiseling, the streams for washing and drinking, the trees for cutting and burning. Eufemia's people performed their ceremonies in the open air, surrounded by the spirits. The Christian God was worshiped in buildings constructed by clever, intelligent masons who deformed the stones with tools and logic.

He glanced at the woman who had concluded she should marry such a man. Her head was bent and she sniffed herself, making a little grimace. Long fingers plucked at the cloth over her breast, pumping it slightly to let air flow. He had driven the cart off the road at sundown yesterday, not worrying whether there was water nearby, but he knew it was not the day's sweat that she smelled so distastefully.

She noticed him looking at the swells appearing and disappearing beneath the puffing cloth and straightened in her ladylike way.

"Were you imprisoned all those years?" she asked to divert his attention.

"Nay." She had been the first person to ask outright. Not even Raymond had sought the details. Everyone assumed he had endured horrible, heathen tortures that were unfit for discussion.

"Then why didn't you come home or send word? Everyone thought you were dead and look at the problems it created. God's crusade or not, you had duties and obligations here."

"For a woman determined to escape her duties and obligations to me, you are sharp-tongued enough in reminding me of mine to everyone else."

"Do not be ridiculous. You were born to your responsibilities."

"As you were born to yours. Tell me, how was it learned that I was dead?"

"When the others returned to Barrowburgh. The knights who had joined you. They came back with the tale that you had fallen during one of the campaigns, during one of the r . . . r . . ."

Lost in that swamp, the French fool leading them having no idea where to go. "During a *reise*. It is a German word. The Teutonic Knights who led the Baltic crusade are mostly German."

"They said that you had been cut down. One saw you fall."

Horses pouring at them from every direction. The enemy whom they had been running down for days suddenly materializing en masse, swords and spears ready, possessing a determination the haphazard collection of crusaders could never match.

"But they could not be sure I was dead." *Which one had seen him fall? Who had been with him that day?*

"Only a few escaped that attack. They said that even if you had only been wounded the pagans would kill you as they always did the fallen crusaders."

"It is the Teutonic Knights who kill all the defeated. Women and children too. Not the pagans." *Not one of our spears, Eufemia had said. The wound is the wrong shape.*

"If they would just convert, this would end," Moira said, articulating the logic of all of Christendom.

"If they convert, they do not lose only their gods. That crusade is not just about Christianity, but about land. The Teutonic Knights have a kingdom stretching for hundreds of miles out from their city of Marienburg, all of it taken when they defeated tribe after tribe, and they seek more. They give the land to crusaders who fight for them. They even gave me some, to compensate me for my ordeal. But now they have met a people who will not be easily conquered, and a king as shrewd as any Teutonic Knight or Roman pope."

It just poured out, unexpected, thoughts never before articulated since, freed by Eufemia, he had suddenly seen that crusade in a different way. In Eufemia's way. Back with the Knights, no longer needing the illusions that had sustained him for six years, the scales had fallen from his eyes during his final *reise* into the Wildnis. It had been a campaign of personal revenge when he embarked, but riding his horse through the carnage of bodies in that first defenseless village, he had known that he could never do it again.

He expected Moira to look more shocked. They were pagans, and one did not defend them. Instead curiosity lit her eyes. "What ordeal? They gave you land, you said, to compensate you for your ordeal. If you were not imprisoned, not captured . . ."

"They are a slaveholding people. They trade in them, sending most of them east into Rus'ia or south as far as the Saracens. They make slave raids into neighboring lands. I was captured, but not imprisoned the way you think. For six years, I was a slave. I was not traded, but kept by one of their priests." He had sworn to tell no one in England about that degradation. Perhaps this peace had its dangerous side.

Her blue eyes sparked. "You lived as a slave, you know what it means, and the first thing that you do upon returning is force me back into bondage!"

"It is not the same thing. I was not born to it, and you

are not a slave. A slave does not ride in the cart, but pulls it. A slave does not own property, but is property. A slave does not speak to her master as you do to me without being punished."

He had not meant it as a threat but she retreated as if he had, as well she might. A serf did not speak to her lord the way he allowed her to address him either.

"Still, one would think . . ."

"One would think that upon his release a man once enslaved would want to free the world? It does not work that way. A man brought low wants to raise himself up, and make clear the distinction between the past and the present."

"So you use me to remind yourself that you are no longer as I am. I enhance your self-worth, much as Darwendon does. I trust that when you get Barrowburgh back and are drowning in status and property and serfs that you will no longer need me to feed your pride and remind you of who you were born to be!"

He doubted that it would turn out that way because he did not keep her for those reasons. Her explanation made much more sense than his, however, so he did not correct her.

She turned her body away and did not speak for hours. Her annoyance could not affect the peace, and he was not much given to talk anyway. Angled this way he could look at her without her seeing it, so he did not disturb whatever thoughts occupied her. On occasion he saw her repeat that private sniffing.

He should have thought about that yesterday. Almost all those slave women reacted the same way about that part of it. After being used they would want to wash. He kept a lookout for a stream or pond.

"Did you have a family there? Is it permitted with their

slaves?" she asked suddenly, as if hours had not interrupted their conversation.

"It is permitted, but not freely chosen, and of course
there is no Christian marriage. Another way in which
slaves are different than villeins."

"As you said at the hallmote, only because the Church
has interfered."

The sun had peaked and begun to fall when he left the
woods behind and scanned the countryside. He spotted
the glitter of water not far ahead and drove the cart
toward it, angling off the road and down a low hill toward
the small lake.

Moira climbed off the cart, stretching and sighing with
exaggeration to let him know that he had waited too long
to stop.

"The lake looks shallow. Go and wash if you want. I
will stay here with your cart," he said.

She looked at him with surprise and then suspicion.
He stretched himself out on the hill behind the cart where
he could observe the road. She must have realized that he
could not watch her from that position, because she rummaged in a basket, then walked down to the lake.

He stripped off his buckskin tunic. The thin leather was
cooler than wool but still too warm for the summer sun.
Lying back in the grasses, he closed his eyes and tried not
to imagine the lush body being uncovered thirty paces
away.

That proved impossible, since all morning a part of his
mind had been divining the various parts until it had constructed a fairly complete image. Full breasts, high and
firm, enough to fill his hands, probably with velvety brown
tips. The rest creamy in color, like the round buttocks he
had seen, much lighter than the tan of her face. Elegant
curving lines where torso tapered to waist and then flared

to those womanly hips. Long legs, with thighs . . . Having her in London was going to be very uncomfortable if the condition of his body right now was any indication. Her presence might bring peace to his soul, but the price would be torture of a different sort.

Slapping water joined the sounds of birds and wildlife. Moira could find no place in the little lake that would be invisible from the road, so she refrained from stripping as she wanted to do. Instead she bunched her skirts up around her thighs and, turning her back to the cart, scrubbed her legs.

Untying the lacing across the top of her bodice, she slipped the gown off her arms and shoulders. The smell of those men had wafted to her nose for over a day now, reminding her of the experience. This stop would delay them a good hour, but she was grateful that Addis had made it. He still limped and presumably needed to rest his hip, but she suspected that he had guessed that she wanted to wash. In small ways like this she had seen a few cracks in the hard facade.

It would be nice to believe that one day the whole shell would crumble away and the old Addis would emerge, but she doubted that could ever happen. She wasn't even sure she would want it to. He may have grown hard, but also thoughtful and sharp, and that might serve him well in the months ahead. Her own maturity had also given her the wisdom to admit that the youthful Addis had not been without flaws. The girl in her might wish the young squire would return, but the woman rather preferred the man.

She splashed water on her arms and neck. Glancing over her shoulder she could not see him, and so she lowered the gown and washed her breasts. Aye, she rather liked the man, but she could do without his silent self-

BY POSSESSION ✦ 67

possession. It had not been just his years in the Baltic that
had done that to him. His life as a slave may have forged
the hard privacy that armored his person, but the internal
changes had begun before he left. Probably they were why
he had left, and Claire lay at the root of it all.

Beautiful Claire. Elegant, charming, radiant Claire.
Frivolous, spoiled, vain Claire. She had loved Claire with
acceptance the way a sister might, but had always known
what she had in her and had marveled that no one else
ever noticed how little of substance lay beneath the light.
Certainly not the men. Definitely not Addis, but then he
had been spoiled and vain too. They had been born for
each other, two perfect, self-centered children who assumed the world had been created as a setting for their
idyllic love.

She remembered them at their betrothal, looking like
figures who had stepped out of a tapestry. She had been
awed like everyone else. Who could not be? Addis stood
so tall and strong, the perfect knight, his dark, deep-set
eyes ablaze. Claire appeared ethereal, floating in silk and
virtue, secure in the belief that in Addis she had gotten
what she obviously deserved.

Then the dream had ended, the idyll had shattered, and
the world had intruded with its harsh truths. And Claire
had been unable to even look at the resulting wreckage, let
alone touch it. Moira knew more about Claire and Addis
than anyone else. Much more than Addis suspected. Far
more than she would like.

A flurry of activity on the lake crashed through her
reverie. Birds and waterfowl suddenly took to noisy flight.
She turned to see Addis striding through the shallow
water, naked to his waist, creating violent eddies and
splashes, coming right toward her with a dangerous expression.

Woman's instinct screamed a warning. She looked down

and saw naked legs and thighs and a wet garment clutched to breasts, barely covering them. Frantic about her vulnerability, and not liking the determination with which he hurried toward her, she turned and tried to run, her thoughts scrambled by her alarm.

Why now? If he planned to force her he could have done so anytime. Last night, even yesterday.

"Do not run away." He did not shout but the command carried clearly over the water. His lordly tone did not reassure her at all. Holding the gown made movement awkward and she let the skirt fall. A mistake, that. The fabric served like a wick and immediately she was dragging heavy sodden drapery.

He was upon her in an instant, grabbing her around the waist. She twisted and squirmed and pushed with the arm not clasping the gown to her body. She opened her mouth to scream but a rough palm gagged her. "Cry out and I will hit you," he growled.

He began dragging her toward the bank, saying something she didn't hear while she blindly struggled. How could she have been so stupid! Of course he wanted his bondwoman with him. More convenient than seeking out whores.

She leveraged an elbow sharply into his stomach and he spit a curse. The lake and bank blurred past while he turned her around, lifted her, and slung her over his shoulder.

She poured desperate arguments onto his back. "Release me! Do not do this! You are an honorable and chivalrous knight—"

"Be silent!"

"I won't! Think of your soul. My God, you went on a crusade. You are probably guaranteed salvation. Would you risk that for a few moments—"

"Hell's teeth, woman, I just told you . . ." He climbed up the bank and dumped her down beneath a tall bush. She rolled and scrambled to crawl away, still clutching the wet gown to her chest. Firm hands grabbed her hips and dragged her back, then flipped her. She watched in horror as he descended on her, immobilizing her with his body.

"Spread your legs."

She beat at his shoulders and face with her free hand. "You had better kill me, you animal, because if I live I will not be silent. I will go to the royal courts! I will see you burned or castrated!"

"Spread them!" He pressed her flailing arm up over her head with one hand and yanked her legs wide with the other and pushed the wet skirt up to her thighs.

Oh saints! How could she have been so wrong? How could she have been so foolish as to ignore what he was capable of?

He grasped her hair, forcing her face to meet his. "I said I am not going to hurt you! Listen!" His tone and eyes brought her panic up short. He glanced over his shoulder, across the lake. "Listen."

Gasping shallow breaths, she turned her attention in the direction of his gesture. Sounds of horses and talk rumbled across the water. A different alarm replaced her fear.

"How many?"

"Between twenty and thirty."

"Colors?"

"White and scarlet."

"Simon . . ."

"Perhaps not. No doubt you think I should have stood in the road and hailed them to be sure first."

"We are a long ways from Barrowburgh though."

"But we are close enough."

She could see the road over his shoulder. The first riders appeared in view. What would they see if they looked down to the lake? A basket maker's cart and donkey, and a man and woman coupling under a bush. Better than a half-naked woman bathing and Addis de Valence sleeping on the hill, especially if they came from Barrowburgh. Or an unattended cart which might tempt the overbold. A cart *with her ruby in it*.

"Can you see a banner or standard?" Addis asked quietly into the crook of her neck. Despite her attention on the road, his warmth and breath unsettled her.

"Aye. One passes now. A banner. Scarlet, then white. A gold falcon crosses the colors."

"Simon's."

"Do you think that they head to Darwendon?"

"No way to tell. Would you have me go and ask?"

"The horse . . ."

"He grazes nearby, below a rise. They may not see him and if they do there is nothing to say he is mine. The sword is not even a knight's weapon."

She embraced his shoulders with her free arm. She doubted much more was visible than the entangled forms of two people and a woman's naked legs, but if they looked this way let them assume a craftsman and his wife had paused to dally.

They were noticed. She saw a hand point and heard low laughter and a few ribald comments. "A few are stopping."

"Then forgive me, madam." He leveraged his weight slightly and pressed his hips forward. She closed her eyes in humiliation at the evidence that their ruse was not entirely a fabrication. Well, if he didn't react to being held between a woman's thighs there would be something wrong with him.

"They are moving on." She kept her eyes peeled until the sounds began to grow faint and the last man passed. "They are gone," she said, smiling up with relief.

The face looking down mere inches from hers caused her to go very still. His expression looked severe and intent and devoid of any concern for passing soldiers. Their physical connection abruptly shouted for attention.

She grew acutely aware of her arm embracing the straight shoulders hovering above her and the feel of his warm skin beneath her hand. Stripped of the fear she saw him anew striding through the water, the slabbed muscles in his chest glistening in the sun, the buckskin soaked against his hips and thighs, his dark hair flying behind him. The images carried a perilous appeal.

The silence became heavy. She tried to ignore the erotic nature of their positions, but instead she was stunningly conscious of every inch of him and the expression in his eyes spoke his awareness too. He slowly looked at her brow, her nose, her jaw, and then tilted his head to examine the shoulders and chest all too visible above the hand still holding the garment to her breast. Her skin flushed beneath his meandering gaze, making it impossible to pretend she was indifferent.

"You would go to the royal courts, Moira? To have me burned or castrated? You are a vicious woman." He smiled. The second one that she had seen. "And here I thought that you at least were not afraid of me."

Not like the others are, but I am afraid. Expectant apprehension scampered through her with a vengeance now, strangely delicious and full of a stimulating quality. It filled her belly with a curious weightiness and made all her senses unnaturally alert. *Nothing but trouble, nothing but shame,* her conscience warned, but even as it did her body began relaxing beneath his of its own accord, molding to his strength, welcoming his pressure. Could he tell? Did he feel the warmth tingling her? A power poured off of him that said that he did.

"I have this ridiculous tendency to get hysterical whenever a man throws himself on me and orders me to spread my legs," she said dryly, hoping to push them both back from the chasm they seemed to be hurtling toward.

He shifted his lower body off of her, releasing her legs, but he didn't move away. His eyes examined hers thoughtfully in that invasive way, demanding an invisible connection. "If you had stopped fighting for a moment you would have heard me explain."

She could get away now. She had only to push at those shoulders and it would be over. She would never be able to pretend it had been otherwise. But his maleness intoxicated her and his power and mystery compelled her, and her whole body felt anxious and waiting in a way she had never experienced before.

It took him forever. Time pulsed in silence with their heads a hand span apart, their eyes locked in a mutually naked gaze. Long after her breath had quickened and her confused heart had accepted it, he waited. They both knew she would not stop him before he lowered his mouth to hers.

Who would have thought that hard mouth could kiss so softly? His lips pressed and moved and bit in a slow, luring dance, as if he tested her taste and checked her compliance. From what Claire had described she had expected a burst of violent passion, not this courtly, almost boyish restraint. Those delicious, searching kisses summoned the remembered heartache of a girl watching from the shadows and the breathless desire of a woman too long without a man, and her complex, poignant response to the joining stunned her. Was it the girl or the woman who impulsively embraced his shoulders, pulling him closer?

His arms circled her body and arched her up to him and the next kiss wasn't nearly so careful. It consumed with possessiveness that grew primitive. His tongue seduced an opening and then explored with a gentle intimacy that rapidly transformed into demand. The warmth of his chest burned through the cool dampness of the gown barely covering her breasts, teasing her skin with the contrast. Memories and emotions and thrilling sensations merged into helpless acceptance. She stretched her hand into his hair and joined him in an ascending passion that blotted out everything but the astonishing urge to give and take.

He ended it, not her. The tension of control slid through him like an eddy of water. He eased the embrace and, separating slightly, trailed his mouth over her neck and shoulders, making little patterns of heat on her water-cooled skin that seemed to sink into her blood. A groan of affirmation almost escaped her when he began exploring her body, learning its shape with a firm hand that wandered over hips and belly and found the thighs buried under the sodden drapery.

She had learned something of lovemaking with her second husband but she had never wanted like this, had never trembled from small touches or waited with such concentrated anticipation for that possessive hand to move on. And that townsman had never taken this long just to kiss and caress, and had never made her body experience such delicious, trickling desire.

He peeled down the cloth plastered against her chest, exposing her breasts to the dappled sunlight. He caressed them and she gritted her teeth at the breathless craving his touch and gaze created. When a thumb curved up and grazed a tight nipple, her whole body reacted with an instinctive stretch of offering. He stroked her softness with his face and then rose up on one straight arm.

"Not here," he said. He covered her breast totally with his hand, the palm pressing the hard nipple and the fingers spreading down its sides. He watched his hand move down her body, curving around waist and hip, splaying over belly, lining down and up thighs. He finally cupped her woman's mound with a subtle pressure that caused hungry thrills of sensation. The long, studied caress pronounced possession claimed but delayed. "Not now."

He kissed her, a mere brushing of lips, and turned to rise. The muscles in his back stretched and corded while he leveraged to his feet, leaving her arms empty and her body tight with discomfort.

Conflicting emotions assaulted her. A vague gratitude that he had shown restraint but strong disappointment that he had gone no further. A prickling resentment that he had denied her the one time she had wanted this thing.

She glanced to the water and the road and reality slashed into her dazed perceptions. She realized with a shock how exposed they had been.

He reached down a hand and she looked up the length of his arm. She suddenly saw them as others would, a half-naked bondwoman lying at the feet of her lord. In fact, that was undoubtedly how *he* saw them. The assumptions implicit in his last words echoed. A devastating knowledge that she had just made a horrible mistake closed in on her.

She reached through the echoes of yearning and found her common sense. Not now? Not ever. She pulled her gown up and struggled to her feet. She turned away from him with embarrassment.

"Do you have other garments?" he asked.

"On the bank . . . near where I was standing . . ."

He left and fetched them and brought them to her. He strode off into the water and she nipped into the trees to change, listening to the splashes of his washing. She slipped on the blue gown thinking that in the future she would also wear a shift despite the heat. She set a veil low over her hair and pinned the wimple around her neck even though the headdress would be uncomfortable while they traveled.

Encased from head to toe in cloth, she ambled around the edge of the lake until she joined him near the cart. Water sparkled off his hair and tanned chest and soaked his lower garment against his hard legs. His dark eyes carried the intensity that had unsettled her from the start. Their message seemed very obvious now, and she wondered how she could have been so ignorant.

He hadn't played fair. Why couldn't he have leered and groped like other men so it *would* have been clear? Why couldn't he have been a total stranger and not someone who old memories insisted was incapable of seeing her this way? She would have insisted on returning with that wagon that passed instead of staying with him. Now they were traveling to London together, and this other thing would stand between them the whole time creating saints knew what problems. He had probably intended for her to serve as his lehman while there and now he assumed that she had agreed to it. It was going to be very awkward, very difficult, and maybe very dangerous.

She began climbing the hill. The sounds of the cart followed her. The danger, she admitted with chagrin, came from herself as well as him. The offer of childish dreams fulfilled pulled the reins behind her. The promise of passion and warmth walked nearby, beautiful in form, slicked by water, glistening in the sun. The suggestion that maybe it would be worth the shame and ruination stuck one finger into her mind, horrifying her.

Dear saints, what had she done? She knew the answer with groaning certainty. She had jeopardized everything, her chance for a decent future, her plans for a marriage and family, her right to respect, even her own resolve, for an intemperate flurry of kisses and caresses.

"I will walk a while," she said over her shoulder when they reached the road. The cart followed. She glanced back and saw that he rode in it. She looked again some time later and noticed he had put on the tunic, which helped some, but that the sun lit beautifully on his face, which didn't help at all. In this light his tanned visage was all sculpted planes and ridges and angles, and the deepest shadows held eyes that studied her.

Nothing but trouble. She sighed. She had been carrying a bowl very full of emotional oil the last few days and now some had spilled out and she didn't know how to mop it up.

She must have walked an hour before the cart pulled closer and the donkey's breath warmed her shoulder. "Get in now," Addis said. "You are slowing us down too much."

She just plodded forward. The cart stopped. A few moments later arms lifted her up. He carried her past the animal and dumped her on the seat, then climbed up and took the reins. "Do not be a child. I am not going to devour you."

She perched as far from him as possible and settled her draping gown in billowing, abstract mounds. Addis watched the preparations with both annoyance and amusement. Did she really think that shrouding herself would make a difference? He had only to look at her and his memory replaced her wary expression with the sparkling passion he had seen a short while ago. His mind easily stripped away the blue garment and examined again the strong body and full, begging breasts. Her strict, unmoving posture now could hardly obliterate the feel of her languid stretches and trembles of pleasure.

Her serious mouth only reminded him of her warm, bonding kisses.

Wonderful kisses. He had forgotten how long it had been since he had just enjoyed kissing a woman. Years. Since his youth, now that he wondered about it. There had been little kissing with Eufemia and none with the whores before her. Kissing was something he had done as a squire, little milestones on the way to goals often unattained with those servants and village girls who substituted for the virtuous Claire. If they hadn't been in full view of the road he might have lain there for hours just kissing Moira's lips and body.

She regretted it. She would have walked all the way to London if he hadn't let her know that she had made her point. His annoyance said he should have given her more to feel so guilty about. Just claimed her there in the dirt by the lake, instead of worrying that she would feel degraded by a quick coupling in full view of the road. She was a bondwoman, *his bondwoman*, and he had retreated as if she were some lady virgin needing feather mattresses and velvet bed-hangings. From the look of things, getting her willing again would not be easy.

He glanced at the water-blue eyes fixed resolutely on the road ahead. Not easy, but compelling. He would have to seduce her though. Something else he hadn't attempted since he had been a squire. Could he even remember how it was done?

He would wait until after Barrowburgh. His restraint should reassure her, and success would be unlikely with her skittish like this. It would also be very unchivalrous to seduce her and then immediately get himself killed.

She caught him contemplating her. Her look darted away and she flushed as if she had read his calculations. He smiled a smile that she didn't see.

You fear that you have made a strategic mistake, little Shadow, and you are right. I would have assumed that you did not want me and settled for the comfort of your presence, but desire thus encouraged can never really be denied again. Now this ends only one way. Sooner or later, you are completely mine.

CHAPTER 5

C<small>UT IT</small>."

Addis held out the well-honed knife. Moira regretfully examined the raven locks cascading thickly over his naked shoulders and back, waving slightly, more beautiful than most women's. They were the first words he had spoken all morning while they broke their fast and prepared to decamp. He had barely acknowledged her, as if all his sight had turned inward. Darkness tinged his mood.

"Do you really need to?"

"No knights in England wear it thus."

"Raymond does."

"Raymond was always more vain than even Claire about his hair. Do it. I will not ride into Barrowburgh looking like a barbarian."

Her hand snatched away from the blade. "Ride into . . . you cannot intend . . ."

"Do you think I came just to gaze fondly upon the walls of my home?"

"You are mad! He will kill you!"

"You should hope so. You will be free then. Brian will hardly insist upon your bondship." He took her hand and smacked the knife's hilt into it. "Now, cut."

She lifted a thick section and the blade slid through it as if it were silk. Beautiful hair. Just like God to waste it on a man. The waves grew more pronounced while the heavy strands fell to the ground. When she finished Addis ran his fingers back from his forehead. Without a word he went to his saddle, removed garments from a bag, and disappeared into the trees.

She set about replacing the stools and baskets into the cart from where Addis had removed them so that she could sleep. After what had happened by the lake two days ago she had worried about the nights, but he had acted as if nothing had changed when they finally camped that day. And so she had been spared having to bombard him with the denials that she had practiced all afternoon.

In fact, he had been exceedingly courteous these last two days, talking more than normal, behaving with a rather indifferent politeness and acting, if the truth be told, a bit more like the old Addis. It was clear that he also recognized that their intemperance had merely been an imprudent response to the embrace forced on them by danger. Yesterday she had slowly grown less wary. When they had traded some reminisces about two comical guards from Hawkesford she had finally laughed herself into relaxation and accepted that her transgression hadn't created the problem she had feared.

Their brief talk about Hawkesford had produced a new intimacy, born of the acknowledgment that years ago they had lived lives connected by that household. The ease with which he spoke of it startled her since he had never mentioned such memories before. She had waited within that warm connection for him to ask the questions that surely he must have about Claire and Brian and all the rest.

Instead he had lapsed into his stony silence, burning the little bridge they had built. He might jest about a bow-legged guard but would not discuss the important things. If he hadn't just mentioned Claire before she cut his hair, one might easily wonder if he had forgotten that she ever existed. Had her name surfaced now because they were a mile from Barrowburgh, and that was where the worst of it had occurred?

She should not judge him. Claire's story had never rung completely true and even if it had been as she said, Claire had not been blameless. What had she expected? Moira knew the answer to that. Claire had expected her own way. She had always gotten it before.

He emerged from the trees. Her heart made a flipping little thud at the transformation. He no longer looked like the displaced barbarian, but very much the son of Patrick de Valence. Hair fell back from his face in thick waves the way it had in his youth. The face itself suddenly looked distressingly familiar, only weathered and seasoned and forever marked by experience. He wore black leather hose and a short blue cotte bound by a knight's belt, and golden spurs flashed at his boot heels. She had seen neither symbol of his status before, and guessed that he had procured them on his trip with Brian. The only other signs of wealth were two gold bands circling his forearms, but every inch of him proclaimed the birth and blood that decreed his right to Barrowburgh.

He began readying his horse. She watched, feeling oddly disconnected from him, as if their small friendship had evaporated with the morning mist while he dressed. She sensed determination in him, but also still that unsettling something else.

"The sword is here in the cart," she said, starting to lift it out.

"I will not take it."

"You go without arms?"

"I will not need them."

"You are a fool."

He swung up onto the horse, shooting her a warning glance that made her shrink. Much harder to speak boldly to this Addis than to the man who had sat beside her in the cart. "I have no armor, and that sword is not the blade of a knight. Weapons and plate will avail me little if Simon chooses to kill me. Let everyone see that I ride in with no sword then, so my death will be known as murder." He looked to the treetops. "Come here."

She moved close to his leg. He bent until his head was near hers and pointed up. "Wait until the sun moves just behind those high branches there. If I have not returned, take the cart and go back up to the Roman road and head east. You should make Waverly by nightfall."

"For a man so sure that he is not in danger, you certainly cover the eventuality of your death with prudence."

He straightened. "One never knows."

"Indeed. Then let us be thorough. If you do not return, I will head west, not east, to fetch Brian. Where is he?"

"He is safe, and no longer your concern."

"Nay? Then whose concern will he be? Do those who care for him know what to do if you die? Will they understand that Simon must never—"

"If I die no one will ever find him."

"He will be frightened and think he has been abandoned by everyone. Tell me and I will let Raymond know and we will get him and keep him safe. I will go live at Hawkesford and care for him."

"Would you go to Raymond's bed for Brian's sake? You

must know that is the only way that you can ever return to Hawkesford."

Would she? Raymond had never used her love of the boy against her, but if that became a condition of having him back, would she accept it?

"If I am dead again, things are no different than they were a month ago. He would not be safe at Hawkesford, and Simon will search at Darwendon as well now. Better that he grow up where he is." He turned the horse, and headed toward the path that would connect with the road to his home. At the woods' edge he paused and looked back at her. "Come here," he ordered again.

She walked over. He looked magnificent on that horse. No banners or retinue would announce his honor, but his presence commanded attention and managed to exude authority anyway.

"Do not think to run away, Moira. I will find you if you do, and will be displeased about the time it takes."

"Saints, we certainly would not want you displeased, my lord." She spoke flippantly to hide her worry about his safety and her annoyance about Brian. And her dismay that she hadn't even considered the chance for escape that his absence would create.

The Lord of Barrowburgh did not find his bondwoman's sarcasm amusing. Rough fingers cupped her chin and tilted her head up. "Nay, you would not. I indulge you much, but do not misthink my will on this. A part of your lord's soul no longer lives by Christian chivalry or embraces the customs of this realm. He knows full well how to enforce obedience if it is necessary. You are smart enough to know that this day of all days is not the time to challenge me. Pray that he kills me if you want, but be waiting here if he does not."

He kicked the palfrey and disappeared into the woods.

She watched the forest swallow him. With a horrible intensity she experienced anew that severing certainty of loss that she had felt when he and Brian rode away from Darwendon. Was it talk of the boy that did this to her?

She busied herself packing the remaining items on the cart, seeking distraction from the strange mood. She *should* pray that he died. Hadn't she left Darwendon deliberately intending to end one life and begin another? One sign from Simon during the next few hours and she would be free.

She suddenly pictured it happening with an eerie clarity. She saw in her mind Simon greeting Addis like a brother, offering him wine, subtly making the signal that brought a sword down. A silent, visceral scream shook her while the weapon fell. She saw his eyes, placid and accepting, and something like relief pass in them while the lights were extinguished.

She blinked away the image and whirled to stare at the spot where he had disappeared.

Suddenly she recognized the emotion darkly edging his aura all morning. A small part of him hoped it would happen that way. She just knew it, even if he did not. She had felt it in him once before, like a force urging him toward a despair that made the abyss alluring. It might gain succor from what he would find at his home, and spread until it weakened his vigilance and dulled his instincts. She should have known it sooner for what it was, and said or done something to thwart its insidious power.

Cursing her stupidity, she fished for a knife in one of her baskets. Kneeling, she cut the thongs tying her coin purse beneath the cart's planks. Then she pulled out her sewing basket, stuck the little sack inside, and walked into the trees. Finding a thick patch of undergrowth, she buried it.

He had ordered her to remain here and threatened

punishment if she did not, but she could not sit and watch the sun move until time's passage announced the worst. She had to be there. She could not help him if something went wrong, but she could bear witness. Let at least one person in Barrowburgh be willing to speak the truth.

She quickly plucked a variety of baskets from her cart, stacking them inside others with handles that she slung over her arm. She looked down at her blue gown, suitably frayed and a bit dirty from the last two days. Anonymous in her craftswoman identity, she hurried down the path after him.

The town gatekeeper stepped aside without a word of challenge, mouth agape with astonishment. No one raised a cry, no runners preceded him, but almost immediately people began edging the main lane to ogle while he passed. Simon might already know that he still lived, but the townspeople of Barrowburgh gawked at the resurrected Addis de Valence.

He took his time, knowing that word would reach the castle long before him. He wanted to give Simon time to decide what to do. The lane grew thick with onlookers as the houses and shops emptied. Some in the crowd began to follow. By the time he passed the manor's ovens and dovecote, a large retinue of townspeople had joined him.

The castle gate stood open. Carts jammed its outer yard, where merchants and craftsmen sold their wares. Scarlet and white flew from the battlements and colored the livery of the guards and knights mingling with the sellers. The din of bargaining lowered while he pushed through to the inner wall.

This gate remained closed. He brought his horse up close and waited. A guard scanned his animal and body for weapons, and then gave the signal to permit his entry.

The townspeople had followed behind him and they choked the yard. When the gate rose and he passed beneath, they surged along, making it impossible for the portcullis to be lowered again.

He rode to the keep's stairs. His eyes immediately lit upon the burly dark-haired man waiting at their summit in a rich red robe decorated with gold thread and yellow jewels. Beside him stood a pinch-faced woman of middle years and a handsome red-haired young knight.

Simon's florid, bearded face broke into a broad smile when Addis neared. Lifting his arms in greeting, he descended the stairs. "A great day, brother, and one blessed by God! I wept with hope at the rumor that you still lived, but now that I see the evidence of its truth, I am overcome with joy!"

So that was how it would be. Addis dismounted and accepted his stepbrother's embrace. "It is good to walk English soil and breathe English air again," he said, picking up the pretense.

"By the saints, you look well! Thinner, but none the worse for your ordeal."

"As do you, brother. Thicker, but content and happy. It brings me great pleasure to find you thus."

"Aye, a tad too thick, I fear." Simon laughed, smacking his barrel chest. "But come, come." He gestured to the stairs. "Our mother has been anxious for news and nagging me for days now. See, she grows impatient."

Addis looked up at the forced smile on the woman swathed in rose silk. His heart held nothing but distaste for Lady Mary, the manipulative widow who had played on Patrick de Valence's grief after the death of Addis's mother. By the time Patrick had emerged from mourning, Mary had already established herself and her son at Barrowburgh. Within a year Patrick had comprehended the error which could not be undone. Lady Mary must have grown too old for effective dissembling, because her own stiff greeting carried none of Simon's effusiveness.

"And you remember Owen," Simon added, presenting the red-haired man. "He was Sir Theo's squire back then."

Addis studied the young knight. Sir Theo's squire back then, and Simon's favorite now. Sir Theo had been one of the other knights on the Baltic crusade.

Simon draped an arm around Addis's shoulders, turning him toward the doorway. "We have much to speak of, brother. Some of it very sad, I'm afraid, and I am sure that you have many questions. Our mother has given instructions for a feast fitting to celebrate your return, but let us go up to the solar, where we can talk freely."

Addis allowed himself to be guided into the large hall, a space that he knew so well that he could walk from one end to the other blindfolded and not trip over a stool or loose stone. Its lighting and cool scent assaulted him like a suddenly remembered dream full of ghosts and nuanced emotions. Snippets of memories flashed while he moved through it, obscuring the flow of pleasantries poured into his ear by the man beside him.

The sensation grew stronger in the solar. He gazed around the chamber that had been his father's. Finally standing here again contained the eerie quality of being both unreal and acutely real at the same time. Only when Simon sat in the lord's chair did his perceptions partly right themselves.

Owen settled himself against the hearth wall opposite Simon, behind an empty chair. Addis noted the vulnerability of the position being allotted to him. He glanced at his stepbrother lounging comfortably, smiling peaceably, calling for wine. *He is well content sitting in my father's chair. In my chair.*

He calmly took the one facing and proceeded to ignore

Owen's presence. "I did not see your wife. How fares Lady Blanche?"

"Died last year in birth. A mercy perhaps. She had been a sickly girl, and too weak to carry a child to term. Lost four babes over the years. Well, such is the will of God. I am negotiating a new marriage contract right now. A kinswoman of Hugh Despenser. You must attend the betrothal."

Addis nodded as if Simon had not just inserted an unsubtle reminder of the power behind his hold on Barrowburgh. Raymond had not known of this convenient death of Lady Blanche.

"Tell me of my father's passing."

Simon had the decency to look mournful this time. "There was a bad fever in the land that year. It carried away many. He did not suffer overmuch, and your wife tended him, but I fear, in the end, her long hours weakened her and may have led to her own sickness after she left. My heart broke when he died, but I must be honest with you, Addis, and say that perhaps that was a mercy too."

So many merciful deaths. God was very compassionate while he cleared Simon's paths for him. "How so?"

Simon's lips folded in thoughtfully. He became the image of a man uncomfortable with discussing unpleasant truths. "Do not be angry when I tell you this, and know that I do not say it to dishonor that good man. But Lancaster's rebellion was the devil's doing, and when our king suppressed it he knew no mercy. There was hardly a crossroad in the realm without a body hanging on its gibbet. Your father had been too generous toward the traitors in his advice on how to deal with the uprising, and suspicion fell on him. If Patrick had lived . . . As it was, the king spoke of confiscating the lands because of treason. It was only because of my friendship with some of his councillors that I was able to keep it in the family."

"But you are not de Valence, Simon, nor Patrick's son. But for your mother's marriage, you are in no way family."

"Which is why the king was amenable. If it had not been me, it would have been some distant baron of no relation, to whom he owed a favor. At least this way his wife has been cared for, and his retainers maintained. The lands remain whole, and not broken apart and dispersed."

"What was the evidence against my father?"

"His friendship with Lancaster. Some meetings during the year before the rebellion broke. I heard there was more, but since no trial was held . . ."

"I have heard that no trials were held for any of them. That men close to the king used it as an excuse to rid themselves of enemies and grab rich estates."

"The king's councillors are honorable men, who offer him much-needed guidance," Simon said testily. "You know how it is with Edward. He needs strong men beside him. He has little interest in matters of governance."

"All kings need strong men beside them, and good council. But I have heard that Hugh Despenser is more than that, and that his influence over the king is of a more personal nature. It is said that he is another Piers Gaveston."

Simon's face flushed at the mention of the young Gascon knight reported to have been Edward's lover when the king was a young man. "Those are scurrilous lies, and always have been."

"If you say so. I only met Edward once and wouldn't know. Are you saying that Barrowburgh was given to you without any formalities? A family is not disseised of its rights so easily."

For the first time Simon looked less than wholly confident. "The realm was in an uproar. You were dead. . . ."

"I was on crusade, and a knight's rights and property are protected while he fights for God."

"You were seen cut down. There was no reason to believe . . ."

"And the boy? What of the boy?"

Simon's expression froze. "What of the boy?"

"Without my body, who could be sure that I died? Under the circumstances, until fact or time proved my death, I would think that the lands would have been held for Brian. You might have been named guardian until he came of age, but it is peculiar that the son of a crusader was so easily disinherited. Do the customs of the realm mean nothing to our king?"

Simon had never been a stupid man, and he knew that Addis was laying out the ambiguities that threatened his hold on Barrowburgh. "Our king faces treason at every turn, and his rights supersede all custom. As for the boy, I looked for Brian, to give him a home and care."

Addis smiled. "That was very generous of you. But my wife's brother saw to his care. You will be relieved to know that he is safe and well, hidden where only I know, and secure from any strife that may develop."

He let his words hang there, and watched Simon absorb their implication. A sharp, speculative stare met his and a palpable tension flowed in the air between their chairs. The silence stretched with Simon examining him, taking his measure. The silent presence of Owen suddenly loomed large, alert and waiting.

Just how confident are you of the king's favor, Simon? Enough to have me slain here in your solar? Addis felt the dangerous contemplation of the man facing him and the tense preparation of the one behind. He glanced around the chamber, at the table and bed and tapestry, each in the place it had held for generations. The sense of unreality swelled again, and with it a numbing indifference for the peril surrounding him.

"Where is the Barrowburgh sword?" he asked, noting the empty wall where the heavy weapon used to hang. When the last king had insisted that all his tenants in chief document their charters to their lands back to the time of King William, Addis's grandfather had pulled that ancient sword from the wall and presented it as his evidence.

"Lost. Stolen."

Interesting. How does one lose a sword? He still felt Owen behind him like a hovering angel of death. Prudence dictated that he appease Simon's suspicions for the time being as he had planned, but he suddenly didn't care much about such things. Instead he felt a profound urge to provoke him.

"You must know that I cannot accept this."

Simon's eyes flickered with surprise that the pretense would be so boldly dropped. Then they narrowed in the shrewd, cold way Addis knew well from their youth. "You will gain naught unless you do."

"I will gain naught *if* I do. Or is it your intention to step aside now that you see I am alive?"

"When the king gave me these lands, the issue of your death was barely considered. The fact of your life will not matter either. Your father's treason lost Barrowburgh."

No longer "that good man," but a traitor now. "My father's convenient and merciful death lost Barrowburgh. With my absence there was no one to speak on behalf of our family, but what has occurred can be undone." He rose. "Now I must take my leave. Apologize to Lady Mary that I could not attend the festivities that she planned in my honor."

Simon stood, no longer the affable brother but an adversary who had just been given fair warning. Addis turned to Owen. "You were with Sir Theo on the *reise* where I fell. Did Theo survive?"

Owen shook his head.

"But you did. How fortunate for you."

Owen colored at the insinuation that cowardice had saved his life in a battle where most had died.

"Do you return to Darwendon?" Simon asked while they descended to the hall. Addis perversely arranged it so Owen walked behind them. That dreamlike sensation had expanded, surrounding him with an entrancing mist. A small part of him dared Simon to give the signal to his henchman, because it really wouldn't matter. He could hardly be killed if none of them truly existed in this time and place.

"Nay. I do not think I will be at Darwendon for some months hence."

He floated through the hall being prepared for a feast that he would not attend. Late morning sunlight blinded him for a moment when they emerged from the keep. He stood looking down on the townspeople and merchants milling in the yard. The colors of their garments appeared too bright. The details of the walls and battlements looked too sharp. Something jostled his elbow and he glanced to see Simon turning slightly, communicating silently with the red-haired man whose presence warmed his back. He knew his danger with a calm certainty, but also experienced an odd irritation with Simon's reticence. *Do it*, a corner of his mind whispered. *Think of the trouble it will save us both.*

He stood at the top of the stairs longer than he ought, immobilized by that small voice while waves of nostalgia and weariness and resignation inundated him. The formidable strength of the fortifications loomed all around, the walls of the home he would have to destroy to regain. Fearful, shielded glances from guards and townspeople met his gaze. He felt Owen move, and sensed the hand easing up to the belt where the dagger hung. He did not react, tempting them still, blindly scanning the crowd below.

And then, like sun breaking through fog, he found himself alert and aware again in an instant. His gaze swung back to where it had just passed, to a woman near the gate peering up at him over the shoulder of a merchant to whom she showed her baskets.

The danger howled. The dreamy lethargy vanished. Stepping abruptly, he placed Simon between Owen and himself.

"Fare thee well, Simon."

He turned and walked down to his horse.

CHAPTER 6

HE JUST STOOD THERE, a nod or a wink away from death. Moira watched while she showed the merchant her best baskets. She wished that she could fly. She would wing up those steps and give him a good shake and wake him up to the danger increasing with every moment of delay.

You could feel death in the air, as if the tension growing among the three men had settled over the whole yard, stilling the breeze and slowing time. Even her oblivious merchant had been affected. He kept peering about himself curiously, as if his spirit knew something was not quite right.

Addis looked magnificent. Simon, for all of his jewels and gold, could not compete and appeared a vain and pompous man who neither liked nor comprehended the commanding nobility beside him that garnered so much attention. Her heart swelled with both pride and sorrow at the image Addis presented. So right. So inevitable.

Her own rightful place among the lake of commoners flowing below him also struck her with force. She did not resent the reality of it. One might as well resent the movement of the sun or the change of the seasons. She watched him survey the walls and crowd, oddly at ease despite his danger, comfortable in the place he would one day stand again by force of his own will. When that day came Moira the basket maker would be a shadow again, a dim memory of a bondwoman who had served him while he decided his course.

Her eyes never left him and she answered the merchant's questions without really hearing them. She thought that her head would split from the suspense. She observed with trepidation the silent conversation between Simon and the red-haired knight, noted Simon's wavering hesitation, watched the knight's stance of preparation. If he used a dagger he could drag Addis back into the hall before anyone knew what had occurred.

You push too far, Addis. He is going to do it. Move now!

As if hearing her silent urging, his dark gaze slid past her, halted, and snapped back. For an instant they looked directly at each other. Just as Simon made the vaguest gesture to the knight, Addis moved to his brother's other side.

"Thank God," Moira cried softly, exhaling the breath she had been holding.

Not too softly, because a knight in scarlet livery turned. She had not noticed him take his place nearby. He stepped closer, angling his bald head to peer at her. Moira tried to ignore him by giving the merchant more of her attention, but she kept one eye on Addis's progress to his horse.

"I know you," the knight said.

"Nay, surely not. I am not from these parts."

"At Hawkesford. I saw you there." His dark eyes

squinted over sharp cheekbones while he searched his memory. The merchant had decided to take all the baskets and she clasped his coins in her hand while she walked away.

A heavy hand came down on her shoulder. "Now I remember. Lady Claire's little friend. 'Tis your eyes, and they don't change. Can always remember a person by the eyes."

"You are mistaken." Addis was on his horse now, aiming for the gate. The knight grabbed her arm and pulled her into the shadows of the wall. While she resisted his grip she glanced to the stairs. Simon still stood there watching Addis with a dark expression, but the red-haired knight had disappeared.

The man pressed her against the stones, hovering his body so she became invisible to anyone in the yard. Not a young man, but the years did not appear to have blunted his strength. "Are you with him?" he asked.

"Who?"

"Do not play the fool with me, girl. Did you come with the lord? I saw you look at each other just now."

"You saw wrong."

He gave her arm a firm shake that jerked her whole body. "Listen you now, and listen well. If you are with him, tell him Sir Richard advises he go to the village of Whitly, near the abbey of St. Dominic. Our reeve there, a man named Lucas, will give him shelter this night, and I will come in the morning."

Addis was passing not fifteen feet away. He looked for her, but could not see her against the wall with Sir Richard blocking her from view. "Tell him yourself."

"And have that wolf watching from the stairs see me do it? Nay, girl, those loyal to him are no use if they are dead."

Simon did watch. His eyes might have bored holes into Addis the way he watched. Moira nodded, and pushed Richard away. Where was the red-haired knight?

She glanced to the gate through which Addis had just passed. The crowd in the outer yard separated, creating a lane for him. Simon remained on the stairs, as if waiting for something to happen.

She scanned the people, looking for that red hair. Impossible to see much in this crowd, but then he could do nothing down here. She peered up at the battlements, pushing into the yard's center for a better view.

A red head moved along the wall walk, heading back to the keep. She turned in the direction from which it had come. A guard bent in the shadow where the wall met a tower. Panic split through her. She stared at him sighting his crossbow, and then pivoted to see Addis approaching the outer gate, a slow-moving target.

She did not hesitate. "Look!" she cried, pointing to the bowman. "Up there! Look!" She yelled this time, using all of the force of a voice that had sung in large halls when she was a girl.

Bodies and faces turned. She kept pointing and yelling, and other hands and voices joined her. Excitement and confusion rippled through the yard. Dozens of fingers led hundreds of eyes to the guard preparing his shot.

The noise distracted him. The bolt flew and Moira heard its high whistle despite the din. Addis's horse reared while he twisted and looked back to the battlements. The bolt missed its target but everyone had seen and all hell let loose in the outer yard. Hands swung out to smack the horse's rump and, willingly or not, Addis galloped out beneath the portcullis.

Moira turned away with relief, only to find angry, cunning eyes glaring at her from atop the stairs. Another hand pointed, this time Simon's, this time at her. The red-haired knight began descending toward her.

"Out now, and run, girl." Sir Richard muttered, walking in front of her. "I'll see you get through the gates."

Blood pulsing with fear, she turned on her heel and dodged through the buzzing crowd. In the outer yard the crowd slowed her progress, but she elbowed and nudged and squeezed to the gate. Popping through, she could not see Addis on the lane ahead. Despite the excited stream of townspeople pouring around her, she decided it would be safer to skirt along the back lanes in case that red-haired knight still followed.

She darted behind the ovens and aimed for the town buildings, trying to stay in the shadows beneath eaves. Would Simon send men after Addis now? The whole town was in an uproar, and people spilled into the side lanes where she sprinted.

Shouts and yells began piercing the general noise. Horse hooves clamored on paving stones not far away. Addis on a horse might get through the town gate before Simon ordered it closed, but she on foot might not. She wondered what Simon did to people who foiled his plans and felt a renewed surge of panic.

The sounds of a horse grew louder, trotting down a side lane in her direction. She ran for her life. The hooves followed in pursuit.

He was upon her in moments, cutting off her path with the bulk of his animal. She heaved breaths of exhaustion and closed her eyes in resignation.

They opened to find a strong forearm bound by a gold armlet stretching down to her. She looked up at the dark head limned by the bright sky. "Up quickly," he ordered. "Unless you want to grow old with me in one of Barrowburgh's dungeons."

She grabbed his arm and he swung her up behind him. She had barely landed before he spurred the horse to a gallop. People gawked and peeled out of the way while they flew through the narrow lanes.

"Do they follow?" she yelled into his back while the horse's rump jostled her.

"Damned if I know. Would you like to stop and see?" he shot back. His angry tone reminded her that his delay while he searched for her had increased his danger. "Not yet on horse, if they do. None saddled in the yard for them to use."

He turned into the main lane and headed for the gate. Its portcullis was just beginning to lower. People saw them coming and many raised arms and cheers while they passed. Addis streaked beneath the descending iron edge and out into the silent countryside. Moira's whole body went boneless with relief.

He didn't slow until he entered the woods. They trotted along its paths until they came to the clearing where her cart waited. Addis swung his leg over the horse's neck and jumped off, then grabbed her and hauled her down.

"I told you to wait here." A tight fury poured out of him. He grasped her firmly around the waist and she angled away in resistance.

With relief had come her own annoyance at his foolish boldness. Now his tone made her patience snap. "You also told me that he would not try to kill you." Her mind saw it all again and his carelessness made her livid. She smacked her hand into his chest to relieve her exasperation. "What were you doing up there? Standing forever like that? You know his mind! Tempting the devil, that's what! I'll wager that you challenged him directly when you spoke too, didn't you? Told him outright that you would come for him one day. Gave him fair warning, like the chivalrous"—*smack*—"noble"—*smack*—"stupid man you are!"

He caught her hand and whipped it behind her back, pulling her closer, arching her body. "You could have gotten us both trapped in there!"

She flattened her free palm against his chest and pushed back from him. A firm arm circled her waist and forbade her release. "You were safe enough once you got through the castle gates. And that bolt was your own fault, daring him like that with your conceited boldness. Do not blame me for any danger you faced today."

"Should I have ridden out and left you within those walls? That is all I need now, for Simon to discover who you are and use his hold of you against me."

"If he had caught me, what would he have had? A bondwoman. One serf more or less will not affect the outcome of this, and that man is smart enough to know it."

She glared at him, hot with anger. She wanted to smack him again, but her free hand had become imprisoned between her body and his chest. Gold lights flamed down at her from absorbing eyes embedded in a stern face.

"That man is smart enough to surmise that you are much more," he muttered, forcing her closer, sealing her against his body. His mouth claimed hers with a punishing kiss.

Surprise made her resist and she twisted her head away. His mouth scorched her neck, finding spots where its heat seemed to flow directly into her blood, arousing visceral sensations that channeled the anger and worry into emotions just as tempestuous but offering a different release. He liberated her hand but captured her head, holding it to his assault, commanding submission. Blood already riled by excitement burned hotter, pulsed faster. Their shared danger and heated confrontation had left her raw and exposed. The relief and worry and anger of the last hours

BY POSSESSION · 101

merged into a blind need for reassurance and she mindlessly relented and joined his passion and the venting it offered.

He took her mouth as if he sought to consume her, but her own spirit responded with something more than passive consent. She broke her arms free from his domineering hold and circled his neck, bowing against him. Her tongue and lips met his in contention, continuing their argument with a wordless sparring, refusing subjugation. Desire prickled her skin, weighted her belly, and pulsed above her thighs. Her mind dulled to everything except the feel of it all and the reality of him, alive and whole. Their passion ascended to a savage peak before slowly subsiding into a clouded valley of vulnerable connections.

She found her head against his chest, his arms wrapped around her body, his lips pressed against her temple. "Offer your life to him or anyone like that again and I will strangle you," she whispered.

He laughed quietly. "I said before that you are a vicious woman." He gently separated from her. "We must go, Moira."

She did not want to leave their embrace and lose that brief, wordless joining of friendship and desire. She moved away reluctantly and forced her emotions into sensible order. "Do you know the village of Whitly?"

"Aye, it is just across the border into the lands of the neighboring Dominican abbey. Some of our people live there."

She told him about Sir Richard and his advice. Addis nodded. "Richard was my father's steward. If anyone at Barrowburgh can be trusted, it is he. And if Simon follows, he will not risk the uproar that an attack on an abbey village would cause." He looked to the cart. "We cannot delay by bringing it. Get what you need, and we will try to have someone retrieve it later."

She ducked into the trees and found her sewing basket. She plucked some clean veils and shifts from one of her trunks and stuffed them inside. He mounted the horse and took the basket from her, then extended his arm again. Once settled astride behind the saddle, she slid the basket over her arm. Holding on proved a little precarious with her burden, and she tottered with the animal's gait.

Addis took the paths leading to the road south, then moved to a faster pace. She looked at the strong back in front of her face, knowing that she had complicated things again by permitting that kiss.

Do not let these feelings overwhelm you, she chastised. Remember who he is and will be and what must happen a few months hence. Picture him on those stairs, and never forget what it means. He will stand there again someday, and at his side will be another Claire. Whatever passion he shows for you now is the result of danger and proximity and convenience. Have no illusions about this.

She continued laying it all out, her common sense forcing harsh reality atop her heart's quandary. She felt confused and emotionally naked, and very glad that she would not have to speak or meet his eyes for a few hours at least.

After a few miles Addis left the road and headed across country. She was sure she would be bounced off the horse now. Unexpectedly, he reached behind and lifted her right hand from its grasp on the saddle. Pulling gently, he led it around his body and placed its palm on his abdomen.

The movement brought her forward against the support of his back, and after a few moments she let her shoulders and head relax against him. She succumbed to the comfort of listening to the muffled beat of his heart. The new position steadied her and made the horse's gait less uncomfortable. He did not release her hand, but kept it flat under his throughout their journey, pressed to his body.

✦ ✦ ✦

The sun hung low when they approached the village of Whitly. Addis paused at its outskirts.

"Three manors share it, but it is on abbey lands," he explained. "Close to half the people are ours."

Moira peered around his shoulder at the longhouses and cottages. "Help me get down, please. I am sore from riding."

He offered the support of his arm while she slid off her perch. She smoothed her skirt and stepped away. He knew that it was not soreness that had made her dismount. She did not want to ride in behind him and face the assumptions that might raise. He glanced to her careful expression while they moved forward. He would have trouble with her still. She did not accept it yet, did not see the inevitability of it.

The houses emitted sounds of families eating their supper but they were noticed at once. Men appeared in doorways and women at windows. A few boys darted up the lane. By the time he stopped his horse near the church a knot of men was waiting.

"I seek Lucas Reeve," he said while he dismounted.

A white-haired man lumbered over from a nearby threshold, wiping his beard on his sleeve. "I be Lucas."

Addis turned. He let the gray eyes examine him and watched the shock of recognition when the gaze slid along the scar. "I am just come from Barrowburgh. Sir Richard, my father's old steward, suggested I stop here tonight. He said that I would find a welcome in this village."

"Saints be praised," Lucas muttered with widening eyes. A broad smile slowly broke across his weathered skin. "Saints be praised!" he hooted. He threw out his arms to the growing crowd. " 'Tis the lord's son, the one what died!" He flashed a toothy grin and winked. "Of course, I'm hoping you didn't die for real since you be standing here now and if you are dead that makes you a ghost or demon, don't it?"

The villagers swarmed and word passed up the lane. Lucas gestured Addis toward his house. "Come and eat and drink. There's food waiting and there will be more once we get the women cooking again. We will feast your return and pray our thanks to God for delivering you and sending you home to us. The people of this land are badly in need of you, that's for sure." He ushered Addis into his house and pressed him down onto a stool. "Come from Barrowburgh, did you? I'd have given my eyeteeth to see that devil's face when you rode in those gates." He pushed a wooden bowl of soup at him. "Meat, wife! Send the boy out to kill some fowl."

Men followed and the chamber became cramped. The next few hours filled with ale drinking and food arriving from neighboring homes. Lucas's wife held court by the hearth, supervising the celebration. Addis could tell from the meager offerings that Simon's greed had left these peasants with little to spare. Still, sounds of revelry filled the building and its croft and toft. The sun set while the villagers squeezed to the table to fill Addis's ears with complaints about Simon and his oppressive fees and corrupted hallmotes and disregard for common rights.

To refuse the hospitality would be an insult to these people, and so he suffered it. Moira had melted away from his side at the church, and now she sat among the women. More than a few curious glances had slid her way at first, and Addis had no doubt that she had read the question of everyone in the house. She answered it by ignoring him. Her garments made her a part of them, but her lady's manner and speech set her apart, and to be on the safe side they finally decided that she must be the latter.

The ambiguity that she successfully established regarding her relationship to him was borne out by the smiles eventually cast his way by a tawny-haired girl named Ann. Inviting smiles, and eyes that focused on the right side of his face and managed not to see the left. The village slut, he surmised.

"My daughter and her husband have gone to a fair, and their cottage is empty," Lucas explained at one point. "They would be honored, I know, if you made it yours. 'Tis the new one at the far end of the lane, and I'm sure that all is right, but we will see it is prepared for you."

The last thing Addis wanted was the whole village accompanying him to that cottage. Nor did he want Moira's disinterest to convince them that she was so separate from him that she required a bed in one of their homes. Suppressed desire simmered in his body and he maintained his patience with these peasants only through concentrated effort. "My woman will take care of it," he said.

Lucas glanced to her. The ale made him bold. "She is . . . ?"

"She is a bondwoman of my manor at Darwendon. She has business to the east and I escort her since I head that way too." It was the God's honest truth, but he trusted Lucas to get the message.

Lucas absorbed this without comment but his gray eyes flickered. No villager would approach that cottage this night or next morning. A sharp glance from the reeve and the slut's expression dulled. Addis turned his attention to a man asking the lord to bless his children.

There were rules regarding hospitality that one could count on in any village, and Moira waited for the offer of a bed or pallet in one of the women's homes. When the night wore on and the offer did not come, she admitted that despite her attempts to convince them otherwise, these people had reached certain conclusions about her and Addis. Her own behavior had been indifferent toward him, so the only explanation was that Addis had said something to the reeve and Lucas had silently passed the word. She resisted believing that because of what it implied, but the petulant retreat of tawny-haired Ann provided the final evidence.

Despite her averted eyes she had been very alert to him the whole time and now the knight at the table began to press on her awareness. The knowledge of what he planned to do to her began to intrude on her thoughts with astonishing explicitness. Despite the seductive memories attached to those images, despite the man commanding her attention through the sheer power of his presence, the shadow and bondwoman sadly recognized the disaster for her life that his intentions would create.

She tried to rehearse the denials that she had worked out two days ago, but in light of that kiss today she doubted that they would carry much weight. She could explain away that first transgression as an accident. Today had been something else. Welcome. Necessary. Born of an uncontrollable euphoria that had existed separate from the practical plans that she had made for her life.

What could she say to him? *I lost my head because I was relieved for your safety.* Partly true. That had possibilities. *If you think about it, it was merely a kiss of friendship.* Aye, and pigs have wings. *I will not do this thing with you, Addis, I am most firm about that. My resolve is like steel.* Unless, of course, you kiss me again, in which case I will melt into a puddle of lust and abandon every shred of common sense.

The memory had her melting already. A heady warmth tingled in her hips and flushed through her limbs. Hollow, hungry sensations streaked through her core. She quickly looked at the handsome face and saw it again above her while he summoned her passion as if it were his to demand at will. He had not given her any more attention than she had him this evening, but she had sensed his consciousness of her over the hours as surely as if they still faced each other in that embrace.

She turned and found Ann eyeing her critically, as if she measured the competition. I forfeit, Moira responded with her eyes. Truly. Do not listen to Lucas. Be bold. Think of the benefits to you and your family if you please the lord. He might even let you live in the castle until he marries again.

Moira looked over to see Addis bending his head toward a man but his eyes found her. His gaze struck her as invasive as ever despite its shielded warmth, and more than a little dangerous. For a few beats of timelessness the whole chamber emptied of everyone but the two of them and his expectation of what lay ahead. An unwelcome thrill spiraled down from her neck to her loins and a low, fearful excitement blotted through her.

Ann, deciding the lord's largesse was worth a few risks, ended it by stepping between them, carrying some ale. His attention shifted to the lithe young body approaching. Moira felt like a cornered rabbit suddenly liberated by the hunter's distraction.

Ann was well practiced in getting a man's attention, and her breasts grazed his arm while she smiled vivaciously and filled his cup. Addis's lids lowered. A few of the men smirked. Moira's good sense heaved with relief, but her heart felt a foolish spike of jealousy.

"Pity, ain't it?" a voice said quietly at her shoulder. Lucas's wife, Joan, had closed in for some confidential gossip. "His face, that is. He was the most beautiful boy."

Moira never noticed that scar much, at least not as something so unusual. It was just a part of him, like his eyes and hair. Of course, she had seen him when the wound truly cut his face in half, so this remnant appeared to her a minor thing.

"They say the hip is worse," Joan continued, bending closely to encourage confidences. She had drunk her share of ale this night. "I know some of the women who tended him when he returned. Horrible, they said. Sure he would die, they were."

She had seen that wound at its worst as well. "Not so horrible if he walks and fights still."

"Aye, a miracle of sorts. Perhaps his young bride prayed for him and God listened. Didn't do much else, from what is told. Rarely saw him all those months, and never helped with his care. Surprised us all that the wedding was held at all. A proud and selfish girl."

"Not so proud. And young and frightened. Lady Claire was my friend."

Joan pursed her lips, sorry to lose that topic to misplaced loyalty. "They said he'd never walk right again."

I know.

"Better off dead, some said."

Aye. Including Addis.

"But even before he was healed, he ordered them to help him stand. As soon as he returned here. Despite the pain, he would walk the length of his chamber holding on to servants, several times a day, back and forth. They cried describing it, those men who helped him did. Like watching a man being tortured, they said. Would beg him to stop, but he would not. Some say the hip healed different because of it, that it kept him from being crippled. I say it was the prayers of his father that done that, and maybe of his lady, if she bothered to pray for other than herself, that is. He went on that crusade before he was whole, you know. Still weaker than he should be, and the wounds still mending inside. Said he went to repay God for sparing him."

Is that what he said.

Joan looked at her meaningfully, hungry for details.

Moira could not oblige her even if she wanted to. She had not been at Barrowburgh during those months, had not even come for the wedding. The last she had seen of Addis had been his broken, bandaged body lifted into the wagon that would take him home. Beside him had sat Claire, her face a mask of duty and obligation. *Not proud. Young and frightened.*

She did not want to talk about this. She groped for a way to change the subject only to realize that she didn't want to talk about anything. In fact, she didn't want to be here any longer. Ann had managed to squeeze herself among the men at the table where she could give Addis her full attention. Lucas looked a little embarrassed by the girl's boldness. Addis neither encouraged nor discouraged her.

"You don't mind?" Joan asked, glancing to them both.

"It is not for me to do so."

"Nay, with such a man . . . still, a woman has feelings."

"I do not mind." That was not true. While she had no intention of giving him what he wanted, she still resented the idea of his bedding Ann instead.

Well, she couldn't have it both ways. Her good sense had been praying for deliverance since she got on that horse even if another part of her had not, and now redemption from her own weakness had been sent in the form of an eager girl with tawny hair.

Joan had told her about the daughter's cottage, and Moira stood abruptly. "I will go prepare the house," she said, wondering if Addis would bring Ann there and if she should just bluntly ask Joan if there was a pallet in another house that she could use.

"She and her mother have their own place a few doors down," Joan explained kindly, lighting a candle and handing it to her.

Moira slipped through the crowded room toward the

door. At the threshold an invisible connection touched her like a hand on her shoulder. She looked over her shoulder to see those dark eyes noting her departure.

She found the little cottage without difficulty. Its new thatching and clean plaster announced it the home of newlyweds. She opened the door and her candle's flame pierced the gloomy interior. Finding the window over the bed, she threw open the shutters to the moonlight.

Buckets stood by the hearth. After lighting a low fire, she collected two and made her way back to the village well. Sounds of revelry still poured out of Lucas's house. She carried her burden back to the welcome silence of the cottage and set the water near the hearth.

Lucas's daughter was an impeccable housekeeper, and the cottage needed no preparation. In fact it possessed an organization and cleanliness that made Moira uncomfortable. It reminded her of her own cottage at Darwendon, and nostalgia for those four years with Brian flooded her.

It had been almost like having a real home and family during that time. She sat by the hearth, using some of the warmed water to wash, fighting the bittersweet mood that those memories evoked. A real home. A secure place. She hadn't had either since she was thirteen years old. A child to love and care for. A spot of stability and warmth in an indifferent, angry world.

The thoughts weighed on her, emphasizing the loneliness that she had known in her life so often that it had become predictable. Worse after Edith died. Excruciating with Claire's passing. Unassuaged by that brief marriage, but wonderfully dulled for four years by caring for a child.

She wanted that balm again. She yearned to feel centered and grounded in one place, with a purpose that mattered and a small world that belonged to her forever. Not the Shadow, but, for a few people at least, for her family, a source of light.

The reflections saddened her and she tried to cast off the mood. When that didn't work she walked out of the cottage to escape its strange power. The little house stood at the edge of some fields, and just past its croft she spied the high roof of the open structure that protected the hay mound. She picked her way through the neat garden toward it.

The sweet smell of hay wafted to her on the cool breeze. She shifted some this way and that, making a ledge on which to sit. Lying back in its springy support, she could watch the half moon and the starry dots sprinkling the velvet darkness.

She began counting those little marks of brightness and her mind wandered through memories recent and old. Her heart grew full and vulnerable. She became isolated from everyone and everything except this little ledge of hay and that vast sky propelling her consciousness freely through space and time.

CHAPTER 7

NOT PROUD, JUST young and frightened . . .

The passageway smelled cool and damp and the stones absorbed the faint scuffle of her shoes. No sounds here, like so many places in the castle this day. The whole household had grown subdued, holding its breath, waiting for death.

She had already tried all of Claire's other hiding places. The chapel, the east tower roof, the nook beside the hall hearth. Now she peered into the shadow under the stairs rising from the kitchen. Her candlelight reflected off a cascade of blond hair draping a huddled body.

A head moved and blue eyes looked up, wide and frightened and then relieved. "Thank the saints it is you."

She bent down over her friend. Two years older than she, but a child again suddenly. "You must come."

"I cannot," Claire breathed, shaking her head slowly, looking to a spot on the floor.

"You must. Your father sent me to find you. . . ."

"I cannot!" She glared up. "Have you seen him? Have you?

Cut to pieces. My God, he had no face left, and his body . . ." The words sliced, full of horror. The tone was close to hysterical.

"Wounds always look worse at first. My mother says it is the bruising that deforms his face, that no bones were broken. She will tend him. There will be a scar, but all knights have scars. . . ."

"He will be crippled and he looks monstrous." She said it bitterly and her eyes glazed, looking inward. What did she see in her soul? A betrothed girl lacking the strength to do her duty toward her intended? A spoiled girl angry that fate had played such a trick on her? Both most likely, but a man suffered upstairs and Moira found that she had little patience all of a sudden with Claire's delicacy and selfishness.

"He is asking for you. Whenever he becomes conscious he says your name. You must—"

"I must, I must! Who are you to tell me what I must? Go back and tell them that you could not find me. Say that you did but I am ill. Do whatever you choose, but I will not come with you. I cannot bear to look at him." Her body began shaking, a slow shiver at first, but then jerking movements that made her cross her arms over her belly. She shook her head and careened like a mourner, heaving dry sobs. "Oh, my Addis. My beautiful, beautiful Addis . . ."

Moira gave her one last glance. So, this was love. What a thin, fragile, self-centered thing it could be. She turned on her heel and ran back up the stairs.

Sir Bernard paced outside the chamber, as worried as if the young man behind its door were his own son. "Where is she?"

"I . . . she is very ill. Prostrate with pains in the stomach."

His eyes narrowed angrily and he glared down the passage at the void where his daughter should be approaching. Shaking his head, he took her arm. "Your mother is going to open and purify his hip. God willing the pain will put him out, and he is mad in his head from the fever, so perhaps . . ."

She resisted, not wanting to go in any more than Claire had.

His fingers closed more tightly. "Stand by his head, girl, and speak to him while it is done. Maybe he will think it is she."

She found herself pulled into that torture chamber. Her mother looked up expectantly, then pursed her lips when she noted Claire's absence. Moira pleaded with her eyes to be spared this horror, but Edith was all business suddenly, laying a dagger in the coals of the low fire.

The space smelled of corruption and sweat and the noxious odor turned her stomach. Raymond and two other men stood alongside the bed. She forced herself to walk around them and look at the man lying there.

Bandages swaddled half his face where Edith had sewn the cut. They covered part of his swollen mouth and so his fevered ramblings came incoherently. Pain and bruising distorted the face she could see, thinner than she remembered, the bones looking very sharp, the youth looking suddenly old. Sympathy for his agony shredded her heart and her resistance.

They had stripped him, and she glanced down to the festering wound slicing diagonally from his waist through the top of his thigh. Someone had sewn it roughly on the field, to cover exposed bone and hold his stomach in, they had said. Edith suspected the sword had nicked the gut, causing the corruption to set in quickly.

She moved close to his head. Raymond shot a questioning look at his father, who remained stoically nonexpressive. Edith rose from the hearth and came forward with the dagger, its hilt wrapped in a thick cloth.

Someone had placed some water on a table near his head. She dampened a cloth and wiped the battered face as gently as she could, hoping she could give some small relief, feeling his pain as if her own body had been ravaged. Oh, Addis. My beautiful, beautiful Addis.

He felt her touch and grabbed her arm. The unbandaged eye opened to reveal a dark pool aflame with golden lights burning out of control. He peered at her and something like rational *awareness flickered over his expression. He looked down his body at the men flanking him, and the hideous wound, and Edith with her dagger. His jaw stiffened.*

Someone brought a stool and she knelt on it. She leaned forward and stroked his hair, cradling his head against her chest. "I will stay with you," she whispered, hoping he would think she was Claire but knowing from that look that he would not. Still, the comfort seemed to soothe him.

Bernard nodded and four pairs of hands pressed down to hold him. Addis pulled his right hand free and sought hers and grasped it tightly to his chest. Edith bent over the hip.

He twisted his head toward her violently with the first hot cut and clutched her hand like a dying man. She pressed her lips to his temple and battled for composure and whispered prayers and poems and songs of love while he smothered his screams in her breast.

She became aware of his presence slowly, sensing it before the body leaning against the post took form in the shadows. He did not startle her. His reality simply emerged out of her thoughts like a seamless continuation suddenly given substance. How long had he been there?

Not now. I will have little strength now.

His shoulder pressed against the post and his arms crossed his chest. She might have been dreaming into the sky but he had been contemplating her and his attention created a disturbance in the breeze that had alerted her to him. She did not speak to let him know she had seen him, but waited desperately for the perilous mood of her memory to pass.

"I thought that you might have fallen asleep," he said.

How could he be sure she hadn't? He could not see her face well in this darkness. Perhaps he heard the slow, hard pounding of her heart.

"Do you think to stay out here all night?"

"I had not planned to, but since . . . why aren't you with Ann?" It just blurted out, sounding more petulant than she felt.

He did not answer at once. He just stood there, filling the night with a subtle danger, making this hay mound a much less peaceful place all of a sudden. "I am not with her because I do not want to be."

"It would simplify things if you did."

"Would it? I don't think so. For this night perhaps. No more."

She sat upright on the ledge of hay and looked out to the dark fields. His arrival had started a visceral throbbing in her that seemed to affect the whole night, as if the air and the crops absorbed a rhythm from her. The sensation was both unsettling and alluring. He hadn't moved, but his own pulse became noticeable in the space between them, as if his life force were adjusting to hers, seeking to join it beat for beat. Instinct mumbled warnings in her ear, but her spirit, hungry for unity of any sort, responded with an astonishing yearning.

"What do you want with me, my lord?" She sighed the question, emphasizing the *me*.

"You have not called me that before. Do not start now."

"I think it best if I do. It is a reality that I forget at great cost."

"As your lord, I forbid it." He walked toward her. Common sense demanded that she jump away from him. She didn't.

He settled onto the hay beside her and all of her senses snapped alert. She should have made the ledge larger so she could scoot away and his hip and shoulder would not graze hers like this, raising that horrible, wonderful friction.

"Right now I want only to sit with you in this perfect

night under this glorious sky. It has been a lifetime since I have shared such peace with a friend." He angled back a little, relaxing against the hay. She could not see his face now, but she felt his warmth a mere two hand spans away from her back.

"When I was in the Baltic, I would sit under skies like this, knowing the same moon and stars shone above England. There was both comfort and pain in the notion."

She could well imagine the loneliness he had endured there and empathy twisted her heart. "Does it work the other way too? Both comforting and painful to know that this sky looks down on those people?"

"A little."

She had surmised as much. "They enslaved you."

She felt the slightest pull on her scalp. He had found one of her errant strands of hair falling down from under her veil and must be touching it. She could not feel his fingers, but their casual movements prickled up to her head, causing tiny shivers to echo through the skin there.

"Aye, and it makes no sense. It is a strange thing, what happens to one in that situation. The first year my whole being was full of hate and anger and scorn. I planned escape after escape in my mind at night. I saw only their barbarism and all of the differences from us. But one can live like that only so long. In time, the strange becomes familiar. Life finds a pattern. I never surrendered to the slavery, but I could not remain separate and angry for six years. The similarities started becoming apparent. We have our barons, they have their *bajorai*. We have our priests, they have their *kunigai*. We burn our heretics, they burn their sacrifices."

"We have one God, and they worship many."

"Their gods and our saints have much in common. The distinction we make is lost on them."

"And on you? That is heresy, Addis."

"I merely came to see it how they saw it. Oddly enough, it is coming home that has made me understand them more clearly. I find that I walk through the land of my birth much as I did at first through that land, like a stranger encountering odd things. Customs and ideas that I took for granted I suddenly see afresh."

He still absently fingered the hair. Her neck had become alive from the emanating sensations. His pulse had met hers now, as if their blood beat in time together and the whole night joined in. The intangible connection was more dangerous than a caress and its compelling power mesmerized her. "And you, Moira. What of your life during those years?"

"My life? What a question! No adventure there. I lived a typical life, not at all notable."

"Raymond said that you married a gentry knight."

Still that gentle play. Her shoulders quivered from the subtle contact. She felt an appalling urge to circle her head and purr like a cat. "You knew him. Sir Ralf, who had a minor holding from Bernard. Bernard arranged it so I would be cared for. He even gave me a dowry. Bernard got it back, of course, in return for my swearing away the widow's dower. It was only right to handle it thus, since Ralf died at the wedding banquet, so it had not been a true marriage."

"Did Bernard also give you to the second man?"

"Nay. That was after he died. Raymond was lord then, and . . . well, I decided it was best to leave Hawkesford, although Raymond permitted both my mother and myself to stay. Edith was sick already, and my own place there had become awkward. James was a wool merchant from Salisbury. He would come after the sheep were shorn every year. He seemed a decent man, and demanded no dowry, although he knew about Edith's house and field and expected it to come to him through me. He had a grown son, so the contract left little for me if he died and I was childless. Still, with no dowry . . ."

"Raymond said that you were not married long before he also died."

"Aye. He fell ill a month later and died soon after. I tried to mourn him and felt guilty that I could not, but he had been much a stranger still. And if my motives had been practical, his had been more so. I think that he had calculated that the cost of keeping a wife was cheaper than the hiring of a servant and the buying of whores. But for the fact I wanted children, I might have found a way for him to continue doing the latter."

"Did he hurt you?"

"Nay. He bored me. What a terrible thing to say of the dead, but it was true. He sought to be a very pious man. He would pray all evening and then come into bed determined not to succumb to the sins of the flesh but his piety sometimes failed him. Sharing his bed was not loathsome, just . . . tedious." Why was she telling him this? Now she was the one being tedious. And yet, somehow, in this night with the rhythm of the whole world tying them together, it seemed natural to speak of it.

"I put up with it because I was his wife and because I wanted children. Not because of the security their birth would bring me when he died. I wanted a family. And my own home, I liked having that too. Simple things really, what every woman has. There was little affection between us in so short a time, but I was contented. I should like to know that contentment again."

So here she was after all, broaching those arguments that would underpin her denial of their passion, and he had led her down the path to do it. It came out easily though, a confidence between friends.

"Caring for Brian made you delay that."

"Aye, but I do not regret it. I do not resent one whit

those four years. But now it is time to make a life for myself."

She expected a retreat from him with this more blatant implication, but instead his hand wound more obviously in the long strand of hair.

"With a freemason."

"Or another such man. A good man, who will be a good husband and father and make a home with me. Such a man will not have me if I have been bedding another."

It had to be said and faced, but she felt something in the aura behind her change in response to the bluntness of it. A small flaring of power that made his presence surge and surround her, shuddering with . . . what? Protection? Possession? Anger? She did not understand it, but it felt as if he had thrown an invisible cloak over her. Within that cocoon their mutual rhythm continued, but his beat pounded steadily stronger, taking control, timing the pulse and demanding that hers conform. The sudden shift astonished her and she sought in vain the strength to cast off his effect.

"Not all men are so pious as James," he said as if nothing had changed.

Why did it sadden her to explain it? She hesitated, reveling for one hungry moment in the way their spirits adhered to each other. "Nay, but all men are proud. They do not want wives whom others whisper about. Do not want a woman who has been the lord's whore. Whoever he is will probably ask about you just as James asked about Raymond. I want to be able to answer truthfully next time as I did with him."

He straightened and sat flush beside her. The movement startled her and she almost jumped away from the warm body looming tall beside her now.

"And what did you say to James when he asked?" His tone sounded light and curious, but something else was happening below the banter of this conversation and her body and soul knew it. Wariness swelled, commanding her to get away. Her feet dangled just inches from the ground, and it would be an easy thing to hop down and run. Run to where though? That invisible cloak seemed to swaddle her tighter, holding her in place beside him. She couldn't move. She could barely find her voice, let alone respond in her own casual tone.

"I said that I had never been in Raymond's bed."

"That sounds very imprecise. An intelligent man will spot the other possibilities. Considering the time we will have spent together, you will have to be more blunt with your mason."

She felt her color rise. "I will say . . . Addis de Valence was never my lover."

He laughed softly. "Still a bit vague, Moira, and in part a bit untrue. Nay, you will have to make it very clear. You could say, for example, that my lord has never had me."

That laugh heartened and reassured her a little. Perhaps her caution had gotten the better of her. "Or get most precise yet. Swear that I have never fornicated with you."

"That should do it."

She laughed herself. "You are a kind man, Addis. To understand and even to jest about this."

He did not respond. She turned her head to find him looking at her. Despite the dim moonlight she read, nay she felt, his expression, and her heart turned over with an alarming jolt.

"Is that what you think this has been, Moira? A jest?" His arm slipped up her back and eased her toward him. "Nay, lovely lady. It has been a negotiation."

His lips took hers before she could marshal any resistance. Gentle but firm, that first kiss spoke a determination that said nothing less than a pummeling struggle would stop him. Weak objections briefly drifted through her mind before she succumbed to the sweet beauty of it. That invisible cloak wrapped them both now, so comforting in its warmth and protection. The delicious connection overwhelmed her, and the careful explanations just articulated disappeared along with all of her thoughts, carried away by the night breeze.

His tongue entered her, probing, savoring, controlling. He dominated that pulse, drawing hers into his. Flushes of heat cascaded through her, burning away any remnants of denial and resolve. She embraced him, anxious for the feel of his solidity, and he pressed her closer until her breasts crushed his chest with tantalizing contact. The speed with which her passion vanquished her solid sense frightened even as it exhilarated. She lost control, helpless to the dangerous sensations and yearnings trembling through her body.

He ended the kiss and caressed her face, his fingers drifting behind her ears to the pins holding her wimple. He slid the cloth off and pressed his mouth to her neck before carefully going to work on her veil.

"You asked what I want with you, Moira," he said while he kissed and bit and licked her ear in ways that made her shake. "I want everything. I would know every inch of you, every part and thought. I want to take you every way a man can have a woman, and I will not pretend otherwise." His hand moved down her body with a firm caress that articulated his desire. "But I do not seek to seduce you to something against your will. I do not deny that I want you completely, but I will settle for less."

His bold words summoned shrill streaks of desire. She barely heard the offer of restraint as he submerged her in another kiss. Long. Absorbing. Demanding. His hand pressed her stomach as if it could feel the blood strumming there.

His arm encircled her neck, his hand slipping down to the lacing of her gown, meeting the other at the knot. He kissed her temple and hair while his fingers worked. She looked at the crossing strands being pulled through their holes, level by level, down past her breasts. The memory that she should not permit this flashed and she stiffened.

"Nay, Moira," he chided, gliding his fingers along her collarbone and down her chest. "I only take what you have already given to me."

His hand slid beneath the fabric to cover her breast and all of her senses reeled with the warm contact. Engrossing kisses and confident caresses methodically eroded her pitiful defenses. She tensed, struggling not to lose everything in the absorbing pleasure flooding her. His fingers began playing with her nipples in devastating ways. A throbbing hunger awoke between her thighs. A low moan escaped her and she lost her hold then and became cast adrift in rising swells of passion. Only Addis existed in this world of sensuality, his presence more real than her own, his strength a raft to which she tethered herself.

He slipped the garment down her shoulders, easing the shoulder bands of her shift along with it. He pushed the fabric down her arms to her elbows so that her breasts were exposed. The cool breeze tickled her skin like a teasing breath. The garment restricted her arms, binding them against her sides, leaving her to accept his kisses and caresses without a return embrace. His captivity of her body both aroused and frustrated.

He bent low, his body obscuring the night sky. His breath mixed with the cool breeze before his mouth warmed her breast. His arm supported her wanton arch of offering. Her whole body shuddered with indescribable cravings while he licked and kissed and drew on her.

No thought now. No yesterday or tomorrow. No sense

and no plans. Just sweet bonding and high-pitched pleasure and piercing, growing need.

He grazed her nipple with his teeth and her little groan
melted with the sounds of the night. He took her in his
mouth and sucked and her rapid, frantic breaths filled his
ear like an audible voice counting the beat of his heart.
The whole night joined in. The sounds of insects, the flow
of air, the spirits of the rocks and trees acknowledged their
primitive intimacy.

He moved them both, resting against the hay and lifting her onto his lap with her back against his chest so they
could both watch the night sky and he could see her
moonlit face. He took both her breasts in his hands and
her lids lowered and lips parted. He teased at those dark
tips and felt every movement of her body's response. The
rhythmic pressure of her hips and buttocks. The sinuous
stretching that asked for more. His joy in her pleasure
astonished him. The comfort and peace of holding her
awed him. The stars seemed to sparkle with the pattern of
her sighs. Amidst them the half-moon glimmered. *Go find
your own woman, Menulius. This one is wholly mine.*

Her rising passion produced little groans of need. Her
legs had parted and he bent his knee so that she rode his
thigh. The intimate pressure completely undid her. The
garments still bound her but one hand flailed, seeking
contact. She gripped his other thigh while her whole body
pressed into his and a begging cry warbled low in her
throat.

He wrapped his arms around her, holding her close
with his lips pressed to her cheek and his crossed hands
still arousing her breasts. Sanity debated with hunger. If
he took her she would not deny him now. The soft trembles beneath his arms said that much. It had been his intention, even while he cajoled her with promises of
restraint. Suddenly, however, he did not want to mar the

perfection of sharing her passion. He needed her completely willing. He did not want to face her regrets afterward.

The stars and breeze swam around him. The spirits urged him to finish the rite of possession. His own body echoed the demand. Menulius gazed down, his vague shadows forming a mocking half smile.

He shifted and slid his arm under her legs. "I am taking you to bed now, Moira." He lifted her and carried her through the croft to the cottage, away from the spirits and elements telling him to use her.

Low lights, cool and warm from moon and hearth, filtered through the shadows. He laid her on the bed beneath the window and she appeared ethereal in that light. He sat beside her and kissed her while his hands went to work on her garments. A small sound of protest emerged while he pulled the gown down her legs. The smallest frown puckered her brow, as if the bed and undressing reminded her of her objections. He shamelessly caressed her back from the intruding denial, playing at the sensitive peaks of her breasts until she slid the straps of her shift from her arms so that she could embrace him.

The sensation of her hands on his shoulders and back immersed him in bliss. He rested his face against her breasts for a moment, reveling in the serenity she brought. Then he pushed the shift down, his kisses following the linen over stomach and hips and thighs. He paused there, inches from the scent of her arousal, and resolve wanted to crumble. Somehow he leashed the animal hunger and rose from the bed.

He gazed at her while he removed his belt and tunic. She looked so beautiful. Moonlight washed her pale form and reflected off the clarity of her eyes. Despite the shadows he saw confusion looking back at him. He pulled off his shirt and lay down beside her.

If she demanded it he would find contentment just sleeping with her in his arms. He would try to hold her to him with that intimacy alone, but he wanted more secure bonds. He had learned a thing or two during those years of competing with a god for Eufemia's passion. He knew something about the power of pleasure and how it worked on a woman's soul.

She embraced him, but he felt hesitancy in those arms. He caressed her length and wariness and embarrassment tinged her shudder and sigh. If he left the choice to her she might well sleep on straw in the croft. She did not know what she wanted and needed, did not comprehend what waited for them if only she accepted it. He made the decision for her with possessive finality. He would not take her, but he would have her.

He used his hands and mouth until she rocked against him, clutching his back, burying her cries in his shoulder. He took his time, enjoying endless kisses, riding the torturous pleasure with her. With searching hands he explored her body, here firm and taut, there soft and yielding. In her aching need her own hands moved, first shyly but then with more confidence. Her fluttering caresses burned into him and the heat of his blood rose to a blinding level.

He pressed her against his length and caressed to the top of her thighs. With his first touch she lost all control. Beautiful sounds of pleasure and need poured out of her until she spread her legs with abandon. She hung around his neck and clawed a hold on his shoulders when the convulsive end neared. A violent tremor quaked and a shocked cry erupted. She grasped him like a fearful child seeking shelter as the release shook her.

He held her huddled body and buried his face in her hair while her slowing breaths soothed his own painful need. She lay silently, nestled in his embrace, with the night air cooling their ardor.

"Why didn't you . . . ?" she finally mumbled against his chest.

"I said I would not."

She burrowed deeper, as if facing him would embarrass her. "At the end . . . why did you do that?"

"To show you that sharing my bed will not be . . . tedious. Didn't you like it?"

"Aye. Too much. But even so, I will not be sharing your bed, Addis."

"You are sharing it now."

She raised her head and looked around the cottage. "Not your bed. Not the lord's bed. Much more like my bed at Darwendon."

She looked so captivating with the moonlight making a little glow along her profile. If she wanted to believe that she could contain this within this cottage and this night, he would let her think so for now. "Aye, not the lord's bed. This night it is just Addis finding solace with Moira."

He sat and removed his leather hose and cast them aside. He stretched out wearing only his braes, letting the breeze cool his skin. Her warmth contrasted deliciously and he pulled her against his chest and legs, alert to every inch of connection. Her palm stroked his face, firmly caressing along the scar as if that thick ridge of damaged flesh did not exist. Shifting slightly, she embraced his shoulder with one arm. Instinctively, naturally, as if he had done so a hundred times before, he rested his head against her breast and an indescribable peace rinsed his soul.

He slept deeply, but she did not. She lay holding his body, looking over his shoulder out the window at the beautiful sky, thinking it was painfully sweet to be close to someone like this, if only for a short while.

Her fingers drifted over the muscles of his shoulders. A strange man and a stranger night. She doubted that this lovemaking had brought him much solace despite his last words, even if he slept like the dead now. She had given her whole life, and she recognized giving when she saw it.

Not selfless though. Nay, not without a charge. He probably already knew what she slowly accepted while she held him. A woman cannot do that with a man and remain aloof. She cannot sleep naked like this afterward, holding him all night, and pretend that nothing binds them in the morning. This strange lovemaking insinuated that he expected something far more dangerous than her services as his lehman. It would take all of her strength to refuse him now, whatever it was that he wanted from her.

The reasons for doing so seemed very distant. Common sense and carefully laid plans counted for little in this intimacy. Confused thoughts scrambled through the fitful sleep that finally claimed her.

Dawn's light woke her. She lay on her stomach under the wool blanket Addis must have thrown over them both. His arm was slung over her back. She opened her eyes to find him awake on his side, head propped on hand, watching her. His raven hair fell around his head in a thick cloud disheveled from sleep. The bronzed shoulders and chest lay a hand span from her nose. The gray light cast his face in severe planes, emphasizing the slash of mouth and the long ridge of scar, making him look stern. She remained motionless and her soul instantly understood his expression.

He rose up on his forearm and slid the blanket off her body revealing her full nakedness to the early light and his eyes. He bent kisses to her back, creating a thrilling trail of heat. He stroked down to her buttocks and his fingers grazed the cleft with startling intimacy. His eyes met hers. "I had six years to learn lessons in continence, but seeing you this morning destroys my resolve of last night. I am going to take you this time. If you want to deny me, you had better run away now."

Deny him? That would take a voice and hers had disappeared because her heart was in her throat. She would need a body that could move, and hers had become immobile with screaming anticipation. He did not wait long for her to decide. Turning her over, he moved on top of her, dominating her with warm strength and hard flesh.

No restraint this time. A different Addis with a different intention. Kisses and caresses that bespoke his need and prepared her to accommodate it. He led her up a rapid spiral into a primitive, hungry passion.

Drumming quietly echoed in her head. It took a while to realize that it was not the beating of her heart or the pulse of his power. It did not even emanate from within the cottage, but poured in the window above them. She tried to block it out, but it only grew louder.

"Hell," Addis muttered, looking over to the front of the cottage and the sounds of a small troop reining up in the lane.

The aura of bliss split as if someone had slashed it with a knife. The door burst open and a blond youth appeared in its light. "Aye, this be it!" he called, backing out with a laugh. "But we came too early. He still be topping a whore."

The men were in high spirits and ribald shouts of encouragement filled the air. Moira shut her eyes to the reality bouncing its sounds around the walls. This night of beauty was to be followed by a dawn of shame. Her good sense suddenly rose tall, stiff from its long subjugation to her impulses, and filled her with scolds. It really wasn't fair. She hadn't even done the crime but she would still pay the price.

She found some composure and raised her lids to find

Addis looking down at her, reading her embarrassment. He rested his palm on her cheek to soothe and reassure her.

"It seems Sir Richard did not come alone." He swung up and reached for leather.

She dressed quickly, pulling on shift and gown and hiding her disheveled hair beneath a veil. Away from his embrace and the bed, she experienced a growing awkwardness with him. The morning air began to dilute the scents of their intimacy. The rising sun burned away those sweet connections. She watched Addis don his garments and fasten the knight belt low on his waist, assuming again the lordly presence of yesterday. She glanced around the little cottage, foreign now in the light of day and looking starkly, relentlessly *real*.

He turned to the door but she hung back. He came over and held her head to a kiss. "You either walk out at my side as my woman or in my shadow as my slut, Moira. Let it be the first way. They will show you respect in order to honor me."

He took her hand and led her through the threshold. Sun gleamed off armor and weapons. Men and horses and wagons jammed the lane. A quick silence fell when they emerged. Seven pairs of eyes scanned down to where Addis still clasped her hand.

Sir Richard strode forward, flickering an apologetic glance to her. While he passed the men his hand swung out and without even looking he cracked the blond squire across the face so hard that the youth staggered. Not missing a step he advanced until he stood an arm's span away and beamed a teary smile up at Addis.

"Well, now, 'tis a glorious morning, 'tis it not, my lord."

Addis released her to accept the embrace of his father's

steward. She eased along the shadow of the house, away from the male drama.

Richard gestured to the others. "Alan and Marcus insisted on coming. And that there's Small John, Big John's son. As true as his father, I promise you. There are others, but we left them back there. Might be more useful inside, and I like the idea of that bastard worrying about whom he can trust." He walked to the carts. "Come see what we've brought you."

Moira realized that the rear one was hers. "Found some villagers bringing it here this morning," Richard explained with a point. "But look you here. Your father's armor and such. And some coin. Not much, since that whoreson found most of it despite my hiding it in ten different places. And we've Patrick's destriers down the lane a bit. Still the devils they ever were and just as hard to control. Ah, and there is this." He reached into the cart and pulled out a long, heavy weapon. "The family sword. I took it when your father died. Thought maybe Simon would try something, what with you dead and the boy just a babe. Figured he might take the land but I wouldn't let him have the rights."

Addis took the old Norman sword in his hands. His face was a severe mask of composure, but Richard was not so contained. He grasped the hilt below Addis's fingers. "We here never swore to him, not in our hearts. Only to the lord, and he was never that."

Addis hesitated. They all stood like a frozen image. He looked across the knights and squires, seeking until his eyes met hers. He glanced at the cottage, through its doorway into its dim depths, and then back at the sword pointing down at the ground. Resolve set his expression. Resolve, and maybe resignation. He lowered the weapon. Sir Richard followed, kneeling to swear his oath of fealty.

She slipped back into the cottage, blinking away stinging tears. Well, that was that. It had begun, and it would end with him dead or triumphant. She was glad that Sir Richard would be at his side. He appeared a man whom Addis could depend upon. He would need such a friend with him.

The sounds of other oaths drifted to her while she busied herself tidying up the cottage, trying to fill her sudden hollowness with practicalities. When she had finished she looked around the little space. A broken pitcher held some wilted flowers on the crude table, and she darted outside to pick some new ones without anyone noticing. She smoothed the coverlet over the bed, noticing the careful stitching of its piecework. Other details, like the carefully scrubbed floor and the neatly stacked crockery, absorbed her attention.

She had no trouble picturing the young couple who lived here. They loved each other. One could just sense it. Happy despite their poverty of goods. Secure in their hold of each other. It had been the ghost of that love that had unsettled her when she first entered last night.

She found her basket and thumbed a shilling out of the leather sack and slid it under the pillow. A body obscured the light from the door and she turned to see the blond squire standing there.

"My lady, my lord said to tell you that we are ready to leave."

She faced him, holding her basket against her stomach. He had addressed her the safest way, but he eyed her curiously, wondering just who and what she really was.

"I am not a lady," she corrected, reminding herself of the essential fact of her relationship to Addis. "My name is Moira Falkner, and my mother was serf born."

CHAPTER 8

THE ROAD BECAME CROWDED when they neared London. Travelers moved in both directions, forcing their retinue into a long line. Moira drove her cart at the rear and Addis rode far in the front. She had planned it that way.

The four-day journey had been a quiet hell presaging her future as the lord's whore. Addis had made his interest clear, and the knights and squires showed their respect for him by ignoring her. They helped her in a formal, guarded way, but no one spoke with her much. It struck her as the way men had treated Edith when Bernard was nearby, and reminded her of the very different way they often treated her when he was not.

Sometimes she would find one of the knights looking at her with an expression that indicated the respect for Addis did not truly extend to her. It is so because he wants it thus, those eyes would say, but you and I both know what you really are. A woman like you could as easily be mine this night as his, and when he tires of you it might yet be so.

Sir Richard demanded all of Addis's attention, but then in this troop of men she hardly expected him to bother much with her. They exchanged no more than a few words each day, and from early dawn until they made camp each evening nothing distracted her from thoughts that debated the alternatives awaiting her at the end of this journey.

If he had left her alone completely she might have felt calmer about what she had decided to do. But the second day she had woken to find him beside her in the cart where she slept, squeezed to her side under the blanket while he held her. Each night he came again to lie by her side. She had clung to him last night under the starless sky, wishing she could hold him forever but knowing in her heart that she could not. His world would never permit that, nor had he ever indicated that he even wished that it would.

It will be much worse later if I wait, she reminded herself firmly while she carefully drove her donkey amidst the other carts crowding her sides as the road widened.

The town walls could be seen now and she scanned their endless breadth with astonishment. London was huge. She had heard as much, but never expected anything like this. The town had outgrown its walls, and spread along her road in a collection of inns and houses of every size and description. Noises and smells increased with each step until all of her senses were assaulted by the density of people and activities. A massive, sculpted gate loomed at the end of the road.

Addis and Richard neared the gate and some guards emerged to meet them. The line of travelers began halting and bunching. A wagon pulled up alongside her and the old man driving it rolled his eyes at the jam developing. "Damn knights," he muttered.

"What is happening?"

"Don't like armed retinues coming in, even small ones. City is on the outs with the king, and doesn't want too many of his men inside at once. Just bide your time, woman. They'll move 'em out of the way soon."

The guards gestured Addis and Richard over to the wall of the fortifications. "Will they refuse them entry?" she asked as the crowd inched forward.

"Depends on who they be, don't it? Have to ask their questions first and such."

More guards had arrived. A general confusion cramped the road. Moira looked at Addis being peppered with inquiries. Blinding yearning swept her. Emotions she had harbored for half a lifetime almost made her turn her donkey. She locked her gaze on him and branded her mind with the sight, losing herself in anguished regret.

The jolt of her cart jerked her alert again. Travelers surrounded her, separating her from the squires, and the line began edging toward the gate.

She forced her eyes away from him and faced the square hole of freedom. His knights and squires pulled aside to join Addis and Richard. She stayed in the line and let the crowd move her on, away from him and the alluring, disastrous passion he offered.

The shadow of the gate fell across her and she faced a guard, but his attention found the little altercation alongside the wall more interesting than her. His arm swung out and she passed through the wall.

The incredible confusion on the other side stunned her and she almost turned her cart around and headed back to Addis. So many people and lanes and shops and animals. Screaming children and squealing pigs and barking dogs kept darting into her path. Colorful signs swung over her head and buildings loomed and jutted above them, some three or four levels high. Carts and stalls jumbled with foods from gardens and hearths, with craft work and leather, clogged the spots where the main road absorbed little side lanes.

She felt immediately lost and overwhelmed, and sighed with relief when she spied the tall spire rising above it all in the distance. In Salisbury the cathedral served as a general meetinghouse and marketplace, and she assumed it would be thus in London.

The street widened in front of the cathedral. The square was full of vendors and people of every degree doing trade or just passing time. She jumped down and led the donkey into the milieu. She skirted the edges, looking for a friendly face.

A fat woman selling baskets eyed her cart and frowned. "Not near me, you don't."

Moira examined the woman's simple but neatly woven wares. "Nay, I have not come to trade today."

The woman's curiosity got the better of her. She huffed around her own cart and peered into Moira's. "Fancy weaves. This one is interesting. Not exactly round, is it, but deliberately not." She lifted it out and turned it upside down. "How do you get the colors? The red and purple?"

"Berries. I make a tub of juice and water and soak the reeds."

"Ach! Well, no berries growing in London, that's for sure, or for miles around except on the king's hunting grounds probably. What there is gets picked and eaten. You'll be wanting a pretty sum for these. Have better luck over in Westminster where the court ladies walk about. They come here too sometimes, and there's merchants' wives who would pay your price, but these be ladies' baskets if you ask me."

Moira stored away the advice. Their common trade had formed a bridge and the woman seemed kind enough. "Can you tell me of an inn where I might find a chamber."

"There be inns aplenty in London, and across the bridge in Southwark. Depends on the kind you want. Some's for ladies and some's for pilgrims and some's in between."

"A clean place, where I can have my own chamber. Run by honest folk."

"Well, if you have the coin there is a small one run by Master Edmund's wife. He is a tanner, and the place smells a bit since his trade is there, but then all of the city smells, don't it? She is a God-fearing woman and runs a clean place. Usually gentry types stay there when they are in town, but you talk and walk like one so maybe they'll take you."

Moira asked for directions to Master Edmund's place. "You take care," the woman warned in parting. "Pretty thing like you in this city better watch your step. There's lots of wolves in this town glad to take a bite of country chicken."

Within an hour Moira had settled herself into the small, plain room leased to her by Goodwife Elsbeth. Her cart and its belongings were stored in a stable in back. Edmund had assured her they would be safe since the city quickly hanged any thieves, so few took up the vocation.

Sitting on her straw mattress, she collected her thoughts. She doubted that Addis would look for her, and if he did he would never find her in such a large town. It would not be necessary for her to hide, but perhaps for a day or two she should avoid the main streets and market-places just in case.

She tried not to picture his face when he realized she had run away. How would he react? With the anger he had promised? With surprise? With indifference? Perhaps the last. Barrowburgh would occupy him now, and in this city he should have no trouble finding a woman willing to share a knight's bed.

The city din breezed through her window and she pictured him all the same. Not angry or indifferent, but looking down at her, his eyes alight with warmth, turning his head to kiss her. An aching hollow emptied her. It had been a delicious dream, sharing his friendship, tasting that passion, touching that spirit. Had it been thus for him too? If so, would he understand that she rejected heaven in order to avoid hell? She doubted it. Men never understood the cost of these things to women, because no one ever asked them to pay the same price.

The emptiness filled with a wash of loneliness and fear. Her good sense had never made her this miserable before.

Elsbeth called up, inviting her to share some ale, and she went down to the kitchen, grateful for the distraction.

"You plan to live here then?" Elsbeth asked while she poured out the ale.

"Aye."

"You brought more coin than I saw, I hope. 'Tis a hard town for them's that's aliens, not citizens in the law, and doubly hard on a woman alone. No shop for you. If you mean to sell those baskets, it will be on the street."

"I have some more coin. Not much, but enough, I hope." The leather sack and ruby were stowed in her sewing basket in her cart. Safer there where Edmund could see who entered the stable than in her chamber. "This inn of yours is very attractive. What does such property cost in this town?"

Elsbeth settled on a stool. "You think to buy property? Your husband must have been good at his trade."

"James was a wool merchant in Salisbury."

"Wool merchant or no, I doubt he left you enough to buy a house like this. One hundred and fifty pounds this one cost. My man saved long for it, close to twenty years."

Moira thought the ruby was worth that much. She had always intended to use that jewel to help Brian establish himself. The plan had been a simple one. He would train to be a knight with Raymond, and she would provide the funds for his horse and armor when he earned his spurs. Now she would use the ruby to establish herself instead, and property made the most sense. A man would understand the value of an inn that earned income more readily than the vague worth of a small red stone.

"Now a craftsman's house in a north or east ward, maybe you could get one of those for fifty. We are near the Cheap and the river, which makes a difference. And if you want to lodge pilgrims, your best choice is to go across river to Southwark. That's where the pilgrims stop on their way to Canterbury."

"I knew a woman who came here a few years ago. She spoke of working in a pilgrim's tavern owned by her cousin. Would that also be across river?"

"Aye. The city discourages the pilgrims coming in. Too many of them. They mostly stay in Southwark."

She had intended to look for Alice after she settled herself, but if finding her might prove easy perhaps she would do that first. In the rare event Addis should find her it would be good to have Alice's testimony about Bernard's freedom. And although she and Alice had not been close friends, it would be reassuring to have a familiar person to turn to in this busy, strange town.

"You come looking for a husband?" Elsbeth asked bluntly. "If so, there's plenty of men looking for a wife. With enough coin or property, you could even get one with the city's freedom, a citizen. The going dowry is one hundred pounds with them, but you have a craft of your own and are pretty enough, so for you maybe it would be less."

"I am not looking for a husband." Her response surprised her. Of course she was. Quite specifically. Confiding as much would ensure a steady stream of eligible men to this house. The notion of facing that right now, the very insinuation of what marriage meant with that unknown man, vaguely repulsed her. She had always assumed that she could tolerate bedding her next husband just as she had tolerated James, but now . . . She would find Alice and then a property and make some more baskets. Later she would place herself on the marriage market. By then maybe Addis would be dead to her again.

She returned to her room, feeling tired but also reassured. Things should work out fine. She had managed in Salisbury, hadn't she? Not nearly so big, but a town was a town. She laid down to rest, sorting her plans for tomorrow. Images of Addis at the gate entered her head, and she wondered if he had even gained admittance to the city.

Southwark was no London. It possessed a transient, unstable mood, as if no one on the streets had been born there or planned to stay long. Haggard pilgrims swarmed amidst footloose squires and apprentices looking for strong drink. It did not take Moira long to guess the profession of the many women who strolled the lanes and sat at windows of certain houses.

Elsbeth had explained that Southwark was not part of London but a separate town, and one with loose laws and a bad reputation. She had advised Moira not to go at all and to guard her purse if she did. Thinking it could not be that bad, Moira had come anyway but brought only a few pence with her.

She had thought that she would find Alice in a snap. After all, how many taverns could she need to visit? Dozens, it turned out. She popped out of one late in the evening, thinking that she should have begun this search earlier in the day. She had waited until late afternoon in the hope that crossing paths with Addis or one of his men would be less likely then. But it had taken longer to reach Southwark than she expected, in part because she kept pausing to examine houses that might serve as likely inns. Now she hesitated in the street and noted dusk's arrival. She would have to come back tomorrow.

She walked back to the stone bridge and made the long crossing. Guards were closing the city gate just as she slipped through.

She retraced her way back to her inn, lost in her thoughts, following her route without much real awareness of anything more than the darkness and the silence. And so, when she turned a corner and stepped right into a pool of dazzling brightness, she gasped in surprise.

Three men carrying torches stood chatting by the side of the street. They heard her and turned.

"Well, now, what do we have here?" one of them said.

She tried to walk past but they blocked her path.

"Coming from a job then?"

"You be a long way from Cock Lane, girl," another said.

She glanced from face to face in confusion. They peered at her in the torchlight, looking very stern and official.

"Let me pass, please."

"Now, we can't do that. It's our job to patrol this ward and be sure the likes of you stay where the city has put you. When you came through the gates you knew the risk if you were found," the first one said.

"I just returned from Southwark. I live inside the gates."

"Do you now? The wardens will want to hear about that. Whores aren't allowed nowhere in the city but Cock Lane." He took her arm in a firm hold.

They thought that she was a . . . it was too ridiculous! She had seen enough whores this day to know she didn't even remotely resemble one. "My good men, you are quite mistaken. I am simply trying to get to back to my inn."

"Ooo! She's one of them fancy-talking ones who goes to the job instead of him going to her."

"Don't be absurd. Do I look like . . . like a . . ."

"In the dark all women look the same. You should know that."

This was taking a preposterous turn. "See here—" she began in annoyance.

"Nay, you see here," he said. "You are walking the streets alone after curfew against city law and in my experience there's only one reason a woman does that. It's Tun prison for you."

Prison! "This is outrageous."

The man who gripped her arm eyed her more closely. He hesitated, then shrugged. "Aye, well, you explain your story to the magistrate tomorrow. My job is to collect the nightwalkers and whores off the street and you be both as I see it. So, let's go. It's a bit of a ways to the Tun."

"You cannot be serious," she cried as he began dragging her away.

"Don't give me trouble now."

"Unhand me," she said lowly. "I will walk with you. Do not dare to touch me again."

The man looked back at his companions and laughed. "She's good. She's very good. Has that snooty tone down pat. I'll wager that this one's expensive."

Moira peered at the eyes glowing in the torchlight. They belonged to the head guard of Tun prison, the round fortress where London incarcerated those arrested for night crimes. The guard had taken one look at her and ordered her brought to this windowless chamber instead of a prison cell.

Grateful for his consideration, she accepted the ale he offered her and then poured out her explanation of why she had been walking the streets after the city curfew. "I told the night constable about Elsbeth and asked him to send for her," she concluded. "She knows that I am new to the city and its ways."

"He will tell her if he can find her. Doesn't mean she will come, does it? You have kin or such here? Anyone else who can pledge for you, or bring the coin so you can stand surety?"

She would rot in this place before she asked anyone to look for Addis. Besides, he might not even have been allowed through the gate.

The guard leaned against the wall behind his bench and patted his thick girth thoughtfully. "The thing is, and it is amazing I tell you, but none of the women brought here are really whores. Night after night the city makes the same mistake and rounds up some females and all of them, every one, have stories much like yours. It grieves me to see what is done to them on the morrow, the ones who can't get out during the night."

"What happens to them?"

"Well, if the magistrate doesn't believe them, and he almost never does for some reason, the woman is put in a cart and dragged through the streets for public mockery. All the way to Newgate, which is on the other side of town. The crowd can get a little rough, I tell you. Then she's left on Cock Lane outside the gate with the other bawds."

That didn't sound *too* bad. Not like a public flogging or being locked up in this damp, stinking place for months.

" 'Tis worse than one would think, being humiliated

like that. Branded a whore forever, she is. The whole city
has seen her face. And there's records kept too. The city
likes to keep records on everything. 'Tis a long way to
Newgate, and the men sometimes get lewd on the way,
especially the young ones, though the women ain't much
better to my eye. And she can't return to the city. If a
woman is found more than once plying the profession
here, the next time her head is shaved before she is
carted." His bright eyes appraised her. "We guards here
hate to see it. We do what we can for the poor things."

Moira recognized the opening ploy for a bribe when
she heard it. "You said that some women get out during
the night. How is that permitted?"

He flickered an appreciative glance. "Sometimes someone comes and makes a pledge and offers to pay a fine.
The way we see it, it saves the city a lot of expense and
trouble that way."

"What is the fine?" She had all of three pence.

"For you, I'd say it would be about two shillings."

Two shillings!

"You look to be an expensive sort. You tell me your
man's name, and I'll send word to him. He'll pay it. 'Tis
his job to do so. No point in sharing with a man if he
doesn't come up with the coin when this happens."

He hadn't believed a word she had told him. The door
to the chamber was closed but the acrid smells of the
prison managed to permeate the walls. Nausea churned
her stomach and helplessness overwhelmed her. "I have
no man. I am not a whore," she said, burying her face in
her hands.

She waited with resignation for him to call the other
guards and have her taken away. Somehow she would get
through this night and tomorrow.

"Well, now," the guard said in a smooth tone that caressed the silence. "If you've no coin and won't send for

your man, there's another way. You've a lady's way about you, and a body most men only touch in their dreams. Might be worth two shillings at that."

Her empty stomach heaved with disgust. She forced down the bile before she raised her head. "Nay."

Two sparks of lust flickered in the torchlight. If this man decided to force her she would have no escape. Collecting herself, she faced him down with one of Claire's noble gazes. Absorbing that manner had served her well over the years with men of every degree, but she worried that if this one dreamt of bedding a lady it might only prove provocative.

Anger and insult flared but soon subsided. He stood and took her arm and dragged her to the door. "Have it your way, woman. We'll see how proud you still are when you get to Cock Lane."

CHAPTER 9

ELSBETH CAME THE NEXT morning but with one glance Moira worried it had been a mistake to ask for her. The tanner's wife bore a hard expression that spoke her embarrassment at being summoned to a whore's trial.

No hallmote would judge her and the others waiting for swift justice. Only two bored magistrates who looked as if they had heard every story before waited to decide her fate.

They barely glanced at her and considering her condition she was just as glad. A night in Tun prison had reduced her to a snarl-haired, half-broken, stinking image of the basest type of person. The prison held one large cavern for all the women, with no benches or stools to sit on, just foul straw on a filthy floor. During the night, one by one, the real whores had disappeared when their men paid their bribes. By morning only she and one other woman remained.

They let her plead her case but no one asked any questions. She finished her tale and it even sounded thin to her. She hopefully identified Elsbeth as someone who could pledge that she spoke the truth. The magistrates called the goodwife forward.

"It is as she told me," Elsbeth conceded.

"Do you have any independent knowledge that it is true?"

"Sounded true enough at the time. An odd manner, I thought. Too refined for her degree. Alone, that was sure. Asked me how to get to Southwark. Said she knew a woman who had gone there a few years ago."

One magistrate pursed his lips and glanced knowingly at the other.

"Asked about buying a house in the city," Elsbeth continued helpfully. "One with chambers enough to serve like an inn."

"Indeed," the magistrate mused sourly.

Moira groaned at the conclusions these men were drawing. Better if the goodwife had stayed at home.

Elsbeth recognized the interest her revelations engendered. She warmed to the attention. "Said she wasn't looking for no husband. *Very* sure about that."

Moira got the impression that that fact, more than any other, sealed her fate. She listened to the punishment meted out, so tired that she almost didn't care.

They brought her to a chamber until the rest of the cases were heard. At midday a guard took her and the real whore out into the yard where two carts waited. A group of men carrying timbres and pennants and drums collected near the wall.

The gate stood open and people drifted in to watch the preparations. While a crowd gathered someone draped a smelly yellow-and-white-striped robe over her shoulders and placed an unlit candle in her hand before pushing her up into the cart.

A sea of attentive faces assaulted her. Unfriendly

expressions of scorn and mocking interest examined her. Hooded eyes glowed with self-righteousness and lascivious speculation.

An unfamiliar horror woke her numb spirit. This was going to be much worse than she had imagined. They were all strangers, but by the time it ended, the humiliation might prove devastating. A public flogging might be preferred.

She tried to steel herself but the sleepless night had left her with little strength. The pointing fingers and knowing nods of the crowd seemed closer. The cart had not moved but already she felt something inside her crumbling.

"You should have told me it only took some coin to assure your compliance, Moira. I could have been using you for weeks now and I did not even realize it."

Addis. She swung around and her heart jumped with relief and then thudded with fear when she saw his expression. Her throat tightened in response to the fury leashed beside her.

She suspected that his mood had little to do with finding her like this and everything to do with her running away in the first place. Her depleted spirit could not bear this now.

"Will you enjoy watching the woman who refused to be your whore displayed as one to the world? I have had all night to contemplate the jest and it ceased to amuse me many hours ago."

"Your memory fails you. I never offered you a whore's price. And you refused me nothing."

"Go away, Addis."

He grasped her chin. "Right now it is unwise to speak with disrespect to your lord, woman."

She needed no reminders of the trouble she faced with him. It leaked out of his body and shot from his eyes. She turned to see the whore ready in the cart behind her. A

guard sidled up and gathered the reins of her donkey, preparing to lead the little pageant of shame. The mummers
with their timbres and pennants took up positions.

Addis strode forward and his hand landed on the
guard's shoulder. The man cringed when the strong fingers crushed his flesh. "Go and get the magistrate," Addis
ordered.

The guard hustled off. Addis returned to her. "Did you
really think to hide from me in this town?"

"It is a very big town."

"Not big enough. Nor will it be the next time if you
think to try again." The crowd had begun making protests
about the delay. "Perhaps I should give you to them,
Moira. I tire of your rebellion. Perhaps this day I should
let you taste the freedom you insist is your due. It will be
easier than convincing the magistrate that an error was
made."

"Could you do that?"

"Give you to them?"

"Convince the magistrate."

"Noble blood counts for something even in this city."
He tilted her chin up with one finger so she looked at him.
"You will have to behave like the bondwoman I tell him
you are though. And you must swear that you will not run
away again."

The mummers swung pennants and tapped timbres to
appease the crowd. Through the gates Moira saw bodies
lining the street, leaving only a narrow path for the carts.
Some guards parted the mob to permit the passage of one
very annoyed magistrate.

"Swear it," Addis ordered.

"I will not run away again. I swear it," she whispered.

The magistrate huffed up alongside the cart. "What is
this? I am told a knight demanded I come. What is your
interest in the whore?"

"I am Addis de Valence, Lord of Barrowburgh and kinsman of the late Earl of Pembroke. This woman belongs to me. She is serf born, and bonded to my land at Darwendon."

"Then you can have her after the city is done with her."

"Does the city punish innocent women just to entertain its people? She arrived here yesterday in my company and became separated when we were delayed at the gate. She is no whore, but only a country woman ignorant of city ways."

The magistrate sneered. "Separated, eh? Run off, more likely, and looking to find a bed the easiest way women know how." He turned to her. "What say you, woman? You did not speak of this before, even to be spared punishment. This cart may not look so bad if you ran away and he takes you now."

The people nearby had quieted while they strained to hear the conversation at the cart. If she were not so dirty and tired and numb she might have refused this public declaration, but in her current condition the protection Addis offered carried a wretched appeal. "He is my lord," she whispered, her throat burning with suppressed tears.

The magistrate pulled the robe from her shoulders. "Then show these people that he is so I don't have a riot on my hands because they think we let some knight buy a whore's freedom."

It took a moment to understand what he meant. Too spent to care overmuch, just desperate to be done with all of this, she dropped the candle, climbed out of the cart, and walked around to Addis. Blocking out the staring eyes and refusing to look at Addis himself, she knelt in front of him.

"Take her, and be sure she behaves while she is within these walls," the magistrate said, scowling. Addis hauled her to her feet. Sir Richard appeared out of nowhere to take her other arm. The two of them dragged her through the crowd.

Some in the mob were not to be denied their sport. Shouts of "whore" and "harlot" rang out, and other voices urged Addis to punish her with a rod or strap. Ripe fruits flew and one landed with a squashing thump on her back. Only after they got through the gate did the mob forget her, and then only because the other cart began to roll.

They pulled her to a side lane where two horses waited. Addis grabbed her waist and threw her up on the saddle and then swung up behind. Richard mounted the other horse but turned to ride in a different direction.

They began trotting through back lanes.

"How did you find me?"

"I talked with basket sellers at the markets." His cold tone made her cringe. The Lord of Barrowburgh would not quickly forget the trouble she had caused and the insult she had given him. Certainly not before they arrived at his house. "I assumed that your wares would have been noticed by them, and I found a woman who had spoken with you yesterday. She sent me to the house of Master Edmund, and he told me where his wife had gone this morning."

That simple. Stupid of her to think that she could disappear even in a town of this size. "My cart is still with Edmund and his wife," she said, suddenly worried about her belongings and especially the sewing basket. The biggest danger of being carted to Cock Lane hit her. If she could never reenter the city, she would have lost everything, including the ruby.

"When Richard returns I will send him for it. The city would allow only the two of us in. The others stayed across the river last night and he must see to their board."

He rode through the low gate of a long two-leveled house and into a small yard. Stables flanked the paved court on the right and a long hall faced it on the left. The overgrown mess of a neglected garden rose up in the back, surrounded by the remains of a stone wall.

She twisted to look back at the block of the house facing the lane. Of good size, with at least five or six chambers, she judged. Her first reaction was that after some desperately needed repair it would make a fine inn.

Addis pulled her off the horse and dragged her by the hand into the hall. She tripped after him while he strode to its end and barged through a door. He swung her forward and she stumbled into the kitchen. An old skinny woman stirring a pot in the large hearth rose in surprise at their abrupt entrance.

"Give her a bath, then send her up to me. Burn the gown," he ordered.

And then he was gone, his retreating boot steps echoing through the hall.

The old woman wrinkled her nose. "Where'd he find you?"

"Tun prison."

"Ach, that explains it. You smell like a devil's fart."

"Since I spent the night in hell, I am not surprised."

"Made a lot of trouble you did, Moira Falkner. My man is still out searching the city for you." She thrust a thumb toward the door. "*He* be ready to kill you, I think. Brave of you to cross a man like him." Stupid of you is more like it, her expression said.

"Who are you?"

"I'm Jane, my man's name is Henry. We were his mother's people. Stayed here after Sir Patrick died, though everyone else left. Not of Barrowburgh bond, but of her family's lands, and besides, we'd been here long enough for the freedom." She bent her stiff body for some buckets. "Come and get some water with me for this bath. Won't help you much if we keep him waiting on you all afternoon."

Moira took several buckets and followed Jane through a side door that gave way into the garden. A well stood a few feet away and they filled their buckets and returned. Together they rolled the big wooden tub away from the wall, toward the hearth. Jane set her buckets to heat by the low flame while Moira emptied hers into the tub. She made several more trips for water, then waited with Jane for the water to warm.

"How have you lived?" she asked Jane.

"Was a bit of coin hidden and we found it. That lasted a while. Mostly we've been selling pieces of furniture. 'Twas some nice chairs in the hall with backs and they brought good coin. Lived off each one for four months. Didn't want to strip the place, but we had to eat. Sold things what wouldn't be missed much. No shame in sitting on benches even in the best halls. I kept telling Henry, What's the point? The house had been forgotten. He wouldn't hear me. Insisted on doing his best to keep it up, but he's old and so the wall's half down and the stable needs a roof and . . . well, you'll see soon enough what's what." She glanced in the direction of the house. "*He* ain't noticed yet. Showed up in a black mood 'cause they wouldn't let his men in but mostly 'cause you'd been lost. Worried at first, then angry in a cold way when he decided you'd run off. You be in for it, Moira Falkner. 'Tis a rash thing you've done."

Moira grimaced agreement and tested the water in the buckets. She poured them into the tub and began stripping off her garments, glad to be rid of their filth and stench.

Jane appraised her body while Moira climbed into the tub. "Well, with that loose robe gone it makes more sense, don't it? Wondered why he had brought a bondwoman all the way from Darwendon, Henry and I did. Curious that he stopped everything to find you, we were."

Moira sank low in the tepid water. "Do you have any soap?"

"A bit. You'll be wanting to wash that hair. Looks like a rat's nest. We'll get you clean and pretty again and maybe it won't go too badly for you."

Moira did not want to contemplate what awaited with Addis nor how badly it might go. Maybe very badly, but she felt little fear. The only emotions her battered spirit could muster were an edgy resentment and sad resignation. She had publicly declared him as her lord and sworn not to run away, and had thus accepted the shackles that she had vowed never to wear again. She had entered Tun prison still secure in who Moira Falkner really was, but had left with that identity repudiated. He had exploited her weakness and vulnerability to make her do that, and it said a lot, too much, about what existed between them and what did not.

Living in Claire's shadow had given her ample opportunity to observe how men like Addis treated women for whom they held affection, and how they treated all the rest who merely caught their eye, highborn or base, wives or villeins. Affection tempered a knight's inclination to dominate and possess, to subjugate and vanquish. She almost hoped that he would beat her as the mob had urged. It would put that night firmly behind them. Maybe it would force her to hate him a little. She was counting on his helping her to do that and from his mood she suspected that he would not disappoint her. The only question was the means by which he planned to demonstrate her submission.

She scrubbed her hair and ducked under the water to

rinse. Her head emerged just as Jane gathered up the gown and shift from the floor and tossed them into the hearth.

"Nay!"

"He said to burn them."

"They are all I have until someone gets my cart."

"I'll get you a blanket. Bit warm for it today, but better than those. Not fit for a beggar, they ain't."

"Could you lend me a gown, just for today? I am larger but if it is loose, at least . . ."

Jane turned with hands on hips. "Look you here. You may disobey and run away, but that's between you and him. I ain't seen that man since he was a boy but I know something of lords and that ain't one to cross. Where would Henry and me go if he got angry and turned us out? If he says burn the clothes I burn them. Unless he says to give you one of my gowns, I don't do it. Only have three and as I see it one of two things is going to happen when you go up those stairs. He's going to beat you or force you and either way any gown won't come out in one piece."

She could do without old Jane so bluntly laying out the options that she herself had refused to face. Perhaps it need not come to that. Surely she had not completely misjudged him when she saw a kinder side.

Jane brought over some ale and bread. "You eat something. Will make you feel better."

The food revived her a little. "Tell you what," Jane soothed while she handed her an old linen towel. "There's some strawberries out in the garden that I found yesterday. You come here after and we'll have some. I've some salves too if you need them. You dry yourself now and I'll use my comb on that hair."

She sat on a stool and stared at the charred remains of

her gown while Jane worked the comb. It had been over an hour since she arrived but she doubted that Addis had forgotten about her.

Jane fetched a blanket from the house. Moira wrapped herself in it. The billowing wool reassured her a little, and the bath and food had returned some strength. Deciding that she could not avoid this confrontation any longer, she followed Jane's directions through the hall and up to the solar.

He was not there. She sighed a prayer of thanks. Deciding that she would wait a few minutes just so that she could honestly claim later that she had, she stepped inside.

The solar was really more of a large bedchamber. At least one chair had not been sold by Jane and Henry, and it faced a table near the window overlooking the street. A curtained bed and some stools and chests made up the other furnishings.

She slipped over to the window and gazed down at the city. She wished that she were back at Darwendon where people knew her. London was too big, too busy, too cruel. But she was stuck here now, cut off from every life she had ever known. She had sworn not to run away.

If she gave the ruby to Addis and bought her freedom at the high price he had set, would he agree that ended the oath she had made? Free women do not run away, they just leave. What then? Free in this city with no property and little coin, how would she live? How could she get back to Darwendon alone, and if she did, what kind of life awaited her there? Darwendon had been a place to protect Brian and plan the future. Could she live in that cottage forever, without the hope that the red jewel had always provided?

He would not insist on keeping her forever. With only two old retainers in this house, he needed her now, but that would end one day. Perhaps in time . . .

A sound broke through her thoughts. She swung her head and then jumped back with a start when she saw him standing on the threshold. She moved from the window into the wall's shadow, as if she could disappear as she had done so often in her life.

"You do not have to be afraid," he said.

Aye, I do, she thought desperately. For she had seen the expression on his face while he watched her, and had known in that instant that if she was not very careful she might never be free again.

CHAPTER 10

"YOU DO NOT HAVE TO be afraid," he said, but she did not believe him. She had caught him watching her, and had seen the emotions that the relief of having her back could not completely appease. She pulled the blanket closer and hugged the wall. He smelled her fear and it sickened him to admit that she did not worry without reason.

He had spent the last hour trying to purge the dangerous tumult that wanted to control him. A day and night of worrying about her safety and seething over her flight, of facing the ghosts of this house without the anchor of her peace, had almost made him a madman. In the darkest hours his resentment that she had abandoned him had revived the scathing memory of another abandonment by another woman. Finding her at the Tun had incited him anew with the evidence that she had chosen to face the city's scorn rather than call for his help.

Not trusting himself near her, he had left her in the kitchen and strode out into the city, hoping to walk off the worst of it. His pacing had brought him into a little square faced by the parish church. It was an ancient building with thick walls. He had entered the deserted cool nave barely lit by a few splotches of light falling through the high small windows.

It smelled of the incense and rituals of his youth, pageants of faith and reconciliation in those days. Desperate for a breeze of grace to calm his turmoil, he walked to the altar and waited.

What had he expected? Light to break through the stone and a ghostly hand to reach into his heart? The vision of the church's saint telling him that all would be well? He did not know, but he had counted on leaving that shadowy space less disrupted than when he entered. It did not happen that way. He stood there hungering for the old reassurances. Instead he only experienced that eerie sensation of being a man out of place and time, now visiting the temple of a foreign cult.

He had returned to the kitchen and listened through its closed door to the sounds of water splashing. He pictured the lush body hunched in the tub, sleek with water, clear eyes turning to his approach. And then other images showing acts of love and punishment, of tender pleasure and harsh profanity, crashed through his mind. He had almost entered and thrown Jane out so as to assert his possession and demand her submission as his blood raged to do.

Instead he had forced himself from the door and walked outside to where the garden once spread in neat beds and pruned orchards. In its current condition one could imagine it was a field far from this city. Weeds reached his thighs while he strode to the back, as far from her as possible. The sounds of town life dulled here, and the buzz of bees and scratching of rodents could be heard. He lay down in some grass and wildflowers and looked up as he had done on days during his enslavement when he sought to pretend that he was home.

The sky god Perkunas's endless domain had stretched cloudless like a serene lake, a cool eternity that could absorb any earthly strife. Slowly, imperceptibly, like so many inaudible murmurs, the spirits of the garden began their rhythmic chorus. Not dead or silenced in this land after all, as he had learned that night in the hay mound. Just so restrained that only a soul open to them would ever feel their presence. Their whispers soothed him, like old friends accepting his fury without argument and thus gently defusing it.

Not an abandonment, he had finally acknowledged. Not like Claire. This one owed him nothing except a serf's obligations which she had never even accepted as his due. A quiet voice carried in the breeze said to let her go, that he could bind her no more than garden walls could hold these spirits, but the last hours had proven that he could not do that now. His physical hunger might be relieved by some other woman, but his soul would find solace with no one else. Recognizing the weakness of his need alarmed him. He had survived six years of enslavement because he had learned to need no one and nothing, and now that he was free and restored to his homeland, unexpected chains weighed him more surely than any slave bonds had done.

He had finally climbed the steps to this solar, following the wet footprints that marked her recent passing. The hunger and rage still trembled but its roar was low and contained now. He had found her standing near the window, limned by soft light while she watched the city street, draped like a mendicant in her brown blanket. He had watched her while she contemplated her private thoughts, realizing that he did not know what to say to her. And then she had turned suddenly and caught his naked gaze and seen more than he would have liked.

She looked so beautiful and vulnerable there with damp waves cascading to her hips. She clasped the blanket together above her chest and only a small triangle of skin showed at the bottom of her neck. Bare feet and ankles poked out below the flowing folds. He had never noticed before how lovely her feet were. Slender and delicate like her hands. Her clear blue eyes watched him cautiously from the shadows.

Part of him still wanted to vent his outrage that she had insulted and betrayed him. Another part wanted to ask how she could have left him bereft of her comfort and peace. But the man who had been a slave knew the answer to that already, not that he would ever admit the dependency that the question revealed. The resurrected Lord of Barrowburgh might be furious, and the knight adrift in his homeland might be injured, but the slave of the *kunigas* understood her far too well. She had seen her chance for freedom and had taken it.

She moved one step forward, a brave woman prepared for the worst. "Let us be done with this, my lord."

"Be done with what?"

"Whatever your reason for demanding my presence here. If you intend to punish me, let us be done with it."

"I said that you do not have to fear me. I never thought to punish you," he lied.

"Nay? Then you perhaps want to command me in my service to you. I can see that this house needs work as you thought it might. It will take time, but with Jane and Henry's help I will get it in order so that it befits you. Do not trouble yourself that I might not understand my duties. I know my place."

"It is good that one of us does. Is that why you think I have you here? To punish or to command?"

"I pray so."

"You pray in vain."

Dismay broke her composure. She licked her lips and lowered her eyes. "Aye. I feared as much. I beg you then not to misuse me, my lord," she said softly.

Her sudden fragility and deference wrenched something inside him. Her plea had been an old one spoken since time began by the weak to the powerful, but hearing it from this proud woman tore at him. "What makes you fear that I plan to, Moira? I have not done so before."

She passed a hand over her eyes, as if her vulnerability embarrassed her. "Perhaps it is because I stand here naked but for this blanket, at your insistence. Jane would not loan me one of her gowns after she burned my clothes."

He had been so absorbed in just looking at her that he had not realized that she was naked, nor wondered why she had wrapped herself in a blanket on a summer day. "I will have your cart gotten soon. Are there garments in it?"

"There is a gown. Between today and that day when those men . . . my others have been ruined, but I have a little coin and will buy some cloth."

With the cost of cloth, it would take whatever she had to buy some. He walked to the chests along the wall and opened one. "Come here."

She hesitated, then emerged from the shadows and obeyed.

"This chest holds some of my mother's things. Take what you need. Take it all."

She knelt beside him. She curiously lifted the edges of folded cloth, then bent and began methodically stacking the garments aside, examining them one by one. The movement caused the wool to creep down her shoulder, exposing the top of her creamy back an inch from his knee.

"It is all too fine. Silks and such."

I would see you in silks and jewels every day. "Better they are worn than that they rot."

"They will not rot if cared for. When you marry, your lady will be glad to have them." She began putting them back in order. She still clasped the blanket with one hand, but the other arm moved back and forth, causing a gap to form. Little flashes of breasts and thighs fluttered beneath the moving edges of wool, inflaming him.

"If I marry I will have the wealth of Barrowburgh with which to buy more. Take them. I do not have coin to waste purchasing simpler things if we can use what we already have."

She knelt back with a linen robe in her hand, considering it. The loosened blanket fell back off her shoulders. Skin and chestnut hair hovered beside his thigh, mesmerizing him. He lightly stroked the bare shoulder with his fingertips.

"I do not think to punish or command or misuse you, Moira. I would have you at my side by day and in my arms at night."

She stiffened, then rose quickly and faced him, casting the robe aside. "Better to punish, my lord. The strap's sting ends."

"You speak coldly for one who was so recently an affectionate lover. Has one day of freedom changed your heart so much?"

"Nay, because in my heart I was always free. 'Tis a few hours of bondage that have chilled me."

His hand still rested on her shoulder. He drew her forward. "Then let me warm you."

Something at his core groaned with relief when his arms closed around her. Her feminine softness seemed to absorb the worst of the sharp emotions that had been driving him this day. He splayed his hands over the hills of her curves and tasted the fresh cleanliness of her pure shoulder.

She *was* chilled, whether from the bath or exhaustion

she could not say. The strength and warmth of his arms promised an enticing comfort. She tried to squirm in resistance against the sudden embrace, but somehow the movement transformed into a pliant molding against his chest.

Lips brushed her hair and temple and cheek with careful gentleness, as if he sought to prove that the danger she had glimpsed did not really exist in him. A soulful yearning cried inside her when he pulled her closer. Firm palms caressed her bare back and found her skin through the gap in front while he pressed kisses to her neck and finally her mouth.

She let him, reveling in a glorious, final taste of what could never be. She let the sensations cascade through her body, evoking the bittersweet longing one feels at any parting.

"I have spent the hours since I rode through that gate to find you gone asking if I had misunderstood somehow," he muttered into her hair.

She closed her eyes to savor the strokes of his hand raising wonderful heat on her thighs and buttocks, sorry that he had spoken so soon. "You misunderstood nothing, but I want us to stop this," she whispered, blinking back tears.

He pulled away to look at her, but he did not release her. "Can you say that these hands misuse you, Moira, and that you are not willing?"

She sorrowfully extricated herself from his hold and stepped back. She hitched the blanket back on her shoulders and grasped it closed. "I am weak to the pleasure, but what you offer me will someday bring misery and I will not endure it. I swore when just a girl that I would not be any man's whore, least of all one to a knight or lord."

Gold fires flamed. Dangerous fires, that spoke of more

than thwarted desire. "You say that often, and insult me with it. 'Tis you who misunderstand, and who think the worst of me without cause. Those garments are not meant as a bribe to buy a bedmate for a few nights. I do not seek to make a whore of you."

She had suspected as much when she saw him at the doorway. Better if he did only want her for brief pleasure. "What you call it will not matter. All others know such women for what they are."

He paced away, his face set in stern planes of confused annoyance. He shot her a glare over his shoulder that flashed with those emotions she had glimpsed when he entered. "What of Edith? She lived with her lord in affection. All could see what was between them. Is that how you knew your mother? As Bernard's whore?"

"It is how *you* knew her, do not deny it. What you and all the others called her, if not to her face then among yourselves. My mother knew more than affection, she knew love with Bernard. She was his leman but she had more than most wives do of her man's heart. She had it the best that such a woman can ever have, but still she was shamed."

"None will shame you if they want to keep their tongues."

"They need never say a word for me to know their minds. Please listen to me and hear what I say and try to understand. You cannot even give me what Bernard gave my mother. Bernard had his son and was growing old. He had done his duty to his family and honor and chose not to remarry. He could treat my mother as his lady because no real lady presided at Hawkesford. It will not be thus for you and you know it. The Lord of Barrowburgh is no Lord of Hawkesford, but the king's man with a position of superior prestige and no serf-born woman can sit at your high table. And you are still young. If not for more sons then for the alliance that will secure your hold on your honor you will marry again, Addis."

He could not refute the truth of it and she was grateful that he did not try.

"She will accept it. She will have to."

"*I* will not accept it. I will not be the woman kept in the south tower, waiting for the lord to steal time from his family and duties to lie with me. I will not be the lehman whose children are bastards, desperate for the lord's recognition."

"Can you doubt that I would care for any child of my blood?"

"I will not be the bondwoman fretting while she ages that the lord's eye will be caught by a younger woman, or growing jealous of the affection that he shows toward his wife."

"I too will be aging, Moira."

His insistence threatened to erode her resolve. "I will not be denied a home of my own, a place in which I know love and security. I have lived on the margins of other people's lives too long, Addis. I will not knowingly choose to do so again, not even if that life is yours and not even for the passion you can make me feel. I am tired of being the shadow."

He walked to the window and gazed out, crossing his arms over his chest. When he finally turned back to her she looked in those deep eyes and knew that he understood, but that it counted for little in whatever compelled him.

"Do you expect me to accept this, Moira? To forget the peace and contentment that I find with you in my arms? To ignore the hunger I have had since I first saw you in that cottage?"

"If you cannot accept it then let me leave! Send me

back to Darwendon at least. Release me for good and forget about me! Some other will give you that contentment soon enough."

"You go nowhere but with me!"

"Then what, my lord? You put us into an impossible position. Or will you force me and thus corrupt the affection that we have shared?"

He did not offer the reassurance she desperately hoped for. He only looked at her so long that she began to feel naked despite the blanket. Her arguments suddenly seemed meaningless as that gaze grew invasive in the old way, summoning memories old and new, demanding that she remember their intimacy and passion, raising images and sensations that her tired spirit tried to reject with little success.

She was waging a battle that a part of her did not really want to win. Her body responded to that probing connection with a flush of warmth and anticipation that both frightened and seduced. Her fortitude began crumbling. Yearning filled her reckless heart.

"I do not think it will come to force," he said, as if he had seen into her mind and assessed the weak forces commanded by her good sense. He held out his hand. "Lie with me now, Moira. You will see that all will be well."

The order jolted her with shock and something terribly like excitement. She looked away from the strong hand reaching for her. "Nay."

"Remove the blanket and come lie with me. I would see you and take you in the full light of day."

Saints help her, she almost released her hold on the wool. "I will not invite what I have just rejected."

"Should I command you as your lord so that you can blame your compliance on obedience instead of desire?"

A little flare of resentment reinflamed her prudence. "I am grateful to you for reminding me of who we both are, my lord. As I once said, I forget it at my peril. The free woman foolishly succumbed, but the bondwoman will not."

"They are the same person."

"Nay, they are not to my eyes. I do not deny that I felt the sweetest pleasure with you. But the heaven that you offer is a form of hell, especially with such chains attached. You have bound me to you with an oath and submission that I cannot undo, but it will not be as you think. Unless you force me, it will not be so."

She really thought that he was going to come and test the truth of her brave words. Tension shrieked between them and her body responded in a shocking way that said the future was out of her hands because if he crossed that space there would be little forcing to it.

He turned away and she almost collapsed with relief. "Then let us both pray that I learned continence in the Baltic as well as I thought, Moira. Take some garments and leave now."

She heard a warning in his order and did not wait for another. Plucking the linen robe from the chest, she hurried from the chamber. The last vestige of strength deserted her on the steps. She clutched the wall, struggling to choke down the sob strangling her throat.

She did not see much of Addis the next few days. He left the house early with Sir Richard to ride to Westminster in daily missions to see the king. Sometimes they did not even return for the midday meal, and she and Jane and Henry would take their dinner alone at a table in the cavernous hall while they rested from the day's chores.

They worked sunrise to dusk. Jane and she scrubbed all the chambers and laid down new rushes. She and Henry managed to mend the holes in the stable's roof and patch and whitewash the plaster on the buildings, but the stone wall and hearth needed a craftsman's hand. She decided to delay asking Addis for the coin since his time at Westminster usually left him angry and silent. He did not speak of those visits with anyone except Sir Richard, but she knew from his mood that they were not going well.

The house had four chambers besides the solar. For her own space she took a tiny one on the first level, far from where Addis slept. Sir Richard had retrieved her cart and she set the few belongings along the walls. Her labors exhausted her sufficiently that sleep claimed her instantly when she retired. She was grateful for that. It would have been horrible to lie there thinking about the man above debating his options regarding Barrowburgh and Simon and all the rest.

A week after their arrival he returned from Westminster in time for dinner. He entered the kitchen with Richard, looking for some ale.

"He avoids it, I say," Richard remarked, continuing a conversation as if she were not present.

"Perhaps. Or he has never been told."

"Do you believe that? You go and wait every day for a week and the man does not even know you are there? You are not some bachelor knight whom his clerks can ignore."

"The Despensers and their people are thick around him, like circles of walls guarding a keep. I think that none enter the gates unless that family permits it. If Hugh Despenser is Simon's friend I may rot sitting in that anteroom."

Richard shook his head. "Fine thing we have in this realm, if the son of Patrick de Valence . . ."

"It is because I am the son that I will rot. Who knows what stories Hugh poured in Edward's ears when he arranged for Simon to get Barrowburgh? Who knows if

Edward is even aware it has happened? It is said he has no love for governance, that he prefers tilling soil like a yeoman and rowing on the fens to attending to state."

"Fine thing we have in this realm . . ." Richard muttered again with disgust.

"I will have to find another way to meet with him, that is all."

"Impossible if those gates are manned as you say."

"I must find a way for the king to order them opened."

"You could petition when the next parliament meets."

"I will not wait on a parliament. I will know where Edward stands before then."

Moira and Jane hustled to lay down the meal in the hall. Addis and Richard sat with them, continuing their conversation at one end of the table. Moira munched her bread and salmon stew and examined the luminous walls of the chamber. She and Henry had finished painting it this morning and it gleamed fresh and clean. She doubted that Addis had noticed the changes in the property.

"There is a tournament seven days hence," Addis mused.

"Edward seeks to appease the barons with sport and a large purse. Stupid, if you ask me. A chance for like-minded men to meet."

"But under his eye and with the Despensers' spies everywhere. Not so stupid maybe."

"Think you of entering?"

"I have already done so."

"Will be good sport, but all for naught if you don't win. You'll just be one of a score of combatants then. Even if you are the champion, there's no saying it will get Edward's attention. He does not care much for weaponry, and will pay little mind even if he is present. Once the pageantry is over he will most likely nap."

"If the king enjoys pageantry, then perhaps one should try and get his attention during the pageant," Moira interjected.

"Oh, aye," Richard mocked. "There will be riches aplenty displayed, girl. A royal tournament is not some country melee. The knights bring their finest garments and gold-painted armor and long retinues of squires and grooms. The Pope himself would get lost in such a fete, and Addis has not even a squire to lead his destrier."

"Then perhaps one should not compete with such richness," she said. "Perhaps simplicity is the way to stand out. Or novelty."

"You suggest that if I ride in that pageant dressed like a simple knight the king will notice? I think not," Addis said.

"Not as a simple knight. As a Baltic crusader."

Addis looked quizzically across at Richard. The old steward shrugged. "Could work, couldn't it? Men always talk of joining the crusade but never do. There is prestige and glory in it, and stories of adventure to be told. Edward may be intrigued."

"The question is, how do I show that I am such a man?"

Moira learned the answer the next day when Addis sent Henry to fetch her to the solar. She found him standing near the bed, wearing the buckskin garments that he had not put on since Barrowburgh. Colorful cloth was strewn around the chamber. She recognized the silks and wools from his mother's chest.

He lifted a red surcotte. "You have not used them as I told you."

"I took some of the simpler things. One does not clean stables wearing velvet."

His jaw twitched. "You should not be cleaning stables."

"If not me, who? Henry is too old to do it all himself. Please, my lord, enough of this. Serfs work, it is why lords have us. Now, is there some way that I can serve you?"

The red silk flowed from his fist. "I do not need you to serve me, but to help me. You suggested that novelty might gain the king's attention. When I attend the tournament, I will be very novel indeed. A knight dressed like a barbarian should at least raise some talk and speculation."

"You will go thus?"

"Aye. Richard has honored me by offering to carry my weapons, but I need someone to lead my horse." He raised in question the scarred eyebrow.

"Will ladies be doing so for the others?"

"Not this time. More novelty."

"I am no lady and all will know it. I will look a fool, as will you."

"You will look beautiful, and when we are done you will look exotic as well. It will be a spectacle that the king cannot ignore." He thrust out the silk. "Put this on, Moira."

She took the garment and held it up. She had no intention of changing her clothes in front of him. " 'Tis not a gown, but only a surcotte."

"Aye. No sleeves. The daughters of the *bajorai* dress thus in warm months." He looked at her thoughtfully. "Your hair unbound, I think. You will cut some of the amber from this tunic to make a headdress to hang across your forehead."

She would appear more barbaric than he. Most likely she would look like a war prize brought home by the conquering crusader.

"Will you do it?"

When she proposed the idea she never thought to be asked to play a part in it. Still, it might work and get him an audience with the king. Until that happened things were at a stalemate, for Addis would never move independently until he knew for certain that Edward had abandoned his family.

"I will do it."

He stepped forward and slid the gold armlets off, then took her hands and pushed one, then the other, far up her arms. "You will wear these as well."

She gazed down at the thick bands etched with intertwining serpents. Pagan images on barbaric gold. Their worth would support her longer than the ruby if she disappeared during the tournament. It disturbed her to realize that he believed her sworn oath enough to trust her with them. "They are beautiful. Where did you get them?"

"The daughter of a priest gave them to me."

Not a Christian priest if he had a daughter. He had said he was enslaved by a *kunigas*. That man's daughter then.

"She helped me to escape," he added.

The meaning of the gold bands seemed very clear. "She must have loved you very much."

"The daughter of a *kunigas* cannot love a Christian slave."

She lifted the silk surcotte from his hands. He stripped off his tunic so that she could take it to cut the amber. He looked very primitive suddenly with the buckskin sheathing his legs and his bronze chest bared. The long scar marked him like a painted line worn to increase his fierce appearance.

The priest's daughter had seen him thus every day. Had they been lovers? He spoke of continence learned in the Baltic, not abstinence. She felt a peculiar jealousy toward that unknown woman, but also deep gratitude that he had not been completely alone during those long years.

Memories of their reunion and journey, of that day

near the lake when she last saw him thus, invaded her. The flat muscles of his chest, the sinewy strength of his arms, the cords of his abdomen . . . she realized that she was looking at him too long, and that he had noticed. A warmth glimmered in his eyes, inviting her, nay, daring her, to reach out and touch the body a hand span away.

"I will try to look as barbaric as possible," she muttered, turning away from him and temptation. So easy to misunderstand the meaning of passion. A woman's soul yearned to do so. Men had probably exploited that since time began.

He was right. The daughter of a *kunigas* cannot love a Christian slave. And the son of an English baron cannot love a serf.

CHAPTER 11

ADDIS DUCKED THROUGH the threshold of the tavern and surveyed the throng of pilgrims. Ale had been flowing for several hours this hot evening. The crowd of petitioners heading to the tomb of St. Thomas at Canterbury had long ago drowned the restraints of their disparate degrees and collected into a noisy, high-spirited party.

He walked over to the keg. The man guarding it thrust a crockery cup into his hands. "Two pence."

Addis paid. "I am looking for a woman. I was told that she lives and works here. Her name is Alice. I wish to speak with her. It is worth her time."

"She be in back, through that door there, washing."

He carried his ale to the back chamber. A stout woman bent over a tub of murky water, swishing cups and mugs. Heavy dark brows bridged a prominent nose. Wisps of black hair escaped her kerchief. It had taken Richard almost a week to track her down amidst the taverns of Southwark.

She straightened and turned and peered at him. He moved closer to one of the candles lighting the chamber. Shock widened her eyes.

She crossed herself three times in a row. "Holy Mother!"

"I am not a ghost, Alice."

"Holy Mother!"

"I wish some time with you."

She backed away. "I have been here the year and a day!"

"I do not seek to return you to Hawkesford, but if I did you could have lived here ten years and it would not matter once you were back there." He let the threat sink in, then set a silver mark down on a table next to the candle.

"I don't do that anymore. I have a man now, and he wouldn't like it. There's women out in the tavern though. . . ."

"I only wish to talk."

She made a face indicating that sounded most peculiar to her. Addis settled himself on a stool and after a cautious hesitation she took another one.

"You left Hawkesford after Claire died?"

"Seemed as good a time as any. My cousin had gone some years before and I knew he was here. Raymond is not a bad lord, but with Claire gone I wouldn't be serving a lady anymore, just be one of the regular women again, so I left."

"You were present at Bernard's death?"

"Aye. Claire had gone home to see him before he passed. I traveled with her from Barrowburgh."

"And what did he say while he lay dying? About Edith?"

" 'Twas tragic to see their love and sorrow. I was pulled in to witness his words to her. Gave her and her people the freedom. About time, what with him setting her above everyone like a lady when we all knew she was no different than the rest of us. Should have done it years before if he meant to. What good was the freedom then, with herself sick already and not long for the world?"

"Was a priest present?"

"Aye. And we all made our marks on some parchment."

"You are very sure that he included Edith's people? Her daughter?"

She nodded. "Spoke of Moira like his own. Wanted her free. Makes sense. She hadn't lived like us for some years, had she? Hard to go back to that once you know better. I certainly couldn't, for all the work here."

He thumbed in his purse and slipped a shilling next to the mark. "You are very sure that he included the daughter?"

Alice looked up in surprise.

Another shilling topped the other. "Positive? You could swear it?"

She licked her lips. "It was some years ago. Whether I could swear it . . ."

A third shilling joined the stack.

"Seems that wasn't so clear, now that I recall. Spoke of it, but it wasn't on that parchment, I don't believe."

Addis nodded. She slid out a plump hand to scoop up the coins.

He grabbed her wrist before she got them. "I think that you should join the pilgrims traveling to Canterbury."

"Make a pilgrimage! There's too much to be done here. I might be gone a month, walking all the way down to the shrine and back."

"Think of the benefit to your soul. There is coin enough there to pay someone to help your cousin while you are gone."

She considered that. "Aye, well, I've always wanted to make the pilgrimage, if truth be told. One hears of such wonders from the others. It is said the cathedral is like heaven itself."

Addis added another shilling to the pile. "Perhaps you will say a prayer for me at the shrine of St. Thomas."

"Certainly, my lord." She glanced to the coins. "Will that be all? I've these cups to wash and . . ."

He pushed the candle closer to her. Not a clever woman, and too frightened to lie effectively. "Nay, that is not all. I want you to tell me about Claire's time at Barrowburgh after I left. I want to hear about Brian's birth and my father's death."

The thick brows shot up into half circles. She met his gaze warily. "Not much to tell."

"All the same, I will hear it."

"Better to let the dead lie in peace."

"Start with the boy. Did she show affection to him while she lived?"

Her eyes narrowed to slits. "As much as could be expected. He was conceived in violence, wasn't he?"

He heard the condemnation that even her fear could not hide. "Is that what she said? If my wife confided that to you, perhaps we need to start earlier. I would hear what Claire told you. I would learn all of it."

Addis stared at the stack of coins on the solar's table. He had found them beneath a stone in the hearth, in the hiding place his mother had once shown him as a boy. Joan and Henry had missed this little cache.

Thirty pounds. It would not go far in hiring an army.

His thoughts drifted back to the coins left in the tavern with Alice. A high price to pay for a woman he could not bed. The mark alone would have hired a knight for a month. Well worth it though, if it got Alice out of Southwark for a month or so. He should feel guilty about bribing away Moira's pledge about Bernard, but his need for her would not let him. The story did not release her of her obligations to Darwendon for the reasons he had explained at the hallmotte, but he did not want to tangle over legalities with her now.

Alice had not wanted to speak of Claire. She might easily betray Moira, the bondwoman who had been raised above her natural place, but she had not wanted to discuss her lady. Nor had he wanted to hear it. He had only suffered it because he needed to know now. He had already surmised much of the story and little that he had heard this evening had surprised him. He should have felt more sympathy when Alice described Claire's loneliness and isolation, but a part of him had been glad to hear that the woman who had let him face hell on his own had seen something of it herself.

He let himself picture her for the first time in years and the memory of her beauty almost seduced him into understanding. A woman whose appearance could devastate the strong had little need of internal strength. The Claires of the world took without asking because everyone insisted on providing whatever they wanted. Small wonder that she had no practice in giving, and had been incapable of it even under the demands of duty.

The memories created a bitter taste in his mouth. He turned back to the coins and his calculations of how many men they would hire and for how long. Selling the gold armlets would make a considerable difference, but if the king failed him and he had to lay siege to Barrowburgh he would need war machines and a large force and possibly many months. Even so, his chances of success were slim, and any victory might be short-lived if Simon procured aid from the Despensers.

A woman's sharp scream suddenly shattered his contemplation. He listened alertly but heard nothing more. It had sounded like Moira. He was out of the chamber and down the stairs even before he had decided to move.

In the torchlight of the courtyard he saw her by the gate. She twisted in an unnatural way and it took a moment to realize that a man held her body, with his hand over her mouth. Addis strode toward them, reaching instinctively for his absent sword.

"Unhand her," he ordered.

The man looked up from where he had been speaking in her ear. He wore long dark hair tied back at his nape and the plain garments of a London townsman.

"I could not risk her slamming the gate," the man explained. "My apologies for frightening you, madam, but tonight's business will not wait for morning."

"Release her," Addis warned again, tightening his fist in case the man refused.

A bright smile beamed. "Pity to have to. She is a nice armful at that. You will not scream again, will you, madam?"

She shook her head and the man stepped away. "You are Sir Addis? I must ask you to wait here a short while. I need to get the others."

The man slipped back out through the gate. Several minutes later he returned leading five men. One dressed in clerical garb led the others. "Addis de Valence?"

"I am."

"My name is Michael. I am clerk to John Stratford, Bishop of Winchester. Myself and the others would like to speak with you. I apologize for the hour but it is essential that none other knows that I am in London."

"Let us go into the hall. Moira, have Jane pour some ale for these men."

"She has retired. I will do it."

Addis brought the men into the hall. They settled themselves around a table. "I would know your names," he said. "If you seek me out at night I assume that your reasons are not friendly to the king."

Michael nodded. "You are an intelligent man, Sir Addis. It is a relief to deal with one for a change. Nay, our errand is not friendly to the king but it is most friendly to the realm. There is no harm in your knowing our names, but I must ask you to swear to speak to no one about this meeting and what we discuss here."

If they wanted an oath it would be treason that they discussed. He should send them off at once, but his days of waiting for the king's attention had not left him in a very loyal mood. He swore as they wanted.

Michael pointed around the table. "This is Sir Robert, Lord of Cavenleigh in Yorkshire. Thomas Wake, son by marriage to Thomas of Lancaster. Peter Comyn, cousin of Elizabeth Comyn, who is one of Lancaster's heirs. Sir Matthew Warewell, once of the king's royal household."

Addis noticed that the man who had held Moira was not introduced, and sat a little aside as if he were not truly a part of the group. When Moira arrived with the ale he got up to help her. The cleric's servant, he guessed.

"There are many others," Michael said. "You are not alone in your dissatisfaction with events in this realm. Robert here was forced to sign a note pledging that he owed Hugh Despenser twenty thousand pounds in order to keep his land. Peter's cousin was imprisoned until she made over a similar obligation and relinquished two estates. Sir Matthew's brother was executed even though he played no part in the rebellion. Unfortunately his lands adjoined those of a Despenser favorite. The king's men flout all sense of law and custom and know no shame. It will be the same for you."

"Perhaps. I have not spoken with the king yet."

"You have tried for several days. We know of your efforts. It will come to naught. Look at what happened to your kinsman Aymer. The Earl of Pembroke spoke for compromise and tried to influence the king to the right path. He became an inconvenience and was murdered while he sat on a privy."

"I am aware of all that you describe. I have not sat in the king's anteroom and walked through this city with my ears covered. I also know that it is not just the barons who are disgusted, but the town burghers and the common people as well. No one is pleased with Edward's choice of friends and the influence that they wield over him. If you have come to tell me about my country and warn me about these men, do not concern yourself."

Michael spread his hands. "I can see that you are a man who likes to get to the point. Let it be so. I am just come from Hainault, where the bishop is in exile with Queen Isabelle. He is there like the bishops of Hereford and Norwich because his life was endangered when he was made bishop over the king's choice, and because he spoke for decent governance to men who do not know the meaning of the word."

Addis had learned all about the exiled bishops. Stratford was an ambitious man, but he was known for good counsel. He had tried to support the king until circumstances and conscience demanded that he speak out.

"The queen has betrothed her son, Prince Edward, to Philippa of Hainault, the daughter of the count. In return the count has promised aid to Isabelle. She has said that she and the boy will not return here while the Despensers are in power. We got rid of them once, but when the rebellion failed the king brought them back and their influence is greater than ever. The return of the queen and the prince cannot be effected until the Despensers are removed again, but a parliament will not achieve it this time."

Now they were getting down to it. Five pairs of eyes searched to see his reaction to this overture.

The long-haired man still sat aside, drinking his ale. Moira entered from the kitchen and set some fruit on the table, then disappeared back through the door. The disturbance at the gate must have pulled her from her room while she prepared to retire because her hair was unbound and uncovered. She wore one of his mother's linen robes, a simple green one that scooped at the neck and stretched across her breasts before flowing freely. The servant's quiet examination was not missing any of it.

"I trust that you are not going to ask me to kill Hugh Despenser," Addis said, trying to ignore the attention Moira was provoking. "It would be almost impossible, and solve nothing."

"Nay," Sir Matthew blustered. "If any kill him, it will be me, and Lancaster's brother, Henry, will hone the ax."

"We only ask if you are with us should other steps be taken," Michael said.

"That depends on the steps."

"Isabelle is raising an army. The Count of Hainault is aiding her. Some time soon she will be ready."

"You speak of an invasion? It had better be the largest army known to man."

"Perhaps not. Edward has lost the confidence of the barons and the townsmen. It is a small group who still are loyal to him. If the country welcomes Isabelle . . ."

"Do you think that Edward will not fight?"

"There is no standing army. He will not have time to call a levy, and if he does few will come."

"You speak of deposing a king."

"We speak of setting aside an incompetent, corrupt ruler, and placing his rightful heir in his place."

"Let us consider frankly what that means. The prince is underage. If a way is found to depose the king and crown his son, there must be a regent. It is said that Isabelle has openly taken Roger Mortimer as her lover. Even when I was a youth he was known as a grasping, ambitious man. If he is regent, or she, we could have another Hugh Despenser."

"It will be a council, not one man, who advises the young king. Any power Mortimer accrues will be short-lived. The prince is fifteen," Thomas Wake said.

"It is a rash thing that you propose."

"It has been done before. There is precedent. Did not his own father set aside a king of Scotland?" Thomas asked.

Addis considered the audacious plan. If the people supported it, it could work. If it failed, everyone who touched it would be cut into pieces and hanged from crossroad gibbets. They had all better be reading the mood of the country correctly.

"We came for a reason," Michael said. "You are not known as one of us, and we will see that you never are. We have need of someone who can move about without being followed. In two weeks Isabelle will send word saying where and when she will land. The messenger needs to be met on the coast and the instructions brought back here. We thought that you might do that."

"Why me?"

"It will be a man from Hainault. A merchant. He will not know any of us. Your scar . . . it cannot be faked. If I say only speak with you, he will know if it is the right man."

So someone had finally found a use for his badge of identity.

They did not press him for a decision. The conversation shifted to more descriptions of the Despensers' excesses and to stories of families destroyed by their greed and injustice. All the while Addis contemplated their request. His father would not have approved. Patrick had believed in diplomacy and took his oath of fealty to heart. But Addis had never sworn to Edward, and would not do so unless Barrowburgh was returned to him.

Moira arrived with some bread and cheese. The long-haired man observed her subtly as she bent to place it on the table. Addis shot the man a warning glance which he did not see as he angled to watch her walk back across the hall.

"Will you do it?" Thomas Wake asked.

"I will consider it."

"When will you know? Michael must leave in three days."

He would give Edward whatever time was left. "I will let you know before then."

Michael looked dissatisfied with that. Out of the corner of his eye, Addis saw the nameless man rise casually and meander away toward the kitchen.

"Who is he?" he asked Thomas Wake, gesturing to the now empty stool.

"His name is Rhys. A London citizen. He knows the lanes well and moves us about at night. The mayor is with us, but we do not know all the constables and he can get us here and there without torches and such."

"He has proven helpful in other ways," Sir Peter added. "He works at Westminster and he has a way of hearing things while going about his craft. There are those who don't notice servants and such and things get said. He heard the king himself swear to kill Isabelle when first he sees her again. Carries a knife in his boot just for that."

Addis twisted a look at the closed door where Rhys had gamely pursued Moira. "He is a craftsman?"

"He works on the fabric of the new chambers at Westminster. Serves the master builder and does the window tracery."

Serves the master builder. Carves the window tracery. Addis twisted and glared at the door again.

Damn. The man was a freemason.

Moira contemplated half of a meat pie left from supper, wondering if there was some way to cut it into seven pieces without having the offering look too poor. It was embarrassing to have knights and barons arrive at the house and have nothing with which to show hospitality.

"Is your well water good?" a voice asked. "I have had enough ale for the day."

She looked up into the blue eyes and friendly smile of the man who had barged through the gate. She bent for a bucket. "Aye, it is good. I will get some for you."

He took the bucket from her hands with a questioning look. She pointed to the door leading to the garden and returned to her deliberation of the pie.

"You are a kind mistress to let your servant sleep and do her work for her," he said when he returned. On his own he found a crockery cup and dipped out the water.

"You misunderstand. I too am a servant."

He propped himself on a stool, as if he planned to stay awhile. He examined her with curious eyes and she wondered how she could ever explain the peculiar, confused life that had brought her here as a bondwoman but also given her the manner that made him think her mistress of the house.

"My name is Rhys. What is yours?"

"Moira."

"You are new to London."

"Is it so obvious?"

"I live in this ward. I have not seen you before."

"I go out to market, little else. I do not like your city much, Master Rhys." She had no idea if he was a master, but counted on his correcting her if he was not. He looked old enough for it, close to thirty years old.

"It is big and noisy, but full of interesting things. With time maybe it will not frighten you and you can enjoy its pleasures."

"I do not think that I will have time for that. It is only me and two old servants here, and there is much work to do." She considered the pie, and then the nice man keeping her company. "Would you like some? There is not enough for everyone."

"Thank you."

She cut a large slice and handed it to him. "You could have just asked entry tonight. You did not have to push your way in."

"I did not want to be seen at the gate overlong. I am sure that Sir Addis will explain to you later that this visit never happened and that those men were never here." He smiled charmingly. A nice-looking man, she decided, with shoulders and a chest that spoke of physical labor. While he held her she had felt the strength in him. Not a merchant then.

"This house had been all but empty for several years," he said, glancing around. "There have been those in the ward who sought to buy it, but the old man here said it couldn't be sold."

"It was neglected. Addis was gone on the Baltic crusade, you see, and then . . ." She halted and flushed. Rhys had blinked a subtle acknowledgment that she had not referred to Addis as "my lord" or "Sir Addis," but in a familiar way. "I have known him since I was a little girl," she added too quickly.

He rose and came over to her. "Can I have more of the pie? It is very good."

She gave him another slice, grateful that he had cut off the prattling, confused excuses and explanation that had wanted to tumble out of her mouth.

"If you live in this ward, you must know the tradesmen here," she said, moving to a stool near his.

"Almost all of them."

"Then perhaps you can advise me. The stones in the wall and hearth need work, and the stable requires a whole new roof. Can you give me some names of men who would do this for us?"

"Wood is expensive. Probably better to secure the frame and then thatch the roof. I know some boys who will do it for you. As for the wall, it will take a mason. That is my craft, as it happens."

A mason. "If you move with such men as are in the hall, you must be very established. Such simple work as this . . ."

"I am established enough, and employed right now at Westminster. But in the evening I have some time before it turns dark. I will come tomorrow and see what needs to be done." He swallowed the last of the pie. "If Sir Addis only has you and two old servants, he must be short of coin. But a house such as this should not be left in ruin. Tell him that I will do it for supper. Someone here is a good cook."

"And your wife is not? She will not appreciate your staying away because our meat pies are better."

He smiled and brushed his hands, then rose. A nice-looking, soft-spoken man. "I have no wife, and I tire of eating in taverns. I will come tomorrow."

He began to leave but Addis entered first. He appraised Rhys and the mason returned his own measuring examination. A strange silence pulsed that made Moira feel a little ridiculous.

"They are ready to go," Addis said.

Rhys moved to the door, then hesitated at the threshold. "Sir Addis, a small retinue arrived this day at Westminster. White and scarlet banner, with a gold falcon. I was told it was led by one Simon of Barrowburgh."

"How large a retinue?"

"Only four knights that I saw. No doubt they came for the tournament."

"No doubt. Did one of the knights have red hair?"

"Like flames."

"I thank you for telling me this."

Rhys shrugged, flashed a warm smile at Moira, and walked out with Addis in his wake.

Addis saw his visitors off and then returned to the kitchen. Moira was wiping the cups and pretended not to notice him.

"Does he know who you are?" he finally asked.

"He asked my name and he knows that I am a servant here."

"Does he know that you are mine?"

She carried the cups over to the wall shelf. "He will fix the wall and hearth and asks only supper in return."

"Very generous for a freemason who already assists master builders."

"Aye, it is generous."

"You will tell him that I do not need his services."

She faced him across the kitchen, her back against the wall. "You do need his services. The stones are half down and anyone can enter. If those men came to discuss what I think they did, you may well need a strong high wall around this property. If Simon followed you here, you most certainly do. I can clean stables and patch plaster, but I cannot mortar stone."

Three strides brought him over to her. "You will tell him who you are."

She glared a challenge up at him. "I will tell him that I am a bondwoman, if that is what you mean. He already thinks so anyway, since I am not of London."

He pressed a hand against the wall near her head and hovered closer, his face a hand span from hers. Something flickered in her eyes. Alertness to their proximity. Fear of it. After seeing her smiling at that mason he didn't give a damn.

"You will tell him that you are *mine*."

"I will not. It is not so."

"It *is* so." His other hand braced the wall so that he entrapped her. No part of their bodies touched but her warmth easily filled the tiny space between them, alerting his skin, summoning responses that he barely kept in check even without this closeness.

He looked down at her, forcing her gaze to meet his. The interest shown by the mason had provoked a primitive possessiveness and he let her see it. She returned his stare belligerently, as if she dared him to try and make her submit. It inflamed his body and blood with a furious desire and he held on to his control by only a single, thin thread.

Her expression changed, softening. A vague tremor wobbled through her. She suddenly looked fragile and vulnerable. He sensed her own arousal, and her fear of it. It only made him want her more.

"Do you think that I will stand aside and let some man woo you?"

"You speak nonsense. He only wanted some water."

"He watched your every move. He has already found a way to come back."

"Even if you are correct, you have no right to interfere."

"I have every right."

"You do not!"

He couldn't help himself. He dipped and his lips brushed hers. A gentle caress, no more, but his whole body yelled an affirmation that staggered him. The need to clarify his possession ripped with a slashing determination. "I have every right. You are mine. Your passion is mine. Do you think my forbearance has meant it is not? I only wait for you to accept it."

"Nay."

"Nay? Let us test the truth of that. Let us see how indifferent proud Moira has become."

He kissed her again, tasting and biting and urging her open. She tried to twist away and he held her head in both hands so she could not. Something broke in her, as if a rod of resolve had snapped. With an anguished sound of dying protest she accepted him, parting her lips.

He probed her soft mouth and pulled her to him and clung to her soothing warmth. A submerging flood of needs rolled through him. He cupped his hands over the curves of her buttocks and pulled her against his swollen phallus and took her mouth again in unrestrained exploration.

"Please do not . . ."

Her whispered protest sighed between the gasping breaths of their fevered kisses. Her passion joined his even while her words denied him, and his hunger ignored the little plea. Holding her limp body in one arm he sought the full softness of her breasts with his hand. Hard peaks pressed his palm. He circled gently and her hips flexed against him. His arousal roared at the familiar rhythm.

Little thought now, and no constraint. He bent and grazed a nipple with his teeth. Her whole body, whole being, stretched in response. His mouth wet the cloth until it adhered to her, a thin obstruction through which he sucked until her lovely low moans sang.

He carried her to the table and sat her on its edge. Her head lolled against his chest while he unlaced the gown's back. Fire glow gleamed off her skin as the fabric fell down to her waist. He pushed her hair back and looked at her.

Beautiful. Lovely. Skin taut over shoulders and inviting breasts. Passion made those clear eyes sparkle with incredible lights. He slid his hands up her dangling legs, bringing the skirt high, and caressed the softness of her exposed thighs. He brushed the curls of her mound and pictured her lying back on this table in the dancing firelight. Bending those knees to accept his body. Clinging to him in pleasure as she had in Whitly, only with him buried inside her.

Accepting him, all of him, and the union still left incomplete by her pride. Wholly his.

He held her breasts and flicked caresses with his thumbs until she closed her eyes and bit her lip against the sensations.

He bowed her back and teased with his tongue while his hand sought her thighs again.

He began easing her down, lifting the skirt yet higher.

She resisted, grabbing on to his arms.

"Then come up to bed, or into the garden."

She looked up with parted lips and blurring eyes, the image of a woman entranced. Even so, she shook her head.

"Did that merchant leave you in fear of it? There is pleasure in the joining too, Moira. I will not hurt you."

Her forehead sank against his chest and he held her

with one arm while he caressed close to her intimate warmth with the other hand. Wetness touched his fingers and the scent of it drifted around them like a musky fog.

"It is not that. You know it. Do not pretend that you do not," she muttered with a wavering voice. "You said in Whitly that you do not seek to seduce me against my will, but you do so now."

He heard her accusation and admitted its truth, but a part of him angered and darkened at this denial. He wanted her to the point of madness and yet even when besotted with pleasure she held to her damn pride. The hunger coiled dangerously inside him. He stroked the cleft of her mound.

Despite her sharp inhale, her hand stopped his and tried to pushed it away. He pressed his lips to the top of her head and felt her quick heart against his chest. He kept his hand to her, gently exploring and probing the soft folds. Shivers of pleasure spread through her with his touch.

She really could not stop him unless he let her. Afterward she would see the rightness of it. Of them together. She belonged to him, after all. By the time he was done she would not call it force, or even seduction.

His better half reasserted itself, aghast at the path he justified. An ancient one, well trod over the ages by lords and their bondwomen. This was Moira, not some serving wench of no account.

If you do it this way, you will never really have her.

He resented that voice of reason. He glared at the arms strained against him with their weak resistance. He suddenly hated the births and blood and pride and realities that kept them apart. He could sweep them all away and make a new reality. She could not stop him and didn't really want to. She would accept it.

Two minds and two souls battled inside him, and the

urge to own and possess and hold her forever began to win.

She lifted her head and moist, clear eyes looked right into his. A regretful, quavering smile turned up her mouth with an expression that said she had no concerns about which way he would go. Her trust reminded him forcefully of who she was, and what she meant to him, and what he really wanted from her. The danger began uncoiling.

"Let the mason come," he muttered. "Let him know you and see the truth of it, even if you do not."

He turned and left abruptly as if angels drove him away.

CHAPTER 12

RICHARD HAD BEEN RIGHT about the wealth and honor gathered for the tournament. Jeweled surcottes, painted saddles, colorful pennants, gleaming armor . . . the richness overwhelmed the eyes. In the midst of it all Addis's animal skins and exotic woman stood out as a distinctive oddity, making the knights and crowd curious.

Moira had practiced with the dangerous destrier whose reins she held. Addis had decided to forgo a palfrey and so sat atop it, controlling the animal with his legs more than she did with her hands. Behind him Richard carried the weapons and shield of Barrowburgh, a knight of high status in his own right proudly assuming the role of squire for his lord.

Among the combatants and the nearby crowd it was working. Whether a king jaded by novelties would notice was another thing.

"Stay nearby after we pass through the lists," Addis said. "As it is, half these men will be following you home like so many dogs."

He sounded annoyed. She thought that took some gall on his part, since it had been his idea to display her thus. The red surcotte reached to mid-calf, leaving part of her naked legs exposed. The silk's soft flow implied more of her body than was immediately apparent, and the scooped neck and sleeveless cut looked indecent without a gown beneath it. All of the other women wore veils over bound hair, so her flowing locks alone were startling. Little lines of amber beads beat on her forehead, a thin gold chain stretched across her chest, and the armlets circled her upper arms. Addis had placed all the wealth on her, and she had glanced in a polished plate and admitted that she looked very exotic indeed.

The pageant moved forward and they took their place among the retinues. She passed in front of the crowd. A blue pair of eyes several heads back caught her glance and she realized that Rhys was here. He had come to the house for two evenings now, working the stone before partaking of some supper in the kitchen. Yesterday she had told him about her role today and he had expressed mocking, exaggerated shock when she described the costume. Now he smiled in a reassuring way and she was grateful for that.

They moved slowly toward the tented raised gallery where the royal family and retainers sat. A shock of red hair caught her eye. It moved and dipped at the back of the platform and she stretched to see better. Her blood pulsed as she recognized the knight from Barrowburgh, and beside him none other than Simon himself.

She looked back anxiously at Addis and he gave her a calming nod that said he had seen as well. Then he turned and formally acknowledged his king.

Edward appeared royal enough, but she had expected a man larger than life, not the very ordinary face and short

beard and normal brown hair. His garments were sumptu-
ous, but then so were all of the robes and tunics surrounding him. He sat with no lady, but between two men who
were clearly related. One was of middle years, and the
other appeared to be his father. She guessed that they
were the Despensers about whom Addis had spoken.
Edward examined the barbaric-looking knight passing by
with obvious interest, pointing and speaking quizzically to
the younger man on his right.

They proceeded on to the tents in the field where the
knights would prepare for the combats. Richard had already secured one and the armor and lances waited within.
Addis jumped off the destrier and Moira gladly relinquished the reins.

"Do you think it worked?" she asked.

"Aye. Whether it worked enough for him to ask for me,
we will see later."

Her role finished, she turned to walk away.

"Stay here, Moira."

"I want to watch the tournament."

"Before my turn Richard or I will take you there, but
do not go alone."

"If you worry about the gold, I can leave it here."

"It is not the gold that might get stolen."

She went to sit in the shade of the tent. She had not
raised *that* much attention and interest. This was her first
tournament but it did not appear that she would have the
day of fun that she had anticipated. She had counted on
mixing with the crowd and enjoying the vendors and entertainers who ringed the field, not sitting for hours under
Addis's watchful eye.

She wondered if he had seen Rhys in the crowd. Let
him come, he had said, but she was never alone with the
mason in the kitchen. Jane or Henry always managed to

have some work that required their presence. She strongly suspected that Addis had instructed them to act as guardians.

She glanced up and caught him looking at her. She suddenly felt very exposed in the red silk. Since that night in the kitchen he had treated her with restrained courtesy, but his deep gaze would catch her sometimes like this and summon that intense connection that seemed to charge the air between them. She should resent this other hold he had on her. She should especially resent the knowledge he had demonstrated that night of how little of her will really stood between him and the passion he wanted from her.

He turned away. She ruefully admitted that her burning face and pounding heart had nothing to do with resentment.

He had chosen forbearance that night. He had known that the hands halting his caresses would not do so for long with that aching pleasure seducing her. He had stopped, but these looks said that he merely had decided to wait for her to accept that she was his. His contemplation of that filled the house whenever he crossed its threshold.

It was a long, hot day. Because of the hours needed to fit Addis's armor before his turn, she only got to see four knights meet in the lists. She tagged along when Addis himself fought and watched from amidst the squires with Richard close beside her. He cuffed a few bolder ones who tried to speak with her.

"You need not hover near me like a nursemaid, Sir Richard. Those boys are hardly dangerous," she muttered while she observed Addis ride into position and face off against his first opponent.

He wiped his sweating bald head with his sleeve. "Nay, but my lord is. Almost did not let you come once he saw you today. Came close to giving up the plan right there and then. If the day wasn't so damn hot he'd have you swaddled in a cloak, he would, or sewn up inside that tent. Wouldn't do at all if he saw something he didn't like and rode over here with that lance instead of where he is supposed to tilt."

"He exaggerates the allure of a few beads and some red silk."

"He exaggerates nothing, woman. Take it from a man who is not too old to notice. Now you stay by me or these young stallions will be holding a different type of tournament to impress you."

Addis unseated his opponent on the second pass and Richard nodded approvingly. "Pray he keeps it up or it will take one of those armlets to buy back the forfeit of his horse and armor."

He did keep it up. She watched proudly as he triumphed in tilt after tilt. Eventually it ended and his name was placed among the finalists who would compete the next day.

A royal page approached their tent while Richard finished unstrapping Addis's plate. Moira was returning with some water for washing and observed the brief conversation. She set the bucket down just as the page left. Addis sluiced water over his head.

"Well?" she finally asked with impatience.

He shook the water off and accepted a towel from Richard. "The king sent a summons to visit him before the jousts tomorrow."

"It worked then. That is good news."

"Aye, it worked."

"You do not appear overjoyed."

"I will be asking for justice from a king who does not understand what the word means, Moira. Hugh Despenser will stand by his side, speaking in his ear, and Simon will stand behind Hugh. The king may not know why I have come to Westminster, but Hugh and Simon do, and they have been working on his mind. Edward can give me justice, but I think he will not do so."

"Still you must try."

"Aye, I must try."

"And if he forsakes you?"

He gestured around the field. "There is much discontent here. One feels it in the air. Meetings are being held in some of these tents. Rumors spread among the squires and grooms. The strife is deep, and many have stories like mine. Hugh Despenser and his father have gone too far in their greed and Edward is helpless under their influence. I have heard that in some regions there are those who pray to Thomas of Lancaster as a martyred saint. If the king forsakes me I will have much company."

"I have heard grumbling when I go to the markets for food. It seems that no one speaks of Edward with any warmth or loyalty."

"He curtailed some of the city's freedoms," Addis explained. "A stupid man as well as weak. Londoners are inclined to support their king against the barons unless they find themselves threatened. We will see what the morrow brings, Moira, but I am not optimistic."

He would not speak of it to her. Danger awaited him if the king refused his petition. Horrible danger. He had not told her what transpired that night when those men came, but she had heard enough and surmised even more. The situation with the king had reached the point where unthinkable alternatives had become acceptable. One smelled it on the streets and read it in the unspoken words underlying vague comments in the market. Everyone was waiting for something, much as she had waited that day in the courtyard at Barrowburgh.

Would he join those men? She watched him prepare to

depart, contemplating thoughts he did not share with her. If Edward rejected his claim, he might decide that he had nothing to lose.

She tried not to think of the cost if he joined a move against the king and lost. She had heard of the horrible deaths such men faced, and had seen the parts of bodies hanging from gibbets after the rebellion. Sick dread turned her stomach at the image of them desecrating his body that way.

Richard emerged from the tent with some plate and weapons and began to pack them on the extra horses they had brought. Addis shrugged a tunic over the padding that he wore beneath his armor. He swung her up on a saddle to begin the ride home.

"You looked beautiful today, Moira. It was you who captured the king's attention." He took her hand and kissed it, startling her. "I thank you. For all of the ways that you help me."

Addis twisted on the bed, unable to find rest. The choice that he had always suspected he would face would be met tomorrow. In some ways it had already been made but for the king's decision. Only if Edward proved worthy of loyalty could he give it.

Tomorrow one of two doors would open, and a man whom he did not know, a man reported to be unfit for the crown that he wore, held both keys. His spirit churned with deliberations about the imminent decision facing him. At times like this he wished that the old prayers still sustained him.

The night was hot as the day had been. He stripped the sheet from his body and lay naked, seeking a breeze. He stretched an arm across the empty space beside him to where the linen felt cooler. He thought of the woman who should be lying where his hand rested and his body tightened, adding a new torture to this sleepless night.

He wanted her. Hell's blood, how he wanted her. He had tried to be satisfied again with the contentment he felt just having her nearby, but it was not enough anymore. He would sit down the table from her, eating his meal while his mind engaged in elaborate, detailed loveplay. He had mentally taken her in every chamber of this house, in the garden, at the well, in the bath, everywhere. He constructed sophisticated arguments to refute the practical realities she had thrown at him, but they were not sufficient to sway her so he did not speak them. She had decided that the cost of what he wanted was too high for her and his conscience ruefully acknowledged the truth of that. He suspected that even if he had Barrowburgh again and could gift her with pearls and jewels she would still find the cost too high. Just his luck to hunger for a proud woman with so much common sense.

Who would have expected the quiet, plump girl to see so much from her shadows? Children should not be that perceptive. She should have been delighted with the betterment of her life and enthralled by the luxury brought by Edith's place with Bernard. Instead she had seen the hooded looks, the silent scorn, the isolation of a woman plucked from one world and put in another merely because she pleased a man.

Bernard's whore. Had he ever called her mother that? Most likely. But the daughter had not read every mind and look accurately. She had seen the veiled disapproval and heard the squires' lewd snickers, but she had missed the envy many felt when they saw the joy Bernard shared with his bondwoman.

He glanced down at the prominent evidence of his arousal, and threw himself from the bed. He pulled on the

buckskin leggings and strode from the chamber and out to
the courtyard. The utter silence of the city assaulted him.
So strange that the hellish confusion could disappear with
the sun.

Faint lights glowed through some windows in the
house from night candles in the chambers. He had deliberately not learned which one was hers because he did not
need to be imagining her there, but now he paced back
into the house and the short passageway on the ground
level.

He knew instinctively that she was at the end, as far
from him as possible. The choice of a woman afraid, but
of what? That the lord might claim her service in the
ancient way? If so, that night in the kitchen probably
had not reassured her much. Nor him. The son of
Barrowburgh was sometimes still tempted. With a different woman it might resolve things, but this one would
only be embittered, even if he cajoled her to pleasure and
passion. He wanted her willing, which she might never be.

He pushed open the low door to the tiny chamber. Her
chests and stools cramped the walls, and her pallet lay in
the position her bed had at Darwendon, with its foot near
the door. An empty bit of floor stretched near her head,
where Brian would have slept. She lay serenely, naked beneath the old sheet that made shadowed valleys between
her breasts and legs in the dim light.

She slept deeply, not stirring at all. Did she dream of
that mason? Intelligent and skilled and on his way to becoming a master builder. Just the man she had described
as her ideal. He was proving smooth and skilled in other
ways too, timing his work to end after the household had
eaten so he could have her attention in the privacy of the
kitchen where Addis could find no excuse to be. He had
resisted the urge to warn the man off, but every time he
saw that dark hair emerge from the garden to wash at the

well he had wanted to. Rhys courted her for marriage, of that Addis had no doubt.

The silk surcotte was folded neatly on top of one chest. She had looked stunning in it and he hoped she would keep it. His footsteps did not disturb her as he walked around her pallet to look at her face. Sliding his back down the plaster wall, he sat on the floor in Brian's spot and calmed within the serenity that she gave unknowingly and he accepted without questions.

The page led him through stone passages and chambers to a door giving out on an enclosed garden. Courtiers dined from plates of fruits and pheasant beneath neatly pruned trees and beside tidy hedges. A few women enjoyed the meal, but only men hovered around the king, who sat on a low bench topped with turf.

Edward glanced up with his approach, at first with confusion and then disappointment when he noticed that Addis did not wear the barbarian garments. He had attended this meeting as Patrick de Valence's son, and his surcotte bore his coat of arms.

Hugh Despenser had been speaking with a man near the wall, but he eased over to arrive near the king when Addis did. Edward accepted Addis's greeting and raked his appearance with his eyes.

"Your face. It is a cruel scar. Did you get that with the Knights?"

"Nay. I have marks enough from those years, but I brought this one with me."

"It is a badge of honor if won in battle, but I expect the women do not like it much."

"Like children, most women find it frightening, but a few have not minded overmuch."

"Aye, but then some women like to be frightened." A

few courtiers laughed obligingly when Edward grinned as if he had made a joke. "Sit and tell us about it. How goes the crusade against the pagans? Hugh here speaks of going next year but I have explained that the realm cannot afford his absence."

"The Knights would be grateful for Sir Hugh's valor," Addis said. Men like Hugh Despenser never went on crusades, especially ones in the Baltic where the Teutonic Knights took all the spoils and land. He settled himself in the grass in front of Edward and spun a half hour of adventures, ending with the fatal bravery of the crusaders in the *reise* that led to his capture.

"You were held by them? The pagans?" The notion fascinated Edward. He lowered his lids suspiciously. "Did you recant your faith to be spared martyrdom?"

"They never asked me to. It is the Christians who seek to convert the conquered."

"Still, you must have seen things. Witnessed rites that no Christian should." The idea of forbidden rituals titillated him.

"A few simple rites. No one required that I attend any rituals or offerings."

"It is said that they burn men. Knights whom they capture."

"I saw one such sacrifice. The knight was in his armor and on his horse. He had been drugged and did not know his own end."

"But they did not burn you."

"Nay. Their gods do not like scarred faces any more than women and children do."

Edward looked around at his entourage. "We must find a way to honor Sir Addis. He has suffered much for God's war."

"I seek no new honor, but only that which is mine by my blood and my birth," Addis said carefully.

Edward appeared confused. Hugh Despenser bent and whispered in his ear. His words only made the king ill at ease.

"Your father, Patrick, was one of the contrarians who rebelled against us," Edward said sympathetically, as if breaking bad news that Addis had never heard. "His lands were forfeit."

"He unfurled no banners against his king."

"There are witnesses who say that he did," Hugh interrupted.

"For coin and land men often bear false witness. Did they swear to this before the peers?"

"Your father died. There was no need, not that such formalities are necessary with such blatant treason," Hugh coolly instructed.

"The charters say they are always necessary," Addis responded directly to the king, ignoring Hugh's usurpation of the conversation.

"Not if a man takes up arms against his liege lord," Hugh tartly inserted.

"That is so," Edward nodded. "The rebellion threatened our person and the realm. The barons received God's justice. My councillor says the lands were not broken apart, that they remain whole, and given to your brother. We have been more generous than warranted."

"He is not my brother, but the son of my father's second wife, and not of our blood. I petition you to undo the injustice."

Edward's eyes glared with sudden anger. "Injustice? Injustice? These barons presume to demand I relinquish royal prerogatives. They dare to instruct *me* in whom I choose as my councillors. They draw up charters and lists of rules for me, and seek to put men I neither like nor trust at my right hand. God's breath, they murder my dearest friends in the name of rights that derive *from me*.

They ferment rebellions and raise armies against me, and then speak to me of *justice*? Lancaster and the others received their justice as ordained by God when I was anointed king!"

His own outburst seemed to surprise him. He calmed under Hugh's hand on his shoulder and continued whispers in his ear.

" 'Tis a grave misfortune that your father forsook his oaths to his king while his son fought for God. A brave man should not suffer for the sins of his father, but it is always so. Darwendon is yours, however, secured by your marriage. And there is a manor in Wales that we will give you, to honor your valor and ordeal in God's holy war."

Wales. Despenser territory. Addis doubted that he would ever be allowed to enter that manor's gates. He would refuse to do so if it meant swearing fealty to the self-satisfied man pulling the king's strings.

He rose, experiencing a new tranquillity about his course. He had learned what he needed to know and the king's decision liberated his conscience. "You are too generous, for a true crusader asks for no reward but what God might deliver when he dies." He smiled. "I am grateful that you heard my petition. I must ask your leave now, with your permission. I should prepare for the tournament."

His courtesy brought a warm smile back to Edward's face. "Fare you well, Sir Addis. I will watch for your performance today."

He turned away and saw Simon standing near the garden portal, stretching to observe the conversation near the turf bench. "You have come for the tournament, Simon?" Addis greeted him when he neared.

"Aye, and who thought to see you here, Addis? In truth I come to visit my future bride, but the festivities drew me as well."

"You do not compete, however. Nor does Owen."

"Owen longed to, but I have other duties for him."

"I am sure that you do."

"Who was the beguiling woman who led your horse yesterday? A fetching piece."

"Just a woman whom I know."

Simon gestured toward the king and leered a grin. "He spoke of nothing else at the evening meal. You should have brought her today."

"I do not think that Edward found her so beguiling as that, Simon. He may have got four children on his wife, but that ordeal is over."

Simon's face fell. "It is treason to insinuate thus."

"Then the whole realm is treasonous. I care not whom or what any man beds, but it should not affect his judgment."

"You are displeased with his judgment?"

"As you knew I would be. Your friend Hugh will tell you all, I am sure."

Simon held out his hands. "You seem becalmed all the same. Let us put this behind us, Addis, and join hands like brothers. It is not my doing or my fault that things happened thus."

Addis gazed down at the outstretched palms that would as easily grasp a dagger as offer reconciliation. "Go and find your bride, Simon. The friendship of a man like Hugh Despenser needs constant vigilance."

"That purse will help," Richard said as they led the horses down the lanes toward the house. "Appropriate that a crusader won. Maybe God has finally decided to repay you a bit on this earth."

"They arranged for me to do so, and you know it."

"Now, I'm not so sure about that. . . ."

"They permitted the king's champion to advance to the

final round even though three knights could have defeated him earlier. He was still half-drunk from a night of debauchery, and my guess is that they arranged that too. They wanted the king's man to fall to the son of a family whom Edward had broken. The message may have been lost on the king, but not on Hugh Despenser."

"If they chose to do so, just as well it was you. Like I said, that purse will help, and paying the forfeit of horse and armor certainly would not."

"Exactly. Another message. One of friendship and this time to me."

Old Henry hurried over to take the horses when they entered the courtyard. Both Addis and Richard joined him in unpacking and grooming the animals. Twilight was dimming when Addis finally emerged from the stable. He and Richard had supped at a banquet on the field, and the household would have eaten by now. "See if the mason is in the kitchen," he instructed Henry. "Tell him I would speak with him."

While he waited he strolled over to the garden. Someone had begun trying to clean out the growth. A bed near the front had been weeded so that the summer flowers could spread and the surrounding hedge had been cleaned of grasses. Moira, trying to impose some order on the wildness, just as she kept the least tame of his own inclinations in check.

Rhys took his time coming. Deliberate, that. A wordless reminder that as a citizen of London he need answer no lord's call. He finally emerged from the hall and sauntered over to the garden's edge.

"You know how to find Michael, Stratford's man?" Addis asked.

"He is in the city. I know where to go."

"Tell him that I have agreed."

Rhys turned to leave.

"Why do you do this?" Addis asked.

"Do what? Help these men or woo the woman you want?"

Now that was blunt, and either very brave or very stupid. "Help these men. The city cannot protect you if things go wrong."

"Nor you. Before they come for me half the barons in the realm will be drawn and quartered."

"Our grievances are heavy ones."

"And ours are not? I may not have lost a great estate to these men, but I have my reasons for wanting them brought down. We all do."

They stood facing each other, the growing darkness dissolving their forms. Rhys did not move, as if he waited for the rest of it. For some reason he had invited the confrontation and Addis could not hold his tongue.

"You know that she is bonded," he said.

A smile flashed in the night. "So she says. An accident of birth, just like yours and mine. She is a proud woman with a strong heart. A man could do worse."

Much worse. "When I leave here, she will return with me."

"Perhaps."

"I will not release her."

"I did not think so. Still, there's things you can control and things you cannot, even as a noble and a baron. Her birth and yours are two of the latter, and so is her character. 'Tis her body and eyes that catch a man's attention but her pride and honesty that keep him coming back. Those are what will form her decision, and it does not bode well for you, does it? Your birth means that you cannot offer her the dignity that she counts more valuable than pearls. I do not think that you have bought her yet, nor will you when this is over. Such a woman would not be swayed by half of Barrowburgh as a price."

She already has half my soul. Half of Barrowburgh would be an easy gift.

"A part of me hopes that you force her," Rhys said, turning to leave. "It will end whatever hold you have on her more surely than death."

He disappeared into the night. Addis circled the garden and entered the kitchen through the open well-door.

Moira sat with her back against the hearth wall, lost in thought. She wore a weary expression, as if she contemplated something that saddened her. Dark hair fell around her body and he wondered if she always displayed her glory while the mason ate here. Jane was nowhere to be seen.

She heard his step and looked over with a resentful glare. Suddenly Addis understood. The man had touched her, kissed her. *It will end whatever hold you have on her.* Rhys had sensed what existed between them.

He dropped the king's purse on the table. A smile lightened her expression. "You won? You were the champion?"

There had been little satisfaction in the competition, but he took pleasure in the sparkle that the news brought to her eyes. "Aye. Take what is needed to pay the mason."

"You will need the coin, and he said . . ."

"I know what he said, but I will not be indebted to him. Use some of it to buy what is needed to make this a proper house for the Barrowburgh honor. We may have visitors in the future. And hire another servant."

"Jane and I can manage."

"Hire one." *Hire ten, damn it.*

"And the king?"

He shook his head. "He offered me a manor in Wales instead."

"As big and rich as Barrowburgh?"

"You can be sure it is not. Still, if he had not accused my father of a treason that he did not commit, if I did not feel the ghosts of my father and grandfather reminding me of my duty . . ."

He felt a soulful need to hold her in his arms all night and tell her about it. Choosing one's course did not mean the journey would be easy.

She came over and lifted the purse. "How much is it?"

She stood so close that he could smell her scent. And another's. "Fifty marks."

"A lot. But not enough?"

She did not miss much watching from the shadows. "Not enough."

She opened the purse and plucked out three coins. "There will be a way. A marriage alliance perhaps."

He gritted his teeth. Proud, practical Moira. "If it comes to that, do not blame me for it," he muttered.

"It would make more sense to blame the wind for moving the leaves, my lord. It is always thus for those of your rank. In some ways you are less free than the villeins who till your fields."

She spoke as if she articulated an argument that her mind had been weighing. Had she been debating the realities of their respective births when he entered? He wished that he knew what had transpired in this kitchen between her and the mason this evening. Just how practical had she decided to be?

"Are you going to do it? Help those men who came here with Rhys?"

"Aye."

She inhaled a deep, composing breath. "I fear for you, Addis."

Addis. At last, his name again. "I have nothing to lose now. All the coin in the realm would not secure Barrowburgh while the Despensers rule in the king's place."

She kept looking down at the purse, poking absently at it with her finger. "Still . . ." She faced him abruptly with glittering eyes full of warmth and concern. Suddenly they were just Moira and Addis again, separated from the world, riding a cart alone through the country. "You will tell me? When you must do something dangerous, if you might not come back . . ."

He brushed the hair near her face with his palm, relishing the moment that she would not let last but that he yearned to stretch into eternity. "I will tell you."

She looked up at him with a trembling lip and puckered brow. He took such joy in her worry that he thought his heart would burst. "You will not do anything stupid, will you? Rash and noble and brave like at Barrowburgh? You will not . . ."

"Nay." And it was true. He would not. He would carry the expression in her eyes with him to ward off the insidious temptation he had felt at Barrowburgh. No matter how weary his spirit might be, he could not know such reckless despair again while she was in his world.

He sensed her pulling back from the sweet unity threading them together. As if she feared it. He battled the urge to embrace her and demand its continued life. *It is so. I know it and the mason knows it. Why don't you?*

She held out the purse. "I have what I will need for now." When he made no move to take it from her, she let it drop back on the table and walked away.

CHAPTER 13

MOIRA SAT SURROUNDED by the riot of late summer color filling the garden. She pulled a reed from a vat of water and nimbly wove it into the basket taking form on her lap. The patch of ground where she rested still shot high with overgrown grasses, but the rest of the garden had been cleaned, its hedges pruned and its paths redug.

Addis had worked this transformation. No longer required to spend his days in the king's anteroom, he had joined the efforts to improve the house. The morning after the joust she had risen early to help Henry in the stables, only to find the work already done. Day by day the garden had emerged from the weeds. It was not fitting work for a knight and Sir Richard was appalled but Addis did not seem to care. She suspected that he merely sought activity to occupy his body and mind, but it had relieved her of the most strenuous chores and so she was grateful.

She had time now to make some baskets and would come out here after the midday meal to rest. She found

herself drawn to this back section which Addis had inex-
plicably left wild. It seemed removed from the house and
the city, a little spot of open country within the civilized
garden.

She turned the basket and worked the pattern, singing
to herself, losing awareness of the city sounds outside the
wall as the strands of her craft and voice spun a private
world. And so she did not notice him right away.

He stood in the shadow cast by a tree near the wall. He
was dressed for riding. She looked to the courtyard and
saw Henry and Richard and two horses. The day suddenly
lost some of its warmth. Her voice died away.

He seemed preoccupied by distant thoughts and a
slight frown hooded his eyes. He could not have been
there long, but she knew that he had been watching and
listening for a while.

"You do not sing much anymore," he said, stepping
closer and settling on the ground beside her. His tone
carried speculative undertones, as if he had just realized
this change from years past.

"That is not true. I often sing. I used to sing Brian to
sleep every night. I sing to myself while I work."

"But not for others."

"I sang at Darwendon."

"A religious song. Not the romances like you often did
at Hawkesford. And only because I commanded it."

"I sang at Hawkesford because Bernard wanted it, but I
never liked doing so." That was a blatant lie. Those moments in the hall had been the only recognition she had
received in that household and she had savored them. But
she did not want him asking her to entertain during their
dinners here. She did not want to sing love songs while
Addis de Valence sat at the table.

"So it is a private thing now, something that you own
that cannot be taken from you."

"Aye. A private thing." With private memories attached to those melodies and words. Hidden yearnings and childish dreams, mostly, but also some heart-wrenching emotions that the sounds could both evoke and soothe.

She could see Richard peering toward them. "You are leaving?"

"Aye. I said that I would tell you."

"How long?"

"Three days. Four. No more than a week."

"I am glad that Sir Richard goes too."

"He insisted."

She lifted a reed and began plying it so that he might not see her worry. "If someone found out . . . if this journey became known to the king . . ."

"No one should know. Few have been told, and their own safety would be at risk if they were indiscreet. There is some danger, but not much."

She wished that she could believe that. "You are not going to tell me where Brian is, are you?"

"Nay. He is safer than you could ever make him and I'll not have you living your life protecting a child who is not your own."

"The choice should be mine."

"Perhaps, but I have made it for you anyway."

She forced a smile. "I may live my life resenting the choices you keep making for me."

He laughed. "Few enough, Moira. For a bondwoman you are not so easy to control." He leaned forward and kissed her, holding her head so his lips could linger. It was a sweet kiss of farewell and nuanced longing that could break a woman's heart. "If something goes wrong, you will not be harmed. Bondmen are not punished for their lord's actions," he said while his mouth brushed her cheek. It sounded more like a reassurance to himself than to her.

He rose.

"Fare you well, Addis. Take care and be safe."

He looked down a moment, then left to join Sir Richard.

She watched him until he passed through the gate, and then picked up her basket and resumed her work. Full of emotions and fears that she dared not acknowledge, she began absently singing a love song from her youth. It was an old one that she had not sung in many years. She thought that she had forgotten the words, but they just emerged without thought, undamming the poignant memories attached to them.

She sat in the shadows, half-alert even while she dozed. Restless movements on the bed had become normal sounds, and so she jerked awake when they stopped.

She peered toward the body dimly limned in gold from the single candle, its left knee bent and propped over a pillow. Her gaze moved up to eyes gleaming in her direction, and elation surged. Finally, after four days, he had woken.

"Who is there? Come here where I can see you."

She approached the bed and he gestured for her to move the candle closer. Doing so quelled her happiness. The watery shimmer of his eyes said he was conscious but not really awake. The flushed dryness of his skin indicated the high fever still raged. This sudden recovery was an illusion, merely the brief tranquillity at the center of a storm. If he survived he might not even remember it.

"Ah, it is Claire's Shadow. Did my wife fear her prayers would disturb my rest?"

"She just left. I took her place while she went for some sleep."

"Do not lie to me, little one."

"Truly, she has—"

"She has never been here. Did you think I would not know

it? Even when they butchered me, a servant woman held my head and hand. I remember not who it was, but I know it was not Claire."

She could find no response to that, so she poured some ale and moved to lift his head to the cup.

"Help me to sit."

"You cannot. The wound—"

"I am stiff from lying here, damn you! I will sit."

"Perhaps I can raise your head at least." She found a blanket and together they bunched it under his shoulders so he only half-inclined. He looked down his sheet-shrouded body and yanked the covering aside.

She had seen him naked many times while she helped Edith care for him, but not with him aware of it. Her presence became insignificant, however. He examined the bandage tied at torso and thigh, covering most of his left hip. He flipped the sheet back with a sound of disgust.

"Sit. Nay, not over there. Get the stool and sit here."

She obeyed and settled beside the bed. His gaze seemed both to see and not see, to scrutinize and to wander. Eyes half-conscious and half-mad peered over the brim of the feverish sea that had submerged him. They both existed as part of a wakeful dream. How long before the waves pulled him back down?

"How fares the lovely Claire?"

His bitter tone made her wary. "She is not so well, Sir Addis. Weakened from worrying and praying for you."

"You lie well, little Shadow, but not well enough. If she prays, it is for my death."

"That is not fair."

"Such loyalty. She is fortunate to have such a friend, but I hope that you do not expect similar loyalty returned. Has she spoken with her father yet?"

Claire had indeed spoken with Bernard and had pulled Moira along for support. Images of that horrible meeting flickered through her mind, scenes of Claire imperious, then *pleading, finally hysterical as Bernard for the first time in her life refused his daughter her request.*

Addis read the conclusion in her eyes. "He would not agree to annul the betrothal?" The bandage had been removed from his face and the raw sewn cut twisted with his vague grimace. "Nay, Bernard will not seek to undo that which has been consummated."

She blinked in confusion, which amused him. "I have bedded her. Before I left. We were neither of us too discreet. Bernard knows. The whole household knows. The one time in her life Claire was generous, and it has led her directly to hell." He glanced toward the destruction hidden by the sheet, then lifted his fingertips and traced the thick line on his face. "Poor Claire." Bitterness again, but a note of sympathy too.

He looked away with eyes glittering so brightly she feared he would succumb to madness. Enough time passed that his voice startled her when he spoke again. "This I can live with." He gestured to his face. "But the hip . . . it pulls so I cannot straighten my leg. Will it always be thus? Am I condemned to walk bent forever?"

"No one knows. No bone was broken, but the fiber . . ."

"Remove the pillow."

"It is not yet healed."

He stretched to reach down and his face tightened in pain. She quickly pulled the pillow from beneath his knee.

He ripped the sheet away again, and tore off the bandage, exposing the ghastly scarlet wound that carved his stomach and belly along the line of his hip from waist to the middle of his thigh. The sight of it made him pause. "Can't say that I blame her," he muttered. Gritting his teeth he slowly pressed his leg to straighten it. She could see the threads along the wound stretching, pulling, resisting his efforts. His eyes darkened but he persisted until she could not bear it any longer.

"Nay! You will tear it open!" She rushed to the end of the bed and pressed her weight against his shin, forcing him to stop.

He sank back, closing his eyes against the defeat. She waited until she believed he would not try again, then replaced the pillow under his knee and covered him.

The stressed breaths calmed and his eyes remained closed. She hoped that he had fallen asleep, but in time the lights glimmered at her again. Not all golden this time, but mingled with black fires in an expression that disturbed her.

"Has he had you yet?"

The question stunned her. "Had me?"

"Raymond. Are you yet a maid?"

"Of course. You are mad from the fever. Raymond is like a brother to me."

"He may be like a brother to you, but you are not a sister to him and he knows it. He saw you with new eyes when he came home last year."

Addis de Valence had barely spoken to her over all these years, and this sudden personal conversation unsettled her. He was in a delirium after all, just articulate instead of rambling. He spoke what entered his mind, oblivious to normal restraints.

Something in his aura bothered her too. A strange mood emanated from him, like a heavy presence born of dark emotions. Hatred for Claire?

"He is to wed soon," *she said, trying to shake her sudden unease.*

"Aye, but the lady does not suit him. He will do it as Bernard requests, but she is not his choice. He thinks to find better pleasure with you, little Shadow. He would have you like Bernard has Edith."

"You are mistaken."

"He watches and waits, Moira, but you are what, five and ten now? You will have to decide soon. He has told the squires that you are his, and the village boys."

She had noticed Raymond warning boys off, but had assumed it was a brother's protection. "You are wrong, but if you are not it will not be so."

He shrugged. "You are probably wise. Raymond is a good man, but such women have no rights. A man's mind changes and his lehman is cast adrift, scorned by her own people and forgotten by his."

She needed no instruction on that. A lehman's daughter knew the same insecurity.

"Should you not rebandage it?" he asked, gesturing to the hip.

She fetched the basket of clean rags. He watched as she washed the gash and pressed cloths along it. He held the basket while she found lengths to cut for binding and took the knife from her when she had finished with it. That indefinable dark presence seemed to grow, like something thick and misty exuding from him. She bent to tie the binding around his thigh and his phallus swelled with her close touch.

"Damn," he muttered. "Still, it is good to know that the sword did not unman me."

Face burning, she quickly finished her work and covered him. He did not seem embarrassed at all.

"Too much to hope that my wife would come ease me." He smiled. A strange smile. Hollow. He watched her carefully and she did not like the dark fires taking over now. "Do you know Eva, the whore who lives by the foundry? Go and tell her that I ask her to come."

"You cannot . . ."

"Go and get her, girl. I will find no rest now."

"You are very ill."

"I am damned uncomfortable and since Claire is praying and you are a maid . . . go and get her."

The fever had made him irrational. "You cannot move. How can you . . ."

"She will use her mouth, little fool," he snapped.

She swung away with shock and embarrassment.

"I am sorry. I am not myself and forget you are a good girl. But go and get her, Moira. It is my bidding."

If it would ease him and bring rest, who was she to lecture on virtue? Reluctantly she nodded and walked from the chamber. At the door she looked back and saw him staring blindly at the ceiling with a peculiar, determined expression.

In the passageway, free of the oppressive air of the chamber, she saw that expression again. It loomed sharply in her head while she began descending the stairs. Suddenly, as if a door opened, she understood it, and understood too that odd mood that had been issuing from him. He did not really want Eva. He wanted her gone so as to be alone!

Turning on her heels she ran back.

She found him leveraged up on one arm, the sheet cast aside, the bandaging knife grasped while he pressed fingers to the inner flesh at the top of his crooked leg, seeking the mortal vein.

"You will not!" she cried.

He glared at her, then continued his search. "Be gone, girl."

"Nay!" She lunged, throwing her weight against the arm that held him up, grabbing at the hand that held the steel. It swung away and the blade flew, skittering across the floor when it landed. He thrust her off and collapsed, cursing her.

She cowered on the floor beside the bed, choking on tears of shock. An awful silence filled the chamber.

A hand touched her head. "Go and get it for me," he ordered softly.

"Nay," she mumbled into her knees.

"It is better this way. Normally such things are handled by comrades on the field. How many crippled knights have you seen?"

"You do not know that you are so badly maimed. Your leg was straight when Edith sewed the wound. Once the skin heals, maybe it can be straight again."

"You will not help me? Then go and get Claire and tell her what I want. For this she will come."

She raised her eyes to his and shook her head. Dark fires consumed him. He pushed up despite the pain and swung his good leg to the floor. She jumped up and forced him down and he proved too weak to resist for long.

"I will not get her. Nor will I leave here again, unless my mother takes my place. You are too sick to know your mind and too weak to fight despair." She sat on the bed beside him, her arms imprisoning his shoulders. "Rest now."

"Damn you!"

"Rest."

He stared with anger but slowly, under their connected gaze from which she would not flinch and with which she announced her determination, the dark fires extinguished one by one. It seemed half the night had gone before the last one died.

"Maybe it can be straight again," he said into the silence. "We will see." He closed his eyes. "Sing, Moira. Not a religious song though. I am not feeling friendly to God this night. Lie beside me and sing. Perhaps I will rest then."

Her voice could fill a hall, but now it only traveled the small space between their heads. She stretched alongside and embraced his shoulders and sang about love until his fevered face nodded against her breast and he sank back into his oblivion.

She shook into awareness. The basket in her hands was finished and she did not even remember completing it. Through blurred eyes she examined it for mistakes.

A movement. A presence. A man intruded on her dreamy mood. She looked up into kind blue eyes.

The wrong man.

Her smile of welcome hid her sigh. She had never known living could be this hard.

Rhys handed her a small sack and she quizzically looked inside. "Cherries! Where did you find them?"

"Best not to ask. They should stain your reeds as well as berries though."

"I dare not waste them so. Jane and I will make them into a pie and you must have some."

"They were for your baskets, but a pie would be nice."

He sat beside her. "Do you not rest on Sundays, Moira? Even peasants do."

He subtly criticized Addis with the question. "Peasant *men* do. Someone must still cook and clean. Besides, I am resting now. These baskets are not work."

He stretched out on his back, his wiry strength propped on his elbows. For the hundredth time she examined him and told herself how fortunate she would be to have such a husband. Decent and good and sober and skilled. She should welcome his attention and look forward to these visits that had continued even after the repairs were completed. He still came despite that night in the kitchen.

His embrace and kiss had turned her to stone. She had wanted so desperately to want him that she had invited the intimacy, only to experience no warmth at all when it happened. She might have been the virgin bride in James's bed again, passive and objective and embarrassed. Feeling some excitement would have simplified many things, but her lack of response had been so obvious that she had not even had to ask him to remove his hand from her breast. He had simply done so, separating just as Henry entered with Addis's summons.

They never spoke of it, but still he returned.

"He has left?"

"Aye. You knew it would be today?"

He nodded. "It will get dangerous from here, and this journey is the least of it. What will you do if something happens to him?"

"I have a freeholding at Darwendon. Perhaps I will go back there. I will probably look for Brian. He is a child I cared for when we thought Addis was dead. He has hidden him, and will not tell me where."

"Sir Addis's son?"

"Aye."

He hesitated thoughtfully. "And yours?"

"Nay." She told him about her place at Hawkesford and Simon's threat, and how she came to live with Brian.

"That explains much, but not everything," he said. "I came here today for a reason, Moira. I knew that he would be gone and thought that you might speak freely. I have been thinking that you would make a good wife, but I sense that your place here is not the normal one. I would know the truth lest I make a fool of myself. What is between you and Sir Addis?"

A gentle way to ask the question, much kinder than James's blunt query. She had answered with indignation to James, but she could not do so with Rhys.

She thought of the responses she and Addis had playfully tested that night in the hay mound. Only the last would suffice. "We have not fornicated."

He appeared amused, which relieved her tremendously. "An odd answer. Amazingly precise."

"It is, isn't it." They might never wed, but she could not lie to this man.

He swung up to sit cross-legged in front of her. "Moira, you are not a girl and I am not a boy. It is not lack of a home or work that has left me unwed, nor greed regarding a dowry. I have bided my time because I sought no ordinary woman. I like your manner and honesty and I think that we could make a good marriage. I would have offered already, but for Sir Addis."

"It does not sound like you offer now either."

"Nay, I do not. It is not a judgment, Moira. I expect no explanations and hold you to no blame." He took her hand. His was strong from grasping a mason's tools. "For good or ill, what begins with his journey today will resolve very quickly. A month from now we will be either dead or victorious. The chance for the former is reason alone not to offer. If by some fate I live and he does not, this may be an easier thing. I will even accept the boy Brian into our home if you wish it. But if he lives, he will leave here soon after and you may have to make a choice because then I probably will offer. I will make this marriage happen if you accept me, no matter what his claims on you."

She smiled at him with true affection. A clever, honest, understanding man. He meant what he said. He would make it happen somehow, even if it meant giving Addis one hundred pounds. No words of love though. Nay, Rhys would not lie to her any more than she would lie to him.

There was nothing for her to say. She merely nodded, and he lay back down and talked to her about simple things, a practical man tilling soil for which he might one day have seed. A patient man biding his time, counting on her pride leading her to the only sensible decision.

CHAPTER 14

MOIRA WAS KNEADING BREAD DOUGH when Richard entered through the garden door. She stared at him and then at the empty threshold, straining hopefully to hear the approach of another man.

"Where is he?"

Her voice conveyed her concern. He had been gone longer than she had expected, longer even than the week he had said would be the limit of the journey. She had not slept well the last few nights while she agonized over fantasies of him cut down on the road or being tortured in Westminster's dungeons.

Richard lifted a reassuring hand. "He was wounded but he lives."

"Wounded!"

"We were attacked on the road back."

"Why didn't you bring him here? If you left him I will—"

"He lies in a house in Southwark. He thought it best not to enter the city gates right now. He asked that you come."

Asked that she come! As if the entire King's Guard could keep her away!

"Carry a basket and pretend that you go to market, Moira. I will wait for you at the pier west of the bridge."

He left and she hurriedly washed her hands and scrambled to decide what she should bring. Had his wounds been cared for? Were there salves in that house? Did he need clean garments? She cursed Richard for disappearing before she could quiz him.

Stuffing a few washed garments into the basket along with a salve to ward off corruption in cuts, she hustled to the courtyard. Wounded. How badly? Not too badly if he was giving orders. She knew that wasn't true, that a man could suffer mortal wounds and still be conscious, but she clung to the piece of illogical comfort just the same. Not that it helped much. By the time she found Richard at the pier she had become a mess of agitated excitement.

She jumped off the boat even before it had been securely moored at the Southwark docks. Richard escorted her past the small houses of the stews in which prostitutes conducted their trade. Marcus lounged outside one near the end and stepped aside so they could enter.

"Small John and Marcus knew of this place," Richard explained. "It is a ways from the town, and easier to defend."

"He is in danger then?"

"We do not know yet."

The house was crowded with knights and squires and two women, all relaxing with drink and gaming. Passionate sounds came from behind a curtained corner. Richard flushed and glanced an apology and gestured her to a door leading to a back chamber.

Addis reclined on a bed and a skinny blond woman of middle years sat beside him, feeding him soup. His arm was bandaged and his left leg rose bent under the sheet.

The woman placed the bowl aside, rose to test some water warming by the low hearth, and then returned to continue the meal. She leaned closely and whispered something to Addis that provoked a stiff smile. Some soup dripped from the spoon onto his naked chest and she bent down with a sly smile and licked it off.

Moira instantly felt ridiculous for those nights of worry.

Richard cleared his throat loudly.

Addis looked over and muttered something to the woman. The whore raked Moira with her eyes and rose. When she and Richard had left, Moira walked over to the bed.

"You look comfortable enough, my lord. Very comfortable, in fact. I feared that you might not be receiving proper care but I can see that I fretted for naught." She crossed her arms over her chest and paced around him, nodding with approval. "Aye. Well fed, well bathed, and well rested."

He grinned. "Well enough."

"Indeed, these ladies seem to have you very well in hand. Completely so. Is there some reason then why you called for me?"

"Not to bathe and feed me."

"Clearly not." She faced him with hands on hips. "If I learn that you have been lying in this pleasure house for days while I worried across the river, that arm will not be all that needs healing."

With a laugh he grabbed her wrist and pulled her to sit on the bed beside him. "I only arrived this morning, and I called for you because these women are so soft-spoken and gentle and obliging that I feared they might be angels. Your sharp tongue reassures me that I am still on earth among the living."

"No doubt such a place is a knight's idea of heaven."

He gave her the warmest smile she had ever seen. "Not mine."

That flustered her so much that she lost hold of her annoyance. Relief and joy flooded to take its place and she felt embarrassed at having greeted him so poorly.

"I am heartened to see you alive and whole."

"Not entirely whole."

"You said a week, and when you did not return . . ."

"The wound slowed us."

She gently touched the bandaged upper left arm. It had been bound with strips of cloth to the side of his torso. "What happened?"

"An arrow. Some men were waiting as we returned."

"Then it is known why you went? If so, even this house will not be safe. Perhaps you should go back to Darwendon."

"We will learn soon enough what was known. No one in London has been taken, which is odd. It is possible that Edward plans some elaborate trap, but maybe some other game is being played. I will stay here a day or so and then return to the city if nothing develops. Whoever is behind this received word I had not died, several days before Richard and I got back. Time enough to send guards to arrest me on the road."

"You are not making much sense."

"The more I think about it, the less sense it makes. The men who attacked intended to kill me. Edward should want me alive, to learn what I had been told about the queen's invasion. So perhaps it had nothing to do with the king at all."

"Simon?"

"Or someone else."

"How many were there?"

"Five that I saw. But I sensed a sixth one hiding in the trees."

"You are wounded but Richard is not." The implications of that sunk in. Richard would fight to the death to spare his lord one scratch. She narrowed her eyes on him. "You met them alone, didn't you?"

"Do not scold, Moira. I had no choice. I sent Richard away. One of us had to try and get back with the message, and to warn Thomas Wake and the others that they might have been betrayed."

"It is a miracle that you are alive, isn't it? You walked into a trap not knowing what would be faced. Noble and stupid and brave. You promised me. . . ."

"It was not like that. Not like Barrowburgh," he said softly, touching her cheek. "It was not."

The full impact of the danger that he risked in this scheme hit her. Five against one. It truly was a miracle that he was alive.

The warmth of his hand touched more than her skin, adding an anguish to her relief with its tangible reminder of what had almost been lost. She had grieved for him once. She had almost had to grieve for him again. She might yet grieve in the days ahead. Her eyes began to blur. She hid her reaction in an examination of his arm. "Has it been cleaned and sewn?"

"A physician tended it. It had become so useless that I thought the bone had been hit, but he said it had not. He bound me because he did not trust me to keep it still."

"He must be a good physician if he knows a knight's mind so well." She turned to the bent knee. "Another arrow?"

"Nay. Just a blow like on the road from Darwendon, but worse. My insides have knotted. It has happened before. I can not straighten it, and it will be thus for a few days. Warmth helps."

"Then we will give it warmth." She fetched the heated water and some cloths and moved a stool beside the left side of the bed, glad to find some way to help him that would also busy the hands that wanted only to touch him and revel in the reality of his safety.

She pushed the sheet up the side of his hip. For the first time she saw the remnant of the wound that she had tended at its worst. Like the scar on his face, it might have shocked her if she had not seen its raw, corrupted birth. Now the long jagged welt of damaged flesh did not dismay her, but the large discolored bruise surrounding it did. She gently caressed the damage with her fingertips.

The hand of his bound arm grasped her wrist, stopping her. She flushed and reached down to dip a compress into the hot water. "I am not surprised you cannot walk."

"It is not the bruise but the muscle underneath."

She laid a towel alongside his hip, then pressed the warmth to his skin. "The blow could have broken the bone, just as the arrow might have shattered your arm. For all of your scars, Addis, you have been lucky in your wounds."

"That is true, Moira. I have been lucky."

She dipped the compress again to renew its warmth. He watched her with a serious expression. She smiled, just enjoying the quiet pleasure of being with him again.

"Has he had you yet?"

The question stunned her. It took a moment to remind herself of their current time and place. "You have no right—"

"Has he?"

"You lie here in a bawd house being licked by a whore and you question my virtue? You have a lot of—"

He grabbed her wrist again. *"Has he?"*

"Nay."

He released her. "Not for the lack of wanting you though. Did he take full advantage of my absence?"

His insistence exasperated her. "He only visited a few times. Once the day you left and then recently. Since I was sure you were dead I found the distraction welcome."

He missed her sarcasm. He cocked his head with a curious frown. "How many days passed without your seeing him?"

"Five . . . six . . ." She suddenly saw the meaning of his question. "You cannot think . . . Nay, Addis, surely not."

"He knew when I left and where I went. He knew it all. The men who attacked me were hired swords and not very skilled. The man who sent them did not fight himself. Hugh Despenser could afford better and know where to find them."

If I should live and he dies, it will make this easier. "You are wrong. He is a good man, and would not betray the plans being laid over this."

"Even good men will dare much to clear a path to their goals."

I will find a way to make this marriage happen. "You do not understand. It is not like that. There is not such between us that would make him kill. The goal is not that important to him."

"We will know soon enough."

"I will not have you harm him because of me."

"If he paid those men to interfere with my return, whatever his motives, I will be the least of his danger. I will not accuse him, but Wake will learn soon enough if he left the city."

"He has been here? Thomas Wake?"

Suddenly he looked ill at ease. He glanced away too deliberately. "He came to learn the message I brought back."

The oddest emptiness trickled through her, like a brief

echo of what she had felt when Brian departed. "Only for that?"

He looked down, lips slightly parted, and remained silent so long that she thought he would not reply. The sensation trickled again and again, like rivulets of loss wanting to form a hollow sea. Finally he raised his eyes to hers.

"He also came in friendship, and with an offer of help."

The emptiness engulfed her, filling her whole chest, choking out her breath. "With the bond sealed in the usual way? With a marriage?"

"Moira . . ."

"It is a wonderful thing, my lord. Such a man and family . . . I said some way would be found, did I not? Thomas Wake is married into Lancaster's family, isn't he? If this plan succeeds they will be as powerful as before. I am relieved to know you will have the alliance needed to regain Barrowburgh."

She prepared the compress again even though the water had cooled. Her methodical actions masked the unexpected devastation ripping her apart.

This was the last time she would help him. She would serve him at the house, but that was not the same. When he left London she would beg him to let her stay, and even turn to Rhys if she must, but he was not so cruel as to expect her to serve him in his marriage. In a matter of weeks he would be dead for her again, and this time she would not even have Brian to care for in his memory.

Her eyes stung and she stared at her hands holding the cloth to his flesh, grinding her teeth and willing composure. Perhaps if she were not so raw from worry she would not react so strongly. She had known this must happen eventually. She had been the one to remind them both of it. But eventually was later and this was *now*.

His hand closed over hers. "Enough now. It is feeling

much better, but whether from the warmth of the water or the comfort of your friendship, I do not know."

And she was the one who had denied them both the full comfort that friendship could have brought. It had been a sound decision, as this news clearly proved. She let the cloth drop into the bucket and sat miserably on her stool, gazing blindly at her lap, wondering if she hadn't been far too sensible. But how much harder to hear these words if she had acted differently? Then again, maybe not harder at all. She had never guessed that the pain of this inevitable reality would slice her into pieces like this.

"Come and sit beside me, Moira. Over here on my good side. I would rejoice in being alive with you for a while."

She looked up to find him smiling. She really thought she would weep then. Forcing a smile of her own she circled the bed and settled beside him.

It seemed the most natural thing to ease down under the arm that circled her shoulders, and lie alongside him in the still afternoon. They lay in the sweet connection she had not known since the night before London, and its poignancy both eased and deepened the pain.

"I think that I envy your mason," he said.

"Sometimes you speak nonsense."

"His simpler life has a kind of freedom. No ghosts of ancestors whisper in his ear. His choices are for now, not the past and not the future. But it is not just that. I envy him because he is whole."

"You make too much of a few scars."

"I am not speaking of scars or wounds. I think I was bitter about them once, at the beginning, but that was long ago. Nay, he is whole in other ways. Complete in himself. It is that I envy."

She turned on her side so she could see his face. It also brought her closer to his body and pressed the skin of his shoulder against that of her cheek, which felt very nice. "You are complete."

"Nay. I feel as though there are two half men inside me, two worlds and two souls. I am only whole sometimes, like now. There is no peace without that completeness."

She only partly understood him, but she sensed the peace of which he spoke. They lay together with a quiet contentment that produced a type of bliss. Even the anticipation of loss that shadowed her heart possessed a certain beauty. He had said that he wanted to rejoice in being alive with her and she felt very alive and unnaturally alert to each specific precious moment.

She turned her head and pressed her lips against his skin, wanting to taste his tangible reality. She laid her hand on his chest, touching his heartbeat. She inhaled deeply, memorizing his scent. *Probably never again.* She snuggled closer, savoring his physical closeness. Aye, she rejoiced even while she cried.

Her hand edged along the bindings tying his arm to his body. Her searching caress traced the hard muscles of shoulders and chest and abdomen, branding the details in her senses. She rose, absorbed in the nowness of him, no past or future whispering in her ear, free in her choice to know him as completely as possible before losing him again.

"Moira . . ."

She ignored him and bent to kiss his chest, letting her lips follow the meandering explorations of her hand. She licked as the whore had done so that woman would not have known more of him than she did. A profound stirring saturated her, richer than mere excitement, a pleasure that filled her heart and overjoyed her soul.

She moved and felt and kissed and absorbed, not thinking about anything at all except knowing him, *having* him for this first and last time. His fingers caressed tensely into her hair. She glanced to his watchful eyes and returned to her discoveries.

She slid the sheet away while her mouth followed the scar's line down and the heat of her breath offered comfort the way the compresses had. She kissed the damage as a mother might when trying to ease a child's pain. Her fingers pressed and learned the sinews of his thighs and knees, his hard belly and hips, finally the smooth surface of his erect phallus.

Total knowing. Completeness. Brief possession. She did not think or question or consider. She explored and learned, the evidence of his pleasure bringing her astonishing happiness. She felt the want pouring out of him, hungering and waiting, and her own arousal spiraled. Aye, total knowing. Her kisses followed her hand as if the progression were essential.

His sharp breath penetrated her constricted awareness. She let his subtle reactions guide her and immerse her. His tension encompassed her, straining beneath his grasp on her shoulder. She sensed it shaking, crumbling. "Enough," he gasped, pulling her up, pressing her mouth to a fierce kiss while the release flexed through him.

She drifted in the moment, tasting him, suffused still with the heady passion of it, feeling his tautness seep away.

A tilt of his head separated their mouths. She opened her eyes to see fires blazing at her.

He was furious.

He kept her head so close that their noses almost touched. "What was that? My betrothal gift?"

"I only wanted . . . I needed to . . ."

"You wanted? You needed? I have been wanting and needing for weeks, Moira, and now when half my body is crippled you serve me this passive, solitary pleasure. I will not take gifts from you any more than you take payment from me."

His anger could not make her regret it. "Do not yell at me, Addis. The gift was to myself. Besides, you could have stopped me."

"A man does not stop a dream come to life, even if it is incomplete." His hand pressed against her head, drawing her still closer to his severe, intent face. "Then let us finish it, to the extent you have left me capable. You look well content with your control of this want and need you had. I do not plan to leave your passion so contained."

He kissed her again with slow deliberation, provoking her sensual stupor to a sharper alertness. He would not let her move, but kept her breast crushed to his chest and his fingers splayed on her scalp, holding her while he carefully ravished her mouth and neck and ear. He was right. She was content in her containment of her need. She was not sure that she wanted this. She feared the pain waiting on the other side of ecstasy.

"Better if you did not . . ." she said.

"You would have me take pleasure and not give it? You are too generous, Moira," he whispered in her ear while his teeth and tongue explored ways to send her body trembling.

" 'Twas not generosity. Not really."

"Nor is this. Not really. Do not worry. You are safe from me for a while at least. Your mouth took care of that too well."

"Then it makes no sense for you to . . ."

"Ah, but I want to. Need to. Like you." He caressed around her arm to the outer swell of her breast, defeating her protests with suggestive strokes that raised anticipations of sensations that she remembered far too well.

She capitulated. Angling across his chest she accepted the kisses turned to her mouth. Shifting on her side she invited the deft touches on her breast. Her body treated the delicious feelings as if it nibbled at a savory. Soon she was thinking of nothing and just experiencing the building intensity of it.

"Take off your gown."

"I don't think—"

"*Do it.*"

He helped her sit on the bed's edge and untie the lacing along her back. She slid the loose gown down her body until it sank to a pile at her feet. She sat a moment, her eyes closed, trembling with an expectation that pierced clear through her.

He caressed along her thigh to the hem of her shift. "This too."

She looked at him. His eyes burned with desire of a different kind, with a passion only partly physical. She understood it. Recognized it. Not generosity. Not really.

She slid the shift off and sat naked beside him, the small of her back against his waist. He gently stroked down her back and she bowed into the heady contact. With two clumsy shifts he eased his body over, making a bit more room for her.

"You are so beautiful, Moira. Kneel here so I can see you and touch you."

She climbed beside him and knelt, sitting back on her feet. Examining her as she had him, he traced along her edges and curves, drawing her body, exploring hills and valleys, crevices and swells. The journey of his hand raised such pleasure that her eyes blurred and her throat dried. Impatient craving trembled its demand in her breasts. Thick moisture dampened the pulsing hunger growing between her thighs.

He eased her toward him until she had to brace her weight on hands flanking his head. She bent a kiss to him while he continued to arouse her hovering body, flicking and rubbing her nipples as if he heard their demands for attention.

Her conscious world began to constrict to just him and her and the crying desire titillating her with its sweet torture. Her passion broke out of any containment. He sensed it and began driving her mercilessly higher until she mindlessly uttered small cries that marked the rhythmic need throbbing through her. The passivity of her position both frustrated and excited her. Only the immobile arm and bent leg kept her from straddling him and pressing herself against his length. Except for the dulled memory that she had rendered him incapable, she would have sought the joining that her body demanded.

He pressed into her back, moving her down and forward until he could take her breast in his mouth. She gasped in relief and then dissolved into sighs and cries. The pleasure became twisting and tense and sharp. He licked and sucked and teased while his caresses moved to buttocks and thighs, to belly and back and she became frantic for more. He gave it to her, sliding his hand between her thighs. She parted them for him and groaned when he ventured where her whole body begged him to go.

Drawing on her breasts and tantalizing with his hand he led her from frantic to desperate and into delirious until the want and need overwhelmed her. The desire started stretching, seeking, reaching. . . . He released her and she rocked back, burying her moans in his shoulder. He used a touch that sent the exquisite release crashing through her like a cataclysm.

She collapsed, managing to remember that half his body was infirm. He pulled her into the comfort of his arm, her cheek and hand sealed against his chest.

They lay there for hours, neither sleeping nor moving, adrift in a little world of sweet comfort and peace. They barely spoke the whole time, as if both knew that words had no place or reason in this precious "now."

It is love, she thought. *Denying its name does not dull either the beauty or the pain.*

She nestled closer and watched across his chest as the afternoon sun grew long shadows on the chamber's walls.

CHAPTER 15

Mathilda Wake was beautiful, small, and frail, with a pale radiance that illuminated the spot of courtyard where she stood. She kept her eyes lowered modestly while Thomas introduced her. Addis frowned down at her elegant blond head. His first reaction was that the girl accepted her duty but knew her worth far too well.

His second was that she reminded him of Claire.

Her creamy lids fluttered and she scanned up his length. It was a slow, long journey before her pretty head tilted back and she saw his face. Thomas must have warned her about the scar, but her smile still wavered.

"You are very tall, Sir Addis."

He had to admire her clever recovery. "And you are quite small, my lady."

"It is thought that I might yet grow, but I do not think that you will shrink."

"If you would prefer that I do, I will try." The banter

flowed easily. He knew how this game was played. He'd once been a champion at it, a lifetime ago.

"Oh, I do not think that I would care for a small knight, Sir Addis."

Thomas beamed beside her. The father's obvious pride interested him more than the girl's obedient demeanor. Did Thomas indulge her? Could she bend him to her will? If she begged to be spared from this match, would Thomas relent?

The possibility should make him concerned, but he found himself hoping it was so. The side of himself that acknowledged the need for this alliance kept battling the side that resented the coercion of duty. A perverse temptation to find ways to frighten her kept pricking at his better intentions.

He led the way into the hall. Pleasant smells floated up when their feet crushed the herbs mixed with the rushes. Summer flowers hung in abundant clusters from the beams and window headers. A crisp new cloth covered the head table and the chair from the solar had been moved down to the lord's place. Piles of colorful fruits substituted for more costly adornments but added to the hall's fresh, cool effect, as if someone had decided silver would be too heavy and formal on this late summer day. Three musicians sat on stools in a corner.

He had ignored the impending visit but Moira had not. She had demanded to know the day and then had prepared for it, badgering the coin from him to purchase the food and objects and services befitting a dinner where he met a kinswoman of a great family, economizing where she could and spending where she must. She knew from her years at Hawkesford that one did not stint on such an occasion. Every detail would be a manifestation of his honor. He scanned the delightful results and wondered if the child by his side could even appreciate the efforts a bondwoman had made on her behalf.

She was not in sight, nor would she be. She supervised in the kitchen, he guessed, or maybe rested out in the garden now that all had been prepared.

He wished that she were present. If Thomas saw her lush body and clear eyes he would wonder and eventually he might ask. Then he could let the father know that which the daughter must eventually accept, that the bondwoman who served him in London would always be with him. That when he sought friendship and comfort it would be with the Shadow and not the tiny sliver of light to whom he was bound. If he had his way he would seek more than that from her, not that he expected success there.

A bittersweet mood had tinged their last week together. She visited the Southwark house every day that he lay there but the intimacy had never again turned physical. The night that he returned to London he had waited, hoping that she would come to him, all the while knowing that she would not. He supposed he had known even while it happened that her passion had been a final, sweet acknowledgment of what had occurred and what might have been.

Thomas had explained that Mathilda was fourteen but she barely looked that old despite her elaborately plaited hair and costly gown. Addis hoped to God that no one would expect a quick marriage between him and this child. Perhaps he would entertain her with explicit descriptions of his scars and how he had attained them. That should help delay things until she matured more. Maybe it would delay things forever.

Henry and a hired servant delivered the food in stages and Thomas's squires served it. The musicians played softly. Richard and a widow lady he had been courting joined them at the table. Mathilda graciously accepted the choice meats that Addis offered her along with his attention.

She talked a lot. She managed to turn every topic back to herself. Claire had been like that when a young girl. Later she had acquired the finesse to make others gladly do the job for her. He wondered if this child was clever enough to figure out the shrewdness of permitting that.

He learned all about her pony, who had run off in the spring, and how half the estate had searched for five days before finding it. He was treated to an elaborate description of the new silks her mother had recently purchased. She reassured him that she prayed often to her favorite saints, but that her special devotion was for the Virgin Mother.

Between her disorganized stories and Thomas's commentary he managed to receive a complete list of her many virtues and womanly skills. He reflected that he had learned more about Moira during the long silences of their journey from Darwendon than he could ever acquire about little Mathilda from all these words.

Moira. What was she doing now? He considered complaining about some dish so that she would be obligated to show herself. He could use her soothing presence. Little rumbles of resentment in one of his souls kept threatening to fracture the courteous composure of the other one.

"The musicians are skilled," Thomas commented toward the end of the meal.

"Aye, they are," Mathilda agreed. "It is too bad there is no minstrel. I so love to hear song."

"Then the next time I will be sure to steal the best from the king's court," Addis said, smiling.

"Methinks one of the best is right here in this household," a squire said absently while he poured wine. His lord glanced sharply at the lapse of etiquette and the youth flushed.

"You've a minstrel but he does not perform?" Mathilda asked. A petulant frown showed her hurt that the man trying to impress her would not offer every pleasure at his disposal.

"I have no minstrel, I assure you."

Thomas appeared confused and twisted to his squire. On the spot now, the youth flushed more deeply. "Not a minstrel. My apologies, my lord, but I heard the lady singing in the garden and it was very sweet and I . . ."

"A lady?"

"Not really a lady. The servant woman from the kitchen."

Mathilda decided to test the sincerity of Addis's interest with this point. He well understood the little pout, the intimations of unhappiness, the signs of a girl checking just how malleable her charm could make a man. An expert had used these ploys on him many times.

It was Thomas who succumbed. He patted her arm. "If it is a singer you want I am sure that this servant will agree to it. Is that not so, Addis?"

He looked at his intended. After they married she was in for some shocking surprises regarding his susceptibility to women's wiles. "She is not a performer."

"But we are a small group," Mathilda cajoled, venturing a touch on his hand. "If you require it she must do it."

Thomas smiled expectantly and Mathilda widened her eyes in a beseeching way. To them it was a small thing. Refusing the child her simple pleasure would seem surly and insulting. He got the sense that the future of Barrowburgh hinged on his giving in to the spoiled girl on this first, small request.

The resentment thundered. If Moira were agreeable to singing she would have planned to do so. It was a private thing for her now. He hesitated long enough that Thomas's face fell. At the other end of the table Richard rose. "I assume it is the woman Moira whom you want, my lord."

Addis glared a glance at him and Richard returned one of his own. Will you risk so much for this? the steward's eyes scolded.

Would he?

Richard did not wait for his agreement. He strode to the kitchen. Thomas reassumed his smiling demeanor. Mathilda seemed very pleased with her small victory.

Richard returned alone and Addis wondered if Moira had refused. No doubt Mathilda would expect that he go beat her.

"She wants to wash first," Richard explained.

The conversation moved to other things and so when Moira finally entered the chamber no one noticed her at first except Addis. She had bound her hair in a thick plait that dangled along her back from beneath her veil. She wore no wimple and the light color of her headdress and linen gown contrasted with the bronze of her skin. Eyes as clear as rippling water pierced him with resentment.

"It is the Lady Mathilda's pleasure to hear you sing," he said when she approached the table.

"I am honored, my lord."

"She is devoted to the Virgin Mother. Do you know a song about Our Lady?"

"Of course. At least twenty. Is there a preference, or may I choose on my own?"

"As you prefer."

She retreated to the musicians and spoke to the lute player.

"I thought she was a peasant," Mathilda said. "She doesn't look like one. She doesn't look much like a servant either."

"Do the women who serve you look like peasants and servants?"

"Nay, that is true. But then, they serve a lady and there is no lady here."

Aye, there is. As noble as you will ever be. "In her life she has been closer to ladies than your maids are to you."

Mathilda pondered that while her mind tried to reconcile the dignity and linen gown of the kitchen maid preparing to sing. Addis turned to Thomas Wake and knew that man had drawn certain conclusions that would explain everything. He shot Addis a man-to-man look of forbearance and understanding.

Moira sang beautifully even though she did not put much effort into it. He could tell that she was uncomfortable and resentful at having the attention focused on her. She sang two songs to the Blessed Virgin, the second a very long one that surely should satisfy Mathilda's devotion.

"We must get a woman singer," Mathilda said to Thomas. "The minstrels are not nearly so lovely of voice." She looked slyly at Addis. "Does she only know religious ones? Something gayer would be nice. A love song perhaps."

"I do not think . . ."

Mathilda rose and gestured. "A love song now, Moira. To raise our spirits."

"I do not think the woman knows any. See how she hesitates, my dear," Thomas said quietly.

"Of course she does. Everyone knows them."

Moira nodded. "If it would please you, my lady." She said something to the lute player and they began.

Except for overhearing her briefly in the garden that day, Addis had not heard Moira sing the romances in years. She did not look at anyone in the chamber. Rather she fixed her eyes on a spot near the windows while she let her voice flow.

More emotion and expression colored this song. It displayed her voice's beauty in ways the religious works had not. Addis listened and a very strange sensation suffused him. It had been years, but still he sensed that he had heard her sing thus very recently and very frequently, that he knew every nuance and detail in the way her voice touched the notes and enunciated the words.

Somewhere, tantalizingly out of reach, vague ideas and ghostlike images wanted to attach to this melody. Soothing memories stirred in some hidden corner where they slept. That made no sense at all. Moira had sung at Hawkesford at meals he attended with Claire, and recalling Claire never brought peace. The experience unsettled him with a gnawing, groping sensation that he should be remembering something.

Her voice mouthing those loving phrases undammed a saturating serenity. He felt his face against her breast and the warmth in her arms and the contented solace of care and love. He stared at her profile pointing toward the window, his whole essence stretching for the memories that would explain if her music called up fantasies or facts.

Sing it to *me*. Somewhere in my dreams or my life you once did so. I can feel it. Forget the others and do so again. One glance only, so I know that you feel what I feel, so that I know that you accept it is so.

She finished without turning her face, leaving him with a profound disappointment. He had lost awareness of his guests and so the girlish voice to his right startled him. "Her voice makes one want to cry or swoon." Mathilda clapped with delight. "Another!"

Moira tensed.

"I am sure the woman has other duties," Thomas said.

"Oh, surely one more."

"It is enough, daughter. I tire of song now."

She tried a halfhearted pout but decided not to bother. "Please, some coin so that I may gift her."

Thomas thumbed ten pence out of his purse and Mathilda called Moira over. "This is for you, in appreciation for sharing your lovely voice." She pressed the coins into Moira's hand. "Perhaps I will have many opportunities to listen to you in the future," she added in a whisper that everyone heard.

Moira looked at the specie and then at the lovely child beaming at her. She smiled kindly. "You are too generous. It was my honor." She addressed Addis without looking at him. "May I take my leave now, my lord?"

He gave it gladly, wishing that song had left him as self-possessed as it apparently had Moira.

She huddled in the garden, balled up behind the largest tree, listening to the sounds in the courtyard of the Lady Mathilda departing. Uncontrollable sobs racked her body and she buried her face into her knees to smother them.

She had finished her duties before collapsing into this overwhelming grief. Somehow she had held together through the nightmare of singing that love song for the two of them. She had directed the final service and even helped Jane with the washing. She had left the sounds of talk and laughter in the hall while the guests took their leave and had walked beneath the afternoon sun, toward the wall, telling no one where she had gone.

It wouldn't stop. The cries ravaged her to where she gasped for breath. Her chest would surely burst. She grasped her legs so tightly that she hurt herself and tried to will her body back into control.

She had prepared this day for him even though he had resisted it. She had tended to the food and flowers and musicians, but she had sworn that she would not see it. She had arranged things so she need never enter that hall and meet the young maid who could give him back his honor. She would help him as she always had when she could, but she refused to watch with heartache from the shadows again.

She peered over her knees at her hands and slowly opened the one that held the ten pence. The coins marked her palm from being grasped so hard. She stared at them through blurring tears and thought of Mathilda's words to her.

She couldn't do it. Not just the singing. She couldn't do any of it. Serve them. See them. Watch their children born.

He did not intend to release her. She just knew it. Lehman or not, he planned to keep her with him. It made no sense. The girl was beautiful, radiant, cheerful. He had never looked to the shadows beyond Claire's light. Why should he want to now?

The sobs calmed to choking bursts amidst deep breaths. From the courtyard she heard the sounds of horses finally moving. Some boot steps scraped the stones and silence fell.

She trusted that he would not look for her. He had plans to make and a marriage to consider. She prayed that the regretful expression on Richard's face when he came for her would be the only apology she would ever receive for being commanded to sing at this feast. If she faced Addis again today she would fall to pieces once more and he would see it. She could not bear that humiliation.

Calmer now, she rose and peeked around the tree. The garden and courtyard were empty. She skirted the flower beds and walked to the house, seeking the privacy of her chamber.

Maybe later he would change his mind. Maybe, after he married, after he had Barrowburgh, he would relent. But she could not endure this that long. As a girl she had done so, but she had little choice then. She was a girl no longer, and she had the means to end it.

She sat on her pallet and pulled her sewing basket into her lap. Ripping at the lining, she plucked out the ruby. She had thought to buy an inn and a husband with it, but her mason had talked of marriage without asking her dowry. Rhys would not miss that which he never expected to get.

She stared at the soft brilliance of the jewel. So costly and so small. Valuable because it was rare. Desired because it was beautiful. Like some women.

Enough, then. Too many years had been spent on a childish infatuation. Too many memories imprisoned her. Enough of the past. Let it go.

Addis looked for her in the kitchen and garden and concluded that she had probably gone to the market to replenish the food stores. He left word with Jane to inform him when she returned and then retired to the solar. He hoped that she would not be gone long. He wanted to thank her, and to apologize.

The feast had tired him in indefinable ways. The girl had made him feel old and world-weary. More than years separated them. A lifetime of experiences that she would never learn about lay like a chasm between them. He doubted that passion or time or even children could bridge it, mainly because he had no desire to do so. His body might join with hers to sire sons, but his soul would never be able to bond with her. Not because she was young and vain and a lot like Claire. Not because of who she was at all. The real problem lay in who she was not.

He paced to the window overlooking the courtyard, hoping for the flutter of light linen that would say she was back. He saw again her gracious acceptance of Mathilda's coin and her stiff composure while she sang that song. She had not looked at him during those love lyrics, even though every fiber of his being had urged her to. Just as well. It would have drawn attention to his reaction. As it was he suspected Thomas had noticed.

He threw himself on the bed. He felt empty, adrift, as if he could not connect his mind to his body and his body to this chamber. The little storm of resentment kept churning and rumbling. In some ways he had been a freer man when a slave. No duty set his course for him there. Yokes set upon your shoulders were easier to bear than responsibilities born in your blood.

He found himself wishing that he had met Moira then, that she had been captured in a raid into Poland and brought to the slaves' compound. Would he have been able to love her during those cautious years? Would the peace have been there then, peeling open the heart hardened for survival as easily as it had done upon his return? If offered his chance for freedom, would he have forgone it if it meant leaving her?

A scratch at the door broke his reverie. Jane poked her head in.

"She is back?" He swung off the bed to go to her.

"Nay." Jane stayed near the door, twisting her hands in her skirt. "She said to wait until tomorrow before giving it to you, to say she rested in her chamber this evening, but I thought as how you might want to know now."

"Know what? Give me what?"

She appeared fearful enough that foreboding began dripping through him. She scooted over and dropped something on the table.

"She said to tell you she's buying the freedom. With this. She said to tell you it should cover the price you set. Said she is not forswearing her oath because a free woman does not need to run away."

He strode quickly to the table. A ruby twice the size of a robin's egg lay atop the parchments.

Jane licked her lips. "She said it'd be more use to you than her now. Said you could use it to hire archers and such."

"Where is she?"

"Said to tell you she cannot do it, whatever that means. Said even in friendship and love she could not, and that—"

"*Where is she?*"

She jumped back. "Don't know. I swear, my lord, I do not. She left awhile ago and said she'd send for her things later. Just took a big basket is all. I should have come at once, I know, but it took me a time to realize what she meant and what she planned to do and then Henry said I should . . ."

He stared at the ruby, not hearing the explanations flowing from Jane beside him. An astonishing pain strangled him.

He gestured blindly. "Leave."

"Do you want Henry and me to look . . . ?"

"Just go now."

She ran off. He fingered the jewel. Its deep brilliance and shadowed planes mesmerized him. Rich color, dark depths, subtle lights. Beautiful. Solid despite its clarity. Like her.

Where had she come by it? From Edith, undoubtedly. From Bernard. She had possessed it all this time. While at

Darwendon and on the journey here. It was her dowry, but leaving him had become more important than going to a husband with such a marriage prize.

Tell him that I cannot do it.

Nay, she could not, any more than he could. If someone said that he must watch her daily with another man, he could not do it. Not even if she needed him nearby. Not even in friendship and definitely not in love. Perhaps even while he demanded that she admit the love they shared, he had been counting on her never accepting it. He could ignore the hurt he planned to give her if she kept denying it.

Admitting that left him raw. He took the ruby over to the chest where he stored the coin. He lifted the lid and the two gold armlets glimmered at him, glowing as if they demanded his attention. He picked one up and fingered it, examining the engraved serpents. Moira's words in this room haunted him suddenly. *She must have loved you very much*, she had said of the priest's daughter.

Eufemia's face loomed in his mind. Had she? He saw her sitting by her house and her passion illuminated by the moon. He remembered her bony frame walking away and her last look from amidst the reeds. After six years of looking at her, he saw her truly for the first time. And in her solemn, controlled expressions that obscured the emotions that he did not share, he saw Moira too, but not just the woman. Moira the girl, watching from the shadows.

His throat burned like fire and the ruby blurred in his hand. He knew everything, just sensed it, even though the history and details were lost to him. Holy God, in his selfish need what had he been doing to her?

When he fantasized about meeting her when a slave, he had asked the wrong question when he wondered if he would have forgone freedom if it meant leaving her behind. Eufemia had demonstrated the real strength of love and friendship. The true test would have been whether he could have sent her away to her freedom if meant staying behind himself.

Jane did not know where Moira had gone. Well, he did. He strode to the door. It would not do at all if a pagan witch woman showed more fortitude than a Christian knight.

CHAPTER 16

EVERYONE IN THE WARD knew Rhys and she found his house easily by asking for directions. It was a modest dwelling on a short spur of a lane. No one answered her scratch and she settled down on the door stoop to wait.

Skinny tall houses crowded shoulder to shoulder around the little finger of pavement. A furrier and a weaver worked at windows across the way. They examined her, as did the women and children milling by doorways. She hoped that Rhys would arrive back before nightfall. She certainly did not want the constable finding her here.

He turned onto the lane an hour later, carrying his tools in a sack over his back. He noticed her immediately and she pushed to her feet.

He showed pleasure at seeing her, which helped enormously. The emotions that had driven her here had dulled a little and the logic of coming did not seem so clear now. He had not visited since Addis returned, and she knew that he had been questioned about the attack on the road from Hastings. If the interrogation had been rough he might blame her for it.

"I brought you some supper," she said, lifting the basket.

He took it from her and opened the door.

He did not need the front chamber for a shop and so the table and stools were there. The house looked comfortable enough, but was furnished sparingly. It struck her as exactly what she expected for an established mason who had not married yet, but who intended to someday. At a loss for words and suddenly shy, she unpacked the food from the basket.

"It looks like someone had a feast," he observed as she set out the white bread and hare stew and venison pie.

"Aye." She carried the stew over to the hearth. Rhys relit a low fire and she set the earthen bowl nearby to warm.

"Thomas Wake visited." She knew that she did not have to say anything else. He had been to Wake's house. He would know about Mathilda and would guess the reason for the feast.

"I trust that your lord's wounds are healing? Sir Thomas sought me out last week. Wanted to know where I had been the last days."

"He asked it of all of you who knew where Addis had gone."

"But Sir Addis thought that I was the one who followed, didn't he?"

She nodded.

"And what did you think, Moira?"

"I told him it could not be you. That you would not try to see him harmed."

"You give me more credit than I deserve. I will not say that it did not cross my mind."

"I know that you did not do it." Actually she did not

know that for sure at all, since the evidence did not indicate that it had been the king or the Despensers who sent men after Addis. She just did not believe that he cared for her in the way that might drive a man to kill.

He shrugged. "Nay. He carried important information. This chance may not come again."

"Do you think someone else betrayed you all? That the king knows?"

"Possibly. It may be that when we leave this city to join the queen a whole army will await us on the road."

She did not want to contemplate that danger again. It had not been far from her mind the last week while she tended Addis in Southwark and lay awake into the nights listening for the sounds of soldiers at the gate.

When they sat to the meal she did not eat much. She kept trying to picture herself here, sitting with him every evening, living in this space, bound to him.

"Are you going to tell me why you are here?" he asked while he poured some ale.

"Perhaps I just wanted to share my supper with a friend."

"Perhaps. But you are not sharing the supper and you look distraught."

"I am just tired, that is all."

"You prepared this feast today?"

"I was glad to. It is an important alliance that he makes with Thomas Wake. It will get him the help that he will need." She tried to say it lightly but the words wavered just enough that he looked at her very intently.

She still walked a narrow precipice in holding on to her composure. She took a deep gulp of ale. "I bought the freedom today. He had set a high price, but I paid it. I had saved enough . . . I had hoped to . . ."

"How high?"

"Too high."

"You need not have done so."

He meant that he cared not whether she was bonded or free and she felt grateful for that. "I did need to. I had sworn not to run away. Anyway, it is done."

"Do you think he will accept this?"

"He set the price and I paid it. A son of Barrowburgh does not go back on his word."

"I wonder if he will view it so plainly, Moira. You see a different man than I do if you believe that."

She did not want to debate Addis's character. It would be best not to think about him at all right now. Even the mention of his name set her tottering on the brink of tears.

She chastised her foolish heart and plunged forward with resolve. "Despite what I paid, I still have some coin. I also have my freeholding at Darwendon. It is a whole virgate, and a cottage and its croft." It did not sound like much now that she listed it.

He poked some bread at his stew. "Are you explaining your dowry, Moira? Have you come to propose a marriage?"

"I hear that the dowry for citizens is one hundred pounds. I doubt the virgate is worth that much. For a mason like you who owns a house and works at Westminster it is probably a lot higher. Scores of fathers probably approach you all the time."

"Aye. Scores." He grinned. "Hundreds."

"But I have my craft too. Ladies pay good coin for my baskets. And if you marry, you would not have to eat in taverns anymore."

"That is certainly worth something."

"And while this is a fine house, it is not really a home for you. You might even take on apprentices if you had a wife to care for things."

He propped his head on his hand, amused with her

recital. "You need not convince me of your worth. I told you that I had been thinking to offer for you myself. I had already decided that whatever dowry you brought would be sufficient and that I could use a wife. Nay, the only problem that I see is a different one."

"What is that?"

"You do not want to sleep with me. There are few things that will turn a marriage bad as quickly as that."

The blunt statement left her speechless. She had not expected to actually speak of that. She dropped her gaze to the table planks.

"I was not married long and am still inexperienced in these things. A new man's touch still startles me. But I was an obedient wife to James even in our bed."

"I do not want obedience. If that is the dowry that you bring me I will not take it."

The day had exhausted her and now the last of her wobbling strength broke beneath a gust of discouragement. It had been a mistake coming here. He did not want her. She should have realized that the end of his visits meant he had reconsidered.

She rose to go, dreading returning to Addis's house. Maybe she could avoid him and after she slept she would be able to think clearly about how to live in this city on her own.

He reached for her arm and stopped her. "Is that the only way you can know a husband, Moira? In obedience?"

"It is what men want."

"Not me."

Nay. If this man only sought a dutiful wife he would have married years ago. Too emotionally numb to know embarrassment, she spoke her mind.

"I am here, aren't I? I came today of my own choice. I do not know if I have what you want, or if we can make a good life. We neither of us loves the other but we have friendship which is as much as most couples ever find. I thought we might begin to see what could grow between us. I had not intended to go back, but I will if I must."

It just poured out, sounding more desperate than she wanted. He examined her thoughtfully, then got up and came around to her. "Nay. You will stay and I welcome you."

His head dipped and he kissed her. It was an offering of friendship as much as passion. She accepted the brief warmth and tried to ignore the quiet cry that filled her chest.

He carefully embraced her and she let herself relax into his arms. The wrong arms, but she drew some comfort from their strength. She half hoped and half dreaded that he would do more than kiss and embrace. She would begin to discover pleasure with him, she resolved. With time she might find a passion that would obliterate all those memories.

A shadow slid over them, distracting him from another kiss. They both turned their heads to the doorway.

Addis stood there, looking dangerously tense. His eyes flashed over them and whatever coiled inside him seemed to suddenly wind tighter.

Rhys released her but only so he could thrust her behind him. "Do violence in this house and you will answer to the city courts."

"I only come for what is mine."

"She is a freeman now."

"Not yet."

She could see Addis and had no trouble reading his mood. She knew that taut conviction and where it could lead and a breathless alarm seized her. "Nay, Rhys, do not . . ."

His arm swung out to prevent her walking around him.

"If you go back he will not let you leave again. Even if it means your death, I think."

She placed her hand on his arm. "That is not true. You do not know him. He is not dangerous to me."

"Nay, I am not," Addis agreed, stepping inside and unsheathing his sword. He lifted it until the point rested on Rhys's throat. "But I am dangerous to you. Do not interfere. You can have her when I am done with her."

"You are already done with her. She is done with you."

"Not yet. Come, Moira."

Turmoil poured out of him and she feared what he would do if Rhys continued this confrontation. "Put up the sword, Addis." She pushed Rhys's arm out of her way and walked to him. "You have no argument with this man. You know that I came here of my own choice. You will not harm him because of me."

He glared at Rhys with a primitive hostility. She stepped closer and placed her hand on his sword arm. Pressing against its resistance, she coaxed him to lower the weapon.

The worst of his fury unwound from his body. She could feel it loosening. After a few moments he resheathed the sword.

He still glowered at the mason, who still stood his ground.

"You will come with me, Moira. Sleep where you wish tonight, but you will come with me now."

Rhys shot her a look of warning. She returned one of reassurance. He means it, she tried to convey. Trust me. I know him. Rhys's reaction displayed neither understanding nor acceptance.

Her gaze swept back to Addis. He looked away from Rhys and their eyes met. His expression almost stopped her heart. Anger still, but also a pain that she never thought to see in him again. A deep, soulful awareness of loss that matched her own fierce grief.

Rhys ceased to exist. There were just the two of them looking at each other, acknowledging what had been and what must end. The declarations never spoken now flowed inaudibly between them. She knew that whatever his reasons for following her here, it had not been to force her back to him. She ruefully admitted to both gratitude and disappointment in that.

She stepped toward the door. A quick movement made her turn in time to see Rhys lunge for Addis. His arm swung and Addis answered the challenge, landing a blow on the mason's face that sent him stumbling back against the table.

He grabbed her hand and pulled her into the street. With long strides he dragged her into the main lane. She stumbled after him, struggling to lift her skirt so she would not trip.

"You did not have to hit him," she snapped.

"I'm glad he gave me the excuse. He got off lightly. I almost took his head when I saw him embracing you."

She resisted his pull, but to little avail. "You lied then. You said that I could go where I would."

"I did not lie. When I am done you are free to go back to him. But knowing he has you is different than seeing it, Moira. I can be excused some jealousy, I think."

He hauled her along, never slackening his determined pace. She realized that he did not head back to the house.

The street disappeared into an open square. She looked up in confusion at the high towers rising in its center from the huge mass of the cathedral. Addis pulled her across the stones toward the portals, through the remnants of vendors closing down their stalls.

Inside the nave he paused, surveying the tables at which

scribes and lawyers offered their skills. He gestured for a cleric passing nearby. "Go and ask one of the priests to come."

He led her over to a table against the east wall. The man working there had begun to gather his parchments.

"You know the law?" Addis asked.

The balding, plump man nodded. "I do."

"I want some documents. Legal and binding."

The lawyer hurriedly set out his quills again. "Certainly, sir. What must the documents convey?"

"I am Addis de Valence, Lord of Darwendon, and this is Moira Falkner, a bondwoman of those lands. Write the language that gives her the freedom."

The lawyer began scribbling. "You will need three copies. One for each of you and one for the Church."

"Do it then."

The cleric returned, leading a member of the cathedral chapter. The priest advanced with curiosity. "I am giving this woman the freedom," Addis explained. "I would have a priest witness it."

They all waited silently for the half hour it took the lawyer to pen the documents.

"It will be legal this way," Addis muttered at one point.

"Aye. Best if it be legal," she mumbled back. She avoided his eyes and carefully studied the cathedral decorations. Being near him kept chipping away at her fragile hold on her battered self-control. She had known many partings from him, but this final voluntary one promised to be the worst. A horrible sensation filled her, similar to what one experienced during a death watch.

The lawyer presented the copies for Addis's acceptance. He read every word on each one, then put his name to them. The priest and lawyer witnessed and Addis rolled one and placed it in her hands, formally declaring the end of his hold on her.

She stared at it and the tears wanted to flow so badly that she dared not move. The priest drifted away, but Addis turned to the lawyer again.

"I need another document now. A charter this time, for property. It is to transfer ownership of a house in London from me to Moira Falkner in return for a jewel, a ruby, which she has given me."

Her mouth fell open. "That was for—"

"The price was cruelly high and even so its purpose failed. I sought an amount you could not find. Since you found it anyway, there is no point in insisting on it."

"Still, it was yours to set. You need not give me the house."

"I could just return the jewel, I suppose, but it will be easier to sell than the house, and for you the property makes a better dowry."

"They are both your right to keep."

"I will not take a single pence for your freedom, Moira. If I had not forced you to resume the bonds you would never have known them again. And I will not see you go to him with less than other women could offer. The house will be yours to keep or sell." He turned back to the lawyer. "Write."

It seemed that they waited a long time for this document. The lawyer conferred with Addis on occasion and she waited to the side, awed by an anguished melancholy that refused to permit any other emotion. She looked at his face as he bent over the parchment, and thought that she saw sorrow in him too. That only made it worse. He was giving her the freedom and her inn and a freemason waited to take her to wife. Everything she had planned and wanted would come true soon. Instead of satisfaction she knew only nostalgia and heartache.

Finally it was done and she wished it were not. She would live in this nave forever if it meant not having to walk out those doors and have it truly end for good. In some ways his death had been easier to absorb than this.

He walked beside her to the portals. She tried to revel in the reality of him one last time, but the awareness was so colored by pain she could not bear it. They paused on the porch, standing so close that their bodies touched, holding the scrolls of parchment that documented the ties he had severed.

He looked down at her. She saw his face through a wash of tears. So handsome. Not a cruel mouth at all, but kind and generous and gentle in its kisses. If only . . . She sighed. So many if onlys stood between them.

"You do not have to go to him," he said. "You need not if you do not want it."

"It is time to make a life for myself. To start anew."

He looked around them with a blind, frustrated expression. Something broke in his face, as if an internal battle had just been decided and he was relieved for the victor.

"Start anew with me then. Say the words and make your life with me."

She looked at him in confusion.

He smiled and gestured to the portals. "This is where it is done, isn't it? By the peasants and townsmen. At the church door. There is a priest inside if you want his witness, but we do not need it. We only have to join hands and say the words that make the sacrament."

She thought that she would break apart from the love and sorrow that ripped and clashed through her. The tears flowed, rivers of saltwater streaming down her cheeks.

He gently brushed their wetness with his hand. "Say the words with me, Moira."

She clutched his hand to her, turning her face to taste her tears and his skin. "You know it can never be. It means turning your back on your place, your blood, the means to regain it all."

"I will live with it."

"I will not let you. The regrets will be a weight all your life. You could not be satisfied with Darwendon any more than I could be satisfied in bondage."

He began to argue. She placed her hand on his mouth to stop him. "It is impossible, Addis. But I will love you forever for asking."

She turned quickly. Her feet moved beneath her. Somehow her body followed. She tore herself from the portal and from the steps. From him.

She wandered for some time before seeking the way back to Rhys. She licked at the love filling her, savoring both its quiet joy and poignant sorrow. She immersed herself in it while she blindly walked the lanes. Finally, when the evening grew old and the buildings cast long shadows, she kissed the sweet memory and then carefully placed it in a chamber of her heart and closed the door.

Rhys was not alone. She entered his house to find a blond woman dabbing at his face with a wet cloth while he sat at the table. She paused in the threshold and they both noticed her. With a sharp look in Moira's direction, the woman handed Rhys the cloth and walked toward the back of the house.

"She is a widow who lives next door," he explained blandly, pressing the cloth to his face. "She heard the argument."

Moira decided to accept that, although the woman's look had implied more than a wall existed between the neighbors. She sat beside him on the bench and placed the parchments on the table. "He would not accept any payment for the freedom. He gave me the house in return for the price I had paid."

"It must have been a very high price."

"It was."

He put the cloth aside and fingered the parchments. The blow had raised a bad swelling on his face.

"I am sorry that he hit you. You only sought to protect me."

"You keep giving me more credit than I deserve. I did not go for him only to protect you."

They sat in a stretching silence that unsettled her. She began to feel like an unwelcome intruder in a stranger's home. He looked at her in an intent, hard way that made her even more ill at ease.

"Why did you come back here?"

The question startled her. "I thought we . . ."

"So did I. But I saw the way that you looked at him, Moira, and now I do not think that we can. When I asked you what was between him and you, you did not answer as precisely as I thought. I had not seen you with him much, and that was a mistake I think."

She began emptying out, as if everything between her neck and her toes started to disappear. "It is over. Completely." She held up the parchments in a crushing grip. "I have the freedom! I have more property than any of those fathers ever offered. He is gone from my life and has no hold on me!"

"Is he? Doesn't he?" He rose with a disturbingly cool deliberation and stepped behind her. She felt his warmth close to her back and then his hands on her shoulders. She stiffened against the intimacy. He caressed down and cupped her breasts and she gritted her teeth.

"Doesn't he? The wrong man, Moira. The wrong hands."

He spoke the words that her heart felt. She broke. Collapsing with a horrible misery, she buried her head in her arms on the table and succumbed to the sobs that vanquished her exhausted control.

He sat beside her and patted her shoulder and said something soothing which she did not hear. The flood of emotion began retreating. She straightened and wiped her face with her hands.

"You are not being fair. With time I am sure—"

"Perhaps, but I am not inclined to take that chance. I did not expect love, but I would prefer to marry where it is at least a possibility. It is a lifetime that we speak of. I am not so foolish as to wed a woman whose heart is owned by another man."

She wished that she could refute him. She could not. He was right. Addis did own her heart. He had for half her life. Eight years of being dead had not loosened those bonds and she could not claim that time would destroy them now.

A crushing bleakness immobilized her empty body. She foresaw a future of existing half-alive, of moving and eating and tending her inn while a part of her, the part capable of love and joy, slept an eternal rest. Rhys was right. Even if she made a marriage and gave some man her body, a part of her would never be touched again.

"I do not know what to do," she mumbled.

He shrugged. "You are free and you are wealthy. You do not need a marriage to secure your future. You need no man to feed you. You can do whatever you want."

"Whatever I want."

"I cannot imagine you ever being more unhappy than you are right now, Moira. If I were to know such pain, I would want it to be for a reason."

For a reason.

Footsteps treaded on boards back in the kitchen. The sounds of the widow moving a pot clanked in the silence.

She turned to him, her lips still trembling from the tears that wanted to spill. But slowly the emptiness began filling with a peaceful, glorious possibility.

He smiled kindly at her. "If you find yourself with child, you can support it. This city takes such things in stride. You will not be the first woman living thus."

A spot of wetness snaked down her cheek. She wanted to weep still, but for different reasons. A wonderful lightness suffused her as she closed the door on her pain for a while, and reopened another that would give the grief reason and meaning when it emerged again. A shared love, at least for a while. Memories to complete the others. Maybe enough happiness to sustain a lifetime.

He placed the documents in her hands and rose. He walked to the passage leading to the kitchen where the widow waited. Stopping, he spoke without looking back at her.

"Go home, Moira."

CHAPTER 17

I JUST TOLD THE MEN to come in one by one over the next few days, and now you are saying that we leave and go to them. You are not making any sense," Richard said.

Addis continued packing his belongings into horse bags, trying to suppress the chaotic thoughts and seething frustration racking him.

Damn her pride. Damn her relentless realism. Damn her!

Dark had fallen. Was he undressing her now? Holding her full, perfect breasts? Licking their hard tips, or other places where his own tongue had only ventured in his imagination? Would that mason take the time to give her pleasure, or just use her the way the wool merchant had? Would she truly give herself to him, or just permit her body to be claimed?

"Why pay for a Southwark inn when there's all this space here? If it's because you want to avoid seeing the child Mathilda, you needn't worry. Wake is sending his family out of the city till all this is over."

He saw her tears glimmering, increasing the clarity of her water-blue eyes. Like tiny pure pools they looked up at him, reflecting his own awareness of loss. So sad and so happy that last look had been. He saw her trembling smile while she pressed his hand with lips he wanted so badly to kiss. She had walked away straight and strong, taking with her the only thing that truly mattered to him, leaving him with the first declaration of what they should have admitted weeks ago. *I will always love you for asking.*

He wiped his mind of the torturous images, wishing he could purge his heart as easily. Nothing left but duty. No course but to complete his responsibilities to the same blood and honor that formed an iron wall between them. He would see it through in the name of his father, but he did not really care if he succeeded or failed right now.

He opened the chest with the armlets. "It is time to trade these for coin. Did your lady know of some merchants who will give an honest price?"

"I asked her, as you wanted. I've the names. Now, about this sudden notion to go across the river, it is not smart. Think about it. If nothing else, it means we have to cross back once things start just to ride north and there's just a few bridges and they can be blocked. Better to be in the city anyway, especially if something goes wrong."

"I am not some green squire who needs lessons in strategy."

"Of course not, my lord. Just I don't understand this sudden decision."

He handed Richard the armlets, then dropped the ruby amidst them. The temptation to keep it, like a token from her, struck him. Best to let it and the memories go. "This too. Tomorrow at first light, sell them all."

Richard frowned down at the riches in his hand. He plucked up the ruby. "One of your mother's jewels? Should have told me you had it. I've been recruiting the men to pay with the gold is all. This will make a big difference."

"Not my mother's. Moira's. I traded this house for it."

"Moira's! Who would think a bondwoman would possess such a thing! Doesn't seem right, somehow."

"She is not a bondwoman. I gave her the freedom today. And the house. I think that she plans to make it an inn."

"If so, she should be glad for us to stay. What with the others, we will fill the place."

"I doubt that she would be glad to have *me* stay, and I know that her future husband would not."

"Future hus . . . you mean the mason?"

"Aye."

Richard chewed on this revelation. "Seems to me that you are making plans as if you know that woman's mind in ways you might not. Perhaps you complicate things for nothing. Better to stay here, and you know it."

"I know her mind on this, I promise you. We leave at first light."

"Well, if you don't mind, I think I'll check with her just to be sure. If she intends to make this an inn, her feelings may be hurt if you take your trade elsewhere."

"You'll not find her. She has left."

"What are you talking about?"

Addis shuffled together the parchments on the table. His hand paused on the newest ones. "She is with him."

"Nay, she is not. Hell, I saw her just before I came up here."

He froze. "Where?"

"In the courtyard. She'd just run in and we jested

about how she almost got caught out after curfew again and—"

"Was she alone?"

"From what I could see, but I was just passing by the gate."

"How did she look?"

"Hell, she looked like Moira. How should she look? 'Twas dusk and hard to see, but she appeared normal enough to me. Bit out of breath is all. What is this about?"

Addis strode to the door, arguing against a desperate hope. The place was hers, after all. She had every right to return. He was the intruder and she probably had expected him to be gone by now. Rhys had most likely come with her. They probably planned to enjoy the luxury of the solar's bed tonight. He had no trouble finding many reasons for her reappearance, none of which had anything to do with him at all. Still the hope spread like a childish excitement that he could not control. He probably should not go to her, but of course he had to.

Richard's voice followed him down the stairs. Out in the silent courtyard he looked around. Instinctively he knew that she was not in her chamber nor in the kitchen. He walked to the edge of the garden and peered into the darkness.

A light figure moved in the back, gliding ghostlike between the trees. He walked quietly along the wall, trying to see if a man strolled beside her.

She was alone. He stopped and watched her from the shadows while she paced thoughtfully, fingering a leaf here and plucking a flower there. Her hair fell around her body, making dark streaks down her pale gown, swaying to veil her face when she bent to smell a rose.

She appeared very serene in her solitude. She looked

276 ♦ Madeline Hunter

like a woman well contented with how things had turned out. The hope crashed into a wall of disappointment.

Even so, her presence soothed him and the turmoil and regrets of the last hour receded. He would stand here a while and savor the gift of peace one last time and then fetch Richard and go.

The soft flow of the pale robe stopped. For several heartbeats she did not move. He had the sensation that the whole garden had halted in time. Then she plucked another flower.

"I have been in love with you since I was twelve years in age."

She spoke it as if she merely continued a conversation that needed finishing before they parted.

He moved toward her, grateful to have an excuse to be closer. She paused on the path until he drew up beside her. Neither hope nor disappointment now, just comfort in walking beside her for a while.

"It was cruel of me not to see it back then, Moira. I fear that I hurt you without even knowing it."

"There was more joy than hurt in it. I will not deny the pain of seeing you and Claire at times, but I was happy for your happiness. And for hers. Even with the heartache, I embraced the love. It gave my young life purpose in a way."

"I find myself wishing that you had said something."

"Claire's Shadow declaring her love? You would have laughed, or treated it like the childish thing it probably was at first."

"Maybe. I would like to think I would have been kinder than that."

They reached the far wall and she rested her back against it. She fingered the flowers of the little bouquet she had gathered. "The whole time you were gone I loved you. I did not contemplate it much, but it was there.

Strange, isn't it? I expected it to fade once you had died, but when you came back I knew it was still in me. A dangerous thing, love. It is that that I ran from as much as the bonds."

And what she ran from still.

"Did he come with you?"

"Rhys? Nay. He decided that he did not want me. Even the value of this house could not sway him."

"He is a fool."

"Not at all. In fact, he may be the most sensible man I have ever met. He knows that I still love you. He knows that no jewel can buy freedom from that."

He leaned his shoulder against the wall, wishing he could see her expressions. He felt both anguish and pride in hearing her speak so calmly of loving him. Her voice sounded even and controlled, as if she spoke from some inner resolve. His own blood and emotions were churning. "If a lawyer's document could settle that freedom the way you wanted, I would gladly procure one for you."

She laughed and poked the flowers at his nose. "I think that you would."

"There will be another man. You are beautiful and now you are well propertied. And you have a good heart. There will be plenty of men who will count themselves fortunate to have you."

"I do not think I will be marrying anyone, Addis."

So there it was. The statement that killed the small chance that she had reconsidered his offer at the cathedral. He could not believe how empty it made him again. Proud, practical Moira. Describing in one breath an endless love and reaffirming in the next its impossibility.

It would be hell to walk away, but staying any longer promised a worse torture.

"I thought that you would not be back tonight. I had

planned to leave before you returned tomorrow, but Richard and I will go now."

"There is no need. The solar is yours, now and whenever you are in London. Besides, it would be very unchivalrous of you to leave after I have set aside my pride and good sense and come back."

He stared at the profile sniffing the flowers, trying to see her face in the darkness.

He almost dared not ask because he feared the answer. "Did you come back to your property or to me?"

She turned her head in surprise, as if the answer should have been obvious. "Oh, I most definitely came back to you." She placed her hand on his chest. "For whatever time we have left."

Gratitude and relief washed in a torrent. He lifted her hand and kissed it, then grasped her into his arms. Sweet perfume rose as the flowers crushed between their bodies. He buried his face in her hair and savored the feel of her fingers against his chest. Her last words tempered his joy for a only a moment before the sheer pleasure of holding her again banished the concern for a later time.

She tilted her head to invite a kiss and the willing gesture undid him. A hunger more soulful than physical drove his hard response. The sweet taste of her lips sent a ferocious desire tensing through him. The tip of her tongue swept his in symbolic acceptance.

He surrounded her, afraid she might disappear if he loosened his hold. He wanted to bind her to him, seal their bodies, absorb her into him. His exhalant phallus pressed against her belly and he probed her mouth in a simulacrum of the joining he craved. With a sharp gasp she broke the devouring kiss but slid her arms from between them to join the embrace.

He ate down her neck until he found the heavy pulse

beneath her ear. His mouth locked on the hot beat, connecting her life rhythm to both their hearts. She gasped again, rising on her toes with an abandoned stretch.

"I want you. Need you. Completely. Now," he muttered against her skin.

"Aye."

Her breathless affirmation made him burn. He almost pulled her to the ground. "Where? Your chamber?"

"The solar. Your bed."

"Your bed now."

"Our bed now."

He had to release her to get her there. He took her hand and led her through the garden, not bothering with the paths, tromping over flowers and pushing through hedges.

She tripped along behind his determined stride much as she had on the way to the cathedral. Her gown caught on a bush and a courtyard torch dimly lit his expression when he turned and snapped the branch with his fingers. Her heart lurched. She had felt very bold and secure while she ran back here and spoke her love in the garden. Seeing his desire and expectation made her excited and nervous and not very self-possessed at all.

He handed her up the stairs and followed a step behind, his tension warm on her back and a guiding hand on her hip. She entered the solar and walked to its center, noticing the packed bags and tied weapons. Despite her decision she felt self-conscious suddenly, and a little fearful. He closed the door and looked at her, then took the candle from the table and dipped its flame to several others in the chamber.

"You do not have to be afraid," he said with a vague smile. "I am not going to devour you."

"Do I have your word of honor on that?" She laughed.

He cocked his head thoughtfully, then shook it. "Nay."

"Well, no one can ever accuse you of not giving fair warning." Giddy and wobbly, she sat on the edge of the bed and watched flame after flame briefly illuminate his face, exaggerating the hard planes and the golden-lit eyes. He wore the Baltic animal skins and she was glad he had changed from the lordly garments of the feast.

"You remind me of my obligations under chivalry. I suppose since you have surrendered that means I should give you terms." He replaced the candle on the table. "But I find I do not feel much like a Christian knight at the moment."

Nor did he look like one. "After such a long and patient siege, I did not expect to get quarter."

"Good."

He stripped off the tunic and she did the devouring, with her eyes.

He walked over until he stood in front of her. Each step quickened her blood, flushing her with excitement.

The chiseled muscles of his chest hovered a hand span from her nose. The smallest gap separated her legs from his thighs. She looked up into his severe intensity. Thudding anticipation tremored through her.

She reached with trembling hands and caressed his chest, admiring his lean strength, loving the sensation of his skin beneath her palms. He let her, looking down. She reveled in the feel of his taut abdomen and waist, and ran her hands along the sides of his hips, splaying her fingers over the buckskin. Leaning forward she pressed her lips to him, closing her eyes, tightening with a strumming expectation.

He stretched his fingers through her hair, holding her face to his body, kissing the top of her head. "I have never taken a woman in love before. Not really."

That was not true, but if time and anger had dulled his

memory of the last time she would not remind him now. "Are you saying that you love me, Addis?"

"Aye, and it needs saying. I love you with both of my souls. I am only whole with you."

He raised her up and turned her so he could undo the closures on the green gown. He lowered the garment, his hands skimming her with titillating brushes while he slid it down her body. He gathered her long hair to her back and turned her to face him. He slipped the shift from her shoulders and it slinked down her curves until she stood naked in the candlelight. He barely touched her while he looked at her, just grazed her softly with his palms. Finally, handling her like a fragile possession he led her onto the bed and discarded the rest of his garments until they lay skin to skin beside each other.

Fingertips and gaze drifted over her breasts and hips and thighs. "You are very beautiful, Moira."

She did feel beautiful. The most beautiful woman in the world. Valuable and rare and perfect in his eyes. The equal of all the Claires and Mathildas of the realm. The love of half a lifetime swelled, filling her with happiness.

He broached her with soft, tasting kisses and slow, contemplative caresses. His hands and mouth moved over her body like he savored the exploration and memorized the passages of pleasure that he discovered. Desire rose in little sparks and tremors, a gradual delicious stimulation. She stretched and arched, thrusting her breasts toward his attention.

"I had planned to spend half the night on this loving, living out my dream, but it appears you may not let me." He smiled, giving the caress she sought. His circling touch provoked heavenly pleasure. "Nor will my own need, I think."

"Next time," she barely breathed.

He gently squeezed her nipple between thumb and finger and bent to flick the tip with his tongue. An arrow of tense excitement shot down to the itching moisture already pulsing its demanding torture. "Aye, next time. And the next. And the next. I had many dreams."

Even so, he took forever, honoring her with intimate caresses, teasing her breasts with his tongue and lips, kissing her with controlled fervor. He guided her into a frenzied tumult of sensuality. She grasped him to her and every spot of her body and consciousness pleaded for more. She reached for him, taking the hard length of his phallus in her hand, using her knowledge of his own body like a challenge against his restraint. He responded by caressing down to the cleft between her legs. A focused heat and hunger burst with his gentle massaging of her inner thighs. She lost conscious control of her body. She undulated with abandon, frantically begging for what he withheld.

He spread and bent her legs, splaying them until the palms of her feet met. Cool air and desperate voracity produced delicious shivers. He touched her open vulnerability and a moan of wonder and gratitude escaped her. He rose up and looked down at her and his fingers began driving her mad. She rocked into the gentle touches and rubs, body and mind knowing only a single craving that pitched higher and higher. The exquisite sensations deepened the hollow hunger that demanded filling. As if he heard its urging he slid a finger inside her and she cried an affirmation, bowing her body in grateful acceptance. The relief was too brief. Almost instantly it became a tantalizing promise more than a fulfillment, making the hunger worse.

"I like to see your need of me," he said. "I like to see you feel what I feel and want what I want."

He sucked on her breast and used his hand very deliberately. She bucked and cried with a delirious burst. Surely she could not bear any more.

He moved over her, settling between her legs, taking his weight onto his arms. She reached down and guided him to her, impatient for completion, almost unhinged with a wanting that threatened to shatter her. She grasped his buttocks and lifted her hips to absorb him. A thread of control snapped above her. He thrust with a force that shook both their bodies and she cried from the startling sensation that she had been split. The shock cleared her senses.

He hovered over her, shoulders and arms tense and expression serious. Her body began to relax, accommodating the invasion. He must have felt it because the veil of concern left his eyes.

"I will withdraw at the end so you do not get with child."

The feeling of ravishment faded, leaving only a blissfully tight fullness, as if he physically permeated every void in her. She caressed his face and pulled his head down for a joyful, welcoming kiss. "Nay. Do not. After all this time, let it be complete."

He moved carefully, easing the fullness in and out of her, emphasizing his possession with controlled retreats and advances, pausing sometimes until her body moved with entreaties for more. The feel of him inside and all around her, the connections of body and skin and intimacy, left her emotions so saturated she wanted to weep. She held on to his strength, accepting, begging, absorbing, immersed in the precious reality of this long-awaited loving.

She thought that he had fed her hunger, but slowly its insistent warmth reemerged, trembling through her limbs, reawakening sensations where they joined. Her sighs of contentment shortened to gasps as her desire escalated again. He sought her mouth in a probing kiss that matched the rhythms of his body, then lowered his head to take her breast in his mouth, sucking hard while he drew her into a higher passion.

He bent her legs and leveraged up to move deeply. Less gently now, he gave her pleasure while finding his own. He answered his own need while summoning hers again. His body ravished hers with quickening rhythm and increasing force. The release of power left her breathless and her consciousness focused on the summit they approached. He thrust harder and quicker. Demanding. Claiming. Profound sensations quivered through her in response. Tension poured out of him, into her, spiraling down to their jointure. Her arousal shuddered with an intense physicality that then soared, split, and spread, shaking her with unearthly exhilaration. He joined her in it, surrendering with a climax that ravaged them both.

His spent body covered her and she surrounded him with arms and legs, holding on to the union and savoring the rippling ecstasy, realizing she had never known such peace and completion. Such wholeness.

I feel as if I am in a new world. I feel as if the earth, the air, every plant has changed.

He rose up slightly with a peculiar look and she realized that she had spoken aloud. His inwardly searching expression passed quickly. She smiled at what she saw in his eyes then. Definitely love. Surely contentment. Undoubtedly happiness. But also something else. Possession and ownership. *Mine*, those eyes declared.

And it was so. His. Not by bonds of birth, but by free choice.

He moved to her side and pulled her into an encompassing embrace. She snuggled against him, still holding him with one arm and leg. They lay in silent peace for a long while before he spoke.

"I think that your wool merchant prayed too well. But for the maidenhead you might indeed have been the virgin widow. You should not have been so impatient. I did not have to hurt you."

"You hardly encouraged patience." She giggled. "James and I wed during Lent. It is why I was called that. He died soon after Holy Week and it was assumed we had forgone consummation until Easter, as is customary. He was not so pious as that, however."

"Nay, not with such as you in his bed. So he succumbed on a few occasions to irreverent pleasure but made sure you did not enjoy the sin. I do not like the man much. Not just because he had you first, although I will admit some resentment at that. Despite what you said in the hay mound, I think that he did hurt you, and not because you were impatient."

"I was his wife."

"Another reason to dislike him." He gave her a mischievous glance. "I should warn you that I am not much given to prayer at all. In fact, you may regret taking a crusader and prisoner to your bed."

"I will never regret taking this one. Besides, you will not convince me that it has been eight years."

"Nay. Only two. Which is too long for any man. But for your gift in Southwark, I might have impaled you against the garden wall tonight."

She looked at his handsome profile. He had the opportunity for all kinds of gifts while he stayed in that bawd house. She had just assumed. . . .

He rose up on his arm. He caressed down her body and his thoughtful gaze followed his hand. "If ever two people belong together it is you and I, Moira. But you are not going to stay with me, are you?"

"I am here now."

"You do not intend to come with me to Barrowburgh though."

"I will come to see you enter its gates, but nay, I will

not live there with you. I have not changed my mind about that, Addis. I will be your lover until you retake it or marry, but I will make my own life here."

"What if you bear my child?"

"Then I will raise your child and be glad for it."

"If it is a son . . ."

"If it is a son he may prefer the life of a craftsman or merchant. Not all born to the blood are suited to be knights. Our king is evidence of that."

"You must let him decide that, Moira. And me."

"When he is of age for service, he and you can decide. At the age when he would leave for apprenticeship under any case. But I'll not give up a child before that, Addis. Do not expect me to." *Do not expect me to give up all that remains of you before I absolutely must.*

He muttered a curse. "I do not understand your pride in all this. You give yourself to me but with conditions of time and place. You will share a bed with me but not let me take care of you as either a wife or mistress. You say that you love me but in the next breath say you will leave me. I do not know if I can accept this."

"You must promise me that you will. You must let me go when it is time. What I said to you that day in this chamber has not changed. Nor has your duty and the life that you were born to live." She caressed his frowning face and smiled. "Let us enjoy the peace of being whole these days that we have. Complete in this time and place, with neither the past nor the future whispering in our ears. For a while at least I am wholly yours. While we can, let us just be Addis and Moira loving each other. I am so happy. Do not let what must occur a month or so hence ruin it."

"So winning back my honor means losing you. It will be a bitter victory then."

She would have trouble with him when the time came. Still, he seemed to accept it, and the kiss he gave her sealed the agreement. The intimacy deepened and he hardened against her hip.

"I said at Whitly that I wanted to know you completely, every part of you. When I said that I wanted to take you every way a man can have a woman, I expected to have a lifetime, not a few weeks. If you will only be mine for a brief passion, then so be it. But no negotiations this time, Moira. No quarter."

He gently turned her body and bent her forward so that her bottom snuggled against his hips. He carefully entered her again and filled her motionlessly. He bent his body around her while his hand cupped her breast.

"Being inside you is so right. Perfect. Better than any dream," he muttered against her shoulder. "Tell me again, Moira. Say that you are completely mine."

It *was* right and perfect. "I am completely yours, Addis."

His kisses on her back and nape and his fingers playing at her breasts quickly had her desire twisting again, seeking assuagement. The sensations of traveling the path to passion with him inside her from the beginning astonished her. With a needful whimper she wiggled against his hips, encouraging the fullness to move.

A firm hand stilled her hip. "Nay, love. Let me go slowly so it lasts."

And it did go slowly. A long, sweet loving full of alertness to each other, her body curved into his as if they made one form. The joining became normal and separation an unthinkable severing. The beauty of it lulled her to something much deeper than pleasure, even when he reached around to caress the spot sure to bring her release.

Three times he took her before they slept, each union a different dream with its own pleasure. After the last she collapsed on top of him, boneless with sated exhaustion. Her last happy memory was lying with her cheek against his chest, his strong arms holding her tightly.

CHAPTER 18

MOIRA SQUEEZED BETWEEN the bodies jamming the wall's battlements and gazed down on Addis.

He stood beside the mayor of London, surrounded by aldermen and nobles, patiently looking down the Strand, toward Westminster. Londoners crowded the wall flanking Newgate, cramping the archers positioned to give their leaders below protection.

She was grateful that he had not ridden north as planned when word came that Isabelle had landed. The mayor had discovered that Richard had recruited over two hundred men from the shires surrounding the city, and decided that this unexpected small army would be more useful protecting London than joining the barons rushing to the queen's side. When he and Thomas Wake had asked Addis to remain and lend his help to the citizen guard, Addis had agreed.

It had proven an intelligent request, but not for the reasons envisioned. The city had received the news of the imminent fall of their king with an orgy of jubilation. But a triumphant people can easily turn into a riotous mob, and only the many armed men wearing the city's colors on their sleeves had helped maintain any semblance of order. Periodically the army of Addis de Valence had been forced to subdue violence. He had been gone long hours the last two days helping command and deploy the watch, only returning to the barricaded house for short spots of sleep. When he came, day or night, she had taken the opportunity to lie beside him while he dozed.

The Strand, the street connecting Newgate to Westminster, appeared deserted. Moira jostled her way next to a tall archer.

"Can you see anything?"

"Nay. Not yet. If he's going to come it will have to be soon though. The last messenger said the queen is only a half day away now."

"Perhaps the king does not know his danger."

"He knows. He's got spies and messengers same as us."

"Maybe he will fight at the castle."

The archer grinned. "With whom? Them that works in the town say as soon as word of the queen's landing reached us, the courtiers began bleeding out of Westminster as if the buildings were on fire. Hardly anyone left with him now and there's no army waiting for his command. Nay, he'll try to find sanctuary in this city."

She gazed down on the raven head of the tall man standing patiently beside the mayor. He had not worn armor and his only weapon was the ancient sword of Barrowburgh strapped to his body.

"Will the mayor and others be safe, do you think?"

He shrugged and patted his crossbow. "The gates don't open no matter what happens down below. Us up here are the best the city has, my lady, and we've orders to take down all of them except the king if the mayor and lords are attacked."

Knowing that Addis would be promptly avenged did not reassure her much. She knew why the mayor wanted him down there. It had less to do with the fact that he commanded two hundred men who helped protect the city walls, and more to do with the fact that he was the son of Patrick de Valence and kinsman to the late Earl of Pembroke, both high nobles with holdings directly from the crown. His blood made him a formidable presence in any confrontation with King Edward. Still, she wished he had not been at the house when the summons came and that he now monitored developments at some other gate besides this one.

"There they be, my lady. Coming slow like, as if the devil wasn't on their tails the way he is."

She did not bother to correct the way he kept addressing her. She had looked the part of a lady for over a week now because Addis had commanded that she wear the silks and velvets folded inside his mother's chest. She squinted at the entourage in the distance.

The group outside the gate had noticed the riders. Addis twisted and looked up, found her amidst the crowd, and made a motion instructing her to move back from the battlements.

She ignored him. She did not plan to lose sight of him for one instant. Her heart swelled with love and worry while she watched the king and his richly adorned councillors come.

It had been a beautiful week of love before the city began to disrupt. For two days it had just been the two of them, before Richard began sending the men over from Southwark. Even then they had time together, enjoying the lengthening cool nights in each other's arms, squeezing a lifetime of passion and talk into the precious time allotted them.

Certain memories made her blush and smile. Those

nights had been filled with incredible pleasure as Addis indeed sought to know her every way a man could have a woman. Sometimes courtly, sometimes primitive. Frequently astonishing. Always careful. He never hurt her but he made no requests either as he commanded her body and her passion and explored the rights ceded to him during this temporary possession.

She had missed him the last two days. She would miss him much more very soon. Even as she stood here, Richard made the preparations for the army to leave the city.

She could see the king now. He rode between the Despensers, resplendent in a long jeweled robe the color of sapphires. He held himself straight on his mount but even from a distance one could practically see the fear and outrage quivering through him.

The whole wall silenced. Maybe fifty riders stopped twenty feet from Addis. Word spread and in the streets behind her the din of celebration noticeably dulled. Beside her the archer pushed for elbow room and sighted his weapon.

A herald hailed the mayor. "The king demands entry to the city."

"I do not advise it," the mayor replied. "Disorder has broken out. His person might not be safe."

"Within your house he will be safe enough."

"I cannot guarantee that. A mob killed his friend the Bishop of Exeter yesterday. Dragged him from his horse and beheaded him with a butcher knife. I fear that no house is secure enough, not even mine."

Edward paled at this news. The elder Despenser became furious. "Open the gates! Your king commands it! I'll find and deal with the murderers of Exeter!"

"The city will deal with them," the mayor said

smoothly. "And these gates do not open. If a war must be fought, let it be fought elsewhere."

Hugh Despenser scanned the walls. "There's soldiers within. I see some," he said to the king. He examined the lords arrayed before him and his gaze settled on Addis. "Your men?"

"My men."

"You dare to raise an army without the king's permission?"

"I expected to have a good use for one."

Hugh chewed his lower lip. "How many?"

"More than enough to deal with the knightly prowess of fifty court administrators."

"No doubt also enough to deal with a citizen guard composed of craftsmen and apprentices. Come stand by your king's side, Sir Addis, where you belong. Your army is already within the gates. Order these merchants to do their duty by their king."

The mayor startled at that, and looked at Addis with concern.

"My king chose to have another stand by his side, but I do not see him there now," Addis said.

Hugh made a face of disgust. "Simon is a coward. Couldn't run away fast enough. Know your blood and put a short end to this foolish pageant. Your kinsman the earl never forsook his king."

"Nor did my father. And it is true that Aymer chose fealty when the opposition moved to rebellion, and even commanded the army that crushed them. His loyalty got him a dagger in the heart."

"By God, man, do your duty by your king! 'Tis treason if you do not. He demands it of you!"

"I have not heard him demand anything of me."

Edward had been silent during these negotiations for

his refuge, but now he spoke. "Barrowburgh is yours again, Sir Addis, and much more if you aid us. I know loyalty to my friends."

"I do not doubt it. But the father and son flanking you now know loyalty only to themselves. Look what they have brought you to. Petitioning for entry to the crown's own city." He stepped forward. "Send them away. They are dead men, but you are yet the king. Give yourself into my protection and I will see no harm befalls you. There are two hundred inside who will aid me at my order. We will escort you to the assembled barons."

"Do not hear him," Hugh hissed. "Men loyal to you prepare themselves. They will rise up and stop this blasphemous outrage."

"None rise up. We receive messengers many times each day. No army musters for you to the west or the south and your queen rides with an army of her own from the north."

"The French she-lion!" Edward yelled. "I will have her burned for such treason!"

"Give yourself into my protection. You will be safe until you see her, and I will hand you to the bishops and not the queen herself."

Edward appeared to contemplate the offer.

"Aye, he will give you protection," Hugh Despenser sneered. "As his kinsman Aymer protected Gaveston."

"The king is not the one who needs to fear Gaveston's fate," Addis said.

But Hugh had hit his mark with the reference to the king's long-dead lover, and his abduction from Aymer's protection and subsequent execution fourteen years prior. Edward's expression tightened into something that almost approached strength.

"We will leave these gates, and remember well the insult to our person by this city," he said. "We will join with the people and barons loyal to us and crush this rebellion like the last. Every man blocking this gate now will suffer the fate he chose with his treason."

He turned his horse. His retinue split to permit him passage and then funneled behind him. Only when the last opulent robe had disappeared amidst the buildings flanking the Strand did the heavy portcullis of Newgate begin to rise.

Moira waited for Addis inside the gate. The mayor held him in conversation a long while before he could break free and come for her.

"He does not want us to leave, but I explained that the worst is over. The people will return to their trades now," he explained while they walked to the house. "This day made the difference. If London had supported Edward, the queen's position would have been made more difficult. It is a foolish king who does not understand the value of this city to his power, and it is said that Edward has antagonized its citizens throughout his reign."

"So it is over?"

"Not over, but done. It will not be over until the barons decide what to do with him."

"Will you follow him?"

"Some suggested that we do, but there is no need. His path west can be mapped by the manors of lords in debt to him and Hugh. We can only hope that whoever finds him remembers that they deal with a man who still is the lawful king."

They entered the courtyard. It teemed with men preparing weapons and packing belongings. In the center Sir Richard shouted orders to squires and servants regarding arrangements for carting food and equipment. The city had found beds for many of Addis's recruits, but fifty men had cramped the chambers and hall and camped in the yard these last few days.

Richard walked over. "I've sent word to the others. We can be off in a few hours."

She turned to Addis in shock. She had known he was leaving, but had assumed it would be a day or two hence.

The arm holding her shoulders tightened in reassurance. "Call for me when all is prepared. I will be in the solar."

When they were out of sight on the stairs he stopped her and cupped her face with his palms. "It will be no easier on the morrow. As it is, I could find a hundred excuses to never leave here if I permitted myself that freedom."

She should have known he would do it this way to try and spare her the anticipation of pain. He had done the same when he took Brian away.

"You have not been here much these last two days. You have not slept a solid night, but only in bits and pieces while you helped this city. Surely it cannot hurt to wait."

"We will ride out to join the queen today. I would have her and the prince see that Barrowburgh is with them."

She accepted the sense of that, but still she felt miserable. He took her hand and led her up.

"Come lie with me, Moira. It has been bliss holding you while I slept my short rests these last days, but now I want to love you before I leave."

It was a heart-wrenching loving. Sweet and slow, with the pleasure suppressed by other emotions. Her soul savored every touch and sensation as much as her body did. When they finally joined he moved as if the pleasure of connection meant more than that of the completion.

She did not find her release with him, but she did not care. She held his head to her breast when he had finished, her arms encircling his shoulders, and just absorbed the nowness of him.

He shifted and caressed her thighs but she stayed his

hand. He rose up and looked down at her. "It would be unchivalrous of me to leave you thus."

"I only need to hold you. I am content."

"But I am not." He twisted her hand off his wrist and stroked her nether hair. "It would please me to watch you in your pleasure, like I did that night in the cottage and that day in Southwark."

She opened her legs. "Well, we would not want you displeased, my lord."

"Nor would we want you ill-pleased."

He watched her but she did not watch him. Her eyes closed with surprise at his first touch. He did not stroke that spot of pleasure but flesh farther down, where they had joined. It still pulsed from the pressure of him. The quick ecstasy shocked her and sent her senses reeling until she was clawing a hold on him, trying to both stretch into and away from the intensity of it, gasping pleas to him and to heaven.

The release came violently, shaking through her, evoking a cry that the whole household must have heard. The extraordinary contractions echoed through her belly long after her body had relaxed.

"That was really wonderful," she sighed, snuggling against him.

"Aye, wasn't it. I'll have to remember that for later," he said, laughing. "Now give me the peace of your love, Moira. Perhaps I can sleep a while before I have to get in the saddle."

He slept but she did not. She embraced his shoulders and focused on the weight of his head on her breast, never loosening her hold, trying to stretch each moment into a lifetime. And so the time passed slowly, but it passed nonetheless. Two hours later she stood by his side while men-at-arms mounted.

"Richard heard that he headed west as expected.

Nowhere else for him to go but to Wales and the Despensers' lands," Addis said while he surveyed the horses bunched in the courtyard. His foot soldiers milled outside in the lane, waiting to march from the city. "Henry of Lancaster will anticipate that and be waiting for him."

He spoke of practical things, as if that would make this departure less significant, but Moira saw in his eyes that he felt what she felt.

"You will follow after all?" She nestled under his arm in the threshold of the hall, wishing this leave-taking could be more private. She wanted to hang all over him and weep and give vent to the emotions screaming below the calm demeanor she tried to maintain.

"We will still ride north to the queen first but then head west to join with Lancaster. Henry hungers for vengeance because of his brother's execution. I will feel better knowing there is a calm voice present when the king is taken. We must convince Edward to abdicate. There is no precedent for executing a king, and if he is killed the whole realm will be torn by war. And while in the west I must stop at Hawkesford and Darwendon and see how things sit there." He gazed around the buildings and smiled. "Your inn will be suddenly empty after being crammed with men. After all of the work of the last week, perhaps you should rest before letting any chambers."

"A few good nights' sleep for a change and I should get my strength back." She grinned weakly, trying to make light of their imminent parting. Their intimacy had left her feeling dreamy and sated but that only added poignancy to the sadness. She dreaded those nights alone without his love holding her. Lonely nights, and days empty of the sound of his boot steps.

He pulled her back into the shadows of the hall and lifted her into an embrace. "I will come back as soon as I can. You said that you are mine until I retake Barrowburgh and I will hold you to it. You will come with me when I go there, so make arrangements for someone else to run your inn."

Aye, he would come back, but many weeks between now and then would pass with him gone. There had been so little time for happiness thus far, and not much more remained. Would it be enough to last the lifetime she faced without him?

"Will you bring Brian back with you?"

"I had not thought to."

"He should see his father's triumph when it comes. He will not get in the way. I will care for him."

A frown creased his expression. "He is safer where he is."

"Please, Addis. I will not see him again after . . . He is your heir. I would think that you would want him by your side when you reentered those gates." He did not look pleased with her request and she hesitated before pursuing it. "Perhaps if you share this with him you can learn some love for him."

His face tightened, but so did his embrace. "Do not blame me if I cannot warm to him. When I look at his face I see betrayal."

He saw Claire is what he meant. Brian had her coloring and face and radiance. Everyone else responded to the beauty with a smile, but she knew the reasons for Addis's scowls. His heart had shut on Claire eight years ago, and he had learned never to think of her. These last days he had spoken of many things, of his crusade and enslavement, of the woman Eufemia, of his father and family, but never had he mentioned Claire and what had occurred between them. Nor had he been receptive to discussions of Brian, who was a reminder of that pain. Hopefully the Lady Mathilda would love the child, because his father never might.

"I will promise that you will see him again, Moira, but I will not be bringing him to a siege camp. It is dangerous. I would not bring you either, but for my need of you."

She tucked her head against his chest and inhaled his scent and relished his breath on her hair. "Will I receive word of you?"

"I will ask that you be told whatever is learned of me, but I face little danger. The whole realm has abandoned Edward. We only have the tragedy of a king hiding in his own country now."

"Still, it is a big country. You might be gone a long while."

"Aye, a long while."

He lifted her chin to a kiss of gentle sadness. "I leave all of my heart with you, Moira. My body will be in Wiltshire and Wales, but my thoughts will be here with you."

She abandoned any pretense of dignity and clung to him while her quiet tears flowed. She looked up at burning eyes moist with yearning. He smiled, caressed her face, and stepped away. Assuming a warrior's expression of duty and resolve, he walked into the yard.

It was Rhys who brought her news over the next weeks. He came as a message bearer but the second time she asked him to stay for supper as a friend. While they waited for the meal she showed him her inn, and the changes she had made to the chambers. When they emerged into the courtyard again he noticed Henry hauling water to the trough by the stables.

"You should think about sinking another well out here. If those ten beds fill with visitors, bringing water for all of the horses will be a burden."

"Aye, and I am saving to expand the stables as well.

Next summer for both, I think, if I have the coin. Right now, with the court disbanded, there is not much trade for inns."

"That will change, and soon. Word is that Lancaster prevented Edward from entering Wales. He and the Despensers are in the western shires, and the net is closing on them."

"Do they have an army with them?"

"You worry for your knight? Nay, just a small group, not enough for a battle. No more than seventy, it is reported, and with Wales closed they lose some every day. Addis will come to no harm."

She leaned against the inn's wall, glad he spoke so easily of Addis. He had hesitated accepting her invitation, but she was happy he had. She suspected he had offered to bring her the messages so as to check how she managed alone, and perhaps to see if she needed a friend. She did.

"You appear happy," he said.

"I am happy. And sad. But you were right. The happiness gives the sadness some reason. He will be back, and I yearn to see him, but his return begins the end, doesn't it? It brings a soulful pain to think about that."

"You have decided to remain here?"

"I will go with him while he fights for his home. He is going to tell Thomas Wake that he wants no betrothal until it is regained, that he will not bind Mathilda to a poor knight, but the match has been agreed to and Wake will lend his aid because of it. But once it is done, once he sits in the lord's chair again, I will come back here."

"Surely he will visit London."

"When he does, the solar is his. And my friendship will always be here for him. But he knows that it ends at Barrowburgh and with his marriage."

" 'Tis a hard course that you set, Moira. Are you sure it is what you want?"

She had been asking herself that same question frequently the last few weeks. "It is the only course that permits me to wish his happiness in the life I will never see. Our love has been beautiful and whole and I'll not live my years grasping at its remnants. Nor will I let the shadow of that love interfere with the contentment he might find with his new family. Aye, it is what I want." She pushed away from the wall. "Now come and see how the cook I hired suits you. It is a man, and he is lately come from a manor is Kent."

Rhys raised an eyebrow. "A runaway?"

She feigned surprise. "Heavens, I wouldn't know! Do you think it is possible? I never thought to ask. I just noticed that his meat pies surpass mine and knew you would never forgive me if I didn't take him on."

He came again the next week to say that the elder Despenser had surrendered at Bristol, but that the king and Hugh had set to sea from Chepstow, just ahead of the advancing army. Word came soon after that both had been captured when they landed in Glamorgan. Hugh Despenser had been sent north to Hereford, but Lancaster was bringing the king east.

She had been living as if in a wakeful dream, going about her duties with a dull spirit and an inactive awareness. Now her heart and body awoke. She knew not how long it would take for that army to travel the breadth of the realm, nor if they came to London, nor if Addis would have other duties that might delay him after they handed the king over to the barons. She only knew that he was coming back. After two long months she would see him again soon.

She waited two weeks before allowing herself to expect him. Then she prepared the solar and took care with her appearance every day, and her gaze drifted to the gate whenever she entered the yard. Time slowed because of how hard she waited.

The last leaves fell from the apple trees. Frost withered the flowers. The first snow fell. The city erupted with stories about Hugh Despenser's execution and Edward's imprisonment.

She waited some more.

CHAPTER 19

MATTHEW, THE NEW GROOM, found her at the well.

"There's four knights in the courtyard asking if we have beds. I told 'em we are full, but they said that they would sleep in the hall if need be."

Moira set the bucket on the ground and pulled her cloak against the biting wind. Rhys had been right about her trade improving. With King Edward imprisoned at Kenilworth, the barons had begun congregating at Westminster to debate his fate as soon as the holiday of the Nativity had passed. A parliament had been called to begin in a fortnight. All of the inns in London and South-wark had long ago filled.

She gazed out at the garden stripped of flowers and leaves and full of winter's chill. Barren, like her life. She bit her lip and valiantly made a decision.

"We will put them in the solar and I will use a pallet in the kitchen."

She had resisted giving up that chamber, but had finally

accepted that the man for whom she saved it would not be returning.

Her excitement had desperately defied that reality. It had not dulled a whit during the additional weeks of waiting for him, of looking for his tall body every time she heard a noise near the gate. But it had never been him, nor Richard, nor anyone with word of his expected arrival.

The anticipation had transformed into worry when she learned that he had not accompanied the king to Kenilworth. After repeatedly badgering Rhys for information, the mason had reluctantly admitted that he had heard that Addis was spending the holy days at one of Wake's manors in Yorkshire. Both excitement and worry had vanished in one horrible heartbeat. With sick acceptance she had drawn the obvious conclusion.

Thomas Wake must have pressed for the early betrothal after all. When Addis had promised to come back he had not anticipated that. It would be madness to antagonize Wake in order to enjoy a few more weeks with Moira the innkeeper. She had decreed there would be an end and she could not blame him if circumstances had forced it sooner than she had expected.

After all, what choice did he have? The course was obvious, sensible, and practical. If asked she would have urged it on him. Of course. Certainly. If it plunged her from heaven into hell sooner than she had expected, that was the cost of such things.

Her heart admitted no anger, just a void of loss. Accepting the sense of it, the inevitability, did not make the disappointment easier to absorb. She carried a grief inside her like a weight, and had begun to wonder if it would ever lighten.

"There should be room in the stable if they have horses," she said, forcing her mind to the practical details on which she now hinged her life. "Tell Jane and Henry to make pallets for the solar."

"When you said that chamber was always mine, I did not expect to share it with other than you," a quiet voice said from the doorway.

She swung around, her heart flipping with a surge of joy that she battled to contain. She barely suppressed the impulse to throw herself into his arms.

She had never expected him to return here so soon after binding himself to Mathilda. She faced him awkwardly, determined to hold on to her dignity.

He stood tall and dark, a simple cloak floating over the buckskin garments. He appeared a little thinner for his travels, as he had when he first came back. Golden lights danced in his deep-set eyes while he inspected her reaction carefully.

"Go tell my men that we will stay here, in the hall if need be. And tell Henry to see that a bath is prepared in the solar," he ordered the groom.

Matthew hustled off and Addis turned to her. "We both knew it would be a long while, Moira."

"Aye. I did not know it would be this long though."

"Nor did I, but duties kept me west."

Duties.

"I received no word of you this last month. Just rumors."

"What rumors?"

"That you were with Wake and spent the Nativity with him and . . ."

She bit off the bitter sound of her words and blocked her mind from memories of her own lonely feast day, spent with the servants while she pictured him charming little Mathilda in front of a merry household.

This was exactly what she had hoped to avoid. The jealousy. The desperate desire to probe for reassurances. It demeaned them both. She had not realized how difficult this would be, but then she had expected to have more time to prepare for it.

"She is just a child. A pretty, frivolous girl. I found her . . . tedious."

"She is your lady." *And she will have you her whole life! Was it so selfish to have expected a few weeks more before that?*

She hated herself like this. The combination of surprised relief and seething resentment kept her immobile. Addis observed her with perplexed annoyance.

"You are wounded and I am sorry for it, Moira. Let us go to the solar and I will tell you why I was delayed."

The last thing she needed was to hear the details. "The solar is yours as I promised. You know where it is." She lifted her bucket and turned to carry it around to the stables.

Three steps had him blocking her way. He pried the bucket from her grip and threw it aside.

"What is this? Have three months turned you cold?"

"I am not cold. I am joyed to see you, but . . ."

"Has some man been wooing you? The mason again? If so he can damn well wait. . . ."

"Rhys proved a better friend to you than to me. He heard where you were, who you were with, and tried not to tell me."

"I could not refuse to go with Wake, no matter what my heart preferred."

"I know that. I do. But those duties in the west, as you call them, have changed things, haven't they? Do not expect me to live as if they had not occurred. She is your lady now. Do not expect me to pretend she is not, and go on as if—"

He reached for her and cut her off with a firm kiss. "You are still mine, Moira." Not a question. A statement. Actually, a command.

"I told you that I would not—"

He kissed her again. "Come to the solar. You will see that nothing has changed."

Just like a man to think pleasure could heal all wounds. "I will not. You have made the marriage, Addis."

He pulled back with a frown. "I can see that I have some explaining to do."

"Not at all. You need explain nothing. . . . Oh!"

She confronted his face one moment and his back the next as he lithely scooped her up and slung her over his shoulder. They had entered the kitchen before she realized what had happened.

"Put me down, Addis!"

"Nay. I can see that we will talk in circles and if we do, it will be in a chamber where there is a hearth at least."

"I will walk."

"You will argue."

"This is embarrassing."

"This is efficient."

He strode through the hall and she closed her eyes against the stunned looks on the servants and knights. Jane scooted close behind and stuck her face up.

"Matthew said you be wanting a pallet in the kitchen."

"Aye."

"She will not," Addis said, not missing a step.

The man had forgotten who owned this house. "Make one up."

"You waste your labor," Addis advised.

"Do it." Moira commanded, attempting to rise so she did not dangle so ignominiously.

Out in the yard now. The new groom and cook stared gape-mouthed. "Water for a bath," Addis ordered while he breezed by.

Up in the solar he dumped her on the bed. "That is more like it. If this city did not close its gates at night I would have arrived while you were abed, naked as my mind saw you all during the last days of riding."

"Perhaps you would not have found me alone."

It was a spiteful thing to blurt, revealing that maybe she did blame him for those duties in the west after all.

Well, damn it, she did!

His expression hardened. "I would have killed the man, Moira. Do not doubt that. If I learn that some lover has been stealing what is mine I will—"

"I have not been unfaithful," she admitted miserably.

The servants arrived with buckets of water in time to see his anger flickering. Henry smiled a nervous welcome, glanced at Moira for reassurance, and quickly supervised the preparations. They couldn't get out fast enough, and left some water heating by the roaring hearth.

Moira began to rise.

Addis unbuckled his sword belt. "Stay there."

"You will not," she announced testily, very annoyed by his assumptions. She had expected him to argue against their agreement when the time came, not simply ignore it as if he held some lifelong right to her. Letting herself blame him for not delaying Wake helped her maintain her anger. And ignore the simmering excitement of lying on this bed with him standing over her.

"Not yet. I am befouled with a week of horse and camp life. I will bathe and then I will take you."

Just like that.

In a pig's eye.

He stripped off his cloak and tunic.

Three months' abstinence and multiple memories and the hidden happiness of seeing him again combined to shudder desire through her. She mentally caressed the exposed muscles of his back.

He stretched his hands to the fire. "I am not betrothed, Moira. I did not visit Wake to make the marriage."

Relief burst. Love broke free of the restraints she had carefully forged this last month. Only a reprieve, but she welcomed it with giddy exuberance.

"He agreed that the girl should not be bound before I take Barrowburgh. Even with his help I might fail. I went to discuss and plan that help, but before that I visited Darwendon and Hawkesford. I spoke with Raymond."

"How is Raymond?"

"Angry. I told him about us. If he joined me on the field, I did not want him to learn it there."

"And will he join you?"

"I do not know. When I left it did not appear so. In fact, it would not surprise me to find him under Simon's colors."

"I doubt that he was as angry as that, Addis."

"He has wanted you for ten years. The youth's lust turned into something else long ago."

"Not love."

He shrugged. "He would never call it that."

"Nay, Raymond Orrick would never call feelings for a serf-born woman that."

"I cannot speak for his heart. Only my own. If he feels only one tenth of what I do, then it is love whatever he calls it, and he may not forgive me."

"It would be a pity if I caused you to lose his friendship and its aid."

"Not your fault if it happens. Anyway, we will see." He lifted a bucket and poured its warm water into the tub. She made to go and help him.

"Stay there."

Making a face of demure obedience she kept her place. He emptied the rest of the water, glancing to her in a considering way. "I cannot decide," he said, laughing.

"Decide what?"

"Whether to have you serve me in the bath or lie on that bed where I can watch you."

The notion of caressing him with soap sounded like a fine idea to her. "The bath."

He studied the tub. " 'Twould be a long soaking but little washing, I think, and it does not look large enough for us both."

It looked plenty large to her. Now that her misgivings had been vanquished she yearned for his embrace.

He began pushing off his leggings. "The bed, I think. Naked."

He stripped himself and she watched the hard body emerge, imagining its strength under her hands and over her length. The memories flushed prickles down her limbs.

He settled in the tub and washed his hair. He combed the wet locks back with his fingers and cocked an eyebrow at her. "You are still clothed. I said naked."

She knelt and plucked out the lacing along the front of her wool gown. Her breasts itched to be free of the garments and warmed by something besides cloth.

He lathered an arm and her senses vicariously experienced the progress of his hand on his skin. The anticipation of touching all of him, of feeling him with her and in her . . . it was almost too delicious and left her trembling. He smeared soap on his chest. White wetness glistened on sculpted flesh. She itched to draw patterns in it.

She slid the gown down her body and his gaze followed the fabric's journey like a firm caress along her length. She sat and slipped off her winter hose, first one leg then the other, and his eyes slowly traveled the knit stockings' long descent to her feet.

He propped a foot on the tub's rim, not paying

attention to his actions while he observed her. She envied the fingers scrubbing the bent, well-formed leg, moving higher to knee and thigh. Serving him at the bath really would have been very pleasant.

Her hands rose to her shift straps and his lids lowered. She recognized that serious intensity. She surrendered to an urge to taunt him. She removed the straps one at a time so that she could keep her body covered. She lowered the fabric down her breasts as slowly as possible.

"You really can be a vicious woman, Moira," he said.

She smiled and made no effort to speed the process. Caressing him in the bath would have brought quicker satisfaction, but this distant pleasure was incredibly arousing.

Naked at last, she knelt high and lifted her arms to undo her hair. Her breasts spread and rose with the movement and she took her time, watching him watch, enjoying the effect so obvious in his eyes. The long tresses cloaked her body like a tattered mantle through which her breasts and hips poked. She crawled away for a pillow and her hair swung down, revealing another erotic view. She reached for a pillow, set it on the edge of the bed, and stretched out on her stomach in front of him.

Washing movements ten feet away continued, but his attention never left her. "Have you heard any news of Kenilworth?" he asked as if they did not mentally make love across the span that separated them.

"Rumors of the king's health and spirit. Nothing else. It is said he is in a deep melancholy."

His gaze meandered along her shoulders and back, over her buttocks, and down her legs. She propped up on her elbows and he did not miss the side swell of breast she exposed.

"At least there are rumors. That is a good sign."

He wet his chest with a cloth. She fantasized that her

tongue licked along his breastbone. Then lower. "You still worry for his safety?"

"His death would be convenient. Turn over."

She did, lying out, watching him watch. "What will the barons do about him?" It took effort to maintain a conversational tone. Tweaking tremors of excitement preoccupied her attention.

"That will depend on him, I think. He must be very frightened. I would be. He has no doubt heard how Hereford executed Hugh. It was as brutal as the indignities that Gaveston suffered. The Archbishop of Canterbury has finally acquiesced to the inevitable and thrown his support to the queen. He will not be king a month hence. Sit now."

She barely heard him but her body obeyed. Her legs dangled down the side of the high bed. He washed the body invisible under water and her mind's eye assisted. Not long now. She did not think it possible to be this hungry without a single touch.

He left the tub and dried himself before the fire. She feasted on the sight of his body glowing beside the hearth and tingled deliciously at the magnificent evidence of his desire. She could tell from his expression that Edward's problems had disappeared from his thoughts.

"In my mind I held you every night while I was gone. I pictured you thus, on that bed, your eyes bright and your breasts full and hard, waiting for me. It did not do much for my rest, but all day I looked forward to it. Did you dream about me?"

"Aye." She glanced down at the two hard nipples pointing erotically, beckoning him. She cupped her breasts' lower swells, directing their fullness in offering. "I dreamt of you. Your hands, your mouth. Here. Everywhere. I dreamt of everything. All of it."

He cast aside the towel and walked over.

She still held her craving breasts. He grazed one protuberant tip with his fingers. "Like that, love?"

The sensation almost lifted her off the bed. "Aye."

His thumb rubbed gently. "And this?"

Warm tension twisted below her belly. "Aye."

His palm lightly teased while he leaned down to kiss her lips, carefully biting and probing in a display of the restraint he intended. All of this indication of the long lovemaking awaiting only made her arousal spread with a luscious burst.

His head dipped to the uplifted request. "And this?" His tongue flicked over each nipple, then circled one seductively.

She thought she would die. Embracing his waist she urged him closer. "Aye. And this."

Anticipating her, he stood tall. Still it surprised him when she enclosed his hard desire in the valley between her breasts, holding him next to her heartbeat.

"And this." Her tongue teased at him as he had done her.

"Ah, Moira, you *are* vicious," he said, sighing, and he used his hands to show her cradling breasts more attention.

They gave each other pleasure until she was rocking with need. She released and embraced him, rubbing her cheek against his abdomen and splaying her hands over his back. "I cannot wait any longer," she muttered.

He knelt, spreading her legs so their bodies were close. The exposure of where she pulsed only made it worse and she grasped his head and shoulders in an entwining embrace and ferocious kiss.

"I think you will have to wait nonetheless. I had all these dreams, you see. Months of them. Would you deny me the chance to make even one real?" He cupped her breasts this time, lifting them to a mouth and tongue that aroused her without mercy. Impatience gave way to a delirious acceptance and she closed her eyes and experienced the sensations for their own sake.

"You are so warm, Moira." He caressed around her hips and over her thighs, brushing the damp curls almost pressing his chest. "Wet. Ready. Tell me that you are completely mine."

More than ready. Starving. Her body pulsed with astonishing demand, leaving her aware of little else. She told him, barely hearing her own words.

He spread her thighs wider. "Lie back."

She gladly did so, grabbing his shoulders, urging him up to her. He laughed quietly and released her hold. "Not yet. Not until you are screaming for me."

His mouth and hands found the way to make her do so. Soon anxious, needful sounds poured out of her, a chorus of passion muffled by her dulled hearing. Primitive sounds transformed into begging cries. They escalated until he came up over her to give the union for which her body shrieked.

He settled himself and then bent her knees up to her chest. Extending his arms he rose up and looked down the gap between them, watching his entry. Their concurrent sighs quivered their bodies.

"You feel so good, Moira. Perfect."

Again and again he fully withdrew before penetrating again. Forceful waves of relief and anticipation alternated, driving her close to the edge of endurance. The howling first streaks of release began spreading and she urged him down, wanting more.

"I'm glad you will be with me at the end this time," he said, his voice low and ragged by her ear. "Complete together."

316 ✦ Madeline Hunter

His passion broke in a burst of intensity, inciting her own, pulling them into an oblivion of shared sensation.

He stayed on her afterward. Her breasts pressed against his chest and her legs embraced his waist and he savored the contact of her moist body beneath and around him. He made no effort to move off her and she signaled no discomfort with his weight.

He tucked his face into the crook of her neck and breathed deeply, inhaling euphoria along with her scent. This drove his lovemaking as much as the pleasure. It was like a taste of heaven, and the glory of calm and love that the priests said one found there.

He wound his hand in the long tresses streaming over the bed. Love, aye, but with its conditions. He remembered her cool resolve when he met her by the well and felt less peaceful all of a sudden. He had trusted, nay, he had prayed, that she would not be able to turn from him when the time came. Today had shown that she meant what she had said, she would hold him to that agreement she had forced.

He rose on his forearms and looked down at her. Creamy lids fluttered and blue eyes narrowed while she smiled. Her upstretched arms, still encircling his neck, rubbed his jaw. He turned to kiss their soft skin and then stroked his face along the valley of her breasts.

She did not know how much he needed her. If he could find the words to explain it he would try to, but what existed inside him did not have names that he knew. The whole time he had ridden with Lancaster's army he had felt a man apart, watching a dream unfold. His body knew the right moves, his voice said the right words, but his soul felt that by some magic it had been placed in the wrong body. The sense of being a foreigner in his homeland had eased over the months while he was with her. Riding at the head of an army, being addressed as the Lord of Barrowburgh, being apart from her, had made it surge again. Time had not brought the familiarity he had thought. That had become clear when he left this house and city and her.

The worst part was that his soul knew not in which body it really belonged. Not Addis the slave, although the spirits still lived for him. Not the son of Patrick de Valence, even though custom and honor dictated his decisions.

Only with Moira did he possess any secure sense of who he was, and then because his image reflected off her love. He even accepted his duty mostly because she expected it of him, even if success in regaining his honor meant losing her. The two halves did not totally forge into one when he was with her, but the division ceased to matter much at all.

Losing her. His essence rebelled against the expectation of that. It would be like being flayed. He held her face with his hands and tried to peer through those clear eyes into her soul and discover if she truly would find the strength to leave when the time came. He saw only the pure love of a serf-born woman who had been taught by life to expect nothing.

The open way she looked back touched him as it had so often since he entered her cottage at Darwendon. A provocative nameless something nudged at him, as if a friendship older than these past months and a connection deeper than even this love and pleasure bound them. It unsettled him now, poking persistently.

He kissed her with a passion and possession that had nothing to do with desire, then moved aside and, as he almost always did, laid his head on her breast.

He could not let her go, of course. When the time

came, he would find a way to keep her. When she was nearby he lived in a different world. Everything changed. The earth, the rocks, every plant . . .

Her firm arms embraced his shoulders in that comforting habit of hers. His face pressed against the softness of her full breast. *I feel like the earth, the rocks every plant has changed.* Her words, whispered that night after they first made love, confusing him because they sounded so familiar.

His mind stretched for something lost behind fog. He noted again this frequent embrace.

She held him the way one might hold a child.

Or a person who mourned.

Or someone broken by pain or despair.

CHAPTER 20

"THIS IS NOT going to work."

"It appears not. The cot is too small."

"It is not the bed, Addis. Even on the ground . . ." She began to giggle. "Where do you get these notions?"

"In my dreams." He laughed, untangling the confusion of limbs he had created. It took some doing.

She stretched and embraced him over her body and heart. She enjoyed his playful experiments, but in truth they both took a special pleasure in this simplest form of lovemaking.

He settled himself, filling her. Spring's earliest smells seeped into the tent with dawn's first light. "I saw the abbot speaking with you yesterday. Did he scold you again?"

"A very mild scold. Since your army camps on his lands he feels obligated to do his duty to condemn sin. He saves the worst for the camp whores, but even then his heart is not in it."

The profound contentment of being inside her suffused

him as it always did, and he resisted the urge to move. "He wants to be rid of Simon as a neighbor badly enough to overlook much, I'll warrant. He did not argue when I brought the letter from Stratford ordering the abbey to let me use their lands."

She ran a finger up his back, making him suck air through his teeth. "It was fortunate the bishop chose to help you."

"Not just good fortune, Moira."

"How so?"

Hunger conquered his patience. "I will explain some other time."

Later she walked with him through the damp field and crisp air to the top of the hill where six sentries waited. They had caught one of Simon's men last night. Spies from Barrowburgh fanned out through the region daily to try and locate the army that Simon knew must be coming. So far none of the men who had found the camp had been permitted to return and Simon did not know that fate literally waited on his threshold.

Addis sent the prisoner to the abbey's dungeon after questioning, then turned and looked out over the encampment.

"It is impressive," Moira said, scanning the tents and fires stretching into the distance. He embraced her and she nestled her back against his chest and snuggled under his surrounding cloak. Together they watched the bright blur of the rising sun burn away the low mist.

"Impressive, but not decisively so."

"Still not enough? Even with the queen's footmen?"

"Barrowburgh is formidable. Wake should arrive soon but even with the army he brings and the archers sent by Lancaster nothing is certain."

"The aid of so many is an honor to your family."

"In part. But like Stratford's help, it is also to repay me and also, mostly, a bid for my support should I succeed. Already the powers in the realm realign and new factions form. It will be thus until young Edward can wear the crown on his own."

"So even with one king gone and another crowned, nothing has changed." She shook her head. "I felt sorry for them both, the father facing the end and the boy facing the unknown."

She felt sorry because she had seen them both. He had brought her with him when he was chosen to join the entourage that traveled to Kenilworth to press for abdication. Not only nobles had faced Edward that day, but representatives of the entire realm. Priests and monks, peasants and merchants, magnates and craftsmen had urged their isolated king to step aside for his son. Edward had fortunately agreed, but Moira had not been the only one to weep at the sight of a man destroyed because fate had condemned him to be born to a life for which he was not suited.

"The boy faces the unknown, but I think he has the heart for it," Addis said.

"Aye. Only five and ten, but one can see it. I saw him watching his mother and Roger Mortimer and the way they assumed the crown was theirs even though he wore it. He did not seem to miss much."

Nor did Moira. He had brought her to the coronation too, dressed in his mother's velvets and looking as much a lady in grace and demeanor as any lord's wife. She had not wanted to go, but once there the excitement of attending such a great event had obliterated any awkwardness. An accident of birth, Rhys had called a person's status, and it had never been more true than in that great hall or been proven more clearly than by the events of the last weeks.

"He is cut of the same cloth as his grandfather. Soon he will come of age to rule on his own. Until then the queen and her lover will have a council to deal with."

"I do not think they will listen to the council," she said.

"Nor do I. Nor does our new king. He spoke with me and some others. He found a way to pass a few words privately."

She turned in surprise. "You never told me that before."

"He said very little. It was more his expression and tone. In fact he began by admiring your form. He may only be five and ten but he has an appreciation for a pretty armful of woman when he meets one."

She laughed and jostled him with her elbow. "Seriously, what did he say?"

"That my lady appears to have the most magnificent breasts that ever a man—"

"Addis!"

"I swear that I quote him directly. And then he looked at his little Philippa and said that Mortimer had reassured him that although she did not come from a great house and was not a beauty that her broad hips meant she would be fertile. He smiled like an old man and added that Mortimer had misjudged the true value of the count's daughter, which would lie in her loyalty and love, and that his wife would be his first and most formidable ally. And then, having just mentioned allies, he asked how my preparations progressed for Barrowburgh, and offered to ask his mother to provide aid."

She peered toward the tents that flew the royal colors. "You mean it was young Edward and not the queen . . ."

"It was the queen, but at his suggestion. I doubt she knows he mentioned it to me. So she thinks she has bought my loyalty when in fact I know the true source."

He led her down the hill and through the awakening

camp. They stood by the fire outside their tent and he wrapped her under his cloak again. She felt so good and right next to him. He wondered if she had experienced the same bittersweet mood when they made love this morning. Soon this army would move. They never spoke of the parting which she still assumed would occur when Barrowburgh fell, but it was never far from his mind. He had greeted the arrival of every man with a combination of relief and resentment.

A horse suddenly clamored through the quiet morning. A sentry pulled up beside them and pointed south. "A troop. Maybe a mile away. Seems to have circled around from the west."

That would be Wake. "How many?"

"Maybe fifty to seventy."

Addis frowned. Thomas was supposed to bring two hundred at least. Wake had not liked Moira's visibility during the last few weeks in London, but had let Addis know that he understood. Still, although marriage alliances were practical arrangements and many men retained mistresses, Wake might have rethought everything if he concluded that Addis's devotion appeared too strong.

If so, why bother coming at all? Nay, more likely he had split his men so they would attract less attention. Part of him felt disappointed with this obvious explanation. He needed Wake, but if the man himself retreated from the agreement . . .

He gestured for the sentry's horse and the part that secretly wished that would happen and damn the consequences drew Moira toward it.

She resisted. "I will wait in the tent."

"You will come. He knows about us already. He will be in this camp for several days before we move and I will not have you hiding." He mounted and pulled her up behind.

"You are a fool to make such a statement through my presence behind you," she hissed into his back.

Perhaps. But during the time left he'd be damned if he would deny her, or let discretion create any separation, or treat her as less than she was to him.

They trotted through the camp and he waited at the southern edge. The arriving troop broke into view at the crest of a low rise of land. The leader saw them and galloped ahead.

Long blond hair flew back from the rider's head. He slowed when he neared, and paced until he sat along Addis's side. Blue eyes scanned, pausing on Moira, and several heartbeats of utter stillness passed.

Raymond smiled and threw his arm back toward the approaching men. "Could only raise sixty, what with it being near planting time, but at least these men are seasoned in battle. You might consider waging your next war during the growing months like everyone else, brother."

Addis had not missed the reaction contained in that encompassing look. No longer angry, but not approving either. He reached out his arm and Raymond did the same, joining in a clasp of friendship. "I am grateful that you have come."

"Couldn't pass up the chance to see that snake get skinned. Too sly by half. Never liked him, even as a youth, and dreaded whenever we found ourselves at your father's board together. Besides, we both know Bernard would leave his grave to haunt me if our family did not do its duty by yours."

"It is good to see you again, Raymond," Moira said as they turned to ride back to the camp.

"And you. Love makes your eyes even brighter, Moira. I can see this knight suits you."

It was said with a forced joviality but it broke the awkwardness just the same.

"Aye, he suits me well," she said, laughing.

At the tent Moira made an excuse to leave. Raymond watched her walk away. "You must suit her very well if she lets you give her velvet gowns. She would take nothing from me."

"They are my mother's things."

"Do not get annoyed. I am not suggesting that you have bought her. If a few gowns were all it took with her . . . She is a proud woman, is all. It must be a true love if she puts that pride aside."

She *had* put her pride aside. She walked through this camp as if living with a man who was not her husband carried no shame at all for her. Somehow she had decided that this brief time and particular place existed outside the normal world and its rules. He was the one who resented the occasional looks of disapproval sent her way, and the abbot's penitential warnings.

"I did not think that you would come because of it."

Raymond shrugged. "She always said that she thought of me as a brother. If those aren't the most dispiriting words women have ever spoken to men, I don't know what are. And I suspected that she had sworn never to be like her mother. But if she has changed on that with you, I have decided that perhaps it is for the best. Lady Mathilda will naturally prefer her own children when they come. It will be good for Brian to have Moira's love in your home."

"She has not changed. She intends to return to London when I am done here."

Raymond looked over in surprise. "With any other woman I would say that was just talk. You will permit it?"

"I can hardly imprison her." Not that the thought had not entered his mind.

Raymond grinned. "Get her with child and she will forget such nonsense."

God knew he'd been trying his damnedest, and only in

part for the bargaining ploy it might give him. He sensed that she hoped for it too, as if a child would be a manifestation of the union they had known. It would continue then, and live on even if they separated forever. When her flux had come last week he had silently shared her disappointment.

Warriors never talked long of women, and Raymond moved on to questions and discussion of the strategies Addis planned. But the whole time he enjoyed the camaraderie of his old friend, a small portion of his mind followed her through the camp. He knew her pattern of activity as surely as he knew his own, and mentally joined her in it every day while the sun relentlessly moved and the men continued to arrive, all of the routines propelling him toward the victory that he both craved and dreaded.

She waited until he had dressed and left the tent the next morning before rising herself. The night had been sweet and touching, just hours of blissful intimacy while they held each other and talked. He spoke of his plans for the next few days but the subject had not mattered so much as the sharing of warmth and words. It had been, she suspected, his man's way of trying to soothe the tensions that had arisen with the arrival first of Raymond and then of Thomas Wake. Yesterday both the past and the future had intruded on their "now."

Several times last night she had seen that look in his eyes that had appeared more frequently as the days passed. It contained the question that he would not ask and that she could not answer. *Will you really leave and end this?*

Her mind still held to her decision, but her heart had been waging a fierce battle against the good sense with which it had been made. In truth she had been ignoring that anticipated parting so that its shadow would not dim the glory of what they had now. Thomas Wake's arrival had reminded her that the moment would come very soon when her resolve would be put to the test. It would be a specific moment, she did not doubt it. A precise point in time when it was clear she must either leave or walk forward with him.

She put on a simple wool gown and cloak and broke her fast with some bread and cheese. Last night Addis had insisted she sup with him and the others, but she knew that her company, that any woman's company, had become inappropriate. She would make herself scarce today, and use this opportunity to do something she had been planning for some time now.

She brought a basket and stopped at the supply wagons to get a jug of wine, then made her way to the rough corrals where the animals were kept. A groom noticed her and walked over. She explained her requirements. By the time the sun had fully risen she was on her way, heading toward the abbey road in a small cart pulled by a donkey.

It took most of the morning to reach her destination because Addis's army camped in the southernmost reaches of the abbey's lands. She arrived at the village of Whitly just as men came in from the fields for dinner.

Lucas Reeve stepped to his doorway at the sound of her cart pulling up. Delighted surprise lit his eyes. "Joan, it be the lord's woman here!" He tied the reins to a post and helped her down. "Just in time to eat, Moira. Come in and tell us how Sir Addis fares."

She presented the wine and accepted the place of honor at their humble table, but ate sparingly so Lucas's two sons would not suffer from her unexpected visit. When they learned she had spent the last months in London, they peppered her with questions about the momentous events there.

"Well, now, it seems to me that with the king and his friends gone, these lands will have the lord whom God intended." Lucas smiled with satisfaction.

"The king's council has returned the estate to Addis, but Simon has not accepted the decision," Moira explained.

"I'm sure. He's been living like an earl, bleeding the people and the land to feed his luxury. If he hands it all back he is a poor knight again, with nothing. And if there's to be retaliations against the pigs who joined Despenser at the realm's troughs, he is better behind those walls."

"It explains the word we have gotten from the other villages," his eldest son said. "That Simon's been calling up those with guard obligations. Must be preparing for a siege."

Their eyes turned to Moira expectantly.

"It is no secret that Addis will come," she said. "He told Simon that he would."

"Aye, but the question is when," Lucas mused with a grin. "And if you are sitting here now, I find myself wondering where the lord is sitting."

It was why she had come, but she chose her words carefully. "Not on Barrowburgh lands, but near enough."

The information raised their excitement. "God be praised," Lucas muttered. "Has he brought enough? His grandfather built one hell of a fortress there."

"He says with the likes of Barrowburgh there are never enough."

"Tell us where he is and every man who can carry a staff will go to him. I served as a pike in the Scot wars and can do so again despite this white hair. Damn, he should have called for us."

"He will not risk you. If he fails you will be at Simon's mercy."

"We'd rather die like men than slowly starve. Hell, a fever could take us all tomorrow. Word of the king's fall came weeks ago, and people are itching to have it out with the bastard hiding in that keep. Point us to Sir Addis and by morning there will be hundreds on the road offering to tear those walls down with their bare hands."

"I cannot tell you. If word spread, Simon would hear and Addis wants his march to be a surprise. But when he comes you will know it, and if word were sent to the other villages . . ."

"It will be done, Moira. We might not be of much use to him scaling walls and such, but every pair of arms can help and an extra thousand men filling that field will put the fear of god in Simon, which alone makes it worthwhile. Every farmer loading ballast will free a trained soldier for the walls."

She dipped a crust of bread into her soup. "He does not know that I came here. He might not like my interference."

He grinned and patted her arm. "None at this table will say anyone told us to prepare. Who is to know that what weapons we have were sharpened in advance? Lords don't count us as whole men in their wars, but we have made the difference before. You are one of us, Moira, and know that even bonded men have rights worth fighting for. " 'Twill be a fine revenge to stand with Patrick's son, be the result victory or death. He may not expect us or think he needs us, but when we come he'll be glad for it."

Lucas and his sons began planning for messengers and Moira turned to Joan for simpler conversation. Men began passing the cottage to return to the fields but a sudden commotion of horses disrupted the lane.

Commanding voices called families out of their homes. Everybody at the table silenced and tensed. Lucas peered around a shutter and cursed. "From Barrowburgh. Six of them, with that red devil Owen at their lead."

Owen! He might recognize her. She glanced frantically around the small cottage, but there was no place to hide.

"All of Barrowburgh bond out in the lane." Harsh voices yelled the order over and over. "Out in the lane or your home will be burned." Joining the commands came sounds of people being pushed and women screaming.

"Stay behind us all, Moira," Lucas said. "Whatever they want it should be over soon enough."

He and his sons stepped outside and formed a wall to protect the women. Moira eased into position behind Lucas and kept her eyes lowered. She prayed that she looked like any other serf despite her linen wimple and veil and the fine wool of her gown. With luck none of these men would even see her.

Her throat dried as the lane fell quiet and Owen paced down its length. He stopped in front of their little group, but then Lucas was Barrowburgh's reeve in this village. She glanced quickly at the flaming hair and steely gray eyes and tried to shrink still further into obscurity.

"Good day to you, Sir Owen," Lucas greeted amiably, as if six knights roused the villagers every day.

"I am come with a message from your lord," Owen said. "The men in this village are to bring all horses, donkeys, and livestock into Barrowburgh before nightfall. Also any grains left from last year's harvest still stored here."

"It is an odd request, sir."

"Not a request at all," Owen snarled.

"It is not within the customs and obligations—"

Owen's swinging fist cut off his words with an impact that doubled the reeve over his knees. Briefly exposed, Moira lowered her head yet more.

"All that is here is his. Your life is his if he requires it.

BY POSSESSION ◆ 331

Any villager found hoarding will lose the hand that dared to steal from him."

He spoke to Lucas but the villagers had closed in to listen. A thick circle of watchful eyes peered over the swords holding them back.

Lucas straightened and met Owen's glare. "And what would Sir Simon be wanting with all the grain and animals? Does he plan a feast that will mean the starvation of every man who serves him?"

"His reasons are none of your concern. Worry only about the obedience of your neighbors. As the lord's man here you will be held responsible for seeing it is done."

"Aye, it will be done. And you are right. I am most definitely the Lord of Barrowburgh's man in this village, and honored to be so counted."

Moira bit her tongue at the true meaning of that declaration. Lucas's acquiescence eased Owen's belligerence. "By nightfall," he repeated in a calmer voice.

She could see his boots on the ground. They began to turn away. Holding her breath, she waited with breaking relief for the danger to pass.

He paused. It seemed that Lucas and his eldest son tried imperceptibly to move their bodies closer together. The boots turned back and stepped forward. Heart pounding with renewed fear, she gritted her teeth and prayed to disappear.

The boots stepped closer yet. Lucas and his son were yanked apart, creating a chasm of shrieking peril that she suddenly faced alone. A hand grabbed her chin and jerked until gray eyes peered into her own.

His other hand pulled off her veil so abruptly that the pins flew in the air. An amused smile broke across his hostile face.

"Well, now. I wonder what the Baltic slave princess is doing so far from London and her master."

✦ ✦ ✦

It was mid-afternoon before Addis realized Moira was not in the camp. When she did not join him at dinner he had assumed that she had decided to leave the knights to discuss war without a woman present. As was his habit, his eyes had searched for her after that whenever he walked through the camp but she never appeared. He told himself that she prayed at the abbey or visited the sick, but with each hour a gnawing worry grew. It finally led him to the men tending the animals.

There he learned that she had ridden off in the early morning.

Numbness instantly soaked him. Right there in front of the nervous groom his body became a shell devoid of feeling or sensation. The small part of his mind that did not succumb existed separate from any physical awareness.

She would not be back. He just knew it. She had left as she had said she would, but sooner than she had warned.

He had expected to feel anger or pain when it happened, not this horrible vacancy. He stared at the groom, vaguely noting the man's increasing discomfort. His senses scattered and his dulled mind tried to understand why she had not waited the few days remaining.

He should not have left her this morning. He had seen how the presence of Raymond and Thomas Wake unsettled her at last evening's meal and had spent the night trying to soothe her. Both men had been very courteous, but each one stood for something in her mind and he could feel her spiritually withdrawing into the shadows even though she held her smiling composure to the end of the supper.

At least, he thought, both men had been courteous. If he learned that either Raymond or Thomas had said something to hasten her departure, he would kill the man.

Doing so right now would not even raise his blood. Because he had no blood. Or bones. Or substance.

The groom eased his weight from foot to foot, anxious for dismissal. The movement brought him back to some comprehension of where he stood. "Did she take anything with her?"

"Just a basket."

No trunk or garments. Nay, they were his mother's things. She would not take them with her. Just a basket. Knowing practical Moira, she could live for a month out of a basket.

"Did she say where she headed?"

The groom should have asked, and now he shrank while he shook his head.

Addis strode away and his disembodied legs took him to the top of the hill. He scanned blindly, knowing there was nothing to see anyway. She had been gone for hours. He would send a man to the abbey on the small chance she had gone to speak with the abbot, but he knew she would not be there.

His senses began righting themselves. The parts of his body began reawakening, finding each other. Emotion trickled into the void. He narrowed his eyes and peered toward the road she must have taken.

An unholy fury suddenly split, like lightening streaking to the ground. Not a word. Not a sign. She owed him that, damn it! They owed each other that. Even if she had guessed that he would fight to dissuade her, she owed him the chance to do so. Did she think this was only about her life and her future and her choices?

He grasped on to the anger because he knew the danger of the sea in which it served as a raft. He had felt that numbness before. Recently at Barrowburgh. Once in the Baltic lands. Long ago in dreams remembered only as journeys in despair. Not a tempestuous sea but one of

334 ♦ MADELINE HUNTER

seductive calm, warm and welcoming, with eddies so soothing it could lull one into an eternal sleep.

He remembered looking down at her before he left the tent in the morning. She had appeared peaceful and serene, her skin luminous beneath the abundant chestnut hair. She had stirred and noticed him there, and held up a limp hand that he kissed. . . .

If that was to be the last touch and sight of her, he had a right to know it. If last night was to be the final hours, she should have told him so that he could speak of things that had meaning.

He glared at the hundreds of men spread out below him. He had been dreading this battle because victory meant losing her, but now he itched to have it done. He would tear those walls down if it meant being finished with it. He would sit in his father's chair and claim the rights of his birth. He would secure his hold and make his power known.

And then, when he had done his duty, he would find her.

He stomped down to the camp and roused some men to search for her and sent another to the abbey. Hopeless, of course, but he would make sure she had not returned. Seething with frustration and disappointment he circled through the camp, informing the knights and retinues that they would move on the morrow. Like a spoon stirring a pot, his progress churned the army into an activity of preparation.

The anger sustained him until the night, when he found himself sitting with Raymond by the fire outside his tent. His old friend had been smart enough not to comment on Moira's absence or his change of temper. They spoke of the morning and the plan to be executed, until Raymond left.

Addis stayed by the fire. He had not entered the tent all

day and did not want to now. It contained garments bearing her scent and other objects of her life. If he saw and touched those remnants of her presence he might lose hold of the raft.

In the distance a small commotion inched down the hill. Like a tiny whirlwind it entered the camp and scooted between fires and tents. Addis watched it come, distracted for a moment from his thoughts. As it drew nearer it materialized into Richard and Small John pulling a peasant between them.

"Caught another one," Richard gloated, throwing the man to the ground. "Simon must be running low on spies if he's using his farmers. Wouldn't answer our questions. Said he was of Barrowburgh bond and would speak only to you."

The man stared around wide-eyed, his gaze finally locking on Addis. He was a young man, not much more than a youth, and Addis thought he looked familiar. To his surprise the spy crawled forward and knelt.

"I am not from Simon, my lord. I am Gerald, son of Lucas, from the village of Whitly."

"I remember you. What are you doing here?"

"Looking for you and this army."

That was not a welcome answer. "How did you know the army was here?"

"I didn't, my lord. Not for sure. She said it was near and that we would know when you moved and I thought about that and decided it must be south of Whitly if we would know first. . . ."

He froze as the rushed words made sense. "She?"

"Aye. The woman Moira." Gerald thrust his hand beneath his tunic and pulled out a cloth.

Addis opened it over his knees. A veil. One of hers. Relief and fear drowned the vestiges of his anger. "Where is she?"

"That's why I've come looking for you, my lord. She was in the village when Owen came and he recognized her and took her. My father too . . ."

Addis rose and walked into the night before Gerald finished. He pressed the veil to his face and inhaled the shadowy smell of her hair. She had not left, but had only gone to visit the village where it had all started.

And Owen had found her there. Simon had Moira and she knew the army's location. He might use torture to get that information if he guessed that she possessed it.

A profound joy churned in him, mixed with heartfelt guilt that he had so quickly misjudged her and a soul-shaking terror for her danger.

He called for Richard.

"How long to get to Barrowburgh? Just the men. The wagons and supplies can follow. A forced march."

"Five hours about."

He scanned the heavens. The night had begun black with clouds but they had broken to reveal the bright disk of a full moon. "Before dawn then, if we left soon."

"Certainly before dawn, but surely you cannot think to march at night."

"I do think it. Spread the word. I want every man ready as soon as possible. We do not wait for the morrow. We go now and we carry what we need."

"It has been threatening rain and even if it holds off we could lose half the men in the dark."

"The moon has come out. We will not lack for light."

Richard looked close to exasperation. "The clouds could cover it again in a snap."

Addis gazed up at Menulius. "They will not." He turned and smiled at the perplexed steward. "The moon will shine for us this night. As it happens, he owes me this small favor."

CHAPTER 21

SHE KNELT IN THE SOLAR like a supplicant. Simon paced around her in furious frustration.

"He is still in London," she said again. The words came as a mumble through her swollen lips.

His temper flared and he glanced meaningfully at Owen. She braced herself. The knight swung and another slap landed on her face, unbalancing her with its force.

Soon it would be a fist instead of a palm. They had spent hours trying to beat the information out of Lucas while she watched. She had come close to speaking to spare him, but the reeve's eyes had begged her to be silent.

They had carried his unconscious body away and then turned to her.

"She knows where he is," Owen said flatly. He was enjoying this. An unhealthy glow lit his eyes even as he acted almost bored with his duty. "She was his whore in London and if she is here now she came with him."

"Nay," she argued, fighting a wretched fear that urged her to grovel for mercy. "He tired of me and I head back to Darwendon and my home. I stopped to visit in the village, is all, and seek shelter until the morn. . . ."

Another blow cracked across her face. Pain split through her head and she tasted blood.

How much longer until dawn? If she held out long enough, perhaps any move that Simon made would not catch Addis unawares. The army at the abbey greatly outnumbered Simon's forces, even swelled as they were by his anticipation of trouble, but an unprepared army could be devastated by many fewer men.

Simon's eyes raked her. "Darwendon, eh? You are bonded to him then, but you don't appear to be a serf. If he had cast his bonded slut aside she would not still be wearing that wool robe, woman, or linen on her neck."

"They were gifts. He let me keep them. He is not ungenerous."

"Well pleased, was he? Aye, I can imagine he was."

Her blood ran cold at the leering smirks that smeared both men's faces. "Apparently not pleased enough, since I was left to make my own way across the realm with naught but the garments on my back." She tried to look resentful and peeved. "And this gown is small compensation for what he cost me. I lost an entire crop because of his insistence that I serve him in London. If he were anywhere in this shire, I would gladly point you to him."

Simon studied her in his sly way. "Where did you learn to talk like that? Your manner is far above your place."

She could not decide if explaining would help or hurt, so she said nothing. Owen stepped forward and yanked her hair so cruelly that she thought her neck would break. He lifted until her knees left the ground.

"Hawkesford," she gasped. "I lived at Hawkesford as a girl."

"Hawkesford?" The answer surprised Simon. He grabbed her chin and lifted her face. Dangerous, shrewd eyes inspected her. He looked long enough that she saw something inside that gaze. Fear. Beneath his bluster and anger, within these walls and his power, Simon tried to hide the terror of a hunted man. The insight gave her heart.

"Hawkesford," he mused again. "Lady Claire had a friend there who was serf-born. She spoke of her sometimes. Would that be you?"

She refused to answer. He stepped back and smiled. "Aye, it be you. If you were of that household and her friend, I think that you know about the boy. Where is he?"

"What boy?"

Owen pulled her to her feet and slammed her against the wall. Two faces, one pale and impassive, the other florid and impatient, glared down at her. "Her boy. Brian. Where is he?"

She felt grateful that Addis had never told her where the sweet child hid. They might break her but her weakness could never help them ensnare Brian. "I do not know."

Owen slammed his fist into her body and her consciousness reeled. If not for the wall's support she would have fallen. "You waste your time," she breathed. "I am no one. Nobody. A bondwoman of no account. Addis de Valence does not confide to his whore when his army moves and where his son is hidden. You know how it is with such as me. If I knew anything I would tell you and at most bargain for some coin."

Simon's face pressed closer. The smell of onions on his breath and of fear on his body made her bruised stomach heave. "You know. Claire spoke of your loyalty. When she went to bed to birth that boy she asked you be called to care for him if she died. Serf-born or not, I think you knew the doings in the households of Valence and Orrick. I think that you still know them. And if you lie to help him now, I wonder if maybe you are not more than a whore to him."

"You speak nonsense and beat a helpless woman for nothing. Could a woman like me ever be more than a whore to you? His birth is even higher than yours. A son of Barrowburgh has only one use for baseborn women."

"She talks too much while answering nothing," Owen said. "Let me deal with her. If he has come she will tell me."

Simon considered her, debating his options. A prayerful hope gripped her, dangerous because it acknowledged and released the terror she had been fighting for hours. A change in Owen's regard said that his predator's instincts had sensed the new vulnerability that the chance of reprieve had created.

"She will tell me," Owen repeated.

Simon nodded and turned away. "Do not kill her though. She might be useful."

Aye, he enjoyed it. Too much. He proved well practiced in creating suffering without causing the damage that would make her drop. She prayed for unconsciousness but it never quite came. Shallow, methodical blows and slaps quickly drove her to the edge of endurance. Obscene descriptions of what would happen next further assaulted her steadfastness. Pain and weakness began pushing her to the point where she might sell her soul to stop it. Knowing she was about to break, seeing it coming, she found a final drop of rebellious courage. Pursing her cracked lips, she let the bile that choked her rise and she spit into his face.

A retaliatory fist crashed into her. The chamber swirled and the stone floor rushed up. Her mind knew red and then white and then nothing at all.

✦   ✦   ✦

Menulius lit their way, holding back the clouds that tried to obscure his glow. They used no torches, but the feet and horses of six hundred men made enough noise in the still night that anyone looking could easily find them. When mile after mile passed and no raiding parties from Barrowburgh attacked, Addis grimly accepted that Moira had refused to tell Simon what he wanted.

He tried not to contemplate what might be happening to her in that keep. The abuse would not come from Simon. It would be Owen. The Simons of the world always found the Owens who enjoyed doing the dirty work. The image flashed of that flame-haired man hurting her, and he barely resisted the urge to spur his horse and let this army catch up as it might.

He looked to his left and right at the thick shadows accompanying them. Men had silently fallen into step when they had passed Whitly, tromping alongside in the fields. All along the way more had emerged from the trees and hills. No one had asked his permission. A growing sea of bodies had simply formed on either side of the road. Some carried staffs or rough pikes or even scythes, but most merely brought their two hands and legs.

"They have heard about the reeve and the woman, you think?" Thomas Wake asked from the horse beside him.

"Perhaps. It would be the final injustice to a people who have suffered many."

"You should send them home. They will get in the way."

"I do not think they would obey if I did so. They are not in disorder, and appear determined. Simon is their Hugh Despenser. Each of them has made a hard choice as you and I did not so long ago."

"But when we reach Barrowburgh . . ."

"They will not disrupt the plan, and we may be glad of their numbers if we fail."

A cantering horse broke through the rhythm of marching boots and Richard pulled up alongside. "Just a mile more over that hill if we go through the woods." He pointed. "That will bring us in from the west. There's time to rest here for a while."

Addis looked at the sky. Three hours until dawn, he judged. His gaze fell on the flanking shadows pausing and bunching to make a large shapeless ghost.

"A brief rest. We will not stop long."

"You are changing the plan? If we continue we will arrive too early and by dawn he will have deployed his men. Have you decided to make camp after all?"

"Nay, we will still march directly into an attack."

Raymond paced around Wake to join the council. "You are mad, Addis. Even with the moon a night attack is suicide. We'll not see who we are fighting and . . ."

"We go forward. He will not expect it even if he has discovered that we are coming, especially at night."

"Your concern for the woman is impairing your judgment. If he planned to kill her she is dead already," Thomas said.

"And if he did not plan to kill her?"

"Whatever he intended is done."

Raymond threw up an arm. "It will help her naught if you fail because you acted rashly."

"You know that attacking in the dark is a fool's strategy," Richard weighed in.

Addis turned his horse and began walking it toward the shadows beside the road. "That is true, but we will not attack in the dark, old friend. Our way will be lit by all of Barrowburgh's hearths."

What the hell are you saying? Make sense, man.
The harsh voice penetrated the fog from far away.

There's movement out there, near the distant trees to the west. Men and horses.

You say you've seen men by the trees? How many?

Closer now. A familiar voice. Simon's.

Not seen, exactly, my lord, not with the moon going in sudden like. Felt more than seen, though there seem to be darker shadows there, bigger than they should be.

Probably just the night playing tricks on you.

Not just me. The other guards feel it too. I'd not have come if we didn't agree. . . .

Send more men to the gates then.

Will you be coming, my lord?

Awareness of the chamber returned and she suddenly smelled the hearth. Her cheek recognized the hard texture of stone on which it lay. Screaming aches groaned through her body from the spots where she had been hit. Sliding back into unconsciousness held an enormous appeal. She heard movements, but enough sense had returned for her to resist the urge to look.

"I'll go to the top of the keep and see what's what," Simon gruffed. "Get back on the wall."

"What about her?" Owen asked as the guard left. She lay utterly still and hoped that they would leave her in the heap where she had fallen.

"See again if you can wake her."

Liquid splashed her face and she fought her shocked reaction even though she inhaled some of it. Wine dripped down her immobile face, burning her broken lips.

"Are you sure she is not dead? I told you not to kill her."

"She still breathes."

"Leave her. We will see about this ghost army the guard *felt* and then see if she can be revived."

She waited until silence surrounded her before she tried to rise. Her whole body from her neck to her legs felt deeply sore, and it hurt to move her mouth. Despite the pain she reached for the wall and pulled herself up.

She could hardly escape, but she would not wait in this chamber for the torture Owen planned. The guard's report had given her hope. Perhaps Addis had come.

She groped along the wall and peered out the door. Men to the west, the guard had said. She skirted through the passageway to a chamber near the end. Trying to ignore the agony of her knotting torso, she felt her way to the window.

She was high enough to see over the walls to the distant fields and flanking hunt-land. A brisk breeze moved clouds across the moon, breaking them up now and then to permit gray light to spread. During those brief illuminations it did appear that movement occurred near the trees, but probably it was just the night playing tricks on one's eyes, as Simon had said.

She rested against the window edge and closed her eyes with disappointment. Of course he could not come until he was ready, and even then he would not do so at night. It would be rash to risk so much, even if he knew she was here.

Which he might not know at all. When he had discovered her gone, he probably concluded that she had gone back to London. Could he have thought her that faithless? Faced with her absence, he might have found it the only explanation.

Her chest filled with a horrible ache. She did not want to picture that. She turned back to the window and scanned the battlements of the inner wall to distract her mind from images of him angry and hurt, believing she had forsaken him so cruelly right before his dangerous task. The distant fields grew very black as clouds completely obscured the moon.

A flicker caught her eye and a tiny dot of gold appeared far away. It moved. Two dots now. She squinted. Suddenly four. Now ten or more. She watched in amazement as the specks rapidly multiplied and enlarged, like stars emerging and growing not in the sky but on the horizon.

The noise of household and guards suddenly stilled and the fortress went utterly silent. Others had seen. The faintest rhythm oozed toward her on the breeze, and the stars, not so tiny now, continued increasing in number and size. They filled the field and began spreading right and left, encircling all of Barrowburgh. She stretched out the window, unmindful of her sores, and the closest spots materialized into torches and then disappeared from view beneath the mass of the wall. Their light cast a yellow glow in every direction, displaying hundreds of bodies. The brightest cluster surrounded a knight flanked by the banners of Valence.

Her heart lodged in her throat while she watched him come. The sounds of his army crashed through the stillness of the keep. He raised his arm and the movement ceased and he scanned the breadth of the fortifications. Instead of grouping to make camp, the army and the torchbearers lighting its way just waited.

Another gesture and the army suddenly split and men surged forward carrying scaling ladders. Their shouts shocked the whole fortress. She gaped as the hell of war instantly replaced the eerie silence. He was attacking!

He rode his horse back and forth, yelling orders lost to her ears in the din. The torches turned his armor orange, as if he wore steel still hot from the forge. Another man joined him and she recognized the bald head of Sir Richard. The steward took command of the western attack and Addis galloped south to where the wall extended to surround the town.

She tore her eyes from the spectacle, her pulse racing. He had come, but his arrival might have increased her danger. She trusted that Simon would be preoccupied with his defenses now, but she could not count on it. She needed a place to hide.

She turned to run but a thick figure barged through the threshold. Simon strode over and grabbed her arm, twisting her back to the window. His body pressed obscenely along her back and a sour smell assaulted her. Fear. He reeked of it.

"You should be flattered. You must have pleased him very well with that body of yours. He comes for you," he hissed.

"Nay. He comes for you."

"These walls have withstood more than he can have."

"He has over six hundred, all battle-hardened men. And it looks like every peasant man able to walk holds a torch out there. You should yield, and if not you should armor yourself."

"Owen will deal with him. He has killed him before. He will do so again."

"He failed before, and proved himself a coward in doing so. When it comes to facing Addis he will flee or surrender and leave you to face it alone."

"He will not. Owen is more a brother to me than Addis ever was."

"If he never showed you a brother's love it was because he knew what he had in you."

"He was too proud to befriend such as me! To share the wealth of Barrowburgh. I saw at once that I would get naught from him. Owen saw it too. We were all just youths, but it was clear that the son of Patrick scorned me."

"So you stole what would not be given freely!"

"A man either takes or he dies on a bloody field for

someone else's honor." He pulled her through the chamber. "You will come with me while we watch this army founder. He will not breach the inner wall. No one ever has. When this is done I will enjoy taking you, as I have taken everything else that is his."

His grip gouged her and she tried to keep up. "He does not have to breach the inner wall. The animals and grain are outside the first gate. He has only to wait until the provisions within are gone."

Twisting her arm behind her back he shoved her up the stairs to the roof. "And let you starve with us? That is why I would not let Owen kill you. For your sake, woman, I hope that you pleased him well indeed."

"Do we enter?" Raymond asked as the town gate swung wide. Figures scurried away and the torches showed five guards lying in lifeless tangles. "May not be a good idea to get caught inside. It could be a trap."

"Those were not soldiers running away, but craftsmen. The town has opened the gate, not Simon."

"Still . . ."

Addis paced his destrier forward. "The easiest way into any fortress is through the gates, Raymond."

"There's two more after this one and no townsmen to open them. We are close to breaching on the east. Best to wait."

Harsh and shrill sounds poured around them. The outer wall would fall, a casualty of the surprise attack, but the inner one would not be so certain. The thick circle of torches lighting the battle made it appear as if the entire scene took place within a giant hearth.

"If we attack the gate even while they defend the walls it might encourage them to withdraw. And it will force them to cover the south as well." He gestured for Marcus and told him to allow a hundred of the peasants to follow with the wheeled battering ram, then led a small force of knights and men-at-arms into the town.

The lanes were deserted and the buildings shuttered. Nearer the gate he could see the progress on the wall more clearly. Simon's men were greatly outnumbered and no reinforcements had arrived. Simon had decided to sacrifice the outer wall and its guard. It looked as if one section to the east had been taken and secured, but even so the superior position of the defenders meant this could last many hours.

He called the battering ram forward and dismounted. He and the others made a canopy of upraised shields to protect the farmers pulling the huge cylinder of wood. The rest of the farmers stayed out of arrow range, prepared to replace their neighbors as needed.

The repeated impact of the ram created a sound like the world's largest drum, crashing through the night. The sea of peasants surrounding the wall began cheering "Valence!" with each blow and the huge swell of noise seemed enough to crumble the walls by itself. A rain of bolts and arrows pounded into the shields with each surge forward, their whistling melody absorbed into the rhythmic battle song.

Suddenly the arrows stopped. Addis peered up to see Thomas Wake and his men fighting on the gate's battlements, but some guards had redeployed and moved in. He called for ladders and led Marcus and five others up while the ram continued its work.

He did not know how long he fought. His presence on the wall was noticed, however, and at least two archers came close to taking him down. At one point he glanced to the upper reaches of the keep and he saw Simon there, with a woman beside him. Moira. Something like the madness in the forest gripped him then and he knew nothing but the mayhem of blood and swords until a dead calm fell that said the gate was theirs.

The sound of the portcullis rising heralded victory, and any guards still standing surrendered. Addis hurried down to the outer yard while his men poured in.

Richard found him and gestured around the bailey. "Have you seen anything like it?"

The yard was crammed with animals and wagons and stores, collected to sustain the keep in case of siege and to ensure that Addis could find no provisions in the surrounding countryside. Simon would have burned the forests next to drive off the game.

"Have it cleared. Move it into the town. Quickly, or it will be fired from above."

Richard shouted the order and men began pulling the animals out while archers helped cover them.

"Think you to continue now? It will be morning soon and we can pick our time," Richard asked.

"What do you recommend?"

Richard wiped some blood off his head and laughed. "As if you need my council, or listen when I give it. Well, aye, I would take advantage of the confusion. The men are still fresh and can taste victory. And if there's to be help from the inside, it will be easier for them if we move before Simon has time to consider what's what now, and think too hard about who is where."

Addis gazed at the tall walls filling with knights and soldiers. The inner portcullis was solid iron and no battering ram would break it. He could starve them out, but it might take months. And Moira would suffer along with the others.

Let it be finished. Now.

He gave the order and Richard went to organize the attack. He looked up at the keep but could no longer see where Simon and Moira stood. He muttered a prayer for her protection. Would the Christian saints help her, considering the sin of their love?

Just to be on the safe side he made the same request of Kovas, the god of war.

They could see it all from the keep's roof. Like gods watching from a high mountain, they saw the battle peak and then suddenly end when the gate opened. Simon's men pressed shoulder to shoulder along the battlements of the inner wall and shot arrows at the army invading the outer yard, but Moira could tell from Simon's expression that he expected no more fighting this night.

Her eyes never left Addis, even while he fought atop the gate. She saw the moment when he noticed her, and then the savage mayhem that followed.

"He will at least wait until morning to attack again. I expect he will want to parlay first," Simon said while they watched the provisions being pulled out the gate. "It will give me a few hours to discover what makes you so valuable."

She fixed him with one of Claire's haughty glares but it did not dull his leer. "He does not fight for me, Simon. There will be no parlay and no terms, and he will not wait until morning. Do you see any camps forming out on the field? Look you to Owen. He knows it is not over."

The red-haired knight paced around the wall's walk, checking the deployment of the enemy. Simon's gaze found him. "He will see that Addis does not enter, or does not live long if he does."

"You have great faith in your friend. Do you really think he will die to protect your hold on Barrowburgh?"

"Nay, probably not. But he will fight to the death to protect himself from Addis's revenge."

A sudden outpouring of shouts and yells drew their attention back to the yard. A ringing line of men surged forward and the attack resumed.

The fighting was closer now, and the blood and pain loomed horribly real. She could see faces rise above the wall and their expressions when swords dealt the death blows. But more kept coming, and more again, until some bodies breached the wall and the fighting spread along the walk.

It was like a scene from hell. Her blood pounded and her eyes teared from the scenes of carnage. Beside her Simon observed as if he enjoyed an interesting entertainment, but she could smell that fear on him still. She scanned for Addis until she saw the colors of Valence and his swinging sword where he fought for a foothold on the wall near the gate. Raymond fought beside him, and Small John too. They were trying to take this entry as they had the last, but Owen noticed and led reinforcements in their direction.

Addis and the others who had breached the wall found themselves isolated as Owen's men thwarted any further scaling. Outnumbered now, they valiantly held off attacks from both sides.

He would be killed. She just knew it. His sword fell with methodical precision, but there were too many. She silently begged him to retreat, to find a way back down, and looked away to avoid seeing the death blow that would find him soon.

Her gaze fell on the inner yard. Amidst the wavering shadows a group of nine men moved in thick formation, all wearing the scarlet of Simon's knights. They eased along the wall with swords drawn.

They slipped forward. Three disappeared into the gate and the other six mounted to the wall. Her heart almost burst with despair when she realized they headed toward Addis. There would be no hope now.

They joined the battle, but not in the way expected. Suddenly those armored arms were pushing men off the wall, crashing archers' heads against the battlements, clearing a path to the sword fight. Owen glanced over his shoulder and seemed to assume they were with him. When a sword from behind felled the man by his side, he realized the truth.

She had forgotten about Simon, but his livid curses drew her eyes to his astonished expression.

"Sir Richard said some had stayed behind," she said.

"Vipers in my own bed! I'll have them roasted alive!"

"It does not appear you will have the chance. Even I can tell that their aid has turned the tide on that wall and that the gate will be taken soon."

Even as she spoke, the grinding sounds of chains and wheels filtered through the din of battle. Simon's eyes glazed.

"Three went inside. You were so busy watching Addis that you did not notice."

His gaze locked on Owen fighting desperately, his position as hopeless as Addis's had been just moments before.

"Surrender. He cannot help you or even himself anymore. Yield. Addis is not without mercy."

Beads of sweat dotted Simon's brow and the hair of his mustache. A furious desperation lit his eyes and he turned away, pulling her with him. "I'll not be counting on his mercy."

He hauled her down to the solar where he plucked two fat purses from a chest. With an iron grip on her arm he forced her down the stairway. The sounds drifting from the yard changed abruptly. She could hear hundreds of bodies moving and yelling, but no longer the screams of death and pain.

"It is over. He is inside," she said, wondering if Simon had noticed.

He pushed her downward with determination. "Aye, but I will be outside."

"You can move more quickly without me."

"I think that you are a better shield than steel, and so are worth the trouble."

"Think you to walk across these lands and not be found?"

"Horses wait not far away. I had great faith in Owen, but I am not a stupid man."

He pushed open a small door at the northern base of the keep. The yard was shallow here, and filled with shacks for chickens and pigs. High above on the wall Addis's men were accepting the surrender of Simon's.

Simon circled her in one arm and gagged her with his hand. Staying in the shadows of the shacks, he dragged her toward the wall. His rough handling reawoke her sores and she submitted to avoid more pain.

If he got her outside her peril might be even worse than before. Desperate and vengeful, he might kill her when he had no more use for her. A rebellious fear spread. She struggled and fought and he twisted her head cruelly in response. Pressing against the wall, he felt for the postern door.

A string of lights began edging around the keep. Simon shrank farther into the shadows but the glow spread until no shadows existed anymore, leaving the two of them starkly exposed. A tall armored figure strode among the torches toward them. Blood smeared the jerkin draping his body and colored the sword clutched in his hand. He stopped ten paces away.

"Are you going somewhere, Simon? I might consider permitting it if you did not try to take what was mine with you."

She could feel the body pressed behind her shake.

Simon's hand jerked down to his side and the two purses flew onto the ground at Addis's feet. One of the torch-bearers crouched and poured their contents out. Gold coins and glittering jewels flickered in a heap.

"I was not speaking of the wealth you had amassed and hoarded these past years."

His arm embraced her more tightly and the pressure on her bruises made her light-headed. "She will stay with me until I am well away."

"She will stay here, and so will you. You have much to answer for."

"It was a king who gave me Barrowburgh, and a king's council who took it away. I will go and answer to them for not obeying, but I will accept no judgment from you!"

"Your disobedience to the council is the least of it."

Simon's whole body flexed, as if he tried to suppress a huge shiver. Moira couldn't blame him. Addis stood there resolute and dangerous, a blood-aroused warrior who had just accomplished an impossible victory. There was little of the kind knight whom she knew in this man. He had removed his helmet and fury flamed in his eyes.

"Where is Owen?" Simon demanded. "Is he dead?"

"You pray that he is, I am sure, but when faced with the choice he took the coward's way as he always has. No trees or hired killers to hide behind up on that wall. No enemy army on whom to blame the sword or the spear. When it came down to him and me in a fair fight he yielded. And then he talked as if his life depended on it, as indeed it did."

He paced forward and Simon tried to pull her into the wall. "When my father married your mother he did not have to take you into his home as he did. But his generosity only planted greed in you, and plans to take my place as his son. Moira once said I was fortunate in my wounds, and she was right. In his youth Owen proved inept. A squire among my companions should have been able to kill me, the second time if not the first."

She gasped and twisted until she could see Simon's face out of the corner of her eye. He stared wide-eyed with terror, sweat pouring down his face. It was true. It had been Owen who scarred that body, Owen whose spear left Addis for dead on the crusade.

His strangled cry echoed her thoughts. "It was Owen!"

"His sword. His hands. But your idea and your gain. A hungry youth's impatient plan. But even with me dead, my father did not embrace you as his new son, did he? And so Lancaster's rebellion offered a way to make your own fate, without my father's favor." Addis traced the ridged scar on his face. "This I might forgive. Even those years of slavery. But my father's death was from no natural fever, I think. Owen doesn't think so either."

Simon's arm had become a death grip, squeezing the breath out of her, crushing her sore ribs and torso. Little spots of blackness dotted her sight. His other hand fumbled. A sharp edge pressed into her neck and a dagger hilt bumped her chin.

"You will release her," Addis said.

"Nay. You are speaking madness and I will get no justice here. You have no proof on Patrick but it will not matter during the power of your victory."

"Release her."

"She comes with me. If you want to see her alive again you will not follow."

Addis looked away for a moment and then stepped closer yet. Simon's terror surged in a palpable way. The blade pressed, the arm squeezed, and she almost passed out from pain.

"Aren't you forgetting something?" Addis asked quietly. "She does not know where Brian is. You may have my woman, but I have your son."

His words stunned her. She tried to twist and see Simon's reaction but the gesture made the blade burn her neck. She stared at Addis, hoping for a sign that he bluffed, but he did not even acknowledge her reaction. All of his attention centered on the face gasping sour breath next to her ear.

"You will never harm the boy who might be yours," Simon blustered.

"Not mine. And a Christian knight should not harm any child, but I find myself feeling less of one with each passing moment. Harm Moira and there may not be a shred of such mercy left in me."

She could feel Simon's panic. Her own mind veered from thought to thought, trying desperately to accommodate what Addis said and the cold way he said it. Simon's son! He had used Brian as a pawn from the beginning. Her throat tightened from a mournful sorrow, strangling her breath.

"Claire said the boy was yours!"

"She lied, even to you it seems. But you suspected the truth. He would not have survived if you had not, no matter how well Raymond and Moira tried to hide him."

"You cannot be sure. . . ."

"I am sure."

Simon clutched harder, the last grasp of a desperate man. The pain made her dizzy. Through her numbing awareness she felt him resist, hover, and then plunge into despair.

A violent push sent her flying at Addis. Her blotched senses absorbed the impact of his body, the support of his strong arm, and then his own thrust as he hurled her away. She floated to the ground on a pillow of semiconsciousness, only vaguely aware of the furious activity raining down around her.

Suddenly a deathly silence fell. Strong arms lifted her

up and her head lolled against a metal chest. Her insides felt as if they had been bludgeoned by that battering ram. Darkness sped by and she found herself gently laid on a soft bed.

Her tenuous hold on reality strengthened, but she resisted full alertness and the pains it would bring. Voices and movements swirled around her but her mind folded in on itself and followed its own paths through memories and emotions full of joy and sadness. She saw Addis in all of his faces, but most starkly in the new one revealed to her tonight in the yard. A profound disillusionment made her keep her eyes closed even when a woman came to wipe her face and check her wounds.

She pictured Brian riding off beside the man she thought was his father. But he was Simon's son, and Addis had known. That she had lived four years thinking she protected one man's child when in fact the boy needed no protection at all did not dismay her. The joy she had known giving Brian love could survive the knowledge that her great purpose had been a fraud. But the fact that Addis had taken that child from her and hidden him among strangers, had risked leaving Brian abandoned and alone should he die, had severed that spot of light from her life, all to hold a threat over Simon . . . her heart turned from what it meant about him. She did not think she could forgive him for using the child thus.

Sounds intruded more insistently and she realized that she lay in the solar. She could hear men talking and entering and leaving, and Addis's low voice giving orders. She turned her head toward him and forced her eyes open a slit.

He had removed his armor and thrown on a cotte. He sat in the lord's chair discussing something with Sir Richard. He looked as if the chair had been built for him. Proud and strong and powerful. A family like Valence did not hold on to their honor by being weak-hearted, and he was undoubtedly Patrick's son. She had been loving hidden parts of him that could no longer be acknowledged. The man whom everyone else had seen and feared would dominate now.

He noticed her looking and gestured Richard aside. She watched him come until he stood beside the bed. He caressed her cheek. "You are badly hurt, Moira, but the women say they do not think that you bleed inside. You will be feeling better soon."

She did not think she would ever feel better again. "Simon?"

"He came at us both with that dagger. A mad thing, since I wore steel. The blade caught your shoulder, but it is not deep."

"Did you kill him?"

"The peasants killed him. They moved as soon as he did, and he was dead by the time I got through to him." He bent down and kissed her forehead. "I must go down to the yard now, and see that the people get back their animals and such fairly. Rest, love."

"Will you ask Raymond to come? I want to speak with him."

He nodded and turned to leave.

She raised a hand to stop him. "Kiss me, Addis."

"I will hurt you."

"Please kiss me."

He carefully brushed her split and swollen lips with his mouth, and pressed the gentlest kiss on them. Tears burned in her closed eyes, and not because of any pain. He lingered there, her Addis, the vulnerable Addis of confusion and loneliness who had found love with a bondwoman. Their warmth connected them long enough that she almost lost her composure. She savored it, branding her mind with this final memory.

A sound interrupted them. She looked through moist eyes at Thomas Wake standing at the door. Addis straightened, suddenly the Lord of Barrowburgh again, the fearsome warrior who could conquer a fortress in three night hours and hold a child ransom in a game of power. The two men left her alone in the solar.

It was as she had known it would be. The string of his life had been retied. He did not need her anymore, not really. And the point had come, that specific moment she had been dreading, when she must either leave or walk back into the shadows.

The deep breaths with which she fought tears racked her bruised body. She only found some comfort when she forced her thoughts from the past to the future, and to the quest awaiting her.

By the time Raymond came she had made her decision. "You have heard?" she asked.

He frowned and nodded. "He says he is sure."

"Will he give Brian to you? You are his uncle."

"I have not asked yet, but I fear not. The truth of his birth will always be ambiguous. Addis can repudiate him, but there is no proof except Addis's word. When he is of age, Brian can challenge it, and will be a threat to any future son's hold."

"A man would not repudiate his own blood. Surely Addis is right."

Raymond shrugged. "Presumably. But it might be his final revenge on Claire. It is said she forsook him, and I know she fought the marriage. If he hated her for that, he might not want her son as his heir."

Could he do that? He had not warmed to the boy, and said that whenever he saw Brian he saw betrayal. "Do you know where he is?"

"Nay."

Nor did she. But she knew the direction they had gone,

and the time it had taken to bring Brian to his hiding place.

"I want to leave here now, Raymond. Will you help me?"

That startled him. "You are in no condition for a journey, Moira. And Addis—"

"Today, Raymond. Now. As soon as you can arrange a wagon. Some of the farmers will take me where I want to go. You need not escort me."

"Moira, you are wounded and shocked. You loved the boy and this news troubles you. Wait to speak with Addis."

"Aye, this news troubles me, and so does the realization that he will want to leave Brian wherever he is, a child alone with no family's love. But I always intended to leave. I said that I would see him enter these gates and sit in that chair and I have done so. The news about Brian only reinforces my decision."

Raymond sighed and shook his head. "You have always had enough pride for three women, and it is a hell of a thing that you do. He will not forgive you, or me for helping you."

"Will you do it?"

"I will do it. In the name of my sister's friendship for you and because you sacrificed part of your life to help my nephew, I owe it to you. But will you not wait to see him again first? To make your farewell?"

If she saw him again she might never leave, even with the disappointments and misgivings filling her heart.

"I have already said farewell to the Addis I love."

CHAPTER 22

SHE DID NOT NOTICE him enter the chamber. She was bent out the small window, the golden light of the late afternoon coloring her veil and flooding her form, the thin wool of her gown draping appealingly over her rounded hips. He could see her profile from the doorway and watched silently as her blue eyes scanned expectantly, then sparkled when a lovely smile enlivened her face. She lifted one hand from the sill and waved, then straightened and quietly stood like a sentry.

She appeared to him as an oasis of softness in a harsh world, a ray of light illuminating the chamber more than the sunbeams. His two souls had begun to accommodate each other, but her presence produced the old serenity and he welcomed the soothing grace made even more potent by the memories attached to it.

She did not move, but he knew the exact moment when she realized that she was not alone. Even so, her gaze did not leave whatever she watched.

"How did you find me?"

He went to her. "You were not in London and your people there had not seen you since we left together in the spring. You were not at Darwendon, and Raymond finally convinced me that he did not hide you at Hawkesford. Then I remembered that you had lived in Salisbury when you were married, and I wondered if maybe you had figured out that Brian was here too."

He looked out the window. The house backed against the abbey wall, and from here she could see into its yard. A group of boys kicked a ball among themselves. The smallest one's hair gleamed pale and blond.

"The friars would not let me speak to him, but I watch him every day from this window. He knows I am here now, and looks for me when they come out to play. His little face lights with a smile that says he knows that he is not alone anymore."

He looked down on the child whose existence symbolized betrayals far worse than the act that conceived him. It really didn't matter anymore. Nothing did from that time except the love and loyalty and strength that the Shadow had selflessly given.

"He is not mine, Moira. I am not punishing Claire by repudiating him. Raymond accused me of that, but it is not true."

"Nay, it is not. There is nothing of you in him. I see that now. Little of Simon either, for that matter. He is all Claire's son. She lied to me about him. About you. She said that you had demanded . . . before you went on the crusade that you had . . ."

"Forced her. And you believed that?"

"At the time it was not so hard to believe. It was a bitter young man whom they carted back to Barrowburgh, with a bitter girl by his side. You hated her then, I think, even if you do not remember it."

He remembered it. That part he had never forgotten.

"I had known Claire since she was born. Aye, I hated her, but not because she turned from me as a wife and a woman. She turned from me as a friend as well. Those years should have left us with that at least."

"She was young and frightened."

"She was shallow and vain and could only love herself. A woman with your depths and heart probably cannot understand that people can be thus. I had begun to see it as I outgrew my youth. Her radiance could not blind me forever. Her behavior when I was wounded only made me face what my heart had known for some time already." She had not looked at him. She still watched the child. "It troubles me to think that whenever you looked at that boy, you saw a child born from violence. That the memory you held of me those years was of a man who would hurt his wife."

A small frown tweaked her brow while her gaze turned inward. "Not really. She described it thus, but I did not believe you had used violence. She was your wife, and I assumed that you had demanded her duty to you. To her mind it might have been force, but I thought maybe it had just been like James and me."

"It was not even like James and you. I know he is not my son because despite the wedding I never lay with her after my return. I could not undo the marriage, but she was dead to me and I did not want her in my bed."

She nodded, as if he had just confirmed her own thoughts. "I have wondered why she lied about such a thing. To claim the child was yours made sense, of course. But why accuse you of such cruelty?"

"The whole household knew how things stood between us. Perhaps she feared that if she did not give a story that fit those facts some would wonder about the child's parentage. Certainly my father would have found it curious, since he knew we rarely spoke and that I had not touched her. An enraged husband forcing his rights on the eve of his departure would explain the child no one expected to see conceived."

"How did you know he was Simon's?"

"I suspected when it was clear that he had not searched for Brian very hard at all. He knew about Darwendon even if he did not know about you."

Brian gave the ball a wild kick. The boys raced around a corner of the building to catch it. She watched him disappear and finally turned, those clear eyes seeking his. "Could you have done it? Used him in vengeance against his father?"

"In truth, I do not know. If Simon had killed you, maybe so. What do you think, Moira?"

"I think not, but I do not know either. You are a complex person, Addis. You once said you feel as if two souls exist in you, but sometimes I sense many more, and some of them frighten me. There are times when I do not think I know you at all and never really can."

"You know me, Moira. If anyone does, you do. You know me as well as I know myself, which I will admit isn't very well."

She dropped her gaze to the floor between them. "I am glad that you came to explain it to me, Addis."

"That is not only why I came."

She looked a little frightened, and shot glances blindly around the room as if he cornered her and she sought an escape.

"This chamber is overwarm. Come down to the garden with me so we can speak."

"I don't think so, Addis."

He took her hand in his. The delicate warmth made his heart swell with relief and love. He had feared he would never feel her touch again.

She resisted warily. He coaxed her with a firm tug,

gearing himself for a battle more vital to his life than the one at Barrowburgh.

She should not go. She should send him away and not listen to whatever words he had for her. Her good sense chanted this while he led her down the stairs and into the small walled garden filled with young plants.

Aye, she should not go, but she looked at the lean strong back beneath its brown cotte, and the fine, tanned arm stretching to hers, and the handsome face looking back. Her heart flipped as it had since she was a girl, and the part of her that had long ago abandoned good sense with him would not be denied this final, brief time, no matter what raw pain it renewed.

He found a bench against a wall where a hedge hid them from the curious eyes of the goldsmith's wife who owned the house. She pried her hand loose and restlessly smoothed the folds of her skirt. She felt him watching her. Sitting close beside him left her a little breathless.

"Is all well at Barrowburgh?" she asked feebly.

"Well enough. The crops look good and the people are content. Lucas Reeve has recovered, although he lost sight in an eye that night. I gave each of his sons a virgate, and have said they need not pay heriot when their father dies."

"You are a generous and fair lord. The villeins at Darwendon thought so too."

"It was an easy generosity."

"And Owen. What of him?"

"At my encouragement Owen decided to expiate his sins with another crusade. A very long one. And Simon's mother asked if she might retire to a convent and I gave my permission."

"So it is all done then. You have your life back. It is as it should be. I am joyed for you, Addis."

He tilted his head thoughtfully. "It is done. I should be more than content. And yet I feel little joy myself, Moira. I have my life back, and I am not so foolish or ungrateful as to forget the value of it. But that keep is a cold place, full of lifeless shadows. I do my duty as I was taught from birth, but my heart cannot warm to it. Sometimes I feel like a slave again, now serving the ghosts of my ancestors."

She could imagine that and her heart ached for him. Loneliness was something she understood and had come to know again far too well. "It will change. When you marry and have a family, it will be a true home again. Lady Mathilda will bring life and warmth to Barrowburgh."

"When I marry it will not be to Lady Mathilda. Thomas Wake regretfully told me that the girl does not think we suit each other. He knew even when he brought that army that there would be no marriage. Mathilda thinks I am not refined and courteous enough. She wants a knight who will write her poetry and hang on each of her many words as if they are pearls that drop from her mouth."

"She is a silly little goose!"

He reached over and brushed back some errant hairs that had escaped her veil. "Perhaps she suspected that the whole time she chattered in Yorkshire, I was making love to you in my mind."

The light touch and the look in his eyes made her tremble. She barely found a voice. "If so, that really was discourteous."

His fingers drifted to caress her face, gently moving over the flesh as if he were learning its structure. He summoned an anguished love in her full of poignant, impossible yearnings that said she would pay dearly in the days ahead for this visit. In the three months since she left him she had finally learned to dull the pain, but had also learned that the punishment of loving the wrong person lasted a lifetime.

"I want you to come back with me."

"Oh, Addis . . ."

He embraced her with one arm and kissed her into silence, his palm resting warmly on her cheek. "You will come. You must."

So tempting to sink into that embrace forever. "There will be another betrothal, another Mathilda. You speak of only a reprieve, and my heart can take just so many such partings before it breaks forever. You are proof enough that each of us lives several lives before we perish. There is wisdom in accepting when one ends and another begins. I love you, Addis. I always will. But there is no place for me in the life you have now."

"If that is wisdom, then I will never be wise. I do not want a life that has no place for you in it. You will come back with me and take the place that is yours in my heart. No obligations to the past stand in the way. We will marry."

He looked so serious, so determined, as if he spoke logic instead of nonsense. She caressed his face and his head bowed to her touch until they sat with foreheads pressed and palms on each other's face. "It is impossible. You know that better than I do."

"It is not forbidden. Once done, no one can undo it."

"You will be scorned by your own, and mocked for your choice of wife. Even the peasants will think you mad."

"Those who know you will not scorn me but envy me, and I do not care what is said or thought."

"I am serf-born, Addis. It might as well be forbidden."

"Aye, you lived as a serf, Moira, with all that means. But I lived as a slave. My degree was even lower than yours."

"That was an accident. A mistake."

"All of our births are accidents, and yours a mistake. I know we are taught it is ordained by God, but I do not believe it. Of all of the beliefs and customs that I have questioned since I returned, this one I know is wrong and I'll not be bound by it. It seems to me if an anointed king can be set aside, a serf-born woman can marry a baron's son. As rebellions against God's lawful order go, ours will be a small one."

She did not know how to answer him. The offer at the church door had been a rash impulse, but this had been contemplated and planned. The idea was too preposterous. Surely he saw that.

He frowned. "Are you thinking that you could not bear it, Moira? If we are mocked, or there is disapproval? Women can be hard on each other, I know, and it may be worse for you than for me. If you do not think you can live in my life, I can always live in yours. I can give Barrowburgh back to the king and become an innkeeper with you."

Dear God, he was serious. "Nay. Oh, Addis, you are speaking more madness. Think. Your sons will have serfs for a mother and grandmother. What of them?"

"They will have a mother whom they will cherish as I do, and want to protect. A woman loved by her husband, and a grandmother who was beloved by her lord."

His insistence was exhausting her spirit and making her lose hold of the solid truths of her own argument. Her emotions scrambled, and his accepting, loving gaze undid her. She shook her head with a final, vague denial before sinking into his arms.

He held her against his chest with her head tucked under his chin, gently caressing her back. "You will come back with me and bring life to those shadows and warmth to my heart as you always have, Moira. And I will learn to give to you as you have always given to me."

"I would only bring you trouble and shame. You are just too stubborn and willful to see it. There are some things that the Lord of Barrowburgh cannot order to his liking," she muttered, hiding her brimming eyes in his cotte. He could not know how much he tortured her with this hopeless dream. He made it sound so possible, so real, but the blood that coursed in her body had been taught by centuries that it could never be so. He would see that soon enough, and be grateful she had not agreed. But, oh, the thought of it, hanging there right out of reach, tempting her to a ridiculous excitement that truth and good sense could barely suppress. . . .

He tilted her face to his, and thumbed a tear off her cheek. "Are you refusing me, Moira?"

Her throat burned and her lips trembled. He looked so sad as he read the decision in her eyes.

"Then I ask a final gift before we part. I want you to sing for me. One of the love songs, as you did at the dinner. I would have the song be about you and me, so that I think of you whenever I hear it again."

"Nay, Addis. Please . . ."

"Would you refuse me this too? This final memory? It is a small thing."

It wasn't a small thing. It would shred her to pieces and she might never be whole again.

She sniffed and licked her lips and rested her cheek against his chest. Only his heartbeat would accompany her. She found a spot of tenuous composure and clung to it and somehow, miraculously, the melody and words whispered forth.

Her voice could fill a hall, but now it only traveled the short distance to his ears. His lips pressed the top of her head and stayed there. The song both anguished and exalted her, and his embrace supported a body that knew no strength. Images flew behind her blurring eyes as old memories loomed sharply in the heavy mood of the song. A youth mourning in her arms. A knight screaming in pain. A fiery-eyed man stripped of illusions and will.

Her voice faltered several times before the end. The final words were lost in a sob that she buried in his chest. He held her to his breast while she cried out her heart, and rubbed his cheek against her hair as a father might comfort a child.

His own voice came low and rough with emotion. "Do you wonder why I will not live without you? Your love and loyalty sustained and comforted me in ways I did not even know. Even in slavery, I think it was you my spirit sought when I looked up into the stars. You have been my best ally for years, aiding me even in death when you cared for the boy, protecting me that dark night when I lost the will to protect myself."

She huddled in the soothing sanctuary of his arms, and struggled to contain the flood that the song had unleashed. "When did you remember?"

"My heart knew as soon as I saw you again. The memories came slowly, in bits and pieces. They began taking form once I had Barrowburgh again. But I had begun to understand where I had to look for them before that."

She felt so close to him that she thought her very essence had merged into his. She found a blissful serenity there, and a loving warmth that stroked her churning emotions like a reassuring caress.

"Look at me, Moira."

She pulled back until she could see the scarred face, and the perfect other half.

"We belong together. You will come back with me and we will wed and the rest of the world can go to hell if they do not like it. And when our children come I will tell them the story of the bondwoman who loved from the shadows and expected nothing in return."

He was not really asking her to agree. It is how it must be, his expression said. And he was right. Rejecting what they shared would be a type of sin.

A streak of sorrow split the euphoria spilling through her. Her gaze drifted to the far wall that abutted the abbey. He turned her face back and kissed her. "Brian will come with us. It will not be Simon's blood that forms the man he becomes, but your love. He is not my son and I will not have him displace our own children though. He must be told the truth of it, but I will accept him like my own blood. He may decide later that he is suited to the abbey and choose to return here, but if not I will give him the Baltic manor that is mine."

She almost wept again. "That is not easy generosity, Addis. And I love you all the more for it."

"He is an innocent, and I cannot remain cold to anyone you love." He rose. "We will go and get him now, if you want. But I hope there is a spare pallet in this house for him. I do not want to have him in our bed tonight."

"I think we can find a spot in another chamber for him." She would make sure that they did. A very special loving awaited them when night fell.

He looked down at her with such naked love that she thought she might fly to the heavens.

"Then let us speak with the friars. But first we will stop at the church door." He held out his hand to her. "Come and say the words with me, Moira. Be mine forever."

She looked at that gesture beckoning her to their impossible future. Only the greatest love and loyalty would survive what awaited them. Her serf's soul knew that even if none of his souls did.

She placed her hand completely in his.

ABOUT THE AUTHOR

MADELINE HUNTER is a nationally bestselling, award-winning author of historical romances. In 2003 she won the RITA award for best long historical romance, and her writing has been nominated for the RITA three times. Her novels have appeared on the *USA Today* bestseller list, the Waldenbooks mass-market bestseller list, and the *New York Times* extended bestseller list. Her stories have garnered critical praise from *Publishers Weekly*, *Romantic Times*, and numerous online review sites. Madeline has a Ph.D. in art history, which she teaches at an eastern university. She lives in Pennsylvania with her husband and two sons.